W9-ABD-687

THE
TIMOR
MAN

FIC
Collison
Kerry
B.

34M0200135217V

CARTHAGE PUBLIC LIBRARY
CARTHAGE, MO
DISCARD
417-237-7040 (Voice)
1-800-735-2466 (TDD via Relay Missouri)

Published by: Sid Harta Publishers for Kerry B. Collison and Asian
                        Pacific Management Co. (S.A.) Ltd.
                        Telephone: (61) (0 414) 958623
                        fax: (61) 03 9560 9921
                        Address: PO Box 1102 Hartwell,
                        Victoria, Australia 3125

First published 1996 as *The Tim-Tim Man*
Revised Edition, January 1998
Third Printing, April 1999
Copyright © Kerry B.Collison,
Sid Harta Publishers and
Asian Pacific Management Co. Ltd. S.A

Text: Kerry B.Collison
Cover Concept: Guy W. Collison
Final Proof Reading: Judith Bibo
Author's Photograph: Courtesy of Ned Kelly and the
                        Bundaberg News Mail, Queensland

This book is copyright. Apart from fair dealing for the purposes of private
study, research, criticism or review, as permitted under the Copyright Act, no
part may be reproduced by any process without the written permission of the
copyright owners.

Collison, Kerry Boyd

ISBN   0 9587448 1 5

Printed in Australia
by Australian Print Group
Maryborough, Victoria.

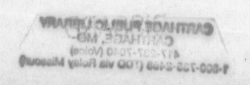

Dedication

To my wife Ni Nyoman Sukasani
and our children Sinta Dewi and
Guy Winston Collison

Kerry B. Collison followed a distinguished period of service as a member of the Australian Embassy in Indonesia during the turbulent Sixties followed by a successful business career spanning thirty years throughout Asia.

Recognised for his chilling predictions in relation to Asia's evolving political and economic climate and as the only Australian ever to have been personally granted citizenship by an Indonesian President, he brings unique qualifications to his historically-based vignettes and intriguing accounts of power-politics and the shadowy world of governments' clandestine activities.

The author's biographical data is available on the Internet at:
http://www.sidharta.com.au

Photo of the author by Ned Kelly, published by courtesy of the Bundaberg News Mail.

"And the beast was captured, and with it the
false prophet who in its presence had worked the
signs by which he deceived those who had received the
mark of the beast and those who worshipped its image.

These two were thrown alive into the lake
of fire that burns with sulphur."

Revelation 19, verse 20
From the Revelation to John
(The Apocalypse)
New Testament, Holy Bible

Acknowledgement

There are many who have assisted with this novel.

On more than one occasion, I wanted to give up and surrender all hopes of finally completing this tale and had it not been for the support of those who believed in me then this book would not be a matter of fiction but merely a figment of my imagination.

Determination is obviously not enough. And by itself, neither is energy. Together they are sufficient to see one through the endless months and in this case, years, of work and self examination.

Often, just one critique is sufficient to break a writer's spirit; I was fortunate to have the critic and the guide who provided the way out of the dark literary jungle I had created for myself. In this respect, I wish to acknowledge the support and assistance of Denise Cox, without whose honest criticism this novel would not have been published.

I also wish to thank Judith Bibo for re-proofing the new release and the many readers who have written to support my work on the trilogy.

Author's Note

The *Timor Man* is a work of historical fiction.

Originally, this story was released with the title *The Tim-Tim Man*, however, out of respect to the East Timorese people I have re-titled the book.

Fact and fiction are often held to be difficult bedfellows. In this novel, I have attempted to weave both into a narrative that general readers will enjoy, readers who have not had the benefit of witnessing at first-hand the incredible changes that have occurred in Asia over the last few decades.

Perhaps some of the descriptions of events and military hardware could be challenged, but for the greater part, the novel is supported by what I believe to be a solid foundation of fact.

In 1965 and 1966, during the time which many of us later understood as the *'Year of Living Dangerously'*, almost half a million people died in one of the worst blood lettings since the Jewish Holocaust.

Later, between the years of 1975 and 1990, almost a quarter of a million East Timorese were killed by Indonesian soldiers. More died, in fact, than were lost in the terrible wars in what are now known as the Former Yugoslavian Republics.

Although this story was not written with a political purpose, I hope it will reach your heart and appeal to your soul. As our world enters the twenty-first Century, we still go about killing each other more than ever before. Human nature doesn't seem to change.

Only the historical facts do.

Kerry B.Collison,
Kompong Som

Contents

Prologue

the present

The explosion erupted through the assembly.

Figures danced momentarily before disintegrating into heaps of lifeless flesh and bone. The blast ripped through the guests hurling musical instruments into the maelstrom of human carnage, decapitating a bandsman.

Then, for an immeasurable moment, silence ...

A shrill cry pierced the quiet, then a cacophony of screams emphasised the full horror of the blasts.

Canberra bomb toll 'horrific' — PM

By PETER JENSEN,

Canberra. Thursday

The Australian Prime Minister has issued a statement strongly condemning last night's terrorist attack which claimed more than 100 lives here in the Capital.

Amongst those believed killed were the Indonesian Ambassador to Australia, Mr. Nathan Seda, the Indonesian Chief of Army Staff, Lt. General Umar Suprapto, the Indonesian Minister for Foreign Affairs, Mr. Abdul Nasution, and the former Australian Ambassador to Indonesia, Mr. Duncan O'Laughlin.

A further 337 people have been reported as seriously injured. Local hospitals where the bomb blast victims are recovering from severe burns have been placed under tight security.

An informed source has stated that the condition of the Papua New Guinea Foreign Affairs Minister has improved but he is expected to remain on the critical list.

Eye witnesses reported that the Indonesian Embassy foyer erupted into a fireball moments after commencement of the Indonesian national anthem.

The explosion was felt throughout the area. Local residents in surrounding areas have reported extensive window damage. Meanwhile, the Prime Minister has expressed deep regret concerning the attack and has sent a personal note to the Indonesian President expressing sympathy and offering Australia's condolences to the Indonesian people.

He stated that he hoped current relations would not be further strained by what he described as "international terrorists and vested interest groups bent on sabotaging Indonesian-Australian relations."

Yesterday's reception was held to celebrate Indonesia's Independence Day in Australia, Mr. Seda's first since taking up his post.

Both Governments had hoped that his appointment would create an air of rapprochement between the countries since relations were strained over the Timor shelf oil disputes and New Guinea's recent border clashes with its giant neighbour.

Border violations throughout the past twelve months have resulted in Australian military units being positioned in New Guinea to assist under the terms of existing defence commitments. A number of Indonesian RPKAD troops and New Guinea soldiers were killed during a recent clash.

At the time, Indonesia claimed that their troops had been on an anti-guerrilla sweep and had inadvertently strayed into New Guinea territory. Political relations deteriorated further when the Australian Embassy in Jakarta was partly gutted by fire during student demonstrations.

It is not known whether Indonesia will now sever diplomatic ties as a result of this attack. Opposition Shadow Foreign Affairs Minister David Carroll demanded that the Prime Minister act to protect Australian interests in Indonesia as students are expected to demonstrate in retaliation to the Canberra bombing.

A Government spokesman has indicated that steps have already been taken in Jakarta but warned that tourists travelling to Indonesia should be aware of possible incidents in response to the deaths of the senior Indonesians here.

A man claiming to be a member of the Frente Revolucionarla de Timor Leste Independente (FRETILIN) party had phoned claiming responsibility for the bombing.

The Prime Minister has instructed the police and security chiefs to mobilise whatever forces necessary to investigate the bombing and pursue those responsible. — AAP

PAGE 3: continues

1975 — Kampuchea falls to Pol Pot, 'Killing Fields' period commences.
1975 — Saigon falls to the Communists.

Konfrontasi — 1958-196
Guerilla-style warfare inve
Malaysia, Indonesia & Bri
Commonwealth countr
includingAustralia, takes p
mainly in Sarawak and Su

Phnom Penh

Vietnam

Ho Chi Minh City (Saigon)

Malaysia

Malaya

Natuna Island
(world's largest natural gas deposits)

Sarawak

Singapore

Kalimantan

Sumatra

Indonesia

Indian (Indonesian) Ocean

Jakarta

Java

Bali

proposed nuclear plants

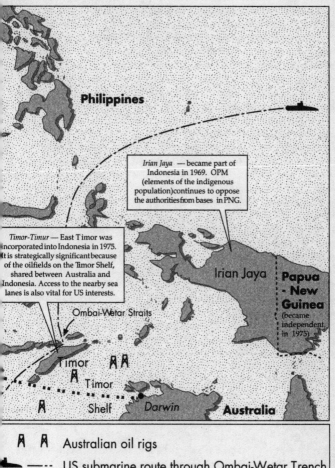

Philippines

Irian Jaya — became part of Indonesia in 1969. OPM (elements of the indigenous population) continues to oppose the authorities from bases in PNG.

Timor-Timur — East Timor was incorporated into Indonesia in 1975. It is strategically significant because of the oilfields on the Timor Shelf, shared between Australia and Indonesia. Access to the nearby sea lanes is also vital for US interests.

Irian Jaya

Papua - New Guinea (became independent in 1975)

Ombai-Wetar Straits

Timor

Timor

Shelf

Darwin

Australia

Australian oil rigs

-- -- US submarine route through Ombai-Wetar Trench

• • • • • route taken by British 'V' Bombers armed with nuclear bombs, 1962–65

Book One

1965

Indonesia in Turmoil

DISCARD

Chapter 1

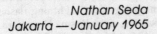

Nathan Seda
Jakarta — January 1965

Lightning cracked yet again, signalling there would be no break in the tropical storm. The city began to choke as rain fell incessantly creating chaos with the traffic. Trucks, buses and cars remained stuck where they had broken down under the deluge, their electrical systems saturated and rendered useless. Scores of drivers waded through the deep and filthy flows which threatened to carry the abandoned cars over the roads into the flooded canals.

The downpour continued throughout the day, threatening to close the capital, as most major roads became small rivers feeding shallow lakes which had suddenly appeared where once there had been parks and fields.

The air was thick with the musty damp smell of the rain. Humidity rose to unbearable levels.

The more congested intersections would remain blocked for hours as children played in waist-deep ponds covering the Capital's pot-holed protocol roads. Electricity flow would have ceased almost immediately rain had commenced. Without power there would be no water — the irony of being without adequate water while rain flooded the city was not lost on the Capital's inhabitants.

The transition from Dutch colonial rule to Independence had thrust the archipelago's one hundred and fifty million people into a political and economic quagmire peppered by religious rivalry and diverse cultural differences.

Soekarno's brilliant use of rhetoric, and support provided by the military, enabled him to take the helm of the world's fifth most populous country, a land rich in unexploited natural resources.

The national philosophy, the *Panca Sila*, provided for five basic principles around which the people were expected to build their way of life. This philosophy eased the racial and religious tensions which otherwise might have caused civil war. Although the country had the world's largest Moslem population, political power was determined more by ethnic rather than religious considerations. Leaders from Java, the most heavily populated island, controlled the country's numerous and politically unstable provincial centres.

The sky remained ominously dark. Lightning flashed again, striking the unfinished skeleton of the Wisma Nusantara building overlooking the British Embassy. *Jalan Thamrin*, Jakarta's main protocol avenue, ceased to function.

Canal water flowed along the footpaths bringing with it unmentionable sewage and the occasional dead animal. Since seasonal maintenance was invariably neglected the *kali*, or drains, could never handle the sudden downpours. Putrid garbage and human effluent flowed into the streets and through the houses. Pedestrian traffic disappeared as the footpaths became increasingly inundated.

Houses built along the avenues adjacent to these canals always suffered the fierce odours from these sewage streams. *Jonguses* waited apprehensively as the rivers of foul waste threatened their masters' residences. Instructions were given to female servants, the *babus*, to stand-by to clean up after the occasional vehicle which passed immediately in front of a residence, throwing small waves into the well kept yards, creating havoc.

Most resident foreigners were members of the Diplomatic Corps. Their houses were grand old Dutch designed mansions built during the colonial times to provide for the numerous Dutch colonists. Now they were occupied by career men and women, many enjoying their first posting overseas.

Expatriates, generally speaking, were provided with vehicles. Transport was expensive and car smuggling was practised in many of the Third World Embassies to compensate for the poorly paid civil servants' meagre incomes. Drivers ferried their masters to and fro, enjoying considerable privilege within the domestic ranks of the expatriate household. The wet season was, however, when these drivers suffered most abuse.

Rain brought floods. Flooded streets caused the *tuan*'s car to stop. *Tuan* would be late for work, or even worse, late for a cocktail function. The 'mister' would then be angry and would surely blame his woes for the day on the driver. It seemed that no one appreciated the rain.

The traffic police disappeared. What could they do? The locals were clever enough to stay indoors and the foreigners, the *orang asing*, were always a problem demanding assistance waving their diplomatic passports whenever their vehicles came to an abrupt halt in the flooded streets. Just four or five stranded vehicles around the Hotel Indonesia circle could create hours of chaos.

Traffic congestion was further exacerbated by the 100,000 *becak* drivers who pedalled their iron three-wheelers everywhere, demanding equal access through the bedlam of traffic. These wiry-legged men were definitely a force to be reckoned with, should one be so unfortunate as to become involved in an accident or any other altercation with them. Theirs was, in fact, the most sensible form of transportation during heavy rain periods as the passenger was reasonably protected from the elements. There were, however, exceptions.

This year's *Idulfitri* contributed to Jakarta's unpleasant appearance. The remnants of that week's festivities floated along the inundated roads. Many who had returned to their villages for the *Ramadhan* feast would soon drift listlessly back to their offices satisfied that their religious and social obligations had been acquitted in accordance with tradition and the Moslem faith.

Idulfitri followed the Moslem month of fasting. Each morning, prior to daybreak, those participating would consume their last food and water until sunset. Initially, most Moslems would follow the dictates of the fast. Many would not have the strength to continue for the entire month and those who felt despondent for not being resilient enough to meet the rigid demands as determined by the holy Koran were not, in general, castigated for their weakness or inability to adhere to the religious rites.

Ramadhan was a time of restraint and abstinence.

Idulfitri was a time of celebration.

It was just unfortunate that this year, the holidays following the breaking of the final fasting period had to coincide with the rain. Most accepted the situation philosophically; the festival advanced by two weeks each year and eventually the holidays would fall during the dry season.

Not far from the central business district stood the splendid obelisk representing Indonesia's freedom from Dutch rule. Positioned in the centre of a large square, *Lapangan Merdeka*, the column could be seen from most points within the city proper. Surrounding the *Merdeka* square were government offices and the Indonesian Department of Defence, HANKAM. The United States Embassy, adjacent to the Republic's military headquarters, enjoyed the benefits of the prominent address, but not the excessive attention it often attracted.

The HANKAM building in itself was a relatively insignificant structure considering its importance. Built by the Dutch, it was a white walled terra-cotta roofed building which reached only to the customary three levels. The Dutch did not enjoy the benefits of lifts and air-conditioning, so consequently they designed their structures so that, having struggled up the stairs to the third floor, they could enjoy the occasional breeze which compensated for the climb.

Louvred windows allowed soft breezes to whisper through the buildings, cooling the self-appointed colonial masters. Security was, at best, cursory. Military police stood as sentries at the main gate checking visitors as they entered in their stately limousines.

The main structure housed two hundred staff, most of whom had very little to do but wander through the deteriorating corridors. Mildew was evident everywhere and leaking water pipes left patterns of moist blotches identifying the piping's irregular path through the maze of brick and cement walls. Cables hung precariously in the air held only by rusting supports. Wires bared to the copper hung threateningly from their two-holed sockets, the inadequate power rarely surging to more than half of its determined voltage. Power variation damaged equipment even more quickly than the tropical heat with its soaking humidity.

Not that power was such a problem, as it rarely worked anyway since the Soviets ceased their financial support three years before. The entire building boasted only three direct dial telephone numbers and the switchboard had virtually no capacity for improvement.

In the rear courtyard, more than twenty Soviet-style Jeeps, Armed Personnel Carriers and trucks stood abandoned and overgrown by grass. Generally speaking, the armed forces were in financial disarray.

A Banyan tree dwarfed the left wing of the complex. Children played in the branches, oblivious to the significance of their surroundings. Not fifty metres from the corner, a long row of two-storey shops and dwellings housed an array of squatters.

A group of Germans had recently acquired a lease to open their own club and construction was under way. This in itself attracted a number of curious spectators, as only occasional building or renovation had taken place during the past years and to see foreigners who were not Soviets actually doing something was quite unusual.

A group of workers waited for their pay, squatting on their haunches beside the remnants of what had been several cubic metres of river sand before the days work had begun.

Another day of drudgery was coming to a close.

* * * * * *

A solitary figure sat motionless, staring moodily across the square through a rain-blurred window from the third level of the HANKAM building.

His office was the typical bleak high-ceilinged room. The walls, stained by the smoke of belching buses and powerful aromatic *kretek* cigarettes, showed evidence of years of neglect. The discoloured ceilings were now a combination of moss-green and moist brown. Surplus ships paint sloshed over earlier leakage stains did little to camouflage the decay. Overhead fans struggled to cut a leading edge through the polluted air, their blades blackened by the endless movement through the heavy, sticky atmosphere.

Photographs hung untidily on the wall adjacent to the military green painted door. General Sarwo Eddie, the hero of the liberation of *Irian Barat*, stood in his typical arrogant style. His picture was placed to the right of the President while Dr Soebandrio sat knowingly in an armchair, holding a pipe, on the left of the Great Leader of the Revolution, placed there obviously by some clerk with a sense of humour considering the good doctor's role in delivering his country to Communism. The office was furnished simply with a desk and two chairs.

The man at the window wore an army uniform. The insignia on his shoulder identified him as an intelligence colonel. His dark, almost aquiline features indicated his ethic origins as being somewhere within the Eastern Nusantara group of islands. He was tall for an Indonesian and his face was completely unlined by the worries of his profession.

To the casual observer, the colonel may have appeared to be mesmerised by the activity in the foreign legation's grounds, the apparent object of his scrutiny. The United States Embassy was not, however, what was distracting him from the unread folders of military documents spread casually across his desk in this third level office.

A roll of thunder interrupted his thoughts, obliging him to acknowledge the unattended, indeed relatively mundane, matters before him.

He sighed. He was bored. Bored with the weather and the overcrowded city that lay sprawled out before him.

Colonel Seda pondered the problems associated with the rain, turned in his chair and returned to his partial view of the outside world. He ran his hand slowly through the curly hair which would soon require attention, his fingers finding a small crusty patch on the hairline to scratch. He examined the small white specks of dry skin under the nicotine stained fingernail. Disgusted with the find, he wiped his hand quickly against his thigh. It was always the little things that caused the most annoyance, he thought.

His driver had not, as yet, returned from Bandung. There was a very real possibility his transport would break down, should the incompetent idiot assigned to him from the motor pool attempt to bring the antiquated vehicle through the flooded streets. Again he sighed. His quarters would be leaking. Every roof in the country leaked. 'Sialan — Damn,' he thought. The country was deteriorating at an alarming rate. Inflation had eaten his salary away to the point where it was practically valueless. At least the monthly rice rations kept everyone going. It was difficult to secure a position where a little extra income could be earned. He should have joined the police force, he mused. Without exception, police, because of their close access to the public, could always extract those little extras whenever they wished. At any time they could just stop any car with a Chinese passenger and squeeze him for a little cash.

Although a minority group, the Indonesian Chinese had a very real stranglehold on the Indonesian economy and were easy targets for extortion. Nobody cared when a Chinese was roughed up a little for they had not integrated with the indigenous races and often manipulated commodity prices to the point where many *pribumi* people starved. Wherever they settled, the world's oldest trading race eventually became embroiled in some form of racial violence and Indonesia was no exception. The Chinese were despised. They controlled the flow of all agricultural products and other basic necessities. They had their own schools. They controlled the shops.

And all that gold they wore!

"*Sialan mereka semua!*" Seda muttered, cursing the whole race as he continued to gaze through the window. Perhaps he should not complain, he brooded. After all, he'd done reasonably well with his life so far, considering that he had been born and raised in a small village near Dili in East Timor. There, life had been excruciatingly hard. His father had died from one of the many fevers that plagued the rural dwellers.

Seda had difficulty remembering much about his father, only his strong, sharp facial features remained fixed in his mind. He had obviously inherited his father's nose, for when he moved to Jakarta as an adult and visited the whores around the *Blok M* graveyard, they often mistook him for a foreigner. He would never know whether these genes were the result of some careless Portuguese sailor or some Dutch seed sown lustfully generations before.

The Portuguese began trading with Timor almost a century prior to any serious attempts by the Dutch to develop a foothold on the island. The division of the island between these two seafaring nations ultimately resulted in the development of considerable religious and cultural differences between the Catholic northeast and the Protestant south.

Although both colonial powers in Timor concentrated their efforts on preventing each other from expanding their spheres of influence, some trade in produce did develop. Coffee became the main export from the two colonies.

Dutch Timor inevitably became part of Indonesia as a result of the Independence movement. It was officially absorbed into *Nusa Tenggara* province by the central government in Jakarta during subsequent provincial restructuring. Kupang remained the provincial capital. For a time, Catholics, Protestants, and a few Buddhists, Hindus and Moslems co-existed without any real racial or religious turmoil. Even the head-hunters put aside their old habits.

When his mother was obliged to migrate to another village across the border, she remarried. Seda became one of seven children in what was already an impoverished family. He slept on a *tikar* mat alongside his new brothers and sisters cramped together on a dirt floor in a one room house which provided only the barest protection from the elements. There were two small meals a day, taken sitting cross-legged on the roughly woven mat. Some days, when his stepfather was unable to find part time work to supplement his pitiful income, they went without food altogether.

He remembered that his mother often stood outside, alone, looking down the dry slopes towards the sea and across to where they had lived when his father had still been alive. Occasionally, he would slip quietly outside so that the other children would not follow and go to her, leaning against her frail body, his head tilted against her hip trying to understand just what she stood and stared at from under the old mango tree.

She would not talk during these private moments but he didn't mind as he always felt a sense of warmth as her calloused hands softly stroked his hair and the side of his face. He knew that she frequently missed meals, ensuring that the children were fed first. She was often sick and he wanted to cry out for someone to care, but he knew, even in his youth, that almost every hut in the dry desolate village housed another mother whose suffering was similar.

Poverty and hunger can be great motivators. When his mother had arranged for him to attend classes at the local Catholic school he grasped the opportunity and studied diligently. At first he experienced great difficulty as the other children were more advanced, having had the advantage of attending classes since turning seven.

Seda was nine before he could read. When he was twelve he had recovered all the lost time and was increasingly being singled out by the priests for his rapid progress in class. These hard working men of the cloth struggled to educate all of the children, regardless of their talents, but their efforts were often severely restricted by a government which favoured non-Christian institutions. During the heat of the day when the classes rested, the children would literally drop to the floor in the school and sleep for several hours, enjoying the cool of the tiled floor against their undernourished bodies.

Schools were inadequately equipped. The population was desperately poor. The Church provided a semblance of basic primary education to many however funds were limited as the government restricted the growth of non-Moslem faith educational institutions. The priests were obliged to be extremely careful and selective when allocating positions in their school.

As a teenager Seda continued to study diligently. Excellent grades created the opportunity for the young student to attend the Armed Forces Academy in Java which resulted in his eventual escape from the provincial backwater. His mother had been delighted that her son had been selected for such a career opportunity. Now, his future would be secure. He would never again experience the hunger of his childhood.

Seda contemplated his humble origins. Although born in Portuguese Timor this was never reflected in any of his earlier school registration documents. Border crossings were frequent and registrations of village births on both sides of the border mainly went unrecorded. He remembered his mother and the tears of joy when his selection had been announced. Her tears were not just in appreciation for the blessing her god had passed to her son. She wept knowing that she would lose him. Once he had tasted the exotic life of the main island she knew he would never return.

* * * * * *

Seda had never been convinced that the army had been the correct choice. In retrospect, he felt that perhaps he should have elected to fly with AURI, the country's Air force. Many of the pilots and technical officers had been sent to the Eastern Bloc countries for advanced training. This inevitably meant additional funds for clothes, travel and other expenses and a chance to travel away from the disorder that prevailed.

Indonesia had entered its most dangerous period. Everything appeared to be confused. The country's leaders had all but embraced Communism yet this strange political ideology did not, in fact, accept religious belief! Bewildering enough for an uneducated Muslim population which followed the teachings of the Prophet Mohammed. The people had been instructed to follow the President's dictates. NASAKOM was the new political order — Nationalism, Socialism, Communism. The Russians had poured in billions of dollars in foreign aid to ensure that the Communist political agenda could be realised in this resource-rich archipelago.

Within a few short years, the country was equipped with tanks and every kind of sophisticated weaponry. Airfields boasted MIG-15s, 17s and 19s. Indeed, Seda had read a report just the day before about the amazing Russian strategic bombers, designated TU-16's, which had the capacity to bomb every major city in the country to the south in just one sortie!

Seda found that there was so much to learn from the new military jargon. IL-28s had been positioned at the Malang and Surabaya airfields. SA-2 missiles were sitting on their launch sites ready for firing from their revetments. There was also talk that the Russians had built a submarine base in Cilacap, on the south coast of Java!

Seda had seen the new steel mill under construction in Cilegon.

All of this, he thought, and still not enough money to feed the hundreds of thousand of troops the country had mustered. Everyone was waiting anxiously for the leadership to prove how the new doctrines would prevent past major food shortages from recurring. Maybe the new ships provided by the Russian Navy would be utilised to bring rice from other nations?

Seda snorted in disgust. He was intelligent enough to realise that the Indonesian people now faced starvation due to the folly of political misadventures by the country's entrenched leadership, and that the days when the country exported rice were over. He did not trust the group headed by Subandrio. The President was too easily swayed by the Communists. Maybe *Bung Karno*, as he preferred to be called, was, in fact, becoming senile and did not realise the dangers of these people around him. The President had spent far too much of his valuable time chasing young women and, to the dismay of his first four wives, his latest acquisition, a Japanese hostess, was set to become the new First Lady!

Seda looked over his shoulder at the photographs and suddenly felt uneasy under the gaze of the powerful trio hanging there as if in silent rebuke. The President was still very popular although there had been several attempts on his life. The political scene created considerable concern amongst the army's generals. Senior naval and air force personnel had joined the Communist Party swelling its ranks under Dr Subandrio's leadership. Considering these problems, it was best not to involve oneself, the Colonel decided.

Rumour had it that the Communist Party would attempt to weaken the Army by convincing the President that only party loyalists should be promoted to senior positions in the services. Their influence had reached into the schools and was evident on billboards and in the press. Seda recognised that the Communists were dangerous. They were dangerous to the nation and they were particularly dangerous to military personnel in positions such as his. Should the President permit their power to infiltrate defence control and policy determination centres, they would succeed in gaining control over the army.

The Timorese shuddered. All those years of study and obedience! These *bangsat* were no better than the blood-sucking Chinese leeches!

Unlike most in his peer group, Nathan Seda really did understand just how acute the problem had become between the Communists and the military in their power struggle during recent years. The President seemed to consider that competition between the two opposing groups was healthy. Seda thought inwardly that *Bung Karno* had lost touch with reality and with the very ideals which had originally brought the Republic together under the red and white flag.

Seda acknowledged that he had to utilise whatever connections he had developed here, at Defence Headquarters, to consolidate his position. He further understood that it was essential to identify himself with the current ABRI leaders who were anti-Communist to avoid possible suspicion of his allegiances. He was convinced that Indonesia's uneasy political climate could easily result in the Communist elements gaining control of the military which would be disastrous for officers of his rank. Being Timorese, he automatically attracted suspicion. Only a handful of non-Javanese would ever make it to the top and with a little skill and a great deal of luck he felt that time would reward him for his patience and loyalty. It was therefore imperative that he maintain his position in HANKAM, avoiding transfer to any other unit where his career could be buried forever, or worse...

The President had seen his war against the Federation of Malaysia as a means of diverting the nation's attention away from the economic and social nightmare created by corrupt and poorly educated leaders. Many of the hierarchy had little better than a primary education and were quite unable to cope with the problems posed by the failing economy. Indonesia's natural resources were mainly undeveloped as the western nations were reluctant to risk their capital in a country whose Communist Party boasted the third largest membership in the world.

The United States and British Commonwealth countries were alarmed when the Indonesian government readily accepted Russian armaments. The CIA often flew missions against the Indonesian forces from Clarke Field in the Philippines. One such mission failed and the American pilot, captured after being shot down, became the charismatic Indonesian President's personal pilot. The British, obliged to provide assistance to the fledgling members of the Commonwealth, prepared for major warfare. RAF Vulcan bombers, armed with atomic warheads, flew regular missions between Darwin and Singapore with their bomb bay doors open over Indonesia.

Australian soldiers served alongside their Malaysian counterparts in the jungles throughout this undeclared war. The Australian public knew little of what was happening as their government smothered almost all attempts by journalists to reveal the facts. Government 'D' notices prevented the release of news which was deemed detrimental to the security of the nation.

Australian SAS troops often carried out cross-border raids into Indonesian-held Irian and Kalimantan, capturing select troops for interrogation purposes and then dispatching them without ceremony. The Royal Australian Navy, whilst on manoeuvres, passed through the Sunda Straits with all hands ready at their battle stations. The fear of Communist hordes swooping down through the archipelago into the land of the Southern Cross was real. Or at least it was made to appear so by the leading politicians of the time.

Poorly trained and suffering low morale, many Indonesian soldiers died fighting against superior and more professionally trained forces. Nevertheless, Dr Soekarno was adamant; the war would continue. And so it did, much to the dismay of both his military commanders and Indonesia's neighbours.

A posting to the '*Konfrontasi*' battalions was considered to be extremely dangerous as the unofficial lists of missing and dead were so unpalatable the figures were never released. A casual observer might be impressed by Indonesia's fine array of weaponry but to a skilled eye, the appalling lack of maintenance was obvious. Sophisticated aircraft and other defence equipment often remained on the ground or broken in warehouses due to the inability of the unskilled personnel to maintain the armaments. Spare parts were lost or misplaced. Although Indonesia had been heavily armed by the Russians, training programs were limited to a select few.

The Communists urged the President to move the military from Java to front line encampments. Their logic was that this would be sufficient to cause the opposing forces to collapse quickly once they recognised the might of the Indonesian military. Dr Subandrio, in concert with his fellow party supporters, urged the President also to consider that this action would bring pressure to bear on those commanders whom they considered were shirking their responsibilities.

The President was easily flattered by Dr Subandrio. As Head of State, Soekarno had himself designated as the Great Leader of the Revolution, President for Life, Chief of the Armed Forces and this self-delusion led him to believe that he would, in the future, lead the Non-Aligned Nations and the New Emerging Forces of the Third World. Soekarno would not heed his army generals when they cautioned him against moving his military support to outposts where they would be unable to support the Java Central Command. The generals were gravely concerned. Deliberate delays were instigated to prevent the main stay of the army's elite forces from being moved away from their direct control.

As a colonel in the Indonesian Intelligence, Headquarters Army Command, Department of Defence, Nathan Seda was privy to national secrets of considerable import. Clandestine meetings were often arranged to permit the exchange of secret memoranda to avoid discovery by the Communists. Reports regarding internal security were often passed, read, then burned.

Seda was not entirely at ease with this responsibility. It rested heavily on his shoulders; however he realised that, correctly used, he could develop considerable power through the accumulation of this sensitive information.

Lightning flashed again, this time followed by a crack of thunder that shook the building. Distracted, he checked his wrist watch, a square shaped Lavina which often opted to stop for no mechanical reason he could understand.

It was time to leave. Seda reflected on his immediate problem with transport then instructed the motor pool not to allocate a replacement vehicle for that evening. He elected to catch a *becak* as the three-wheeled contraptions often succeeded where powered vehicles could not.

Securing his desk, Seda strolled out through the old building into the courtyard, past white helmeted security guards and on to *Jalan Merdeka Utara*. There he beckoned towards the multitude of *becak* drivers who, having sighted the colonel leaving the defence building, edged forward calling out for the fare. He selected one and cautiously climbed aboard.

A Russian-built staff vehicle eased into the courtyard as he departed. The occupants appeared agitated. Probably, thought Seda, from the many stops the vehicle would surely have made in getting through the obstacle course that the congested street had now become.

Buses and trucks blocked traffic as passengers attempted to push their transport, often unsuccessfully, to higher ground. Waves created by the few vehicles which moved through the traffic pushed dirty water perilously close to the top of the *becak's* passenger seat. Seda's trousers became wet causing him to shift to protect the contents of his pockets from the wash. In doing so, he slipped forward and, to his and the driver's dismay, fell sideways into the filthy, inundated street.

"*Aduh, Pak,*" the driver called, his eyes wide, anticipating the angry outburst. "*Sialanlu,*" snapped Seda, pulling himself upright, using the *becak* frame for support.

He succeeded in wading to the other side of the flooded road where the water was shallower, cursing the driver for his stupidity, punctuating the vitriolic outburst with easily identifiable finger and thumb movements, while admonishing himself silently for having lost his balance.

He looked down at his trousers and what he saw angered him even more. They were ripped. His feet were wet and his shoes would take days to dry. He stood silently for a few moments forcing his anger to subside. Remembering the cause of his accident, Seda extracted his wallet along with its soggy contents. Four hundred and fifty wet rupiah notes! Angrily he stared at his identification card and passes. All would require replacement. *Aduh,* he thought, this had been one hell of a day. Resigned to the two kilometre walk and determined not to board another *becak,* Seda headed off in the direction of his quarters, brooding over the bad *karma.*

* * * * * *

The morning summons to report to the director's office had been unexpected. Although Seda was an excellent officer and there was no apparent reason to be alarmed, he still experienced a sense of uneasiness. Despite being self-confident under most circumstances, he knew that this call had to be serious. The director rarely ordered such one-on-one meetings with lieutenant colonels. In fact, Seda had only met the general twice and both occasions were during briefing sessions in the War room. He resisted the temptation to hurry. It would display signs of nervousness.

The First Directorate for Intelligence Operations was at the end of the second wing, secluded in a tight web of security. He approached under the watchful eyes of two KOPASGAT airborne guards. One of them advanced towards him and ushered him directly into an ante-room. The door was closed and locked.

A small desk off to one corner was occupied by a first lieutenant who rose respectfully and offered the Colonel a seat on the hand-carved wooden bench seat. The suite was typical of the decorative carved settees throughout the government offices and, as many a foreign guest had found, they were not designed for long periods of sitting.

The Colonel observed that there were no water stained ceilings here. A hand woven Persian carpet lay spread along side the coffee table upon which had been placed a glass of Java Robusta coffee, covered with the standard aluminium lid to prevent dust and flies from spoiling the cooling thick liquid.

He ignored the offering and continued to pass the time examining the recently printed map which covered half the wall area above the trophy cabinet. The chart indicated that the ocean to the south and west of his country was now named the Indonesian Ocean and that the whole of Borneo and Malaysia bore the same identifying colours as all of the provinces of the Indonesian Republic. Seda resisted the temptation to smile as he was conscious of the young officer's attention.

The General kept him waiting. It was warm in this room. Was it his imagination or did the overhead fan appear to be slowing? He felt the moist droplets forming around his buttocks and then under his arms. The perspiration made him self conscious and a small damp trickle established a line down the centre of his back. He leaned forward, to prevent the sticky drops from saturating his shirt, annoyed that his anxiety would be apparent.

Suddenly the buzzer sounded, startling him. The adjutant rose to his feet to escort him into the general's presence. The large double doors opened into an enormous room. It stretched across ten metres and was at least seven metres deep.

Seda was surprised. He had no idea that such offices were available in the cramped HANKAM complex. He had, in the course of his duties, visited many of the other senior ranking officers' rooms throughout the command but never had he seen an office with such expensive decor. The walls were covered from the floor halfway to the ceilings with polished teak timber panels. The skirting boards were all hand carved as were the joining sections between each panel. The ceiling followed the line of the roof, making the chamber large and impressive, and priceless Dutch colonial lamps were hung in each of the corners. One wall was covered with plaques, pennants and photographs from the general's past military service.

On the opposing wall, a huge Garuda highlighted with gold leaf was positioned overlooking the director's magnificent desk. Directly between its talons, creating an appropriate backdrop to the throne-shaped director's chair, were the words *Bhineka Tunggal Ika*. Unity in Diversity. The Red and White hung on its stand, moving gently to the wisps of artificial breeze blowing from the three, two-horsepower Carrier air-conditioners installed inconspicuously where former windows had been removed.

The imported guest chairs with tanned matching leather seats and chrome tubular steel supports were positioned so that the visitor was obliged to view the general's military memorabilia and photographic record of his achievements. He could feel the authority emanating from the room and its tenant. Seda came to attention directly in front of his superior, saluted smartly, then waited for a response. The door closed softly behind him as the adjutant slipped quietly away.

General Sudomo sat erect in his oversized chair which had been carved to match the front and side panels of the three-metre desk. The impression created was that the man was considerably smaller than normal, perhaps even a dwarf, but Seda knew this not to be the case. He was very aware that it would be dangerous to underestimate the Director, as his reputation for toughness was well known in military circles.

"*Ah Seda*," Sudomo spoke softly, indicating with a gesture for Seda to be seated. He obeyed. An opened cigarette packet had been carefully positioned in the centre of the glass coffee table. He noticed that the General's ribbon collection, displayed prominently on the left side of his chest, had grown since his last intelligence briefing. Seda made it a practice to notice such things. These small yet colourful bands provided considerable information as to the bearer's past and even current movements and activities. In a world of intrigue and power plays it was imperative to have up-to-date knowledge.

For high-ranking officers like the General, the ribbons were literally decorations. At the last count there were just over four hundred generals in the combined army, navy, air and police forces. Both the new decorations were the elite '*Konfrontasi*' ribbons and Seda again felt uneasy at any prospect of his possible posting to an active unit which specialised in border crossings into Malaysia and New Guinea.

Seda had seen intelligence reports before they had been revised for general dissemination. They had indicated that the highly skilled British and Australian troops assisting Malaysia were reducing Indonesia's 'hero squads' to scattered rabble. He had no desire to be a recipient of these distinguished '*Konfrontasi*' ribbons for the majority were awarded posthumously.

"*Kolonel*, I have called you here to discuss a most sensitive intelligence matter," the General firmly announced, then dropping his voice to an almost inaudible level, continued. "*However, there are some grey areas which must be disposed of before your security grading can be upgraded.*" He paused to light a cigarette.

Seda's palms were now very moist. He was staggered. It was what he had dreaded — a posting to a '*Konfrontasi*' unit! He desperately wanted to take one of the cigarettes from the table but knew to do so without one being offered was unthinkable. Instead, he clenched his fists tightly until he could feel the palms aching and then relaxed his grip, permitting the blood to flow freely again.

General Sudomo sat comfortably behind the ornately carved desk observing and enjoying the obvious agitation the Timorese was experiencing. The clinging aroma of the kretek cigarette permeated the stuffy atmosphere within this enormous Javanese sanctum. The general relished the power of his position and had orchestrated the demise of many of his peers from this very office. Now he was one of the few trusted officers close to the President.

He himself claimed to have no political ambitions. He had always believed that the military were the real power and that the day would come when even the over zealous politicians would need the total support of the army to survive their fool-hardy and unworkable efforts to change the inherent character of the peasant class.

Born in the heart of Central Java in a small village not far from the historic Borobudur temple, this son of a peasant farmer had once idolised the man who had become the nation's leader. Politically naive, Sudomo had followed Soekarno's leadership without question, as so many others had over the past twenty years.

He had learned to read at the village *Sekolah Dasar*. He could speak a little of the difficult Dutch language, but preferred communicating in his native dialect, Javanese. Even the national language, *Bahasa Indonesia*, did not flow fluently from his lips.

Although poorly educated, his rapid rise in rank was directly related to his ability to understand and overcome opposition. Prior to receiving his first star he had, in fact, met the President only twice. The first meeting was in Semarang when the *Bapak*, as he was often referred to, visited the local military command to introduce Dr Subandrio's latest innovation, a cadre force of women soldiers. These turned out to be a supply of Sundanese prostitutes for the *Bapak's* private use. These women would follow their leader from town to town ready at all times to provide the President with the creature comforts he so obviously enjoyed when away from the Palace.

At that time there were already rumblings of discontent regarding the President's support for increased Communist activity within the military. The Javanese Generals were secretly concerned that the communists were covertly stripping power from the army as they had succeeded in doing so with the AURI and ALRI leadership.

General Sudomo's second meeting had been in the company of General Nasution who had visited the *Bapak* at his weekend palace in Bogor. Soekarno had remembered his name and from that time Sudomo's star commenced its ascent. Now he headed the army's most secret intelligence bureau, reporting directly to the Chief-of- army- Staff.

His reaction to the young Seda was typically Javanese. Inwardly he despised the minority tribes, while in public he maintained an air of friendliness to all, regardless of their ethnic origins. He had kept Seda on his staff as the man was intelligent and loyal.

General Sudomo leaned back casually, preparing his next words for their greatest impact. The Javanese enjoyed drama. It was an integral part of their cultural make-up. The *Ramayana* saga. The discomfort he was causing the Timorese was most gratifying.

"How long is it since you have seen your brother Albert?" The General asked. The words hung in the air before Seda realised they were discussing his estranged step-brother in Australia.

Seda knew that he should show no signs of nervousness with this man and that his questions should be answered quickly and precisely. A small knot began to form in his stomach as he recalled omitting all reference to his brother in the detailed security information sheet prior to being selected for the Intelligence Corp. A brother, albeit only a stepbrother, who had acquired a criminal record for subversive activities, was not exactly ideal reference material for security clearances, especially in this Corp.

General Sudomo's pleasure increased as he identified the uneasiness evident in the Colonel's posture.

"Well, Kolonel?" he asked.

"Pak 'Domo," Seda commenced using the polite and abbreviated form of the General's name hoping it would ease some of the tension between them. *"It has been many years since he was deported and we were not really brothers."*

The General was completely conversant with the facts surrounding the departure of Albert Seda, his misdemeanours as a student, and Nathan Seda's family. This interview was only a formality. He wanted to appear to be thorough with the Timorese.

The Colonel continued.

"We shared the same mother — I mean my mother married his father after my own father died." He felt flustered having stumbled with the reply. Seda was now embarrassed and angry. His family background was one subject he preferred not to discuss and now yet again it had become an issue in his career.

"As his adik-tiri, I had no influence over him whatsoever General," insisted Seda, anticipating some negative result from his family association with the man. *"I felt that any reference to our family relationship would only have been detrimental to my career and decided to omit all reference to him."* He stared blankly in front of him, resigned to whatever punishment he would receive.

Sudomo, now satisfied that Seda had confirmed his earlier information said, *"It is not necessarily a problem Kolonel."*

"Maaf, Pak 'Domo, I don't understand."

"We will overlook your oversight," the General responded, smiling at his choice of words. *"Your brother has communicated with you recently?"* he asked suddenly before Seda could have the chance to compose himself.

Seda squirmed. Letters usually requesting assistance to forward money to his mother and other family members had arrived from time to time. Surely they would not be aware of this?

"Tidak, Pak 'Domo," he lied. The General's eyes narrowed slightly. He studied his subordinate for what seemed to Seda to be an excruciatingly long time.

'What is this all about?' he wondered, now very concerned as to the direction the meeting had taken. He refrained from speaking further, waiting instead for the senior officer to continue.

"You are instructed to commence communicating with him." Sudomo ordered. *"We feel that he may be of some assistance to us, should you foster the relationship."* Seda was stunned. Surely they were mistaken! What had Albert done to bring himself to their attention? His letters had been brief, courteous, and uninformative. He felt the knot in his stomach return.

"Your brother has achieved a position of confidence with the Australian Government," the Intelligence Director said sharply, focusing on the Colonel's eyes as he spoke. *"He is currently employed as a language teacher for selected government personnel. We feel that his access*

to these people could be of advantage to Indonesia's future."

Seda could not believe his ears. Albert! A position of importance with the Australian Government! It was incomprehensible! He was certain that there had been some mistake. His stepbrother had always been in trouble. How was it possible that he could now be the one suggested by his superior? He thought quickly. Without knowing the General's real purpose he was lost in this discussion. He dare not refuse to assist.

Whether or not Albert's relationship could be cultivated was another consideration. It had been so long since they had last seen each other and even then Seda was happy to see the last of the troublemaker. He did not feel confident of carrying out the orders, remembering the circumstances governing Albert's departure from his homeland.

"You will be required to move your office to a new section created specifically for this task. Your total cooperation is essential to the successful cultivation of Albert Seda. Should you succeed, there will be rewards commensurate with the benefits achieved by your section."

General Sudomo paused ensuring the importance of his words had been absorbed, then continued. *"You are to report directly to me. There is to be a minimum of written communications between your section and others. You will be assisted by two of our former military attaché staff. They are former Siliwangi division soldiers and completely loyal to me."* Seda understood immediately that these two would be the general's watchdogs.

"You are expected to initiate a rapprochement with your brother within the month." The General hesitated before continuing. *"You are being given a position of complete trust. I suggest you go home and consider these things before reporting to this office for further details tomorrow morning."*

Stunned by the sudden change in events and his new instructions, Seda wanted to say something but wasn't quite sure what would be appropriate. He paused for a moment before replying.

"Terima kasih, Pak 'Domo." Seda knew that there was really nothing left to say. He had been dismissed. Standing to attention he saluted and turned to leave.

"Kolonel!" the General called.

Seda turned and his heart sank as he recognised the envelope in the General's hand. It was a letter he had forwarded for Albert some time before. His world began to fragment before his eyes.

The General flicked it across the room towards him. *"No more secrets, Kolonel, do you understand?"*

Seda retrieved the envelope. The contents were missing. He nodded again, dumbly, saluted and fled.

The General sat motionless considering the Timorese Colonel. Convinced that he had made the correct decision he buzzed his adjutant.

"Bapak?" responded the Lieutenant. *"Call Mas Suryo dan Mas Wiryo,"* the General ordered. Immediately, the Lieutenant set about advising the former Military Attachés that the General had demanded their presence. Having completed his calls the young adjutant shuddered involuntarily. He had seen these two watchdogs in action once before.

And they scared the hell out of him.

Chapter 2

Albert Seda and
Stephen Coleman — April 1965

"*Java soldiers, go home! Java soldiers, go home!*" Albert chanted as he marched alongside his friends. "*Come on Didi,*" he called to a classmate who was struggling to carry a poorly inscribed placard as they were jostled. "*Give it to me. I'll carry it for you.*"

"*We'll carry it together,*" his friend responded, moving closer to Albert while raising the sign above the heads of the others.

They continued with the chant and soon their numbers swelled as hundreds of senior school students joined in the demonstration and headed towards the mayor's office.

"*Java soldiers, go home! Java soldiers, go home!*" the crowd yelled in unison as they boldly took their positions directly outside the military official's building. Their spirits were high. They were enjoying the moment and the thrill of challenging the Jakarta officials.

As they continued to chant and call for the Mayor to show his face, the students failed to notice the soldiers move quickly into position. One of the boys threw a rock through the Mayor's front window and within moments others followed with a hail of missiles they had picked up off the road.

A volley of shots cracked through the air over the demonstrator's heads sending the students into a frenzied panic as they broke ranks and ran, knowing that their lives were in danger. A squad of soldiers trained in riot control moved forward quickly with their rifles held out directly in front, the deadly bayonets fixed alongside the muzzle of their weapons. As they were confronted by the mass of youngsters who pushed each other in their attempts to flee, the sharp blades glistened brightly as they moved savagely from side to side cutting through flesh and cloth amidst the screams and cries of disbelief.

When he first heard the shots, Father Douglas was uncertain but when these were followed by the frightening screams which pierced the tranquillity of his small church, the priest knew for certain that the rumours had become fact. The students were demonstrating.

Immediately he feared for them all and crossed himself quickly. They were just children. Foolish children at that, forever challenging the authority of their new colonialists, the Javanese. Father Douglas rose quickly from his knees and ran to the church's side entrance. He opened the heavy teak doors and peered cautiously towards the main street and the incredible noise. He was stunned by the scene before him.

It was as if the streets were engulfed by white, breaking waves as the mass of students ran hysterically, yelling and screaming as they fled from the barrage of bullets and soldiers' bayonets. Two of the youngsters ran towards the church. Suddenly, the staccato sound of automatic fire hammered at his ears and both the students fell to the ground. Father Douglas closed and bolted the church doors.

* * * * * *

Albert Seda had not, at first, been as fortunate as his young stepbrother, Nathan. Bitter since childhood at the injustices that the Javanese soldiers had inflicted on the Timorese, Albert spent considerable time in the company of priests at the local Catholic church. Early on, Father Douglas identified the young man's ability as a student and coached him, helping Albert become fluent in English.

The priest's hopes that Albert might even enter the priesthood were dashed when Albert, involved in the student rally, found himself incarcerated by the local garrison commander on charges of sedition.

Albert had not really planned to attend the group rally. Like many of his friends he was just caught up in the excitement of the moment and the opportunity to protest on behalf of his people. He believed that to be his right. His responsibility.

The students, all teenagers experiencing the first euphoria of knowledge without the benefit of an adult life's exposure to disappointment and frustration, had gathered with placards pointedly aimed at the suffocating economic and military stranglehold the Jakarta-based garrison commanders had imposed on this poor province.

Almost without exception the young boys and girls originated from humble and still struggling rural families whose parents, as had theirs before them, suffered the harsh hand-to-mouth existence of the impoverished farmer. They had seen the soldiers enter their homes demanding and taking whatever they wanted. Forced at gunpoint to stand by silent and helpless, they had witnessed the rape of their mothers, sisters and friends. At least one member of virtually every family in his village had suffered the humiliation and terror of being dragged outside their houses in full public view, where they were stripped, taunted and taken behind the trees where they were abused and left to struggle back home, their spirits broken from the torment and physical violation.

They were angry but they were also naive. Had their parents known of their intent to demonstrate they would have forbidden such a rash and provocative act. There were less than two hundred students in the demonstration. The local garrison duty officer dispatched fifty well-trained troops. The results were devastating. When it was all over four dissidents lay dead. At least another twenty were seriously injured. Only a few of the youths escaped beatings and many just disappeared.

Their parents lived in hope that their children had been taken to another province for indoctrination courses but, in their hearts, they knew that it was unlikely that they would ever see them again. And, of course, they had other and younger children to care for, to protect.

Albert had been fortunate to survive the soldiers' first onslaught. He was knocked unconscious during the first few minutes as the soldiers commenced their methodical and brutal attack. When he awoke, he was shackled and in a dark foul smelling cell with two other detainees. It was then he realised that, although he was lucky to be alive, he had been locked up in the *Lubang Maut*, or Death Hole, underneath the detention cells within the garrison walls.

These fearful cells had been built by Dutch plantation owners. Originally intended to break the spirits of peasants who protested the confiscation of their land, now they were used to deal with

CARTHAGE PUBLIC LIBRARY
CARTHAGE MISSOURI

Timorese freedom fighters — what the Indonesians called political agitators. Now the underground caverns held the children of those who had struggled before them. Now the colonists were Javanese, and they demonstrated their cruelty to excess.

He was beaten repeatedly each morning and, for some perverse reason, always within an hour of being fed the maggot-infested food. He was obliged to urinate and defecate within a one-metre radius of the damp corner to which his right leg was shackled. He was repulsed by the foul smells in the dungeon, suffering nausea and choking convulsions. Soon he sank into despair, punctuated by periods of prayer. Albert had no idea how long he had been detained.

Then one day he was savagely prodded to his feet. A length of rotan was extended towards him at the end of which hung the key for his chains. These he clumsily unshackled, dropping the key into the slime around his feet several times before mastering its use. Even his jailers moved away from their prisoner to avoid the stench. The soldiers forced him to sit in the prison courtyard where he was roughly hosed down to remove the accumulated filth from his incarceration.

He remained silent during this cleansing, his eyes shut tight against the brilliance of the sunlight. He had, Albert later discovered, not been held more than three weeks but he felt as if he had become an old man. Recovery was slow and extremely painful. His spirit was all but broken. His friends had all gone. Only his stepmother cared for him, the others too frightened to admit to his relationship with their family. He spent weeks, sitting quietly alone, living with the fear that the soldiers might return to take him back for further interrogation.

And then, one day, a visitor came. At first he did not know Father Douglas, the blue-eyed priest who had taught him English, but when recognition came, Albert broke down and sobbed uncontrollably. The priest, at his mother's desperate behest, had come to help him escape. Father Douglas had pleaded the young man's case with the local authorities and agreed to arrange to have Albert sent overseas with the Church, should the Commandant arrange his release. Being a man of God did not deter the Father from encouraging the officer to accept a small token of the church's appreciation, without which, Albert's release would have been impossible.

CARTHAGE PUBLIC LIBRARY
CARTHAGE MISSOURI

After a tearful good bye to his family, Albert and the priest took the road to the coast and boarded a fishing boat. It was not until they arrived in Darwin five days later that Albert could really believe that he had escaped and that he was to spend the rest of his life in another country.

Albert was permitted a visa for entry into Australia and commenced studies in Melbourne. Within a year he met a young female staff member in the immigration hostel and fell in love. Two years from the anniversary of his release from prison, Albert Seda married. Immigration officials who investigated his case were satisfied that the union was genuine and subsequently permitted him to stay as a migrant. Initially he obtained casual employment at the hostel, acting as an in-house interpreter.

Three years after his brief detention in the Kupang barracks, Albert was earning a substantial salary teaching Indonesian to Australian diplomats prior to their taking up posts in Jakarta. Father Douglas had been careful to communicate Albert's deep-rooted anti-Soekarno feelings to a friend in government. This made Albert's credentials acceptable and the father's friend then arranged for Albert's security clearance to teach. Suddenly, life was extremely pleasant for the good looking young Timorese.

Albert took advantage of all the opportunities available to him. He eagerly commenced evening classes undertaking a rigorous study schedule. He laboured late into the evenings. He worked through the weekends while others relaxed or played. He was highly motivated.

The young Timorese never forgot the cruel beatings. He stayed away from any involvement with political movements which he associated with too many memories of pain and humiliation. Now he had responsibilities. He was married. He now lived far away from the terror of his childhood and had been given a second chance by God. He would work hard!

Albert's wife, Mary, maintained her position at the hostel, working as an administrative assistant. She was so proud of her handsome husband. She knew Albert worked and studied diligently to ensure their future together although she often wished he would take more time for them to be together.

Mary's father, an Irish immigrant who worked occasionally between dole cheques, despised his dark son-in-law. Like the majority of blue-collar workers in the postwar years, Patrick O'Malley, with a dozen or so beers under his belt, would make the most of any opportunity to parade his prejudices, to sneer at anyone who was not white, Anglo-Saxon and Catholic.

Xenophobia was rife in Australia. Australians feared that waves of yellow-skinned narrow-eyed races would descend upon their Lucky Country and take it all away. The immigration authorities even prevented Asian applicants from gaining entry by introducing a system of discriminatory procedures which presented them with the most appalling obstacles.

Paddy, even when reasonably sober, could not differentiate between the various ethnic groups originating from Asia. Like many other Aussies, he believed that if you looked Asian, you were either a 'bloody Jap' or a 'bloody Chink'. He neither knew nor cared that such derogatory outbursts branded Australians as insecure white racists.

"Bloody yellow Chinese bastards!" Paddy would yell down the saloon bar at this favourite local on Friday nights. "Come down here and seduce our lovely ladies they do, and before you know it the whole bloody country will be overrun by the bastards!"

During the small wedding breakfast organised at the hostel, Paddy, a reluctant guest of honour, drank himself into his usual ugly, inebriated state. Hopelessly confused and adrift from reality, O'Malley, enraged at Albert's impudence in kissing Mary, ordered his new son-in-law outside for a thrashing. Mrs O'Malley, ashamed and embarrassed, attempted to save the party. As she dragged her husband home, he continued yelling and screaming drunken abuse, threatening to feed Albert's testicles to the local shearer's dogs.

Yet Mary loved her father Paddy. She could not understand why he could not appreciate her handsome husband who would one day produce Paddy's first grandchild. Mary's eyes glazed over as she slipped away into one of her frequent daydreams, imagining herself pregnant, and then holding her own baby, nestled calmly between her breasts. Had she realised her father's revulsion at the mere idea of his daughter bearing a half-Asian child, of sullying his family's pure Irish lineage, then Mary might have been a little more circumspect during her father's birthday dinner.

Paddy had invited the local drinking team to help celebrate his fiftieth birthday. If the truth be known, Paddy invited his mates simply because it was traditional for guests to bring more alcohol than they could reasonably expect to consume. O'Malley estimated that the surplus would stock his larder for at least two weeks. The lads were more than aware of Paddy's sensitivities; however they could not resist the temptation nor the opportunity to stir the little Irishman along, to see his nostrils flare with rage.

"Well then, Paddy," Pete Davies commenced, winking in the direction of his drinking associates, "when will we hear the patter of little feet around here?"

"When hell freezes over!" Paddy responded, eyes narrowing a little as the blood pressure rose and his muscles tightened. He did not appreciate this type of talk. Having his daughter married to the Timorese was bad enough; having her procreate with the man would be socially unforgivable!

Mary, unfortunately for all present, happened to overhear the rejoinder and slipped up behind her father, placing her arms around most of his enlarged stomach. "Looks like next year will be a very cold year then dad." Mary insinuated, not realising that she had struck her father straight through the heart in front of all of his drinking mates.

" I will make you a grandfather, yet," Albert added.

There was a hush. The men knew Paddy only too well. He was going to blow, and they did not wish to be on the receiving end of his temper, drunk or sober. His face turned scarlet as his chronically abused heart forced itself into overdrive in line with the adrenalin surge.

O'Malley bellowed with rage. Just once. Then he collapsed. Guests and family alike stood rooted as Paddy's body fell limp to the floor. It was all over in just a few seconds. He had roared once, then died. The ambulance arrived within the half hour and Albert, sensing the mood, left his wife alone with her grief and her emotional family friends.

* * * * * *

Mary and Albert never did begin the family she had hoped for. The guilt of her father's death ruined all chance of Mary and Albert having a normal happy married life. After the funeral the Seda household became quiet. Albert continued his studies, deliberately staying up late to permit Mary the opportunity to go to sleep before he retired.

He was extremely self conscious. He imagined that friends and acquaintances would whisper behind his back regarding his father-in- law's untimely heart attack, saying he was responsible. As months wore on his self confidence returned, and he learned to tolerate the bigoted Australian middle-class attitudes.

He concentrated his energies on his new teaching position. The challenge of preparing the young trainees from the government departments was rewarding and, generally speaking, Albert found the quality of these potential diplomats and consular employees surprisingly high.

He was one of a number of teaching staff selected to train the students in the formal use of the Indonesian language, *Bahasa Indonesia*. He rarely experienced animosity from the students as they identified a genuine willingness on his part to assist. It was this sincerity that enabled him to establish close bonds with them. Albert had found his niche. He was content although his co-workers often remained aloof. He had conditioned himself to ignore the social difficulties which existed between the staff members. Some academics publicly supported full racial integration while secretly concealing their distaste for mixed marriages. Amongst their number there were fathers who cringed at the very thought of their daughters marrying someone like Mary's "Alburp", as Seda was so unkindly referred to when out of earshot.

His recently acquired nick-name stuck when an instructor from the French department grossly embellished an incident which occurred during a formal dinner for the newly appointed finance director. Unaccustomed to the paté, Seda had burped during a lull between speeches and, visibly embarrassed, had then broken wind causing those sitting nearest to pale considerably. Mary had attempted to make light of the matter, but Albert's silence subsequent to the incident indicated all too clearly how deeply sensitive he was to the caustic comments and the general attitude of his fellow teachers. Over a period of time his embarrassment turned to disappointment and, eventually, indifference.

The students continued to warm to Albert. They sensed a sincerity that was not evident with other instructors. He gave his leisure hours to assist them and often ventured into their individual worlds to nourish relationships which soon developed beyond that of teacher and student. Often he would recount his student days in Timor, earning their admiration for his stand against the authorities. He never discussed his internment. This was part of his earlier life's horrors which he attempted to purge from his mind.

The memory could never be completely erased. He resisted the temptation to solicit their sympathy. No, these past nightmares were his, and his alone. Often, when the day's stress prevented Seda from sleeping soundly, the nightmares would recur and he would awaken, screaming, to find himself drenched with perspiration. His nightmares were real; they filled his dreams with the terror of his incarceration in that stinking hell hole in Kupang, the detention centre for subversives.

* * * * * *

Albert was already in his fifth year at the institution. It had grown considerably as a result of Australia's commitment in Vietnam. He taught Malay and Indonesian which, although basically the same languages, were just different enough to warrant separate courses. The 1965 course had commenced two months before, soon after the new year. Twenty students had been accepted from over one thousand applicants. Three were Foreign Affairs officers, and the remainder a mixture from the armed forces and government bodies such as AID and information agencies.

Albert was part of a five member teaching team responsible to the Director of Studies. The director coordinated the language courses and, in turn, reported to the college head, a Defence Department appointee. The courses were designed to produce graduates fluent in the target languages. Very few of the new intake had any previous exposure to the Asian languages as these were not taught in Australian schools.

The *Malay Emergency*, followed by the Indonesian '*Konfrontasi*' movement finally convinced the government of the need to develop an Asian language institution. Premises were located within an existing defence establishment and lecturers were scrounged from wherever they could be found. The need for extensive security inquiries reduced the pool of potential instructors to a small but talented group of men and women who were expected to produce linguists in the incredibly short period of just one year!

Father Douglas had provided the information required to fill in the blanks in Albert Seda's past. Security had been impressed with his anti-Soekarno stand and the priest's recommendations. He was cleared for the low-level security position almost without reservation. There had been some concern that this young man was anti-military; however lengthy discussions with Albert convinced the department that this was not so. It was understood that his animosity was directed at the Indonesian military machine and not the Australian armed forces. Had they persisted, Albert would have admitted that, in fact, he had a deep rooted hatred for all military groups but was realistic enough to realise that he had to say what they wanted to hear.

The Indonesian community in Melbourne was relatively small. Albert avoided his former countrymen and had it not been for an occasional visit to Radio Australia and the presence of two other Indonesian instructors, he would have had no contact at all. Occasionally a letter would arrive from his village. Father Douglas had been sent to Sumatra and his replacement refused to assist to forward correspondence from his family. He felt the sadness the migrant experienced on foreign soil once contact with family is broken. A few requests for funds had managed to survive the inadequacies of the postal system, and these always arrived months after the originator had put pen to paper. It was impractical to send money directly to Indonesia. Rupiah were not available in Melbourne, and Australian currency was unknown and not able to be cashed in Kupang. American dollars would certainly be stolen from the mail and postal notes or cheques were hopeless.

The solution was to entrust cash to a courier, but these opportunities were few and far between. At year's end he would occasionally seek the assistance of graduating students destined for Jakarta. Some would assist, but there were always those who would not, for fear of violating the currency regulations and thereby jeopardising their positions. Once in Jakarta, an embassy official had little difficulty in assisting with such trivial matters.

Albert was reluctant to send money via his stepbrother, Nathan. Occasionally he dispatched letters or small parcels directly to Nathan seeking his assistance as it was unlikely that postal items addressed to a military officer would suffer the same fate as mail bearing a civilian destination. He preferred not to encourage the relationship with Nathan as the Australian Government was unaware of his family association. He was concerned that, as his stepbrother had risen to the rank of colonel, then perhaps they may review his security clearance should the relationship come to light. His earlier declarations would be challenged and he would be dismissed, perhaps even charged, and sent to jail. He was well aware of the Australian paranoia when it came to Asians.

Albert shuddered involuntarily at the thought of being deported. Quickly he dismissed the thought and decided it would not be in his best interests to make further contact with Nathan. He really felt nothing for the man anyway, he justified in his mind. After all, was his brother not one of them now, fighting and killing as the others had done throughout the bloody Revolution? He guessed that Nathan was most probably unaware of Albert's good fortune as previous communications had been formal and uninformative. Nathan had merely been a convenient conduit to Kupang for his remaining family.

Albert rocked his head from side to side, a habit he had developed when alone and deep in thought. He believed that his relationship to Nathan would eventually jeopardise his position, and decided that he would discontinue all communication with his stepbrother; he would write to his family instructing them not to mention him in any of their letters, as an additional precaution. He was aware from a friend in Radio Australia that occasionally incoming mail was opened at the Australian end and not, as it was commonly assumed, by the Indonesian authorities.

Albert did not know of the existence of ASIO.

* * * * * *

Albert turned his attention to the students sitting facing him. Some already showed the strain of these few hard weeks. Others, with a stronger determination, forced themselves along, only to discover the hopelessness of attempting to understand the Asian logic. Every aspect of the languages they were learning seemed to be imbued with underlying alien thought patterns.

A few students actually enjoyed the pressures caused by constant correction, repetition and competition. These were rare, Albert acknowledged, his eyes moving casually from one student to another. There were only two he could identify in that year's intake. They stood out far in front of the rest of the class. Neither had previous language training and neither were members of the military.

Albert was pleased. He did not particularly enjoy devoting his life to teaching soldiers whose ultimate purpose was to kill. Intellectually speaking, he found the civilians who attended these courses far superior to the other students. It was for these reasons that Albert created opportunities to develop closer relationships with the civilians. Albert was wise enough to realise that these were the officers selected for overseas posts who might, in time, provide him with assistance should the requirement arise.

The bell rang announcing the end of the period. Albert's attention returned to his class. The students looked to the instructor who nodded, indicating that time was up. Their expressions reflected the mental fatigue. Written tests often produced this quiet response. As they departed Albert collected the papers and, as it was the end of the school day, he wandered home to the accommodation provided.

* * * * * *

Stephen Coleman rubbed his eyes and immediately wished he hadn't. They felt like sandpaper, irritated by lack of sleep and cigarette smoke. Far too much smoke. He realised that rest was imperative to prepare for the oral test scheduled for later that day. His head ached, the temple pulse exacerbating the pain with a dull throbbing sensation, beating a brittle drum inside his head. He knew that he consumed far too many cigarettes but this was not the time to break the habit.

The course pressure was devastating. Already four students had been removed and they were still only in their first quarter! The course was damn difficult and it was obvious that they were burning people off. They wanted only the best. Previous year's confidential records clearly indicated that most students failed or were removed either early in the course or, surprisingly, during the last days towards graduation.

The latter was a direct result of accumulated pressure for, as the end appeared in sight, some students virtually collapsed with memory loss, unable to remember even the basics of what they had studied through the long and mentally demanding year. The rewards were considerable for those who successfully completed the training. For some, instant promotion, for others a posting overseas with excellent career opportunities.

Coleman lighted another cigarette. Leaning back he viewed his cell-sized quarters. Small, sparse, practical. Almost claustrophobic. The adjacent rooms were occupied by dedicated military types who had considerable difficulty accepting civilians on their courses. He smiled, recollecting the first assembly.

Soldiers marched in, saluting, pivoting and stomping their feet at one another with gusto. The Timorese instructor, expecting students, not toy soldiers, was horrified. Ground rules governing an acceptable standard of conduct were explained. These were received with grunts of disapproval from the army, smiles from the navy and airforce, and cool disdain by the few civilian participants. This obvious contempt for all things military was the hallmark of public servants, which the servicemen found intolerable at the best of times.

Students were given a native name suitable to the language studied. Ranks and service seniority were to be ignored on campus and all were expected to live in the allocated accommodations, separated from family. Quarterly breaks of one week were scheduled. Most students utilised these leave breaks to consolidate their vocabulary while others simply disappeared, escaping the dull monotony of endless study.

Pre-selection for attendance had been announced in the monthly Government Gazette and it was not until the preliminary tests were conducted that Coleman realised that special priority had been given to the training. He observed the number of applicants and was surprised as to the standards demanded for the pre-qualifying examinations.

For some time the Australian intelligence forces had become increasingly alarmed at the accelerated development of military capabilities in some of the neighbouring countries. Indonesia was of particular concern considering it boasted the third-largest Communist party in the world and was well armed with sophisticated weaponry supplied by its Soviet mentors.

The Australian public was deliberately kept uninformed as to size and capability of this immediate threat, as Australian cities were clearly vulnerable to attack from Indonesia's air and sea strike arsenal had their Government been motivated to do so. That was the enigma. The Indonesians never displayed open hostility towards the Australians and yet attacked the very concept of a united Singapore and Malaysia. The two British Commonwealth states had recently formed their own Federation together, and the Australians were unsure of their best course of action.

Defence specialists urged the government to embark on a program which would give greater access, through information collection, to enable more accurate interpretation of the mass of foreign language material made available through Australian embassies and friendly powers. The difficulty lay with the defence sector's inability to source qualified personnel with acceptable security clearances to assist in filling the information vacuum. The decision had been made to provide immediate training in Asian languages to specific branches of the Government ranging from defence to information services.

Coleman was surprised when he was selected for the course. He had studied journalism at college before joining the department, believing at the time that this would provide the opportunity to travel abroad. But it hadn't. As a career it lacked the excitement his contemporaries enjoyed. Life in Canberra had been dull and, more out of boredom than any other motivation, he had applied for language training when the positions were called.

The financial rewards were attractive also, although he believed that few of the applicants were motivated by the considerable salary increases offered. He had not stipulated *Bahasa Indonesia*. The selection committee, having assessed his preliminary aptitude tests, decided that Chinese, Thai and Vietnamese would be too unmanageable due to the difficulties of tonal pronunciation. He had considered their decision and decided that this course was difficult enough. Had he attempted the Thai course there was every possibility that he would already have returned to his desk in Canberra.

The alarm sounded startling Coleman. Five o'clock! He had studied through the night without sleep. He yawned. God how his mouth tasted! His sense of smell was practically nonexistent but he knew the room stank of stale smoke and the partly demolished block of New Zealand cheddar.

He shaved, showered, and dressed quickly. Outside it was light and Coleman left his quarters and walked briskly towards the sea where, to his relief, the tide covered the foul smelling seaweed which could, at low tide, turn even the strongest stomach. He enjoyed these early morning walks.

Coleman reflected on how he had changed over the years. His present success continued to surprise him. He had been a shy and unconfident child! An only child, Stephen Coleman had grown up in an atmosphere filled with intelligent albeit often inebriated debate, and witty but cutting sarcasm, as both his parents were professional people who were often, to Stephen's amusement, fiercely competitive towards each other.

As a young child he experienced an ongoing sense of loneliness. His parents, due to the nature of their work and interests, were basically peripatetic and disliked putting down roots of any kind. They travelled extensively and the inside of his wardrobe doors were lined with post cards from the most exotic places one could imagine. He had spent his adolescent years in boarding school.

At night, when the other boarding students were asleep, he would lie on his bed visualising these faraway places and conjure up some fantasy in his mind to carry him off to those destinations, not necessarily to be with his parents, but to escape the monotony of being a teenager ensconced in the rigid disciplines as determined by the school's masters.

He had been one of those children who could pass through others' lives without being obvious, or apparently special. Not that he had really tried. In fact, although he had the ability, Stephen found the whole idea of attending boarding school relatively boring and conformed just to pass the time. He existed on the periphery of the other students' worlds.

One summer he had the good fortune to spend his holidays in the country at the invitation of another boarding student. He had enjoyed every moment. The host family had gone out of their way to treat him as they would one of their own and in the first week he had already mastered the basics of horse riding and sheep mustering. He had not known until some years later that the two-month holiday had been arranged by his parents. Apparently they had been invited to Banff Springs for the fabulous New Year's Eve formal celebrations and his mother had insisted that she and her husband attend without their child.

Stephen believed that his mother, having never been pregnant prior to his own conception, decided to become so just once for the experience and, once he was born, had decided also that it was not something one should repeat.

He had completed his secondary education without being able to remember even one occasion when either parent attended a prize award evening held by the school. Perhaps, he determined, that was one of the reasons he was not really motivated enough to win, or compete, as there was nobody to encourage his success or applaud his efforts.

University had, at first, been just as unstimulating as school but before the end of his first year he discovered that easy sexual conquests were available to all and he was determined to have his share. This new found confidence with the opposite sex nearly brought about an early end to his tertiary studies.

During the second semester of the following year he was caught in a scandal and his father was obliged to intercede on his behalf in what could have resulted in his premature and permanent departure from the campus. Fortunately the Dean of Students' over endowed and flirtatious wife admitted encouraging his advances and, in the interests of the college and with a little outside pressure, the matter was dropped. Stephen did, however, move from Melbourne to a Sydney campus.

Having completed his formal education at one of the state's finest colleges he felt there was not a great deal left for him to do in the academic sector. His life became directionless. He drifted through the long hot summer holidays surfing, reading and generally just lazily filling in the days alone. His parents, when their complicated schedules permitted, arranged never ending eating and drinking marathons around their pool with stockbrokers, lawyers and what seemed to be an endless list of interstate associates. Stephen should find something to do, they urged.

It was towards the end of February, the summer heat having reached its zenith, when his mother hosted one such reception in their home. Stephen had attempted to avoid attending the party but his mother's insistence obliged him to do so.

It was at this gathering that he first met Mr John Anderson. During the course of the afternoon, as he strolled around the pool stopping occasionally to speak to his parents' guests, he had observed his mother standing close to this charismatic and handsome man. She had called Stephen over to introduce them. He wondered had his father been present, would he have been concerned with the obvious attention his mother lavished on the popular guest, or would his reaction have been one of customary complacency.

Twice Coleman had the opportunity to engage the tall suntanned man in intelligent non-party conversation and to his pleasant surprise, Anderson did not patronise him nor did he avoid conversing with the younger man. They had also discussed the ski slopes of the Snowy Mountains. Stephen had developed his winter skills as a teenager whilst visiting Smiggins and Perisher and both men related their own stories of how they'd had near disasters on those runs, and the exhilaration of speeding down the snow covered slopes alone, challenging the mountain and the elements.

When Anderson had politely inquired as to Stephen's future plans and had discovered that the young man was not only undecided but lacked any direction whatsoever, it was he who suggested, later in the day, that Coleman consider entering government service. At first he considered the idea preposterous. He spent a week recollecting the brief encounter with the intriguing Mr Anderson and then decided to give him a call. Stephen borrowed his mother's Jaguar and drove down to the capital. They met over dinner at the Statesman's Club in Canberra at the request of the older man.

The evening had gone well. So well, Stephen felt as if the meeting was just an extension of the previous week's amicable conversations. He could not remember ever being so at ease with an older person as he had with John Anderson during those moments. It was obvious that his mother's close friend had deliberately gone out of his way to ensure that Stephen was relaxed.

Anderson had talked extensively and Stephen had happily listened, as the man made a lot of sense. Without a great deal of further deliberation he accepted the advice and made a commitment to apply for the position suggested.

He remained for a few days before returning to Sydney. There he stayed just long enough to pack and inform his parents regarding what had transpired as a result of his visit to Canberra. There was practically no discussion regarding his monumental decision although his mother appeared to be pleased. His father's reaction had been surprisingly cool and indifferent. At the time Stephen had shrugged it off and, as he departed, just shook his father's hand without any further exchange or comment, sensing that something had disturbed the man and that it related to his career choice.

Stephen had put his arm around his father's shoulders but there was little response. He seemed distant, almost preoccupied and overly reserved. His father had never really been a demonstrative person. Clever, yes, Stephen had thought but never warm or affectionate towards his son. Stephen could not remember ever kissing the man, even as a child. His mother had fussed as he said goodbye to her. She had held him closely and whispered into his ear, instructing her son to behave himself and phone regularly. It seemed strange. He was only travelling a few hundred kilometres from their home and yet he experienced a strange sensation of one who was embarking on a long journey, away from all that was familiar and loved. He had never experienced this emotion before, not even when he was away at school.

John Anderson used his authority to locate a suitable apartment. These were scarcer than hen's teeth as most were allocated directly according to strict waiting lists. Anderson was good to his word. Within a fortnight Stephen Coleman was accepted into the Department.

Once settled, Stephen easily fell into the routine of government employment. He enjoyed his workplace and the new circle of friends and threw himself into the arduous training schedules. He found the pristine air invigorating but soon discovered that the capital had a downside when the weather warmed. The flies drove him into fits of temper he'd not displayed since his childhood days on the sheep station. They were small and aggressive, attacking the nostrils and ears, causing Canberra's inhabitants to curse the filthy little insects, bred by their own government to consume the larvae of the traditional country fly which infested the rural areas around the capital. Stephen often wondered how the foreign diplomats and their families put up with the pests. Gradually he settled into the new routines and found life satisfactory.

Stephen enjoyed the first months assimilating to the work conditions and also adjusting to the demanding training schedules. He was pleased at having made the decision to enter into the government service. There was so much to learn and the opportunities seemed endless.

He had become concerned during the first weeks however when, for reasons he could not fathom, several of the other Department's officers displayed a coldness towards him, a coldness which was not evident in their behaviour with respect to their other fellow workers. He put it down to a personality clash or basic civil service arrogance and did not dwell on the matter until, during the course of a function at which one of these men having consumed more than was wise, made an offhanded remark that concerned Coleman. He raised the issue with Anderson when next invited to the mountain retreat which now had become a regular monthly excursion.

Stephen was surprised to discover that John Anderson had stood as referee for him. He knew, of course, that Anderson had facilitated his entré into the Department. They agreed that the attitude some of his co-workers displayed was probably resentment at Coleman's swift acceptance into his new position. He acceded to the older man's advice to put what he considered only a minor annoyance out of his mind.

A year passed quickly by which time he found that he was firmly ensconced in the Canberra circuit and continued to spend at least one weekend every month in the quiet of Anderson's hideaway. He still found himself relaxed in the man's company. Apart from the weekends away they met often, dining together and even travelling to Queenstown in New Zealand together for a weekend ski visit. He never tired of listening to John's deep soft resonant voice advise on subjects new to Stephen or lecture him on the idiosyncrasies of bureaucracy in government. He was always attentive to the older man's advice and out of the deep respect he had developed for him had, without hesitation, accepted his urging to transfer to the Information Bureau and broaden his horizons. Except it wasn't really the Information Bureau!

In years to come Coleman would reflect upon his close relationship with Anderson and silently acknowledge that he was not really conscious at the time that it was then he had been recruited, albeit surreptitiously, by the master craftsman. He had entered a new world, sinister and without shape, a world from which few had ever escaped. And now he was back in Melbourne, in literary hell, struggling to stay alive — or at least remain on the course.

Although difficult, the study load suited Coleman's demeanour. He was offered an intellectual challenge and was obliged to

DISCARD

compete as an individual. Initially, during the confusing first days he had questioned his judgment in selecting this training. Critical of his own lack of patience he had, he decided, to persevere and complete the task he'd undertaken. Now, armed with weeks of confidence building results behind him, Coleman applied the necessary self-discipline required to push himself just that little harder, to achieve the level of fluency required to communicate in the alien tongue.

As he strolled towards the soft sounds of the sea and the waves slowly encroached on the narrow strip of the dark sandy foreshore, Stephen's thoughts continued to drift in the early morning hours. He felt tired, but at the same time he experienced a sense of exhilaration at being alive, almost as if he had finally been given some real purpose in life. Stephen found this new energy invigorating. He identified the new motivating forces and was pleased that they were not based on monetary considerations. It would have been relatively easy, he knew, to obtain employment through his parents' connections in a far more lucrative field of endeavour.

The cry of birds overhead interrupted his thoughts. A flock of sea-gulls passed over and Stephen instinctively raised a hand over his head. He stood for a moment observing a small fishing dinghy bobbing up and down a few hundred metres offshore. They were probably from the base, he thought, as it was some distance to a jetty not located within the military surrounds. Coleman stood for a few moments looking out to sea. A figure moved past behind him and called, "*Selamat pagi.*"

Coleman instantly recognised *Pak* Seda, one of his instructors. "*Selamat pagi,*" he responded.

Seda approached, hands in pockets, with the casual gait Asian men have developed throughout the centuries. "*Mau kemana?*" Where are you going? asked the short dark skinned man. Coleman hesitated. He knew he had to select his words precisely as mistakes, even off campus, were remembered when assessing student proficiency.

"*Iseng-iseng saja Pak.*" Just strolling around, sir, he answered. Coleman was pleased he had remembered the phrase. His vocabulary was growing rapidly which increased his confidence.

"*You are up early Koesman.*" Seda observed, using the student's allocated Indonesian name.

"*Yes. I needed the fresh air. Too many of these,*" he replied, indicating the cigarette dangling between his nicotine-stained fingers, his sentences still stiff as one would expect of a new student.

"*Would you like a kretek?*" the teacher offered. Aroma from these cigarettes mixed with clove would permeate every corner of the staff building when Seda smoked. The uninitiated would stand close to a *kretek* smoker only once before discovering that apart from the marijuana grass-like smell, the weed would often explode burning holes in nylon shirts, trousers, or even worse, as had happened one day, to the Director of Studies' sports coat. Seda had almost changed to more orthodox brands after the embarrassing incident.

Coleman flicked his cigarette away before accepting the *Dji Sam Soe*. As he lit it, the taste touched his tongue followed by a cooling sensation of scented smoke flowing into his lungs.

Seda observed the student expecting a response he had often witnessed from inexperienced Indonesian cigarette smokers. When none was evident Seda was pleased and proffered the rest of the packet.

Embarrassed, Coleman refused. "*No, Pak, terima kasih,*" breaking into English, "Thank you, but no. I cannot take your cigarettes as they must be very difficult to obtain here in Australia."

"*Tidak apa apa. It's all right. I buy them from friends who work for Radio Australia. They have plenty. Please. I would be offended if you don't take them.*"

Coleman knew that this was not the case. Asians would not show offence over something so trivial; instantly he felt a warmth for this lonely man who tried so hard to be inconspicuous amongst his peers. Stephen accepted the packet and walked along the beach road, his tiredness forgotten, pleased to be in the company of the Timorese.

"*As a child I used to walk along the beach near my village. I would dream of crossing the ocean to make my fortune and return as wealthy as a king.*"

Seda paused to ensure that he selected words simple enough for the student to understand.

"*In my kampung the people were so poor there was not even one motorbike. We were the neglected island: the forgotten people in Soekarno's dream.*" He turned his head to ensure that his student had under-

59

stood. *"Do you understand, Mas?"*

Coleman had understood but was unsure how he was expected to respond. *"I understand what you are saying but do not understand the ..."* he paused, searching his memory for the correct word. Unable to remember, he resorted to the English substitute, "situation." he added.

"Ah. Yes, for Australians life is relatively simple. What will you do when you have completed the course?"

Coleman felt the thrill of the assumption. He had been reasonably confident of completing the training but this was the first indication, almost confirmation of the possibility from a staff member. *"No doubt I will be sent to Jakarta to assist the Information Bureau there. After two years in the Embassy the government usually sends us back to Canberra where we sit and wait for another opportunity to travel,"* he explained, struggling to find the correct words in his limited vocabulary.

"Perhaps you will have the opportunity to visit my kampung halaman," suggested the guru.

"Insja Allah," Allah permitting, Coleman responded flushing immediately he realised his mistake. He corrected his error with a suitable Christian equivalent and apologised to Albert for his error.

"Tidak apa apa," Albert declared, not wishing that Coleman suffer for his mistake.

The two men walked together each contemplating his own future until the intrusion of the putrid seaweed smell forced their retreat to prepare for the school day.

******

That evening Coleman decided to visit Albert briefly, away from the school, to establish whether or not the teacher would be prepared to offer additional tuition. He believed that, with the assistance of one of the indigenous speakers, colloquial and idiomatic dialogue would be less difficult to deal with once he had completed the course and commenced his tour in Indonesia. The basic syllabus provided only a general introduction to idiomatic terminology as most graduates would, in fact, have little opportunity to actually visit or work in Indonesia. Consequently, those who were fortunate to receive overseas postings would discover to their chagrin, upon arrival in the target language countries, that they would have considerable difficulty with the day-to-day communication.

As he approached the well-kept married quarters, Stephen noticed Albert sitting outside his terraced accommodations. Mary remained inside, apparently preparing the evening meal.

"*Selamat sore, Pak Seda*," Coleman called, pleased with the opportunity to approach the instructor outdoors.

Albert had not seen the young man coming. In fact, he had not been conscious of anything much for the past hour. Startled, he jumped up and prepared to escape from the intruder before recognizing the student on his way up the path. He quickly buried the letter deep into his baggy trousers pocket, then waved, beckoning for Coleman to approach, composing himself as best he could considering the weight of the communique hidden in his trousers.

"*Selamat datang, Mas Koesman. Silahkan masuk.*"

Coleman hesitated, surprised at the initial reaction he had witnessed, then proceeded to address his teacher. "*Maaf mengganggu, Pak,*" he apologised.

"*Come in, come in,*" Seda repeated opening the front door to his bungalow. They entered together. Coleman waited in the guest room while Seda disappeared momentarily, returning with his wife.

"*Selamat sore Njonja Seda,*" Coleman extended his hand to the short homely-faced woman. Her hair was dull red and her skin showed signs of a harsh childhood, perhaps on a farm, the guest concluded.

"Sorry, I do not speak much Indonesian. I leave that to Albert," she explained.

Coleman was amused that Mary showed another of the country's characteristics. Foreign languages were something never spoken and rude if used by others in front of real Aussies!

They sat, talked, and drank strong black coffee. Coleman politely refused the offer to stay for dinner, returning to his room to study. The brief discussion had been rewarding. Seda had agreed to provide the additional instruction Coleman had solicited. Payment had been offered and brushed aside. A schedule was established and both had parted feeling pleased with the arrangements. Seda was particularly pleased that he had been asked. Coleman was delighted that the senior *guru* was personally committed to assisting with the extra-curriculum instruction. Later, as he lay awake, his mind recounted the two meetings with the Timorese that day. Albert's earlier over reaction to being startled now caused Coleman to smile as he recalled the scene as the instructor's behaviour had been almost comical.

Albert Seda also lay awake anxiously contemplating the letter from his brother Nathan. Sleep was impossible. The disguised threats unsettled his stomach. Should some source inform the Australian authorities of Albert's relationship to Nathan, dire consequences would follow for their remaining family in Timor. Tired and agitated the following morning, Albert decided not to attend classes for the day. He had to have time to think, to convince Nathan that it would be impossible for him to do those things that he asked. No, not asked, demanded.

* * * * * *

In the following weeks a further and even more threatening communication arrived and Albert assumed the Asian philosophical approach to Nathan's letters. He decided that he was, after all, of Indonesian heritage and that bore certain responsibilities even though he had not found peace in his country of birth. He had also considered his remaining family in Kupang and the additional hardships they may have to suffer if he refused assistance.

He really had no choice but to submit. He agreed to cooperate and, in so doing, commenced down a parallel path to that of Stephen Coleman, unaware that their respective journeys would eventually twist and turn in opposing directions as each moved forward in search of their own dreams and, perhaps too, their *ajal*.

Their final destiny.

Chapter 3

*Kampung Semawi,
Java — October 1965*

The line extended for kilometres. In some places, the bicycles were four and five abreast as the children free-wheeled down the gentle incline enjoying the lower temperatures and light humidity of the early morning. As they rode, they talked, laughed and flirted, occasionally pedalling, as they coasted down the hill. They were happy, innocent, and eager to get to school.

The girls wore dark skirts, white cotton blouses and thin red scarves knotted loosely below the neckline. The boys wore similar colours, dressed in shorts or trousers, depending on their age, and white short-sleeved shirts without the distinguishing loose tie. The girls held themselves erect, poised like Parisian models, their backs straight, both hands elegantly touching but not gripping the handlebars as they maintained their positions in the column.

Many of the young ladies sported waist length deep black hair. Occasionally, as the bicycles passed under the trees and then out of the thin shadows into the light, the sun's rays would touch the fine long strands causing their well-kept crowns to shine with the care, the brushing and the natural aloe vera applied each evening by their doting mothers before they retired.

Even though their appearance could cause one to think otherwise, these were not wealthy children and they wore sturdy sandals. Some wore white socks but only as an option as these were not a mandatory part of the school uniform. The boys wore an assortment of footwear. Most preferred a sandal not dissimilar to those worn by the girls, but more robust to withstand the perpetual pounding they suffered from the mid-morning and late afternoon breaks when the nearby field became a soccer battlefield.

Occasionally a scooter would pass, and then slow, to permit the driver or passenger to converse with the slower moving two-wheelers. To be privileged with a scooter did not, surprisingly, create peer group animosity as young Indonesians generally applauded others' successes.

Sharing was already a cultural trait well before the Marxist-Leninist philosophies crept into their lives. Thousands of years of cultural development had produced a people who had achieved a special ability to understand the import of preserving their way of life, to appreciate their history and respect their families and, at all costs, to coexist with their neighbours in their restrictive, suffocating dwellings. This same cultural force was also responsible for the occasional but sudden explosions of temper and violence which sometimes caused normally calm souls to run out of control, or run *amok,* often killing at random on a scale not understood in the West. Or at least that was so before militant religious sects eventually gained a foothold in the developed nations.

The road to the school travelled directly through the rich rice fields, the black tar macadam raised several metres above the millions of individually owned *sawah* under cultivation, permitting traffic to pass unhindered. Each plot, some almost unworkably small, would have been farmed by the same family over and over for many generations. Ownership would have passed from father to son throughout the centuries, the unwritten titles rarely questioned or disputed. Often these fields remained as the only real security that these betel nut chewing peasants could really rely upon.

Of course, the occasional dispute would arise as to just how much creepage had taken place when the *padi* fields were worked for it was relatively simple to enlarge ones area by widening the mud retaining walls over a few seasons. The gradual change to the miniature dam wall would go unnoticed as a few centimetres were added here and there until finally, after some years had passed, the plots size could differ in area considerably. If not kept in check, a farmer could conceivably lose land the size of a small suburban front yard over a period of ten or fifteen years.

Coconut groves separated these magnificent green fields from the roads. Flowers grew alongside the pathways and Hibiscus hedges were planted between the small thatched-roof dwellings. The rich volcanic soil provided food for all, including the slow-moving long-horned water buffalo. They were used to till the heavy black mud, producing a bed of fertile ground waiting to be seeded to commence the growing cycle once again. Clumps of banana trees grew in isolated spots throughout the sawah, giving shade for the farmers during the heat of the day. During the wet season, children would casually snap a large banana leaf away from its tree and use the branch as protection from the rainy squalls. To the villagers, the banana and coconut trees were symbolic of protection such as a roof may give, although one would be foolish to sit under the latter without first examining the position of the nuts. Young maidens, when courting, would often say to their lover, '*Please don't use me like a banana leaf, to be thrown away casually when its use is no longer needed!*' But often, even these life giving trees threaten man's handiwork. Overhead telephone and power lines, hanging like huge strands of black spaghetti, were often caught up in the trees or tangled between the supporting poles, further exacerbating the already hopeless state of the power and telephone systems.

Traffic was normally light during the early mornings — not that country town congestion was of any great consequence. Most vehicles were registered to the government offices or military and, although fuel was merely five cents a gallon, mechanical transport was used only when really necessary. Kerosene was even more important, for this was the fuel of the nation. The peasants were dependent on this low grade product for some of their cooking and most of their lighting. Charcoal was, of course, more commonly used in the villages; however the townspeople were developing a preference for the new fuel in their more modern kitchens. The country in general did not appreciate that this essential item on the basic commodities list was heavily subsidized as was most fuel, by the government, although not to the same extent.

These, and other economic problems which continued to plague the Republic, were of little concern to the young students as they peddled their way to their respective schools. They cruised together, chatting, discussing what may have been considered banal nonsense to others but, to them, represented essential dialogue. Their lives were isolated from the faster moving city communities.

There was no television in the village. Some listened to radios, but the majority read their books, read them over and over again until the flimsy paper became so worn that pages often needed to be glued back into place as they were passed on down to younger students. There exuded a sense of pride of achievement as many of these children were the very first in their families to be educated to read and write. Illiterate parents were still obliged to stand before an official whenever a signature was required, and first place their thumbs on the purple pad used for such purposes, before affixing their print on whatever document demanded their identification.

The emphasis on education had, understandably, become a priority with both the cities and rural communities. Kampung Semawi was no different. In this village all of the children went to school. One of the families which struggled even more than the others to achieve this aim now had two of its older offspring well advanced along the educational highway. Both had achieved exemplary results and enjoyed a certain kudos within their small community.

Even the old nasty woman (some said she practised witchcraft!), her head tied in towelling, her lips and toothless mouth bright red from chewing betel nut, would no longer whack them belligerently as she had done when they first raced across the small muddy stretch in front of her shanty in the years before. These days she would giggle like some inebriated soul, squatting still as before, but kinder to the two students whose legs would now only attract a token, but still accurate, flick of the willow branch as they passed.

Bambang and Wanti both knew that the village folk were proud of their achievements. They realized also that in an agrarian state such as theirs, the opportunity for advancement beyond secondary school was practically impossible unless one's family had the funds to pay for the university, or a scholarship provided the necessary access and ongoing financial support.

The column continued to grow as more and more students joined the throng. Several of the older male students moved into position on each side of Wanti. Popular at school with both the faculty and her class mates, Wanti personified the concept of beauty and intelligence. She was well motivated and never failed to achieve a leading position in her class. She was rarely outspoken. Wanti's observers were all in agreement that, given the right opportunities, she would succeed easily in life, even without her obvious intelligence, as her soft beauty was apparent even before she had turned sixteen.

On this day she was being teased by two of her classmates for sitting together with an older boy at school.

"*When are you getting married, 'Ti ?*" The cyclist on her left taunted, using the familiar abbreviated form of her name.

"*Ya, ja, 'Ti,*" enjoined the other, "when's the big day?"

Wanti eased her machine slowly to the left forcing the first lad to reduce his speed placing him then behind the much sought after girl. She feigned ignorance of what they referred to and just smiled, pleased that the school would no doubt be abuzz with gossip concerning her. The boy in question was Sutarmin, a close companion to her brother, Bambang, and he was as handsome as they came, or at least Wanti thought so. The taunting continued as the first boy regained his position, although he was now content just to ride alongside without any response from the girl. Both were happy just to be seen talking to her, accompanying the popular student to school. She had become conscious that recently the boys had begun paying more and more attention to her.

She flicked her head deliberately, causing her glossy hair to move across her back. She knew the effect this would have on her two admirers. Wanti ignored the two alongside as she continued towards the school. Her brother would have arrived already to prepare for those meetings he attended each day, she thought.

Bambang, although an excellent student, was far too outspoken and often hard-nosed about his own opinions. He had leadership qualities and had his own small following of young ladies who would just love to snare the ambitious young Javanese. At the end of that semester he would graduate. Bambang was severely disappointed that he would not be attending university. The resentment he felt was not just for himself but also for Wanti and the others in his disadvantaged family.

Tertiary education was only available to those with the finances or political affiliations which would see them through the arduous five and six-year courses. His family, not unlike most of the others from his class, were poor and, although he knew he should be grateful that he had been given the opportunity to reach as far as he had, Bambang still felt bitter that he was limited by what was effectively his caste. He had discussed this with his best friend, Sutarmin, on many occasions.

'Min had the foresight to anticipate his own funding problems and the year before, despite Bambang's heated objections, joined the Young Communist League, hoping that this would enhance his position when applying for one of the several scholarships the Party provided annually to students at their school.

'Min had been lucky. He had been informed just the day before of his scholarship and upon learning this news he'd grabbed his best friend, lifting his well developed body off the ground, and whooped loudly with excitement.

Bambang was, of course, pleased for his close friend but unhappy with himself when he admitted that the slight pangs of jealousy were real, and not just anger at the system, as Sutarmin's grades were well below his own. His friend had acknowledged the reaction and later that day decided that, although it was too late for Bambang it was not necessarily so for his sister. And so, without discussing the matter with his classmate, Sutarmin went in search of Wanti, finding her sitting with friends gossiping between classes.

As she cycled along she remembered with a wry smile that the meeting was not at all romantic as her girl friends had imagined. Wanti was extremely pleased to have a senior approach her and invite her to walk with him to discuss something, in private. Especially when her girl friends, without exception, thought that the handsome 'Min was unapproachable considering the strong competition from the older ladies in year twelve.

Sutarmin sat her down near the teacher's room under the loudspeakers which blasted forth each morning with what had become a very scratchy recording of the national anthem, *Indonesia Raya*.

He was still shaking with excitement.

"'*Ti*," Sutarmin commenced, "*I have won the scholarship!*"

Wanti's eyes opened wide in disbelief.

"*Bohong!*" she responded, accusing him of gross exaggeration as she knew that only two scholarships were awarded at their school each year and that it would be impossible for him to receive such acknowledgment for his scholastic efforts as 'Min was no academic giant.

"*No, 'Ti, I am not lying. I really did win the scholarship!*" he replied, laughing and taking both her hands in his and squeezing them with affection.

"*How is this possible, 'Min?*" Wanti asked, not entirely convinced that it was true, her doubts giving way to laughter at the wonderful surprise.

"The League, Wanti, the League," he answered hurriedly, his excitement bubbling.

Wanti's reaction was mixed. Her excitement at Sutarmin's good fortune was tempered by the mention of the Communist body responsible for his exuberance. Her mood changed quickly as the ramifications of what might now follow dawned on her and she sat, hands still clasped in his, looking into his eyes.

"I am happy for you 'Min," she said but in her heart she had doubts.

"Wanti," he whispered, *"listen to me. Join the League now, and you too could have the same chance next year. With your excellent grades you would certainly be selected."*

She slowly extracted her hands from his grasp, so as not to offend, then sat smiling at her naive friend. It was not necessary for her to respond, as both knew that what he suggested would be impossible. Her brother's anti-League activities in the Student National Front would exclude her from selection. She would have little chance unless Bambang ceased his damaging activities on campus and even then it would be highly unlikely that the League would be that forgiving. Wanti smiled again and turned to see if her friends were still watching them together.

"I must go now, 'Min." She tried to sound bright. *"I am really very happy for you."* Smiling, she rose and waited for him to leave before returning to her girl friends, all of whom were now giggling together, anxious to discover what had taken place between the couple in private conversation. To their dismay she simply refused to be baited, electing to smile and leave the rest to their vivid adolescent imaginations.

That evening she had discussed Sutarmin's scholarship with Bambang without mentioning that he had encouraged her to consider joining the League. She did not sleep that night and, unknown to her, neither did Bambang. Both deep in thought, their eyes wide awake as they considered their futures, imagining *'what if?'* and the extrapolations of these possibilities and their nebulous consequences.

When morning came neither spoke again of Sutarmin's scholarship. Both realized the doors were permanently closed to them and it would be best to resign themselves to the fact that neither would ever see the inside of the famous university in Jogjakarta, the object of many a student's dreams. Or at least, in their case, certainly not as undergraduates. Neither should have had such grand designs, they knew. They were farmers' children and should therefore contain their ambitions. These serious yet despairing thoughts passed sluggishly through Wanti's mind as she and her group finally arrived at the *Sekolah Menengah Atas*, her high school.

The red dust was their only welcome as they pushed their bicycles into the grounds. There were no gates. There was nothing to steal here. The class rooms were inadequate and the demand for learning was so great that classes were organized on a shift basis so that two full sessions could be run each day. Unfortunately, the same poorly paid teachers were obliged to cover both the morning and the afternoon classes.

* * * * * *

Bambang had mixed emotions when the reports first spread through the school. He, like many of his contemporaries had become instantly excited while many of the other students were just a little frightened and confused. They had gathered together to listen to the *Voice of America* on the short-wave band, quite in violation of the government's ruling regarding foreign broadcasts, when news broke internationally for the first time.

Often the youngsters would use the village head's old cabinet set to listen to the overseas broadcasts. Its valves were always running hot, threatening to destroy the entire apparatus. Foreign pop music was just not available anywhere at that time and the boys (girls were banned from participating as they could never keep a secret) prided themselves on being able to recite the words to such fabulous songs as the Beatles *A Hard Day's Night*. They all, without exception, adored the wonderful music. Life was dull in the village and these clandestine gatherings added untold excitement to their young lives. The *lurah* would leave the boys alone in the care of his son Sutarmin, as he disliked the strange sounds and could not understand what the young men saw in the racket which blasted from his Grundig with its thirty centimetre speakers.

The old Bedford truck and this radio were the prized possessions of the village head — even he couldn't remember how both these antiquated items originally turned up in their village. Not that it really mattered. These items were his, a *warisan*, left to him by his father and no one in the *kampung* questioned their origins nor their use. The villagers would always know when the headman was returning from an outing as, during the dry season clouds of red volcanic dust would trail behind his noisy truck, distinguishing it from the government machines of Soviet manufacture.

When the old man drove down the four kilometres to the sealed highway he would load the truck with children, their parents, and their produce, and a large number of caged chickens for sale at the roadside markets. He was a good man. A simple man. But he was not a Communist.

There was a small foot track from their *kampung* which cut the distance by half to the main road and the outside world. The children took this path when walking as all they had to do was step carefully along the hardened tops of the mud-caked walls separating the paddy fields and, within the hour, they could reach the small market. When the heat was intense, just before the storms which heralded the beginning of the 'Wet', the old man would stop and load the school children, some with their bicycles, up into the remaining space after his trip into town. He knew they would be near to exhaustion, hot and in despair climbing the last few hundred metres over the small knoll and down to their hidden corner of the world. He loved all of the village children and certainly didn't object to their using his wireless.

On this day, as he brought the Bedford to a halt he could see a large number of them, more than usual, crowded outside his hut. Immediately concerned, he approached and heard the intermittent foreign voice fluctuating across the air waves. The radio squawked sending out a signal piercing the young listeners' ears.

They sat silently trying to comprehend the words as the broadcast continued. Only Bambang and Sutarmin, due to their constant use of the radio, were capable of understanding the general gist of the commentator's message. One of their group, frustrated with not understanding the broadcast reached across and moved the large tuning dial throwing the program into another frequency, which happened to be broadcasting music, the oscillating sound waves providing a much distorted Jerry Lee Lewis singing *Shake, Baby Shake*.

The smaller children laughed. Bambang whacked the errant member and quickly re-established the correct frequency. They all sat huddled together, transfixed, as Sutarmin interpreted what he understood from the foreign broadcast. And long after the news was over they continued to sit there in silence, dumbfounded, as Bambang, reality slowly sinking in, glared angrily at his close friend.

The report they had just heard was not specific with detail but the message was very clear. The Indonesian Communist Party had made its move. They were taking over the country's leadership.

******

Bambang, unlike his sister Wanti, was regularly involved in political rallies so he was used to political disturbances. Was it not correct for students to do so, to lead the uninformed village people through to better lives, to attempt to achieve a standard of living that was all but an impossible dream to his *nenek mojang*, his forefathers, under colonial rule?

Ah, the Dutch! Bambang would sit for hours listening to his parents rhetoric recounting the *Revolusi*. Heroic tales of untrained soldiers armed only with bamboo spears fighting the Dutch Army stabbed his heart until he, in chorus with the other children would cry out in unison *'Merdeka!'* 'Freedom!' each time the story gave an opportunity for their participation. Their dislike of the Dutch turned quickly to hate as each tale they heard depicted the horrors and cruelty of the War of Independence, which raged from 1945 until early 1949, and there would be tears on the cheeks of all when they listened to the sad tales of incarceration suffered by *Bung Karno*, their leader.

Bambang was the only male child and consequently cherished dearly by all. Often in trouble, but always forgiven, Bambang managed to survive his mischievous childhood ways, becoming serious with his studies as he entered senior high school. He developed into a handsome young man. Diligent at school, he was regularly selected to accompany the *gurus* when they attended political meetings. Almost without exception they participated in the President's guided democracy policy of NASAKOM - Nationalism, Socialism and Communism.

Wanti was determined to succeed. If nothing else, at least she would be able to escape the potential trap of being obliged to marry while still very young, bearing a multitude of children and remaining in an almost destitute state for the rest of her life.

Although the eldest of the children, she had started school behind her brother. Wanti had no desire to participate in the political groups. Chided by her brother, she would feign interest; however her ambitions lay elsewhere. Wanti's aim was to finish high school and hopefully study a part-time course at a secretarial college. As in most village families, money was almost never seen in their household.

The postwar economy was sluggish due to lack of investment and corruption. Wanti realized early in life that to survive she would need to leave the village and find employment in Solo — perhaps in a *Batik* factory or even in the government service. To achieve this end she would require high grades at school and some political influence in order to be accepted. Competition was enormous on this small island as the population grew dangerously close to sixty million. Her classic face and figure would not burden her and being of Javanese descent was a distinct advantage.

* * * * * *

Wanti placed her bicycle in line with the hundreds of others and moved slowly towards the main school building. That day her first lessons were history and geography. She was pleased with this as Wanti enjoyed the opportunity to daydream of other places and other people. The bell had already been rung loudly, calling the children to their classrooms and she had followed, talking to others as they entered the overcrowded halls.

She had been uneasy during the morning class when rumours spread throughout the school of massive political unrest in the capital, Jakarta. The school was abuzz with excitement. None of the students understood what it all meant to them. Jakarta seemed a far away place, one that only a very few from their village would ever have the opportunity to visit. The previous evening they had listened, mesmerized by the charismatic idol, President Soekarno, as he harangued the masses packed into Freedom Square. Tears were evident — tears of pride and in some instances, fear, as their Great Leader of the Revolution, President for Life, screamed "*Revolusi kita belum selesai!*" Our Revolution is not yet finished! just moments before collapsing on the rostrum witnessed by hundreds of thousands of his faithful followers.

What happened next is history. An extraordinary and significant series of events changed the nation's course and resulted in the deaths of some half a million souls. The children had no idea at the time that they had witnessed the beginning of a very dangerous era which would scar their lives forever. Few would ever forget the events that followed.

Wanti wondered what these rumours would mean to them and their family if the reports were true. She went in search of her brother for reassurance. He would know, she thought, just how serious the rumours were. After all, was not Bambang a popular political activist himself? She hurried through the maze of corridors until finding her brother in the headmaster's office grouped with his classmates and teachers listening to *Radio Republik Indonesia's* broadcast. They were all very quiet, their eyes glued to the speaker fixed to the wall above the President's photograph. A solemn voice made the announcement over and over as throughout the country the people listened in shock.

The President had fallen ill, they heard, and might even be dead! Acting swiftly, Communist elements had initiated action to take control of the country. The capital was in turmoil. There were riots. Armed groups had taken control of the communication centres. A *coup d'etat!*

There was an abrupt, crackling interruption, then the broadcast ceased. The students sat in silence, stunned. Fear gripped them all, immediately. Even this far from the city there would be trouble.

Familiar with political violence, the teachers urged the students to flee the school for the security of their homes. The younger children were ushered out bewildered by the urgency, and soon the whole school was deserted. The inherent ability of the Chinese shopkeepers to identify danger was signalled by the closed and boarded shops. Within minutes, the Chinese had retreated into their houses fearful of retaliation. For whatever historic reason their race always suffered the brunt whenever violence erupted. The simple fact that they were Chinese was usually sufficient to warrant the wrath of rioters and looters.

People everywhere returned to their homes and waited for the unknown to happen, as they knew it would. Electricity was immediately cut off to the villages and, by nightfall, an uneasy quiet descended upon the *kampungs* everywhere, throughout the nation.

The terror had begun.

* * * * * *

In the weeks that followed, life developed a limbo quality for the people of Indonesia. Gangs from the cities gathered to avenge the savage deaths of their country's generals, whose bodies had been grossly mutilated. The Communists were held responsible and so too were the Chinese. None were safe to leave their homes and many were butchered without any comprehension of what their misdeeds may have been. Many groups led by students formed vigilante squads to burn out the Chinese and Communist sympathizers. Totally misguided, these groups, often supported by the military, murdered hundred of thousands of simple farmers whose only wrong was often a matter of simply being related to or merely being acquainted with a Communist follower.

General Sarwo Eddie was misquoted, or misunderstood, when he reportedly stated that the Communists should be driven from the land and their roots torn from the ground and destroyed. Tens of thousands of innocent young children were then slaughtered.

Wanti heard stories of entire villages being razed to the ground and that tens of thousands of innocent young children had been slaughtered. She realized too that Sutarmin's membership in the League and his recent scholarship would just about guarantee him a death sentence unless he could hide. What originally he had thought would be a blessing now amounted to a deadly threat to his life and family. Maybe even the village also, she thought desperately. The country had gone crazy.

Two agonizing weeks passed. Bambang and Wanti were instructed by their parents to visit the neighbouring *kampung*. Word had reached their village that rice stocks had been plundered by marauding gangs, creating shortages throughout the countryside. Without delay, the two eldest children were dispatched to bring their grandparents to safety.

They left quickly and quietly followed the small paths which zig-zagged between the paddy fields and through small streams until Bambang decided to rest close to a tall stand of thick bamboo trees. Neither spoke for fear of being overheard and shortly thereafter they continued with their journey. They were hot and thirsty but knew not to drink from the small streams.

Wanti couldn't understand why she felt so tired. Distressed at having to leave the safety of their village they plodded on, each with thoughts they wished would leave their taunted minds alone. It had never seemed this far before, they thought to themselves. Why is it taking so long to arrive? Were they being watched and would they be safe? They were tormented by fear with every step away from the safety of their own village.

Suddenly Bambang stopped, and Wanti almost slipped down the wet slope to avoid stepping on his heels. She stifled a small cry. Her brother was frozen in his tracks. He opened his mouth to scream but nothing came out.

Lying across the well worn path, half hidden in the grass was an outstretched arm facing upwards, fist clenched. *"Wanti, stop there,"* he hissed.

"What is it Bambang?" she called but her brother merely waved his hand urgently, ordering her to remain still. Slowly he bent down and with both hands cautiously pushed the long grass aside which covered the body. He gasped as his gaze fell on the headless corpse and he released the grass, quickly jumping to his feet, bumping heavily into Wanti.

"What is it?" she shrieked, her view of the body remained blocked by her brother and the tall grass.

"Someone's had an accident," he lied, turning and grabbing her hand, moving quickly away.

Wanti closed her eyes as she was dragged past the grotesque scene, only opening them again as she almost fell on the slippery path. Alarmed, they hurried towards their destination. Three kilometres from their first gruesome discovery they came upon worse horrors. Stacked on the side of their path were more bodies. Some had been young men.

All had been hacked to death with *parangs*.

The quiet terror of death caused Wanti to cry out. They broke into a run, fearful of being caught up in the nightmare of butchery. They slipped as they ran, now urged on by the possibility that they too would be slaughtered, running faster and faster until they fell in total exhaustion together down the slippery slopes into a small deep stream besides a field of near mature corn.

"Bambang. Save me, Oh Tuhan save me!" Wanti screamed as she struggled to claw her way out of the wet muddy bog. She continued to scream while Bambang unsuccessfully attempted to calm

her racking sobs of fear.

"*Djangan panik, Wanti! Don't panic! It will be all right. Our grandparents' village is close by. Be calm, please Wanti, be calm.*" Bambang whispered urgently. He was terrified that they may be heard by violent marauders roaming nearby.

They sat wet, dirty, cold and afraid on the edge of the *ladang*. Bambang held his sister close, whispering soothing words of comfort while his own insides churned with fear. Hours passed and, after what felt like a lifetime, evening fell. But the darkness brought little comfort as Bambang could see the sky ablaze with night fires. He understood the terrible danger they were in. To proceed to the next village would invite certain disaster. To return home would be as dangerous as it was now apparent that the gangs had reached out as far as even the most isolated *kampungs*.

Bambang explained to Wanti that he had decided they should stay where they were until morning. Wanti cried, urging Bambang to take her home, but he refused.

"*We'll sleep here until morning and then the killers should be gone,*" he told her.

"*I don't want to go on Mas, please don't make me go!*" she cried.

Bambang thought for awhile. "*Tomorrow we will return home,*" he promised.

"*Then we don't have to go to Nenek's village?*"

"*No,*" he answered, "*we'll go straight home.*"

She whimpered, trying to choke back the tears, petrified that her sobs would give their position away to the killers out there in the darkness. Exhausted, finally, she fell asleep in her brother's arms until awakened by the sticky damp surrounds and discomfort of the Indonesian outdoors.

* * * * * *

The two children stood exhausted, staring with disbelief at the carnage. Bodies lay twisted grotesquely wherever their murderers had cut them down, their life's blood making curious patterns around their mutilated corpses.

Bambang vomited out of control, his stomach heaving long after it had emptied itself. Wanti had stood in shock, motionless, the full impact shutting down her mind to assist her to cope with the death that lay before her.

Her three sisters lay sprawled in the garden. Beheaded. Her parents had been hacked into pieces now almost unrecognizable as once being human bodies. As she turned, the carnage continued to be evident. Bodies. Everywhere bodies. Over there an infant no more than a few months. What was her name, Elly? Or was it Atun? No, it was not Atun for Wanti could see Elly's body at the base of the brick wall against which she had been thrown. Death had snatched her from the hands of those twisted minds which had slaughtered over three hundred of her fellow villagers in this small *kampung*.

Their world had been destroyed.

Hours passed. Bambang led Wanti into the forest taking whatever food and clothing he could carry. His fear had now been replaced by hate and anger. His first concern was to secure a safe camp until the madness had ended.

As night fell they hid in the *alang-alang*, the long grass offering temporary refuge. They remained there, arms locked together in dread of being discovered until finally, exhaustion overcame fear and they slept.

A bird screeched loudly close by. Bambang awoke, startled. He turned his head slowly observing Wanti. His sister remained undisturbed, almost as if she had ceased breathing, her body was so still. He looked closer, panic rising in his chest. '*Oh Tuhan*,' he thought, '*what if she is dead?*' He raised his right hand to her neck to see if she was still warm. His face twisted in horror as he recognized the disgusting slimy body of the *lintah darah*, the leech, attached to his hand. He jumped to his feet examining the rest of his body.

It was worse than he had feared! The bloodsucking worms covered his body. He moaned and writhed pulling at the disgusting creatures undressing as he wailed. Then he remembered his sister!

"*Wanti! Wanti! Bangun, wake up, quickly!*" he screamed.

Wanti jumped to her brother's command, instantly overcome with fear, expecting to see the killers approaching. Seconds passed before she was sufficiently conscious to identify the reason for her brother's panic. She screamed.

"*Aduh! aduh!*" she wailed pulling at the leeches stuck to her arms.

Hurriedly, they had both stripped, pulling, brushing, occasionally assisting each other until their bodies were free of the terrible sticky animals. They inspected their bodies thoroughly and discovered that there were ticks as well, full now from their bloody diet. They slowly checked again. Their mother had told them that once a tick had entered the body, certain death would follow. Bambang vowed to sleep away from the damp ground in future. Later, he could not coax his sister into bathing in the small *kali*, which flowed nearby, for fear of the slimy creatures.

They stayed in the jungle for several days on the assumption and with the hope that the marauding gangs would have left their district, having already destroyed all of the local kampung settlements. Their village was one of perhaps twenty in the area spanning a radius of some ten kilometres. Wanti wanted to remain hidden a little longer but Bambang had convinced her that they must seek help from the army detachment billeted at *Kampung Kawi* just twenty kilometres to the north.

Wanti had reluctantly agreed, insisting that they cut through the mountain forest to avoid running into the gangs. Her brother felt certain that the murderers would have moved in a direction away from the Army, not wanting to engage a well armed force.

He discovered his error the following day when they almost stumbled into their camp. His fear was so great, Bambang felt his bowels begin to betray him again. He turned, grabbing his sister, and fled, not once looking back to see if they had been detected. They ran for what seemed to be an eternity, oblivious to the direction their legs carried them. They rested. Wanti complained that her feet were tired and sore so Bambang agreed to rest there through the rest of that day. They were hungry, and nearing exhaustion but still they couldn't sleep for fear of being discovered.

Bambang was not to know that this was not just one short spell of terror. Throughout the Archipelago, villages were raided and old scores were settled — the spark which ignited the countryside flared from home to home, village to village, town to town, and island to island until the number of dead blocked waterways and roads, corpses floating far out to sea where passing ships witnessed the bloated bodies by the thousands.

Muslims killed Chinese; Balinese killed Javanese; Sumatrans killed each other; and so the madness continued until one strong man emerged to take the country's helm and correct the savage course it had taken.

The new leader, an unknown, acted quickly and managed to restore order. As the country's leadership had been all but eliminated, General Soeharto assumed full control. He placed President Soekarno under virtual house arrest where he would remain for five years until his death, a hero in disgrace with few remaining followers.

Bambang and Wanti survived the holocaust physically, but spiritually they became just empty shells. They passed from *kampung* to *kampung* begging for food, working when they could until they arrived in Jakarta, destitute. Without identification and, more importantly, a letter certifying their good conduct and non-involvement in the abortive *coup* it was legally impossible to obtain employment. They found shelter on the outskirts of the city amidst thousands of other refugees who were camped along the canals, their homes also destroyed, many having suffered a similar fate to that of the young brother and sister from Kampung Semawi. Within months, their numbers increased until an outbreak of cholera convinced Bambang to risk entering the Capital in search of safety from the disease and constant violence now evident in the growing shanty town.

Slowly they made their way through the outlying areas of Ragunan and Kemang, along the unsurfaced roads until finally they spent the night resting amongst the old tombs in the Pattimura graveyard. The following day they were chased by passing police but managed to escape. Bambang took his sister down to an area behind the Asian Games complex where many thousands were also camped, sleeping at night under the derelict military vehicles that had been unceremoniously dumped there when spare parts had become unavailable. There were many soldiers camped inside the sporting complex and, as Bambang spent time around their billet, some of the younger Javanese soldiers befriended the pair, offering them an occasional meal of rice and vegetables.

As they became more familiar with their surroundings and less intimidated by the size of the city Bambang and Wanti learned to survive. As did another half a million itinerants who had flocked to the capital for safety. Many did not find the security they had hoped for as troops had inundated the city, bullying the terrified inhabitants.

Time passed slowly as the city moved to recover from the

terrifying year of civil war and its aftermath bringing an air of hope to those who had survived the slaughter, starvation and disease. A new government was installed. The years of undeclared war with the Federation of Malaysia and Singapore known only to the Indonesians as '*Konfrontasi*' was declared over and quickly forgotten. The capital's inhabitants breathed a sigh of relief as the Military gradually moved its tanks from the centre of the city to the outskirts and regular police commenced patrolling the suburbs in an effort to reduce crime. Law and order appeared to be restored. The New Order was now completely ensconced and the Chinese reopened their shops.

Life had returned to normal in Indonesia.

Chapter 4

The screaming prisoner curled his body in the foetal position, in terror, pressed hard against the wall, holding his hands at first around his legs and then quickly up before his face to protect his head from the blows. The other prisoner lay groaning on the floor as the interrogator took his knife and swung the bladed weapon with the skill of a butcher, severing the man's left ear and two fingers, cutting the soft bone and tissue with a quick slicing motion of the wrist.

The prisoner remembered being struck. The severity of the blow brought him to his knees as the wind gushed from his lungs. He knew he should have anticipated the elbow to the stomach; *Allah* knows he had learned enough to understand the dangers of silent insolence; the failure to accept total subjugation at the hands of those in command at the detention centre for political detainees.

These guardians of the malcontents, runaways, perpetual troublemakers and other lost souls were hand selected for their unswerving obedience and callousness. Mean and extremely vindictive, they vented their frustrations on the inmates, most of whom were guilty of no greater crime than that of ignorance.

How many times had he already been struck? Twenty? Thirty? The pain was extreme. He dry-heaved momentarily then, agonizingly, dragged himself upright. His eyes were partly glazed but reflected the hate he felt for his new found jailers. His stomach heaved again. More blows. Then more pain followed by a vicious onslaught of kicks to the back and thighs.

To his right were other custodians. He knew there would be no respite should he react to the guards' onslaught. Obedience was the key and one might survive only if perceived to be subservient.

Opposition was for fools and would be counter-productive. He knew this much. He had sufficient experience as an interrogator to appreciate the hopelessness of his situation. God how quickly the transition had occurred!

Another kick. He groaned with the pain. And then another, this time causing him to fall again. He knew that he should not remain on the ground. This would only invite further punishment. His mouth was dry and his mind confused. He knew from the force of the blow that someone had kicked him in the head as he fought to maintain consciousness. Somewhere in the back of his mind he could identify what was happening. He had seen it before. He knew he had seen others struggling in fear, attempting to avoid the inevitable.

But now there was something wrong. He was the prisoner and someone else was delivering the cruel blows! It was a nightmare. Next would come the interrogation. Followed by total submission. He knew. It had been his duty before; in another lifetime. Blood filled his mouth. He was losing consciousness again. Next would come the final interrogation and the ultimate loss of one's self respect as he would be obliged to plead for his life. Total submission. The pain would far exceed the requirement placed on one's honour and he would accept the inevitable. He tried to grimace but his jaw was broken.

Honour! He wanted to scream. What would they know about Honour!

Another dogma instilled during one of those courses — which one was it now, the Code of Conduct or the Interrogation Techniques Course? His chest heaved, convulsed, and finally slowed as he forced his mind to maintain control over his battered body. Then he lost consciousness. His custodians instructed other inmates to drag him through the yards, his boots drawing almost identical snail-like tracks in the ground. The semi-conscious body was dumped unceremoniously on the floor in a solitary cell. Someone doused him with water. The surrounds stank of the previous tenant and those before him, for this was the ultimate in seclusion, and he slowly recognized the hopelessness of his predicament.

The beatings recommenced. He screamed and cursed as he willed his body to maintain consciousness, fighting off the waves of darkness sweeping over his body urging him to surrender, to sleep. He had been observed. The silent figure stood there watching the intense beating, watching every blow delivered as the prisoner's body jumped and bucked, involuntarily spasms twisting the torso, reflecting the excruciating pain as the punishment continued on and on, in one final attempt to break the man's spirit. Occasionally the stranger drew heavily on his cigarette to disguise his own disgust. He had to know if this prisoner could be the man he had searched for: his instrument.

The beatings continued. The punishment was inhuman but he didn't interfere. He had to know. The nauseating stench of the cell was more than offensive. Yet it was not just the accumulated human waste which offended the nostrils.

It was the smell of fear. Of death.

The punishment ceased momentarily. Some minutes passed and the prisoner groaned. Somewhere in the darkness of his mind he thought he heard someone speak. The voice had that deep-throated pitch, the resonance almost soothing as he tried to identify what was being said. His fatigued mind groped for reality. He knew someone was talking about him. Maybe there to do a body count. He raised his head a fraction and was unable to establish whether he was in the cells, or dead, and if the body men were perhaps waiting quietly to take his mortal remains away. He fainted.

Somebody coughed. The prisoner awoke. His surroundings had changed. He was positioned on a chair, his head resting on an old table. The room was poorly lit. A light hung low, perilously close to his face. He opened his eyes, moaned, then passed back into semi-consciousness. The shock of the cold water thrown over his head and neck partially revived his senses. The guards retreated, leaving him to his misery. He collapsed into sleep, exhausted, only to be awakened by the quiet. He had no idea how he had slept but when he moved, the shooting pain signalled that it had not been long enough.

* * * * * *

He was aware of the presence of another in the room. His swollen eyes would not permit clear vision as he squinted in the general direction of the shadow. The silent observer's breathing was the only indication of his presence. The man moved slowly from the dark corner of the interrogation room and, lifting the prisoner's head slightly, observed the broken features, then permitted the beaten skull to fall listlessly back onto the table.

"Your life is in my hands, Major. Do you wish to live or end the suffering now?"

The beaten officer again attempted to lift his head to identify the threatening voice. He cried out in agony as he succeeded in pushing himself up and away from the table. The figure in front of him was blurred. He realized that he had to respond — or die!

"Mati atau hidup, terserah!" he cried out weakly, almost insolently.

As the shadowy figure moved closer the prisoner prepared for the blow which did not come. The intruder observed the beaten body before him and admitted in his own mind that the officer's resilience to punishment had to be admired.

This was the man he wanted! This was the soldier he had to have and control to carry out his demands without question. Without remorse! He had searched the prisons for months, examining the scum imprisoned awaiting their executions for the role they played in the failed *coup d'etat*. For most there would be no time-consuming trial, just interrogation and execution.

He needed a man who had this one's talent. One who had lost everything and yet was prepared to accept an arrangement which would wipe the slate clean, so to speak. He leaned over close to the battered face and spoke quietly to the semi-conscious criminal.

"I will send you for re-indoctrination Major, conditional on your swearing on the Holy Koran that you will serve me faithfully and comply to my every command. Do you understand?"

The Major could barely comprehend the words of his benefactor. He turned his head slowly immediately wishing he hadn't as the pain shot quickly along the side of his bloodied neck and shoulders, signalling him to move his head no further. He looked out through the corner of his half closed left eye, the other now completely useless from the earlier beating. The figure there was difficult to distinguish from the other silhouettes in the interrogation room. The man was in uniform. Too difficult to determine which, in the dim light.

His spirit near broken, the Major accepted it was time to listen to what this stranger had to say. He had finally come to terms with his predicament and understood that he was close to death. He had lost. No doubt all or most of his men would by now have met their *ajal*, or predestined time of death. Although a Communist unit, all of his troops were Moslem by faith. This, unfortunately, would not have saved them from their executioners.

He tried to respond but his voice was hoarse. The visitor moved forward to give him water from the filthy dish. The major gratefully grabbed and gulped before it could be taken away.

"*Sudahlah*," he whispered hoarsely, finally surrendering all remaining resistance.

The shadowy figure moved back quickly to the broken man's side and, with a slow movement so as not to indicate a blow, he placed his gloved hand at the base of the Major's neck and, leaning to within earshot, he whispered his message to the exhausted body in front of him.

"*You will be rehabilitated and then escorted to a special training camp. You will be taught that strict obedience will be required at all times. I will personally keep your arrest and charges file to ensure your loyalty. I have the power to have you returned to this or a similar centre at any time. Should you fail me at any task you are given then you may expect a continuance of what you have suffered here in prison. You are fortunate as I don't believe there are many officers who sympathized with or supported the Communists who have managed to survive the firing squads.*"

"*Terima kasih, Bapak*," was all the broken-spirited soldier could muster.

"*Your name is to be changed. We will find something suitable to fit the records. You are to completely disassociate yourself with your past, family and friends. Is this quite clear to you, Mas?*"

The Major staggered to his feet, grunting with pain. He wanted to stand erect to indicate his acceptance and obedience but he could not.

"*Saya sumpah, Bapak*," he managed, swearing a holy oath.

Colonel Seda smiled as he considered the irony of a Communist army Major now swearing allegiance to a Christian with a Moslem oath. He approached the Major and stood very close examining the subordinate. The badly beaten officer could see, for the first time, the unsmiling features of the taut skinned face, as his benefactor turned and silently departed. A cold shiver caused the soldier to tremble as he collapsed back into the chair. He knew, in that instant, he had only traded one hell for another, as he recognized the look he had identified on the Colonel's face. He had seen

that expression many times before. It was the mask of death.
'*Aduh*,' he moaned inwardly. '*Aduh, I will still surely die!*'

* * * * * *

Seda leaned back in his chair, gripping the report now almost illegible from continuous handling. His face was a mask but inside he was consumed with rage with each review of the document.

It was an interrogation report. The dark smears were dried blood. Unlike the Major that Seda had recruited from prison, this soldier had died, beaten to death for his part in the atrocities listed. He had been a member of a small group of Communists who had seized the opportunity within days of hearing reports that the central government had fallen. They had been trained in Java. They were of Javanese stock. They had opened their cache of Chinese weapons and swept through the Timorese villages executing their ill-prepared plans to seize control and impose themselves as caretakers until one of comrade Aidit's teams could arrive with support.

Hundreds died that day. Many men, many children and, caught in the crossfire, Seda's mother, left for dead by the animals who had burned the village.

He returned the document to his wallet. He could not permit what had happened to interfere with his plans. If anything, his resolve would now be stronger. It was essential, he recognized, that he be patient, regardless of how long it may take. He would use the Major as his instrument. The knuckles on his hands were white as the inner rage was contained.

He would have his revenge, one day.

The Javanese would pay...

Chapter 5

Jakarta — 1966

Somewhere in the back of his head Stephen Coleman could hear the noises. They sounded like people moaning but amplified as if sent to torment him. He believed he was dreaming but on carefully rolling over, knew he wasn't. The waves of nausea struck, making him instantly aware that he was in danger of throwing up. The wailing continued and he slowly came to the realization that it would not go away, even if he phoned downstairs to the reception and asked them politely to turn whatever it was, off.

The nausea prevailed.

He rolled back hoping to compensate for the bilious effect of whatever he'd done the evening before. This obnoxious feeling in his head, stomach and somewhere in the lower reaches of his body, was all too familiar. The bile made an attempt to rise but he fought it back. He had been poisoned, he thought wildly but knew, in reality, that he had overindulged the night before, and was now paying the penalty for his indiscretions. Ill as he now felt, recollections of the previous night's activities flashed through his thoughts.

He could remember being met at the Kemayoran Airport. It was a relatively cool reception which developed into a one night indoctrination attempt by the man who would soon be referred to as his predecessor. Alan someone or another. Alex, that was it! Alex Crockwell. What a nice piece of work he turned out to be.

As dead memory cells were replaced by more active and not so alcoholically influenced ones, pieces of the previous evening's activities began to filter through to his brain and then, with a rush, everything flooded back to him.

He turned around quickly looking for the girl, and seeing no apparent sign of her, attempted to recall his last movements before returning to the Hotel Indonesia. He tried but could not remember. Sitting on the double bed with its hand-woven embroidered bed-cover still not turned down he leaned forward and placed his hands so that they would support his head. He really felt terribly sick.

The basket of welcome fruit, still wrapped in a cellophane cover, sat on the coffee table directly in front of the bed. The card stated something to the effect that the management welcomed him to the hotel and trusted that his stay would be memorable.

The phone rang shrilly, the sharp tones piercing his throbbing head.

"*Selamat pagi, sir, this is your wake up call*," the tinny voice announced.

He raised his arm and peering through one bloodshot eye checked his watch. It read six-thirty. He dimly recollected booking the call for an hour earlier! Again he checked his watch, thanked the operator and pushed himself up into a sitting position.

He got up and the room swam before him. He knew he must get to the bathroom quickly, not through commitment to attend the office on time, on his first day, but more to avoid the inevitable disaster that would occur if he didn't, as he felt that the queasiness surging through his stomach could no longer be ignored.

Coleman headed for the bathroom knowing what was to follow.

He retched.

The heaving convulsions forcing him to his knees as he clung to the chrome grip alongside the bathtub, his head cradled by one arm over the toilet bowl. Minutes passed slowly and Stephen dragged himself upright and stepped into the bathtub, turning the cold faucet on to maximum. Leaning with one arm against the ceramic wall he steadied himself.

He remained in this position, the tropical cold water stinging his body, assisting with the slow recovery process. He then altered the water flow and filled the huge American Standard bath to its brim. He lay still in the bathtub contemplating what would lie ahead on his first full working day in the capital.

He had arrived over the weekend, much to the disgust of the staff delegated to meet and escort him to his hotel. He had completed his customs and immigration checks and identified the embassy official. He was obvious. Alex Crockwell stood alone with his hands clasped behind his back, apparently oblivious to the surrounds.

"Coleman?" he called out, raising one hand, finger pointed in the air as if he was about to hail a taxi.

"Stephen," Coleman answered, lowering both cases and extending his hand.

"Leave those there, the boy will carry them for you," he said and turned, leaving Stephen with no other choice but to follow.

"You couldn't have picked a more difficult time to arrive."

"Sorry?" Coleman called to the disappearing figure, not entirely certain that he was following the right person. The young and pretentious man had not even bothered to introduce himself. Moments later he caught up as the embassy officer had stopped and turned, almost impatiently.

"Put those in the back," Crockwell ordered the driver who had jumped from the Holden and raced around to open the door for the embassy official. Coleman watched without saying anything.

"Thanks for the reception," Stephen offered as they drove away from the dilapidated terminal.

"My turn on duty roster, I'm afraid," Crockwell replied. He then went on to explain that he had missed a wonderful opportunity to spend the weekend away in the mountains but, as Coleman's arrival coincided with these plans, he had to cancel. Stephen was surprised that the embassy officer actually raised the point that personnel movements always seemed to take place on weekends, apparently spoiling some event or other; Canberra really should be more considerate and realize that Indonesia was a difficult post, and should not expect the limited resources of the Embassy staff to sacrifice their own time to meet and escort others, when they should be recharging their batteries.

"I suppose you will want to have a look around later after you've freshened up?" Crockwell asked. The tone of his voice implied that Coleman should refuse the halfhearted invitation and, having enjoyed a few drinks during the eight hour flight, he was tempted to tell the escort officer to get lost and leave him to his own devices. But he didn't.

"Yes," Coleman replied, "it's still early and I would appreciate a quick tour. How about I check in, dump my gear and you show me around for a bit?"

Crockwell was visibly disappointed and sat silently for the rest of the ride to the hotel. Coleman decided he really didn't need the other man's company but would insist just out of bloody-mindedness. Crockwell waited impatiently in the lobby while Coleman slowly showered and changed. Visibly annoyed with having to wait, Crockwell displayed a show of childish temper by snapping at the driver as they left the hotel.

Coleman managed to restrain himself until later in the evening. He remembered enjoying himself in the bar with the women hanging around his neck, when Crockwell again made some comment as to the lateness of the hour.

"Hey!" Coleman had snapped. "Why don't you just piss off then and leave me here?" There had been an argument and, although the temptation was there, Coleman had resisted smacking the other man around the head as he rightfully deserved.

Stephen groaned. Damn! He hadn't even set foot in the office and already there would be at least one person gunning for him!

Slowly he towelled and waited for his body to adjust to the room temperature after the bath. He selected the pin-striped suit with a maroon tie. Conservative enough, he decided.

Venturing down to the expansive lobby Stephen immediately remembered the lingering smell he had identified when first alighting from the aircraft. It hung heavily in the air like the aroma of ageing fruit which was about to turn, and yet there was something about its scent, something exotic, which made one feel that it was a permanent part of the general ambiance.

Coleman viewed the traffic confusion from the hotel foyer. No briefing could have prepared him for the awesome spectacle of Jakarta's traffic crawling around the *Selamat Datang* column located directly outside the Intercontinental Hotel Indonesia. Bedlam would be an appropriate description, Coleman mused.

Thousands of *becaks*, the Indonesian trishaw, congregated at the entrance. He knew that the drivers often lived in these contraptions, earning barely enough each day to purchase a meal of *nasi putih* before collapsing exhausted. They would curl up in the passenger seat, breathing the foul diesel fumes as they slept. Undernourished and prematurely aged, these men would be lucky to live longer than thirty-five years. When they departed, a hundred others would scramble for the opportunity to pump their legs, strain their hearts and finally die, maybe even to die harnessed to their iron monsters, as had so many before them.

Competition was fierce. The city boasted one hundred thousand of these car-scraping, traffic-congesting, back-to-front pedicabs. He would take a ride in one of these *becak* at the weekend, Stephen Coleman decided. Until then, the Embassy had provided him with a light blue air-conditioned Holden, complete with driver.

Driving! Coleman shuddered at the thought. Part of his briefing had been an information sheet describing action to be taken in the event of an incident when driving oneself. The instructions were basic. In the event of involvement in an accident, regardless of the condition of any third parties, the foreign driver was to return immediately to the embassy grounds and report directly to the Consul. To stop and render assistance could result in the driver's immediate departure to a more heavenly highway at the hands of the violent crowds which, within moments, inevitably appeared at the scene of any altercation in the Far East.

Facing him across the roundabout lay the freshly gutted remains of the British Embassy. To his left, the Press Club stood as a reminder of the Asian Games held a few years earlier. The large vacant block adjacent was the site for the new Australian Embassy. A few tanks were still positioned nearby to the new city centre. Troops in battle-dress paraded around stopping vehicles, demanding cigarettes, and generally terrorizing the pedestrian traffic. Billboards once displaying socialistic slogans now featured garish artists' impressions of cowboy and James Bond movies. The government's Police Command had the territorial zones renumbered so that the Jakarta area could be allocated zero zero seven. Jakarta's finest now sported belt buckles, Texas size, with the three numbers blazoned across the front.

Coleman found this desire for Western identification totally in conflict with the paranoia towards imported customs which, he had read, still persisted at senior government levels. Indonesia had severed all diplomatic ties with mainland China, accusing them of precipitating the abortive *coup d'etat*. Hundreds of thousands of Chinese fled the country taking with them the very funds the economy so desperately needed to continue to operate.

The Post Report and other economic data made available prior to his departure were all very negative. Inflation was out of control. The rupiah was devaluing on the black market at a rate of twenty percent each week. American dollars were in great demand. Communications were practically non-existent. The country was on the verge of economic collapse.

Coleman pondered these things. In his capacity as a Second Secretary, Australian News and Information Bureau, his effectiveness would be reduced considerably due to the absence of modern communication facilities. Urgent messages were dispatched by telegram through the PTT which often required several days before delivery could be effected. These difficulties were further exacerbated by the government's inability to provide a constant supply of electricity. The PLN, *Perusahaan Listrik Negara*, often had major power failures for days on end severing communications domestically and internationally. The Embassy provided each of its staff with diesel generator backup systems - essential to the preservation of meat and occasional dairy supplies which managed to survive shipment via the harbour of Tanjung Priok.

Living under these conditions was a demanding task for foreigners. To operate effectively one required patience, cunning and stamina supported by almost unlimited financial reserves to survive the corruption, disease and frustration of day-to-day existence. The older expatriates would caution newcomers with regards to their health.

Disease was rife, ranging from the plague, cholera and all forms of hepatitis, to the more common 'revenge' series of disorders such as the bug, Soekarno's revenge; the bug had successfully permeated Jakarta's drinking supplies. The *Koki*, or cooks' revenge, was a similar bug caused by the unsanitary habits of the domestic staff and it was often the more devastating of the two. And then, of course, there was the frightening venereal wart which expatriate wives claimed was their revenge on unfaithful husbands. These excrescences grew to a huge size and were common amongst Jakarta's one hundred and twenty thousand prostitutes or *kupu-kupu malam*, the night butterflies, as they called themselves.

Coleman had suffered the discomforting after effects from the mandatory series of injections prior to his departure. The gammaglobulin was painful and, disappointingly, had proven ineffective to many who had suffered the long needles. His cholera and typhoid cocktail shots had caused light fevers and swelling during his final weeks in Melbourne.

Albert had been sympathetic but insisted that, even with the added protection of these injections, Coleman should never drink un-boiled water in Indonesia. Asians are often shy and avoid describing ablutionary problems to Westerners. Coleman could now understand Albert's reluctance to describe the filth he now observed before him. The open storm drain which ran east to west under the roundabout towards the hotel was crowded with Java's itinerants. What the foreigners' minds did not wish to comprehend, their senses were obliged to perceive as the sight of *becak* drivers squatting on the edge of the *kali*, defecating alongside women washing their clothes while others bathed, was all too real.

There were no public ablution blocks in Indonesia, this former Dutch and temporary British colony, yet it contained the world's largest Moslem population, which required its followers to clean before each of the five daily prayer periods. Coleman was reminded of his error in using a Moslem supplication during his early days with Albert. The Timorese were Christian and despised the Islamic teachings. He acknowledged his debt to the *guru*. There was no doubt in his mind as to the real reason for his success in studying the language. He had been informed that due to the political crisis in Indonesia his posting was to be effective immediately upon completion of the final examinations. He had excelled. Each evening he had spent hours with Albert and their relationship had quickly grown beyond that of student to *guru*. His vocabulary and style improved in fluency until he felt almost as comfortable in *Bahasa Indonesia* as he was in his own tongue.

Mary never accompanied them whenever they left the campus. Albert would attempt to explain the Asian philosophy by taking Coleman on field trips to farms, where in-situ exposure to agricultural life could be utilized to teach him the more delicate interpretations of idiomatic usage.

"*Never forget, Mas Koesman, Indonesia is and always will be an agrarian state. It is therefore imperative for the complete linguist to first of all understand those things which are of most importance to the people. Europeans have little knowledge of our staple food. Rice. As you have now learned, we use a variety of terms to describe the state of that mystical crop. We do not call it just rice. You may consider me a pedant. I am not.*

Nor am I attempting a lesson in semantics, for rice to Asians is life and life is God's gift to us. It therefore follows that, to a logical Asian mind, rice is a life form with its own soul. You must understand that, for Asians, acceptance of animism is common and is often intertwined with religious philosophy to become one belief. There are no rules governing what man should accept unto himself in terms of personal belief. Those barriers exist only within religious dogma itself."

Coleman had listened intently. In a country as populous as Indonesia, it was obviously a mammoth undertaking to feed the newborn millions each year.

"Do other basic crops command similar respect and therefore name changes from planting to consumption?" he had asked.

"Only some, and not in Indonesia, however I would expect so in China. Those people will eat anything."

The student was now accustomed to the occasional slight directed at the Chinese, for even a Christian Timorese who had grown up in poverty could still be expected to harbour some animosity towards the more affluent members of the community. The Asian staff at the school rarely proffered political opinions nor did they openly cast aspersions on other ethnic groups. Albert's comment was merely indicative of just how close the two had grown. Their time together had been mutually rewarding.

Stephen might have viewed their friendship differently had he known that Albert had forwarded his name to the Chief of Indonesian Intelligence — Nathan Seda. Albert felt satisfied that he had fulfilled his ongoing commitment to Nathan by advising him of students' names, military background, and postings upon course completion. He felt little remorse for these people were occidental and could not begin to understand the orientals' obligation to family. The mere suggestion of threat to his father and family was sufficient motivation for Albert. One is born with a greater loyalty than friendship and this was enforced by his belief, *thou shalt honour thy father and thy mother.*

He did not look on what he had done as disloyalty, but he did not deny that his strengthening bond of friendship with the young Australian tempted him to confide in Stephen.

His predicament had no immediate solution. To divulge his secret to Coleman and trust him not to alert the authorities was too much to demand of any friendship. On the other hand, once in

Jakarta, his friend could convince Nathan of Albert's impossible position. These alternatives frequently crossed Albert's mind; however he feared that an officer such as Coleman would be obliged to inform his superiors if he became aware of Albert's extra curricular activities. He had, wisely, discarded the idea.

They had parted at the end of the course with feelings of mutual affection and respect and, as Stephen had bid his farewells, Albert immediately felt the void of loneliness in which he was left. In the months that followed they had not communicated. Both had been too preoccupied with the demands placed on their lives during that time.

Coleman's fond memories of Albert were abruptly interrupted as he identified the CD-18 number plates on the Holden. The driver ran around the vehicle and opened the door before he could do so for himself.

"*Selamat pagi, tuan,*" Achmad, the smiling Sundanese driver greeted him.

"*Selamat pagi, Mas,*" responded the Australian, much to the surprise of Achmad.

"*Tuan bisa mengerti Bahasa Indonesia?*" Achmad inquired, amazed at Coleman's grasp of the language.

"*Bisa saja,*" Coleman replied.

The driver sat quietly concentrating on his driving. He was pleased that he had been sent to meet the new *tuan*. None of the other drivers would believe this when he told them. A new *tuan* who could already speak their language! Surely he must have lived here before. Ah, decided Achmad, then of course he could be Dutch and just pretending to be Australian. Achmad decided to scrutinize the newcomer to look for visible signs of his being Dutch.

Not that Achmad would know for he had never seen one of the former colonists. He was born during the Japanese occupation and the Dutch never returned to his province after the war. Those who had stayed on after independence left when Soekarno annexed West Irian in the early sixties.

Coleman could see that Achmad was not concentrating on his driving as well as he should. Instead, his small brown eyes darted continuously to and from the rear vision mirror observing the *tuan*. What for, Coleman could not fathom. They continued in silence for the short drive to Cikini where the Embassy building stood, set back from the railway some seventy-five metres. Coleman's heart sank.

The building was the obvious remnants of some colonial family mansion built in the latter part of the last century. To some it would have antique charm. To others, who knew that the ageing exterior often indicated a complete state of interior ruin, such dwellings were best demolished.

Alex Crockwell, the embassy officer who had been delegated the task of meeting him at the Kemayoran airport the previous evening had not discussed working conditions in the Embassy nor had he mentioned the poor state of the premises. Coleman assumed that it was not an oversight as the man most probably considered the dilapidated building's appearance romantic.

He was not unhappy that Crockwell would leave as soon as their hand-over was completed. Stephen disliked the petty, almost officious character, as he had seen many like him during his stay in the capital. He knew that there were many small-minded bureaucrats whose relatively unimportant positions provided the breeding ground for their moody dispositions and deep-rooted animosity for those who had real power.

Achmad the driver left the engine running as he raced around to open the *tuan's* door. Stephen adjusted his suit and started up the steps admiring the magnificent *beringin* tree to the right. The highly polished brass plate affixed to the small roman column on the right announced that they were entering the Australian Embassy. Coleman thanked his driver and entered the foyer, surprised at the apparent lack of security. He was relieved to observe that the structure had been air-conditioned with large banks of window units, each humming its way through a surprising range of mechanical noises, as the power fluctuated through lows and peaks that would have destroyed lesser machines.

"Ah, there you are old chap." a voice boomed from the other end of the reception area causing Stephen to turn quickly, immediately wishing he hadn't. The sharp stabbing pain near his temples returned with a vengeance. "Welcome, welcome," the rotund figure continued, extending both hands as he waddled towards the newcomer. Coleman thought the man looked like some giant duck.

"Have a good trip, did we? Are they looking after you at the *Ha Ee*?"

Stephen was to learn later that this sound like a banshee wail was the abbreviated form for the Hotel Indonesia and that not knowing so identified one immediately as new blood in town.

"My name is Geoffrey Dickson, Dicky to my friends, and I am the Consul in this fine establishment. You, of course, must be Stephen Coleman!"

Stephen smiled and immediately relaxed at the warmth of the man.

"Yes, and thank you Mr Dickson, Stephen Coleman is correct," he said extending his hand to those of the Consul.

"Dicky, man, Dicky," he intoned, taking Stephen's right hand between both of his, pumping ceremoniously and beaming sincerely.

"I will take you around this fine establishment and introduce you to its erstwhile tenants," the jovial Consul announced, sounding more and more like Robert Moreley.

"That's very kind of you, er, Dicky," Stephen responded, his left arm now under the control of the surprisingly strong grip of his escort.

"No need to worry about registration and all of that nonsense right now, old chap, you will have ample time to complete the formalities tomorrow. Come along now," he ordered, almost lifting the taller man off the ground with a sudden spurt of speed Stephen would not believed him capable of making.

"This is Bobby; he is the Assistant Consul. Totally superfluous in my opinion but the Post staffing requirements demand that his position be filled even though he has less than nothing to do," he said, his twinkling eyes and trace of a smile showing that he was not serious. "Bobby, say hello to our newest addition, Stephen Coleman."

The junior stood with an outstretched hand while removing his glasses for the introduction.

"Robert, Robert Thornton. Welcome to Dicky's Den," he said. The emphasis on the Consul's name indicated that this part of the complex really did belong to the fat career civil servant.

"Thanks, Robert, look forward to having a chat with you later. Maybe you can help me unscramble some of my advances and docs. Okay?"

"That's what we're here for, mate, that's what we're here for.

Come back when you're settled and we'll have a look at what you've got," with which Bobby sat down again and resumed his examination of the long list of financials in front of him.

They continued on through a lengthy corridor, down the centre of which was a length of thick wine red carpet, held in place by highly polished brass strips.

"You must close your eyes now, my dear," Dicky joked, as he extracted a large ring of keys from his back pocket attached to which was a chain tied carefully to his belt.

The door was unlocked, and again Stephen was speedily lifted off his feet by the Consul as he ushered his new man inside, Dicky ceremoniously re-locked the doors with a double turn of the strange looking keys. Stephen was surprised, as all that was visible was another corridor. He had expected something quite different, not sure exactly what, but certainly not just corridors! Dicky increased his pace and Stephen was a little troubled by Dicky's vice-like grip, which had remained on his arm since they were outside in the foyer.

"Won't be long now," he said, and suddenly propped before pushing at the wall between photographs of Her Royal Highness and Sir Robert Menzies.

Stephen was mystified. Why was there no handle on this door that had been made to appear to be part of the wall? He didn't ask. They entered another corridor, and now Stephen began to feel as if Dicky was playing some practical joke on him, a common trick back home when someone commenced their first day in a new job. Dicky sensed the younger man's resistance to continue and moved his grip further up Stephen's arm closer to his shoulder, without reducing his incredible speed.

"Ah, here we are," he announced, coming to the end of the corridor and opening yet another door with one of his countless number of keys. He pushed the door ajar, gestured with his left hand and, with a slight mocking bow, indicated that the newcomer should enter. Stephen did so, amused by his escort's antics.

They had entered the second level of security. The first had not been obvious but did, in fact, include the reception and the entire consulate area. Systems had been put in place to ensure the safety of the personnel and the security of the embassy's contents; however, these were deliberately not evident to the eye of the casual visitor. There were six or seven offices directly off to his left as he had entered, the upper sections of their partitioning constructed with glass to permit visual contact between the offices while affording soundproof cubicles.

"Why all of the subterfuge, Dicky?" he asked, not yet comfortable with the first name basis this man had insisted apon.

"Riots, my man, riots," he answered as if Coleman would automatically understand, but before he had the opportunity to delve into the idiosyncrasies of the passages with their strange access, Dicky was already opening the doors to the cubicles and introducing him to the officers at their desks.

"This is David, and that empty seat belongs to Alex Crockwell," he indicated with another wave of his hand. "They are with the remnants of the Colombo Plan section and assist with Australian aid and information. I believe you have already met Alex. Where is Alex, David?" he asked, lips pursed not expecting more than a token response, and then deciding he would answer his own question.

"Of course," he exclaimed, snapping his fingers, "you have already met our Alex. He was rostered as the duty officer to pick you up from the airport. I trust he took good care of you?"

"Yes, thanks Dicky, I certainly appreciated being met and assisted with the hotel check-in," he lied, but somehow feeling that this man already knew more about Crockwell's attitude than he let on.

The introductions continued as they passed from office to office, most offering no more than a cursory polite 'welcome' and displaying impatience at wanting to return to whatever they were engrossed in doing before being interrupted by the gregarious Consul.

"Well, that's about it for here. Except, of course, your desk, which is over there next to the First Secretary's. You can have Alex's when he leaves. Bit cramped here, I'm afraid, but you'll soon get used to the hang of things and once the new Embassy is built then we won't have these problems of space, will we?"

"Where are the Military Attachés' offices?" Coleman asked.

The Consul snapped his head ever so quickly back and his eyes narrowed considerably. "We will come to that shortly," he answered, as if miffed.

Coleman immediately regretted his question. He should have

remembered that the consulate section had limited security access and this had always been a bone of contention between the diplomatic service and consular offices since the first overseas emissaries were sent from country to country eons ago.

Consular officers were basically there to care for the citizens of the country they represented, whereas the main body of the Embassy housed not only Aid and Trade offices, but also sensitive sections such as the Military Attachés representing army, navy, and air force contingents. Even Federal Police sometimes maintained a presence as part of the international effort to prevent the flow of drugs from country to country.

The Ambassador, of course, as formal etiquette required, was equated to the rank of a Four-Star General in the host country. His authority was final. This is why the position was designated Ambassador, Extraordinary and Plenipotentiary. The Military Attachés naturally resented having to report to a civilian who probably did not understand their world of armaments and fighting, and often the mood during briefings reflected these differences.

When the need for the first Ambassadors became apparent more than a millennium before, they were sent as emissaries bearing gifts, offering peace and goodwill. They were trade representatives, not political officers. Somehow the two became confused as one, and this made it necessary for Ambassadors to carefully juggle the needs of both their country's merchant houses and the militant forces waiting impatiently behind them.

"Another officer will take you through," Dicky pouted, leaving the surprised Coleman uncomfortable, standing alone not quite sure of what he should do next.

As the door was pulled tightly closed by the departing Consul (if he could have slammed it, he would have happily done so!) another man appeared through yet another access adjacent to the last cubicle.

"Coleman?" was all he said, holding the door slightly ajar assuming the gesture was sufficient for him to follow.

"Yes," was all he had the opportunity to say moving quickly to follow the man with the serious face.

He stepped inside and once again he heard the familiar click of another exit being locked behind him.

"I'm Peter Cornish," the man stated, not extending his hand

very far from his body.

"Stephen," he responded. His surname would surely be known in here.

"Okay, Stephen, let's go. I'll introduce you around. Hope you smoke, everyone here does and there's one hell of a lot of pressure on right now."

Coleman nodded, quickly evaluating what he saw.

There were five Australians present. Two were women. The outer section was relatively small. It was effectively a barrier. Keys were required to pass through the mini-reception which consisted of an observer's window so that the inner-sanctum officers could identify the visitors without their being aware that they were being observed.

Past the double locked security door and to the right were a number of telex machines. All clattered away, out of synch with each other, creating a staggering amount of mechanical noise as they force-fed themselves information that had been retyped and converted through the deciphering monsters buried further inside, locked away from the scrutiny of even these operatives.

He passed several desks and continued down through a maze of filing cabinets into an area which housed two large refrigerators and an electric stove. Stacked to the ceiling on both sides of this walled-off section were cases of malt whisky, Jack Daniels Bourbon, Gordon's Gin and Bacardi Rum. There were no soft drinks or sodas evident.

Squeezed into this already tight area was a desk on which a new Remington blazed away at unbelievable speed, its extended carriage holding oversized pages unlike anything Coleman had seen before. The young woman operating the machine, a desk officer, momentarily looked up and smiled before returning her attention to whatever it was at hand that demanded her full attention.

"This is Margaret. She knows who you are. Margaret is the senior secretary in this section," he said, his voice almost monotone. "This is the First Secretary's office."

Coleman followed him into a cramped twelve-square-metre box. The desk, small as it was, carried more paper than Stephen believed possible. He looked around and asked, "Where is the First Secretary?" raising his voice more than he wanted, out of nervousness.

"That's me. I'm the man," Cornish answered, almost impatiently, then continued, "and you didn't actually get off to a good start in this city did you?" he snapped, gesturing to Coleman to sit on the typist's chair, which doubled for guests, rare as they were in here.

Coleman responded, surprised, "What the hell do you mean?"

The other man had by now taken his position behind the mound of files and, swivelling on his chair, lit a cigarette without offering one to his visitor, then swung back and hit the small cleared space over the blotter with his open hand.

"What the hell do I mean?" he shouted, then repeated himself, "What the hell do I mean? For Chrissakes, you haven't been in town more than twenty-four hours and already you've been out humping around with this lot!"

Stephen was stunned. Cornish didn't even bother closing his door as he continued.

"You young bastards come up here, full of your own shit, and forget everything you've been taught as soon as some tart opens your fly!" He flicked the imaginary ash onto the floor. "What's more, weren't you bloody well briefed by that little cock-sucker Crockwell when he picked you up from the flaming airport?" he demanded.

"No," Stephen stammered, "he didn't brief me on a damn thing except the fact he would rather be away for the bloody weekend than have to escort someone from the airport."

Anger now pumping the necessary amount of adrenalin, he continued. "Who the fuck are you to get on my case anyway?" he demanded, his hackles rising as he started to move out of his seat; aware that his temper had taken control of his better judgment but did not care, as his head ached, his stomach was in turmoil and now he was faced with some sanctimonious bastard who was having a bad day and quite obviously prepared to take it out on the new boy. It was not lost on Stephen that part of his response was in retaliation to being reprimanded within earshot of the young woman just outside the Secretary's door.

Suddenly, he was determined. 'If this arsehole wants to get his jollies off berating others within earshot of his staff then he can find someone else to take a shot at, and now!' he decided. He leaped to his feet and started to leave the office, when the secretary outside leaned across and closed the door brusquely, not even giving him a second look.

"Get back here, Coleman!" the voice barked. "Sit down and shut up." He was about to respond when Cornish raised his open palm and glared at the newcomer not to talk. "Just shut up and listen," he said.

Shaking with anger Stephen turned and glared at the First Secretary who was standing behind his desk, his anger obvious. Moments passed. He shook his head in disgust and returned to the seat.

"I am sick to death of seeing you young upstarts coming up here and carrying on as if you were the proverbial gift to whatever it is these days. You have only been here two days and already you are in shit up to your eyeballs."

Coleman sat still, listening partly out of shock and partly also because he was captivated by this man's performance.

"What the hell," the First Secretary continued and then, with a sigh of exasperation, pulled a cigarette from the box of Rothman filters and offered the packet to his new assistant. "Man, did I cop a bollocking because of you when I came in this morning," he said, his voice having dropped its venom. "Ten minutes with the boys out the back threatening to down grade our security in this section did not, I assure you young Coleman, offer the best start to my day!" He leaned back in the chair, placed his hands behind his neck and, with the cigarette still hanging from the side of his mouth, blew smoke from the other side contemptuously. "They will want to see you in fifteen minutes so I guess we'd best get on with the rest of the introductions."

Stephen still sat there, stunned. He didn't even know what the hell he had done but decided to wait for the 'boys out the back' to enlighten him as the atmosphere in the room was still hostile.

"Okay, thanks," he offered, "sorry about the outburst."

The older officer stared directly at his assistant's eyes for what seemed an eternity before unclasping his hands and leaning across the desk. He held his hand out which Stephen readily grasped, relieved that the bumpy start had a chance of being overcome. It was only then that it also dawned on Stephen that this man either had two offices or he had misheard Dicky point out the First Secretary's desk in the adjacent section. He was about to ask when there was a brief knock, the door opened and, not waiting for permission to enter, Margaret stuck her head into the room and said, "Time to move, boss, the animals need feeding," with which she left the door ajar and Cornish beckoned to Coleman to follow.

Turning to the others sitting around the larger office he said, "Listen up, everyone, this is Stephen Coleman. He will be on our team but will be seated outside until we can come to some other arrangements. He's coming with me now to the zoo so don't raid my stocks while I'm away!" with which he half waved while there were audible responses such as 'Hi, Steve' and 'Welcome, mate', but the one which caused him to be even more curious than ever was the girl's voice as she called back to her boss. "The animals sound hungry boss, better tell Stephen, to keep his hands in his pockets!" which attracted several guffaws from the men.

He followed his new superior back through the maze of doors and corridors towards the reception and consulate offices. Leading off in another direction from the area he had just visited was yet another passageway which led into a small guest area containing a number of chairs, coffee tables and book racks, creating an atmosphere not dissimilar to that of a dentist's or doctor's reception. There was a buzzer positioned at almost eye level above which the instructions advised those requiring to enter need only to push the button twice. They did so and were ushered into an area which contained at least a dozen offices, each tagged with the occupant's name, rank and official position, and a warning that access was strictly for authorized personnel only.

Stephen was taken around the outer office first and introduced to the three non-commissioned officers who acted as personal assistants to each of the three Military Attachés. He was then taken in to meet the attachés, one by one. He observed that all desks had been cleared of files and loose documents.

There was one remaining office apart from the others which had no designated name or any other information to identify the occupant. Only the warning regarding unauthorized entry was evident on the door. Peter Cornish knocked and waited. When the door was finally opened, the tall man extended his hand to the surprised Coleman.

"Welcome to the Zoo," said a smiling John Anderson.

* * * * * *

During the following days he met most of the remaining members of the embassy staff. Their reception was warm and Stephen was amused to discover that he was the only fluent Indonesian speaking Australian in the Embassy. Most of the others had acquired a smattering of what sounded to Coleman's ear to be basic kitchen pidgin. However, he reminded himself not to be overly critical as he understood only too well the problems these Australians would have experienced taking up temporary residence in a country where even most of the local inhabitants used their national language poorly, not to mention the absence of spoken English.

Where possible the Australian Embassy had purchased or rented houses in adjacent suburbs. He had not expected a palace neither had be been provided with one. *Jalan Sidoardjo*, Number Two, consisted of a one bedroom apartment-sized home surrounded by high brick and bamboo walls. The sliding iron gate was so heavy that the *jaga* appeared close to rupturing something each time he was required to provide access to the garage. The previous tenant had apparently used only embassy hire vehicles and was not particularly concerned with security. Previous guests were obliged to park their cars outside where there should have been a curb had the government of Jakarta both understood the necessity for such conveniences and, of course, the funding to build such infrastructure.

The area where he was now domiciled was known as Menteng. The homes were all of Dutch vintage and desperately in need of care. Lawns were practically non-existent as servants could never bring themselves to understand the reasoning for growing grass around one's house, cutting it regularly then throwing the cuttings away. You could not eat it and the effort in maintaining fine grass in the tropics was excessive. As a result, houses in Jakarta rarely had lawns but, instead, cleanly swept areas of dirt which, when the *tuan* was away, always managed to double-up as a badminton court.

Coleman inherited three servants. This did not include the *jaga* whose basic function was to provide security around the quarters. As the driver carried his suitcases into the house the servants ran around bowing and wishing him welcome. They had already heard of his linguistic ability. Surely life would be much easier with this new *tuan* who could actually speak to them avoiding the confusion which reigned with the previous tenant! He spoke to them for a few minutes and then set about familiarizing himself with the house. The *jaga*, an East Javanese, presented poorly. His demeanour was arrogant and Coleman identified the product of too close an association between employer and employee. Several questions to the cook confirmed his suspicions. The previous *tuan* had been dependent on the *jaga* for his girl supply and often shared his liquor with the man.

Stephen discharged him immediately to the dismay of the other servants. A replacement was found within the hour.

Another problem was the fasting period. He had arrived the week the religious observance had commenced and was now well into the *Ramadhan* cycle. Although the majority of Indonesia's Moslems commence the fast together, very few manage to continue for more than a few days. The general lethargy in the workplace becomes impossible to deal with by the end of the second week, at which time tempers have a tendency to become more volatile than usual.

As *tuan* of the house, his responsibility was to ensure that when the fasting period ended and the celebrations had commenced his staff would each have a set of new clothes and an additional ration of one month's rice, or *beras*, as it is called before cooking. He was politely informed by the cook that *tuan* should give them sufficient funds that day in order that they have adequate time to instruct the tailor to sew the new clothes.

He agreed and immediately there were requests for loans, holidays and salary increases by all. Coleman suggested that they were overdoing their demands and reminded them of the *jaga* who had been replaced. *Koki* agreed that the others had been greedy and ungrateful and undertook to reprimand them herself.

Christmas was a nightmare as it co-coincided with the *Ramadhan* period. Home-made firecrackers prevented all but the very deaf from sleeping during the fasting period. There were many parties but one had to risk the possibility of being stranded at another's home due to the curfew imposed nationwide. Liquor from the Embassy's duty-free canteen was extremely cheap and, as there was very little else to do, most of the foreign community drank — in most households, to excess.

The New Year was quickly followed by the *Lebaran* holidays. As Moslems celebrated, the country was inundated with the wet season's first rain. The conditions were not as Coleman had expected. Humidity caused discomfort demanding constant showering and a slowing of one's physical pace. Offices closed at two-fifteen providing workers with the opportunity to take their lunch then sleep through the hottest part of the day. Expatriates emulated the locals. They too slept through the afternoons. Most evenings were occupied with cocktail parties, national day celebrations and endless dinner parties. Weekends were often spent in the magnificent Puncak Hills bungalows area, where cool evenings often required a log fire, due to the scenic area's altitude of five thousand feet.

Coleman easily settled into the swing of the routine and soon enjoyed the self-confidence of an old hand. Local staff warmed to him when they understood that he had taken the time to learn to speak their language prior to his arrival. The drivers joked with Achmad, now Coleman's warmest admirer, for the rumours he created regarding the new *tuan's* Dutch shaped head, incorrectly designating him as a descendant of the former colonial rulers.

Achmad had suffered the embarrassment of their jokes until being requested through the driver pool manager, Sjaiful, to become the new Second Secretary's permanent driver. He was ecstatic as this removed him from the uncertainty of not only his work hours but also provided him with the opportunity to deal only with a *tuan* who understood his language. He was so very pleased that evening when, having completed his ritualistic prayers, he prayed also for the health and good fortune of his new *tuan* who had come from that faraway country of weapons they threw into the sky called kangaroos and cuddly little bears they called dingo. He knew all of this as he had listened to the other *tuans* and their *njonjas* discussing such things and laughing, happily about their country with its strange habits and practices. Although culturally confused, he was a good driver.

Achmad's position in the world improved overnight.

Ah, he had thought, he must ensure that his children have his advantage of understanding a second language!

Direct communication permitted Coleman access to government circles never before open to the monolingual embassy personnel. His willingness to assist others soon endeared him to the other

Embassies for few of their staff could match Coleman's fluency. His face could be seen at all the major social and diplomatic functions as the *Corp Diplomatique* suddenly discovered that they could invite senior military and cabinet representatives to their function without fear of their being left out of the conversations.

* * * * * *

It was at such a function Coleman first met Louise. Embassy functions were not designed to entertain. More so, these events were orchestrated to continue to highlight both one's country's and one's own presence on the cocktail circuit. Most parties commenced at the evening hour of six-thirty and rarely continued for more than two hours. Dress was normally formal and it was obligatory that all members of the host Embassy attend the Ambassador's residence where the functions were normally held.

Coleman had dressed slowly to avoid perspiration spots. He just could not get used to the depressing heat! The black tie and cummerbund made him feel self-conscious when he was first required to wear the dress suit but now, his confidence was such, the thought of wearing the Singapore tailored outfit made him feel more presentable. During his first formal reception not long after his arrival, he had discovered that almost without exception the other male guests were as uncomfortable as he in the tropical heat wearing the white dinner jackets, and yet they all persevered with the inappropriate attire just because of tradition.

Most of the time, the talk at these functions was mundane. One woman would complain of boredom, poor servants, bad stomachs and the heat while another would compete with stories of rashes, cockroaches and petty theft amongst the servants. The men bragged of their latest excursions to Mama's Bar where they drank hot *Bir Bintang* and paid the equivalent of thirty cents for a short time hooker out in the rear toilets.

Coleman soon discovered that eating the *paté de fois* was dangerous at these events. He restricted his diet to the occasional chicken saté as the electricity, and therefore the refrigeration, was not completely reliable.

He viewed the assembly which, as the alcohol took effect, appeared more like a flock of penguins gathering than the elite of the diplomatic establishment. It was Australia Day. Unfortunately, it was also the Indian National Day but tradition had it so that the Indian Ambassador would first attend the Australian function and delay the commencement of his own so as not to draw upon each others' common guests.

He was bored. Even the champagne was warm and he found himself restless. He was about to refuse yet another glass from the attentive *jongus* and leave when he saw her moving through the garden towards the steps.

She was wearing a full length white evening gown and her blonde hair was cut just above her suntanned shoulders. Lifting the hem of her dress between thumb and forefinger, and with very little effort, she covered the four steps back into the crowded, hot and noisy main reception hall.

Coleman removed two glasses from the waiter's tray and stepped into her path.

"I think you may have misplaced this," he said, holding one of the glasses towards the young woman.

She stopped. Casually casting her eyes over the now noisy gathering she returned her gaze to Stephen.

"Thank you," she smiled in response, accepting the flute. "I knew I'd left it here somewhere."

Stephen was surprised to see an unattached and yet attractive European alone. Especially one as beautiful as this!

"Coleman. Stephen Coleman," he offered.

"Louise," she answered, "and thank you for the champagne."

"Would you prefer to move away from the crowd? It's safe, I can assure you," Stephen offered, indicating an area in the corner garden.

She hesitated and then turned without speaking, leading the way back down the steps to the fountain and impeccably maintained garden. Raising her glass she said, "Saluté, Coleman, your timing was perfect!"

Stephen laughed and touching her glass with his own, paused momentarily to observe her place the crystal glass to her lips and sip the champagne before he followed, drinking the flute dry.

"Well," she teased, "you're either from the liquor suppliers or very thirsty," referring to the speed at which he had consumed his drink.

"No such luck, I'm afraid. Just a thirsty civil servant," he joked, feeling the alcohol working its wonders as he stood there bewitched by this beautiful woman, her fragrance more intoxicating than the wine he had consumed.

"Well, civil man, how would you like to be my servant and take me away from all of this?" she bantered, tossing her hair with her left hand while flashing impeccable teeth.

Stephen admired her beauty as she stood there, the party lights playing tricks with the colour of her fair hair and golden skin. She was immaculately dressed, her make-up highlighting her beautiful features. Taking her by the hand, he led the way through the now inebriated mass of diplomats and the portals of the white-columned entrance.

Always alert, Achmad spotted his *tuan* and soon had them both in the Holden speeding away from the celebrations. He was almost as excited as his boss that the beautiful woman now sat in the rear of the vehicle with her head on his *tuan*'s shoulder.

* * * * * *

There had never been any question that they would make love. She had opened her apartment, and within moments had disrobed standing naked in the room as if it were quite natural to do so. Coleman had followed — an urgency now taking charge as he held her, feeling her warmth and then her hands slowly stroking, encouraging him to the floor as she dominated the love play.

He felt his heart thumping as his body moved in concert with the slim soft stomach and firm breasts on top of him. Her perfume permeated the air and, as she called encouragingly he found his body moving to her commands, moaning together as they held each other tightly until the waves of muscular spasms urged by her orgasm caused him to ejaculate, draining his energy in total. She took his hand and slowly kissed his fingers, then his palms, his wrists and finally his mouth until he clung to her body passionately, unable to respond any more through sheer exhaustion.

They rested together, in a lovers' embrace, oblivious to the outside world. He dreamed. It was a peaceful dream and when he awoke he was totally rested. Coleman lay on his back savouring the clove cigarette. Louise's radio clock had turned itself on and he rested in the double bed listening to the Voice of America's music segment. He found himself humming along with Buddy Holly's

'Heartbeat' although he didn't know the words. He was happy! And as the song continued, he hummed, *"why do you skip when my baby kisses me?"*

Totally relaxed, at peace, and resisting the floating sensation merging on drowsiness he'd rarely experienced after previous sexual encounters, he smiled as he dragged on the sweet cigarette. This nothingness, this lack of 'afterglow' should have a word more descriptive of how he felt, he mused. His lips compressed into a thin smile as he mentally envisaged a definition for this lack-luster feeling. They smoked marijuana; his first. And now he was suffering from post-coital depression.

He laughed. He turned his head just enough to observe her beautiful body, the soft lines of her milk white breasts and pink aureoles dominated by the tiny nipples standing lazily overlooking the lines falling away to the firm stomach and shapely thighs. He remembered the warmth of her tongue and the shuddering spasms which followed. They spent the entire weekend together, making love, sitting on the large cushions which lay carelessly thrown onto the floor over the broadloom carpet, listening to her collection of LPs and cooking for themselves while Louise's two servants looked on in dismay.

She played the guitar and sang, and when Stephen had tried to accompany her she threw the smaller cushions at him, pulling a childish face while mocking his poor voice. They wrestled and they showered together (Louise insisted that the two of them just couldn't squeeze into the bath!) and Stephen taught her how to play Five-Hundred, a card game he had picked up back in his boarding school days.

Late on Sunday evening as the unfinished bottle of Medoc stood on the floor, accompanied by two partially finished glasses of the soft red wine, Louise suddenly leaped to her feet and ran into the bathroom where she stayed until Stephen could coax her out. He knew exactly how she felt. As the weekend came to a close it was as if each would lose something extremely precious that they had shared together.

He held her closely in his arms and whispered to her until the tension of the moment was broken, and he tried to sing the Johnny Horton ballad she loved, softly into her ear. She collapsed to the floor laughing and then he knew they would be all right. They

113

CARTHAGE PUBLIC LIBRARY
CARTHAGE MISSOURI

were in love. And neither wanted to say it for fear that they would break the spell.

Louise asked him to leave before morning. He didn't understand but he unhappily agreed to her wishes, leaving the apartment compound where she was billeted in search of a *becak* to take him home. To his amazement, Achmad was standing outside beside the Holden with a broad grin on his face.

"*Selamat pagi, tuan,*" he said, pulling the rear door of the sedan open for the young foreigner.

"*Ya, selamat pagi, Achmad,*" Coleman responded, alerting the driver to the fact that he was not all that happy to be going home.

* * * * * *

Monday was hell in the office. Everybody wanted him for something or other. He phoned her office before lunch and then again late in the afternoon. He had left several messages for her before leaving for an official visit to Medan. When he returned he was disappointed to discover that there had been no reply at all.

The second week dragged slowly and Coleman felt that had Louise really wanted to respond she would have returned his calls. He was depressed. A few more weeks passed and he decided to get on with his work and, if necessary, put the affair quickly behind him. He tried, unsuccessfully, as Louise totally dominated his thoughts. Stephen had been required to attend yet another reception. He was averaging more than five per week due to his linguistic skills and was becoming more than a little testy with the over-demand on his time. He understood the cause of his moody behaviour and was determined to put her out of his mind, once and for all.

The evening had commenced well. He had accompanied the Ambassador's wife to the function at her request as she despised being alone and admired the young Coleman's knowledge of the local people. Her husband had been unable to return from Pontianak on time as the aircraft was grounded with engine trouble leaving his wife to carry on to represent them both.

Actually, she was quite pleased. Normally she found these cocktail parties as boring as hell but never indicated to those around her that she felt so. Tonight she would not be obliged to stand behind or to the side of her vociferous husband and listen to him

CARTHAGE PUBLIC LIBRARY
CARTHAGE MISSOURI

carry on about the Commonwealth's interests being eroded in this hemisphere or how *that* man in Singapore was really a Communist, and so on.

Stephen held her by the elbow as he escorted her up the few steps to the formal reception line. He had developed considerable social skills and, dressed in his white jacket, attracted more than one second look from the ladies, most of whom were married and led very dull lives. The reception had been under way for just a short time when he spotted her. The other guests were moving around quickly, almost in a frenzy, snapping up the hors d'ouvres before the fresh Sydney rock oysters all disappeared. It had been quite a culinary coup for the New Zealand Ambassador to have a visiting RNZAF Hercules crew bring the ice packed shellfish on their visit in time for his function.

Peering over the heads of the crowded room he could see her standing talking to an Indonesian officer. He sauntered over to join in their conversation. As he approached, Louise's blue eyes sparkled as they had that first night they'd met and when he heard the soft laugh he felt the fist grab at his stomach. He moved in closer to them and was about to say 'Why the hell didn't you answer my calls,' when their eyes met and he instantly felt foolish.

"*Selamat malam, Bapak Seda,*" was all he could muster, hoping at least his use of the language would impress her.

"Good evening, Mr Coleman," the general replied in English as a courtesy to the young lady. "Have you met Miss Louise?"

"Yes, sir, I'm pleased to say," he acknowledged adding "but I was not sure that at the time I hadn't been dreaming."

The general looked at them both quizzically not understanding the connotation as the beautiful young woman flushed red with embarrassment. Louise regained her composure almost immediately and asked, "So, you are friends with General Seda?"

Coleman looked distantly into her eyes. Why hadn't she returned my calls he wondered? "We have met once or twice," Seda replied before Coleman could. "Then I am sure you will have something to discuss. Please excuse me," she said, smiling at the officer and quickly leaving to speak to another group she had spotted near the temporary bar.

Seda took mental note of the mild social skirmish and then he too excused himself leaving Coleman feeling like some disbeliever who had just been discovered in the midst of a holy gathering.

He headed for the bar and not finding Louise, settled down to enjoy the champagne.

Stephen did not go unobserved as he downed the Moet, too quickly, the bubbles forming an airlock in his throat. Louise stared at him, with mixed emotions, from the far side of the room while the Timorese casually observed them both. He reached for another glass from the silver serving tray as the *jongus* passed by. The house servants were always careful to ensure that this man always had their attention for more often than not, his presence in a household inevitably meant that the domestic staff were in trouble as he was the man who could speak their language and they knew they should watch him carefully.

Nathan considered the smartly dressed Australian. His dossier had been completed with additional input from Albert. He had identified some reluctance from his stepbrother when pushed for the information but eventually the data had flowed through. Nathan was surprised with his brother's glowing report and foot-note concerning their apparent friendship. Albert had emphasized that his relationship with Nathan had never been disclosed.

Nathan had smiled when he read this annotation. Albert was no fool as he obviously realized the consequences that such disclo-sure would have brought to them both. Nathan's dedication had earned him the coveted star on his shoulder bringing him to the Attaché Corp's attention immediately. His job function under the newly reorganized HANKAM was described as Intelligence Pro-tocol. This enabled Nathan to mix with the foreigners easily. His English was poor as he had forgotten most of what he had learned under the priests. To his delight, conversing with this new Infor-mation Attaché Coleman was, indeed, a pleasure.

Believing that he had inadvertently caught the young man's eye, he signalled. Coleman noticed Brigadier General Seda's wave and he returned the gesture. The General had been particularly helpful with assistance travelling to remote areas which still required mili-tary escort. Central Java and a few of the outlying provinces were unsafe for foreigners. In diplomatic terms this indicated that the Central Government was still mopping up some of the so called communist remnants in those areas.

Coleman had witnessed the execution of one hundred and

twenty seven peasants near a small *kampung* in the Blitar region. The Captain responsible for the turkey shoot proudly paraded some fifteen rifles, the total armoury captured, hoping the representative of the Australian News and Information Bureau would congratulate him, perhaps even send photographs of this heroic soldier to Australia for inclusion in the newspapers.

There it would be picked up by *Antara* and perhaps included in the Armed Forces News. This would result in a rapid promotion for the cowboy Captain. Coleman understood this dangerous mentality and used it to improve his own position. Coleman praised the Captain, his men and their efforts to assist eradicate Communism. At first Coleman felt disappointed with himself for the hypocrite he had become. As the months passed and the horror of what had occurred in this beautiful country became apparent even he developed an affinity towards the hundreds of thousands of innocent victims who had been imprisoned on islands such as Pulau Buru and Nusa Kambangan. Rehabilitation camps appeared throughout the country and virtually a million men, women and children were 're- indoctrinated' into the *Panca Sila* way of life.

Along a dusty mountain track south of Blitar Coleman was disgusted to see pre-school children being instructed in the ways of the New Order, the *Orda Baru*. As his four wheel drive Toyota passed the newly erected *kampung* huts, row after row of little children were forced to stand with their right arms raised in a Hitler-style salute, yelling *Merdeka!* Freedom! in unison. These were the orphaned children of executed communists and it was here that the New Order practised its grass roots policy of indoctrination.

The sins of the fathers. He remembered the text from his boarding school days when at least two hours each week were dedicated to the scriptures.

Although Coleman realized he was becoming drunk he decided that another drink would give him something to do with his hands. He heard his name being called and turned towards the guest responsible.

"Ah, there you are Coleman," called the British Ambassador. "I wonder if you would mind interpreting for me for a moment old chap." Coleman disliked this Ambassador intensely. He was, at best, extremely patronizing and excessively colonial in nature and, in Coleman's view, a poor choice to send to this country.

"Not at all Ambassador. To whom do you wish to speak?"

"Why, this chap here of course," announced the gnome-like figure of Maxwell Westaway, in his deepest baritone, indicating the Asian figure to his left.

The object of the Ambassador's attention stiffened and turned to avoid what could presently become an unpleasant incident caused by the obnoxious diplomat. The British Ambassador would not be thwarted and he grabbed the man's arm.

"Just a moment old fellow, I would like to ask you something. This chap here speaks your lingo so don't run away." Ambassador Westaway had, by this time, secured the embarrassed Asian with his left hand while gesturing for Coleman to approach closer and assist with the dialogue.

"Coleman, be a good fellow and ask this chap if he had that dinner jacket made here or in Singapore. I'll bet it's a Singaporean product if ever I've seen one. Very stylish. Very stylish indeed."

The Asian gentleman diplomatically checked his anger over the Ambassador's obvious lack of finesse but the glint in his eyes suggested that he intended scoring off the pudgy British Queen's representative.

Turning to Coleman the Malaysian First Secretary asked in his own language, *"Are there very many more like him in Jakarta? My name is Ali bin Noor and I am the new First Secretary at the Malaysian Embassy. I overheard you speaking to our Ambassador in Bahasa Indonesia and I must admit, I'm impressed. Do you have difficulty with the slight differences in our two languages?"*

Coleman played the game.

"I should apologize for the Ambassador. He is the epitome of the sort of racially bigoted Englishman even we Australians have come to despise."

The Malaysian smiled and shook Coleman's hand warmly. He then turned to the Ambassador and announced, in precise English, "Actually, I purchased the jacket in London. If you wish, Mr Ambassador, I would be only too pleased to phone my wife in Kuala Lumpur and ask her to send the address to you." Smiling broadly, he then excused himself winking to Coleman as he passed behind the embarrassed diplomat.

Brigadier General Seda had overheard the exchange and he too winked at Coleman. He approached the Australian and assisted his escape from the now visibly furious ambassador. They conversed in Indonesian. *"Mas Stephen, I have something I wish to discuss with you."*

Cautiously blended with the correct tone of respect Coleman replied. *"Pak Jenderal how may I be of service to you?"*

"I have observed you and am pleased that you show simpati towards my country. One day you may need friends who are able to assist you for it seems that you are a good man. It also appears that you are not so adept at making friends amongst your own?"

It really was not a question that required an answer. The General continued.

"There are those in positions of strength who could be of assistance to you should the need arise. Everyone needs friends, some more than others."

"Does the Jenderal include himself as one of those who may wish to assist if the need arises?" Coleman was not sure which way this conversation was heading however he intended playing the game through.

"Yes. In particular ...." the General hesitated, and then decided to change his approach. *"The request I have really is just an idea. You speak our language so well whilst we have great difficulty with the English speaking foreigners. Watching you tonight I though what an opportunity we have for you to assist us with our English speaking courses. What do you say, Mas, would you help with some of that spare time I hear you foreign visitors have so much of here in Jakarta?"*

Coleman was conscious that the request was not necessarily being made for the General. He decided to play along, accept the challenge as he could always drop out, if it became too involved.

"Yes, of course, I would be pleased to participate in such a program. Why don't we discuss it formally, next week?"

"No. I don't think so. I would prefer an informal discussion to define the possible areas of cooperation before proceeding to an official level."

Coleman now knew he was entering dangerous ground. Informal discussions could easily be misconstrued.

"Perhaps then, if you would provide me with the opportunity I could visit you in your office Pak Jenderal"

"Bagus!" he replied. *"Let's leave it at that for the time being. I will arrange for a meeting next week."*

Satisfied that they had concluded their arrangements both men continued with small talk until eventually drifting into separate groups. Coleman felt uneasy with the General's oblique approach. He gave no more thought to the discussion and, considering the possibility of the protocol soldier's motives being not what they seemed, he decided as a precaution to report the incident directly to Canberra in his weekly report. He returned to the bar having strolled around the remaining guests looking for Louise. Where could she have gone?

Coleman was confused and angry that she had ignored him. He couldn't understand her attitude as he knew he'd done nothing to upset her! He remained at the bar, drinking heavily. He could vaguely remember one of the other guests suggesting he'd had enough. Each time the *tuan's* glass was empty the *jongus* refilled it quickly. Finally, somebody took him home but when he awoke in the early hours of the morning in the unfamiliar room he realized instantly the stupidity of his actions.

In the darkness the Ambassador's wife moaned and rolled towards him. Naked, her breath foul from the cigarettes and far too many Jack Daniels, Coleman's eyes opened wide with surprise as he saw the white mound edging towards him. Quietly, he crawled out of her bed, dressed quickly and searched for the security gate. The old man dressed in his white safari jacket, proudly displaying the gold buttons with the Australian crest, pretended not to notice as Coleman slipped past him into the night. He stood outside under the ageing elms, feeling foolish, dressed in his tuxedo at three o'clock in the morning on a deserted street.

Achmad, of course, was nowhere to be seen as the previous evening Stephen had had the benefit of the Ambassador's limousine. And, apparently, also his wife!

He walked to the corner and woke one of the sleeping *becak* drivers to take him home to his own bed. He needed more sleep. His body was already sending him alarm signals over the abuse he had heaped upon it. Still partially drunk, his anxious house-boy helped the swaying *tuan* into the bedroom. Exhausted, he kicked off his shoes, removed most of his clothes and dropped onto the bed.

* * * * * *

He'd had difficulty at first, drifting off to sleep, the ceiling spinning slowly and even when he closed his eyes he still imagined the nauseating motion through his eyelids. When he finally succumbed Stephen dreamed he had been pushed into a *kali* by a beautiful naked blonde who laughed as he was slowly being sucked down in the stream's filthy quagmire.

The dream was confused with others also laughing as soldiers threw bodies of children into the canal while Albert stood high on the embankment sagely shaking his head at Coleman's futile efforts to retrieve the bodies and throw them back to safety. Occasionally he succeeded, only to have the children scream as they were again bundled back into the cesspool. A tall soldier, his uniform covered in blood stood yelling at Coleman to do his duty and teach the children the words in English so that the soldiers could understand that they really did not want to die thereby saving them from his stupidity.

As he groaned and cried out in his sleep the house-boy banged on his *tuan's* door. He feared that something dreadful had happened to his master. Coleman was partially conscious of the pounding on the door but believed it part of his nightmare until finally, he awoke, crying out, his body smothered in sweat in the cold air-conditioned bedroom.

Sukardi, the *jongus*, raced into the room to help the young *tuan*.

"*Tuan, tuan, ada apa? What is it tuan?*" screamed the house-boy now feeling the terror in the room.

Perhaps the *tuan* had been bitten by a *krait*! No! That is preposterous he admonished himself. How could a snake enter his master's bed when he himself just hours before had prepared the room?

"*Tuan, tuan, please tell me what it is that is wrong with you,*" he pleaded.

As his master's consciousness returned 'Kardi put his arm around the younger man's shoulders assisting him out of bed.

"*Maaf tuan, maaf tuan,*" the servant apologized for placing his hands on the *tuan*. No sooner had Coleman regained consciousness than he doubled forward as the sharp stabbing pain ran down through his lower abdomen signalling the cause of both the nightmare and the screaming. Coleman had been initiated with his first attack of Soekarno's revenge.

As a result of this illness and its debilitating effect both physically and psychologically, the concerns he'd felt for General Seda's obvious attempt to recruit him and the guilt of spending part of the night in another man's bed diminished with the days, as he lay listlessly in bed recuperating from what he hoped would be his last encounter with the dreaded disease.

He had made a mental note to discuss his interpretation of the General's approach with one of the Military Attachés when the opportunity arose once back at his desk. His real concern was what his reception would be back in the Embassy considering his blatant indiscretion. And, of course, his career!

One very long week passed slowly and, lighter but now stronger, Stephen returned to work. He'd tried to contact Louise from his home to see if she would accept his call to discuss whatever it was she seemed to have on her mind, and obviously the cause for her behaviour towards him at the party.

The Embassy operator was impatient with his insistence that the call was extremely important. He insisted that she connect him to her extension. Finally, after numerous attempts, he was informed that Louise had been very specific in her request to the switchboard. They were not to accept any of his calls. That was it, then! He decided he couldn't understand her attitude — at least she could accept just one call to explain her position. He was deeply disappointed and became even more depressed.

Fortunately, the incident involving the Head of Mission's wife became more of a joke around the Chancery than an impediment to Stephen's career. Straight-laced Dicky had waddled past him during the early days when the rumour mill was in full swing, and merely 'tch-tched' him indicating his disapproval of the indiscretion. He had no idea how the gossip managed to spread as quickly as it did but, by his second day back at work it was obvious that he'd become the centre of attention within the Embassy's community.

The clearest signal was when he entered the main office area and all conversation ceased, the men with knowing smirks while the women looked at Stephen, almost with admiration. He had stood in the centre of the office and with a sombre voice and hands up-raised had said, "Not guilty," and left it at that. Unbeknown to the young attaché, the Ambassador's wife was responsible for the story travelling at such speed as she blatantly admitted having the romp with Stephen, during the weekly tea session all the Embassy wives attended.

Exaggerating the brief encounter, describing his sexual prowess directly from her vivid imagination some of the younger ladies had giggled nervously, one spilling her tea, while others laughed at her rendition of how eventually she had cried 'enough, enough,' and dispatched him on his way before he completely wore her out!

Stephen would have been very uncomfortable had he known that many of the looks he now received from the opposite sex were, in fact, an appraisal of the good looking man and curiosity as to whether his 'one-nighter' with madame was as sexually extravagant as she had insisted. He knew that if he could get through the following days without any clear indication that his career was to suffer then, by all accounts, he believed that the story had not and would not reach the Ambassador's ears and perhaps then his future would not be jeopardized by the foolish error in judgment.

* * * * * *

Brigadier General Seda arrived home and elected to work in his study until his wife decided to sleep. She was heavily pregnant and the soldier found her condition sexually repugnant. As a Christian he had only one wife whilst his Moslem peers sported as many as four wives and numerous *cewek* on the side.

He had married a Javanese hoping his Timorese heritage could somehow be overlooked by his superiors. Divorcing her would be out of the question unless he could find a woman whose family could influence his career to his advantage. Perhaps he should be satisfied with an occasional visit away.

Bandung — now there was the ideal opportunity for a man who had needs! The city boasted a major divisional headquarters and was literally over- run with poor young ladies financing themselves through school. He considered the options and decided he may invite the young Australian to accompany him on such a visit. He reflected on their casual but pointed conversation; however he remembered that, at the time, the Attache's attention had been somewhat distracted by the attractive American. He made a mental note to obtain further information on her, also. Seda was determined to move slowly with the embassy officer as he had detected the reluctance to meet privately when discussing the possible mutual advantages of cooperating together.

Control was important to the General. Although his salary was officially equivalent to only a few dollars each month, his position in the community provided access to the business sector which could not operate without the assistance of senior military personnel, such as he. The more important consideration was, however, to gain control over General Sudomo's slush funds, acquiring control of the clandestine operational accounts which, reportedly, ran into millions of dollars each month. He desperately needed access to these funds if he was to survive and grow. To build a clandestine power base required money, and he knew it was only a matter of being patient before he had the key.

The tall Timorese undressed then showered. Without reflecting further on these matters he slipped quietly into bed, cautious not to awaken his wife.

Indrawati, his wife, legs curled up so that her knees touched her enormous belly smiled contentedly. Her husband had returned home. How considerate he was not to awaken her and demand his rights! She imagined the other wives were envious. Her husband was handsome. She was an only wife. The first wife of a General!

She was pregnant. She was happy, deliriously happy. Tomorrow she would insist he couple with her as she understood only too well the dangers of an unserviced husband. That would surely please him, she decided, as he had not had many opportunities these past few months.

The room was not air-conditioned. The still, musty air, slowed their breathing. Had Seda's wife had any insight into her husband's covert activities which were so secret that even his superiors had no information regarding his machinations then, in all probability, Indrawati would have delivered her child there and then. Seda was building his network He was now a very dangerous man. Totally oblivious to each other's thoughts, their minds drifted until they finally achieved a deep, comforting sleep.

* * * * * *

BAKIN — Jakarta

Another year passed quickly. The city changed dramatically whilst in the villages the people had already put most of the horrifying past behind them. There had been tears and recriminations but nothing had really changed. The peasants still rose with the first rays of the sun and worked until exhausted from the day's physical toil, returning to their village huts to sleep only to awaken the next day and do it all over again with monotonous regularity.

Nathan Seda was pleased with his new appointment. General Sudomo had passed away, creating the opportunity for the ambitious and still relatively young soldier to tentatively occupy the sensitive post.

He had followed the career of the American, Hoover, and emulated some of this powerful man's control over others by developing an information base regarding their personal activities. Since the abortive *coup* attempt he had ensconced himself solidly within military as well as political circles.

Many of the former military officers had retired or passed away. Some were dispatched overseas as Ambassadors. A number still remained under detention for their part in the abortive *coup* or their affiliations with Communist elements or sympathizers. Some just had the misfortune to be in the path of another more ambitious player resulting in their disappearance or secret incarceration until whatever they had or knew had been surrendered. His star was rapidly on the ascent.

Military Attachés frequently wrote reports advising their respective Governments that Seda, although neither Javanese nor a Moslem, should be considered to be an integral part of the nation's New Order and not to be underestimated. He was well received amongst the *Corps Diplomatique*. He often assisted facilitate access to senior government officials and generally presented himself as a loyal, intelligent, and dedicated officer with no apparent political aspirations. His youth was not considered a handicap.

Even the Chief-of-Air-Staff and Minister for Air, *Laksamana Madya* Roesmin Nuryadin had been appointed by the President at the incredibly young age of thirty-eight! Informed sources suggested that Seda had not only slipped into Sudomo's chair but had also succeeded in accessing the funds used by the intelligent services for their clandestine activities.

The Indonesian counterpart to the Central Intelligence Agency occupied a prominent complex of buildings at the southern end of Jalan Jenderal Sudirman. This organization, BAKIN, *Badan*

Koordinasi Intelijen, received more than adequate funding for the many nefarious activities considered essential to the nation's security.

Seda relished this position of power. He had finally accessed the enormous amount of capital previously hidden away by his predecessor. The funds at his disposal were even more substantial than he had envisaged! Now he could build and develop his plan. He was secure.

There was virtually no financial reporting as the Ministry of Finance was under civilian control and, providing he spread sufficient funds around in the correct quarters, there would be no questions to answer as he now dispersed these funds. All of his predecessor's aides and administrative support staff were either posted to other commands or pensioned off to ensure positions for his own people.

He had both the Sudomo watchdogs ordered to Irian Jaya where they suffered, at his request, before the tribesman removed their heads. He had set about initiating a special operations team responsible for highly sensitive duties and it was at the head of this team that he appointed Captain Umar Suharjo.

Even in the BAKIN building there were whispers regarding this silent unsmiling Javanese whose past career details remained vague. He was a man to be avoided and the more hardened amongst their number did so, willingly, as the soldier's cold almost blank eyes could penetrate in the most chilling manner. Some said that he had been trained in a special camp; others declared that he had served in the anti-Communist sweep which accounted for several hundred thousand dead during the post abortive *coup* clean-up campaign. Whatever was said or whispered, there was, in fact, no accurate data relating to the Captain's past.

Only Seda had the key. The man would disappear for weeks at a time and no one dared inquire as to his whereabouts. Suharjo was Seda's secret coordinator, bag-man, go-between and, on occasions, executioner. He had killed so called enemies of the State, blackmailed members of the government and even orchestrated the recent demise of one of the other BAKIN operatives who accidentally discovered information dangerous to both himself and *Bapak* Seda.

He never questioned his instructions. He received his orders directly from the General. His life was simple, uncomplicated, and suited his talents. He had no family and no friends. Just the General. He never questioned his superior's instructions. He did not care. He had become the perfect soldier.

And he belonged to the Timor man.

Chapter 6

Canberra — Australia

John W. Anderson briefed the Prime Minister with the Attorney General in attendance. As the special adviser liaising between ASIO, the Australian Security Intelligence Organization, and the Prime Minister's office, it was his responsibility, *inter-alia*, to ensure that the country's political leadership remained current regarding security matters. The session had not proceeded well.

The Prime Minister had exploded when the Attorney-General had dropped the bomb shell. "Jesus bloody Christ!" the politician hissed menacingly. "Jesus bloody Christ!" he repeated.

"Prime Minister, we will have an update within a few days and hopefully the report will not be as grim."

The most powerful politician in the country glared furiously at Anderson. He despised cloak and dagger operatives even more than the career bureaucrats who controlled the public service.

"Are you telling me Mr Anderson that we will not have an update regarding critical defence information for at least another forty- eight hours?"

The liaison officer responded affirmatively. The Attorney-General folded his arms and looked disapprovingly across the room at the senior departmental head.

"It's not good enough John. Not good enough," he intoned.

Anderson was not to be intimidated. His position was more or less permanent. Politicians come and go. He just wished that this one would go sooner than later.

"We have been successful in intercepting communications from an extremely high-ranking officer in Indonesia. We anticipate further intelligence regarding this source imminently, Prime Minister," Anderson offered. The response was a cold accusatory glare.

"Get the Chiefs of Army, Navy and Air Staff here immediately," the Prime Minister demanded.

Anderson smiled inwardly. Everything was always immediate when the shit hit the fan. He sat waiting for someone else to make the calls.

'Damn!' he thought, if only the government was run by qualified people. He had never understood how the archaic Westminster System had survived so long.

'Why weren't these people required to have qualifications for their positions as other government employees?' he had often asked himself. It would be highly unlikely, he knew, that an executive would be appointed to head a major corporation anywhere in the developed world without having first demonstrated the necessary qualifications and experience applicable to the position. And yet government had no such established criteria! He felt contempt for these politicians, running around in their first pin-striped suits as if they were ordained, rather than simply being representatives elected by an ignorant public. Anderson remained seated.

The Attorney-General left the office and issued instructions via the Prime Minister's personal secretary. Drawing a deep breath, John Anderson then followed as it wouldn't do for him to be so obvious, so apparent, especially in the presence of the one politician who had the real power to create difficulties for his organization. He stood within earshot of the Attorney-General and clasped his hands in a submissive stance, as if now awaiting further instructions.

Less than thirty minutes had passed when all three senior officers summoned were sitting together with the Prime Minister, the Attorney-General, the Director of ASIO and Anderson. The Prime Minister listened while the Armed-Forces Chiefs discussed the information which had earlier been passed to him.

"In short, the armaments have been confirmed as having been shipped from Timor. We suspect that the consignments were received and rerouted via Dili," informed the Chief-of-Air-Staff in a calm, matter-of-fact tone.

Anderson noted the four rows of campaign ribbons which, in the Commonwealth, reflected real time, unlike their non-Commonwealth counterparts.

"Who is responsible?" demanded the Admiral who felt that the navy should, as the senior service, control all activities relating to defence. It was an ongoing battle to maintain the Navy's position as resources had been chipped away, little by little ever since the Australian aircraft carrier had sunk one of its own ships, the *Voyager*, with an incredible loss of Australian navy lives. Incredibly, the tragedy had later been duplicated and the carrier had sunk an American warship during a similar manoeuvre. As always, while lost in his own thoughts, he was answered.

"We have been unable to determine that at this point in time, however the 'think-tank' lads in Defence have offered the following scenarios," responded the Air Marshal, happy to retain the floor and assert his authority in the presence of the P.M.

"The first assumption is that the weapons have been financed to provide indigenous groups in West Irian the opportunity to prove they have the ability to resist the substantial influx of Indonesian troops prior to the United Nations controlled plebiscite, or *Act of Free Choice* as the general public refer to the vote. I believe that all present would agree that to give untrained villagers sophisticated weapons is, in itself, a seductive move. If the Irian people wished to become pro-active in their quest for independence it would be more beneficial to their cause not to resort to armed conflict against Indonesia's superior forces. Should sufficient passive resistance occur perhaps world opinion will support a rethink by the United Nations to prevent the territory from continuing under Indonesian control. We should consider that there is considerable support for a free and independent West Irian. This has come about not just because ethnically they are not related to the Indonesians but also this support stems from the regional concern that Indonesia may eventually wish to swallow the rest of New Guinea, once they are firmly ensconced in the western half of the island.

"They have been more than a little expansionist over the years and we should remember that *Konfrontasi*, had Soekarno succeeded, would have resulted in all of East Malaysia, that is, northern Borneo, falling under their control. Next would have been Singapore and perhaps even an attempt against the southern islands of the Philippines which have always been in dispute."

The Air-Force officer paused, taking a glass of water, before he continued.

"As we are all too painfully aware, should Indonesia, or any other foreign force attempt to enter Papua New Guinea, then the Australian people would be obliged to send troops in to protect the country.

"There is also a high probability factor that the Indonesians are testing our resolve by positioning armaments along our northern corridors and may even be willing, God forbid, to push into Papua New Guinea if we appear to be overly receptive to their move.

"These, gentlemen, are the questions that this meeting must address and," he added, "ask ourselves, why the Indonesians are sending weapons into the area, and what is their strategy behind utilizing these newly sourced arms supplies which have shown up during our own reconnaissance checks."

There was stunned silence. The soft hum of the air-conditioning became evident as those present were struck by the import of what had just been imparted to them.

'No,' they all thought, refusing to accept the information, 'it was just not possible!'

Although the Chiefs-of-Staff had been briefed, none had actually paid any real credence to the initial reports. All present now knew that it was time to re-evaluate their earlier appraisals.

Again, they had been caught by their own complacency! They had erred by basically arriving at the same conclusion as the first scenario had offered, that small groups of armed tribes people were being supported by external interests. This is what they preferred to believe as this option was more palatable. However they had not been convinced that there was any real threat just because the Indonesians were pouring significant numbers of troops and equipment into the area. The possibility that the Indonesians themselves were positioning armaments from non-traditional sources and suppliers with the intent of a possible swing across the border was, to say the least, unthinkable!

"Why would the Indonesians not just send their own equipment in, assuming you are correct, instead of purchasing additional supplies?" inquired the Admiral. "Surely they could justify such a move?"

The Army General decided it was time for him to assume the role of senior spokesman.

"Obviously this is part or could be part of the overall deception." The General continued. "Should their strategy be to infiltrate across the territorial lines terrorizing the inhabitants of the disputed border villages then they would be clever to use weaponry not associated with the ABRI, or Indonesian Armed Forces, as this would suggest an intrusion by yet a third party which, in itself, the Indonesians would claim as being provocative and maybe then march in under such a pretext to protect their borders!"

The veteran was enjoying himself. In fact, he almost relished the thought of the possibility of an Australian military intervention.

"The Indonesians have maintained for some time that they believed that both West Irian, or *Irian Barat* as they call it, and Papua New Guinea will eventually become targets for communist subversive elements," he lectured.

"It is possible that the Indonesians will use the weapons themselves to incite some of the border tribes in an attempt to frustrate the plebiscite, push these ignorant indigenes across the New Guinea border and then rush after them as part of a terrorist sweep."

The General paused for the greatest effect. "Then, with great difficulty, we would be involved in two police actions simultaneously," he warned referring to the Vietnam commitment the Australian politicians had so foolishly entered into.

"Are you telling me that a second-rate, uneducated, third-world bunch of coconut eaters have the ability to sit down, plan an excursion into a neighbouring country with the forethought to embroil Australia deliberately into a regional military mess such as the scenario you have just suggested?" snapped the Prime Minister testily.

"May I suggest, gentleman, that at this time we do not have sufficient evidence to substantiate the conclusions or possible outcome suggested here today," intervened the A.S.I.O. Director.

"Then what do you propose?" demanded the statesman.

"If I may ...?" the Air Marshall offered.

"Let's hear it then," the politician sighed, feeling the murky grip of this one already around his ankles.

"Prime Minister. We don't have the resources to keep track of the weapon movements. Nor would we have the materials nor the supplies to support a prolonged and systematic campaign of aerial and ground surveillance over the next nine months leading up to the plebiscite. My recommendation is that we inform the Americans if they don't already know and request satellite surveillance. In the meantime, we should endeavour to ascertain more concerning the source of supply of the weapons and develop some strategy to either prevent further shipments or at least, slow them down."

The Air Force officer completed his last sentence by first raising his hand and then slowly pushing it down demonstrating how he would resolve the supply flow.

"Shouldn't the Ambassador in Jakarta make some attempt to determine the extent of the Indonesian military's involvement?" suggested the Admiral.

"That will be attended to," warned the Intelligence director.

The last thing this agency wanted was some career diplomat identifying an opportunity to ingratiate himself with the Minister, yelling insults at Adam Malik, Indonesia's Foreign Minister.

The Australian Intelligence Agency, ASIO had no charter to operate overseas and was, to some extent, similar to the Federal Bureau of Investigation. These delicate matters of foreign inquiry were best left to those authorized.

The Prime Minister examined the faces of the men around him. He felt a wave of tiredness beginning to creep up from his feet indicating that he was not convinced that they had resolved the major problem, merely postponed the hard decisions. Still, he thought, that was how one often survived. Do nothing, appear to be doing everything and most party observers would applaud the non-decision making process as an integral survival tactic of the politician.

"Keep me informed," was all their leader demanded which indicated the end to the security discussions.

As the group departed, the Prime Minister indicated with a cursory nod that he wished the Intelligence director to remain.

Alone, the Prime Minister commenced issuing his instructions to one of Australia's most powerful non-public departmental heads. Unlike many other western nations, the head of Australia's Intelligence Service was not approved by consensus but more appropriately, by selection, *in camera*, of the most qualified candidate. He was responsible personally to the Attorney-General. It was not unusual for the Prime Minister to communicate directly with the powerful director.

"What do you really think?" he inquired, the tiredness in his voice apparent.

"The Chief-of-Air-Staff is a good man. Sensible. I would go along with his suggestions for the time being," the Director advised.

"Is there something else I should know?" the politician asked challenging. "You didn't appear convinced that we understood the real substance of the reports."

It was always difficult when asked for opinions relating to information collected by the intelligence gathering apparatus. So often the information was just a red herring; and yet, more often than not, when there was detail such as he had examined but not released to the other departments in relation to these arms shipments his sixth sense warned him, as it had in the past, that there was a subtlety behind the strategy that they had missed.

"It's tricky. We are missing something but it eludes me," he explained. "I just can't put a handle on why the shipments are coming out of Timor through Indonesian waters when it would have been far more expedient to dispatch via the Philippines if there actually is third party involvement and, if not, why not just move it directly from one of the closer ports?"

"The Americans are probably still our best bet for a quick answer. In the meantime I will arrange to activate one of our operatives."

"Don't get caught!" instructed the politician not comfortable that they were exceeding the organization's charter.

The Director smiled weakly. "We won't," he responded realizing that he had included the Prime Minister in his undertaking.

* * * * * *

That evening the Prime Minister attended a formal state function and noticed the Indonesian delegation across the room. He was tempted to orchestrate an encounter but his political experience warned him to wait for developments to occur.

"Damn the little bastards," he muttered under his breath before turning his thoughts to the argument taking place behind him regarding the Second Test cricket series.

* * * * * *

Merauke — Irian Barat
Indonesian New Guinea

The weapons were moved out of the safe houses during *fajar* as this was when the villagers were least observant, engrossed in going about their own morning ablutions. This had been the eighth load, as the inventory had to be broken down into manageable shipments. Another four, maybe five days and the entire group could vacate the premises pending the next cargo's arrival.

"*Awas, lu!*" the leader warned as the heavy box containing South African semi-automatic rifles began to slip from the lead man's grip. "*Cepat, cepat,*" he urged, encouraging them to hurry. The team of Timorese struggled and groaned as they carried the crates out to the waiting vehicle. "*Cukup dulu,*" enough, the leader hissed, "*kunci pintunya dan jaga baik-baik!*" ordered the Javanese, to ensure that the security locked the premises and guarded the armoury well.

"*Besok saja kembali,*" he advised, undertaking to return the following morning. The dilapidated four wheeled drive Russian version of the American A-2 Jeep then departed, carrying the officer and the remaining two team members.

They headed east for an hour and then stopped. Another vehicle was waiting for them. The weapons were transferred to the other vehicle. The men all worked silently.

No one spoke. This had been one of their instructions, and the teams now always adhered to their leader's orders. They had all witnessed the execution of two of their number for ignoring orders. Before departing from Dili they had been warned. Now they obeyed. The transfer completed, the men returned to town and slept in the *losmen*, remaining in their rooms until being called.

They repeated this procedure over the following four days until the *gudang* was empty of any remaining evidence that weapons had been stored there. On the fifth day they boarded a small coastal freighter and returned to Dili. There were now seven thousand rifles stored in twenty hidden armories throughout the New Guinea border area.

* * * * * *

Jakarta

The Ambassador was furious. The Military Attaché had, *en passant*, mentioned the visitor to the Head of Mission. He had not been informed. As ambassador he had absolute authority over all communications and any other activities which involved the Australian Embassy in Indonesia. He dictated a strongly worded message and instructed his secretary to ensure that the Communications Centre expedited his inquiry at level one traffic priority. The response to his tirade was immediate.

MOST SECRET

FROM: MINISTER EXTERNAL AFFAIRS.
FOR: ADDRESSEE ONLY.
ADDRESSEE: AMBASSADOR/AUSTEMBA/JAKARTA/INDONESIA
YOUR COMMUNICATION RECEIVED AND APPRECIATED. YOU
ARE TO ASSIST IF REQUESTED AND SUPPORT THE INITIATIVE AC-
TIVATED BY THE ATTORNEY GENERAL'S DEPARTMENT.

THIS AUTHORITY ORIGINATES DIRECTLY FROM THE PRIME MINIS-
TER'S OFFICE AND YOU ARE FURTHER INSTRUCTED NOT TO EN-
TER INTO ANY FURTHER COMMUNICATION REGARDING THE
SUBJECT.
COURIER DIRECTED TO NON-DIPLOMATIC RECIPIENT.
MESSAGE ENDS.

EXAFF/REF/PM
CODE:173224. NO ACKNOWLEDGMENT REQUIRED.

MOST SECRET

* * * * * *

John Anderson had not ventured into the field for some considerable time. His seniority and knowledge of the subject matter demanded his personal participation. The director had no choice but to elect to keep this particular activity strictly covert in nature. The Prime Minister was explicit. He would accept no responsibil-

ity should it fall, as they say, 'off the tracks'. He had slipped surreptitiously out of Canberra, travelled via Hong Kong and Bangkok and was now in Indonesia. Upon arrival at Kemayoran Airport, Anderson went immediately to the old Hotel Duta and used
the archaic telephone. Reaching his party he delivered guarded
instructions for the meeting then, settling back in the rotan chair,
removed his tie and waited.

Twenty minutes passed and his contact arrived not in an Embassy vehicle but in an old Mercedes 190. The black pirate taxi
pulled into the driveway adjacent to the beer garden where the
passenger alighted, paid the fare, and waited for the cumbersome
vehicle to depart. Identifying the visitor sitting on the patio, he
then approached, obviously agitated.

"Hello, Stephen," Anderson said, rising perfunctorily to shake
the annoyed Attaché's hand, "you made good time considering
the appalling traffic."

Platitudes, always platitudes, Coleman thought. He really didn't
need to be called out at this time. He was already up to his neck in
other assignments and was angry at being dragged away from these
tasks. Even by his director!

"It wasn't all that far," Stephen replied, anxious to cut through
the pleasantries quickly to discover the nature of Anderson's visit.

He was surprised to receive the call and was concerned when
he identified the voice. They had not communicated directly for
some time.

"Sorry about the surprise. We decided not to advise you via the
Embassy channels as this visit is strictly on a need to know basis."

'Aren't they all?' Coleman thought, annoyed that he had been
dragged out in public to meet at the Duta Hotel, of all places.

He looked anxiously at his watch. The older man understood
the gesture and wasted no time in imparting his instructions.
Stephen would understand the urgency once he had been briefed.
The director knew that.

Anderson continued. "Not even Foreign Affairs has been informed, however I will need to appear at the Embassy to speak to
the Military Attaché briefly. He will be advised that I am travelling
informally and I will treat the meeting as a courtesy call."

The soft spoken Intelligence Liaison Chief than dropped his voice
to a level at which even Coleman had difficulty hearing. He bent

forward and listened. Occasionally he shook his head or merely nodded to indicate agreement. They continued in this way for almost an hour before Coleman took his leave, disappearing into the pedestrian traffic as inconspicuously as he had appeared. The director watched him leave concerned that Coleman showed signs of stress. He ordered more coffee, paid the *bon* and waited for his change while carefully scrutinizing his surroundings. Confident that sufficient time had elapsed since the other man's departure he also left, following Coleman's steps.

Thirty minutes later Anderson arrived at the Embassy and asked the reception if he could speak with Colonel Wilson, the Military Attaché. He was ushered upstairs to the third level of the new building. The butterfly roofed four storied structure was often mistaken for the Japanese Embassy which stood alongside, all twelve stories, most of which were their Trade representative offices. The Japanese had understood, even then, how to impose their presence and economic grip on neighbouring countries.

The Warrant Officer escorted the visitor immediately to the Colonel's subtly furnished office, offered coffee, then returned to his own post. He had taken weeks learning not to stamp his feet with every movement in this undisciplined environment. It was a difficult habit to correct. The officer, even when he sat, exuded military bearing. He was just ten months off retiring and enjoying the pleasantries of his final posting. The Colonel didn't need any problems in his comfortable life at this time. Not this close to retirement! He was counting off the days to when his handsome pension would commence and when he appeared to forget, his wife would remind him that soon he could look forward to doing nothing more than having coffee each morning together, taking long walks, and doing whatever they had always wanted to do when he retired.

The ageing Colonel could not think of anything he would really enjoy doing with the woman who had been his wife for thirty-five years. Especially sitting and talking together. He smiled at the civilian whose very presence caused him concern.

The Colonel remembered being escorted down and through the underground labyrinth which contained the highly secret section. There, isolated from other sections of the Department of Defence, he was shown a list of names of operating agents and personnel cleared to access the sensitive information relating to the service.

As the Senior Military Advisor, it was essential that the Colonel be briefed prior to his departure for Indonesia and taking up his post as Military Attaché. He was, to say the least, flabbergasted.

All of those years in the army without any knowledge whatsoever that his government had been running such a clandestine operation. At first he was excited at being included on the list of less than seventy personnel. Then he worried that this information would compromise his career, and his pension. He knew the man in front of him by name. It had been high on the list.

"Well, this is a very pleasant surprise, John!" he announced, with as much sincerity as he could muster. "When did you arrive?"

Anderson smiled warmly at the older man. "Just this morning. This time it's unofficial as I am heading for Singapore for a little, and much overdue, 'R and R'."

"I am pleased that you took the time to drop in," said Wilson, adding, "had you sent us a cable we could have had you met at the airport."

The visitor's eyes twinkled. "Travelling with company I'm afraid, and I suggested that I leave her shopping down at Sarinah while I drop in just to say 'hello' on my way through."

"Touching base, so to speak," the civilian added.

The Colonel nodded thoughtfully. Must be discreet! He could understand this sort of reasoning and, although uneasy, he was pleased that this senior officer had made the time to drop in.

"Can I offer any assistance while you are here. Maybe dinner tonight?" the officer offered.

"Very kind of you, Peter," Anderson answered using Wilson's first name, "however I plan to leave for Singapore tonight. Maybe a rain-check?"

"Of course, of course, John," both now relaxed with each other's use of Christian names, the Attaché considerably relieved that there was no official demand being made on his office.

"I thought that I should report in just so they are able to keep track of me down South. You know how they are about our travelling abroad, Peter."

The Colonel nodded knowingly. He called the Warrant Officer. "Have a signal, Warrant. Take it down for my guest please and dispatch the message by routine. What classification John?" asked the Attaché.

"Oh, just send it as a standard restricted notification to my department that I have dropped in and am departing today for Singapore." Anderson said, now enjoying the discomfort the military duo were experiencing.

"Would you care to write the message yourself, sir?" the Warrant Officer inquired, not knowing the guest's official designation..

"Surely," Anderson responded, taking his pen, reaching for the Colonel's blank pad to draft his message.

Minutes later the simple message was being encrypted by the registry clerk also on the third floor for obvious security reasons and, within the hour, the brief and enigmatic signal was being read by the Deputy Intelligence Director in Canberra.

Anderson departed for Singapore later that day on the MSA flight, inter-connecting with the Cathay Pacific service into Hong Kong. There he briefed the Resident Officer who, due to the nature of the Colony's status, decided that it would be inconvenient to accommodate their activities in the High Commission.

John Anderson went immediately to The Lodge upon his return to the Australian Capital. The Prime Minister had sat silently, listening to how the mechanisms now being put into place would resolve the looming crisis.

'Or, God help me, even bring down the government!' he worried Looking out through the row of pines partly obscuring the fine view of the well planned city he felt the dread of being alone, unable to impart or discuss the secrets for which he had become the nation's keeper and he knew that, whatever the outcome, lives would be lost and few would ever know.

The Prime Minister also understood, and accepted, that he must live with the knowledge that it was on his authority and his alone that the order had been given.

'Is it the politics or the burden of responsibility that makes one age prematurely in this job?' he wondered momentarily and, not wishing to dwell any further on the possible demise of others, turned back to the papers he had been working on when interrupted by Anderson's visit.

"God save the Prime Minister," he muttered rubbing his weary eyes.

Chapter 7

Jakarta – Irian Barat

General Seda sat comfortably, legs crossed, listening to the Australian describe his recent journey through Sumatra. The Timorese continued to be fascinated by the Attaché's linguistic ability. He had almost developed the fluency of a native speaker.

"You seem to be quite taken by Sumatra, Mas," the host teased, *"maybe you were smitten by the beautiful cewek there?"*

"Of course one could not avoid noticing the beauty of the ladies throughout the island," Coleman acknowledged diplomatically. Some of the guests present were of Batak and Aceh origins.

"Perhaps you could give us your opinion how the Sumatran girls compare with the East Indonesian ladies?" challenged Njonja Seda, herself of Javanese extraction.

"Sayang, saya belum pernah kesana," apologized Stephen explaining he had not had the opportunity to visit the area.

"Kenapa tidak?" demanded another lady whose features varied considerably from Seda's wife.

"Why not? Well, for one thing I have not had the opportunity and another, visits are restricted due to the instability of the area," he answered, looking directly at the Timorese searching for a response.

"Surely you're not suggesting that travelling in Indonesia is unsafe, Mas?" asked the unfamiliar lady, *"Is this possible Bapak Seda?"* she addressed her question coquettishly in Coleman's direction' not really soliciting a response from the host.

"Unfortunately, at this time, there is considerable unrest in the eastern provinces. There is consistent subversive activity, particularly in Irian Barat, at this time," the host informed the gathering.

"Perhaps when things have settled down we can arrange for you to visit informally," suggested the young Foreign Affairs officer from

Surabaya.

"*Ah well, until that time the ladies of Ambon and Kupang will just have to wait,*" Coleman suggested lightly.

"*Why wait, Mas?*" again teased the General, "*we are surrounded by many of those areas' beauties right here!*" indicating politely with his right hand the young woman who had questioned travel security through the distant islands.

Coleman was visibly embarrassed. His face flushed slightly, much to the ladies enjoyment, and the other men's amusement.

"*Jangan, dong!*" ordered the hostess urging her husband not to tease their guest, although she was also enjoying Stephen's discomfort.

"*Tidak apa-apa,*" Coleman responded, recovering his composure.

"*As I am from Ambon perhaps the General would permit me to escort you to the region,*" suggested the taller young woman with curly and wiry hair.

Joining in the banter and responding now with ease the Australian replied, "*Asal Bapak Seda juga ikut,*" proposing acceptance conditional on the General's participation.

"*Mungkin juga, mungkin juga,*" offered the host in a non-committal manner leaving the door open to the possibility.

The afternoon drew to a close and the guests had all but departed when Coleman rose to thank the couple for their invitation to join them in their home.

"*Tunggu dulu, Mas, saya mau bicara sesudah yang lain sudah pulang,*" the General advised, sotto voce to avoid being overhead, suggesting that his guest not depart until the others, as there was something he wished to discuss. The time dragged on for another hour before Coleman was now alone with the Timorese.

"*Mas Stephen,*" began the older man in a friendly tone. "*I wish to discuss the possibility of that visit you suggested.*"

Surprised, Coleman was about to interrupt when Seda raised his hand indicating that he wished to finish speaking. "*These are not conversations that should be held with the ladies present as they have a tendency to gossip without considering the consequences. For example, most of the women present this afternoon would have made several telephone calls upon arriving home either bragging about their visit or simply gossiping to impress.*"

Seda paused, then continued in a manner accustomed to the

authority he had acquired.

"*I will arrange for you to visit providing you are able to secure your Ambassador's approval. We will require a formal request via the normal Foreign Affairs channels.*"

The Attaché considered the Intelligence Officer's offer, surprised by his directness, completely unaware of this influential man's motives.

"*I would be very pleased to visit Irian, Pak Seda,*" he responded, "and I will discuss this opportunity with the Ambassador first thing in the morning. Thank you. Pak."

Coleman paused, and then asked, "*Kenapa dikasih pergi, Pak,*" inquiring as to the reason for the offer to visit the area.

"*Because there are things that our Government needs for the West to see, yet don't understand how to proceed to disclose these situations without the outcome resulting in confusion. Or worse, embarrassment.*"

"*There are those of us who feel that Australia is not just our neighbour. Australia is our friend and we wish to maintain that relationship. Perhaps if you were to report the truth of what difficulties we are having with the primitive tribal groups then public opinion would not be so critical of our efforts to stabilize our half of Irian.*" Coleman was not surprised that the general had been a little presumptuous as to the outcome of the forthcoming plebiscite.

"*Then why not just open up completely and permit the Press to visit and inform their readers of the events there?*" he asked.

"*The government had considered this but came to the conclusion that it would be far, far too dangerous. The area is riddled with extremists and we could not guarantee the safety of large numbers of civilians tracking around in the undeveloped villages.*"

Coleman was not too impressed to discover that he had been invited to venture into areas where killings occurred frequently. He was no coward but travelling unarmed, even accompanied by military security through fire-fighting hot spots was not, in his opinion, within his job description.

"*Also, Mas,*" the General added looking directly at Stephen, "*we believe that most of the journalists likely to be selected would have preconceived ideas regarding our treatment of the indigenous and, consequently, such a visit would be counter-productive. We believe that your position would be objective.*"

The General paused before continuing, gauging the foreigner's reaction. *"Of course, we would prefer to have others accompany you, preferably of another nationality as this would add weight or more credibility to your findings if they were to be verified by an independent observer."*

Coleman slowly nodded his agreement. It would be disastrous to open old wounds. And what the General had said was accurate, he understood all too well. Sending another foreigner who could substantiate his own findings would be the politically correct thing to do.

The majority of Asia's rulers could not understand why the Australian Government permitted the free press to operate as it did. Having journalists sensationalize the Irian village resistance groups leading up to the plebiscite would not only endanger the successful outcome of the *Act Of Free Choice* but could also create a substantial rift between the two neighbouring countries. He was aware that the Australian Government's policy was to support Indonesia's taking control over the underdeveloped country. Coleman had assumed that steps had been or were being taken by their giant neighbour to ensure the desired outcome. Tens of thousands of non-indigenous Indonesians had been transmigrated into the former Dutch colony. Military strength had been considerably increased.

Neither Australia nor Indonesia wished to see the potential Indonesian province as an independent state, threatening the security of not just Indonesia's borders, but also Australia to the South and New Guinea to the east! No, Australia would not accept such a development even if this required turning a blind eye, so to speak, concerning reports of atrocities carried out by Indonesian troops.

Coleman studied the Timorese. The newly promoted General wore his rank well. An air of confidence surrounded this man who had developed an incredible power base within a very short period of time. It was clear that a close relationship with this man would be of considerable benefit to the Australian.

"I believe that it is a sound idea, and certainly a wonderful opportunity for me personally, Pak."

Seda smiled, pleased that his offer would be accepted.

"We will find someone suitable to join you on the tour. Our preference would be for a non-journalist but certainly a person with acceptable credentials. Anyway, we will sort that out only after you have spoken to

your superiors."

"Baiklah, Pak. I will discuss this at length with the Ambassador and be in contact with your office when I have his response."

Seda smiled again and, holding his hand out to Stephen, indicated that the discussion was over.

Looking back over his shoulder and offering a friendly wave as Achmad drove along the magnificent *Jalan Teuku Umar*, Coleman felt an exhilaration that had been absent from his life for some time. He'd felt that his work had become mundane, the monotonous regularity of submitting weekly reports making him stale, and that somewhere along the line, he had lost his edge. This trip was exactly the remedy he needed! Turning down into Mohamed Yamin and around the corner towards his small residence Stephen was comfortably relaxed and already looking forward to the excursion into one of Indonesia's more primitive areas.

The General watched the light blue Holden with the diplomatic plates drive slowly away. His face muscles tensed as he considered the danger of what he was about to do, and the risk of exposure should his arrangements not be perfect in every way. Time was running out for the Timorese.

He was now committed to this new course of action and he believed the opportunity should not be wasted. Should his tactics prove successful then his ultimate ambition would be realized that much sooner and, in the event that his plan fail, only time would be lost. And a few lives. Either way, General Seda was convinced that his actions would only bring a further consolidation of power to his position within the military and, with that, he would be one step closer to realizing his dreams. He would use this foreigner to enhance the success of his strategy. He had thought it through thoroughly prior to the invitation being arranged for the Information Attaché to visit his home. He was sure that the inquisitive Australians were keen to take a peek into whatever the Indonesian military was up to in Irian and would most probably jump at an opportunity to investigate, should one arise.

An untimely terrorist attack killing the young Australian Attaché would create considerable damage to the implementation of the plebiscite, and may even result in its postponement. This, in turn, could inflame the entire indigenous population in Irian providing the regional instability he required to achieve his ambitious plans.

* * * * * *

Coleman considered the wording of his report and prepared its transmission personally. He was pleased that events had resulted in the opportunity to reconnoitre the Irian area and was amazed at the timely coincidence. The invitation fitted his brief perfectly.

He had informed Canberra immediately. His coded communiqué was deciphered and collected by an appropriately security cleared secretary for delivery to the Director. The Intelligence Chief discussed the contents with his Deputy. John Anderson then made the necessary arrangements for the Department of External Affairs to approve the visit. Canberra advised their Mission in Jakarta that the invitation had been offered through the Indonesian Embassy in Australia for a responsible journalist to visit and had, in response, suggested the Second Secretary Information, Stephen Coleman for their approval. The Indonesian Ambassador himself had phoned to confirm Coleman's acceptability.

Stephen had been summoned by the irritated Head of Mission. He was acutely aware that events were taking place without not only his concurrence but also his knowledge.

"Coleman, you have been selected, for whatever reason, to be given the opportunity to visit Irian as a guest of the Indonesian Government," he puffed. "There have been numerous mutterings within this Mission as to your qualifications for this tour, however. Your name was obviously picked out of the hat without any prior consultation with the department."

"Perhaps it was a decision relating to my language qualification Ambassador," he gibed.

The Ambassador rose to his feet, his face red with anger. He was incredibly short and attempted to compensate by lowering his deep resonant voice into a bellow. He reminded Coleman of the Wizard of Id.

"Whatever the reason young man, I do remind you that you are accredited to this Embassy and will maintain some semblance of respect when addressing this chair!"

"Yes Ambassador," the younger man responded wearily.

"You will be briefed by the Military Attaché as they require certain information you may be able to obtain during your trip into the wilds," he informed facetiously.

"When arrangements have been completed, you are also to be briefed by the First Secretary. Do you understand?" he demanded in a low growl.

"Perfectly, Ambassador. Is that all, sir?"

"That's it. Get to it. Don't screw it up!"

With this last order the rotund diplomat turned his back on the subordinate member of his Mission indicating that the interview was finished.

Coleman turned and left the room, smiling, as he enjoyed antagonizing the supercilious and egotistical Ambassador who so obviously suffered severely from the small man complex. He winked at the secretary whose office was adjacent to the side entrance of her boss' office.

"Not in a particularly good mood today, are we," he joked, pointing his thumb back in the direction of the man he had just left.

The secretary responded with a cool smile. "I hear you're going to Irian, Stephen?" she asked in response. Not surprised, but pleased that the fine looking Melbourne girl had at least attempted to be civil to him, Coleman's face broke into a grin.

"Yes," he answered, "I've just been informed."

"We will all miss you," she announced and turned her attention back to her typing. He immediately recognized the insincerity of the remark. A strong bond existed between the secretary and her Ambassador.

"I will try to keep my head," he quipped sarcastically as he left, displeased with himself for letting the remark get to him. He retreated to his office on the first floor and commenced preparations. He informed General Seda of the positive response and requested details for his journey. Satisfied that he was moving in the correct direction, Coleman settled down to prepare for his departure for Irian.

* * * * * *

He had never enjoyed flying. His hands were wet with perspiration as the attacks of fear kept him clinging to the sides of the canvas seat. The old C-47 bounced around continuously at around twelve thousand feet. The pilot appeared to be looking for a gap in the weather as he needed to drop down to a lower altitude. The first leg had taken almost five hours from Jakarta to Tuban airfield.

Coleman was aghast when he saw that several of the volcanoes were actually thousands of feet taller than the maximum ceiling this old aircraft could reach. The air was thin and cold. He felt no nausea, just fear. The transport dropped again and Stephen gripped the bars on each side covered with canvas until his hands ached. He had visions of the aircraft hitting the side of one of the mountains, never to be found in the dense jungle, even if he was fortunate enough to survive such an impact! At least his nervousness had taken his mind off his travelling companion who now sat across and directly opposite, apparently not at all bothered by the inclement weather, and resulting yawing effect the heavier than air machine experienced.

He'd been surprised, and then overcome with anger when he walked into the small asbestos-walled departure room reserved normally for crews and recognized her standing there, talking to one of the crew about her baggage. His travelling companion was to be Louise.

Furious, he had dropped his own case and stormed up to her.

"What the blazes are you doing here?" he demanded not even waiting for her to finish talking to the orange suited airman.

"A simple 'hello' would suffice, Stephen," she responded stiffly.

"You're not on this flight, surely?" he asked incredulously.

"On the flight. On the mission. Yep, guess you could say that cowboy!" she answered, deliberately exaggerating a deep-southern accent.

"And in what capacity, if I may be so rude as to inquire?" his face flushed with controlled anger.

"As an observer. Courtesy of Uncle Sam and however they refer to the Indonesian Government department responsible for the farce they have the audacity to call a plebiscite."

"You're the other foreign national sent to substantiate my report of this visit?" he asked, knowing that she was going to respond in the affirmative but not wanting it to be so.

"Correct." She hesitated for just a moment before adding, "and, it would be the mature and professional thing to do if we were to establish some ground rules together now, before we depart. Don't you agree, Mister Coleman?"

Stephen glared at the woman for whom he'd once held such deep passionate feelings and was suddenly lost for words.

She was as beautiful as ever. How could you be angry with a woman who looked as good as this? he wondered.

"Okay, Louise. Or is it Miss Louise, or, considering your newly developed accent, Missy? I'd heard you'd taken up with the good doctor over in your patch but I didn't realize that he was from Georgia!"

There it was. He'd said it. It had just slipped out, his mouth faster than his brain and immediately he'd regretted the barbed innuendo regarding her social life. For a long moment they looked at each other. He thought she had smiled first and he misinterpreted the sign, stepping closer to her, almost sheepishly.

"No, Stephen. Not now, we'll talk when we're airborne."

With which, he was obliged to wait. He was curious to discover why this woman had exited his life so suddenly, so mysteriously. He now had the opportunity or would, during the tour, to confront her, alone and away from the cocktail circuit.

They had seen each other at functions. She had always avoided him and, after some months, Stephen had finally accepted that they had no future together. He had never understood what had happened. He knew that their brief affair was more than some temporary fling. At least it was to him. Stephen resented the mixed emotions he immediately experienced when she turned up as his travelling companion. Stephen recognized that he still held strong feelings for Louise. But that was now all in the past.

Life had gone on for both. He had an occasional relationship, but without developing any real feelings for the partner he'd taken at the time. On the other hand, he knew that Louise was seen regularly on the arm of one of the USAID doctors, also an American. He let it all pass and after a time believed he'd put it all behind him. And now she was here, together with him, and he felt the old familiar stabbing sensation which had plagued him before. They were now both approaching the end of their tours and he did not want her to disappear again, or at least, not without a reasonable explanation. A reason, even an excuse. Something you could give to another who had once opened the window to their soul and believed the softly whispered promises that had been made.

A sudden drop dragged his thoughts back to the present. The air turbulence persisted on throwing the Dakota around as if it were made of paper. He probed his memory to recall whether or not he may have revealed his terrible fear of flying to her during those few exciting days together. Stephen was angry with her. She just sat there reading a bloody book! He wanted to unbuckle and move across to sit alongside her but fear kept him strapped into his canvas seat.

Again the aeroplane dipped, lifted slightly then dropped bringing a silent scream to his lips. And then the plane broke through the lower cloud cover and there, off the port side, Coleman could see the white beaches and coconut palms of the Island of the Gods.

Suddenly, it was as if there had never been any threat of falling, or fear of dying. He slowly regained his composure and smiled at Louise. She was preoccupied with the landing formalities and, as this was a freighter, double checked her straps and gear.

"Good flight, hey?" he called nonchalantly over the engine noise as they banked towards the small and narrow strip with ocean at each end.

She smiled in response. "Of course, I've had worse but out of ten, this was an eight," he offered, now full of bravado as the aircraft's undercarriage shook when its tyres leaped from zero to seventy-five miles per hour within a fraction of a second, hitting the hot tarmac and screaming as rubber tore away.

"Stephen," she said sharply, leaning towards him still buckled tightly, "shut up!"

It was said without venom. He realized then he'd been obvious and that she'd known he'd been terrified the whole time. He felt foolish.

The crew wanted to refuel then continue on through the rest of the afternoon to Kupang but he was adamant. He simply refused to fly any more that day. He was already tired and needed to regain his composure after the dreadful aerobatics he had experienced for most of the past few hours. He looked to Louise for support. "What about it, shall we take a break here?" he asked as the aircraft taxied to a halt.

She appeared indifferent as she sat looking at the pale blood-drained face. "It's your tour, Stephen but, to be honest, I wouldn't mind a hot tub after that last leg."

He was relieved that she'd agreed and immediately sensed the stress flow outwards from his body. The crew acquiesced, finally agreeing that an evening's stopover in Bali wouldn't be all that bad. As it was unscheduled, and at Stephen's request, he offered to pay for the meals and accommodation for the evening. The crew willingly accepted. They pocketed the advance he proffered and then disappeared into the free messing facilities available to them as members of AURI, the Indonesian Air Force. He was too tired to squabble over a few dollars.

The airfield was practically deserted. Together they hired an old left-hand drive Plymouth Belvedere taxi and proceeded to the Hotel Bali Beach in Sanur. Settling down to the 'welcome drink' in the Baris Bar Coleman recovered from his ordeal. Later, having showered, he attended to his equipment before phoning Louise's room. There had been no answer. He was disappointed.

That evening he dined alone. Well, as alone as one can be, Stephen thought, with more than a dozen staff observing his every movement in the under-occupied four-star resort. He searched high and low but could not locate Louise anywhere. Even the reception staff could not help when he pressed them politely, inquiring if she had gone out sightseeing, or taken a stroll along the thin strip of sand which separated the hotel grounds from the onslaught of the fast moving tides of Sanur. He sat in a deck-chair beside the pool overlooking the ocean. The setting was magnificent and, he thought despondently, wasted! There were less than ten guests in the hotel. The airport had yet to be upgraded to accept wide-bodied aircraft and, consequently, only a few visitors were able to enjoy the serenity of the warm hospitable people, their culture, and unbelievable scenery.

He had returned to the Baris Bar off the foyer and was entertained by observing a colourful character, an American, dressed in Bermuda shorts working very hard to sell what looked like Indian blankets. The man ordered drinks for the bar. Five, in all counting Stephen. Then he had opened the beautifully woven cloths to demonstrate their magnificent colours. The man was an absolute salesman, Coleman acknowledged.

Within minutes the old couple from the States had succumbed to his outrageous story of how he had smuggled these priceless and rare materials from right under the nose of the headhunters in one of the outer islands. Stephen had seen the same cloth in the small back streets of Pasar Baru in Jakarta selling for around three dollars. Before permitting his fellow countrymen to know the price of these rare and unique hand-woven works of art the overweight fellow insisted that they be his guest and enjoy yet another round of martinis which, of course, the elderly and now slightly tipsy couple readily accepted. Coleman knew when not to interfere. Anyway, he was enjoying the show and it was none of his business if this strange character found it necessary to flog village cloth to unsuspecting tourists.

He attempted to buy the man a drink. Surprisingly, he refused.

"That's my limit, man, got to fly tomorrow. Taking a quick run over to Surabaja but I'll have the bird back by sixteen hundred hours if you want to try your luck then."

Coleman looked at the American.

"I'm the chief pilot for Mutiara Airlines," he announced, his speech now more slurred as the martinis supposedly took effect. "In fact, I'm the only goddammed pilot," he laughed, holding both his arms out demonstrating to the bar that he obviously knew what aircraft wings looked like. "Haven't been paid in five months. The arseholes!" Looking directly at the couple he said, "Reduced to selling bric-a-brac to pay my way. What sort of life is that for a man who flew missions all over Indochina for Air America?" the words slurred more.

"Tell you what. As you're from back home, fifty bucks will do it!" he said, rolling one of the pieces up slowly over his arm and placing it in the woman's hands.

"Are you sure?" she asked, feeling guilty that they were taking advantage of one of their own, lost in the backwaters of civilization, probably without any real food.

"Ma'am," he started, "if I charged you any more I wouldn't be able to live with myself in the morning," and turning to the Balinese barman called for the check.

"Please," the old man was out of his chair, moving towards the bar. "Please let us at least pay for the drinks?"

Coleman quietly smiled. This guy was really good!

"Sir," he replied, almost sadly," you are a gentleman, and I thank you." With which he turned to the barman and instructed him, in Bahasa Indonesia, to put all the drinks, as usual, on the tourist's check. Having been paid he then disappeared.

* * * * * *

Stephen stayed for a while longer then strolled back outside into the balmy tropical evening air. He could hear the small waves and, occasionally, spotted their white crests as they broke onto the gentle sloping beach. Removing his shoes, Stephen walked down to the water's edge, deep in thought. In the distance he could see more lights and wandered slowly towards them.

As he approached he could hear the music long before seeing the dancers. A Balinese *gong* was performing, the sharp distinctive sounds emanating from the bamboo *gamelan* accompanied by drum and metal being beaten, the orchestra piercing the serenity of the night. They were performing for themselves. Perhaps a rehearsal, he guessed.

Stephen moved in closer to the artists and watched as they carried out their intricate dances, the beautiful young girls bending, twisting their bodies, while well rehearsed movements of their fingers and eyes not only displayed incredible discipline and control but provided the onlookers with a sense of participation in this rich and vibrant culture. Occasionally, as one of the musicians tapped the *cengceng* cymbals in concert with the beat of the *rencang* Stephen believed he could almost visualize the mythical characters depicted in the *gamelan's* sounds.

He was intoxicated with the night fragrance of the frangipani flowers and totally engrossed in the scene, this private view of the village collective, the *gong*, when he was startled by a hand touching his shoulder.

Turning quickly, he saw the silhouette of her head and shoulders, the shadows partly hiding her face.

He stood transfixed.

"Shh," she said, placing a finger to his lips. "Don't spoil the moment, Stephen."

Alarm changing quickly to surprise, he felt her arm slip through his, standing quite still, as if mesmerised by the unfamiliar noises coming from the village play performance. He could feel the warmth of her hands and recognized her perfume as they stood together, fascinated by the skilled dancers carrying out their intricate routines casting a spell over the Balinese night. The tantalizing rhythm continued, captivating the two, urging them together, locked in their own magical trance as they witnessed the soft brown figures moving gracefully to the sounds and the story of the

Ramayana Epic.

He turned to her and slowly moved his mouth towards hers.

She responded.

As she raised her lips to his, their soft touch produced a flood of memories. Holding each other with a tenderness long forgotten, Stephen tasted the bitterness of their long separation. And for a long time they embraced, without talking.

"I'm so sorry, Stephen. So very, very sorry!"

Her eyes reflected the sadness she felt and, suddenly, tears trickled down her face.

He moved his hand softly over her cheek, wiping the tears away as he kissed her gently.

"What ever happened to you, Louise?" he whispered, holding her close as if she would suddenly disappear again as she had before.

"I can't," she started, and then buried her head into his shoulder,.

"I must know," he spoke softly, encouraging her to continue.

"No, Stephen," she whispered, "not tonight," and looking into his troubled eyes she promised, "we'll have enough time together, I promise. Let it be, just for tonight."

He looked deep into her eyes, trying to understand, and silently agreed.

Suddenly she turned away from the ceremony and led him back down to the beach.

They sat quietly for awhile. He wrapped his arms around her and kissed her softly, first on the eyes and then gently on her lips. She leaned back, her head resting on the white sand and he kissed her again, passionately, her response signalling her desire to continue. There, in the cool of the tropical night, accompanied only by the sounds of the sea and the mystique of a Balinese night, they made love, tender love, unlike anything he'd ever experienced before. They stayed together until morning, touching each other tenderly, caressing, and whispering endearments until the soft cool morning sea-breeze alerted them to the coming day. Together they sat on the damp sand silently admiring the beauty of the sunrise.

As the morning's first rays stole silently from below the sea into the new pale sky, dancing though the jagged peaks of Gunung Agung teasing its occasional puffs of volcanic smoke, they made their way back slowly, reluctantly, through the coconut grove. They had not spoken again of the past. But both realized they would have to do so. And soon. Louise squeezed Coleman's hand tightly as they parted without speaking, each to their unused rooms to prepare for their departure.

Full of remorse she flung herself desperately onto the bed and buried her head in the pillow.

'Damn! Damn! Damn!' she screamed into the soft thick kapok filled cushion, hitting the bed with clenched hands. 'You stupid, stupid woman!'

She admonished herself for permitting it to happen, again. Their relationship should not continue. It was not the same as when they had first met.

This time she knew!

* * * * * *

Louise's own section head had shown her the file and advised her, no, instructed her to discontinue their relationship immediately for fear of her being compromised by Coleman. This limited brief merely contained a restricted advice to all section and department heads listing other foreigners attached to the multitude of embassies and consulates throughout the country. The confidential memorandum advised that those whose names were listed in the brief were to be treated with considerable caution. It did not elaborate.

When she scoffed at the innuendo, her chief had considered her emotional involvement sufficient to speak to his own immediate superior and the following day the young Attaché was summoned to the offices of what her friends referred to as the 'shadow people'. At first it seemed that the security section wished to discuss her file and clearances again. This was not unusual, as often these were checked and updated at regular intervals as promotions flowed, and postings changed the government employee's domicile.

She had not expected her relationship with Stephen to demand the attention of these people. Louise was astonished at the Langley file copy which she been obliged to read while sitting directly under the close scrutiny of the Embassy in-house 'spook' as they were referred to by the other civilian agencies. He had asked her to sign the declaration as Louise had done on many previous occasions when viewing restricted and sensitive material. This time she was surprised to see the additional marker flags on the top and sides of the folder containing the document, designating CIA-sourced intelligence.

The first photograph showed a group of young men talking together. Innocent enough, she thought at the time. The second series of photographs was taken with a telephoto lens but the clarity was enough to identify the man dressed in combat fatigues undertaking training exercises. The description was chillingly cold and brief.

Stephen Charles Coleman. Field operative Australian Security and Intelligence Forces. Active agent. Refer all CIA coded reference Top Secret 23519-68.

She listened quietly as the officer ordered her to discontinue the relationship; however, he suggested, his people would have no objections should she see Coleman casually, preferably in the company of others, as they understood that chance meetings both socially and professionally were almost unavoidable; such situations should be handled sensibly. Louise was then asked to confirm that she would accept the instructions given. The veiled threat was apparent.

Had she refused then there was no doubt in her mind that the following day someone else would be handling her official chores while she winged her way back home to the good old US of A!

She had no real choice. For days she suffered periods of depression and was bitterly distressed at not being able to explain to Stephen why they could not continue their relationship. Oh yes, she remembered, saddened by the memories, they had seen each other from time to time, at parties and receptions, but they never talked.

Louise could remember the cold look of bitterness she'd seen on Stephen's face during the first encounter, some months after she'd ceased accepting his calls. She had dated other men and had even started to see a colleague, an USAID volunteer doctor, regularly, but there just wasn't the same electricity she'd felt with Stephen and she ceased going out with him as well. At the time she felt that Stephen understood the reason for her behaviour and often wondered why he had given up so easily. She was a mature person for her age. Even as a teenager she did not accept that people could just fall in love, that quickly, so suddenly. And yet it had happened to her and Stephen!

She sat cross-legged, her favourite position when alone, her head resting thoughtfully on the palms of her hands. An hour passed. And how could she tell him that she knew? Another hour ticked away slowly.

She made her decision.

Distressed by what she was about to do but certain that there was no alternative, Louise asked the hotel operator to place a call on her behalf to Jakarta. Twenty minutes later she slowly placed the handset back in its cradle. Louise continued to sit, staring at the cream-coloured receiver. She wiped the tears away, angrily, as they blurred her vision as she started to write the message. She now knew she had made an error in judgment phoning her departmental head at his villa in Jakarta.

"Are you mad, Louise?" he had yelled down the line at her. "Even if you resign then there is no guarantee that you know who won't have your pretty little butt out of there so goddamm fast your head will still be spinning when your feet hit the ground in Washington."

He had been furious and, although guarded when discussing her situation on the open line, he still managed to convince her. His instructions had been explicit.

She really had no choice but to obey.

* * * * * *

Stephen waited in the foyer for thirty minutes. She had missed breakfast in the Barong Coffee Shop and he was becoming impatient. He phoned her room but there was no reply. Again he questioned the reception staff and they assured him that Miss Louise had not yet checked out of the hotel. He rode the lift to the seventh floor and moved quickly to her door, knocking several times, without any response. He returned to the reception and demanded that they open her door to see if she was all right, concerned that perhaps she had taken a fall in the bathroom and needed urgent assistance.

Embarrassed, a young girl dressed in the traditional *kain kebaya*, seeing the concern in his eyes, handed Stephen an envelope. He

KERRY B.COLLISON

tore it open immediately, already experiencing a sensation as he read the hand written note. Louise had decided not to continue the journey to Irian. She could not give him a reason, at this time, but would when he returned to Jakarta, that is, of course, if he could forgive her for not remaining with him for the remainder of the tour.

He couldn't believe it!

As he finished reading the brief note he noticed that most of the lobby and reception staff had been observing his reaction to the letter. Stephen was not to know that they genuinely felt saddened for him, as the entire staff had known the beautiful romantic story of their interlude on the beach, the evening before. There were no secrets on this island.

When a woman refused to meet face to face with her lover, sending a letter instead, it was always bad news.

They felt *sedih* for Stephen but their pragmatic oriental minds knew, and both the young men and female employees agreed that, as he was also young and handsome, his disappointment should not last too long.

Several of the young ladies smiled even harder, as he settled his account. Stephen ignored their kindness, engrossed in his own unfortunate affairs. Anger now displacing disappointment, he didn't answer the note, departing brusquely, almost rudely. As he believed that her refusal to continue with the journey could also affect the outcome of his own observations, Coleman permitted this aspect of her decision to distort the magnitude of her unexpected change of heart. Moody and almost belligerent, he checked out of the hotel and was driven off in the same antiquated American car as the day before.

He cursed the driver as they plunged off the narrow roads twice. It was strange for Stephen to be sitting behind a driver who steered the oversized sedan along the small partially bitumenised tracks sitting on the opposite side to what he was accustomed to. Many of these old vehicles had been brought back by former diplomats who never concerned themselves with moving the steering position to its correct side. The perilous ride helped distract his attention away from his disappointment. After nearly hitting a Brahman bull and killing several unlucky chickens, Stephen finally arrived at the airfield, just before nine o'clock.

160

The crew were all sitting around waiting for him. Unsmiling and resisting the temptation to unleash his foul mood on others, he mumbled the basic courtesies as he threw his baggage up before him into the old aircraft.

The crew acknowledged Coleman with a polite *selamat pagi* and quickly boarded the freighter.

Fifteen minutes later they were grinding along at eleven thousand feet. There were no clouds. Coleman was relieved. He spent most of the flight time thinking about the previous evening and, conscious of her absence, occasionally looked across to the empty seat.

He shook his head in disappointment.

It was almost as if their meeting on the beach had not happened. A dream even.

Strange, he thought, she had just about convinced him of her sincerity and now she was gone again. Just like before. Stephen suddenly realized that he really didn't know Louise at all. The longer he thought about it the more confused he became. When two people hit it off the way they first had you would expect them to know more about each other. He tried to recall their conversations and could not remember ever discussing their families, their work or any intimate detail about each other's lives. He wasn't even sure what she did in the aid section of the American Embassy as they really hadn't had the time to discuss these things. Maybe he should have encouraged her to discuss her job, her work, and her friends.

He considered these passing thoughts and decided that had he engaged Louise in such conversations then she too may have asked the same questions of him. And he would have had difficulty with that. Not that Coleman was unsure of his work, it was the constant deceit he had difficulty with. Had Louise asked he knew he could never reveal his true function in the Embassy, covering the truth with easily practised lies. He had never been comfortable lying to close friends about the nature of his employment. Suffice to say, he was a competent journalist and carried out the responsibilities of the Information Section with considerable energy. It was the other, more secretive responsibilities that often gnawed away at his conscience. It seemed obvious, he thought, that a permanent relationship would be near impossible anyway, considering the constraints of his covert activities which, he suddenly admitted, kept him fully committed to his masters.

His mind drifted back to the previous night's love making and he smiled. She had said in her note that it was an evening she would never forget and hoped that he wouldn't either as it had been so very special to her. Yes, he agreed, permitting images of their bodies pumping urgently together in unison on the beach to occupy his mind, distracting him from the aircraft's movements. It had certainly been a special night! Alone, the only passenger, and for the first time since he could remember, Stephen slept undisturbed whilst in flight.

* * * * * *

The aircraft droned on. And on. Finally, they arrived in Kupang, refuelled then continued on to Ambon. Having enjoyed the last sector, Stephen now felt slightly more comfortable with the knowledge that he was still faced with a substantial distance left to cover by air. During the break he sat away from the nauseating aviation gasoline fumes as several ground staff hand pumped the load from two hundred-litre drums. It seemed to take forever and yet, during the time required for the refuelling, their conversation was inconsequential, the exchanges stiff and awkward.

After the next leg of their journey they rested for a day and, to Coleman's surprise, changed crews. The following two days saw the aircraft forced down onto an unkempt, unsealed, World War Two runway with engine problems. They had picked up contaminated Avgas during the last refuelling stop. The Captain radioed ahead requesting assistance as he decided against flying with the possibility of ongoing fuel problems. When help finally arrived, it was in the form of a fishing boat dispatched from a coastal village nearby. The seas were unseasonably rough and Coleman stoically faced the turbulent conditions. Towards the end of the first day he was horrified to discover that the wind had increased its intensity, the waves smashing over the ship's bow as the crew fought for control.

Then the Australian suffered the humiliation of seasickness. His body ached all over from the constant heaving. His rib cage felt bruised and his throat was tender. He prayed that the vessel would soon arrive at its destination. He did not believe that he could survive another few hours of the waves' pounding motion. The boat rocked from side to side almost in a corkscrew motion. One moment the bow would lift high into the air and the next it would go crashing down amongst the waves, dipping below the horizon forcing the bile to erupt as he struggled to control his stomach. The vessel was battered for two days by the severe conditions. Exhausted, he crawled into the foetal position and collapsed, his body tossed around the deck oblivious to the pain as his limbs were bruised and cut by the hardened timber.

A solitary figure viewed the limp body with disgust. He made no attempt to assist or relieve the young man's discomfort. He merely watched to ensure the foreigner did not die, at least not here, as it would not fit the plan he had been given. He spat over the side and continued to observe Coleman as he lay, curled up, occasionally moaning in his fatigue induced sleep. *'Pity we couldn't just dump him over the side here!'* the man considered, *'would be safer and not as complicated!'*

The dark Javanese considered his current mission. He had received his instructions directly from the General. He always did. No one else could be trusted with the tasks he carried out for the Timorese. He was provided with more than sufficient funds to carry out his orders. He discovered that, if he was careful, he could retain a considerable portion of these monies and did so, turning the cash into gold and burying the proceeds. Not that he needed money. He had no life other than that ordered by Seda. He merely obeyed. This was just another mission which he would complete and then report back to the General.

He started forward to grab the sick passenger who was in danger of falling overboard. The Australian somehow unconsciously managed to avoid this catastrophe and, satisfied that he was out of danger, the observer stepped away from the ship's rails. As the seas grew calm and the wind softened Stephen slept. The old fishing boat chugged along until reaching their destination late in the afternoon of their third day. The crew laughed quietly at the prostrate figure lying on the deck. They secured their fishing boat.

Some villagers were called and the foreigner was carried into the *lurah's* hut. As headman, he would be responsible should the stranger come to harm. There Stephen was examined by one of the women then left to sleep through the night. He awoke several times, thirsty, and was given water after which he drifted back into an exhausted sleep. The following morning he was awakened by the sounds of the village coming to life. He bathed and went in search of a familiar face as he had no appreciation of his whereabouts. He was advised that the crew had returned and that the village *lurah* was to escort him to the military post some twenty kilometres by road.

Upon checking his belongings, Coleman discovered that everything was intact. He was given food and then asked to accompany the village head to the next destination. Transport had been organized and he was relieved to see that the rest of his journey would be over dry land.

* * * * * *

Towards noon, the jeep bumped along the track leading into the army post. As they moved into the clearing where the soldiers had established their base camp, Stephen estimated that there were about two hundred men stationed there. They were fully equipped. This, obviously, was not a training camp, and the look on the men's faces reminded him of the Blitar operation. He could tell that they had already experienced action. There were no smiles for the visitor, in fact, their arrival was almost ignored. A solid framed Javanese Major received them in his hut. "*Selamat datang,*" he welcomed them.

Formalities completed, the officer advised him that he had been in radio contact with his headquarters and informed Coleman that he would take him on an inspection of several tribal areas where patrols had encountered surprisingly hostile and well-armed groups of what he termed terrorists. They discussed the mission. He was shown a map of the target areas and was advised regarding procedures to be taken should they encounter hostile forces.

Coleman was instructed not under any circumstances was he to wear anything resembling a uniform as, they agreed, it would be unlikely that he would be targeted if the enemy identified him for what he actually was: a non-military observer. Hopefully, he would be mistaken for a United Nations representative although, to date, there had been none venture this far into the hinterland. The following day, accompanied by the Major, Stephen departed for the first contact zone. The object was to demonstrate to him from a distance, if possible, the considerable military hardware that these isolated tribes had been armed with, and had learned to use with a reasonable amount of success.

The small convoy progressed slowly. The drivers of both trucks engaged the four-wheel drive mode as the tracks were wet and slippery. Stephen estimated that they had travelled approximately forty miles before they rested. It was difficult going. They had commenced with fifty soldiers and, when they stopped the Major instructed a corporal and five others to stay behind with the vehicles as the remaining distance could only be covered on foot. Almost within minutes the landscape changed, from light undergrowth to bush, and then into jungle. Nettles stung Coleman's face, neck and hands while thorns tore at his clothing. The mosquitoes were unbearable!

He was wearing jeans, boots and an old light weight jacket which zipped all the way through. Anticipating identification problems Stephen had selected this particular apparel as it was bright orange in colour and was unmistakably non-military clothing. He did not wish to be shot by accident and hoped that these precautions would be sufficient to guarantee his safety.

They continued pushing along small tracks which the Australian assumed were recent as the foliage on both sides had been freshly cut back to permit the contingent passage. The ground was covered with leaves and grass indicating that these paths had been in frequent use. They walked in single file. Coleman had not yet removed his camera from its protective cover. He needed both free hands just to maintain his balance.

It started to rain. The Major beckoned for Stephen to keep pace a little closer to the soldiers in front, as he was falling behind. He obeyed. They progressed a few kilometres then rested again. The Major indicated that in another hour they would camp. The thought had not entered Stephen's head. Camp! Out here? He groaned with the thought of spending a night in the jungle being bitten by every insect known to man and the possibility of the tribes people slipping into their camp and removing a few heads, as they had been known to do!

These primitive people had accounted for many a famous explorer in the past. Coleman tried to remember if this was where the young Rockefeller was murdered.

* * * * * *

When the time arrived, the soldiers moved swiftly establishing their perimeter defence, and protection from the never ending rain. Coleman crawled into the small area which offered some respite from the elements. He was tired and felt that every muscle and joint in his body was calling out for him not to continue with the trek. Aching all over he tried to rest as best he could. They handed out *dendeng*, their version of beef jerky.

Coleman ate what he could. The *dendeng* was tasty but he had no appetite. Instead, following the soldiers actions, he rested, saving his strength for the following day. He slept. It seemed that he had only just closed his eyes when he felt the rough hands on his shoulder. The young Lieutenant was shaking him.

"*Tuan, tuan, bangun,*" he called, waking the foreigner. Startled, Stephen jumped to his feet and immediately felt the rigours of sleeping in the jungle. He attended to his ablutionary needs and finished the remaining dried beef.

They marched on for two hours until the tension began to grow amongst the men. Coleman noticed the change and decided that they were obviously approaching some known point of danger. He could almost feel the absence of wildlife. He remembered that only a short distance back the jungle was alive with sounds as the birds and other animals called to each other, warning of the possible dangers brought by man's presence. Suddenly they stopped. The point man waved silently to them, indicating that they should crouch and remain silent. They had arrived at the top of a rise and the Major beckoned for Coleman to follow him quietly. He did so, half crouched, half crawling, being guided by the experienced veteran.

They had left the main body of their troop some seventy metres behind. Coleman was instructed to copy the officer's movements. He lay beside the Major, accepting the field glassed offered to him.

"*What am I looking for?*" he asked.

The officer indicated a clearing below and roughly one-hundred metres away from their position. There was a group of perhaps twelve to fifteen men dressed in a mixture of khaki and tribal dress. They were armed. Coleman removed his camera and adjusted the telephoto lens. He shot the roll of twenty-four exposures, replaced the film and returned the camera to its case.

"*Okay, Pak, let's get the hell out of here,*" he pleaded.

The officer smiled, shook his head, gestured for the civilian to remain where he was and waved for the Lieutenant to advance.

"*You're not going to engage these men down there, Major?*" Stephen asked in disbelief knowing in his heart that this soldier was surely going to do just that!

"*Mas, kamu diam disini sajalah,*" he ordered, instructing him to remain there in a tone that Coleman could not argue against.

"Shit!" he muttered, surprised that he was, within minutes, to witness an attack on the guerrilla group he could practically touch from where he lay.

Minutes passed. The Commander had left two men with Coleman. The remainder followed him down the slope, crawling, until they had reached the point the Major had determined.

Suddenly, the air erupted with the ear shattering sounds of rapid fire. Bullets seemed to pass frighteningly close as he heard the air rupture when the small missiles passed by. Stephen wanted to bury his head in safety but was captured by the fire fight, observing the men running down towards their target, firing from the hip as they descended into the enemy's camp. The engagement continued for what seemed an eternity. Coleman lay as still as he could hoping it would all be over quickly. But it wasn't.

The attack continued for at least fifteen minutes, followed by sporadic fire. Angry voices could then be heard. These were followed by more shots and then the jungle became quiet, only the smell of the fierce exchange remaining. An hour passed. The soldiers accompanying the Australian directed him to follow their lead which he did, descending down the slope in a half-crouched position.

He was reminded of his early childhood, when Guy Fawkes celebrations were still permitted. On November the fifth, bonfires burned throughout the night. For days before and after, firecrackers could be heard exploding and the air held the same acrid pall of gunpowder smoke. Cautiously, he followed the soldiers.

Suddenly, he noticed a body. Then another.

Coleman was stunned. These were Indonesians! He had, for some reason, not anticipated any of his own group being injured, let alone killed! He was taken to the centre of the clearing. The

Major was sitting close by, resting up against the trunk of a tree. He started to move towards the man, at the same time calling to the officer.

"*Pak Major*," he began but did not complete the sentence as the young Lieutenant grasped his arm and turned him away. Bewildered, Coleman brushed the hand aside and once again addressed the Major.

"*Tuan*," the Lieutenant called softly, "*tuan, dia sudah mati!*"

Stephen stared at the Major unwilling to accept what the Lieutenant had said. He approached the silent figure and looked more closely, moving around to face the now lifeless body of the Commander. Coleman stood in shock, unable to move. The bullet had struck the Major's head around the left eye socket, tearing through the flesh, ripping bone and muscle away then exploding through the back of his crown.

His legs weakened. He had to sit down.

The Lieutenant moved quickly, assisted by the more experienced Sergeant, clearing the area and reorganizing his new Command. "*Tuan, bangun, cepat,*" the officer ordered, instructing the Australian to get up quickly. Another soldier assisted him to his feet.

The Lieutenant barked out commands and the survivors regrouped. Carrying their fallen comrades' weapons, they departed the battle scene leaving the bodies where they fell.

* * * * * *

As they retreated up the slope they were observed closely. The shooter replaced the binoculars and lifted the high powered snipers rifle. He checked the PSO-1 scope to make sure that it was exactly in the condition required for the remaining and more difficult shots he'd have to make.

The weapon was a Soviet SVD, weighing only four and one half kilos and had a muzzle velocity of two thousand seven-hundred and twenty feet per second. The killer enjoyed this weapon more so than its American counterpart, as the Soviet sniper's rifle had the advantage of being considerably lighter to carry. And over these distances and terrain, that was a major factor when determining which weapon to use, especially considering that both the American and Soviet versions were practically identical in all other aspects.

The weapon felt like an extension of himself as he settled the rifle comfortably into the shoulder, resting his right cheek against the stock as his left eye peered across at the magnified images. He was pleased with the accuracy of the earlier shot which dropped the Major. It wasn't necessary but he justified the killing for the additional confusion it had created.

He adjusted the telescopic sights marginally. Aiming at the figure towards the front of the line retreating back up the hill, he compensated for the angle of the shot, the differences in height, then took a bead on the centre of the man's back.

'The power of the small missile will tear the target's heart out through the front of his chest,' the sniper speculated.

Gently he squeezed the trigger and the bullet leaped from the weapon hitting its target even before the sound of the shot could be heard. The startled Lieutenant turned and, as Stephen started to crumple, immediately recognized what had happened. Assisted by the other soldiers, he dragged the young Australian's body away from the line of fire.

* * * * * *

Umar Suharjo was satisfied with his second kill. But he was annoyed that the third target had not appeared. *You can't kill someone if they're not there!* he thought, his mind racing as he knew that the General would be displeased that he hadn't also executed the American woman. He searched the field of view until he was convinced that none of the soldiers had established his position. He scanned the scene one last time to be absolutely certain then turned and crawled back into the thick undergrowth. He stashed the weapon under the trees, covering it with a thick mound of decaying leaves.

And, with the expertise of the silent killer, he quietly slipped away, unnoticed, and made his way back to the coast where the pre-arranged vessel took him aboard, for Jakarta.

And Seda.

* * * * * *

Louise had stood outside the hotel. *Why hasn't he left, already?* She'd waited for Stephen to emerge from the Bali Beach and finally, she saw him stride out purposely, almost angrily, and slam the door of the old battered sedan. The staff had done as she had asked. By now he would have read her letter. And no doubt, hated her for her what she'd done. Again! Louise watched Stephen driven away in the old sedan, and out of her life, forever. She waited several minutes then returned to the reception where her luggage had been placed behind the cashier's door. The staff smiled at her, thanked the young lady for her generous tip, and watched her depart with the *gendut*, overweight American pilot whom they despised. She'd little choice but to take the Mutiara flight as Garuda Airlines had nothing going out that day.

The pilot had changed his scheduled flight to Surabaya to accommodate her, agreeing to fly directly to Jakarta and return via Surabaya instead of the other way around. It really made little difference to him anyway, he'd said, and so Louise had decided to fly with her fellow American.

As they approached Tuban airfield she felt relieved to see that Stephen's flight had departed. Louise searched the horizon for the aircraft unsuccessfully. Her driver passed through the unguarded gates leading into what would have been a restricted area in other airports in many parts of the world, and drove directly up to the only plane parked on the small concrete surface outside the hangers.

Several men working around the port side ceased what they were doing and assisted the American woman with her baggage. She boarded the twin-engined C-47, the same vintage as the aircraft she had taken just the day before, knowing from its appearance that this machine had not been maintained as well as she had hoped. There were crates of tools and other mechanical items stored slightly forward in the cabin. These had not been strapped down and, judging from the condition of the rest of the aircraft, Louise thought that it was unlikely there were even any straps available to secure the heavy boxes. Grease remained smeared along sections where recent maintenance work seemed to have been carried out, and she had to be careful not to brush against these areas when taking her seat.

There was some activity around the tarmac area and Louise could see two men sauntering casually across in the direction of the plane. She recognized the American and assumed, correctly, that the other man was part of their crew. Both boarded and went forward to the cabin, mumbling as they dragged themselves into their cockpit seats, acknowledging her presence with merely a cursory nod.

Louise didn't have much of an opportunity to see their faces, particularly their bloodshot eyes, as they had half stumbled past her as she sat already strapped into the flimsy seat; but if she had, there is little doubt that the aircraft would still have enjoyed her company for the remainder of the trip.

Jack was in a mean mood. His head was thumping from the late night and his co-pilot, one of the few Indonesian men who drank hard liquor, was not feeling too much better for the same reason. First one engine was fired up and then, within a minute or so, the other coughed to life; as the decibels affronted her hearing, the high screaming mechanical pitch causing Louise to cover her ears. The old aircraft wobbled around as it taxied out from the hard-standing area in front of the maintenance building, as if it were trying, or testing its wings.

Suddenly she wished she'd not phoned Jakarta and followed her heart instead of her mind! The aircraft stopped momentarily, the engine revolutions reaching an almost unbearable pitch, before it suddenly lurched forward and commenced its attempt to breach gravity.

No sooner were they airborne when the unshaven pilot unlatched the cockpit door and left the controls to his Indonesian co-pilot. He stumbled back into the mixed cabin and cargo area, lurching around until he located the small and dirty overnight Pan Am bag which had dislodged itself during takeoff. He pulled an aluminium flask from the side pocket, unscrewed the cap, put it to his mouth and took a generous swig of the contents. The pilot then looked back at Louise. She could see that he was unshaven. His puffed face and eyes were of immediate concern to her, and she was about to ask if he was well enough for the flight when he belched loudly.

"God damn, I really hate flying!" he laughed, sucking at the container for a second time. "Would you like a hair of the dog?" he asked, not really expecting his only passenger to accept.

Louise eyed him coolly. She was concerned. "Sure," she replied, unexpectedly.

The surprised pilot passed the flask to the young woman, eyeing her now more closely. "Don't drink it all," he suggested, "it's a four-hour haul to the next one."

'God,' she thought, 'four hours to Jakarta with this cretin!'

She sipped once, smiled and extended the flask, deliberately permitting the bourbon to fall to the deck.

"Christ!" he snapped, lunging forward to retrieve the hip flask.

Jack managed to salvage a little of the contents. He eyed her coolly and thought, 'bitch,' as he returned to the cockpit, fuming. "Just what we don't need right now, a smart-arsed woman on board," he called to the other man as he levered himself back into the port side seat while using his co-pilot's shoulder for support.

Had she witnessed this man's clever act of the previous night then she may not have been as concerned, assuming the drinking was part of a routine the former civilian war pilot played out for his guests. But she hadn't, and this was no act, as the man always drank when flying. He'd developed the perilous habit along with many of his flying buddies in 'Nam. On occasions he'd been known to drape a pet carpet snake around his shoulders when on the flight deck, but unbeknown to him, the other pilots at Mutiara had willingly disposed of it, under instructions from management. The man had a vicious streak and all were subject to his mean temperament when he drank.

Alcoholic haze and reality have no place together in the cockpit of any aircraft, and this flight was no exception. Considering the added aggravation of the incident involving the alcohol, Louise was concerned but not frightened, as she knew there was another pilot sitting forward, obviously competent, as Jack the blanket-seller had permitted the other flyer to take the controls while he went in search of an instant remedy for his hangover.

The aircraft droned along for an hour. Jack was, by now, well down the path of one of his fantasies which had, some eighteen months before, resulted in his contract not being renewed in Indochina. He'd not been lying when he boasted of his previous employers and his unusual background.

Jack had, in fact, flown for Air America for some time but suffered burn-out and was terminated before he killed someone. He'd managed to park two aircraft in unusual positions hard against the side of hills which, fortunately for him but not his other crew, were covered with thick vegetation at the time. Although the majority of the pilots were similar to Jack in nature, often taking uncalled for risks endangering their lives in the pursuit of the hefty pay packets these hazardous missions demanded, he was considered over the top with his weird antics as he scared the hell out of even the less stable flyers in the group.

After the second crash nobody would fly with him any more. He'd taken his pay and headed for Guam but, somehow, ended up in Bali with a job, flying the three former Australian C - 47s which, when they first took delivery, had almost zero engine hour time and full airframe clearance. The former owners had even added disc-brakes to the aircraft which were in almost perfect shape for these tropical conditions and would remain so, providing they were carefully maintained.

Now, suffering continuous neglect, these machines, once admired in aviation circles for their safety, had become very dangerous and should not have been cleared to fly. Two of the three planes had already been stripped for their parts, leaving the small feeder-service unable to maintain schedules and, more importantly to Jack, also unable to pay crew and ground staff salaries which had fallen seriously into arrears.

He drank here because that's how he'd flown in 'Nam, Cambodia and hell, even Laos when he dropped in there with a load of weapons to pick up the white powder from the pudgy little General who always paid for his deliveries in that way. There was never any difficulty in finding a buyer for the heroin although he drew the line at taking any himself. An occasional puff on the ganja sticks was okay, he thought, but that white powder, it would make your brains rot like shit! And besides, he could probably drink a fifth of Bourbon on every leg and not miss a marker, he often boasted.

* * * * * *

He recognized the familiar coastline of Java over the city of Semarang. In the distance he couldn't help but identify the incredible slopes of Gunung Semeru, its smoking peak reaching over twelve thousand feet into the sky, dominating the world around it, sometimes spewing sulphurous clouds over low-lying villages or hurling thousand of tonnes of volcanic rock and ash over all it viewed.

Air becomes very thin around twelve thousand feet and this aircraft type was not designed to climb much above that ceiling. Jack decided to take the smart-arsed lady on a detour to show her some of his skills. He corrected the course slightly changing the new heading in line with the volcano and winked at his fellow crewman.

"We'll have a quick look," he laughed, pointing his thumb back in the direction of the rear.

His co-pilot just nodded, all too familiar with Jack's flying antics. He peered ahead and identified the backdrop of cu-nimbulus and muttered to himself knowing that the sensible thing to do would be to avoid these instead of playing around with the mighty clouds. The American smiled as he returned to the rear section of the plane, this time opening what appeared to be a tool box, but in fact contained yet another bottle of his favourite bourbon. Jack had never wondered why it was that he drank so little when on the ground but consumed such incredible amounts when airborne! He tore the cover off, unscrewed the top, and lifted the bottle to his mouth.

Louise understood the macho play and smiled at him when he'd finished taking the equivalent of two or three direct shots from the bottle. She returned to her book, electing to ignore him, not showing her concern which had grown considerably, as now Louise had really become worried by his behaviour.

He took another long swallow, and then moved forward to take over the controls.

'Bitch!' he said again, silently to himself.

Another half hour passed and the mountain was directly up ahead in their flight path. The alcohol now stimulating his brain, Jack commenced his tour around the active volcano, moving the stick across, placing the slopes seemingly within grasping distance. He was determined to either impress the young good-looking babe in the back or at least demonstrate his flying skills even with the bourbon under his belt.

'Who knows?' he thought, maybe I'll get lucky tonight!

He corrected the plane's altitude, increasing its climb and moved the compass bearing for a new heading to the port side of the huge mountain. He intended to position the machine up as close to the summit as possible for a look-see into the crater if he could find a hole in the low weather which partly covered the peak. But even his clouded brain acknowledged the aircraft's altitude limitations.

Fifteen minutes later Louise felt the change in the aircraft's attitude, as it started to jump around suddenly, startling her. She looked out the starboard window quickly and was surprised to see the magnificent mountain slopes covered with trees seemingly scratching at the heavens, their tall trunks piercing through the rich undergrowth in search of more light, their crowns a mass of thickly leafed foliage offering haven to the numerous families of birds nestled there.

The scenery was incredibly beautiful. And disturbingly close!

The mountain seemed to disappear above her, far up to the right of the aircraft, the upper slopes now smothered in a blanket of cloud. There were no people or villages to be seen. It was as if the green walls of this enormous geological structure had forbidden man to enter, protecting its secrets under a veil of soft cloud and dense jungle. She was in quiet awe as the aircraft continued to encircle the mid-slopes of the mountain, staring at the jungle below as it smothered the lower view, offering its protection to the life forms which survived in the strange environment.

"Well, what do you think of that ma'am?" the voice interrupting her thoughts.

"It's stunning," she acknowledged

"Thought you'd enjoy the detour," he laughed, holding the now refilled flask towards her.

"No, thanks." Louise refused quickly.

"It's okay. Got the boy up the front taking care of things there."

He stumbled and fell as the aircraft dipped suddenly. "Goddamm!" he cried out as his knee came directly into contact with the leading edge of a case of tools tied down near where he was standing.

The aircraft dipped again, as the unusual air currents played with the intruder. Within moments they were engulfed by cloud. They had zero visibility. The co-pilot over-corrected as the starboard wing dipped.

And then it happened.

As the plane hit the treetops with incredible velocity, the fuselage disintegrated and the wings sheared off. The aircraft exploded into unrecognizable twisted fragments, and pieces of wreckage fell to the forest floor below.

Jack and his co-pilot didn't even feel the impact. The unbelievable force ripped them apart, taking their lives before their startled brains could acknowledge the fact that they were going to die.

Louise also died instantly. Her remains and those of the crew scattered onto the treetops and then down to the forest's floor.

Within minutes of the tragedy, quiet returned to the mountain and the jungle which covered its slopes. It was as if the accident had not happened and there was really nothing much there to indicate that it had. Pieces of the disaster blended immediately into the landscape, undetectable from the air as the disturbed birds returned to their nests high among the very same treetops which had stolen three lives just moments before. The C-47 had been well off course and the SAR parties would never consider looking there for the lost aircraft.

Not on the slopes of this volcano.

THE TIMOR MAN

Book Two

1975

The Timor Invasion

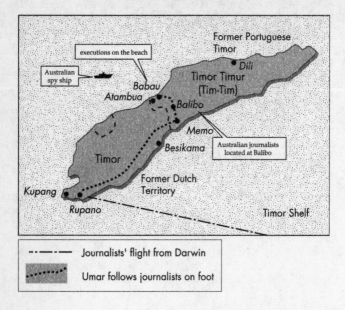

Former Portuguese Timor

executions on the beach

Australian spy ship

Babau

Atambua

Balibo

Memo

Dili

Timor Timur (Tim-Tim)

Australian journalists located at Balibo

Besikama

Timor

Former Dutch Territory

Kupang

Rupano

Timor Shelf

– · – · – Journalists' flight from Darwin

••••••• Umar follows journalists on foot

Chapter 8

Canberra — Jakarta

******

Canberra's winter ambiance suited this city of public servants perfectly. The Capital virtually went to sleep as the severe cold atrophied all resemblance of outdoor social activities other than those associated with Winter sports. The social set which normally thrived on cocktail parties, political functions and royal visits suddenly became subdued as if some local ordinance had abolished all revelry. Government offices closed at five and were, for the most part, deserted by six. Skies remained overcast, further reflecting the depressed social - political atmosphere.

******

John Anderson glanced at his watch. He had arranged one last appointment for the day after which, he would escape to Sydney for the weekend.

When his secretary announced his guest's arrival Anderson smiled remembering that Coleman had always been punctual.

The visitor was ushered in, provided with coffee and then left alone with the well-groomed intelligence chief. They sat quietly for a few moments sipping the hot but tasteless liquid.

"Well, this is it then, you're really off tomorrow?" the older man asked, more as a statement than a question.

"Yes. It's definite," was the response and then, "it's time. . . " the words were left hanging.

"Remember our last discussion?" Anderson started, "whatever you need. . . "

"Thanks. I appreciate the offer," the visitor interrupted.

"When will you return?"

"A week, a month," he answered almost listlessly. "Maybe I will take the full three months and put my feet up on a beach somewhere," he answered.

When Coleman had requested the extended break, citing accumulated leave from his former department, the general consensus was that he should go, although his superiors were not keen on having him return to Indonesia. There was also the consideration of his not having the comfort and, more importantly, the protection of a diplomatic passport as he was no longer accredited to the Embassy.

As far as the public was aware, Stephen Coleman worked with the Australian External Affairs Department's Information Service in Canberra as a desk officer.

Recently there had been a major reorganization of the Australian Intelligence Organizations, including the military within which resulted in the ANIB no longer being used for overseas under-cover operatives. This had the effect of eliminating the requirement of the 'double-desk' subterfuge used during Stephen's tour, as current Information Officers in the embassies were not associated in any way, nor were they aware of the existence of any such covert activity.

John Anderson uncrossed his arms. "We accept that you may need this leave. We don't necessarily agree that returning at this time to Indonesia would be the correct choice of destinations under the circumstances. "

"There is no hidden agenda," Stephen had insisted.

"Even so," Anderson continued, "there is no reason for you to insist on that country for your break. Why not visit Thailand or even the Philippines, Stephen?"

"I wish to take a couple of months and wander around the place as a civilian for a change. Before it was different. I never really had any opportunity to relax and develop a genuine feel for the country. I need this trip John, although I do understand your reluctance in approving my itinerary. "

"If you take the full three months, just spread your time around," he advised. "Visit Malaysia or one of the other countries I've suggested and that will assist you to develop a more objective perspective of your life after what happened to you in Irian. "

"Then you approve?"

The older man had actively discouraged Coleman's revisiting Indonesia. If not for any other reason there was the consideration of his recently upgraded and highly sensitive security clearance. This alone demanded approval for any overseas travel by him as Director.

"No," Anderson insisted, "I agree. There is a subtle difference as you well know."

"Thank you, sir, " Stephen had said, in deference to the man and to reflect his gratitude for the approval.

"No more than three months, Stephen, just three months. Agreed?"

The younger man smiled. "Sure John. Just three months. " The extended break would be more than adequate for him to determine what he really wanted out of the rest of his life. He hoped to take the opportunity to decide once and for all whether he really wanted to continue in his present occupation and, if not, to examine his alternatives.

"Keep us posted. "

"I will," he promised, rising to his feet with his hand outstretched.

"Good luck, Stephen," the older man stressed warmly, taking Coleman's grip and squeezing it tightly.

His visitor nodded, smiled and departed with a casual wave born out of familiarity. He closed the Director's door behind him.

The Intelligence Chief leaned back into his chair, considering Coleman. He'd known, of course, that his protege had filed an application for a visa with the Indonesian Embassy weeks before informing anyone of his intentions. Anderson shook his head slowly and smiled to himself as he heard Stephen's voice.

"Bye, Madge," Stephen called softly, smiling as he departed.

Anderson's secretary watched the clean-cut, handsome and well spoken operative leave. She sighed. The senior secretary continued to look even after he had gone, deep in thought and then, remembering the stack of unfinished correspondence on her desk turned her thoughts back to the job at hand.

* * * * * *

The QANTAS Boeing 707's powerful engines thrust the aircraft along the runway until the nose lifted and the under-carriage could be heard retracting to the in-flight position. The Sydney-Jakarta flight time was eight hours, more than Stephen Coleman cared to spend in an aircraft but, at this time in his life, his fear of flying was of lessser import than it had been before.

He settled back in the comfortable first class seat, a courtesy upgrade arranged by 'Madge the Magnificent' as Anderson's secretary was often referred to by those who knew her well. Stephen accepted a glass of Moet Chandon then removed his shoes immediately sensing the tension dissipate.

He smiled inwardly at being relaxed aboard an aircraft. Life and attitudes had drastically changed, he contemplated as the four-engined jet climbed comfortably away to the deep hum of the four Rolls Royce engines. Sipping the champagne, Stephen's mind wandered back over the last time he was in Indonesia, the artificial friends he had acquired and, of course, that near fatal expedition into Irian.

* * * * * *

Stephen never did understand how he had survived the shooting. The bullet, having struck the soldier's arm first had been deflected upwards ripping into Stephen's right shoulder. He now realized that the corporal who was assisting him at that precise moment had inadvertently saved his life. His recollection of the medical evacuation and the first few days of hospitalization were vague. He did, however, remember the pain. The military team had been poorly equipped to handle extreme medical emergencies.

There had been no morphine or any other pain killers. He had awoken to the searing, burning agony time and time again, repeatedly collapsing back into oblivion. His left hand moved unconsciously to the wound; it had become habit. Long hours of physiotherapy had helped repair the muscular damage but in his nightmares he still saw the grotesque remains of the Commander's head transformed by the assassin's bullet. His shoulder would never be the same again, of course, but this was not evident in his stance.

As Stephen underwent physiotherapy under the watchful eyes of the nurses he had to struggle to meet the demands placed on damaged muscles and tissue. He knew that there really was no choice but to accept the discipline required for recovery. The exercises were difficult and tedious.

His mental well-being also required attention. Though there was no therapy that could help with the loneliness and sleepless nights, Stephen managed to cope with his memories. He was given the opportunity to rebuild his life, an opportunity given by Anderson.

The Director had been a regular visitor before he was discharged from the hospital and even visited when Stephen remained at his mother's home as a convalescent. On the anniversary of his 'accident' he completed his visits to the hospital. The physiotherapist had given him instructions for an exercise routine to maintain muscle development. In the privacy of his mother's home Stephen examined his body in the full length mirror surprised that even after a year the cicatrix remained ugly and red, like some great welt on his shoulder and side.

There were other scars; but these were indelibly etched in his mind. He had almost accepted the shooting as accidental. The Governments of Indonesia and Australia both agreed that the shooting was accidental, that he had obviously been mistaken for a regular Indonesian soldier during the attack by the insurgents. It had then become generally accepted that there had been nothing sinister behind the accidental shooting of the Embassy representative who was on record as having requested the tour. To accept otherwise would have raised too many unanswerable questions.

Coleman believed that it had been a deliberate attempt on his life. The circumstances leading up to his shooting appeared too orchestrated and, whenever he reflected on the events surrounding the attack, he believed that there could be no other conclusion. He had, however, elected to follow the general consensus and accepted that the shooting had been an accident. But only publicly.

Fortunately, the press also accepted the popular version of the incident. The Australian government did not need to issue a 'D' notice to prevent the newspapers from publishing articles detrimental to national interests. Intelligence services from Australia, New Zealand and the United States agreed that there was a substantial arms operation underway prior to the plebiscite. The majority of these agencies were convinced that vested interests had deliberately manipulated the Irian tribes into believing that armed revolt against the Indonesians would eventually lead to their achieving independence from the powerful Indonesian presence, and the United States delivered satellite photography to support these views. The poorly organized rebel movement, lacking in military hardware and training, failed dismally. What started as major outbreaks of resistance soon turned into occasional skirmishes. Opposition diminished rapidly once supply lines had been effectively disrupted. Most of the primitive groups lay down their arms and surrendered. Others regrouped along the New Guinea border vowing to continue their campaign of terror against the Javanese transmigrant colonies. The United Nations moved quickly and, as indications were that the people of Irian Barat wanted to be part of the Indonesian republic, the supervised voting commenced.

The results of the plebiscite destroyed all future hope for an independent West New Guinea. The exultant Indonesian authorities named the new province, Irian Jaya.

The significant events and changes which had occurred over the time of his absence amazed Stephen. He had maintained a watching brief over Indonesia and was restless to witness the changes he'd read about for himself. The people of Indonesia had become even stronger, uniting behind the powerful *Golkar* Party to establish their leader as the most powerful head of state in Asia, outside of China.

The country had commenced its drive towards a full market economy. Foreign investors flooded into the capital signing commitments never thought possible just a few years before. Suddenly, there was a burst of activity and the capital city's skyline started to change. The Chinese entrepreneurs returned and, with them, funds to develop the trading opportunities of this country's enormous consumer potential. Overnight, with its energy reserves, Indonesia became the new investor destination. They came in their thousands with briefcases full of money and promises.

The Indonesia Coleman had left, just two years before, had changed. Even the people seemed different. Senior government players had come and gone already over the short period. The technocrats were now involved. It was an exciting time. Particularly for General Nathan Seda.

* * * * * *

During the second year of his physical and mental recuperation and towards the completion of his intensive advanced intelligence training, Stephen had considered leaving the Service. The months had dragged on laboriously as the monotonous daily routines chipped away at his energy causing him to question his motives for continuing with the department.

He felt as if he now lacked motivation and needed something to stimulate him, to provide an excitement, to generate new energy in his life. Anderson understood the underlying reason, as did Stephan's mother, both annoyingly endowed with some sixth sense when it came to his well being. At times he found it suffocating. They had both, in their own time broached the subject of Louise.

He'd flatly refused to discuss her. Not with his mother and certainly not with Anderson. Stephen didn't believe that either could understand the emotions he'd experienced, the mental torment he had suffered once when news of her accident had been divulged to him. Their relationship was now history and nothing could change the facts surrounding her demise. Most was now just part of his confused memory punctuated with flashes of the shooting, their last night together, and the disappearance of her flight.

He'd been informed while still under hospital care in Sydney. By then the Search and Air Rescue parties had been called off and she had been declared officially lost, one of those incongruous euphemisms, he soon realized, which can be vague enough to provide a small window of hope to friends and loved ones. Even now he refused to accept the loss, although he recognized that part of the healing process was coming to terms with her death. He just wasn't ready to let go. At least, not then.

With the coming of the first falls of snow, Stephen eagerly accepted the opportunity to revisit Anderson's mountain lodge. Although he would need to nurse his shoulder back into the demanding sport carefully, he decided to go. It wasn't lost on him that his mother had been thinking of psychological recuperation rather than physical recovery when she suggested the holiday and somehow secured his Director's consent.

At first he was content to plough around through the white-blanketed setting enjoying the serenity of the Australian Alps during winter, but when he observed the other guests their host had also invited carrying their gear out to the four-wheel drive, he was immediately impatient to ski again.

He commenced with some light down-hill skiing and, although the conditions were poor he had little difficulty regaining the form he had achieved some years before. Stephen discovered that he still enjoyed the exhilaration of speeding down the slopes and, under the observant eyes of the clandestine department's chief, Stephen regained his confidence quickly. Convinced that his mind was back on track he attacked his work with a refreshed vigour, much to the relief of the departmental watchdogs who had become increasingly concerned with their agent's demeanour.

Due to his in-depth in-country experience, Stephen was placed in charge of the Indonesian desk. He was not completely comfortable with the position but understood the necessity of staying behind a desk until he felt *au fait* with the administrative and logistical support aspects of the profession he had entered.

Occasionally he dined with the Chief but other than those rare occasions Coleman kept to himself. This was not considered unusual as most of his associates had also kept to themselves during the intense training. They understood that their social lives would forever be restricted by the sensitive information they knew and avoided developing new relationships outside the group. The identity of members of the elite circle of government operatives was known only to the Prime Minister, his Attorney General and the small number of directly involved personnel. Apart from the demanding field training in Canungra, Stephen spent most of his time inside the Defence Department offices.

ASIS had been designed along the lines of the British secret intelligence services, more commonly referred to as MI6. The major difference between the two was that the existence of the Australian counterpart was unknown to the public and media. Only the most senior foreign intelligence chiefs had access to this extremely sensitive information. Stephen knew from the list he had examined that this included the Director of the CIA and, of course, MI6.

The security clearance alone often required extremely intensive investigation of potential recruits. Many were abandoned by the Department over the most minor considerations well before there was any possibility of their accessing any information whatsoever relating to the existence of the Service.

Coleman had been encouraged to re-enter the cocktail circuit and did so willingly. He was constantly amused by the not so subtle differences in behaviour he observed between the Canberra bureaucrats and the foreign diplomats. It was as if most of the city's population were all on some extended political holiday as they appeared to be always away down the coast fishing or visiting the ski resorts on weekends while their evenings were occupied by the numerous functions listed on the diplomatic calendar.

Occasionally Stephen spent the weekend with his mother in Melbourne. He was shocked to see how she had aged so during the past two years. He came to understand that he had never really appreciated just how much she had cared for him and how proud this elegant lady had become of her son. There had been no communication with his father. Not even when he had been hospitalized. His parents had separated not long after his first overseas posting and dfrifted to their own distant horizons, until finally losing all contact with each other.

Stephen found time to visit his old friend and teacher, Albert, who always reciprocated with a lunch or dinner invitation whenever he came to Canberra. He was pleased for the Timorese. Although his life had also suffered the extremes of love and disappointment Albert now appeared to be quite comfortably settled in his current position as a part-time technical advisor to the government, while maintaining his former teaching position at the Language Academy.

Mary had long deserted their marital abode. The couple had exchanged the necessary papers through their solicitors and now Albert was alone again, although he still received occasional communications from Nathan which, these days, he passed directly to the ASIO officer who arranged to meet with him regularly in Canberra. There he received a brief which he followed precisely upon returning to Melbourne, and the Indonesian community. Although he had asked himself the question many times, Albert just did not understand how or why he had been placed in the unenviable position which now overshadowed his entire life.

Unfortunately for Albert, he had never applied for naturalization whilst still married to Mary. Although the authorities stated that he now qualified in his own right, he could not understand why both applications submitted had been refused without a reasonable explanation. Albert had been informed that immigration checks took time and that he should be patient and persevere until he was accepted. During his most recent visit to Canberra and discussions with his intelligence contact, he had raised the issue and requested their assistance. He had been informed that his application was not necessary as he was already a resident and a further application may just open a Pandora's Box which could even result in his deportation.

Deportation! The very word gnawed at his intestines for weeks. The thought of being forcefully returned to Indonesia threw the fear of God into Albert. He accepted the agent's explanation and decided not to attract any further attention to himself. Albert was worried. He wished he could discuss the difficulties with his old student and now close friend Stephen Coleman. In fact, that is exactly what Albert should have done but he knew nothing of the Machiavellian world of intelligence and espionage and, in consequence, remained but a minor pawn under threat in two separate games.

He felt sad for Stephen when he first received news of the shooting accident. He had phoned his former student's parents to console them and obtain information regarding his condition. Albert journeyed to the hospital regularly as he was most sincere with respect to Stephan's well being.

Coleman appreciated the display of warmth from the Timorese. Their friendship grew and developed a new dimension.

Now Albert was alone again as Stephen, having informed him of his intended departure during his last visit, had bid farewell briefly by phone just the evening before as he waited in the departure lounge at Mascot Airport. Depressed since returning to Melbourne and alone in his empty bungalow, Albert considered his friend and silently prayed for his well being, the constant feeling which nagged at his thoughts ever since he had seen Stephen lying on the hospital bed covered in bandages, a worry to his mind.

There was just something about their relationship which he felt tied them together, driving them towards a common destination, to some form of conclusion. That night he said another prayer to his god, this time he prayed for his friend, Stephen Coleman.

* * * * * *

Coleman could not believe the changes he witnessed driving from Kemayoran Airport. The activity was intense. Roads had been widened, trees planted. New buildings were taking shape and the city's skyline changed from one of neglect to that of a city full of promise. The people even appeared brighter. There was a presence of hope in the air and not the despair he had so often encountered during his first visit to Jakarta. And the motorbikes! Where had all of those machines suddenly appeared from, screaming along in packs, twisting in and out of the traffic at dangerous speeds? He shook his head in disbelief. In just two years the changes had been dramatic. He was excited, the anticipation of seeing the Embassy again and perhaps meeting one or two old acquaintances raised his spirits even further.

When the taxi turned into Jalan Thamrin Stephen could not accept the incredible change that this avenue had undergone in such a brief period of time. Now there were skyscrapers where before there had been empty fields. Previously unfinished buildings, now completed, boasted neon signs on roofs advertising Sanyo, Toyota and other Japanese products. The main protocol road had been reconstructed as a four lane avenue with pedestrian crossings and traffic lights. The military with its tanks and soldiers were no longer evident.

Still suffering the mixed emotions of pleasant surprise and regret that he could no longer recognize the old city, Stephen felt his taxi pull to a jerky halt in the grounds of the new Australian Embassy. The old security guard, Pak Ali, recognized the former Attaché immediately.

"*Tuan, tuan,*" called the withered old man. "*Selamat datang, selamat datang,*" he continued to call as Stephen climbed out of the taxi and pumped the old Pak Ali's hand.

"*Apa kabar, Pak, sudah kawin lagi?*" Stephen asked, joking with the old man and asking him if he had taken any new wives.

"*Enggak, tuan. Pak Ali udah terlalu tua!*" he responded pleased that the tuan had remembered him and responding to the effect that he was now too old for that nonsense.

"*Kawin lagi dong, Pak Ali, bisa kembali muda!*" Stephen bantered, advising old Ali that if he remarried he would feel younger immediately.

"*Enggak, tuan, enggak!*" No tuan, no!, cried the toothless man.

This happy soul had served faithfully through until his first retirement when, at the mandatory age, he had been terminated. Almost everybody in the Embassy was aware that the old man could not support himself and the incredible number of offspring he had so indiscriminately sired and, as a gesture of recognition for his

loyal service, the staff re-engaged him immediately, using a pseu-
donym to circumvent the inflexible regulations which had resulted
in his predicament.

Coleman enjoyed the light banter with the old man. Always
pleasant, smiling and willing to help in anyway, he was considered by some to be one of the kindest men in town. Waving fondly
at the *jaga*, Stephen entered the Embassy foyer and was surprised
to see Australian security manning the reception desk.
Commonwealth Police.

Another change.

He registered his name and requested to see his successor, Phil
Walters. Minutes later he was ushered upstairs to the military's
'mess' quarters, a section of the top and fourth floor dedicated, as
the Naval Attaché suggested, 'to the spiritual pursuits of the military contingent attached to the embassy'. The serviceman had
turned this top security area into their own comfort station, complete with bar. Stephen was ushered into the room and was pleasantly surprised to recognize some of the faces present.

"Embassy still closes at 1430 hours, old chap," the Army Attaché
remarked, rising to greet the visitor, "and we heard you were going to pay us a visit. Welcome back."

Coleman shook the army officer's hand, "How are you Colonel?" he asked.

"Be a bloody sight better this time next week. Going home.
Tour's finished. "

The group had obviously been hard at it for some time as the
noise level for such a small group was unusually high.

"We bent the rules today, young Stephen," called another officer, the Air Attaché, "to welcome you back."

Phil Walters was obviously not completely comfortable as what
the Group Captain had just announced was completely true. These
six servicemen held their own regular and private function in the
Embassy, and it was always located somewhere where security prevented most others from entering. During his tour Stephen had
been called upon more than once to assist these men in their duties, due to his language expertise. He'd never refused their requests even when it involved giving up his valuable spare time
over the weekend to defuse domestic problems with their staff.

They, for the most part, respected the young civilian. After all, he had graduated from one of their most difficult military courses and was so given provisional membership status within their secret circle. These private meetings also provided the opportunity for discussion of sensitive Indonesian military data, access to which had been within Coleman's realm, but not his successor's.

He looked at the small group of hardened but likable professionals and was immediately pleased to be back.

"I'm honoured, gentlemen," Stephen said.

He was then introduced to the faces which were strangers to him. A large Bangka tin mug filled to overflowing with beer was placed in his hands.

"Welcome back, Stephen," again the Army Attaché called, which solicited a chorus of 'welcome' from all present.

They raised their specially engraved mugs in salute.

He hadn't known it, but he was somewhat of a legend amongst the Embassy hands. Having been shot had something to do with that. Coleman toasted them all and, understanding the other civilian's discomfort at being present, drank just two mugs before thanking them for their hospitality and excusing himself from their further activities.

These extra curricular pastimes were mainly restricted to the Sergeant, Warrant Officer and Chief Petty Officer who acted as personal assistants to the three Military Attachés. As their superiors always departed together, these experienced and highly respected men would often remain behind consuming the remnants of liquor before proceeding onto more disreputable pastures.

All three assistants, although not commissioned, received salaries equivalent to that of a field officer as their experience and security classifications alone were second to none. They had access to most files and one of the three would have been painstakingly security cleared to yet a higher level placing him amongst the very few who knew that the service even existed. He spent an hour with Walters before requesting assistance to take him to a hotel.

"Why not stay with me?" his successor asked.

"If I remember correctly, those quarters were claustrophobic at the best of times. No, thanks Phil, I don't mind spending a few days at the Hotel Indonesia."

Walters laughed. "Your old place has been demolished and the First Secretary's position now commands a three bedroom semi-

CARTHAGE PUBLIC LIBRARY
CARTHAGE MISSOURI

detached out at Jalan Wijaya. Come on, Stephen, change your mind. I would enjoy the company. "

Coleman considered the ramifications of staying with this man. He didn't know him personally and did not feel completely comfortable staying with a stranger, even though Walters worked in his former department.

"Phil, I appreciate your offer. Thanks. I would normally accept but I have a few things to iron out first and, if the offer is still open in a couple of days, I may well take you up on it. "

"Okay, Stephen. While you're here, whatever you need, just call and I will do whatever I can to assist. " He hesitated. "That means, anything, okay?"

"Thanks, I'll certainly call if I need assistance."

"How long do you intend staying," he asked.

"Maybe a month or so, I'm not sure at this stage. I'll let you know."

The Information First Secretary recognized the sudden change in the visitor's demeanor. "Stephen, don't misunderstand," Walters apologized, "I'm not trying to keep tabs on you. As far as I am concerned, you're on leave, and what you do here is your business. "

Stephen eyed the man coolly. 'Yes,' he thought, 'on leave, but not from your department, laddie.'

Walters was not privy to the real nature of Coleman's employment nor the existence of his secretive masters.

"I'll still keep you informed," Stephen advised, the tone of his voice suggesting that this line of discussion had ended.

He shook Walters' hand and was escorted out of the building. Coleman had only to travel two hundred metres to the Hotel Indonesia. He walked, dispatching the driver ahead as the traffic flow had changed and the car would need to drive a considerable distance before reaching the roundabout.

Coleman arrived at the hotel simultaneously with the blue Holden. He checked in, showered and commenced checking old telephone numbers. At first he had difficulty as many of the numbers had changed or acquired additional numerals. The operator assisted him with the third number, as the first two were no longer used by the previous subscribers.

A familiar voice spoke on the line. It was *Si Jempol*, a useful

CARTHAGE PUBLIC LIBRARY
CARTHAGE MISSOURI

contact from the old days. Immediately, Coleman replaced the receiver, not wishing to identify himself. He sat on his bed and considered this information. There was no guarantee that the subscriber was at the original address. It was quite possible that the number moved with the original *langganan* to a different location, providing, of course, that the new address was within the original exchange's distribution network. He decided to check it out.

* * * * * *

The street lighting had improved but it was still a brave tourist who ventured too far from the centre of the city at night. Proceeding from his hotel, Coleman walked directly up Imam Bonjol until he spotted the familiar Dutch colonial house with the unorthodox windows. He sat at a *kaki-lima* roadside stall, ordered a hot chilli *marta-bak* and waited. Half an hour passed. There had been no activity that he could see in the house across the quiet and poorly lit street. Stephen then finished the tasty Indian omelette and decided it was safe to approach the dwelling. He crossed the road and noticed a slight movement behind one of the windows on the second storey.

There was no *jaga* apparent. Immediately his body tensed as he found this scene disturbing. Stephen knew that all houses in Jakarta required security. He entered the yard cautiously and knocked softly on the heavy panelled door. Another curtain was pulled back, this time on the ground level, and a childish face peered at him.

The curtain closed. He knocked again. The curtain was again pulled back slightly and a man waved indicating that the *tuan* was not at home. He refused to accept the ploy and knocked yet again, for the third time and, as he expected, the door opened slightly to permit the tenant a better view of the intruder.

Seconds passed. The door was then pushed closed to permit the safety chains to be released, with which the door was opened quickly and he was pulled inside.

"*Tuan, kenapa kesini?*" the voice implored, its owner refusing to switch the lights on, demanding why to know Coleman had come to this house.

"*Mana Si Jempol?*" he hissed, demanding the whereabouts of the man he sought.

"*Udah pergi, tuan, udah pergi!*" the servant lied telling the foreigner, that the man had already left.

"*Jam berapa pergi?*" Coleman insisted, demanding to know what time the owner had departed.

"*Sejak kemarin, tuan, sejak kemarin,*" the servant again lied, advising that the man, *Si Jempol*, as he was known, having lost a thumb in a street fight, had left the day before. Stephen knew this not to be true as he'd identified the voice just hours before when he phoned from the hotel.

"*Suruh dia hubungi saya,*" he ordered, instructing the servant to ask his employer to contact Coleman.

"*Saya tinggal di Hotel Indonesia, kamar 722. Mengerti?*" Stephen left his hotel and room number having ascertained that the servant understood.

He returned to the hotel, and waited. Several long hours had passed when Stephen heard the knock he'd anticipated would come. The small peep-hole located at the hotel room's front entrance helped him identify the caller. He opened the door and gestured for *Si Jempol* to enter.

They shook hands. Neither spoke. *Si Jempol* opened a small case and proceeded to unpack certain items wrapped in used but clean cement bag liners. These bag liners, cleaned and rubbed smooth were as good as a chamois cloth suitable wrapping for delicate items and *objets d'art*. He unwrapped the items and placed them gently on the bed. The four pistols were in immaculate condition.

Coleman examined the Walthers A 9 mm Short and a 7. 65 automatics. He checked the latter's action then looked at the rugged Eurasian inquiringly, with one eyebrow raised.

The man indicated the number with his hands. It sounded a little on the expensive side but considering the weapon's condition he decided not to hassle him on the price. He picked up the second Walther and could hardly see any difference between the two. He opted for his first choice, returning the 9 mm Short, as the former was the more common of the Walther PPKs and Coleman considered the 7. 65 mm calibre as quite adequate for his needs.

He paid in greenbacks while the rest of the items were placed, having been carefully re-wrapped, back in the case. *Si Jempol* extracted a small box from his pocket and passed the container to Stephen who examined the contents, nodded, placed the package on the bedside table then opened the door for the man to leave.

He had not been in Coleman's room more than four minutes. The transaction completed and the merchandise now safely locked away in his suitcase, the Australian retired for the night.

* * * * * *

BAKIN Security had at least a dozen operatives working the Hotel Indonesia around the clock as most foreigners on diplomatic or business visits were obliged to stay at the only four star hotel in Jakarta. Their function was mainly to stand around in the bars and lobbies watching and listening, reporting anything of importance involving the foreign community. The phones in the hotel were all monitored, recording most of the considerable traffic which passed through the system each day, only to be discarded due to the Indonesians' inability to cope with the sheer volume of information and their shortage of skilled technicians.

One of the team leaders observed *Si Jempol* leaving the lobby lifts and casually made a note of the time and date. The normally discreet trader was up too late, the security agent thought. A little too late for the black market gun dealer. Surprised to see the well known figure in such an obvious location the BAKIN agent underscored the time then returned to watching the wealthy foreigners parade around the hotel lobby.

* * * * * *

Coleman awoke early, completely rested and feeling more confident of his decision to return to Jakarta, although uncomfortable with the possibility of being compromised in having acquired the automatic. Anderson's approval for his trip, despite it being organized in his own time, was conditional on his undertaking to secure a weapon and carry it while he remained in Indonesia. He was also instructed to bring the weapon back to Australia upon his return. The service was always in need of foreign unregistered hand guns.

Stephen was concerned with customs but, unlike the United States, there were no metal detectors installed at Asian airports. He had agreed, albeit reluctantly and his Chief had then insisted that he use the contact numbers Coleman had tried upon arrival. The weapon would remain locked in his baggage, he decided.

Chapter 9

Jakarta — the Kongsi

Nathan Seda had known of Stephen's arrival within an hour of his immigration *cap* being stamped into his passport at Kemayoran Airport. He was surprised that the former Attaché had elected to return. Seda considered the Australian's visit and admitted that he found his presence a little disconcerting.

He of all people understood just how fortunate the Australian had been to survive Umar's bullet.

It was not like the man to miss. As it turned out, the wounding was almost as effective as his death would have been. The world press, spearheaded by the Australian media, ran the story for a considerable length of time as Coleman was one of their own and his fellow journalists wouldn't let the story die. This had suited Seda at the time although the eventual outcome had been difficult to accept.

The surrender of the primitive Irian natives enabled the plebiscite to take place. The superior numbers and weaponry of the Indonesians Forces had prevailed. As one journalist had stated at the time, referring to the rebels, it had been an invisible war waged over invisible boundaries, as the primitive tribes of the region had no understanding of the import of political lines drawn by others which restricted their movements within their traditional habitat.

In retrospect, Seda acknowledged that although the desired result of the ambush had not entirely been achieved, considerable experience had been gained from the attempt. He had developed a greater depth of knowledge and understanding of, not only his own military and government leaders and how they reacted to provincial separatist threats, but also the international media and humanitarian groups.

He was committed to continue with his ambitious plans, adhering to the original oath he had sworn, motivated by a myriad of events so complex even he had difficulty sometimes understanding the strength of his own resolve and determination. Foremost in his mind, heart and soul was the one principle in which he really did believe, providing Seda with the necessary motivation needed to achieve this aim.

He swore that one day Timor would be governed only by the Timorese. And if his dedication could assist realize this outcome then he would be a very contented man. And a powerful one.

Even more powerful than he had already become.

Funding his operations was not overly difficult. The secret operational accounts from BAKIN had grown considerably, commensurate with the significant increase of foreign investment capital which had poured into the country over recent years. He had little difficulty in maintaining operations as he easily siphoned more than two million dollars off each year's budget allocations. The General realized that vast sums of capital would be required for his next war chest. Although thoroughly disappointed with the events in Irian Jaya he was determined to be better prepared when the next opportunity arose. Seda had learned to be more patient as he believed that the Irian uprisings were unsuccessful primarily due to the impatience displayed by tribal leaders and their lack of leadership. He would provide that leadership to his own people when the time came.

His current program involved sending specialist units across the Indonesian border into New Guinea where they terrorized the primitive groups and, on occasions, managed to successfully locate remnants of the Free Irian Movement. Occasionally he reported these incursions to the monthly defence and security sessions which he now co-chaired and was applauded for his dedication in eradicating these former terrorists.

The Indonesian Defence Council had received irrefutable evidence that armed bands of terrorists frequently crossed from havens in New Guinea and created havoc. They were more than happy to approve counter attacks and supplied Seda with additional funding to support these efforts. His position had never been stronger.

The Intelligence General realized that he had to be careful at all times, remain diligent and ensure that his position be maintained. The military had always been a competitive arena in the past but was even more so now, he discovered, due to the ever increasing number of commercial opportunities available to senior officers.

Coleman arrived in Jakarta without any request for official clearance and accreditation. This disturbed General Seda. All foreign diplomatic activity information was channelled through his offices. The General examined the dossier once again. Most he already knew as he had memorized the data through repeated readings of the Embassy journalist's information sheets.

He had almost successfully had this man executed. Why would he want to return? And then Seda remembered the girl. What was her name, Louise? Seda smiled darkly. He would have the Australian followed anyway. It was always best to be sure with these foreigners who had obvious government links. He could be troublesome but Seda didn't feel there was any real threat. Suddenly he smiled again, a thought playing to his cruel sense of irony. He would invite the former Attaché around for a social function as he had in the past. Then, first hand, Seda would be able to determine the foreigner's intentions in revisiting Indonesia.

* * * * * *

Seda was pleased with his new home.

His wife had not played any significant part in its planning, having merely stipulated that she wished it to be large and impressive. The mansion was both. The General knew that it impressed as he had observed the envious looks on guests' faces when they first visited his household.

He was selective in whom he invited to his home. At least once each month he would host a formal function at his residence, always arranging for at least two or three foreign diplomats to be present. Rarely would these senior members of the expatriate community fail to attend as to do so would inevitably result in missed opportunities.

The gregarious General was renowned for his generous hospitality and powerful associates, many of whom often appearing unannounced at Seda's functions. Some embassies actually requested that their ambassadors be invited. He enjoyed the power but he had not let it influence his thinking, nor diminish his resolve to achieve his final goal. His recent affiliation with the President's family was dangerous he knew, but essential as he was realistic enough to appreciate that the First Family would be around for a long time to come and to advance his power base any further would require the President's support.

Seda smiled when he remembered his first meeting with one of the sons. He couldn't believe the young man's arrogance and total absence of personality. They had met through a Chinese intermediary and discussed an arrangement whereby a Japanese consortium would be given priority in a military tender due to be called over the following months. Seda had deliberately ingratiated himself and asked for nothing, knowing that this is what the self-centred youngster had expected of him. After all, he was his father's son and Nathan was merely one of his father's generals.

The delicate relationship had paid off well. His shoulder displayed the additional star before the end of that year and it was then that Seda's name had become synonymous with the powerful forces which steered the nation. He had learned the game. When the Palace spoke, he listened. If there was a request, he endeavoured to have it fulfilled. As his superiors unabashedly demonstrated their greed, he helped satisfy their appetites. And, within a very brief time, a day would not pass without his name being mentioned with respect by his peers, in awe by his competitors and in fear by those who were foolish enough to consider themselves his enemy.

Seda had indeed become a force to be considered.

He called his adjutant, explained what he wanted and then informed his wife that she was to invite a small gathering of friends for the weekend. Seda was confident that the visitor would accept an invitation to meet up with an old acquaintance.

'If he was really here in a private capacity then why would he not accept such a social invitation?' he pondered. *'Then again, if he was involved in something covert for his government surely they would want him to accept the invitation as an opportunity to dine with the General Seda, these days, was not something to be scoffed at!'*

There was something about this *bulé*, something which made the General slightly uneasy. Incredibly superstitious, Seda decided that maybe it was an opportune time to drive out to Bogor and visit his *dukun* again. He made a mental note to do so. These days he could not afford to be as complacent as he'd been before, he warned himself, such as when he was involved in orchestrating the disturbances in Irian Barat. The medicine man would offer him guidance and solace.

Feeling that he had resolved the slight annoyance he dispensed with any further thoughts relating to the foreigner and turned his mind to one of the many other problems he faced on a typical day. He looked up at the photograph of General Sudomo, his predecessor, his lips curling into a tight grin as he remembered his first visit to this office and the assignment he'd been given regarding his step brother.

The image of Umar substituting the powerful director's heart tablets with the wrong stimulants flashed through his mind. Without further thought General Seda turned his attention back to his work.

* * * * * *

Stephen Coleman remained in Jakarta until Thursday.

"I'm off, Phil," he advised, "heading for Samudera Beach for a week and then on to Bandung, maybe Jogjakarta. "

"When do you intend returning to Jakarta?" Walters inquired.

"Haven't decided yet. I will call from wherever I overnight to keep you current with my itinerary. Okay?"

"That's fine, Stephen, you're a free agent," Walters responded, with no innuendo intended. "Just have a good time. "

Coleman wanted to catch a bus but just could not bring himself to board one of the speeding giants. It wasn't just that these buses contributed to most of the road casualty figures. They were dirty and unreliable. Instead, he hired a private taxi for the week, departing from the city around mid-morning, finally arriving in the village of Pelabuhan Ratu in time for lunch at the Bayu Amerta.

The small seafood restaurant had been constructed along traditional lines, positioned on the edge of a cliff overlooking the majestic swells of the Indian Ocean. The panoramic view was spectacular. Waves crashed against the rocks below, showering spray high into the air, threatening the open garden restaurant setting. He ordered the swordfish which was served grilled, basted with sweet soya sauce, and placed on a bed of saffron rice. His favourite.

Memories of earlier visits came flooding back as Coleman began to unwind and accept the tranquil atmosphere and ocean air. During his tour he had made several trips to this beautiful resort area.

Once, he reminisced, Stephen had joined with a group from the embassy and hired a bungalow during one long weekend. He had encouraged them to experience the fresh seafood served at this restaurant and, after lunch, they had ventured down to the fish market and witnessed fisherman returning with their catch.

The group were enjoying themselves until one of the Australian girls had cried out in dismay. The inexperienced traveller had wandered off ahead of the others and now stood with both hands held close to her mouth in surprise.

Immediately in front of where she stood a fisherman had taken a long sharp knife and, brandishing the glistening blade was preparing to butcher a porpoise. Imediately, a shout of protest arose from the onlookers causing the bewildered fisherman to pause in his action. Eventually he was persuaded to sell the mammal at a good price to one of the foreigners who asked that it be thrown back into the sea whole. The old and very poor fisherman, now joined by several of his own villagers instantly agreed, not understanding why these naive Westerners differentiated between dolphins and the abundant big game fish found in the oceans.

Stephen had no doubts in his mind that once they'd departed the porpoise would have ended up in its original predicament and perhaps in the villager's cooking pot that very same afternoon.

* * * * * *

During the first days Stephen walked the beaches, clearing his mind of everything except the life around him. He sat with the fisherman discussing winds, tides and weather, and told stories of great storms and winds which often endangered the villages there. Stephen found that he could sit for hours listening to their simple stories of exaggerated catches and tales of sharks so great that even a coracle was once swallowed whole by one of these monsters. He found that the smell of the salt air, the innocence of these hospitable coastal people, and the abundance of coconut trees swaying together on the long white sandy beaches, simply idyllic, and wondered why he had not returned before this. Huge Indian Ocean waves thundered down onto the black volcanic rocks strewn across the shallow reaches, sending claps of thunderous applause at their own mighty strength when they then smashed against the tall cliffs surrounding the hotel, as he strolled along the white sandy beaches. He often found broken remains of swordfish bills strewn along the sandy coast, evidence of the mighty fish which were often captured unwittingly in the fishermen's net, their last dying efforts to thrash their way to freedom ripping the precious nets forever. Stephen enjoyed his stay more than he could have imagined. The simplicity of the people and their surrounds brought an inner peace he had not felt before.

A week passed and Stephen reluctantly called Jakarta. Walters' office continued to act as a conduit for any message traffic as a matter of professional courtesy. The First Secretary was not available however his assistant informed Coleman that he had received an invitation for the previous weekend. She apologized then explained that the telephone connection to Pelabuhan Ratu had been difficult and she had therefore been unable to inform him of the dinner arrangements.

"I did manage to have a letter sent to their house, expressing apologies on your behalf, Tuan Coleman," the efficient woman advised.

"That was very kind of you," was all Stephen could say, not remembering her name. She had not considered it necessary nor prudent to inform the Sedas that she had been unable to contact the *tuan*.

He was surprised when he'd discovered that the personal invitation had been sent by General Seda's charming wife.

"Would you please advise the General that I am not in Jakarta and don't expect to return for some weeks?"

"Certainly, tuan. I will phone immediately."

Coleman thanked her again, not wanting to be stuck there in the lobby waiting for hours to be connected to the Seda household to speak directly to them when the assistant could connect easily through local dialling. He hung up and hurried to the waiting Toyota Corolla anxious to get underway. The lobby staff waved as he departed, impressed with the Australian's fluency in their tongue. The receptionist went immediately to the communications room and typed a telex which, due to the shared lines suffering continuous delay difficulties, did not arrive at its destination until the following afternoon. The communications clerk at BAKIN head-quarters had explicit instructions which he followed upon receiving the message.

He passed it to Major Umar Suharjo.

* * * * * *

The road from the narrow coast rose sharply as it wound its way through the range of volcanic mountains. The soil was rich, providing a lush green countryside of terraced rice fields bathing in the tropical sun. The terraces, stacked one upon another, reached to almost impossible heights. Small streams of life-giving water flowed gently from one paddy to another, maintaining just enough velocity to run from one field to the next. Banana trees grew in abundance shading the village shanty dwellers who lived alongside the pot-holed road.

Stephen passed occasional teams of workers, their lungs exhausted from the toxic fumes generated from heating the two-hundred-litre drums of asphalt to be poured by hand along the road. The weary men waved as he passed slowly, calling for cigarettes or money for food. As the car struggled slowly uphill they often encounted these sun scorched men, their clothes in tatters and their feet burnt from the hot tar they had just laid. Stephen instructed the driver to slow down even more so that he could hand these desolate souls a packet of cigarettes, or a few Rupiah. They always smiled and waved, even when they received nothing from the occasional passing vehicles.

The mountainous road climbed for an hour before they arrived at Sukabumi and although the main street was alive with the morning market activity, he continued through to Bandung, the city of endless students.

Stephen spent only a few days visiting the provincial capital again. As nothing much seemed to have changed apart from the Savoy Hoyman's menu and the introduction of a sleazy disco in an adjacent alley, he left the garden city. He was feeling a little disappointed with the lack of real change or progress that he had witnessed in Jakarta.

Stephen travelled through off-road and well hidden villages, examined the mighty temple, Borobudur, and even Candi Mendut, finally coming to rest in the hills just short of the east Javanese provincial capital of Surabaya.

* * * * * *

He was now into his third week back in-country and discovered to his delight that he was enjoying himself immensely. He had rented an old Dutch Colonial plantation villa which overlooked the valley below. The air was cool and filled with the scent of flowers which grew only at these altitudes. A tea plantation lay spread out like some gigantic green carpet covering the slopes, providing endless pleasure as he sat on the terrace, watching the rows of women move slowly through the bushes, picking the small shoots, careful to maintain the flat level appearance of the tree thereby guaranteeing the continuous growth of the sweeter leaves. This small hill station area had been built for the exclusive use of the former colonial masters. Situated an hour's drive from the city of Surabaya, it was the weekend destination venue for those who wished to seek relief from the heat and humidity of the dusty port. Since Independence, little had changed here with the exception of a few new walls and a small dance-cum-disco bar situated inside the lobby of the dilapidated hotel.

Each morning he walked down to the vegetable markets, purchased several of the small bitter apples and wandered back slowly taking in the vibrant colours of the commercially grown flowers. Twice he had ventured into the hotel's bar and spent most of the evening being entertained by the young girls who were only too eager for his company.

And his Rupiah.

The second evening he took two of the hostesses back to his villa, where the young girls took turns playing and splashing around in the cast iron bathtub filled with steaming hot water, as they had never had the opportunity before and, he guessed, would probably not have again. Stephen was delighted with their frolics. When they appeared from the ensuite bathroom robed only in towels and cheeky grins, he led them to the large four-poster bed and, removing the hand made quilt, undressed then slid in between the soft brown bodies. They giggled and talked then made love then afterwards, called for food from passing vendors before splashing around some more in the ancient tub until Stephen finally fell asleep, exhausted by their energy and effervescence. When he

207

awoke in the morning they were gone.

They hadn't taken anything. And he remembered not giving them any money. He decided to return that night and present them with a gift for providing him with the happiest experience he'd known for too long a time. He laughed remembering their antics and was still smiling when the *jongus* appeared with the traditional thick cup of Java coffee and a small plate of strong cheese and chocolates for his breakfast. He had nothing to be ashamed of and was surprised at just how relaxed he was considering the lack of sleep.

Sitting on the patio of the magnificent bungalow admiring the scenery and enjoying the mood, Stephen Coleman made a decision. He felt at peace in this incredible country. He experienced a feeling of release; a cleansing, and closure.

The memory of Louise was still there, but he no longer felt the sadness which had plagued him over the past two years. He was alive. He would always remember their brief and loving affair as he believed she would have wanted him to. He had not dwelt on her reasons for leaving him on that fateful day.

As for the shooting incident, he decided that too must be placed in perspective with the choices he now made. He understood that it would be impossible to be comfortable with the dramatic changes he was about to undertake should his mind still be clouded by the shadows of his past. Like so many other questions that couldn't be answered he decided to now cast these negative aspects of his life away, and start afresh.

Coleman decided to remain in the archipelago. He realized that this decision had been in the making ever since he had regained his health. Reasonably conservative by nature, Coleman examined the motivation for his decision and conceded that he had been influenced by some magnetic pull which had always been there, tugging away until he surrendered to its mystical power. He spoke the language as well as most locals and believed that his funds would be sufficient to survive for at least a reasonable period. He was pleased with himself, but resigned to the fact that others would not be exactly supportive of his decision.

Collecting his thoughts, Stephen spent the following days composing letters to his family, Albert and of course, a telex to his superiors in the Department. Although he dispatched these from the central Surabaya post office. Coleman also decided to request access to the Embassy's communication channels to advise John Anderson directly and personally of his decision. He telexed the carefully worded message disguising the main gist of the text and addressee's name. This was a relatively simple procedure all field operatives used when obliged to utilize unreliable postal and telegraph services. The message was sent from Surabaya to Jakarta's main post office and then picked up by an embassy driver when running the hourly check for incoming telexes. This in turn was re-routed via Walter's office as there was no overseas link from this eastern provincial capital.

Stephen addressed his resignation to the Head of the Department who, in this instance, was the Minister for External Affairs. He knew that it would reach its correct destination once the Minister had read the communiqué. Stephen realized that he would be required to return to Australia, however briefly, to tidy up loose ends and sit down with his mentor, John Anderson. He was not looking forward to that meeting as he knew how disappointed the Director would be when he realized Coleman could not be dissuaded from his decision to resign.

These thoughts occupied his mind as he boarded the Garuda flight for the short hop across to Bali. Having now made these decisions and informed his department he felt as if a tremendous weight had been lifted off his shoulders, unshackling him for the future, and from his past. Stephen smiled in anticipation with the thought of relaxing at the Segara Village Resort before heading up to the cultural delights of Ubud.

He didn't wish to stay at the Bali Beach. Now that he had finally managed to come to terms with Louise's death he felt it would be better not to stay where they had shared her last evening together. He said his farewell and didn't need to resurrect old ghosts. He wanted a fresh start.

As he drove from the airport Coleman noticed little change here as well. He was pleased. It was unfortunate that progress would come to this beautiful island and he, like many others, wished that day was still far into the future. He checked into the traditionally designed hotel bungalow resort and was presented with the customary welcome coconut cocktail, a combination of rice wine and coconut milk which the staff often spiced with a touch of gin or rum.

Coleman failed to notice the man watching him complete the required registration procedures at the reception desk. All foreigners were required to register when moving around the country, particularly at hotels or guest houses. These alien registration forms were collected each evening by the local police and the data telexed immediately to their headquarters for further dissemination.

Foreign tourism had not yet developed to any extent outside Jakarta and the majority of all hotels were owned, managed or controlled by the central government. When Coleman had left the Samudera Beach Hotel it was this information that had been finally telexed through to Jakarta. He had been the only foreign guest there during his stay on the coast.

The dark-skinned man continue to watch the tourist complete the required formalities. He'd missed Coleman in Pelabuhan Ratu due to the delay in receiving the telexed information. However he caught up with the Australian in Bandung, and had inconspicuously followed him ever since.

Umar strolled across in front of the visitor and passed by without acknowledging his presence. Even had Stephen been more attentive he would not have identified the Javanese who had followed him for almost two weeks. Umar Suharjo smiled arrogantly to himself. He'd even stood outside the villa in Tretes listening to the three occupants bounce around inside.

Satisfied that the foreigner would remain in the hotel to unpack, the major vanished skilfully, to report on Coleman's movements.

'*Strange,*' the Javanese killer had thought to himself, '*the General appears so preoccupied with this one.*'

Convinced that he should have thrown the Attaché overboard when the opportunity availed itself, he grunted an insult to all who were *bulé* and went in search of inconspicuous quarters for himself.

* * * * * *

After three relaxing days in Ubud Stephen felt as if he never wanted to leave this idyllic place, its artists, its beauty and its characters. And yet, the entire time he had felt something strange as if his sixth sense and his training were sending him signals. He was almost certainly being followed. Stephen couldn't prove it, he just knew. Several times he had doubled back from where he'd been to check but there was no one there.

The following day he flew back to the capital.

******

When Coleman returned to Jakarta his reception by Embassy staff was cold and indifferent. The official departmental representative in the Embassy was critical of his actions.

"Stephen, think this right through, man, you sound as if you've gone *troppo*," Phil Walters pleaded.

Coleman let the derogatory remark slide. He would need this man's assistance and decided to permit him his say. They discussed the situation for some time. Finally, realizing that his predecessor was not being stubborn, just determined, the Attaché threw his hands upwards in exasperation.

"All right, Stephen. Why don't we agree to put it on hold until you have spoken to the Minister?"

"You can't very well pick up the phone and just call him on an open line, Phil," Coleman patronized.

"We'll signal him and you could send a safe-hand dispatch with tonight's courier. He would have it before lunch tomorrow. "

"Okay," was the response. Coleman was, in fact, pleased that events were proceeding as he'd anticipated, not that they were any more palatable.

"Where do you now intend staying?"

"Why, with you, Phil. Unless the offer is no longer convenient?" Coleman parried. He had considered the advantages of hotel accommodations and privacy against the cost. Anyway, Stephen had argued, the Attaché would be in his office most of the day and, if these times were anything like those during his own tour, then the evening social demands would keep the residence's occupant actively engaged elsewhere.

"Of course, Stephen, you are welcome," Walters answered, not entirely convinced that was doing the right thing as their situations had now changed considerably.

With that, the two men accompanied each other to the official three-bedroom dwelling in *Kebayoran Baru*. The staff were introduced to the guest, some of whom remembered the Indonesian-speaking *tuan*. His host, having excused himself and agreeing to leave Stephen to his own devices, returned immediately to the Embassy.

Once secure in his office he composed a lengthy message, typed the signal himself and took the report to the registry. There, due to the sensitivity of the subject matter, the First Secretary Information, used his own combination access and encoded the low-level message.

Minutes later at the communications centre in Canberra a ribbon of paper was spewing out from the antiquated Lorens telex machine which received the encrypted signal. There was no lettering on these tapes, merely a series of punched holes, each representing a corresponding pulse on the master decoding tape which, for obvious security requirements, was locked and available only to those officers cleared to receive or interpret such classified material. The duty officer identified the classification and called the designated officer to accept the tapes. Ten minutes later the Minister responsible had read the communication and immediately used his secure phone. A further fifteen minutes elapsed before John W. Anderson read the report and frowned.

Pressing the intercom, he issued instructions to his secretary, "Call the Attorney General's office, and arrange for me to see him. Explain the urgency to his secretary."

Anderson sat deep in thought, chewing the end of a letter-opener.

'The stupid bugger,' he muttered angrily having read the confirmation of Coleman's intentions as relayed by Walters. A response from the AG was received and immediately the Director left the heated office instructing his secretary to cancel all appointments until he advised otherwise. 'Madge the Magnificent' obeyed and proceeded to check the Director's schedule for the following forty-eight hours.

That evening, late into the night, Director Anderson and his counterpart from the Australian Security Intelligence Organization discussed the recent developments and debated the most advantageous direction their two organizations should follow.

Both were in agreement. Coleman could be dangerous if permitted to cut loose without any further commitment to the Department. On the other hand, Coleman's determination to stay on in Indonesia could be beneficial to all, if handled judiciously.

* * * * * *

Stephen was surprised and disappointed. The Charge d' Affaires, in the absence of the Ambassador, had called him into the Chancery, where he was presented with a terse notification from the Department that they had received his resignation and would therefore set about completing his records.

Would he please arrange to meet the Australian Consul and surrender any official documents in his possession? Oh, and of course, his passport would require an endorsement that he was no longer employed by Her Majesty's Government. He was, of course, entitled to retain his passport, however the relevant endorsements were required to be executed immediately. Would he also advise details of his on forwarding address etc etc, to assist with final computation of outstanding administrative matters regarding leave-pay etc etc.

Stephen re-read the departmental letter delivered by Walters earlier that afternoon.

"Sorry, Stephen," was all the embarrassed host could offer. "This does not affect our relationship in any way, you know," he added. "Also, it goes without saying that you are welcome to stay on here as long as you wish. "

Stephen finished sipping the whisky, his third, and slowly shook his head.

"I expected at least a farewell note from someone," he complained. "Not even a bloody thanks for the years of service or a simple goodbye!"

"You must have anticipated at least a little annoyance Stephen," his host defended, "the way I hear it, the powers-to-be had great expectations for you in the Department. "

"Still, it's bloody rude," Coleman complained, the first effects of the alcohol accelerating his aggressive mood.

He resented their distancing themselves considering he had served conscientiously and with considerable merit. Well, he'd asked for it, and now he was on his own. At least the break had been clean. Now he had to get on with his life, reorganize, establish new relationships, find a job.

Find a job? The thought suddenly struck him. He had no employment and, consequently, no income. He poured another whisky, looked inquiringly at his host who shook his head then proceeded to think about his future.

Securing permits and obtaining an acceptable sponsor would be his most immediate concerns. Stephen was aware of the difficulties businessmen experienced establishing their activities in Indonesia, however he'd not given these problems much thought before this. He understood that he must address these difficulties without losing his new momentum. The government was frustratingly inflexible in its implementation of regulations governing the employment of foreign nationals, an understandable consequence of the abortive *coup d'etat* back in 1965.

The Australian embassy had wasted no time in advising the Indonesian Immigration and Foreign Office that his employment status had been withdrawn, even though he was not accredited to that post. Coleman had considered this particularly action as unnecessary. Even malicious.

He poured himself another whisky. Looking up, he identified the unhappy appearance of his host.

"I will arrange to move my things in a couple of days if that's okay by you, Phil. "

"I told you that you are welcome to continue on here as long as you wish. "

"Thanks. Time to wing it alone. "

"Have it your way," Walters replied, as he rose to leave, "Take it easy, Stephen," he warned, leaving Coleman to think his problems through.

"Sure. Thanks again, Phil. See you later. "

Coleman sat alone for a while, finished his drink, then instructed the houseboy to call him a *becak*.

"*Mau kemana, tuan?*" he asked politely, inquiring where Stephen wished to go, not out of curiosity, but so he could pass the information on to the three-wheeler's driver when he asked.

"*Jalan-jalan sajalah!*" the now quite inebriated guest advised the unhappy servant. "Just out."

The other servants giggled nervously when they observed the *tuan* climb into the *becak* as he appeared a little drunk. Still, if that made him happy.

The *becak* driver pedalled around for an hour until the young foreigner fell asleep. He then returned to the man's residence. Coleman was not drunk, just a little tipsy. He had been drinking without having taken lunch and was the worse for it. Feeling a little foolish at having to be woken by the driver, Coleman tipped the man for his kindness. As he undressed he realized that this was the first evening in over five years he could go to bed not knowing what he should be doing the following day. With those thoughts, and assisted by the whisky, he slept.

* * * * * *

At first he thought he was dreaming. He was certain there was something going on nearby, if not in his head. There were sounds from outside. Raised voices. The houseboy was adamant. The *tuan* was tired and could not be disturbed. He, Sukardi, would accept the letter and present it to the *tuan* when he had awakened and showered!

The soldier had persisted.

Sukardi resigned himself to the possibility of incurring the wrath of one or the other and decided that the messenger was far more menacing in appearance than the effect of *tuan's* possible tongue-lashing. Coleman was awakened and told of the visitor.

He checked his watch. It was already afternoon.

Immediately he was irritated, partly from the effects of the alcohol, but mainly because a soldier had succeeded in exercising control over the senior servant in a foreigner's household. Prepared to confront the soldier with more than a few sharp words, he instructed Sukardi to keep the man waiting at the front door until *tuan* had completed his *mandi*.

He deliberately procrastinated. An hour passed and Coleman emerged instructing the houseboy to usher the soldier into the small *ruang tamu*, a sitting room just off to the right from the main entrance.

"*Maaf, tuan*," the soldier apologized coming to attention paying the courtesy of a subordinate, "*saya disuruh Bapak Jenderal Seda. . .*"

Coleman raised his hand cutting the man off in mid-sentence as the General's name was mentioned, waving for the houseboy to leave the soldier alone with him. He felt annoyed at his own stupidity. He certainly could not, especially at this time afford to offend a senior Indonesian, particularly one as important as the General! Having the messenger cool his heels would certainly reach the General's ears and could be misconstrued as a deliberate insult. He gestured for the soldier to sit.

Embarrassed, the soldier remained standing.

'Damn!' thought Coleman, regretting his insensitivity in placing the Corporal in the position of *serba-salah*, a potential *faux pas*, as it would have been incorrect to accept and impolite to refuse.

"*Baiklah, Corporal. You were saying that General Seda had ordered you here. Has my jongus offered you something to drink?*" he inquired.

"*Belum, tuan,*" the man replied, "*but that is all right as I am not thirsty, terima kasih.*"

"*Corporal, I am sorry that my jongus failed to tell me that one of the General's men was waiting,*" he apologized. "*However he will be reprimanded.*"

Both men knew that this would not happen; however the Corporal was pleased that this *tuan* had recognized the fact that it was incorrect to keep the General's messenger waiting for as long as he had.

"*Tidak apa-apa, tuan,*" the soldier smiled, indicating that what had happened was of no importance. He then handed the letter to the foreigner.

Coleman read the invitation immediately. Considering it may provide a window of opportunity and even resolve his present difficulties, he decided to accept. The soldier departed. Coleman changed quickly from the casual attire he had hastily dressed in selecting a blue motif *batik* shirt with dark trousers. The invitation was for cocktails followed by dinner.

The old Dutch grandfather clock indicated he would be late if he did not hurry. He had no vehicle.

As he was preparing to board a *becak* to take him to the Blok M shopping centre, Phil Walters returned, and offered his car and driver. Coleman accepted as the invitation was for six o'clock.

His previous experiences and working knowledge of the country and its people's habits were all too familiar. He was grateful for the extra effort he'd spent studying their customs and idiosyncrasies. Indonesians usually took their evening meal early. Remembering that Seda was not a Moslem, the *Magrib* prayer period would not pose a problem. Christians, Moslems, Buddhists and Hindus alike all practised what was referred to as *jam karet*, or rubber time.

Appointments had to be flexible. The contradiction lay in the fact that for a foreigner to be late was considered disrespectful and inexcusable. It was late afternoon and, as the residents rose from their midday rest, the city began to stir for the second time that day. The former diplomat sped towards his destination as the sun disappeared for the day.

The driver turned into the driveway stopping briefly at the security post. Coleman identified the familiar Czech automatic machine pistols held by shoulder straps as the guards carefully scrutinized the driver and his foreign passenger. The Holden displayed CD-18 series number plates, indicating that the vehicle was an Australian diplomatic vehicle. Not that diplomatic privilege was something these well-trained troops would respect should they consider the occupants a threat to their General, the passenger reflected.

The army would never forget the loss of its generals some six years earlier when the abortive, and first of three coups commenced. Security was now extremely efficient. Just to raise one's hand in friendly gesture too close to one of these military leaders could possibly result in an aide shooting the offender dead. The attendance of senior ranking officers at functions was always marked by a certain atmosphere of apprehension.

* * * * * *

Stephen was astounded at the size of the mansion. Obviously a new structure, the building occupied at least two thousand metres of land and was designed and constructed in a Mediterranean style. The entrance was surrounded by columns. The building was painted white with red terra-cotta tiles adding to the character of the overall design. Stephen was very impressed.

An aide appeared and ushered him into the splendid structure. As he entered, directly to the left of the foyer, two of the most magnificent creatures he'd ever seen strutted close by, their presence totally unexpected. The Birds of Paradise strolled in a natural setting where the late afternoon sun could strike their enclosed plateglassed cage. A pond had been arranged simply so as not to detract from the natural beauty of the indigenous fauna in the enclosure.

The flora too was obvious, several rare varieties of black spotted orchids from Kalimantan being positioned above the artificial waterfall. The decor was pseudo-colonial, the emphasis on size. Twin marble columns on both sides of the reception area created the impression that the upper levels numbered more than were actually built. The walls were decorated with paintings of heroes with Diponegoro gracing one wall on his life-sized white stallion, his sword held menacingly as he screamed in still life at the enemy. Despite the power constraints placed on other households, a brilliant chandelier which hung ostentatiously in the centre of the room sparkled brightly, casting its own spell over the Persian rugs adorning the highly polished marble floor.

"*Silahkan masuk, tuan,*" the aide invited, and Stephen followed, conscious of his own awe at the wealth this residence represented. During his absence from the Capital many new and palatial houses had appeared along this avenue. The President's residence lay not more than four-hundred metres to the north.

This area of Menteng spreading from Jalan Teuku Umar down through Jalan Cendana, was always smothered with armed guards and armed personnel carriers. It represented an elitist suburb for the government and military *bapak-bapak*. There were practically no Chinese in this section of the suburb with the exception of one who was as regular in attendance at the palace as the President's own family. This man had become almost as important to the new government as it's own military support.

Many stories revolved around the little broker who had become wealthy as a direct result of his association with the Javanese who now occupied the Palace. Within a few years, his financial empire placed him as one of the wealthiest entrepreneurs in the world. Acting as the President's financial confidant, this man managed to develop his interests in association with the privileged few until emerging as the financial and manufacturing giant of the Republic.

The New Order was cognizant with the influence this man wielded over the Chinese community and, in consequence, over the entire non natural resources or energy sectors, for the Chinese were the shopkeepers, bankers and manufacturers who, through their *kongsi* arrangements, assisted the economy to survive. Stability was relatively unknown to the peoples of this vast country. Now, with the strength of the new government and it's foresight to introduce a series of Five Year Development Programs it appeared as if political and economic stability could become reality and not just dreams propounded by politicians.

Bitter animosity continued to exist between the Chinese and *pribumi* peoples of the archipelago. The government could not afford to be openly seen to be conducting business with the Chinese minority group. Freedom of the press was perfunctory at best whilst in reality, the government maintained the strictest controls over the media. Anti-government or even defamatory statements directed at senior individuals was considered to be subversive action and treated accordingly. Harshly. The ultimate deterrent, the death penalty, was imposed as an anti-subversive measure and was strictly applied to those who did not toe the line.

Coleman shuddered as he remembered he no longer had the protection of his government. Any indiscretion on the part of his former colleagues could jeopardize his fragile existence in this new environment. Coleman was aware that most foreign governments including his own continually maintained covert listening agencies throughout South East Asia. It was a fact of the times. The outside world was still highly critical and suspicious of this country which was quickly emerging, almost galloping, ahead of its other Asian neighbours. As to who would be recruited for the position he had forgone, Stephen Coleman really did not wish to know. It was imperative that he was seen to be and was, in fact, totally distanced from all government agencies which incredibly, as history has shown, managed to compromise their operatives with amazing regularity, leaving them to extricate themselves from dangerous situations which were, for the most part, not even of their own doing.

* * * * * *

Coleman turned as his host appeared. The General entered the split-level guest area where his young visitor waited. Seda was dressed in an expensive hand-made long-sleeved *batik* shirt, cotton trousers and Bally casuals. He carried an air of power and, as he approached, his gait was that of a man of position, almost of royalty. He smiled benevolently at his guest. It was obvious that he was proud of his new residence.

He had done well since his former director had 'passed away'. Seda's appointment to the vacant post had surprised most Jakarta observers as he was not of Javanese stock and also relatively junior within the military hierarchy. As to the secret of his continuing success, embassy circles whispered stories of how he had saved the Vice President from exposure over his unfortunate association with a former general who was still incarcerated on the infamous Buruh Island. Others in the know claimed that it was because his wife was related to the Chief of Staff. But those who thought they really understood the Timorese's swift rise to power claimed that their sources confirmed it was because of simple Indonesian logic, to promote the man most unsuited at the right time. How else would a relatively junior officer rise so quickly to such a prominent position?

Only a few who moved in palace circles knew he had been personally selected by the President as a direct result of substantial support from his own son, whose recommendations were a direct result of a new corporate relationship which Seda had recently developed. Within the short span of just a few years this arrangement with the Palace and the Japanese yielded untold millions into their offshore accounts in Singapore's newly created ACUs, or Asian Currency Units.

The Singapore banking fraternity had been first to identify the magnitude of hidden wealth in Indonesia and moved swiftly to provide secure and discreet storage for these funds through numbered accounts. Switzerland was too far away, too distant. Jakarta businessmen and other wealthy residents knew that they could not jump on a plane and fly to Geneva in just over one hour, physically sight their gold and cash then return home on the afternoon flight. To the simple yet wealthy corrupt officials, Singapore represented a safe haven, not just psychologically, but a practical one as well.

The sense of security knowing their money was just across the water, and that its secrecy was guaranteed by Singapore was sufficient to allay any fears they might have had. They believed that their offshore positions could never be challenged by any third party, including their own government. Funds could legally be transferred into a numbered interest bearing account into any one of the many prime banks operating in the Republic of Singapore. These funds would be jealously guarded by Singapore law, providing the account holders with complete security and, more importantly, anonymity should they so desire. And most did, out of necessity.

Within ten years these accounts had grown in volume to exceed thirty billion American dollars, most of which represented the result of corrupt deals or were just funds hidden from the taxation authorities. Singapore would eventually displace Switzerland as the world's safe haven for illicit funds.

The new premises, so admired by his guests, had cost the Director (Special Services) Intelligence Protocol, as he was officially designated, the equivalent of approximately one hundred years of his official salary. Nobody questioned his or others in his peer group, how they had acquired their sudden wealth. To do so would not just be foolish. It would be madness.

But in Indonesia corruption was such new stars were spawned by the day. Few were not involved and finger pointing was considered the conduct expected only of foreigners. It was apparent to Coleman that, as no other guests were yet evident, his invitation had been designed to permit his host the opportunity for a *tête-á-tête* and in style.

The General was trying to impress and Stephen was flattered. As the Timorese approached, Stephen could not help but feel how the man had grown, not physically, although there was more to him than before. It was something else. His posture. and self-assurance. The General moved with an air of confidence that had not been present when Stephen had first known him.

Seda greeted Coleman warmly. "*Apa kabar, Mas, you are looking well.*"

"*Terima kasih, Pak. And how are you and Madame Seda?*"

The older man just nodded his head as neither was genuinely interested in his wife's health, both recognizing the obvious opening courtesies required by custom before proceeding on to more important matters.

"*Please,*" he indicated, with all of his fingers extended, showing the guest where he expected him to be seated.

"*Pak Seda,*" Stephen began, "*firstly I wish to thank you for the invitation tonight. Also, I must apologize to Njonja Seda for not attending your earlier dinner party but, unfortunately, I did not receive your wife's invitation and was unable to attend. *"

It was not lost on the host that his young guest had elected to mention that the previous invitation was, in fact, sent in his wife's name, as he had instructed.

The General smiled, the slight gesture of his right hand indicating that it was of no consequence. "*You're here now, that's what is important."*

Seda viewed the Australian.

As did many of his race, he admired these people from the rugged southern country who had fought alongside the Timorese against the occupation forces of the Japanese. There was almost a camaraderie between their two peoples and yet, race colour and politics demanded that this not be so. Seda believed that the young Australian could play an integral part in his overall plans. He knew he could use this man to his own advantage. He had thoroughly considered the opportunity Coleman represented and, having expended considerable energy and time developing an offer which would be attractive to the foreigner, arranged to broach the subject before other guests arrived.

Even though he had put a great deal of thought into the proposition he was about to offer Coleman, Seda still had reservations as to the man's dedication to himself, as distinct from his country. This was imperative as he was about to take a dangerous, but necessary chance on the man's natural human failings.

Avarice and greed.

For a limited time they discussed Indonesia's rapid changing economic and social structure and, satisfied that they had exhausted all other topics unrelated to the real purpose of the meeting and, pressed for time as the other guests were due in thirty minutes, the General raised the question.

"Have you managed to obtain an acceptable sponsor to enable you to continue in Indonesia?"

Having advised the older man *en passant* and earlier in their discussion that he had left the Australian Government and now intended staying on in Jakarta, Coleman had hoped that the conversation would take this new direction.

"No, Pak Seda," he responded, indicating his lack of success with a slight gesticulation of the hands, *"perhaps you could advise what course of action I should take?"*

Seda studied the Australian. His decision had not been made lightly. The former government employee had been investigated both in Indonesia and through the Embassy in Canberra to ascertain this man's real function within the government apparatus. He was not considered a political risk although any journalist's credentials were always of concern to the Indonesian authorities. Con-

sidering absolute proof was impossible, the Timorese was sufficiently convinced of the former Attaché's sincerity to reside in Indonesia for purely personal considerations.

"*I will arrange a sponsor,*" Seda advised, smiling at Coleman as
he extended his hand.

Coleman gripped the hand lightly but warmly, understanding
that Asians preferred not to have their limbs pumped in the Western way.

"*Pak Seda, you honour me with your offer.*"

"*It is the least one should do for one's business associate,*" the General offered the surprised foreigner and, not detecting any negative reaction, continued, "*survival in this environment requires more
than a sponsor, Mas Stephen.*"

Seda's use of his first name and the insinuation of a possible
future relationship caught Coleman by surprise.

Maybe he'd misheard?

"*Pak Seda,*" he started only to be interrupted.

"*Mas, we'll talk tomorrow. Tonight I want you to celebrate quietly, as
what we have to do together will be our secret and to our mutual benefit.*"

"*Tomorrow,*" Stephen again started to speak and was again
prevented from continuing.

"*Tomorrow will be a very important day for you, Mas. We will talk
about many things, but particularly we will discuss a new organization I
am involved with and, as it requires the knowledge of someone, a foreigner, I wish to offer you the opportunity to join with us.*"

"*I have observed you since you first arrived in my country. You are
intelligent, respectful and clever. You are also young and impetuous. However, you have my support.*"

Stephen sat quietly as the General continued.

"*Whatever we discuss tomorrow, regardless of your decision, must be
kept confidential.*"

Stephen became restless. "*Of course,*" he replied, hesitantly.

"*Mas Stephen,*" Seda spoke softly, "*I must have your assurance that
whatever you hear during tomorrow's discussions will remain between
you and me only.*"

It had all been presented too quickly, and Coleman was not only
surprised but confused. He wanted to respond in the affirmative
but felt that he should know more before making such a commitment, even though it appeared that he was being offered the very

opportunity that suited his own personal yet undefined needs.

"*Pak*," he began, "*I agree to keep anything you disclose to me completely confidential.*"

"*I require your word, Mas!*"

Stephen stared at the powerful man. He realized that to hesitate now would lose him an opportunity to really befriend one of the most powerful figures in the country.

Coleman extended his hand. "*I will be here tomorrow, General, and you have my word.*"

Nathan Seda smiled, obviously satisfied.

He would utilize this relationship to achieve his goals. The Australian would be of immense assistance to him. He would place Coleman at the front of his commercial activities, supporting him silently with his financial and political strength. The relationship would be most beneficial to both parties as he was reasonably confident in this man's abilities and unusual understanding of the Indonesian people. Then there was, of course, the question of maximizing the former government representative to access some of those foreign military suppliers who resisted dealing directly with Third World buyers.

They spoke quietly together, pausing only when the other guests arrived. The amazingly brief dinner party *Njonja* Seda had arranged for the small group of guests lasted only one hour. It was apparent to Stephen that the others had been window dressing for his meeting with the General.

They had been left alone again as the other visitors had excused themselves relatively early, obviously to permit the private discussions to continue. The problem of sponsorship was considered further and then settled. Seda would arrange for one of the departmental heads on the Foreign Investment Board to personally sponsor Stephen.

The General noticed his guest stifle a yawn and understood that his new associate had absorbed enough for one night. He reminded Stephen of the agreed meeting scheduled for the following day. The hour being late, Coleman took his leave, his head spinning. Everything had fallen into place for him like pieces in some giant but complicated jigsaw puzzle.

He was driven back to the house on Jalan Wijaya. Physically tired but mentally exhilarated he was unable to sleep for some hours, until finally drifting off, as the faint light encroaching on morning sky heralded the approach of *fajar*.

* * * * * *

Njonja Seda's car called for him at precisely nine o'clock as arranged. Coleman was impressed, not just with the driver being on time in a country which put little store in being punctual, but more with the expensive sedan. It was a dark brown Mercedes 450, the windows heavily tinted, permitting those inside to easily view the outside world while remaining obscured from the onlookers. This gave the German-manufactured vehicle a sinister appearance.

He had received telephone instructions earlier to leave the embassy accommodation and wait to be met outside the Brawijaya Guest House, not more than a five-minute walk from Walters' house.

The impressive sedan had pulled up directly beside where he stood, so close the tyres almost touched the tips of his shoes. The door immediately in front him was opened slightly from the inside, signalling for Stephen to enter. Having done so, the driver sped away without so much as a greeting, guiding the machine dexterously through the maze of *becak* and pedestrian traffic which blocked the road.

They wound their way through this maze of humanity easing into the Kemang turn-off before speeding quickly along the Kemang Raya road towards Cilandak. The surface was yet to be sealed and they accelerated forward, the driver with his palm pressed continuously on the double horns, roadside vendors waving their fists menacingly at the passing vehicle which trailed clouds of red dust.

The driver remained unconcerned, concentrating only on steering the expensive vehicle to its destination. They stopped momentarily at the junction leading off to the Navy's large depot which, for some unknown reason, had been built more than fifteen kilometres inland and south of the city. Here the car turned away from the Navy establishment and then continued twisting and turning, following the red-coloured dusty surface, broken from the constant pounding of oversized military trucks which used this track for transporting their river sand and other building materials.

They travelled for another twenty minutes and Coleman guessed that, by then, they should be somewhere around halfway to the town of Bogor. He couldn't be sure, of course, not having been along these roads before. Their vehicle approached a small village house, inconspicuously simple in appearance. And very isolated.

Guiding the now filthy Mercedes with considerable skill between a number of tall *rambutan* and mango trees, the driver managed to bring the sedan to rest directly behind the building, concealed from all who may pass by. Coleman was again surprised that the surly driver did not alight to open his door, a gesture expected by all *tuans*.

"The General is waiting for you inside," the voice from the front of the car advised.

Stephen opened his own door and proceeded towards the small and rustic dwelling, stepping cautiously as the soggy ground was covered by chicken and duck droppings. He knocked.

"*Masuk, Mas,*" a voice ordered.

He did as instructed and found the General sitting alone drinking coffee. There was a red thermos and several cheap glasses on a teak table. There were no servants evident. He joined Seda, accepting the glass of black coffee, wishing he'd remembered how hot these could be to unsuspecting hands.

"*Let's begin,*" Seda said, opening a folder and placing it so that his new associate could view the documents inside.

They discussed the mechanics of the new arrangements. From time to time Coleman interrupted to ask questions, continuing only when both were satisfied that he clearly understood the subject matter. They worked well together and, by mid-afternoon, they had established a mutual respect for each other's obvious capacity to understand the complicated issues and tasks with which they would be faced. Approaching five o'clock, they were both showing the strain of the tiring day.

Seda's powers of concentration increased as the in-depth discussions and Stephen's briefing led them into areas yet unknown to the Australian. They evaluated everything revealed by the Timorese General, together, and Stephen was pleased that he'd understood the older man's explanations when questioned on points still unclear to him.

It was agreed that Coleman would appear as the sole proprietor of a new company established as a supply conduit to the Department of Defence. Behind the scenes, Seda would manipulate others within the Department to consolidate the new company's position as a recognized and reliable supply source for the military's needs. A series of subsidiary companies would be established in regional capitals such as Singapore and Hong Kong to facilitate the double documentation associated with buyer's commissions.

Coleman listened, fascinated and impressed with the General's thoroughness and the extent of the elaborate plan. As Seda talked, with obvious knowledge and authority, Coleman became aware of the General's superb understanding of commercial matters relating to the Defence Department.

Seda took him through the concept, step by step, explaining his reasoning for the complicated procedures he had insisted on introducing prior to implementation of the project. Stephen thought he'd misunderstood when the General had indicated that his potential share of the company's proceeds would, within three years, exceed one million dollars.

As Stephen sat, stunned, Seda deliberately rolled the figure off his tongue again, more slowly, so that the ramifications of the potential their arrangement had would be overwhelmingly engraved on his mind. He could be wealthy!

The General understood the value of people. But he had a greater understanding of human nature and how values change proportionately to the volume of dollars involved. Recognizing the expression on the Australian's face, Seda was finally comfortable that he had made the right choice in selecting this man. Assured that his new associate understood the consequences of any disclosure concerning their relationship, Seda established a routine for their private telephone conversations which were scheduled to occur on a weekly basis.

They had also agreed that, in the interests of further distancing themselves from each other publicly, all personal meetings or sensitive transactions should be conducted strictly off-shore through nominated safe houses or via such people as the General may wish to designate.

Obviously, there was considerable detail yet to be discussed and resolved. They accepted that it was more important to establish the principles of their relationship and agree on a *modus operandi* for the company's overall activities during this day's discussions rather than attempt to cover too much detail.

"That's just about it then, Mas," Seda suggested in a tired voice, *"we will talk again next week and commence from then. Don't concern yourself about funding, we will have it all in place within a few days or so. You should concentrate on finalizing your permits and other documentation with the immigration authorities. Everything must be done according to the regulations. We don't want you to attract unnecessary attention."*

"Phone this number," he instructed, passing the piece of paper to Stephen, *"and arrange an appointment with Sutrisno. I have already spoken to him, as you know, regarding your sponsorship. It's all settled but he will need to assist you put your applications together correctly."*

"No one's going to refuse his sponsorship," he stressed, referring to the Chairman of the influential Foreign Investment Board.

"He will also provide you with a list of acceptable houses for you to occupy. Select one and he'll have it prepared through his offices. Power, water, telephones, everything. Then you should move in and settle down, preparing yourself for an interesting time," he paused, for the effect, *"and an exciting one, I'd expect. "*

They spoke for a few more minutes but as both were weary and Seda had to return for another appointment, he departed first, leaving Stephen alone in the smoke-filled village house.

An hour passed and he heard the horn blast twice. Coleman was annoyed with the driver's obvious display of contempt. The horn sounded again, impatiently. Coleman appeared and sauntered to the car, slamming the door as he entered, without effect, as the meticulously engineered doors clicked into place. Once again he sat in the rear and in silence, as they returned via a different route. The driver dropped him precisely where he'd waited earlier in the day. As Coleman left the Mercedes he deliberately left the door ajar so that the driver would have to close it.

He didn't. Instead, the car suddenly accelerated forward a few metres, jerked to a halt then accelerated again, causing the car's own momentum to close the door. Stephen shook his head in bewilderment as the brown sedan drove away, leaving him still standing in a hail of small gravel stones thrown by the spinning rear wheels.

The driver circled the block to observe the foreigner. He'd disappeared. Coleman, tired and not keen to walk the short distance home had quickly climbed aboard a *becak* and was already around the corner heading for a hot bath when the vehicle returned. The driver's eyes narrowed. Slowly, this time, he drove away from where he'd dropped the General's guest.

'*One day,*' he muttered, '*one day you'll get it, bulé!*' the thought of which seemed to comfort him as he unclenched his tight grip on the steering wheel.

Umar Suharjo returned the Mercedes to the Seda household. He was angry to the pit of his stomach. He didn't appreciate being looked down on by others. He had skills beyond their comprehension and one day he would demonstrate some of these to the arrogant Australian, Coleman.

Chapter 10

Wantl

Stephen Coleman enjoyed the transition from government to the private sector. He had returned to Australia briefly, spending a weekend with his mother on the Hawkesbury River with some of her friends, enjoying the wines and pollution free air. She had expressed disappointment, as he'd anticipated, at his decision to leave the government and enter the world of commerce.

"I guess there's nothing much can be done now, dear," she had criticized, standing on the Canadian redwood sun deck overlooking the serene river, a flute glass filled with Chardonnay in her right hand, posturing, her head covered with an oversized straw hat. "I doubt you could return to your position now even if you wished to do so."

He knew that this was his mother's way of informing her son that he was practically in disgrace and that someone in Canberra had been talking to her about him. She enjoyed secrets, he knew, but Stephen guessed correctly that Anderson was responsible for her mood.

The following week had not been as pleasant. He'd made arrangements to meet with the Secret Service's Director and was twice left to cool his heels at the designated appointment without meeting the man. Stephen knew the importance of sitting down with Anderson and explaining his position. For that reason and the respect he still had for the senior civil servant, he tried a third time and was relieved when the Director's secretary confirmed their meeting.

Anderson had agreed to meet him for lunch. Stephen had arrived first and walked across the lounge to greet his former department head. He had observed the tall, almost gaunt figure enter, his shoulders slightly stooped from the years of sitting behind a desk examining reports, the gray hair adding a touch of sophistication to the conservatively dressed Director. His handshake was firm but without warmth.

The meal was a disaster. Anderson was reluctant to respond to Stephen's light-hearted attempts at casual conversation.

"There should still be plenty of snow, John," he suggested, hoping an invitation to the last of the season's powdery falls would be offered as maybe a skiing trip would provide him with a more relaxed venue for discussion.

Anderson refused the hint. "Don't have the time at the moment. Seems we are a little short-handed these days," the inference aimed at Stephen's departure.

For a moment Stephen glimpsed an expression of sadness in the older man's eyes, but looking again he saw nothing and knew that he'd imagined it.

"Pity," he said, rotating the ice cubes in his scotch slowly with a plastic stirrer, "your lodge will always be one of my fondest memories. "

"Why, Stephen?'

"Well, because that is where you. . . " he started before being interrupted.

"No!" the other man snapped. "Why did you resign?"

Coleman leaned back into his chair and sighed. He knew it was going to be difficult, but didn't appreciate just how complicated his position had become until then. Only when faced with the man who had been his benefactor, Director and close friend, did he understand how hopeless any argument would be.

He wanted to tell this man, who had been more of a father to him than his own during his formative years, that he no longer believed in the way governments moved silently, secretly, subversively, without accountability. And that the power of the covert organizations was created through fear. He was disillusioned by the lies and corruption that permeated all the other secret government agencies such as the CIA, MI6 and the KGB.

He couldn't find the words to describe the feeling of not being able to go home at night and take a shower to remove the filth of the day's work, and lie awake until morning unable to sleep because of the uncertainties and all too frequent self-examinations.

Coleman didn't say these things because he was sure that this man already understood. He sat across the table and appraised the Director he'd so greatly admired. Anderson looked weary.

It was the stress, Coleman knew.

"I'm out, John. I'm sorry you're disappointed, but it's over for me," was all he found to say, pushing the inconspicuous package across to the other man.

Anderson had said nothing ignoring the rectangular cardboard box placed in front of him. He sat for awhile silently thinking. All around others continued to talk as they dined. Only their table remained silent.

Suddenly Anderson rose and stood erect looking down at the shorter man. "The door is always open, Stephen," he said quietly, then left, the brown parcel containing the PPK automatic held tightly in his right hand.

Coleman watched his friend walk away with his purposeful strides, hoping he would look back, just once, and wave or smile. He waited as the tall well dressed frame passed through the glass doors leading out to the car park and down the wide steps, until suddenly he was lost from view.

Stephen remained at the table for a few more minutes. He knew it would be difficult. It was just the hollow feeling of disappointment he now felt towards the man who had been his friend. He would never forget the final look Anderson had given him, as if he had betrayed their relationship and was no longer to be trusted. Saddened, Coleman paid the check and wandered outside into the sudden burst of sunshine as the Canberra sun broke through the clouds.

For a brief moment he experienced the despair that comes when long-established relationships are ultimately broken, leaving the participants with a moment of regret, even emptiness. Suddenly, as quickly as it had come the feeling was gone replaced immediately with a sense of bitterness. He looked across the avenue at his former offices.

"Fuck you, John Anderson!" he said, lifting his hand in mock salute. Then he turned and walked away from his life as a Secret Service agent, forever.

* * * * * *

He had left for Melbourne the same evening, experiencing a

233

DISCARD

sense of loss. Anderson had been a good friend, he knew, but Stephen had made his choice and was committed to at least giving it his best try. As he looked out the window, the city's lights were evident and he remembered that he must call Albert. He put the earlier events out of his mind and prepared himself for the landing.

Australia's financial centre plays host to most of the country's corporate leaders. Coleman had introductions to several mining companies and an aviation group which wanted desperately to break into the lucrative Indonesian market. He took the opportunity to identify his company's activities and was pleased with the response. During his brief visit his phone rang continuously as more companies discovered his presence in their city. They were eager to discuss opportunities in the newly awakened giant called Indonesia, and identified Coleman as a possible means to enter the massive market without too much risk or exposure.

His credentials were excellent. A former government employee, fluent in the local language, an established office and considerable connections into the host country's government circles were enough to convince his clients that he could represent them adequately in the target area. He concluded several arrangements, in principle, and returned to Jakarta via Hong Kong where he repeated his performance, also successfully. Stephen discovered that foreign companies were desperate for representation to facilitate their way through the maze of bureaucracy found at every turn when dealing with government agencies. His background, contacts and local knowledge were suddenly in great demand.

Stephen selected an address in the 'dress circle' and quickly established his activities in a newly constructed office-cum-residence along the main arterial road of Jalan Teuku Cik Ditiro, which connected Imam Bonjol through Menteng into Cut Mutiah, the administrative centre for the newly formed Foreign Investment Board. His company soon became the preffered alternative to the Embassy's Trade Commissioner's office for most visiting businessmen, as Coleman, courtesy of his silent partner, could offer realistic arrangements and often had greater access than the Embassy.

The city had been transformed into an exciting metropolis due to the government's attractive foreign investment laws. Bars and night-clubs mushroomed supported by the American oil men with unlimited expense accounts. Massage parlours appeared everywhere, in many cases located directly behind male hairdressing salons to permit the customers discreet access. A new race track had been built. Casinos operated around the clock, as did many of the new and more popular night clubs such as the LCC, situated adjacent to the National Monument. The city fathers turned Jakarta into a rival for Bangkok and Macau.

The Governor, a Marine General, shoved Jakarta into the twentieth century with such gusto even his administration could not keep pace with the planning requirements such rapid development demanded. Roads were widened, bridges rebuilt, hotels appeared and all prospered.

Indonesia had become the land of the new gold rush. The Japanese flocked into the country building textile mills and electronic factories. The Americans charged in with their drilling rigs and expertise carving out great sections of concession areas in the rich oil fields of the Java Sea. The Rupiah settled down and confidence was restored in the economy. Evidence of the military had all but disappeared from the streets.

Jalan Thamrin, Jakarta's main protocol thoroughfare, had been raised and then re-sealed, for a third time. Unfortunately, it still flooded regularly, creating chaos as the city traffic had grown at a much greater rate than road development.

The Australian Embassy stood dwarfed by its Japanese counterpart and the Hotel Indonesia, now surrounded by three other international rivals still managed to maintain high occupancy levels. Many major buildings were under construction to provide facilities for the continuing boom. Companies associated with the oil and gas industry increased the foreign population over three years by ten thousand families.

As the government had insisted that only foreign personnel with the required expertise be admitted, semi-skilled local labour was in considerable demand. Typists and receptionists received salaries five times that of a senior government employee and a night club hostess could easily double a Cabinet Minister's annual income in just a month. Or a week, should she be receptive to some 'extra service' so often demanded by the lonely visitors.

Home owners with acceptable dwellings could receive the total value of the premises as an advance payment for a five-year lease.

This introduced a domino effect which created thousands of new Californian-style homes suitable for the foreigners as the landlords would use the advance rental payments to construct yet more villas and the cycle continued.

The foreigners brought their own strange cultures to Jakarta. Restaurants which claimed to be English pubs serving pizza, hamburgers and cottage pies flourished. The expatriates collected in the bars daily to communicate with each other, as other means were totally unreliable. Managers were obliged to use drivers to deliver messages, as this method proved more efficient than the local telephone system.

Businessmen and tourists found the local girls appealing and willing to administer to their needs. Jakarta's street prostitutes moved off the footpaths into the numerous bars and massage parlors, leaving their territory to the transvestites. These *banci*, dressed in the latest fashions, paraded around outside the Kartika Plaza Hotel, dominating the street's pedestrian traffic. Their numbers grew unchecked until the tall deep-voiced prostitutes completely controlled the Jalan Blora district.

The Indonesians found the all too frequent altercations which occurred between drunken foreigners repugnant. They had never been exposed to this alien social behaviour and had extreme difficulty dealing with it. Most simply avoided frequenting those hotels or restaurants which attracted the oil-rig crews.

Many civic leaders claimed that the Western influence was detrimental to the Indonesian people and should be curtailed before the effects were irreversible. The Moslem leaders were particularly vociferous, claiming that casinos and poker machines which were now rife in the city's bars and night clubs, had an anti-social and anti-religious effect on the population, and should therefore be banned immediately.

The Governor of Jakarta pointed out that the greater part of the funding received for the construction of the prestigious Istiqlal Mosque was, in fact, derived from those very poker machines. Teenage school girls cut classes to attend the night clubs to work as part-time hostesses. Drug abuse on the streets was evident for the first time and teenage suicides became a major statistic. Illegal taxis thrived and Jakarta's *cross-boy* hoodlum gangs emerged.

All this, and more, in just three short years! The city was alive with an exciting ambiance. Jakarta's inhabitants were smiling and enjoying life. Opportunities existed where before there had been nothing. The government embarked on an ambitious development program spending many millions of dollars on infrastructure projects and a restructured Defence Department — all of which required a constant supply of equipment and new weapons.

* * * * * *

Stephen Coleman's company thrived on its defence contracts. At the end of his second year, the company boasted thirty-one permanent office employees. Their activities were mainly centred on the provision of military supplies. Although the other areas also provided substantial income, profits from armament and equipment sales to the Department of Defence represented over ninety percent of all earnings.

Seda's system was simple and effective. They had first established a holding company in Hong Kong, using nominee directors. This enterprise appointed Coleman's Jakarta based group to act as official representatives promoting the arms and services offered via Hong Kong. Stephen visited manufacturers and suppliers in the United States and Europe, negotiating directly with company presidents to obtain agency agreements for sales into Indonesia. These corporate heads were informed that he, in fact, was the legal owner of the supply company registered in Kowloon. He also advised them that he represented several well-placed military associates who could guarantee orders should agency agreements be successfully concluded.

At first Coleman was confronted with considerable resistance. Several manufacturers approached HANKAM directly themselves, attempting to circumvent Coleman's proposed supply route. Nathan Seda blocked their every move. Eventually several smaller dealers contacted the Australian and established test orders for the supply of radio broadcast equipment. Delivery proceeded smoothly. Further orders followed. Again the dealers were satisfied, and his reputation began to grow. Within the year the Hong Kong company had secured sales in excess of five million United States dollars. Seda ensured that Coleman was informed regularly as to the Government's requirements and budget allocations for military purchases. They were cautious not to monopolize the market.

Coleman suggested establishing other nominee companies to expand their field of representation however Seda was reluctant to do so. He became concerned with the frequency of their meetings outside Indonesia. The General had become increasingly uncomfortable being away from his power base more often than before. He suggested that they restrict the regularity of their meetings to minimize exposure. Seda insisted they implement a more efficient and less dangerous procedure, one which would remove the need to meet as often thereby reducing their overall exposure.

He proposed the use of a single courier, who would facilitate delivery of sensitive documentation between the two men. They discussed the idea and, although Stephen accepted the General's proposal in principle, he was still concerned with the thought of an outsider being given such responsibility. Both agreed that the only real link in this arrangement would be the reliability of the courier. They understood also that should the documents be compromised at any time then their personal safety would be at risk.

Stephen agreed to use coded communications whenever exchanging letters with Seda, and nominated one of his senior staff, Pasaribu, who had developed a keen interest in the company's activities and had demonstrated his willingness to carry out orders without question. The General had refused his choice as the man was of Batak descent. Seda disliked Bataks.

They discussed alternatives and decided that until such times as the Timorese was comfortable with any of Coleman's immediate staff to fill this sensitive position, Seda would bring in another one of his own.

Umar Suharjo reported for courier duty the following week.

* * * * * *

The school where Wanti worked catered for students at the *Sekolah Menengah Pertama* level. The junior high school had been built only two years before, one of many, to cope with the sudden influx of students from the provinces. Bambang had been able to convince the local educational authorities to accept his sister as a part-time teacher. She had felt so proud on that first day when the other teachers had received her warmly as one of their own.

Wanti had tried very hard, teaching rudimentary subject material. She had no training for the position but her willingness to always do more and the students' immediate acceptance of her as a teacher was sufficient for the senior staff to move her temporary position, into full-time employment.

Wanti was grateful to her brother and the other young women who now shared the simple accommodations not far from the school. She knew that Bambang had pressured his girlfriend to assist with her application and Wanti now endeavoured to repay her kindness whenever the opportunity arose. Sharing a room with her brother's girlfriend was appropriate, she thought.

Often, when at school and during lessons she would feel a strange sense of exhilaration with the work. Especially when the young teenagers treated her more like an older sister than their teacher. She adored them all.

Once, when the school year was approaching the final days after examinations had been completed, the staff and students spent the whole day travelling the thirty kilometres to Bogor. The picnic had been arranged to coincide with the annual flowering of the huge plant the foreigners called *Rafflesia*. Wanti and the children learned a great deal that day as they sat and listened to the guide explain the historical values of the beautiful gardens. She was surprised to discover that the British had, for a brief period, displaced the Dutch and taken over her country. They had sent an English gentleman by the name of Raffles to become the new Governor of the Spice Islands. Wanti would see the results of his tenure in Indonesia. The beautiful Bogor Gardens were designed and built for his wife and, when she had passed away, Raffles had buried her there.

Wanti loved the romantic story. She was amazed when told that the foolish English had surrendered possession of her wonderful country, returning the islands of Indonesia to the Dutch receiving, in exchange, a small malaria-infested island called Singapura and the northern lands of Malaka. As she sat with the other teachers surrounded by students and observed the enormous flower finally open for its annual display of beauty and size, she was shocked that the world's largest flower had been cursed with such an obnoxious odour!

Later, as they returned to Jakarta and the children joked and teased each other, Wanti decided that there must be many wonderful places to see and visit. It was after that experience Wanti knew she just had to travel. At night she would dream of faraway places, conjuring up mythical lands in her mind before falling to sleep and, sometimes, dream of the wonders she had not seen but only read about in the brochures which lay neatly stacked under her bed.

When school finished on Saturdays she would climb aboard a bus and make her way into the city. There she would search out the travel agents asking for brochures for her students. The receptionists knew that the young woman obviously wanted the material for herself, but none could refuse the attractive girl as she was so sweet.

At night, after taking her *mandi* and shared rice with her room-mate Wanti would first attempt to read the brochures to herself before practicing aloud to her friend. She found the language difficult but was determined to persevere. Within a few months Wanti found that, with the aid of an English dictionary, she could actually make her way through an entire brochure in just one evening, understanding the contents clearly. Having mastered the contents she would then insist that her friend sit and listen as she read through the pages.

Wanti wished that her life had more to offer than just teaching simple subjects at school. She dreamed of being given the opportunity to fulfil her earlier ambitions. Wanti wanted desperately to become a secretary or at least a receptionist with one of the foreign firms she was always reading about, and sought ways to improve her chances for such positions. She concentrated on improving her communication skills understanding that knowledge of the foreign language was a pre-requisite in obtaining such lucrative employment.

Bambang had not laughed at her when Wanti explained why the travel brochures were so important to her. They were poor and could not afford the additional expense of books.

Wanti adored Bambang and he in turn cared for his sister above all else. She realized that soon he would be obliged to follow his unit to wherever they were sent, once he had graduated. Then she would be alone. Wanti knew that time was running out and it was imperative that she advance herself in some way. As most opportunities demanded a foreign language skill, the young Javanese girl decided that this should be her first step.

ɔhe would attend a course.

* * * * * *

Wanti viewed her brother's uniform critically. Although two years his senior, Wanti considered her *adik* more of an older relative. He certainly looked impressive dressed in his graduation uniform. Who would have thought Bambang would become such a handsome soldier? She smiled as he adjusted his beret for the umpteenth time.

"At last, their *rejeki* had improved," she thought, considering how their fortunes had changed for the better over the months.

Standing there, staring, not altogether conscious of the dreamy expression she displayed, Wanti's eyes slowly began to glaze over as they had so many times before. She realized that it was happening, again, and attempted to resist the sudden seizure. *No!* Wanti pleaded with herself, willing her body unsuccessfully to control the strange effects of the attack. *No, not now! not today!* she cried out silently, alarmed. Suddenly, Wanti remained very still and her mind slipped away from the reality of the moment into some dark void, as it had so many times before ever since she had witnessed the horrific aftermath of the raid on her village.

The unskilled doctors understood her trauma but could offer no remedy, no therapy to the beautiful but tragic soldier's sister. They had not received adequate training at medical school and had been unable to do anything to treat these self-induced seizures. As her mind retreated into another world closing down temporarily distancing Wanti from the reality around her, she would be transported to another plane. Her eyes would glaze over as she stared unsmilingly into space, breathing slowly, almost calmly. It was as if Wanti was not even present. There was never any panic, or so it would seem to the observer. It was just as if her spirit had temporarily departed leaving its physical semblance intact, waiting for consciousness to return.

To Bambang, who was accustomed to these trances, it was heartbreaking. For others who witnessed the incredible transformation, it was frightening. Outwardly she would appear as if day-dreaming. There was never any apparent physical movement to reflect the torment of the violent imagery flashing across her brain as she experienced scenes from a time long ago, now buried deep in her subconscious. Deep enough, almost, to prevent a total collapse.

As the headless children and mutilated torsos danced in her thoughts distancing her from whatever reality that may have triggered the turn, she would continue to experience the hallucinations and suffer extreme fear while those around her saw only the unusual, placid demeanour of the afflicted young woman.

Her brother Bambang could merely stand by and watch helplessly. She would never remember and could not therefore explain to Bambang the silent screaming terror she experienced with each of these sudden attacks, and even the doctors did not understand what triggered these relapses. Wanti would suddenly awaken, her frail body exhausted, saturated in perspiration, sometimes startling her brother with a shrill scream as consciousness returned. Wanti never had any recollection of the chilling visions.

When the first seizure occurred Bambang was terribly frightened. He'd called to her softly but when she did not respond he thought her brain had snapped like the old woman who lost her son in a bus accident during *Ramadhan*. He had shouted at Wanti to stop. He'd shaken her violently to make her snap out of the trance, but she had remained in the self-induced state. He had taken her by the hand and called her name, over and over, to no avail.

Then, suddenly, she returned to normal, blinked, looked caringly at her brother and smiled softly.

"*Kenapa, Mas?*" she'd asked, curious as to her brother's anxious expression.

At first he'd thought she'd been playing some stupid trick on him until he realized that she was not pretending. Bambang had just let her hand drop back by her side. He didn't know what to do. He prayed that her sickness might go away, naturally, with time. When several more fits occurred, he learned just to shrug them off.

As Wanti's self-induced hypnotic state started to recur regularly, he realized then that it was *Allah's* way of preventing her mind from snapping. *Allah* was *Great* and understood these things.

Bambang was a simple *kampung* boy and being such, was not equipped to understand why these attacks could occur at any time without any apparent trigger. He pleaded in his prayers for this mind sickness to go away. But it didn't.

The frequency of the seizures did, however, diminish. Fortunately Wanti never remembered any of these incidents. Whenever she regained full consciousness and returned from wherever her mind had taken her she would always respond by asking why others were staring at her. *"Kenapa, Mas?"*

After this latest attack he stood with his arm around her tiny shoulders. It had been some time since her last trance. He would not tell her that it had happened today, of all days.

Wanti was suddenly aware that her brother was still staring at her. She detected the concern in his expression.

"What is it, Mas?"

Her brother hesitated, his eyes filled with love and sadness for his beautiful sister.

"Wanti, I am worried about you," Bambang slowly shook his head as he forced a smile, reassuring his sister. *"You are too attractive to take to the graduation ceremony amongst all of those good looking young soldiers."*

She returned his smile. Her classic features warmed his heart for she was truly a beautiful woman.

"Bambang, ada-ada saja, You're too much," she laughed enjoying the flattery. *"Do you think I don't know what you boys really say about your sisters when they are out of earshot?"*

"Ah, Wanti. If only you really knew!" the young Javanese soldier teased, adjusting the angle of his beret again, now pleased to put this most recent attack out of his mind as there was so much to do on this important day.

He looked at her closely and, reassured that she had recovered from the spell, continued to prepare for the ceremony.

"We should depart. I am very pleased you came to escort me to the parade Bambang, but to be late would not represent a good start for your career."

"Ayo, let's go," she cajoled, slipping her arm through his, feeling confident that their luck had, in fact, changed for the better at last.

That evening Wanti was excluded from the boisterous celebrations. Instead, she sat at home and contemplated her future. She understood that Bambang would no longer remain in Jakarta. It was likely that he would be sent to one of the distant Territorial Commands for practical field experience. She had managed very well alone, these past six months separated from her brother, while he attended his training courses. Living with a girlfriend and sharing a room, their incomes as primary school teachers less than that paid to a foreigner's *babu*, the attractive young Javanese girl quickly developed an understanding of how poorly paid they were in comparison to others.

They were all economic conscripts, she thought.

Now that her brother had commenced his career, Wanti understood the necessity in taking positive steps if she expected to drag herself out of these sub-standard living conditions and make something of her life. During her brother's absence she had undertaken free English language lessons conducted by the American Friendship Association. She had found the course difficult as there was little opportunity to practise. Nevertheless, the young teacher persevered and the Americans who taught as volunteers were impressed with her progress. In spite of her undernourished frame, she consistently worked hard.

'*Who knows,*' Wanti wished for herself, '*maybe I will be fortunate and marry well,*' considering that marriage would, after all, be a very acceptable solution to her immediate problems.

* * * * * *

A junior American Consulate Officer had spotted her in the long queue. The Information Section was running an additional program which could lead to most of the successful graduates being employed as local personnel in the Embassy. This was a very competitive opportunity and applications had been keenly sought over past days.

Wanti had waited in the queue until four o'clock on the first day. Applications were required to be submitted in person. There had been only four other girls queued ahead of her when the wire screen shutter dropped indicating that the application window was closed for the day. Her face fell and her lips trembled slightly. She had been waiting in the outside queue since early the day before. To be this close!

Determination brought Wanti back the following morning. She had argued with the others, moving far ahead of her entitled position to within view of the window. Ignoring the abuse, fighting back the tears, the beautiful young woman stood her ground and, before the morning break, was within six positions of being able to submit her application. Wanti refused to leave the queue for food or drink and, when the afternoon session commenced, she had moved forward two more positions.

One of the junior consulate officers had spotted her in the long queue the day before. He'd been disappointed when the attractive girl had disappeared with the others as the Embassy closed down for the day. And here she was again, just as radiant, just as stunning! He was struck with her natural beauty and, slipping into the information office, he spoke quietly to one of his drinking buddies who was responsible for processing the forms, pointing in Wanti's direction.

She had seen, as did many of the silent hopeful applicants, the slap on the shoulder followed by boyish laughter and smiles without understanding that she was the reason for the banter. Unbeknown to Wanti, she had just been guaranteed a position on the course.

Totally unaware that she had jumped the queue, Wanti continued waiting her turn and, when it arrived, she smiled and passed her documents to the young American. Had it been brought to her attention that she had been successful primarily because of her appearance, the young lady would have just smiled sweetly and answered, '*And why not?*' responding with Javanese logic, '*beauty is as much a gift as is one's ability to do things, such as type or manage the complicated telephones, or teach, or work in the fields, and one should not be ashamed at being selected because of that gift.*'

She was pragmatic enough to appreciate that every opportunity must be taken in order to survive. As Wanti left the building her benefactor approached and very directly asked her for a date. She blushed, unsure of how to handle herself with the *bulé*, as being asked so directly by any man let alone a foreigner was a completely new experience for her. Wanti managed to escape with a polite response, hoping that the American would not be offended.

"Thank you, sir," she answered demurely and softly enough to send the young man's heart palpitations into overdrive, "but I am sorry. I cannot do so just now. "

She did not wish to offend. Although she felt there was little chance of her winning the position, Wanti was astute enough to realize that upsetting one of her potential employers would rule out any possibility whatsoever of being selected for this vacancy.

As she walked away the veteran of only two months smiled to

himself and made a mental note of her person. Later he checked her application and wrote down her name. The applicant's pass photo didn't do her justice but he had little difficulty identifying her picture. When Wanti returned for the first lesson he was waiting. Again he asked her out and again she refused politely.

But the American was very persistent. In the end she agreed, accepting an invitation to a function at one of the Embassy residences. Unable to afford new clothes for this special occasion she was, nevertheless, embarrassed to wear her traditional costume. *"Wear it, Wanti,"* advised her room mate, *"show them what a beautiful Indonesian girl should look like when she dresses."* Wanti agreed and spent hours in preparation.

* * * * * *

Her escort had insisted on sending his driver to pick her up prior to the function. Wanti didn't object as she did not particularly wish the American to meet her at their lodgings. It would not do to have a *bulé* hanging around her door for the neighbours to gossip about and she certainly did not wish this fair foreigner to witness her living conditions.

The driver's attitude verged on offensive, but not enough for Wanti to outwardly react. She merely made another mental note concerning the idiosyncrasies of Indonesian drivers who had developed this strange superiority complex because they were fortunate enough to be driving foreign *tuans*, whilst earning as much as one hundred dollars per month.

The American's car was luxurious. She had never felt such comfort. And it was air-conditioned! She would have a story for Bambang when they next met. In fact, the conditions inside the sedan were cool and refreshing, similar to what she had experienced in the mountains in Central Java where, should one walk up the trails to the two thousand metre summit, blankets were required to prevent exposure from the cold.

Wanti shivered. The driver had turned the air-conditioning to maximum knowing this would cause this girl to feel uncomfortable. He counted off the minutes expecting his passenger's reaction at any moment. He was aware that these girls were not accustomed to the cold air and this was his method of punishing them for associating with the foreigners. Wanti realized that the vehicle's air-conditioning was far too uncomfortable but was uncertain as to how to remedy the situation. She refused to seek this arrogant driver's assistance. There were no handles on the door with which to open the windows and momentary panic engulfed her.

Her eyes began to glaze over. Her mind slipped away taking her to another world and another time. It was as if her person had departed, leaving her physical being while her spirit travelled away - away to the picturesque terraced mountain slopes topped with blankets of cloud overlooking the tranquil rice fields spread so uniformly below. Her next recollection was that of the driver whispering urgently.

"Non! Miss, wake up miss!" The driver was extremely agitated and beginning to panic, 'worried that she had fainted or even worse, might complain to the *tuan!*

"Non, please Non. Wake up!"

Slowly her consciousness returned. Her body was no longer cold. '*Aduh,*' she thought, '*we have arrived. I must have been daydreaming again.*'

Regaining her composure Wanti was assisted from the Nash Rambler by the courteous young Marine who took her hand and escorted her inside. When Wanti first entered and saw the large crowd of guests she was immediately intimidated by the scene before her. She was nervous at being alone, not recognizing anyone until she spotted her date amongst the other guests standing in the reception queue. As Wanti was late, he hadn't waited more than a few minutes outside the residence before entering with the other guests, assuming she had elected not to come.

Wanti had walked directly up to the American and stood alongside as all the guests in the line moved slowly forward into the large colonial structure. The premises were located on Jalan Raden Saleh. It was the residence of the United States Military Attaché and the evening's function was to introduce some of the many new Military Aid Advisers. Wanti was relieved to see other Indonesian ladies wearing the traditional *kain kebaya*. Now she would not feel so conspicuous.

Her escort introduced his guest to the host, a very tall Colonel who towered over the assembly. American Marine guards stood stiffly at the entrance their colourful uniforms adding to the atmosphere of colonial splendour. Five hundred guests crowded the stately home, some spilling out into the garden and gazebo where houseboys mixed, then refilled, cocktail glasses at an amazing pace. Trays of *hors d'oeuvres* were offered by the white uniformed *jongus* while others prepared the buffet.

The spectacle almost caused Wanti to cry out. She had never imagined anything so beautiful! It was if she had been thrust into a scene from Hollywood. Foreign Attachés and Ambassadors, French, German, Italian and even Russian representatives were to be seen. It was almost too much for the attractive Javanese as she remembered not to gape at the cocktail dresses and jewellery adorning the wives of these prominent people.

As she was introduced to another group Wanti noticed the young foreigner standing alone, a cocktail in one hand, cigarette in the other. He smiled, and Wanti looked away, embarrassed. She turned to ask her companion if the food provided was *halal*, or prepared according to traditional Islamic Law, but had difficulty in expressing herself.

The American replied, asking her if she was already hungry, misunderstanding what Wanti had said. She attempted to ask the question again, and when the words she required stubbornly refused to flow in the required sequence, she turned away to avoid the feeling of panic which threatened to engulf her. Flustered, Wanti reverted to Indonesian to escape unwanted attention as the other couples in their group were observing her struggle, the women inwardly enjoying this pretty young girl's discomfort at not being able to converse as fluently as the others.

Immediately she felt self-conscious. Exposed. Alone. She wanted to flee, and turned back to her escort for comfort. He was now preoccupied with the platter of *saté* offered by the servant to his left. As Wanti's concern grew she was surprised that the young man who had smiled at her had suddenly joined their group.

He was introduced by the American. Wanti immediately noticed the man's confidence and looks of admiration he received from the women nearby. He stood directly in front of Wanti, squeezed her hand gently and inquired, *"Nona cantik ini, siapa namanya?"* Who is this beautiful young lady?

Momentarily, she could not answer, amazed that this foreigner could speak her language. Wanti stared at the handsome darkly tanned Australian, his green eyes smiling at her surprised expression. Her fears immediately vanished. She looked at Stephen, mesmerized, deciding that he was of mixed extraction as he was darker than most of the other foreigners in the room. Or maybe he was one of those Dutch Christian missionaries she had heard about? Whatever he was, one thing was certain — she had never met a *bulé* who could speak her language so fluently. Confidence returning, Wanti responded in her national tongue.

"My name is Suwanti. Can you really speak Bahasa Indonesia or have you merely memorized a few phrases to flatter the ladies and impress your foreign friends?"

Coleman laughed at her refreshing directness. He decided to converse in her language so that the other foreigners could not follow the conversation and to keep her at ease.

"Bukan main galaknya!" he retaliated, indicating that she was snappish, noticing the instant change of expression.

"Maaf tuan, kalau perkataan saya menyinggung," Wanti apologized for her cutting remark. *"Apakah tuan bisa maafkan saya?"* she requested, soliciting his forgiveness.

"Sudah dong!" Stephen replied with genuine sincerity as he took her hand once more and guided her away from the group and her partner.

"I noticed your concern and decided that you were too pretty to be ignored by your boyfriend."

"Boyfriend? Oh no tuan. He is my English teacher when he is not working at the Embassy."

Coleman grinned. *"Call me Stephen, not tuan. You will make me feel so old with tuan this, tuan that."*

He led her into the garden where the strong fragrance of jasmine hung heavily in the air. Frangipani flowers decorated the tables while orchid arrangements enhanced the gazebo's setting. Candles flickered in their clay temple-shaped holders as harmonious voices blended perfectly with the Tapanuli guitarists' chords.

* * * * * *

Stephen realized that he'd been staring at her only when Wanti suddenly smiled, looking directly into his eyes. He couldn't believe how stunningly beautiful she was, dressed in the traditional costume, her hair rolled into a meticulously dressed half bun which rested gently on her lace-covered shoulders.

Wanti's features were classic. Her bright almond eyes were more oval than round, accentuated by high cheekbones providing just a touch of almost regal strength to her face. Stephen had seen many beautiful women in Indonesia and other countries, but never had he been so struck by the beauty of a young woman as *cantik-molek* as this magnificent Javanese creature.

He knew that the other guests would be observing them together in the garden and, although there were many other couples now mingling in the outdoor setting, he became conscious of the other guests' glances in their direction. They made a handsome couple, indeed, he thought.

Wanti sat where he'd indicated while continuing to admire the decorations. Coloured lights placed along the walls spreading high into the tall *beringin* tree created an almost carnival atmosphere and she was now pleased that she had attended the function. They sat together, momentarily silent, absorbing the serenity of the evening setting. A *jongus* replaced Coleman's drink, asking if the *tuan's* health had completely recovered, genuinely interested in this man he obviously admired.

Wanti was surprised with the sincerity she observed between the men. It was not common to see a foreigner behaving so kindly to those they considered below them. She was again impressed with the man's manner. Her interest in the young Australian grew through the evening as she came to notice the respect given to him by many of the other foreigners and the friendly nature he displayed when dealing with her own people.

He talked to Wanti for a while telling her about the function and the people present, stopping only when interrupted by other guests who had also ventured into the garden. She realized that he had a natural ability to put those around him at ease. Wanti suddenly felt comfortable in his company and was reluctant to return to her original escort, although she knew that good manners demanded that she do so.

"Please excuse me, Stephen. You have been very kind to me but, I should return to talk to my escort. I don't wish to make him angry. You understand?"

Coleman turned his head and after examining the crowded area inside spotted the American.

"Wait here, Wanti," he asked, *"I'll just be a moment,"* with which he rose, patted her hand softly and walked back through the garden and into the main hall.

When he returned, he was surprised that she looked concerned, almost worried.

"Was I gone that long?' he teased, smiling so that she would feel at ease, as before.

"I must go now, really."

"I don't think it's a good idea," he started, *"I have just spoken to your date and he is currently putting the hard word on someone else."*

"I don't understand."

"Wanti, your escort has just arranged to meet with the young lady who is leaning all over him after he has you sent home," he lied.

"That will be all right. I don't mind, he is not my boyfriend and I am grateful that he asked me to come here tonight. I think it has been a wonderful evening," she said.

"Wanti, I have told him that you have agreed to permit me to take you home." He looked very serious. *"It is not correct that you should be sent home alone. I hope you don't mind?"*

"I'm not sure," she hesitated, *"should I speak to him first? Was he angry that we have been out here together in the garden? Have I been rude?"*

"No, Wanti, no," Stephen assured her, taking the long fingers of her right hand and squeezing them warmly. *"He was pleased, in fact,"* again he lied.

"If you're sure, and if it is not too much trouble. I could go home by becak if necessary but it is so far and late at night, not so safe, as you probably already know."

"Well, we should not be in a hurry to leave," with which he took her by the hand and moved around with Wanti attached to his arm, introducing her to many of the guests. She couldn't remember their names and had given up attempting to do so after the first few. It was so difficult. The names were strange and the accents varied greatly making it almost impossible for her to cope. She realized that in no way she did feel intimidated, holding Stephen's arm as they walked slowly around, he shaking the men's hands, introducing her to them and their ladies while ignoring questions regarding the length of their friendship, or how they had met, while she smiled and occasionally responded with a polite

rejoinder.

As the evening progressed she discovered to her surprise that she was really enjoying the party and the guests. They had accepted her as one of them. They had been kind and charming. She looked at Stephen as he finished listening to a story, laughing at its ending as he caught her eye. He grinned and winked at her. Wanti just smiled in response.

One of the other ladies in the small group they had joined put her hand on Stephen's arm as she laughed, and Wanti immediately felt a twinge of jealousy. The woman was dressed in a long white evening gown, her short brown hair cut to permit the expensive earrings to display their elegant diamond settings, matched with the small brooch clipped beside the cleavage exposing her softly tanned but adequately endowed breasts.

Wanti could not understand the feelings she was experiencing, accepting that she had only just met her handsome new friend.

"*Stephen,*" she interrupted, "*may I go home now please?*"

He turned, looked at her and smiled. "*Sure,*" was all he said, taking her by the hand and leading Wanti out of the main reception room, stopping briefly to speak with their hosts.

"*You're tired.*" Although the statement did not require an answer she responded anyway.

"*Thank you Stephen. You have been very kind to me. I wonder why?*" she asked, almost coquettishly, her eyes wide, smiling at her small success in having him move away from the group inside and the attractive foreign woman. She had not expected him to agree to leave immediately and was now not really ready to return home to her dismal surroundings there.

"*Because you are like a fairy princess who's just stepped into my life,*" he answered, smiling kindly, holding her hands firmly.

Wanti laughed. "*Never a princess, Mas,*" unaware of her familiarity in addressing him so, "*never a princess!*"

His car had turned into the brick-paved driveway as they waited on the steps outside and he laughed with her, pleased that she had used the almost intimate form in her response. He drove her to his villa. Stephen knew she would be impressed and was surprised at himself for feeling the necessity for her to be so. At first she had refused to leave the car wishing that he'd taken her directly home.

"*We will only be a few minutes, Wanti. Please come inside. It's okay,*" *nothing will happen to you."*

"If it's only a few minutes then I can wait here."

Stephen shrugged and turned to enter the doorway now open as the *jongus* waited for him. Surprised that the young lady had not followed, he left the door ajar and followed his *tuan* into the lounge room.

"Make coffee, Kardi," he ordered.

The houseboy disappeared and within a few minutes had returned with a silver tray, coffee, two cups and an already poured crystal glass partly filled with Hennessee's XO Cognac and a selection of after dinner mints. He placed them on the long carved teak table and stood with his hands clasped in front of his body.

Stephen looked up and raised his eyebrows. *"What is it, Kardi?"*

"The young lady, tuan?" he inquired, turning his head in the general direction of the front door which remained open.

Stephen thought for a moment. *"Take this out to the car,"* he said, indicating the tray.

Never totally understanding the whims of the foreigners and their strange habits, the houseboy obeyed.

Wanti saw the *jongus* appear and moments behind, Stephen.

"We will have our coffee here, if you find it more comfortable," he said, climbing into the rear seat.

Wanti was speechless. At first she felt embarrassed, realizing that she had insulted this kind man who had been so thoughtful to her all evening. Then, as she observed how relaxed he was sitting back comfortably holding a large balloon shaped crystal glass softly swirling its contents, she started to laugh.

Stephen looked sharply and then, appreciating just how ridiculous it must all seem to the young and inexperienced Javanese beauty he too smiled and then joined with her laughing out aloud. The houseboy watched from behind the curtains. He was convinced that the *tuan* had gone completely mad. And then he too then started to smile. The young lady had stepped out of the *tuan's* car and was heading for the door.

Still laughing together, Wanti permitted Stephen to usher her into the house where they sat together in the guest lounge, sipping the retrieved coffee while listening to Neil Diamond sing his way through an Lp.

They talked and laughed, enjoying each other's anecdotes and other trivia as Sukardi politely entered from time to time, checking their coffee and replenishing the snacks he had hastily prepared when his *tuan* had returned. The hours passed quickly and, as she looked up at the antique clock as it chimed the hour, Wanti suddenly realized that it was already morning. She had stayed out all night. Immediately Wanti was filled with anxiety. She couldn't permit Stephen to take her home.

"*I must go home by becak, Stephen. Please understand. I have been out all night and my reputation will be ruined if the others see me returning with a foreigner,*" she had pleaded. He understood and reluctantly agreed.

Promising to meet again on the following Saturday, Wanti took the *becak* arriving home with barely sufficient time to *mandi*, change and catch the bus to the school where she taught.

All day Wanti's spirits were high. She didn't feel at all tired even with the long hours she had then to spend at the school. And when she awoke the following morning, the strange feeling persisted and continued to do so throughout the day. She sat, observing the young children as they studied their books, aware that it was not just the anticipation she felt for their next meeting that sent her pulse racing — it was more than that.

The young Javanese woman now understood the emotion she'd experienced late into her first evening together with Stephen when suddenly, as he'd touched her hand gently, softly, an overwhelming warmth had passed quickly through her body. Wanti sat, uncomfortably, observing the children as they studied their books, conscious of the strange and unusual sensation she had never experienced before. It was more, much more than she had ever imagined it would be. As she day-dreamed, the unfamiliar feelings caused her to unconsciously adjust her position on the hard wooden chair. Confused but happy, anxious but excited, Wanti thought she might be falling in love.

* * * * * *

Weeks later, stretched out alone on the poolside deck chair Stephen still didn't quite understand exactly how he'd permitted it to happen. He sat up slowly, raised the *cubra libre* to his lips, slowly sipping the Bacardi as he observed the two topless sunbathers across the azure blue swimming pool.

Wanti had not yet returned from her third successive day's shopping. He couldn't believe her capacity to stay away all day browsing through shops, bargaining, missing meals, then returning late in the afternoon flushed with the excitement of the day's purchasing spree. Their hotel suite was already inundated with scores of plastic shopping bags containing shoes, scarves, negligees, jeans and jackets, all boxed and bearing the latest tags. She'd even bought new suitcases, needed to accommodate the range of fashions she'd acquired and an assortment of cosmetics which immediately filled all available bathroom space.

It hadn't been so much a whirlwind romance but more of a whirlwind wedding he thought, reflecting on their impulse decision to marry. Stephen knew that he was expected to settle down sooner or later and cease the debauched life he'd enjoyed as a single man if he expected to be taken seriously within the International Trading Community. Now, he wasn't even sure that he loved Wanti, but decided that it didn't really matter. He was content to have her near as she added a new dimension to his life and, more importantly, she loved him.

General Seda had been pleased when Stephen had asked for his opinion.

"*Do it, Stephen,*" he had urged, "*do it! She is a very beautiful girl and it would do you no harm to have such an attractive, intelligent and loving wife.*" Seda failed to inform Stephen that her being Javanese was probably a greater consideration than her other attributes.

Stephen had not wanted to go through the monotonous ritual of a traditional Javanese wedding. He explained to Wanti and Bambang that, as she was an orphan and as his parents lived so far away, it would be wiser to keep their wedding ceremony small, inviting just a few close friends. Wanti agreed. At that time she would have agreed to anything although later, as the initial euphoria faded, she did have some regrets.

Although he had not insisted, his bride had readily accepted the simple wedding at the registry office in old Kota, downtown China Town. They invited a small number of close personal friends, and Wanti's brother Bambang, to the celebration. Seda had suggested he would not attend.

They had honeymooned in Singapore and Hong Kong. Sitting around the pool at the Hyatt Regency on Scott's Road, Stephen finally came to terms with what he'd done and how impetuous he had been. He was surprised and a little annoyed with himself for the impulsive step he'd taken.

Stephen closed his eyes as the sun suddenly emerged from behind the clouds warming his well-tanned skin. The long Bacardi and Coke rested in his left hand, the ice cooling his palm through the thin glass. He relaxed, watching one of the topless women sit up suddenly and add some more cream to her body. He thought about his new bride. Stephen Coleman knew then that he had to make the best of his commitment. He waved to the white jacketed poolside waiter and ordered another drink.

* * * * * *

It was in Singapore that Coleman received Nathan Seda's couriered letter advising that their operation was about to enter a new phase, incorporating the supply of several squadrons of helicopters and associated armaments. It was a major opportunity for them. The note had instructed him to meet with the General in Kuala Lumpur the following day.

Coleman left his wife with friends who promised her a shopping excursion even his bank manager would never forget. Upon his return they recounted the day's events, laughing as they explained to Stephen how even they had difficulty keeping pace with his excited bride. As she hurried from shop to shop Wanti just couldn't believe her eyes. Meticulously she selected materials, ordering the tailor to copy a cocktail dress she'd seen in his imported catalogues and a smart trouser suit to match the three-inch heels purchased in the *toko* next door. She was like a little child, tearing open the parcels showing her husband what she had purchased barely finishing an explanation of one before tearing open another.

That evening, alone in the darkness of their hotel room Wanti related the story of her life with Bambang and the horrors she had experienced. Wanti finished her story without being subjected to one of her seizures. For the first time, since she could remember, Wanti felt safe.

Stephen held Wanti close to him comforting her as she sobbed choking back her tears while describing the savage mutilation of the many *kampung* children slain dead, as they were held to their mothers' breasts. Her story carried them through the night leaving them both emotionally drained. Only then had Stephen realized what an incredibly strong little woman he had married.

As she lay asleep, her long black hair spread softly across the pillow, the classic aristocratic features accentuated by high cheek bones, her soft brown skin highlighted against the white sheets, Steve Coleman swore an oath that, as long as they were together, he would never permit Wanti to be exposed again to horror such as she'd suffered as a child.

It was then he also decided never to reveal the true nature of his company's activities nor the principal responsible for his success. That he was dealing in arms did not overly concern him, nor did he see this as some flaw in his character. Selling weapons was an honourable profession, he thought. And if it wasn't, then this didn't really matter either. He believed that his ideals and integrity had already been compromised years before when he'd first met John Anderson, and whatever he might do after his life after ASIS, the Australian Secret Service, could in no way make him a lesser person than he had already become.

Stephen softly stroked her cheek admiring her features. He knew that she would be in danger should he reveal his relationship with the General and decided that this would have to be the one secret he would hold from her.

* * * * * *

Married life in Jakarta changed Stephen's life style very little. Office activities occupied the mornings, after which he would lunch with business associates, sleep in the afternoons and spend the evenings with Wanti. She was extremely happy and couldn't wait to be pregnant. As the months passed by she became agitated by the possibility that she might not be able to bear children. Stephen seemed not to be concerned and this also gnawed at her heart.

In Indonesia, as a marriage was not considered truly consummated until a child had been produced, several of Wanti's card playing partners irritated Coleman with their playful innuendos suggesting that she should be careful, as there may be others waiting in the wings. Fortunately, Wanti's brother Bambang visited frequently and his presence had a calming effect on her.

Coleman admired his brother-in-law for the care and protection he had given his sister. The soldier never discussed the events leading up to their departure from the *kampung*. On one occasion, when Wanti appeared to be daydreaming but was, in fact, only concentrating on her schedule for the day, Bambang had whispered her name several times, calling to her as if she had fallen asleep. Bambang's apparent relief at his sister's response had mystified Coleman at the time. He was unaware of his wife's former, frequent relapses and, as her condition had obviously improved since their marriage, Bambang decided not to discuss his sister's attacks with his brother-in-law.

Wanti had only induced the effect once during this time. She had overheard one of her husband's senior employees discussing their *tuan's* frequent trips overseas, joking as to the nature of his short visits away from Jakarta.

"*Tuan must have arranged a regular cewek in Hong Kong,*" Pasaribu playfully announced, waving the air tickets for that destination around in the air. It was one of his responsibilities to ensure Coleman's travel arrangements, or at least those which Coleman permitted his staff to know about as many of his destinations after Hong Kong were kept confidential.

"*This is his third trip this month,*" he said. "*I'll bet she has big breasts and is very expensive,*" he continued, holding his hands out in front of his chest cupping his fingers in an exaggerated manner to approximately the shape he was describing.

Wanti's reaction was to immediately to look down at her own chest. Her breasts were so small!

Wanti accepted, reluctantly, that the conversation she'd overheard was just office gossip and that she should not permit such talk to upset her. Nevertheless her bust was small and she would suggest that Stephen take her on his next trip.

The Sumatran's actions were quite intentional. Pasaribu had positioned himself so that it would appear he had not seen *Wanti* enter the office. Raising the tickets he laughed, waving the travel documents in the air as he insinuated that the boss was obviously not just preoccupied with business when away.

Wanti had immediately slipped back out of the room to avoid embarrassment and drifted away to her private world alone in her bedroom.

The Batak's motives were quite simple; devious, but simple. As he was one of the senior managers, he expected to benefit directly should such a situation arise due to his seniority and fluency in English, which might find him relegated to travelling overseas in lieu of Coleman.

Pasaribu had no idea as to the real purpose of these trips, his employer had never discussed these excursions and he did not appear to maintain records concerning these activities. Curiosity caused the Sumatran to ponder possibilities quite beyond his sphere of responsibilities and influence. Whatever the reason, he suspected that these short journeys to the other Asian capitals were obviously connected in some way to their supply activities.

He was familiar with the volume of material and weapons supplied and consequently understood the staggering dollar value of the group sales to HANKAM, but often wondered why the company did not increase its profits by dealing directly with the manufactirers and bypass the Hong Kong middleman.

He had learned that the margins earned by the sales were thin and, according to the talkative accountant, too thin, as the company's declared profits were surprisingly small. Pasaribu appreciated that, although his role was purely that of employee, the company should endeavour to increase its profitability whenever the opportunity arose. He had also considered that should the company be obliged to pay more taxes he would have the opportunity to take advantage of this situation. His cousin's wife was on the district taxation audit team. Pasaribu believed that he would be able to nibble into any increased monthly payments together with his relatives without anyone being the wiser.

He decided to examine these opportunities more while waiting for a suitable opportunity to manoeuvre himself into a stronger position within the group. Maybe even accompany the *tuan* on one of those business holidays. Pasaribu knew that there were hidden secrets somewhere in the company's files and dossiers locked upstairs in the boss's bedroom. If only he could locate that data he knew that he could be a wealthy man.

* * * * * *

As with the other office staff, the Sumatran was not aware that one of their number had been directly orchestrated into her position as a clerk, monitoring the other employees' activities. She reported everything to the Umar. He paid her thirty dollars every month for her loyalty. But she did it out of fear.

Six weeks after the incident regarding the air tickets Pasaribu's body was discovered, his throat cut from ear to ear and his wallet, wristwatch and other valuables missing. The office workers attended the funeral and, without exception, expressed their dismay that he could come to such a disgusting end, even though it was in the car park behind one of the more notorious massage parlors.

A few days later Coleman's accountant disappeared. Annoyed with losing two key personnel in the same week Coleman decided to look at the possibility of engaging foreign staff to assist with the ever-growing administrative support his company required. He advertised in the Straits Times in Singapore and was pleased with the standard and number of applicants who applied. Many were of Chinese extraction and, in his business, definitely not politically acceptable.

* * * * * *

The following month Coleman employed his first foreign assistant. His résumé had provided the applicant with an almost guaranteed position with the company. He had the correct academic qualifications and background. He was young and appeared to be comfortable living in the fast moving world of armament and equipment dealings. His credentials indicated that he had worked with one of the Australian Small Arms manufacturers and it was this particular reference which influenced Coleman's final decision.

Not that the new employee would have immediate access to many sensitive aspects of the company's activities such as actually arranging purchases and delivery of weapons — Coleman would always retain that responsibility for himself. It was essential to the security of his relationship with Seda that only he be conversant with such sensitive detail. The knowledge of the arrangements already in place would be too dangerous in another's hands.

Not mentioned in the man's curriculum vitae was his expertise as a skilled hand gun expert and dedicated skier. And that he'd fine tuned both of these abilities under the watchful eye of John Anderson. He was an ASIS mole - and his name was Gregory James Hart.

Chapter 11

Jakarta — The Riots

Umar Suharjo was delighted with the riots. Cars and buildings were burning everywhere. Sirens screamed as fire tenders and police raced frantically from one location to the next, unable to keep pace with the deliberate destruction of property. Anything of Japanese manufacture came under attack. All of this excitement and none of it any of his doing!

Tension had been mounting ever since the Japanese Prime Minister's visit had been announced. In just a few short years the Japanese economic machine had moved into Indonesia and virtually dominated the consumer market. There were cries of unfair trade practices, such as buyer's commission and dumping. The Japanese elected to ignore the obvious signs of dissent and suddenly, without further warning, violence erupted throughout the capital.

Students ran *amok*, while soldiers stood by and watched, permitting the chaos to continue unchecked. It was if the government itself wanted this violent display against their economic benefactors. Vehicles of Japanese origin were blocked by the huge crowds and drivers invited to vacate their cars before the vehicles were destroyed. At first many drivers did not appreciate the seriousness of their position and immediately became the first fatalities.

All of Jakarta's major arterial roads were blocked by damaged and burning Datsuns, Nissans and Toyotas as the riots spread out of control. Crowds vented their hate, burning school buses and motor bikes, the violence finally spilling over into buildings displaying Japanese products or neon signs.

* * * * * *

Coleman sat in the rear of the new Nissan. The traffic had slowed,

261

and he could see smoke billowing from what appeared to be an accident up ahead on the junction of Jalan Juanda and Jalan Hajam Wuruk.

"Shit!" he muttered, turning to speak to his co-passenger, "another screwed-up morning. "

He was referring to the previous day's appointments, missed due to traffic confusion and rescheduled for that day. Moments later the traffic ceased to flow completely. Both of the passengers immediately felt the discomfort as the air-conditioner laboured, struggling to cool the stationary vehicle. Several youngsters ran along between the blocked lines of stagnated cars, trucks and buses and, as they passed between the Nissan and the adjacent vehicle, they banged the side heavily with their fists, startling the occupants.

"Little bastards," called Hart, not entirely happy with the situation, his clothes developing moist patches because of the failing air-conditioner.

"Okay," Stephen decided, "let's walk. This jam is impossible. We'll slip down past the accident and grab a taxi on the other side."

Leaning forward he touched Achmad on the shoulder. He turned his head slightly.

"*Nanti, kalau sudah bisa jalan, pulang saja,*" Coleman instructed Achmad to find his own way when the road cleared. The dedicated man who had driven for him when he had first arrived in the country and had resigned from the Embassy to follow the former Attaché.

Stephen and Greg then both left their locked briefcases behind and began walking towards the stagnated vehicles. They were within fifty metres of the intersection when the mob appeared.

At first Coleman assumed that the crowd was moving in their direction urged by traffic police. And then it dawned on him. He called his companion.

"Greg. Quickly! Follow me. And don't panic!" he added urgently.

Hart started to ask why when a team of well organized students commenced throwing stones at selected cars. Startled by the sudden violence he ran after Stephen, following him to the side of the street closest to the canal which divided the road.

"Cross here!" Coleman ordered, a note of alarm in his tone. Hart identified the urgency in Coleman's command. The small footbridge permitted the two foreigners to hurry across the canal, avoiding the coagulated brown mess below. Hart continued to follow his associate now moving quickly back away from the burning cars as the first vehicle erupted with a deafening explosion.

They stopped and stared back at the incredible sight. Bottles filled with petrol were hurled through the air at the expensive cars, exploding upon impact.

"For Chrissakes!" Hart yelled, "they're throwing Molotov cocktails!"

At least a dozen more vehicles caught fire. They were already burning furiously as the mob surged along the other side of the *kali,* screaming slogans, smashing shop windows and torching more cars. Their numbers multiplied by the moment.

"What are they yelling?" the visibly shaken Hart asked, "are we in real danger?"

"Come with me Greg! Take it easy, they're not rioting against us. The chanting sounds like anti-Japanese slogans. "

Hart paled. "Shit, Stephen, we could be killed! For Chrissakes, man, let's get the hell out of here before these bastards decide to widen their parameters!" yelled Hart above the rising crescendo of the swelling mob.

"Don't lose your head! If they see you run or panic they will turn on you as quickly as a savage dog so just bloody well stand here against the wall and shut up!" Coleman yelled, now concerned not just for his own safety and that of his associate, but also for his driver who had completely disappeared from view amongst the mass of rioters and spectators.

He could just see his Nissan. The flames consumed it with incredible speed. He stretched and still couldn't see Achmad. He hoped he hadn't attempted to protect the *tuan's* new sedan. The noise increased as the students moved into shops smashing more windows and throwing furniture onto the fires. Coleman could see that this was going to be worse than the rice riots of 'Sixty-eight.'

He shuddered. The demonstrators were now completely out of control wrecking everything, not just Japanese products, but anything at all as they broke into shops, looting and burning. He had learned from his own experience and from some of the older members of the expatriate community that generally rioters left foreigners alone providing they did not display arrogance, fear, or attempt to offer any resistance to the crowd's destructive actions.

Hart was alarmed by the sudden turn in events. He had never witnessed mob violence before.

"Shit! Stephen! Let's make a dash for it!" he pleaded as the crowd swelled past them, moving dangerously close.

"God damn you! Stay where you bloody well are!" he was ordered.

Hart wanted to close his eyes and permit it all to pass, tensing his body in anticipation of the first blow.

"Take it easy, take it easy," Coleman called loudly to the shaken man. "It'll be over in a few minutes. Keep your cool! The main body of the mob is moving away from us down towards Kota."

Jakarta's Chinatown represented the commercial hub of the capital. Historically, whenever there were signs of civil unrest the Chinese would react instinctively before any other ethnic group, protecting their shops and homes by throwing down the steel grated shutters to prevent looters from entering their premises. It was if their very actions were some form of riot indicator.

"Shit! They are going to burn Kota!" Coleman exclaimed.

"Couldn't give a rat's arse," Hart screamed, engulfed in fear, his voice almost inaudible, "just as long as they get the fuck outta here!"

The main body of the rioters headed quickly down town. As the mob moved, the terrifying yelling and screaming followed. Both men remained where they were, watching the alarming mass move slowly away, continuing on their destructive path towards the Chinese Quarter. Soon there was not nearly as much noise as before. Coleman and Hart remained alert, waiting, as they could still see smaller groups, mainly thieves, smashing their way into the remaining shops which had escaped the first wave of pillaging. The looters remained at work, but these were not as threatening as the screaming mob that had passed by just minutes before.

Coleman watched the ongoing violence around him cautiously.

He waited a few more minutes and then decided it was safe to move away.

"Greg? Are you all right?"

Embarrassed, still shaking, his legs a little weak around the knees, Hart attempted a brave face. "Guess so. "

"Stay on this side of the street," Stephen instructed." Walk quickly, and we'll turn down one of the narrow side roads and head towards the market. Maybe we'll find a *becak* there. The taxis aren't stupid. They won't move out into this mess. "

Hart followed. Moving back towards the junction where the first explosion had occurred, Coleman remained alert, his eyes searching for Achmad. He was very worried. There were people seriously injured everywhere. Some were probably dead.

They walked up to the smouldering wreck of the Nissan. Nothing could have been done for the faithful driver. His broken body lay on the roadside covered in blood and filth. His chest had been crushed by the weight of hundreds of rioters as they had swarmed through the street, carelessly trampling across the fallen driver smashing his ribs. Achmad had screamed out for Stephen as he went down but his cry had been lost in the tumult. In that instant, as a heavy booted-foot had kicked down, Achmad had died.

As the two foreigners passed the wreck it was impossible for them to see the dead driver's body, obscured amidst the burned and damaged vehicles.

"Down here!" Stephen called, indicating a small laneway too narrow for anything but *becak* and pedestrian traffic.

Hart moved quickly resisting the temptation to run. More explosions could be heard in the distance as petrol tanks ruptured throwing lumps of hot steel and other debris back into the crowd of unsuspecting onlookers.

Coleman pulled a thick wad of Rupiah from his pocket and waved furiously at the *becak* speeding past.

"*Where do you want to go?*" the becak driver asked braking dangerously.

"*Menteng!*" Stephen answered.

"*Enggak mau,*" the driver spat, refusing to take them to Menteng. As he pedalled away he called back to the foreigners. "*Lebih ramai disana dong!*' - It's even worse over there!'

Stephen spun around, shocked.

Hart looked at him impatiently. "What is it?"

Coleman turned his head slightly, his face a white mask. "Let's

265

go! Now!" he yelled and commenced to run.

"Stephen," his companion called after him, also breaking into a run as he realized that the other man was not about to stop.

"Stephen," he called again, breathlessly, "wait up, damn it!" as he slowed to a walk, already fatigued.

Coleman was at least twenty metres ahead when he stopped and yelled for Hart to hurry.

"Stuff it! I can't run any fucking further!" he choked, his adrenaline reserves almost depleted.

Coleman hesitated then stood impatiently waiting for Hart to catch up.

Glaring at the other man Stephen hissed, "Run! Run now you bastard or I'll leave you here alone!"

"What the fuck for? The crowds have long passed and we're safe here. " Hart screamed vehemently, disorientated and still terrified of the possibility that they'd bump headlong into another crowd of demonstrators.

"Yes. We are," Stephen clenched his fists, controlling his anger, "but others may not be so lucky. That *becak* driver refused to take us back home to Menteng as he claimed it's burning! The riots have hit there as well, Wanti will be in danger!" he yelled.

Immediately they ran, at first together and as Hart tired he called out to Stephen, insisting that he continue on without him. Coleman refused and, also out of breath, rested for a brief moment. He managed to wave down another *becak* driver, his fist held high full of Rupiah notes. This time he didn't indicate their destination as being Menteng, insisting only that the driver take them to Cikini, not a kilometre from the office.

The driver agreed and twenty minutes later the pair approached Jalan Cik Ditiro on foot, having paid the nervous driver off just two hundred metres from the office. As they neared the premises it was obvious that there had been considerable damage to the building.

Earlier, the screaming mobs had turned off from Jalan Imam Bonjol and commenced their path of destruction along Cik Ditiro. Stephen's complex was on a corner, between the Governor's official residence and the home of a retired Admiral. The former Marine General's house was well protected by armed guards who quickly demonstrated their impatience with the forward line of the approaching crowd by shooting over their heads.

The mob had panicked and split into two groups, one pouring down the smaller side street towards the Governor's home where they were met yet again with a barrage of bullets from another team of marines delegated to guard the city's much admired leader.

Molotov cocktails were thrown. More rounds of ammunition were discharged until finally the rioting crowd could no longer contain their rage, several of their number falling under a barrage of bullets. The frenzied mass of humanity poured forward determined to distroy everything in their way.

The mob was no longer motivated just by anti-Japanese feeling. They were out of control, the participants determined to vent their pent-up hatred of the wealthy, the powerful and the military.

Both of Stephan's neighbour's homes survived due to the diligence of their Marine Guards. Stephen's building was spared as a result of its position between the two senior citizen's well-protected residences.

One Molotov Cocktail had successfully carried its dangerous contents through a side plate glass window bursting into flames in the private dining area only to be extinguished by Sukardi, who had bravely attacked the flames with his jacket. All around on both sides of the street, houses had been gutted by fire and most were still smouldering as the rioters had hit this district first, leaving the carnage behind as testimony to the ferocity of their destructive power.

Stephen viewed the scene before him as he started to run towards his home and office. And wife. Another sedan, this time one of their Datsuns, stood half on the footpath and partly on the road, windows smashed and the body damaged, but not burned. Stephen rushed inside where he found the staff were all standing together, confused as to what they should be doing. They know it would be madness to attempt to venture out and yet it was apparent from the look of helplessness on their faces that they were all very concerned for their loved ones.

"Everybody wait here," he instructed, walking briskly through the office to his private quarters and opening the sliding door which accessed the inner guest area.

He sighed immediately. Wanti was sitting there as beautiful as ever, smiling as he entered.

"*Wanti*," he commenced, washed by a wave of relief to see that she was unharmed, "*Are you . . . .*"

"*Kenapa, Mas?*" she interrupted, continuing to smile blankly at her husband.

Stephen approached her slowly, kneeling in front of the chair where she sat elegantly and whispered softly, taking her hands in his.

"*Wanti?*" he called, stroking the side of her face with one hand, the other clasped tightly together with hers. "*Wanti?*" he called softly again, searching her face for a sign of recognition.

"*Kenapa, Mas?*" she replied, then commenced humming, the soft tone driving a cold slither of fear straight through Stephen's stomach.

Immediately he knew that she was suffering from shock. All around he could see and smell the remains of what had been a small fire. She had been sitting in that room when the bottle of petrol had hurtled through the thick glassed window and exploded into flames. The thick drapes had been open permitting the dangerous explosive to shatter across the room barely missing Wanti as she sat at the table, already petrified with fear as she witnessed the screaming mass move towards her home. The houseboy had saved her life, acting quickly to put out the fire then covering the broken window with a blanket from the bedroom upstairs.

But now Wanti remained still, sitting silently, seemingly totally oblivious to all that had happened. At that moment, Sukardi returned with coffee and placed the silver tray next to his mistress.

Wanti merely smiled. Stephen spoke to her quietly, urging her to rest. He was devastated by the sight of her poised on the chair, unaware of his presence. He sat with her for hours until Wanti unexpectedly rose from her seat and, still humming, walked unaided upstairs and retired to their bedroom.

As she left the room Wanti had hesitated and, for just a fleeting moment, Stephen thought she was going to be all right.

His heart sank when she spoke, then turned and walked away as she asked, again, "*Kenapa, Mas?*" her mind still locked under the spell of her seizure.

Chapter 12

Melbourne

As the wind grabbed at his coat and chewed eagerly at his ears he tried to protect himself from the unexpected cold. Stephen, more accustomed to the tropics than to Melbourne's bitter and deceiving Spring wind, shivered. He kept his arm around Wanti's shoulders, occasionally adjusting the thick woollen cap and scarf to keep her warm. Her near ankle-length coat covering the chic trouser suit provided suitable protection from the sudden gusts of wind. Stephen had taken her into the David Jones store and asked the fashion department supervisor to select something appropriate for his wife. Satisfied that the clothes would be warm enough, he had then taken her for a stroll, walking aimlessly as he pointed out buildings and churches and other historical places of interest. Wanti appeared to enjoy these walks, although there was no real indication that this was so. He just presumed that his wife was content to wander through the shops and parks as he hadn't observed any resistance to these outings. Nor was there any recognition that she understood anything of what he said during the walks.

The City Fathers continued to maintain the country's financial centre amidst never-ending and well-cared for parks and gardens throughout the Central Business District. Footpaths and jogging tracks wound their way through extensive settings of well-groomed lawns and garden beds.

Partly shaded circular beds of Lobelia dwarfed by the garden's tall sturdy palms would normally have warranted a closer look, but the weather was not really conducive to the mood he had wished for as they strolled along. Stephen walked slowly, hoping that she would enjoy the magnificent display of flowers as he deliberately detoured through the park's gardens.

269

CARTHAGE PUBLIC LIBRARY
CARTHAGE MISSOURI

The sky was grey. Not unusual for the State's capital. The weather had never been one of Melbourne's strong points, he remembered.

He slowed, pointing to a monument. As he explained its significance, Stephen felt that perhaps she really understood, as if his wife was in some sort of conscious coma in which she recognized what was actually taking place around her but, at the same time, was unable to respond or even participate in the moment.

As they left the park, Stephen steered her across the street to the two-storey late nineteenth century wooden and stone structure. There were several highly polished brass plates affixed to the front columns informing the public in an almost intimidating manner that this was the address of Doctor Raymond D. Phillips, M. B. B. S. D. P. M. Australia M. R. C. psych. F. R. A. N. Z. C. P.

They had arrived at the specialist's rooms.

He looked at Wanti's smiling face and, as he had often done before, stroked her cheek gently and reassuringly with the back of his palm.

"You don't have to do this, Manis," he said.

Wanti smiled, her mind trapped, locked tight and shut away securely from the real world.

"I will take you back to Jakarta today. All you have to do is say 'yes'," he pleaded.

She continued to smile as if pleased just to hear him talk. Stephen hesitated. He looked once more into her eyes searching for any signs of response. Then he took Wanti by the arm again, leading his wife up the steps and along the corridor to the doctor's reception. He placed her on a chrome and leather chair then attended to the registration details.

"Mr Coleman," the woman began, "how do you wish to arrange for payments for your wife's therapy?" she continued, leaning forward inspecting the uncompleted forms.

"Whatever is required," he answered, offended by the woman's tone and angry that this conversation was taking place in Wanti's presence.

"We accept most major credit cards if it is of any assistance. Or," she continued, rattling off the well-rehearsed routine, "if you're a member of one of the recognized medical schemes we can make the necessary arrangements for you. "

CARTHAGE PUBLIC LIBRARY
CARTHAGE MISSOURI

"Whatever," he responded tersely, counting out two thousand dollars in cash and placing it before the astonished woman.

Stephen was very annoyed and not just because of his helplessness in dealing with Wanti's illness. The couriered letter he'd just received warned him that his absence was jeopardizing the imminent contract Seda had put into place for the Hercules Aircraft refit and spare parts supply.

This was, he knew, a huge order and one which would generate significant profits for their *kongsi*. Stephen could understand Seda's concern over his absence but was irritated by his lack of compassion and how the General arranged his priorities.

The receptionist checked the registration forms and asked that they both wait for Dr Phillips. He sat impatiently.

After some time they were escorted into the doctor's studio room. Wanti remained still as he checked her eyes and reflexes, occasionally speaking to her softly as he carried out his thorough examination. Stephen sat and listened to the specialist then deliver a lengthy synopsis regarding his new patient's condition.

It made little sense to him. He just wanted to get it over and leave. The doctor explained the procedures he would apply and the probabilities of success with the new therapy. The treatment had recently been introduced from the United States Veteran Trauma Centres.

Stephen listened. He was told that it was unlikely that Wanti would totally recover from her latest seizure. The doctor had seen many similar cases of Post Traumatic Stress Syndrome among the returning Australian soldiers from Vietnam. He should prepare for a lengthy and expensive period of therapeutic care.

Stephen just nodded, occasionally looking out through the small dusty window and across the park. He could see a couple sitting there, together, a blanket across their knees as they fed the pigeons. They were old.

As the doctor droned on Stephen listened, suddenly very tired and depressed. He looked over at his beautiful, silent wife. Her eyes were still devoid of any signs of awareness of her situation. The doctor made a few more notes from his observations and promised Stephen that his wife would receive the very best treatment available.

He took her back to the Southern Cross Hotel. In a few more

days he would leave her with Albert, under the care of the specialist nursing service he'd engaged through the doctor to watch over his wife. They had been employed on an open ended arrangement, for an undetermined period of time to ensure her care and guarantee constant surveillance on a full time basis. He had the money. He was wealthy and wanted desperately to provide nothing but the very best for her.

They entered the hotel room and Wanti smiled as he passed her hand to the attendant nurse. He left the double roomed suite and went directly down to the lobby bar, returning only when he thought she would already be asleep. Stephen stayed just long enough to throw down enough double Chivas Regal whiskies to put him to sleep before riding the lift back up to the seventh floor.

He unlocked the door and went to the adjoining room. The nurse looked up and smiled then placed a finger to her lips to indicate that Wanti slept. Stephen returned to the interconnecting room and undressed. He tried but couldn't sleep. And when morning came he still lay awake wondering what it was that this beautiful and loving person had done to deserve her cruel condition.

* * * * * *

The arrangements were then all in place. Wanti had commenced treatment under one of Melbourne's finest doctors. At first, Stephen had considered placing her with his mother, but then rejected this idea. Her distant, almost aloof, attitude reflected her disappointment with his insistence on discontinuing his career with the government. Now, his marriage to a woman of Asian extraction had rendered his mother just another distant observer in his life. But he didn't want to leave her solely under the care of doctors and nurses.

Albert had been quick to make the necessary arrangements when asked and had even offered to accommodate them in his own home. Stephen considered his friend's offer and accepted without reservation.

It was an almost perfect solution. During the day Wanti would attend therapy at the specialist's clinic. When she returned to Albert's home in the late afternoons there would always be someone close by who understood her language and would watch over her. He would be her father, her family, and Stephen's constant liaison with his wife.

Stephen felt deeply indebted to his old friend. He was more comfortable knowing that, whatever her needs, Albert would be there to provide the friendship and attention Wanti would need during her treatment and convalescence. Having escorted his wife to Australia, met with her doctors and discussed the course of therapy the specialist had prescribed for Wanti he felt there was little else he could do. The doctors had agreed that her therapy should assist with the recovery progress and, hopefully, enable her to re-enter the world of reality. After coming to arrangements with Albert and the nursing team he became impatient to leave.

Stephen remained in Melbourne for what had seemed to him a long and painful three weeks. Each day he accompanied his wife to the clinic, waiting patiently for her to complete the sessions before taking her downtown to Melbourne's exciting fashion centres. Remembering her passion for shopping he'd hoped, wildly, that once she saw the array of fine clothes and specialist shops along Collins Street maybe, just maybe, Wanti would acknowledge something or even somebody. It had made little difference. If anything, she was totally indifferent towards her husband, except for her constant willingness to smile.

The specialist had explained that this behaviour could be an indirect result of the fact that she had not known, or perhaps even seen, a foreigner before the tragedy she had witnessed as a child. There could be some association, but it might never be known, as he could not be sure. The doctor had expressed confidence that as Wanti underwent concentrated therapy and, hopefully, slowly recovered, these barriers would disappear. Maybe she would remember the events leading up to her most recent seizure, permitting her mind to come to terms with what had precipitated the total withdrawal.

This was not exactly what Stephen had wanted to hear. He needed to have someone tell him that she was going to be all right. That she would recover. And soon.

He had to return to Jakarta. He really had no choice as his company operations were experiencing difficulties and only he could overcome the administrative mess that had piled up during his short absence. He'd phoned Hart, but there was little his personal assistant could do considering the confidentiality of the off-shore arrangements.

He booked his flight and informed his friend, his dear friend, Albert.

Albert was exceptionally kind to Wanti - and she appeared more at ease sitting quietly listening to his former teacher read in her own language. Whenever Stephen attempted to communicate he was always rewarded in the same manner. Wanti just smiled.

Albert cautioned his younger friend to be patient.

"*Sabar, sabar, Mas,*" he would advise, understanding some of the frustrations the husband must overcome.

"*I just feel so bloody helpless. The doctors have no idea how long she will be like this,*" he indicated, pointing at his wife, now sitting silently as she gazed out the window.

"*It will take time, Stephen. You must be patient.*"

"*I can't be patient, Albert, I have a multi-million dollar company to run. Every day I'm away is a day closer to another major cock-up which, if I'm not careful, could end in one almighty and expensive disaster.*"

"*I must get back and pick up the reins again. It's pointless my staying here unless someone can tell me realistically just how much longer it will be before Wanti can at least show some signs of recovering from the trauma.*"

As Albert looked at his friend he observed that not all of the apparent agitation was related to his company's pressures. The older man sensed a feeling of guilt. He understood that Stephen didn't want to leave her alone, locked in her own private world, which no other could enter. Albert was extremely sad for he recognized that this man had deep and sincere feelings for the woman sitting quietly across the room.

"*Stephen, I will take care of Wanti. The housekeeper is not entirely necessary. However I do understand your concern for her well being.*" Albert then smiled. "*It will be a welcome change having people around the house again. I accept your offer for the domestic staff. It's time someone else washed and ironed my clothes,*" he added, attempting to lighten the conversation. Stephen had insisted. He could well afford the service.

The ladies had been selected from a local suburban agency. He had also arranged for a regular taxi pick-up from both Albert's home and the clinic. Everything had been methodically organized to ensure Wanti's comfort and to prevent her presence from becoming a burden to his old friend.

The two weeks passed quickly and, with mixed emotions, Stephen bade farewell to Wanti and Albert. He returned to Jakarta and was soon absorbed in the increased demands upon his energies. Although his mind constantly flashed images of the beautiful young woman he had left behind, as the weeks passed by, Stephen realized that he too should face reality and accept the increasing possibility that Wanti might never recover.

Time passed unnoticed even as his work-load increased and suddenly Stephen was aware that it had been some seven months since he had seen Wanti. After a year had passed Coleman was convinced that his wife was destined to spend her days locked in her dream-like world forever. At the end of the second year he returned to discuss her condition directly with the doctors and Albert. Even the specialist was no longer confident of a recovery and suggested politely that maybe Stephen might consider having his wife institutionalized.

Albert now doted on Wanti like a younger sister and at his request Stephen agreed, reluctantly, to leave her in his care. The nursing visits were reduced to twice per week. The doctor's visits were discontinued. Stephen and Albert made arrangements for a more permanent stay for Wanti through the Immigration office, having her passport endorsed as a Permanent Resident. As the wife of an Australian citizen she was entitled to do so.

Coleman had smiled thinly when preparing to leave as Albert had spoken to him softly regarding his future.

"*Stephen, this is very difficult for me to say and, no doubt, more difficult for you to accept. However, as we are close friends. . . "* He then smiled kindly at the Australian, permitting his words to trail away, unfinished.

"*Stephen, you will probably never forget Wanti but you should now make plans to get on with your life.*"

Coleman understood what his close and dear friend had so much difficulty expressing.

"*It's okay, Albert,*" he sighed. "*It isn't easy leaving her here like this but you are correct. It is time for me to think ahead.*"

Albert was pleased and put his arm warmly around his former student's shoulder, not needing to say anything more as both understood what had just been said.

As the taxi sped away heading for the airport Coleman looked back and caught his last glimpse of Wanti standing radiantly beside Albert as they raised their hands together waving him goodbye. He felt his heart tearing apart.

It was then he realized just how much he had really cared for her, grieved that now she might never know, her mind no longer capable of dealing with such realities.

Stephen looked back quickly, again, for one final glimpse. They had already disappeared from sight and, as the taxi slowly turned the corner obliterating his last view of the beautiful woman he'd married, he knew, although he did not understand why, she was lost to him forever.

Chapter 13

Timor — 1975-1978

The Portuguese colony was in turmoil and the population felt abandoned. After four hundred and fifty years of trading and more than one hundred years of direct colonial rule, the Portuguese had virtually thrown their hands in the air and walked away from this isolated outpost on the edge of the chain of thousands of Indonesian islands.

In Dili, the capital, violence had already broken out between the inexperienced and politically naive groups including disillusioned expatriate Portuguese who had been caught by the sudden change in circumstances. The confused and bewildered government civil servants who no longer appeared to have any official or legal status to oversee the former colony's administration, looked for leadership, but there was none.

Many Portuguese-trained Timorese soldiers turned mercenary overnight. Others formed armed bands and commenced pillaging shops and raiding outlying farms. Weapons were easily stolen from the poorly equipped armories located in the small towns and from the departing contingent of Europeans, who were ecstatic at being permitted to return home to Lisbon to escape the political upheaval.

The successful and bloodless *coup d'etat* the year before had all of Portugal's military in a festive mood.

A disgruntled group of some two hundred service Captains who, dissatisfied with the long, unsuccessful and drawn-out wars in the African continent as Portugal strove to maintain control over its colonies, overthrew the mediocre regime of Anonio de Oliveira Salazar in the *Captains' Revolution*. The new leadership, the generals who had been catapulted into power as a result of the *coup d'etat* had then set about cutting the burdensome cords to Portugal's colonies.

East Timor was not mentioned in the initial proclamations. As Portuguese Guinea and the African colonies, Mozambique, Angola and the others gained their independence, the embryonic separatist movement in Timor rapidly developed momentum. And outside support.

Almost immediately, Angola was seized by the Marxists who had received substantial military aid from Fidel Castro. The *coup d'etat* in Portugal had resulted in rapid decolonisation of her territories. Unfortunately there had been no transition period and this resulted in the creation of an administrative, political and military vacuum which could not be filled by the inexperienced and poorly trained Timorese.

The region surrounding Timor suddenly became hostile and extremely volatile.

The military leadership of East Timor's giant neighbour, having eradicated Communism less than ten years before, were aghast at the events associated with Portugal's uncontrolled decolonisation process, particularly when militant Marxist groups were permitted to assume power in the former colonies.

The Indonesians were perplexed by the rapid change of events. Suddenly they faced the possibility of a new independent country on their doorstep. And not only a new neighbour, but one that threatened to spread Communism across the borders into Indonesia itself. And their antagonists already controlled more than one half of an Indonesian island.

The unthinkable had happened. Indonesia was suddenly faced with an enemy potentially more dangerous than they had ever known before. The military knew that a consolidated Communist force located within their own country's borders could only spell catastrophe for Indonesia and could even be a threat for Australia.

* * * * * *

Nathan Seda had great difficulty concealing his pleasure. It had finally happened. This was the opportunity he had dreamed of and had planned towards for almost ten years. Now it was about to become a reality.

A free and independent Timor.

He had difficulty controlling his excitement. He knew it was now truly possible and no longer just a dream. These were dangerous times and Seda knew that he must be even more diligent than before. The other Generals would now watch him even more closely, because he was Timorese. He understood that they would no longer be as complacent. Since ascending to their rewarding positions of power under the New Order, as they insisted on referring to the current generation of military strong men, many had grown fat and lazy, their stomachs filled with the riches reaped from others as they easily carved comfortable niches for themselves.

He was not one of them. He wasn't Javanese. Even the Sumatran officers now viewed him with suspicion. But he would play their game. He would bend to their wishes as does the willow tree under a soft wind. He would smile in friendship while in his mind he would visualize images of a new Timor, one in which the children would not suffer as he and all the other village children had suffered. A Timor that could bury the bitter memories of its people forced to endure centuries of misery under the hand of the Portuguese. He would never forget the children lamenting the injustices inflicted by their cruel masters. And the fate of his family.

Seda believed the time had finally arrived. He acknowledged that earlier efforts had been badly organized or poorly timed. The West New Guineans were a miserable lot, he thought and his experiences dealing with these primitive tribes had not been memorable ones.

But this! He was amazed at the reactions he had witnessed from the Indonesian Armed Forces Strategic Committee when attending the urgently called session earlier that day. To think that this mighty country, with its now sophisticated hardware and half a million troops, could be rocked by just the threat of a Timorese uprising. He was astonished that a little sabre rattling had panicked all of them! He wanted to laugh out loud when the decision had been made to send a delegation to Portugal. The mood in the room, then filled with Indonesia's most powerful figures, supported immediate military action.

'Annex the potential danger area!' they had cried. *'Before world opinion can grow in support of the mercenaries, and other militants.'* The general consensus was that there would be little or no resistance if they marched in immediately. The ABRI Chief of Staff even guaranteed that there could be few Indonesian casualties.

But there were logistical difficulties and many of the generals were reluctant to support such an immediate move. The High Command was embarrassed to admit that the basic difficulty was the navy's inability to transport the newly acquired hardware and, as for AURI, the nation's air force, most of its younger or more capable pilots were currently undergoing advanced training in the United States.

The non-military faction warned against occupying the eastern part of the island as, they reminded all present, less than a decade before their country had been accused of being expansionist during *Konfrontasi* when it was unofficially at war with Malaya and Singapore. They recommended that a delegation be sent immediately to discuss the crisis with Portugal's current strong man, Colonel Vasco Goncalves, in Lisbon. The debate continued well into the night and, not surprisingly, tempers flared, causing the Vice President to call an end to the Council's emergency meeting.

The President made it known that he was not supportive of meetings with a pro-Marxist government, even a military one. He had always believed that the Portuguese should have departed from the region with the Dutch, leaving the former colony to its rightful owners. His supporters knew that this meant Indonesia.

The 'Smiling General' also clearly understood from his economic and financial strategists that, as his country desperately needed its ongoing foreign investment dollar flow to continue, any arbitrary decision to ignore the possibility of a negotiated settlement-cum-acquisition of the former colony could be dangerously detrimental to his country's development. Bilateral discussions would be viewed favourably and would be far more palatable for the soft politicians in Washington, the influential heads of the International Monetary Fund and World Bank, than being confronted with the rumblings of Indonesia's military machines from far across the Pacific. He sent his decision to the Foreign Minister, Adam Malik.

The Foreign Minister considered his own national responsibilities and then the United Nation's position. He had enjoyed the exalted chair as President of the Twenty-Sixth General Assembly and did not wish to have his international reputation tarnished.

He elected to follow the path for which historians would commend him, a decision that he knew would earn him acclaim for his objectivity and understanding of world opinion. With his eye on the Vice Presidency, he supported his President's views, although not for the same reasons.

Seda snorted privately at the presidential suggestion. 'To hell with Portugal,' he thought, 'they are out and we are in!' he chuckled gleefully to himself sitting comfortably in the back seat of his Mercedes.

He now maintained a fleet of five almost identical cars, the same make, model and colour with tinted windows. The only distinguishable difference for those with a sharp eye was the Department of Defence consecutive registration numbers.

General Nathan Seda now knew he had the perfect opportunity to implement the plan he'd envisaged for so long. It was the opportunity he had not dared to expect, but now that it had happened, he would take the fullest advantage of the unrest and act decisively, providing his people with the chance to advance their cause for an independent nation. He would drag his people, with force if necessary kicking and screaming, into the twentieth century. The people were still uneducated, almost primitive and desperately deserved a leader who could show them the way. He would be that man.

His mind was full of details that now needed to be addressed quickly to take full advantage of the timing and confusion. There was so much to arrange. Coleman had to be organized. Umar had to be briefed. Shipments had to be dispatched. He must send weapons and supplies to the newly formed separatist groups. They needed his help, desperately. Impatient and eager to facilitate the additional supply of necessary weapons and logistic support to the guerrillas, he urged his driver to hurry as if they were, in fact, already waiting eagerly for his deadly gifts of destruction at some predetermined destination; and he was late.

Seda acknowledged that he had very little time. The opportunity would not last, he knew, as he understood how these Javanese and Sumatrans thought. He could predict exactly how they would react.

First, they would talk. Then they would ask to meet with all the groups with vested interests. These would consist of companies and individuals with existing contracts with the government. Together they would evaluate the financial benefit of agreeing to support any proposed invasion. Future timber concessions would be promised. Infrastructure contracts, perhaps supported by future international aid funds would be pledged and ownership of cement plants and rice silos would be agreed. Only when the Chinese money men were satisfied that their sector would maintain their monopoly of any future expansion into the new territory would they throw their economic support behind the government's leader.

Seda smiled.

There would be, of course, a substantial increase in military supplies required to match whatever the Indonesian forces encountered. This would further swell his coffers. And Coleman's.

He thought about the Australian. Their relationship had been very rewarding. The General had clearly believed, however, that the foreigner would always be the one weak link which could compromise the security of not only his person but also the complicated strategy he had embarked upon years before. This was the primary reason for the ongoing surveillance.

It hadn't been difficult. Not in his capacity as the head of the military's intelligence services. After all, any foreigner involved in supplying the Armed Forces with weapons and other equipment could jeopardize national security at any time. Coleman was watched around the clock seven days a week by a now, expert surveillance team which reported only to the BAKIN office. Umar Suharjo kept a close eye on the reports and advised Seda whenever anything unusual occurred.

The General was sceptical about the need to employ another foreigner, but Coleman had insisted that Hart was not only competent but essential to their overseas dealings. They had agreed that Hart's access to the more sensitive workings of their *kongsi* remain restricted. The General reminded his associate that should anyone else become aware of their relationship then they would both suffer the consequences.

"*You wouldn't even get to the airport, Mas,*" he had warned, "*they would have you picked up and secreted away in some unknown place. They'd have you locked tight where even your Embassy would never find you. As for me...*" he did not finalize, leaving the words hanging in the air.

Seda was pleased to see Coleman shudder at the thought of being incarcerated in some secret place miles away from any possibility of assistance from the Australian authorities. It had happened before, during the post *coup* period. Many thousands had disappeared.

Seda's thoughts returned to the Timor border. He considered the likely reaction of the Indonesian leadership to any provocative or threatening action. Fearing that the small population would swing completely to the Left and threaten the Republic's internal security could, he knew, provide sufficient justification in their minds to strike first. They would panic and move the troops into the Indonesian, and western, half of the island.

World opinion would prevent Indonesia from crossing the border, but would not prohibit Timor from standing up for itself against its giant neighbour.

He extracted a file from his briefcase and opened the aerial reconnaissance reports. Seda brooded over the map. He considered the shipments that were to be increased in frequency now unforeseen events had almost overtaken his own well-laid plans.

Already Umar had positioned more than twenty substantial caches in the rugged eastern part of Timor near the foot of Ramelau Mountain. As many again had also been distributed to the guerrillas. The remaining weapons would be secure, as local inhabitants rarely ventured up into these difficult areas. Only occasionally did the villagers scratch around in the jungle in search of the wildlife for food. The hills were abundant with deer, monkey and the cuscus, which were trapped for sale to the occasional tourist as foreigners were fond of the marsupial.

A further fifteen caches of supplies had been hidden on the slopes of the hilly island of Kambing, almost within view of the fishing village. The small airport had been considered should airdrops become necessary, but Seda vetoed his own idea as the runway would attract too much scrutiny. The new series of Hughes' satellites were now keeping the regional hot spot under close surveillance for the American intelligence community.

He realized that additional shipments needed to be delivered without delay. As the separatists had only now being given limited supplies from some of his secret hoard, he estimated that to arm at least five thousand men would take a much greater logistical effort and a sizable portion of his funds.

Thinking quickly, Seda commenced organizing shipments in his mind, calculating the fire power he could arrange for delivery to Dili, Manatulo and Tutuala over the following weeks.

The company had offshore stockpiles ready for shipment but these would need to be replenished as the number of supporters grew.

'*The Cuban weapons will be very appropriate,*' he decided.

Ever since Angola fell to the Marxists, Cuba had sent, not just sophisticated weaponry to assist with the civil war now well under way in the former Portuguese colony, but also more than five thousand Cuban special forces who had trained in the jungles of South America.

* * * * * *

The weapons Seda considered Cuban were actually Russian and Czechoslovakian in origin. These were not made in Cuba, merely shipped via the Communist country. The Cuban negotiators had also offered to send their own advisers and, at the time, Coleman had burst out laughing thinking that the offer had been made in jest. He was not aware of the intended destination of the weapons under negotiation. Coleman was later surprised to discover that the Central Americans were extremely serious with their offer to provide highly trained soldiers to operate the more sophisticated equipment.

Privately, they had also negotiated directly with members of the Front for the Liberation of Timor to provide five hundred experienced soldiers, directly from the killing fields of Angola. The funding for these advisers was to be provided by the Castro regime as a gift of friendship to fellow Revolutionary Freedom Fighters working together against the Neo-Colonial Powers. When the original offer had been made, one of the misinformed negotiators had incorrectly assumed that Coleman was aware that these shipments would be sent to Dili and other East Timor destinations. Fortunately the Australian had replied, unaware that the arms dealer had committed a serious error.

"Not really applicable, gentlemen," he had explained recovering from a coughing fit, the result of suppressing a laugh, "it is unlikely that the Indonesians would accept assistance from your country at this stage. "

One of the team had stepped forward and jabbed the errant

speaker, warning him sharply in Spanish to hold his tongue or lose it. Fortunately Coleman had not picked up on the man's *faux pas*.

Seda had smiled when Stephen had met briefly with him in Bangkok and related the incident, but was immediately concerned with the possibility of foreign nationals, particularly soldiers, entering the game. The General realized that this could be enough to force the Indonesian military to occupy East Timor should they discover the existence of Cuban troops on their borders.

"Could you believe that these guys were deadly earnest?" he had said to the General, *"they actually believed that they could just drop a hundred or so of their troops into Indonesia if you gave them the order."*

Nevertheless, Seda needed the Cuban shipments and ordered Stephen to finalize the transaction then ship the weapons to Macau pending on-forwarding instructions. Seda had never felt the need to explain the nature of the orders to the Australian and had suggested during the embryonic development of their business relationship that for Stephen to have such knowledge of Indonesian military affairs would not be appropriate.

Stephen had always been under the impression that all of the shipments left Macau for Jakarta. When orders were placed, his instructions were explicit. The consignments were to be broken into smaller shipments for Umar.

The rest had been relatively easy. Seda now had sufficient firepower already in place to start his own civil war. But not enough to prevent one of the scale that was imminent unless he moved quickly. Assisted by the skilful Umar Suharjo and his uncanny ability to select the right time and place to move the secret cargo, the staggeringly expensive cashes of weapons had grown dramatically. The profits from the HANKAM contracts had mounted until even Coleman's share exceeded his expectations. He had become an exceedingly wealthy man. Over five years they had shared rewards of a scale so great even many major companies would have been pleased to see such profits posted in their balance sheets.

And it was all tax free!

This was to be Seda's new war chest.

* * * * * *

The General phoned Stephen in his office, his impatience causing him to violate one of his own strict rules relating to their covert activities. Coleman was not available. Annoyed, he summoned Umar. His partner had been enjoying himself in the Captain's Bar of the Mandarin Hotel when the assistant front desk manager approached and discreetly passed the message.

He phoned immediately. Stephen listened attentively to the instructions and closed the connection by simply answering 'yes' to the other party knowing that this would be sufficient. He disliked using the hotel phones. They were rarely secure. As he turned back to his friends a burst of raucous laughter exploded from the men he'd been drinking with minutes before.

"Missed a good one, Stephen," the burly red-faced insurance consultant belched, wiping the back of his hand across his eyes to remove tears of laughter.

"Tell it again, Alister, we won't mind," urged one of their number.

"It's okay, fellows," Stephen offered, looking at the time, "probably heard it before anyway. "

"Give us another round," he ordered casually, drawing an imaginary circle in the air with his finger indicating to the barman that everyone at the bar should have a drink on his account.

Immediately several of the drinkers changed from beer to scotch or other expensive spirits. Stephen didn't care, he knew most of them reasonably well and it was more or less expected of him. His success over the years had its down side. Petty jealousies and the occasional snide remark no longer offended him. He accepted that this occasional reaction went with the territory of being wealthy. After all, he was born in the country with the worst 'tall poppy' syndrome in the Western world.

He observed Greg Hart. His assistant seemed to be doing really well these days. Stephen appreciated the importance of sound administration but readily admitted his lack of interest in what he described as 'day to day drudgery'. Fortunately Hart's expertise and willingness to focus on the mechanics compensated for Stephen's indifference. Since Hart appeared to relish the monotonous regularity of compiling statistical reports day after day, Coleman was content to leave it entirely to him.

He caught Hart's eye and indicated by tapping his watch that he would soon leave the gathering. The man acknowledged with a slight nod then turned his attention back to the end of yet another story, this time related by one of the better raconteurs their expatriate community offered.

Having missed the story's beginning, Stephen was content to stand back and view their reactions to each other as the foreigners participated in what was almost a tribal tradition, practised during the extended lunch hour. He recognized that most of those gathered around the bar were no longer just social drinkers. They had passed those acceptable barriers years before. Without any self-imposed limitations regarding their consumption the majority were not concerned with the volume of alcohol which passed their lips in an almost dedicated fashion. Every day they would meet, drink furiously, while only consuming a limited volume of solids, and then leave for yet another and probably less respectable drinking hole to fill in their otherwise empty afternoons. And empty lives.

Many of these men had been employed on a two or three-year contract knowing that the clock had started and already their time was running out. Most were unemployable in the more normal working environments. They had developed the skills of the permanent expatriate and with these skills the knowledge that they would never achieve their long forgotten ambitions. Consequently, they were content to float along as the 'token' foreigner, often employed only to make up the foreign investors' numbers required by law to sit on their management boards.

As the noise level had risen somewhat he knew that the group wouldn't miss his presence. Following another peal of laughter Stephen excused himself with a half-hearted wave and called for his car. He was surprised that the General had, in fact, breached their established system of contact. The General had never attempted to contact Stephen, directly, before and he was anxious to discover what Seda considered so imperative that the security of their relationship could be ignored. Agitated by the breach and annoyed at the distance he would now have to travel, he climbed into the red Mercedes and prepared for the long drive.

* * * * * *

Stephen was alone as he steered the manual through the slow traffic. Foreigners generally preferred to be driven and, in most cases it made sense, considering the irregular traffic flow and irresponsible drivers on the city's roads.

He handled the car well although, had it been possible, he would have been very pleased had his old driver Achmad been there for him. He buried the thought as quickly as it had emerged, amongst the other distressing memories.

Stephen had agreed to meet with Seda in his mountain villa, located just over the Puncak Pass. Several hours had passed when they walked quietly together through the garden of the small estate, situated four thousand feet above the muddy capital. The air was noticeably cooler than Jakarta and a chill had already entered the afternoon air. Clouds had formed earlier in the afternoon, blocking all view as the misty and moist forms enclosed the heavily timbered property.

The men returned indoors. They sat inside the high-ceilinged structure directly in front of two oversized sliding doors which led back out onto a patio overlooking the well manicured lawn. A small fire had been burning for some time, Coleman had noticed, its choked chimney now throwing out more smoke than heat as the tea bush cuttings were dropped onto the smouldering embers.

Seda waited for the servant to leave the room.

"Stephen," the General commenced, *"the Government needs to move quickly due to the Timor crisis. "*

Coleman was not surprised that the obvious urgency was in some way related to the distant colony that had featured regularly in the newspapers.

"What is required, Pak?" he asked.

"The problem is more political than logistical," Seda elaborated, *"as there is considerable support for the military to go straight into the former Portuguese colony to prevent further bloodshed there. "*

Coleman was amazed at the revelation.

"The Americans would scream, Pak," he responded, quite surprised at the man's candour, *"and they would be quick to react. Possibly even introduce an embargo as they have on Vietnam which would block further sales to HANKAM. "*

Stephen had referred to the United States trade embargo on the export to Vietnam of all American product. They had sought and received considerable support from other Western nations, including Australia. The crippling economic and social effects had already become evident as the now-united country struggled to drag itself out of the quagmire created as a result of hundreds of years of civil war.

"Maybe," he paused, "maybe. But I don't think so. Vietnam is a Communist country and Indonesia is today threatened by a Marxist group. I doubt that the Americans would pressure us into permitting Timor-Timur to fall to a Leftist regime."

Stephen considered the logic of Seda's statement. The man had developed an uncanny sense of intuition. His inside knowledge of the country's likely response to potential border threats enabled the head of the powerful intelligence apparatus to remain at least one step ahead of his peers.

"The new OV-10 Broncos approved by the Government will be amongst those weapons delayed, Pak," Stephen warned, referring to the state-of-the-art aircraft sitting in the clean, uncompromising air of Tucson, Arizona, awaiting shipment to the West's newest ally.

Two squadrons had been sold to the Indonesian Air Force. It was an urgent yet ongoing effort by the United States Government to compensate for the recent disastrous collapse of the South Vietnamese Government in April of the same year. Russian manufactured IL-28s had subsequently been positioned in Vung Tau, overlooking the oil and gas fields Lyndon Johnson had so desperately wanted for his country and friends in Houston.

SAM missiles had been redeployed from the North to areas around Tan Son Nhat and Bien Hoa. MIG-23s now controlled the skies around the former so-called Democratic State of South Vietnam. The aircraft were within striking range of one of the world's largest gas deposits, the island of Natuna, which for some strange reason of history, fell within the territorial integrity of the Indonesian people. The Pentagon had identified the potential threat as Saigon had surprisingly fallen back in the earlier part of the year.

The oil barons from Houston applied unprecedented pressure to have the island protected at all costs. Natuna had to be theirs! The United States Military Advisory Committee suggested that their government provide strike aircraft compatible to the Russian MIG-23s already deployed in the mouth of the Saigon River. The Armed Forces Select Committee assisted with the push to have the deal done quickly, as the Vietnamese suddenly had the support of the Russians, filling the void created by the American embargo.

The Soviets wasted no time embracing their new satellite. It enabled them to spread their sphere of influence into a new dimension, directly within striking distance of the American Fleet in Subic

Bay in the Philippines. They already controlled Cam Ranh Bay and looked hungrily at the one remaining naval base in the region.

The Indonesians were also to receive Skyhawks once their pilots had completed their high performance training. The sale had already been sanctioned by the US Government. The Senate and Arms Manufacturer Lobby Groups were pleased that the potential expansionist move by the Soviets could be used to justify the sale of the two squadrons of American-manufactured aircraft to their new ally. They promised even more aid would follow.

The sale was approved by both the Congress and the Senate and, within weeks, Indonesia was able to transfer the elite of its young pilots to their advanced training course in The States.

"How will the Australians react?" he suddenly asked.

Coleman was taken by surprise.

"I have no idea."

Stephen decided that the invitation to discuss the Macau consignments may have been a ploy to obtain information. He guessed that Seda always suspected that he had access to more information about Australia's 'interest' in the country than he'd revealed, but this was no longer true. And he would never reveal the nature of his past activities before his resignation.

Coleman dragged the General's attention back to the potential problem of the two squadrons of Broncos. Their *kongsi* stood to make millions from the ongoing supply of spare-parts, not to mention the commissions that would be due once delivery had been effected.

"What do you think the Americans will do with our aircraft contract?" he asked Seda. *"Don't you agree that they may elect not to deliver if the Timor problem escalates?"*

The General thought for a moment regarding this point. *'Yes,'* he pondered silently, *'I should do everything I can to prevent the new squadrons from being delivered, as they would be perfect for the AURI pilots should ABRI decide to ignore world opinion and march across the border anyway.'*

He looked back at his guest.

"That's a calculated risk that HANKAM will consider," he suggested to Coleman.

He shook his head slowly, trying to absorb the information and, at the same time, understand where Seda was headed with the conversation.

"*You were saying that the problem was more political?*"

Again the older man paused before responding quietly, as if he intended no one else to hear what he was about to say.

"*Yes. HANKAM has decided to take delivery of the Cuban shipments.*"

"*Why?*" Stephen was now very attentive at this curious piece of information, obviously offered by the General after considerable deliberation.

Being privy to state secrets made him slightly uncomfortable. There was obviously more. He waited for Seda to continue.

"*They may have to send a small group of two or three hundred across the border just to settle the area down as it is really getting out of control.*"

"*Why then the Cuban gear?*" he asked, confused by what he had just learned.

"*If Indonesia sends soldiers across the border they will be hand selected from surrounding islands and Timor itself, armed with the nonstandard Indonesian issue weaponry and dressed in non-combat uniforms.*"

"*Clever,*" the engrossed Coleman said, surprised at the ingenuity of the plan.

"*And, as there will certainly be some casualties, none will be identified as ours,*" the General explained, "*thereby avoiding any possibility of an international furore.*"

The Australian nodded his head in agreement. The Indonesians could not afford to displease the Foreign Monetary Bodies.

"*When do we ship from Macau?*"

Seda waited for a few moments before replying, as if preparing for the other's expected reaction.

"*Stephen, this is very sensitive situation and on this occasion I don't want you involved.*"

Surprised, the younger man thought for a while, examining the pros and cons of such a variation from standard procedure.

"*I'm not sure that I'd be happy with that, Pak Seda,*" he said.

Not altogether satisfied that the General would place the operation in the hands of somebody competent, Coleman shook his head in disagreement. He was confused as the introduction of third parties could compromise their operations. Their *kongsi*. And their security.

"*You won't be out of it altogether, Stephen.*"

He listened as Seda continued.

"*I would feel more at ease with your involvement, say, from the sidelines although I feel that you should be on hand for the formalities which relate to receipt of the consignments, even if it is for only a day or so.*"

"*When do you require my presence in Macau?*"

Seda didn't hesitate.

"*Can you leave tomorrow?*" he asked.

"*Yes, of course,*" answered the surprised Coleman.

The apparently relaxed General leaned back into his heavy leather chair.

"*Good. It's done then. Let me know when you return and we will makan bersama,*" the General instructed. The suggestion of dining together when Stephen returned caught him off-guard. Considerable time had passed since his last invitation to the Seda residence.

Their meeting concluded, they parted company and returned to the city as they'd come. In separate cars. The following morning Coleman caught the Cathay Pacific Tristar into Hong Kong. He needed a short break, and made arrangements to continue on the ferry for Macau the following afternoon.

* * * * * *

The Rolls-Royce glided noiselessly along the overcrowded streets from Kai Tak airport. Coleman had always enjoyed Hong Kong. He thrived off its pace, its mass of humanity, its opportunities. The Peninsula Hotel sent one of their prestige saloons to meet him.

Having checked in and showered, Coleman phoned several numbers before visiting the bar. The operator would know of his whereabouts, if required — a practice he'd maintained for years. His head office in Jakarta was manned twenty-four hours each day by a very competent number of switchboard operators. They would not know how to reach him, even if necessary.

When Stephen travelled on business he rarely made contact with his office. Should the necessity arrive he would phone his home office and talk directly to his efficient secretary. He paid his staff well but he also acknowledged that they were probably one of the most efficient teams in all of the Capital. Just like the Peninsula Hotel.

Coleman never ceased to wonder at the ability of the hotel staff to remember the names and faces of the multitude of guests who passed through this magnificent edifice so prominently positioned by its founders overlooking Hong Kong harbour.

There was something about standing alone in an expensive hotel, propping up the Lobby Bar by oneself. Everybody ignored you, with the exception of the staff and that is how Stephen preferred it to be. Guests would come and go, some to meet others, some to sit and listen to the pianist playing, for the millionth time, the theme from *Love is a Many Splendoured Thing* as they imagined themselves enjoying their own romantic interlude. Such dreams so easily achieved in the setting and ambiance of the colonial structure, with its mixture of oriental and European intrigue.

He had dressed in a light summer sports jacket, a soft green shirt, without tie, and charcoal grey trousers. He still felt over-dressed. Coleman pushed the large bowl of cashew nuts away to the side. Small, crisp pieces of roasted pork rind followed. He avoided the bar snacks having discovered during his early apprenticeship in the East that many a stomach complaint could be traced to the prolific assortment of *hors d'ouvres* provided in such establishments. Not that he was concerned here. Another reason for his loyalty to this hotel had been its excellent cuisine. He just wasn't hungry.

A small group of wealthy tourists clapped as the song thankfully finished. The woman who had requested what she most probably considered to be Hong Kong's version of the national anthem, had attempted to sing the theme song before losing her way after somewhere 'high up on the mountain'. She then attempted to completely destroy the song by joining the singer pianist only on the high notes.

The tourist wasn't drunk. But she was close to that threshold.

Another request was played and Coleman pulled his jacket sleeve back slightly, checking the time. And frowned. He accepted another Chivas and stirred the ice cubes with his index finger. Stephen turned as this song also came to a close just in time to witness her entry. Most conversation stopped as the tall slim woman glided across the floor and over to the bar.

She was stunning in appearance. Her shining black hair had been cut to a pageboy presentation, its richness absorbing yet reflecting the multitude of rays, split and redirected by the chandeliers overhead. She was tall and walked like a model, her feet dressed in Chanel satin stiletto heels barely evident as the almost floor length body-tight black chiffon evening dress faintly touched the beautifully polished nails of her stockinged feet. She wore simple jade earrings. Her neck was decorated with a matching black choker to the side of which another, but smaller, jade piece had been positioned.

She approached the bar and placed her matching clutch purse on the bar beside him. Stephen Coleman immediately thought that she was the most beautiful woman he had ever seen. Her skin still displayed the softness of care with just a suggestion that she'd been briefly in the sun. Her eyes were brown. She looked Eurasian, and there was a suggestion of Chinese to her features. Whatever the genetic contributing factors had been, their perfect blend had produced a most breathtaking result.

Conversation died immediately at surrounding tables as men admired the magnificent creature who had just entered, while their ladies sat mesmerized with her appearance.

"Sorry I'm late," she said, holding her hand out to Coleman but not so far as to indicate that she wanted it shaken. "Problems with the driver," with which she smiled, displaying her even white teeth highlighted by the thin line of peach lipstick professionally applied across her lips.

"Do it again and you're fired," Coleman said, returning her brilliant smile.

"Fire me and who would take care of the children?" she responded.

"I know it would be difficult but even in Hong Kong I'd probably get lucky," he suggested.

She laughed and the stress of the past days and the long flight disappeared as he admired his date.

"I'm Angelique," she whispered, moving close so others couldn't hear.

"Stephen," was all he could muster, holding his tumbler up to welcome her, suddenly realizing that she hadn't been offered a drink.

The barman returned quickly and, identifying the woman, asked Coleman, "Moet, sir?"

"Of course," he replied, almost choking in laughter at the cheek of the man. "You do drink champagne, I take it?" he asked her, still smiling at the barman's hustle.

"All the time," Angelique laughed in reply.

They waited for the champagne to be poured then raised their glasses touching them together softly, enjoying the identifying ring of the Bohemian crystal flutes before sipping the wine. One of the older waiters serving outside the bar hobbled across and positioned the bar stool for Coleman's guest.

"Are we staying here long?" she asked.

"Hungry?"

"Famished!" she replied, touching the small of her stomach.

"Your choice then," Stephen offered, hoping she would not select some distant destination which would take hours in the Hong Kong traffic.

"Room service?" she suggested, watching for his reaction.

For once he was at a loss for words. He was tempted to agree but there was something in her manner which influenced his decision.

"Room service it is then, but not for dinner," Stephen said, continuing the banter. "For now, we shall sip our Moet and then I'd suggest we dine here in the hotel. "

She was obviously pleased as she flashed another of her incredible smiles first at Stephen and then around the bar to show their observers that she was indeed, with this man.

They finished the champagne and then dined in the hotel's superb main restaurant.

"Seafood or beef?" Coleman had decided to order for them both.

"You choose," she answered, causing her host to flip back to the menu's entree selection.

"Fine then," he said, addressing the waiter, "we'll both have the sultan's cream of tomato soup followed by the smoked salmon. Give us about thirty minutes and then we will have the baked crab."

Stephen then ordered another bottle of champagne.

"The soup here is excellent," he explained, "I have only found one other place that makes it anywhere near as well. "

The champagne arrived and as the waiter poured he explained. "They use fresh tomatoes, none of that canned variety here, and it is cooked almost too thick in texture but that's so the cream can be poured in the shape of a small ring around the centre of the soup. Then, very delicately, they also pour a gracious serving of Gordon's Gin into the centre and serve. "

She smiled as he talked, listening to his culinary description, without interrupting, appearing naturally attentive. They enjoyed their meal, resting between the courses, talking together as if they were old friends. Coleman had changed from the Moet Chandon to a burgundy with his meal but Angelique had politely refused, content to remain with the champagne.

Before the crab was served he'd asked her to dance. There were six or seven couples on the floor and, as they moved slowly around the small dance area, he knew that the others were admiring them as a couple.

"We're being watched," he whispered.

"I know. They are all thinking who is that handsome man that ugly woman has managed to catch?" she whispered back like some co-conspirator.

Stephen laughed, pushing her away slightly, jokingly, to admire her face. The music finished and they returned to their seats.

"Tell me something about yourself, Angelique," he asked.

"Only if you tell me about you, first. Okay?"

During the main course they took turns talking about childhood dreams, where they were born, where they had gone to school and other simple detail as if it all really mattered. Neither discussed the present, each sensitive to the other's unwillingness to divulge the more intimate and private aspects of their lives. They refused dessert and the coffee.

Suddenly Coleman realized that they were the last couple left in the restaurant and, glancing at his gold Omega discovered to his surprise that it was almost one o'clock in the morning. She noticed his expression and leaned across placing her hands on top of his.

"Stephen," she said softly, "time for room service," with which she rose pulling his hands forcing him to follow.

They rode up in the lift in silence. He could smell the tantalizing French perfume, a Guerlain Shalimar, and was conscious of the warmth in her arms as they brushed lightly together.

The suite was decorated in creams and gold borders. The double-lined drapes, when closed, displayed tastefully illustrated scenes of Chinese junks under sail, the mountainous islands surrounding Kowloon as their backdrop. He undressed as she left him to use the bathroom.

The bed had been turned down by the maid service. Stephen softened the lighting before he opened the huge and heavy drapes to gain the benefit of the harbour view.

He lay back on the bed, his head propped against his hand as he absorbed the sight of Hong Kong after dark. He heard the movement and, turning towards the sound saw her naked body silhouetted in the hall doorway, the bathroom lights behind.

She moved slowly towards the end of the bed and stood quite still providing Stephen with the breathtaking sight of her full breasts and womanhood. She moved around to where he lay and bent down, kissing him softly on the shoulder and then on the chest and finally moving her warm sweet mouth to his abdomen from where she used her tongue slowly, side to side across his stomach making a soft, almost snail like trail back up to his neck.

Finally she kissed him softly on the lips, forcing his mouth open with her tongue while pressing forward with her body, moving across to straddle his, the sudden warmth causing Stephen to groan. He lay like this as she prepared him, taking him in her hand and gently stroking his body until sensing the change in his breathing.

She stopped, rolled over onto her side guiding his length through her warm and soft gates deep into her body, moaning softly as he commenced the rhythmic pelvic thrusts while gently stroking her firm and sensitive breasts. Stephen climaxed, the jerking spasms sending an indescribable warmth of joy through his body as he emptied himself inside her.

They lay together, embracing each other until gradually falling asleep, only to awaken and make love again, this time more slowly, giving her as much pleasure as it did him.

The sun pierced through the windows as they had forgotten to close the drapes. They each bathed, ordered a breakfast of juice, toast and coffee and sat silently, sipping their black Turkish coffee together, dressed only in their white bathrobes, enjoying the quiet of early morning. Angelique noticed that he had finished.

She stood and let the robe fall back off her shoulders to the floor. In the light of day he could see that she was even more beautiful than he'd thought the evening before. They made love, again, but this time without the sense of urgency they had experienced during their first coupling. This time they kissed gently, slowly, and enjoyed each other's bodies reaching their climax together. They bathed again and dressed.

Coleman escorted the attractive woman down through the hotel lobby and, having arranged for one of the hotel's Rolls Royces to be standing by at his disposal, said his goodbyes on the marble steps and sent her away. He returned to his room and prepared for the journey to Macau.

* * * * * *

He thought of Angelique as the ferry sped across the choppy sea, and the previous night of love making, her beauty and exotic smell, and the probability that he would not be fortunate enough to have her again. It was best like that, he believed, as he didn't want any complicated involvements in his life right then. Perhaps in the future he would be able to settle down into something solid, maybe. For the time being he was content to survive on the casual relationships such as the electric encounter he'd had with Angelique. If that was, in fact, her name.

As the ferry slowed to prepare for arrival, Coleman made a mental note to phone and thank Mister Lim for his excellent taste. Stephen smiled as images of their bedroom tryst danced quickly through his thoughts. She was certainly worth it, he thought, amused at himself for having gone a little overboard this time with the wining and dining routine.

As the Rolls Royce had glided away from the hotel, she waved, and immediately her client turned to re-enter the hotel. She ripped open the envelope he'd given her as she stepped into the exquisite saloon. The woman who called herself Angelique let out a squeal of delight as she counted the money. She squealed again, having come to the last note in the count, and held it tightly to her chest. Two thousand Hong Kong dollars! She could hardly believe Stephen's generosity.

Remembering the envelope, the young hostess quickly replaced the money and buried the small fortune deep inside her copy Chanel bag, one of the first to be made in Thailand for the Hong Kong market. She would not disclose the gift to her boss, Lim, as he would be furious that she had accepted such an amount from one of his clientele. Instead, she would send the money back to the Shanghai hovel where her mother remained.

Deserted by her French lover, and barely sixteen, the pregnant and destitute girl had been forced to sell Angelique to Lim when the child was but six years old. He had arranged to have her transported illegally across into Hong Kong, hidden along with twenty other young girls, their skinny and fragile bodies caked in filth from the pigs which shared the junk during the rough crossing.

Two days after her fourteenth birthday she was given to a visiting Japanese businessman for the weekend on his friends yacht. She was forced to submit not just to this man but, when he had finished with her at the end of a painful first day, she was then used by three of the others in the party.

Lim had been paid well for the young virgin and he immediately identified her potential. Within four years Angelique had been given new documents, her name, and had completed intensive training directly under the supervision of the infamous Mama Lily in Wan Chai.

She was now one of several stars in what was known in Hong Kong as The Lim Collection. Lim's exclusive agency arranged escorts for wealthy and powerful clients. This provided the Chinese entrepreneur with considerably more than the substantial income generated by the beautiful ladies. Lim also traded in information, and secrets.

Angelique would be questioned at length as to what she might have heard or seen while in the company of the wealthy arms dealer. A report would then be made to those who paid handsomely for the occasional surveillance Lim's girls carried out whenever Stephen Coleman visited Hong Kong.

Lim would personally deliver any such information to the client although he was never comfortable with this chore. Raised in the world of Triads he was all too familiar with the dangers of such covert activities. Lim feared few people but always felt uneasy when alone with Umar Suharjo.

* * * * * *

The lighting inside the old warehouse was limited to one corner where the storeman sat, smoking, surrounded by bundles of documents. Coleman waited for an hour. The air was humid and the dilapidated building had little ventilation. A car horn sounded and he checked his watch. A solitary passenger alighted, paused, looked around carefully then entered through the poorly lit doorway. Stephen identified the courier and nodded in his direction.

"*You're late,*" the Australian admonished.

The Javanese ignored the complaint and walked directly to the storeman's table. He removed an envelope from inside his jacket and dropped it casually onto the desk.

The storeman retrieved the documents and handed them to Coleman who, conscious of the trace of arrogance displayed by the courier, examined Seda's signature carefully to ensure that this man had been delegated the unusual responsibility of accepting delivery of this particular consignment.

The papers were in order. Stephen instructed the storeman to pass control of the shipment to the latecomer. There were no further signatures required. Satisfied that this surly little courier, who had obviously been promoted by the General, could now handle the next phase of the delivery, Coleman prepared to depart.

He watched the Indonesian walk around the stacked cases containing the Cuban consignment, concerned that Seda had appointed this man to ensure final delivery of the weapons. Stephen had met this courier perhaps as many as thirty or forty times over the past few years.

He rarely spoke. Stephen had attempted to be civil on these occasions however the Javanese would merely grunt then surrender Seda's written instructions and depart without so much as one word. Whenever he was around this man , Stephen felt uneasy. There was something about him that worried him, even frightened him.

Coleman turned to leave as the courier completed his cursory inspection of the shipment. Strolling towards the corner table, a *kretek* cigarette now dangling from his mouth, he removed his jacket and sat on the corner of the storeman's cluttered desk displaying an air of arrogant overconfidence. He dropped the almost spent *kretek* and stepped on it with his left shoe.

Coleman now understood the reason for the light weight jacket. The man was armed. The revolver hung menacingly from its shoulder holster.

Umar Suharjo's gaze followed the departing Australian. He spat on the floor, removed a packet of *Gudang Garam* from the jacket and lighted yet another of the aromatic clove cigarettes. Minutes later his team arrived. They had been instructed to wait for Coleman to depart before entering the warehouse. They worked through the night loading the cases onto the fishing trawlers.

The men worked hard, their sinewy arms and legs bulging with the effort of moving the cases from the warehouse. Sweat poured from their bodies. There was no conversation, just hand signals and the occasional grunt as the men moved quickly to complete their task before morning. Umar checked the warehouse one last time to ensure that they had left no tell-tale identification of their activities. Satisfied, he ordered his team to join the trawler crews and prepare for departure. He re-entered the building alone.

Minutes later his men noticed him return. The flotilla departed, the destructive cargo well secured and camouflaged to avoid detection as the vessels headed for the southern Filipino islands in the Mindanao Sea. Behind, in the warehouse, everything was still. And quiet.

The dead storeman's body was not found for three days. One of the Macau police investigators at the murder scene checked the victim's pockets. The contents were placed in a small pile on the dead man's desk. The detective examined the items. With the exception of a few dollars and the victim's ID card there was nothing of value.

He noticed the loose cigarette which the storeman had extracted from his killer's packet left on the desk during the loading operation. Rolling the *kretek* between his fingers and, out of habit, the policeman placed the clove cigarette in his mouth and lighted the only evidence left by the Javanese. Moments later, recovering from the worst coughing fit he had experienced in many years, the investigator recovered the remaining stub.

Convinced that the cigarette was marijuana, he placed the remains in an evidence bag and returned it to the pile of personal effects. The detective knew that the murder investigation would have a low priority as it was probably drug related and his department already had its quota for the month, courtesy of the Triads.

* * * * * *

Seven days passed before the innocent fishing trawlers were

positioned off the former Portuguese colony's coast. The passage had been relatively easy. They had sailed down through the Mindanao Sea and then headed directly for Timor.

Umar Suharjo leaned against the railing scanning the coastline for activity. Satisfied that there was no threat, he ordered the teams to prepare for arrival. Later, under cover of darkness, two hundred men assisted to unload the valuable cargo. Within days, the small band of guerrillas had stashed the rifles, ammunition and grenades in discreet locations surrounding the town of Dili.

The weapons, coupled with earlier shipments of stolen equipment delivered directly from within Indonesia and the numerous caches now buried around the island, represented a substantial armoury for the group which would soon receive international attention as FRETILIN, the *Frente Revolucionarla de Timor Leste Independente.* The Revolutionary Front for the Independence of East Timor.

They were ready.

Chapter 14

Canberra — Jakarta

Albert was struck speechless when it happened. It took place without any warning whatsoever.

He had finished his breakfast and was engrossed in reading *The Age* when Wanti approached the small alcove and sat beside him. At first, he had not really noticed her presence. Until she spoke. Albert's initial reaction was that the nurse had called his name but immediately he realized that this was not one of her scheduled days.

He turned with an inquiring look and the young woman had smiled, leaned across to inspect the newspaper and asked, *"What are you reading, Albert?"*

Tears filled his eyes with disbelief. He took her hands and held them tightly.

"Wanti?" he asked.

Two hours later she sat holding an intelligent conversation with her psychoanalyst. Just five hours later they sat in a Dutch Indonesian restaurant together ordering a selection of dishes from the *rijstaffel*, celebrating her remarkable recovery.

The rapid change in Wanti was incredible and, although cautioned by her doctors, Albert knew that she had finally broken through those barriers which had held her mind chained to the dreadful memories of her childhood. For days Albert waited to see if her recovery continued to show signs of permanency before phoning Stephen. He didn't want to build up his friend's hopes only to discover that after a short time she would retreat back into her secret world once again.

A week went by. And then another. They talked continuously. About Indonesia, her brother, her schooling, while Albert discussed his unsuccessful marriage, the racial bigotry he'd encountered in Australia and his early childhood, deliberately omitting the severe hardships he'd experienced. He was concerned that he might inadvertently trigger some reaction with his tales of the desperate life he'd suffered in Timor.

She rarely spoke of her husband, Stephen. He thought it better to wait for her to raise the subject of his absence. Only twice did she mention his name and even then the subject was quickly forgotten.

Albert doted on her every move. He took time off work to spend with her, visiting the zoo, Phillip Island and as many other scenic places as he could manage, believing that the outings would assist with her ongoing rehabilitation. Instead, they grew closer, and Wanti became dependent on his support and tender attention. Albert and Wanti were content together and went about their lives in a comfortable and orderly fashion as if it were the natural thing to do. It was inevitable. Albert just hadn't seen it happening. He couldn't understand the signs at first but when he recognized what had happened he was overjoyed.

They became lovers.

Albert had never intended for this to happen but it seemed so natural when the moment came. He delighted in the warmth and sincerity of the relationship. He had never really been a very physical person but the tenderness they shared reminded him of the first months of his marriage and the terrible void that had enveloped his very being when the comfort of his first woman was removed from his life. In his mind Albert accepted the possibility that this still quite beautiful young woman had merely slipped into this new role as part of her recovery process. And she was so much younger. He didn't care.

He loved her dearly. He felt no guilt.

Stephen had not communicated with her for some time and it became apparent that he too had developed other relationships back in Jakarta. He was, nevertheless, concerned as to how best to break the news to Stephen.

They discussed their feelings for each other and Albert expressed concerns that, once she met her husband face to face, Wanti may discover that she still loved him. He really didn't want to take that risk but when he had suggested the possibility to her Wanti had held him warmly and reassured him of her affections. She had then agreed to marry Albert. It was decided that they would travel to Jakarta to meet with her husband and settle the matter quickly. Divorce in Indonesia was not a complicated process and Stephen was unlikely to object.

Albert hoped that too much time had now passed for Stephen and Wanti to ever recover their previous relationship, or restore the feelings they had once shared so intimately together. Albert set about making the necessary arrangements for their journey. It would soon be Christmas and he wished to return in time to celebrate with his loving companion as man and wife.

* * * * * *

Coleman was surprised by Albert's telex advising of their visit. He responded immediately, informing his old friend that he would meet them both at Halim Perdanakusumah airport. Although Albert had not advised Stephen of his wife's progress, he acknowledged that it was obvious there had been considerable improvement in her mental health for her to be able to travel back to Indonesia. He hoped she could now at least converse.

Coleman considered Wanti's return and accepted that he would be obliged to make considerable changes to his current lifestyle to accommodate the existence of a spouse once more. A lady of the house. The official lady. It had been so long and he almost resented the intrusion.

Stephen felt a twinge of annoyance. His life as it was, and at this moment, left little to be desired, but he understood that this would change dramatically with her arrival. He made a note to tell Sukardi to clear the rooms of whatever paraphernalia might still remain in his room left behind by his numerous female guests.

It was unlikely that their relationship could ever return to whatever status it had achieved prior to Wanti's collapse. He wondered if she could accept that he had obviously acquired new friends and if this discovery might trigger a recurrence of her illness. He didn't understand why Albert had dropped all of this on him so suddenly. And why inform him by telex? Why not just phone? Coleman sat staring at the message momentarily and, opening his diary, drew lines across the days commencing with his wife's arrival to provide them both with the time they would so obviously require to readjust to each other. He wanted to feel responsible but his heart just wasn't in it.

It was almost the end of another year. His work load, the pressures of the multi-million dollar monthly turnover, and his extravagant life style had started to show. He'd added a few kilos and his over exposed skin had become scaly from the constant damage imposed by the sun's ultra-violet rays.

The weekend cruises were not just all business. Amongst the more affluent foreigners, his was the most sought after weekend boating invitation. Stories of starlets and incredible parties preceded him whenever he attended dinner parties or other social events. Wherever he appeared as he was, unofficially, still considered an eligible bachelor, the younger women, foreigner and Indonesian alike, would become blatantly obvious with their attention, dominating all conversation just hoping for an invitation to one of his excursions to the islands. There had been no shortage of beautiful women. And money.

The company's activities continued to grow, his holdings in real estate alone so embarrassingly significant that his friends in the taxation department became overly friendly.

Stephen was obliged to use nominee names to hold most of the large acreages he'd acquired in the mountains for the new villa development the company had started there.

He estimated his net worth at more than eight million dollars. But it was tiresome and boring work. Particularly the mainstay of their activities, the ongoing defence contracts which provided the enormous cash-flow. He channelled his share of the profits into other ventures.

He had become a sought after figure. His advice was respected. Stephen had come to understand more about human nature and the incredible but superficially based respect people held for those who were successful. He despised them. And there were always problems with the younger women. It just never seemed to end. They went after it all with a dedication even he couldn't believe. They would do almost anything to secure a permanent place by his side. He acknowledged that this had been one of the reasons he'd never really considered divorcing Wanti. She had provided him with an acceptable social shield, protection from the insurmountable number of young females who continuously, he was sure, spent their spare time devising more schemes and more traps than one could consider possible just to get his dollars into the sack or a lock on his collar.

He thought about having a wife who was never present. Many of his friends, and certainly most of the women thought she was some figment of his imagination or a pretext he'd use to avoid being entangled. An excuse.

Slowly Stephen closed the diary and pushed it wearily to one side. He was resigned to the inevitable.

Yes, he had a wife. And she was returning. Soon. Perhaps even to stay.

Although he experienced an uneasiness with these thoughts of her return, he took the decision to provide Wanti with whatever opportunity she required to re-enter his life, even if it meant readjusting his household to provide an acceptable atmosphere conducive to her return. A token marriage. He felt sure that she was still ill, or at least continued to suffer from the traumatic seizures that had torn their lives apart. Those things just never went away. He knew. He'd corresponded with Wanti's doctors regularly at first, and they had all been of the same opinion. It was highly improbable that she would ever again enjoy the realities of the world as others knew it. In short, her mental illness had rendered her incapable of living a normal life, perhaps forever. He reached out and reopened the diary to the place where he had made the entries.

The uneasiness returned. He put it down to the effects of having over indulged the evening before and the ridiculous pool party he'd left sometime in the early hours of the morning. He suddenly remembered. He paged the houseboy and sent a note with a small envelope up to the master bedroom.

Coleman refused to move from the original quarters where the company first commenced its activities. Other offices were scattered throughout the city but this was still the nerve centre for his personal and joint activities with Seda.

He thought of the General. Their relationship had been lucrative. They still kept their distance from each other publicly although, occasionally, for appearances, one or the other would attend a function at the other's invitation.

Coleman was not a superstitious man but the sense of foreboding he experienced made him uncomfortable. Acknowledging that the sensation could have been precipitated by the unexpected news of his wife's pending return, he rose from the teak executive desk and placed the ribbon marker between the pages indicating the arrival dates. He would advise his staff that he would only be available for limited access during the initial period of her visit. Or return.

Greg Hart had become a most competent executive and was well versed in the general operating procedures of the company. Even Seda had agreed that the man's mastery of administrative matters was exceptional. He ensured that communication between the operational and administrative aspects of the *kongsi* flowed smoothly, almost mechanically. Coleman could confidently instruct his assistant to assume temporary control over the activities for the week. Having made his decision Stephen decided to lunch at one of his old haunts, The George and Dragon.

In the following week FRETILIN declared independence in the former Portuguese colony of East Timor.

Chapter 15

Canberra — East Timor

The panic in the air was ominous. The Prime Minister's office resembled that of a football locker room as one by one the senior department bureaucrats came and went hurrying along the corridors as the news spread from office to office. The relatively inexperienced leader glared furiously at his subordinates gathered to discuss the incredible news.

"Why in the hell don't we have adequate intelligence regarding their strength and basic political intentions?" the tall articulate politician's voice boomed across the room.

"We have no representation there, Prime Minister and at this moment we're dependent wholly on isolated reports originating from the missionary posts in the area."

The Attorney-General contemplated Anderson's predicament. He was already working out possible scenarios whereby he could pass the responsibility for this screw-up down the line to Anderson. This could mean the end of his career.

What was the point in maintaining covert operations overseas if they were unable to provide current and crucial intelligence information when it was needed? The limited budget allocated to clandestine operations prevented reliable intelligence sources from remaining current and the lack of suitable communication centres in the vicinity of the Timor group of islands made information gathering very difficult. They had sought the assistance of an Australian hotelier who had established a small operation in Dili but, as the man was an amateur and followed everywhere by Indonesian and former Portuguese agents, his services were practically useless. And then, of course, there was that poorly trained Consul and his uninformed opinions!

Funding such operations were also extremely difficult. Due to the nature and sensitivity of the work involved, the number of support personnel or those who needed to know of the covert activity was always kept to the bare minimum. As it was, ASIO's Chief regularly complained that his own domestic operations now suffered as the funding for the overseas activities could not be acknowledged publicly. For obvious reasons, these expenditures were hidden within the domestic budget.

When the Prime Minister came to power he and his colleagues wasted little time taking control of the Intelligence Services. He was shocked to discover that Australia had been running a clandestine department for years under the direction of the Attorney-General's office and, as files had been kept also on members of his own political party due to their affiliations with the Left and other Socialist or Communist groups sympathetic to Australia's enemies, he was rightfully outraged. The Deputy Prime Minister had been vocal in suggesting that Australia withdraw its troops from Vietnam. Upon winning power, in one of its first announcements, the new Government signalled its intentions of carrying out a full withdrawal from the war-torn country. The Americans were furious.

Australia's allies had been concerned with its swing to the Left and had, for a considerable time, kept regular surveillance teams operating in the country observing some of the more radical elements in the leadership Down Under.

As the votes had been counted and it became quite apparent that the Conservatives would lose power to the Socialists the lights in Canberra's offices burned well into the night as the shredders worked overtime clearing the decks of all compromising material. Anderson had personally overseen the destruction of at least four hundred files. Having destroyed the last vestiges of damaging evidence collected over the years, he had felt relieved at the time but later, along with many others within the Defence and Intelligence community, he was not entirely convinced that he had acted in the interests of the nation.

There had been considerable soul searching within the walls surrounding the highly sensitive security department. He'd even contemplated resigning his position, as he didn't believe that any of the incoming rabble could even understand the importance of maintaining the Service's secrecy, let alone support its covert overseas activities.

It was quite clear to him that the success of their teams depended not just on their abilities as operatives but also the necessity for them to function in a world ignorant of their existence. It appeared that this would no longer be, as already the list of those who were now aware of the secret operations had been dramatically increased to include senior party rank and file members who, just months before, had also been listed on the department's surveillance sheets.

Anderson felt disgusted with the unprofessional approach the incoming Attorney-General had taken regarding accessing the most secret files. The AG had almost been cavalier about whom he added to the list. The Director believed that it was now only a matter of time before the department's existence became public knowledge — that is if it hadn't already been compromised by one of the new members whose name now appeared in the highly classified file.

He looked up into the Prime Minister's red-jowled face, his pulse now evident above the cheek lines as it pumped with the rising blood pressure.

"Are you telling me that we don't have any bloody idea whatsoever what these, uhm, FRETILIN terrorists are up to?"

"Sir, our reports indicate that they are only interested in maintaining sovereignty over the former Portuguese colony. "

"What about the American intelligence that they have showing satellite proof of Russian weaponry?" demanded the Minister for External Affairs.

"What?" the Prime Minister exclaimed, paling considerably at the news. "Are you telling us that these bastards have actually been stockpiling Communist war supplies without our knowledge? And why in hell have I not been informed of this development? For Chrissakes!" he yelled, slamming the palm of his hand hard down onto the desk to his right.

"The reports were sent to us by the Americans just hours after the FRETILIN announcement, sir, and we have not had the opportunity to disseminate the material to all departments. "

The leader's face turned crimson. His voice was deep and he spoke slowly, glaring icily at the Attorney-General.

"Your office was aware of the contents of the report. The External Affairs Ministry was aware also of the report. Why wasn't the information passed to my office?"

The men shuffled their feet. Several coughed.

The Chairman of the Joint Intelligence Services viewed the politicians around him with disgust. If he had had his way, none of these incompetent bunglers would have access to any of the intelligence communities' information. He believed that this group represented everything that the previous Government had warned against during their many years of office but, unfortunately, complacency had ruled, thrusting the Left into power for the first time in many years. As a result of an indifferent middle class vote, the Socialist Party had finally broken the Conservative grip on Australian politics.

The JIS Chairman looked around the room and identified several of those present who had vowed to dismantle the very political system which had brought them to power. The Chairman was certain that anarchy was only one step away.

The Australian military establishment had understood that their budgets would be slashed and their power base eroded commensurably. They believed that the country would slip back thirty years in terms of its capacity to defend itself, with a government in power that didn't believe in the existence of any real threat to the Australian people reportedly now sitting to the north of the country they now governed.

"Prime Minister," the Chairman commenced, "the information indicates the weapons originated from Cuban sources and are of Russian manufacture. We cannot at this time be sure of the size of their armories. However indications are that they have been stockpiling for some considerable time. "

The speaker looked around the office knowing that he had delivered a considerable shock to those present. What they did not realize was that a select number of highly-cleared Intelligence masters had prior knowledge of the information only now released to the assembled group. The intelligence chiefs had agreed that as they apparently could no longer determine just who could access the highly classified material, then they would initiate their own system of controls by retaining the information on a 'Director's Eyes-Only' basis to maintain its integrity. Those in the room who had knowledge of this tactic were pleased, as it had obviously worked.

"Furthermore, we have unconfirmed reports there have been

small numbers of Cuban observers identified around the town of Dili," the Chairman added.

"Cubans?" the Prime Minister gasped, shocked at the incredible news. "Cubans?" he repeated shaking his head disbelievingly, "have you all gone stark raving fucking mad?" almost choking with the invective.

"We can't confirm the sighting, however we believe that as the weapons probably originated from Castro's own arsenal there is little doubt he would have sent advisers and other technicians along with the equipment."

"What sort of weapons do they have?" the Prime Minister asked, reluctantly, expecting the worst.

The General stared directly at the nation's leader. Pausing to achieve the maximum impact, he slowly shook his head and spoke authoritatively.

"The FRETILIN and other armed groups will have the latest in rifles and small arms. The general consensus is that they will have a considerable supply of AK-47s, anti-personnel mines and, unfortunately, maybe even some small missile capability."

Those present who had not been privileged with this information prior to the General's announcement, were stunned. For moments no one moved. The politicians remained speechless, mouths agape, staring wide-eyed at the Military Commander who had, in one brief moment, delivered the most incredible statement they'd ever heard. Even by these Members of Parliament.

"AK-47s? Missiles?" the Prime Minister commenced his question, stammering, "wh. . . what type of weapons are they?"

The General again sighed, faced with the senior politician's ignorance.

"The AK-47 is a Soviet assault rifle used widely throughout the Communist world. The rifle is both semi-automatic and fully automatic, with a cyclic firing rate of six hundred rounds per minute. The weapon has been around for some time and the Cubans have stockpiles large enough to support armies of insurrections in at least half a dozen separate theatres.

"It's what the North Vietnamese regulars have been using against our boys," he added.

The room was filled with more silence.

"And the missiles?" the leader asked quietly, dragging the words out slowly.

"We don't know. "

"What?" the Prime Minister bellowed, "what do you mean we don't know? For Christ's sake man, surely we must have some information?"

"If the Yanks have this information off their satellites then they have not, as yet, been forthcoming in providing the data nor permitting our access to the material. "

"Jesus bloody Christ! Missiles!" the politician exploded again, slumping back into his heavy leather chair.

"The bastards!" he shouted, jumping back to his feet, "the dirty stinking bastards!"

The assembly watched their leader, surprised at his apparent loss of control over the situation. It was totally out of character. Several minutes passed and, regaining his composure, he looked back at the military men whom he now also despised for wrecking what had been a reasonable week in office.

"What is the estimated range of these missiles that we do not know whether they do or do not have?" he demanded sarcastically.

"If they have taken delivery say, of a Russian Guideline series surface-to-air missile then these could deliver a devastating effect to aircraft within range. The Russians have been modifying this missile and you may remember its effectiveness during the Six Day War when the Egyptians used it successfully against the Israeli Air Force. These birds can fly at three and a half times the speed of sound and will hit a target up to sixty thousand feet," he answered, almost proud to be a member of the world's military machine that could manufacture and deploy such sophisticated weaponry.

The General stopped to ensure that this was all sinking in as it was imperative that these civilians understood the ramifications of what was to follow.

"But these Guidelines are not our real problem." He now had the attention of every person in attendance.

"The major danger, gentlemen, is the distinct possibility of our own Cuban-styled missile crisis!"

Slowly all eyes turned towards the large man seated behind the Victorian desk. He was ashen and sat motionless except for the slight shaking movement of his greying head. The Prime Minister, as were those around him, was in a complete state of shock.

"My God!" he exclaimed softly.

"How?" he inquired, in a soft almost inaudible whisper.

"Gentlemen. We are all aware of the crisis precipitated by the Russian deployment of the Russian IRBMs in Cuba in 1962. These missiles were of the Sandal series which have a strike range capability of some one thousand two hundred miles." The General rose and approached the wall on which now hung a map of South East Asia down to the Commonwealth of Australia. He pointed at Timor and, removing his ball-pen, drew a circle around the island.

"Gentlemen, this is the potential strike range of the Sandal missile. Let's hope that they will not be able to deploy these or any other IRBMs for, as you can see, such a strike range puts most of Northern Australia, New Guinea, the Philippines and, of course, Jakarta and half of Indonesia, well within the targetable range of these missiles."

Several of the Cabinet Ministers had now approached the map and were examining it in disbelief.

"Good grief!" the Minister for External Affairs exclaimed, astonished at the revelations he had just heard, "they could wipe out Darwin and maybe even Perth!"

"And probably Cairns, Alice Springs, the three secret American installations, also Port Hedland and Mount Isa," added the Cabinet Secretary.

This announcement brought the Minister seated across the room immediately to his feet.

"Are you sure? Mount Isa?" his lip trembling as he darted across the room to determine for himself that his own electoral seat could be obliterated by one of these incredible monsters.

"There is no doubt, gentlemen," the General continued, "should the Independence Movement succeed, with the obvious political ties they have already established, we should all assume the worst. There could quite possibly be a small independent Communist nation sitting just off Australia with the capacity to throw nuclear warheads into our and everybody else's backyard in the region."

Immediately the room lost all semblance of decorum and broke into shouts and cries of panic.

"Gentlemen!" the Prime Minister called. "Gentlemen, let's have some order, please, this is not the Floor of the House! Settle down.

Now!" he demanded.

The nation's leaders returned to their seats. They all stared numbly at each other; several of their number had lowered their heads and closed their eyes, as if they had already been struck by some alien force.

"We cannot allow a hint of this situation to reach the press or the public. Attorney-General, please advise all present of the gravity of permitting such a leak to occur. "

The Attorney-General rose slowly and stood visibly unhappy with the task of warning his own colleagues of the penalties of the Official Secrets Act.

"As the Prime Minister wishes," he commenced. "I should request that we all maintain complete communication silence regarding these developments and, as the subject has been classified with the highest grading, the penalty of any such breach could earn the responsible party up to thirty years in prison. "

"I really don't consider this at all necessary, Prime Minister. If anything, it is a little insulting to suggest that any of us present would consider such irresponsible action," intervened the piqued Chief of Navy Staff.

"Nevertheless, that's the way it will be, gentlemen, and you will be informed as to where and when a further general discussion will be called to address the crisis," the leader announced. "General, I wish for you to remain, along with the Attorney-General, and Mr Anderson."

The room all but emptied within a minute.

Anderson observed the nation's leader drumming the desk with his pudgy and oversized fingers. Alone with the three men he had instructed to remain, the Prime Minister observed each of them, in turn, determining in his own mind that only his elected political associate could really be trusted completely.

"General, what is the suggested course of action, or remedy to resolve this situation?"

Anderson observed the Senior Army Officer as he considered the question. The man was almost as large as the Prime Minister. Both men had reached the pinnacle of their careers and, as is the case with most powerful men, each considered the other to be inferior and of lesser achievement. The General's obvious meteoric rise had been a result not just of his war service record and outstanding capabilities, but also his family's close association with the previous political moguls who ruled the Australian classes uninterrupted through the Fifties, Sixties, and early Seventies.

"My opinion is that we should encourage the United Nations to occupy the former colony immediately with troops for at least five years until such time as the people are able to govern themselves and convince the island's regional neighbours that its amenable to some non-aligned movement. Failing that, Prime Minister, either we go in ourselves, or we orchestrate for the Indonesians to enter the colony as it is, after all, just the other half of an island already occupied by their country."

The politician turned to Anderson.

"Would you agree?"

Anderson had already discussed the possible scenarios with the Army General. Although they were basically in agreement as to what action should be taken, they were very conscious that the politician with whom they were dealing was astute and could easily detect any possible collusion on their part.

"Sir," he commenced, "the obvious dangers of yet another independent state coming into being in the region oblige us to seek a course of action which will not just offer a short term remedy but also enhance Australia's own position with its Asian neighbours."

The statesmen slowly began drumming on his desk.

"The Indonesians will not tolerate an independent East Timor and we should avoid, at all costs, any confrontation with them over this issue. In fact," he continued "we should encourage them to enter the arena guaranteeing our political and, if necessary, our military support in this crisis."

"How will the Indonesians react?" he asked.

"Historically, the Indonesians believe that the whole archipelago belongs under one flag. Their action in West Irian has proven that political stance. I believe that they will jump at the opportunity to acquire East Timor as part of their country."

"General?"

"They certainly have the fire power to march in and wrap up the FRETILIN quickly. The danger is that the Cubans may have already firmly entrenched themselves and this would then become a United Nations issue which, eventually, could result in the creation of an independent country with substantial Communist backing. "

"Then you are both in agreement. The Indonesians should be approached immediately and advised of our position?"

Both men looked at each other and nodded their approval of such a gambit.

"General, the Indonesians would be receptive to someone of your stature approaching them with such a proposal. I feel that you should contact their ambassador immediately who, if I'm not mistaken, is also a retired officer of senior rank. "

The General's eyebrows rose quizzically.

"Also retired, Prime Minister?" he asked.

A semblance of a smile appeared on his lips. It was not the smile of mirth but one of sarcasm. He had nothing to be pleased about.

"Prematurely put, General. I'm sorry. "

"Thank you Prime Minister," the career officer responded without any sign of warmth. He despised these socialist politicians. "I will contact their Ambassador immediately and advise you of the outcome. "

"Thank you, General. "

Anderson prepared to depart with the officer but the huge framed man indicated that he was to remain.

"John. Tell me what you really think will happen, totally off the record," he asked when they were alone.

Anderson took a long slow breath and settled back into the comfortable guest chair.

"The Indonesians will grab at the opportunity, but world opinion will not be kind to them as Portugal has already recognized the declarations of independence in other former colonies, such as Angola and Mozambique. "

"Well, we all know what's happening in Angola,"the Prime Minister said unhappily.

"The way I see it, it really is a matter of how well we in Australia support the Indonesians and keep the press off their backs. "

At the mention of the newspapers the Prime Minister's nostrils flared. There was little love lost between his office and Australia's press moguls who denigrated him and his colleagues at every opportunity. They were all too aware of the government's philosophy and the party line regarding the press and the power its owners wielded. He had agreed prior to taking office to settle a few old scores should the opportunity arise.

"I will speak to them myself," he advised.

Surprised, Anderson's expression amused his superior.

"Everybody needs somebody sometime, John, you of all people considering your profession should understand the necessity for compromise. It's not just politicians who prostitute themselves, you know."

Embarrassed at the comment Anderson remained silent.

"What would happen if we suggested a Kennedy-style blockade of the island?"

"Nothing. We don't have the fire-power and neither do the Indonesians. It is unlikely that the Malaysians or the Singaporeans could muster enough shipping to assist. And I wouldn't recommend that we even suggest this alternative to the Filipinos as any participation on their part would agitate the Indonesians and we could well end up with an expanded regional conflict."

"You realize that in my capacity as Prime Minister I am privy to all the activities of your department?"

"Certainly. We never burned any files."

The Prime Minister looked coldly at the bureaucrat.

"No one is suggesting that your office did. However, you are aware that there is considerable pressure from within the Attorney-General's Department to isolate these activities and bring them directly under the control of defence?"

Anderson had anticipated the possibility, although he dreaded any such action.

"That would cost us the integrity of our operational arm, which has taken considerable time, funding and effort to establish, Prime Minister."

"What can you do with this team to assist alleviate the current crisis over Timor?"

"We could certainly improve our lines of communication which, as we've observed today, are totally inadequate due to insufficient funding. We could position a vessel close enough to act as a communications centre and place a team on the ground."

"How would you execute this plan?"

"We will seek the assistance of the so-called 'Press Barons' as cover in exchange for the direct flow of non-essential information to the newspapers."

"You believe this is achievable?"

"I will put something together immediately."

"John."

"Sir?"

"Don't screw this up. We don't want any bodies and we can't afford any more skeletons."

Anderson nodded slowly as he rose.

"With your permission, I would like to liaise with the General."

"No. I don't feel comfortable with that. If the requirement arises, deal directly through this office."

Anderson agreed, excused himself and returned directly to his offices by commonwealth car. Ignoring the PM's instructions, he had his secretary leave a message for the General to contact him urgently upon his return from the Indonesian Embassy, then settled back to devise a plan which would place his clandestine section in a more secure and potentially powerful position for the future.

* * * * * *

Later that day Indonesia's Ambassador to Australia sent an encrypted radio communication from Canberra to Jakarta. The message was picked up by one of the Defence Department's listening posts, recorded, and dispatched to Melbourne for deciphering.

The Indonesian codes were simple and often a transcript of a coded message would be on the desk of the duty officer at the operational centre of Anderson's headquarters even before the Indonesians had received their own radio message at BAKIN in Jakarta.

The message read:

MOST SECRET BAPAK DJENDERAL NATHAN SEDA DIREKTUR/ COVERT/OPS BAKIN DATE: 28 NOV 1975 FROM AMBASSADOR INDONESIAN EMBASSY/CANBERRA. TEXT: AUSTRALIAN GOVERNMENT DEEPLY CONCERNED INSTABILITY CREATED BY FRETILIN UPRISING AND THREAT TO REGION PEACE. AUSTRALIANS CONFIRM THAT THEY WILL SUPPORT INDONESIAN ANNEXATION OF TIMOR-TIMUR AND ADVISE THAT AUSTRALIAN PUBLIC OPINION WILL ALSO SUPPORT SUCH AN ENTRY INTO TIMOR-TIMUR. THEIR PRIME MINISTER HAS ADVISED THAT THEY OFFER MILITARY SUPPORT SHOULD WE REQUEST SAME. MEETING HAS

BEEN REQUESTED WITH BAPAK PRESIDENT SOEHARTO EITHER
HERE IN AUSTRALIA OR IN INDONESIA. SIGNED: COLONEL
SUPRAPTO N2337339 ON BEHALF OF AMBASSADOR. MESSAGE
ENDS: MOST SECRET

* * * * * *

Nathan Seda considered the communication now on his desk
looking mockingly back at him. This was developing into an impossible situation. The Australians were acting out of character involving themselves in what he viewed as a simple case of a sover-
eign state declaring itself independent. Should the contents of the
message become public knowledge then this would encourage the
Indonesian High Command to march directly into Dili without fear
of international condemnation.

For Seda and the FRETILIN forces this would be a major catastrophe. They did not have the manpower to defend themselves against
the might of the Indonesian combined Armed Forces. He could
not accept that the Australian Government did not support the Declaration of Independence nor did they recognize the Portuguese
announcement that their former colony must not be annexed by
Indonesia.

Something was dreadfully wrong. He had to think. There had
to be a way of slowing the Indonesian attempts to seize the other
half of Timor without interfering with the process of establishing
the new Government quickly. Then there was the other signal he
had received. The Americans were discussing putting a hold on
the squadron of Broncos due for delivery.

This was favourable news as the OV-10Fs were equipped with
twenty millimetre canon and air-to-ground missiles. These aircraft
were an obvious choice for AURI to use in the event the Government declared war on the FRETILIN army, as the Broncos were a
superior counter-insurgency strike aircraft which, Seda knew, had
been modified for the Indonesian Air Force with the latest laser
controlled missile launch systems. Should the Indonesians succeed
in convincing the American Government to deliver these aircraft
then resistance, he knew, would be futile against such machines.
The Australian Sabres AURI acquired would need urgent modifications to handle the new air-to-ground missiles if they were also
to be used.

What was confusing was the change of attitude on behalf of the Australians as his sources had confirmed just days earlier that the Royal Australian Air Force had refused any assistance with a refit to the Sabres to provide for missile capability. He had come a long way and could not permit this opportunity to lapse. There had to be some way of keeping the Australians out of the conflict.

Seda realized that the Indonesians would mobilize quickly once they understood that public opinion was not against their entering its small neighbour's territory. He had to eliminate this support. He must prepare a plan with immediate effect.

Seda sat deep in thought. He continued to do so through the evening and well into the next morning. He did not sleep.

It wasn't until another week had passed that an idea began to formulate in his mind and, after considering the ramifications of the bold step he was about to take and when he believed that the timing was appropriate, Seda put the plan into action.

The General called Umar Suharjo.

* * * * * *

Bambang was proud to be amongst the soldiers whose units had been selected to protect the Indonesian Timor borders. He could see that the others felt the same way from the gait in their walk, and the confidence they exuded. This is what they had been trained to do.

They had all been briefed. A group of terrorists calling themselves the Front for the Liberation of East Timor had run amok across the border, butchering women and children, and were now threatening to cross the border *en masse* and destroy the Indonesian villages there. They were soldiers and their duty was to protect their country. He was not afraid. Bambang wished his sister, Wanti could see him now. She would be so proud of him!

The C130E transport had lifted them out of Surabaya for the long haul across the East Nusatanggara Lesser Archipelago, crossing over Bali before continuing on through hours of monotonous airborne travel until finally disembarking at Kupang.

The landing was, in itself a feat, considering the unsealed landing strip! His colleagues had joked with him in the mess where they hurriedly gulped down a large serving of steamed rice and *rendang*. The officers and men in this Command ate exactly the same food.

The airstrip in Kupang had a bad reputation and, in fact, should not have been used for aircraft the size of the Hercules which he now found himself in, winging his way towards his first real military adventure. The others were equally excited. One thousand soldiers had already been airlifted and rumour had it that there would be as many as twenty thousand KOPASGAT, the elite quick-action commando troops, to backup the ground forces. They had a history to live up to. Theirs had been the forces first to strike fear into the hearts of the Malay soldiers when they had courageously attacked the superior forces during the *Konfrontasi* period under *Bung Karno*, their first President. And they had also been with the forward troops when their Command had bravely jumped from the ancient C-47s into West Irian to liberate that province from the Dutch soldiers. This action would be just as swift, perhaps not even lasting one week!

There wasn't a command within the Republik as competent as theirs! They were well equipped.

The senior officers had told them that the basic training the men in this command had undergone was as superior as that of the British commandos.

Their training had kept them all fit and Bambang could not understand the necessity for sending so many of their superior number against a raggedy bunch of peasant rebels from across the border in what was known to be one of the poorest areas in the region.

He rubbed the two gold stars on his shoulder for luck as they prepared to land. As the enormous transport bumped along the grass runway the soldiers cried out in unison *"Merdeka! Merdeka!"* Freedom! Freedom! and sang their battalion's song of courage.

* * * * * *

The aircraft landed with a squeal of burning rubber as the tyres took up the momentum of the aircraft's touching down on the red, hard baked clay airstrip. As Bambang followed the other young soldiers, his eyes opened in incredulity as he counted four more of the massive transport planes also disembarking troops and supplies. Across the fields he could see the already erected tents of the different divisional encampments. He had never seen so many troops in one place anywhere before.

As they strutted across the hard-standing surface jammed with jeeps, crates of supplies and platoons of soldiers working on their delegated unloading and loading assignments, one of the non-coms barked an order from behind and immediately the paratroopers broke into double time.

As *Letnan Satu* Bambang and the other junior officers filled with excitement, he never even considered the irony of the date of his own arrival in Indonesian West Timor. It was the first day of October, 1975.

Exactly ten years to the day when Indonesia suffered the abortive Communist *coup d'état*.

And its bloody aftermath under Soeharto.

* * * * * *

Anderson was annoyed with the arrogance of the media baron. He was rude and manifested the ruthlessness for which he was renowned in every movement, in each gesticulation he made as he waved his arms from the elbow down, in pontifical manner, ignoring the cigar's threatening path as he demonstrated his point.

"Tell him to shove it!" was his reaction to the offer.

This man was tough. He acted tough, played tough, and had a reputation second to none for achieving his aims when it came to corporate acquisitions. There had been rumours, only rumours, that he also had direct links with the underworld element, but there wasn't a soul in either Sydney or Melbourne who would allude to this publicly.

He was feared. Often when negotiations got out of hand he was known to reach across the table and lash out directly at whoever on the opposing team presented him with the most resistance. He lived to gamble. The amounts he'd laid on horses were legendary. He even owned his own stables on several continents.

The final choice had been left to Anderson. The Government had enough problems of its own just maintaining its authority over Parliament without the added complications of the approaching regional conflict.

'Bloody self-serving politicians,' he'd thought when delegated the tasteless task of finalizing negotiations with this man. Anderson was exasperated by the knowledge that they were blinded by their own self-serving interests and their domestic difficulties to the extent that, if they weren't careful, the problem would escalate until finally becoming unresolvable. Under pressure, he'd agreed to finalize the arrangements. John Anderson had elected to run with this choice of the major players out of those who owned the tabloids in Australia. He had feared that the others may have rejected the proposal out of hand due to political differences with the new leadership in Canberra.

The man sitting in front of him was basically apolitical. Except when it came to amassing his ever growing fortune.

Anderson anticipated that in the event that the operation came unstuck, he could count on this man's greed and general absence of morals to bury the remains of the operation before creating any embarrassment for either his department or the Prime Minister. He recognized that it was essential that he maintained a stable working relationship with the Australian leader. Without him, it would be practically impossible to fund the covert operations and operate without the same bureaucratic procedures which had stifled ASIO's growth and thwarted so many ASIS operations over the years.

Anderson looked across at the media giant and waited. The heavy set square-jawed entrepreneur sneered at the suggestion that his assistance would guarantee him a closer working relationship with the Government's 'powers-to-be'.

"I couldn't give a shit about those mongrel bastards in Canberra. They are a bunch of wimps who'd sell their souls to whoever provides them with the key to the House. "

"Whatever," was Anderson's response.

"Do we have a deal then?" he asked.

"Let's just get it straight for the record then. "

Anderson repeated the arrangements, hiding his dislike for the bullet-shaped head towering over him.

"You provide the vessel, we provide the crew. We use it as a communications centre for relay purposes. You get to send some of your journos into the arena. We dissect the military sensitive material and your papers have the first opportunity to run the rest directly from the front line. At all times it must appear to be a private operation and you are not to lend your name to the ship's presence in the area. Also, the journos are your responsibility and in the event that they do suffer any injuries, we are not to be held responsible in any way. "

The Intelligence Chief assumed that tacit agreement had been arrived at discreetly between the PM and the entrepreneur and whatever the additional *quid pro quo* might have been, Anderson was certain that details would never be disclosed.

"Is that the lot?" the gruff bullying tone demanded.

"No," Anderson answered, determined not to permit the other to dominate the meeting. "As agreed, your papers will support the Indonesian position. And, as discussed, your television licensing applications will, in turn, receive the Government's support. "

"Set it up with Charlie. He will act as the intermediary between our offices. "

"Good. That's it then. I will inform the P M. "

"You can shove it up his arse as far as I'm concerned. Just ensure that the bastard keeps his word. "

Anderson nodded and left the powerful brusque figure standing, peering through the window of his office, surveying the influential empire he controlled.

That afternoon John Anderson reported back to the Prime Minister who, having received an assurance that the arrangements were completed and, recognizing the commitments made on his behalf, sighed and just motioned him away.

Within days the ship departed from Sydney late at night and headed directly to Darwin, where it took on additional fuel and victualling supplies before leaving for a position off the Indonesian island of Timor.

The security officer and the ship's Naval Commander were unhappy with the additional 'crew' which had boarded just an hour before departure from Garden Island. As it was, anchoring the civilian registered launch in the RAN's station had been difficult enough without the additional complication of having civilians passing through the restricted area.

On board was a team of specialist technicians trained in communications, deciphering, and their own collection of encryption devices.

The security officer in charge of the modifications hastily installed prior to their departure was first to discover that these recent and late arrivals were journalists. To his further dismay, the Captain informed his officers that the journalists were to be given instruction in the use of the ship-to-shore mobile radios as they would take several sets with them when they disembarked.

The ship's Commander was surprised when the group suddenly decided to discontinue the voyage once they had arrived in Darwin. All six of the men had suffered from seasickness and had requested that arrangements be made for them to fly the last leg of the journey. The Lieutenant Commander sent a priority signal and, several hours later, received confirmation that they were to proceed without the media personnel, and re-establish contact once the vessel had taken up position in the target zone.

The crew were relieved to have them out of their hair.

* * * * * *

The South Australian-based aerial taxi company had positioned both of its Cessna 310s in Darwin. That's how the contract read. They had requested urgent clearance for their flight into Kupang and, having waited three frustrating days, the charterers had become impatient as news of the military build up had spread quickly. As the flight path entered Indonesian territory, a 'diplomatic clearance' was required under the Geneva Convention and, although not strictly adhered to, it was always prudent to be able to produce some form of written authority when landing in the host country.

At 0630 hours on the fourth day the first of the two flights departed, followed at 0730 by the second Cessna. Neither aircraft had approval to enter Indonesian airspace nor did they have any authority to land on Indonesian soil. Both applications had been deliberately held, pending a final decision, on General Nathan Seda's desk, at BAKIN headquarters.

On board the first flight several of the group went about checking their gear. Cameras and bags of film were packed safely in the event of turbulence as the aircraft droned on towards the island of Timor. An hour behind, the second aircraft was making up lost time, having been delayed by one of the reporters who had insisted on making one final call back home, to his estranged wife Shelley, to see if she had returned the divorce papers he had sent her.

They were all young. And excited. The assignment was going to be a dream. The brief had been simple. Get amongst the action, they had been told by their boss, photograph whatever they could and radio report on an hourly basis everything that they observed on the frequencies provided. Their instructions had been emphatic. Radio report every hour. Everything!

Some time almost a week after leaving the launch which had taken them from Sydney to Darwin they were spotted. The crew of the ship had waved but the passengers were too high to see the friendly signals as they passed overhead.

The ship's Captain observed and noted in his log that the first aircraft had been followed some time later by another similar aircraft. As he watched the second aircraft pass and then fade into the distant light he wondered why they were in such a desperate hurry to reach their destination on the tense and primitive island. Two hours later the six journalists radioed that they had all arrived safely in Timor.

* * * * * *

The hot, moist, and debilitating pre-monsoonal conditions continued. The men had not encountered weather this severe even during their training exercises into other unfamiliar areas of the country. It was, as if by command, all cool breezes had been redirected to another world. As temperatures soared early in the tropical heat of the jungle the men had to be more disciplined than before in observing their water rations. Already a number of his own platoon had come down with the dreaded stomach cramps they had been warned about during their arrival briefing.

During their first week in Timor Bambang's regiment suffered from the prevalent diarrhoea more so than the earlier arrivals as they were bivouacked beside a running creek already fouled further upstream. Two of his men were evacuated with cholera symptoms just days after they drank from the small river. Most of the others suffered the debilitating cramps and the all too frequent latrine stops while out on patrol. At the beginning of the second week they had difficulty moving equipment as the first heavy deluges turned the dry fields into quagmires of mud.

The mosquitoes were enormous. Sleep was almost impossible.

The men who were not already weakened by the distressing symptoms which cursed the young soldiers became restless with the inaction.

They had come to fight. Instead, they had arrived and done nothing except clean and maintain their equipment and occasionally wander out through the jungle after the Hughes 500 choppers dropped them in relatively unsafe landing areas. The helicopters had been appropriated from the Pertamina fleet which had, in turn, left angry drilling crews stranded on their rigs for days beyond what their contracts demanded of them.

Bambang's platoon, or what was left and still capable of participating in the patrol, had been dropped two days before, but not by choppers. They had jumped from the rear of a Hercules transport as their target was considerably further away from their base camp than their earlier patrols had been. They could see the mountains up frighteningly close as the huge aircraft banked then settled down for the final run. The few veterans amongst them realized solemnly that the real test of their training would come when they plunged into the surrounding jungle below, into the foothills of Tata Maila mountain.

The Captain who led them had instructions to set up a forward reconnaissance camp to assist future incursions penetrate further into the enemy's territory. There had been fifteen such camps established on the same day. All across the border. Having secured the area and established radio contact with their base camp, they then waited for further instructions. And they continued to wait. Time passed very slowly for the young soldiers.

They had been in place for weeks and the men were already disillusioned with the conditions. Jungle rash had broken out, covering their bodies, festering under their arms and between their legs, spreading over their genitals, as they scratched continuously, further exacerbating the painful itch. They ate from their cold ration packs. There were no fires permitted. They knew that this wasn't just an exercise. This was for real!

Bambang had recovered from his most recent attack of stomach cramps and now lay around listlessly with the other men in their patrol and, although he didn't feel much up to it, he did attempt to set an example for the enlisted soldiers. He didn't complain but he really hated doing just nothing. Waiting. Just waiting.

* * * * * *

The Indonesian Command had decided to initiate two separate missions approximately six hours apart. The general purpose of these incursions was to create the impression that the raids were the responsibility of the pro-Indonesian East Timorese soldiers and, accordingly, the crack paratroopers were obliged to change their camouflaged battledress for less conspicuous military apparel.

A Company of almost one hundred of the well trained soldiers crossed the border as night fell and positioned themselves for the planned assault. They waited until the target area appeared to be secure for the night before proceeding through the densely wooded hill, avoiding the main track, just before 2300 hours. The shelling by their ships was supposed to have prepared the area for their attack and they could hear that the loud thudding bombardment had ceased some hours before.

Their Captain issued the command and the raiders entered the peaceful compound on the run, shooting at the small huts and everything else in sight. To their surprise they were confronted by a well-equipped force of regular troops who succeeded, much to the chagrin of the Indonesian Commander, in preventing the invaders from advancing any further. There was no evidence of the two days of bombardment reportedly delivered by their navy nor was there any sign of the *Apodeti* support groups who were supposed to have provided the local back up if needed.

The officer radioed his position and reported the resistance they'd encountered. He couldn't be sure if the enemy was FRETILIN or not, although judging by the professional tactics he'd seen, it was unlikely that they were entirely responsible for the surprise outcome of the engagement. The Commander was instructed to withdraw leaving none of the wounded behind. Each time he called for his men to pull out and regroup they suffered more casualties as the enemy pursued the poorly trained Indonesian soldiers.

The fire-fight continued for another half hour. The Indonesian losses were distressingly high. It was as if the enemy had known of the assault in advance and had been just waiting. In ambush.

The Captain called for his men one final time to retreat as he could see that their numbers had been reduced to but a few by the enemy's incredibly accurate fire. As he led the handful of survivors away he screamed as a bullet pierced his lungs, throwing his body to the ground. Reports of the number of dead, more than seventy men, were radioed by the wounded signals operator after they retreated. His Commander had been killed, shot in the back as they fled with the remnants of what had been a proud force of soldiers just hours before.

The village of Balibo experienced its second attack in less than five hours as another two companies entered the area anticipating the same fierce resistance that their comrades had encountered and paid for dearly. To their disappointment the enemy had already fled the area and it was assumed that they had headed towards the coast. The Company Commanders regrouped and were preparing to follow when, to their surprise, a number of foreigners suddenly appeared.

Across the mountain and less than sixty kilometres away and still at sea, the second team of raiders prepared to board the small motorized dinghies which had been tied alongside after the ship's guns became silent. Some had experienced the nausea of sea sickness as they were unaccustomed to the ship's motion. They were part of a the two-pronged attack, and although the task of storming beaches was normally left to the *Korp Komando*, the responsibility for the operation had been given to them. The officers understood the necessity for maintaining the small task force as a regimental operation. The two forces had planned to meet up on the coast at Babau, not so far from where they now prepared to leave their ship. The Navy had been softening up this area for several days.

This raiding party was also of Company strength, one hundred men and, as they stood on the deck holding the wire ropes to steady themselves as the ship moved under the slight swell, news of the incredible losses suffered by their comrades was passed to them by their officers. The fleet's radio operators had been responsible for relaying the information they'd picked out of the air waves to the contingent's Commander. The officer in charge was aware that this devastating news would otherwise only have been passed on hours after their own assault and deemed it necessary that his men be informed.

The soldiers reacted with dismay. Many of their friends were in the fateful operation and they now would have to wait for days before they would know who had survived and who had not. They were told that it had been an ambush. These young and inexperienced men felt bitter and angry. Bitter because the enemy obviously knew in advance and had waited for their comrades to walk into their trap.

The Commander knew only too well just how compromised their communication traffic had become. Even during the preceding days while searching for the Radio Indonesia broadcasts his Communications sergeant had picked up an Indonesian language broadcast and, thinking it was their own, listened to the news program on the short wave band. He remembered the looks of concern which passed over the Colonel's face when, to their complete surprise, as part of the news bulletin the commentator made explicit reference to the Indonesian troop buildup and actually identified the Divisions, their strengths and movements.

As they continued to listen, the broadcast language medium changed to English as the station identification was announced closing off the news broadcast and, to their astonishment, they believed they heard the voice advise that it had been a broadcast service from Radio Australia! They knew immediately that the information on the air waves could just as easily be picked up by the enemy. Almost every village in the region had at least one short wave radio and a large number were tuned into the Australian broadcasts. Still, they had wondered, how could the information be passed from the active front across thousand of kilometres to the distant city of Melbourne? With this information resting heavily on their minds they boarded the twenty dinghies and headed ashore.

It was still three hours before dawn. They too were dressed in an assortment of apparel made to appear as if their number originated from the East Timorese sympathetic to the Indonesians. They expected to arrive on the outskirts of Babau village just before dawn in preparation for their attack.

The small flotilla of Zenith rubber dinghies moved quickly towards the shore. None of the soldiers spoke as the small craft, each carrying up to six men and their supplies, moved like a swarm of large bees towards the shoreline, pushed efficiently by the Evinrude outboards. Foremost in their minds was the tragic loss of life suffered by their Battalion. They were convinced the foreign broadcasts had alerted the FRETILIN forces. As they moved closer to the shoreline the Commander checked his watch. The luminous hands and numerals glowed brightly in the moonless dark of the predawn day. It was almost 0430. On 16 October 1975.

He couldn't see the expressions on his men's faces but he knew what was in their hearts. Their fear had now been displaced by hate.

* * * * * *

Umar Suharjo had carried out his instructions exactly as directed. FRETILIN had been substantially supported with regular arms shipments and access to the hidden caches in the hills. The results were greater than the General had anticipated and, in turn, he was pleased with the Major's efforts rewarding him accordingly.

Umar was confident that the Jakarta Armed Forces Chiefs had no idea whatsoever as to the immense amount of weaponry they had prepared in anticipation and support of the armed revolt the Separatist Forces continued to organize. They had appealed for international understanding of their cause but, it seemed, only Fidel Castro was prepared to listen. Although there were others who continued to watch, observing the accelerated changes in the small town's defences through the advanced technology of Satellite Imagery Enhancement.

Umar was suspicious of the bearded men who, to him, appeared to be Italian. He wasn't too comfortable with the presence of the Cubans. He guessed that out of the original two hundred men transported via Macau, no more than half a dozen had been killed in the action to date.

They were very good. Experienced and extremely cruel. He was pleased that they had no wish to mix. Often they would spit at their Timorese comrades and then break into laughter while babbling in a tongue only they could understand. He thought they were like monkeys. But, he acknowledged, they were very good soldiers. Their tactics were clever. Umar admired their patience and cunning. They would lay traps for the unsuspecting Indonesian soldiers and just wait.

Although the Indonesian fire-power was superior in numbers, their troops were far from home and poorly trained. And they had never been in combat before whereas these hardened veterans had accounted for more heads than one could imagine during their tour in Angola.

The Cubans scared him.

It was because he had not yet learned their ways, and when he did, he smiled with the thought, they would then be scared of him! They were intelligent and seemed to understand many languages. Each day at least two of their number would sit in front of their radios listening and writing furiously for hours.

Umar's lips curled, the closest he could bring himself to smiling. And then, of course, there was the free intelligence offered by the Australian news broadcasts. Although these created considerable bewilderment at first, the reports were now considered an integral part of each morning's briefing as they had proved to be totally accurate and dependable.

Umar was not convinced that the FRETILIN forces could withstand a full frontal surprise attack should these reports cease, and that was the question at hand. He was often confused by the commands he'd received and had long ago given up all attempts to understand the man to whom he had become an important extension.

His executive executioner!

Again Umar curled one lip as he enjoyed his own definition of his relationship with one of Jakarta's most powerful figures. The General had decided that time had come to increase international pressure on his own government. Umar was annoyed at not being able to second guess the man, although he rarely could. This latest directive appeared to contradict the basic plan. Or at least, as Umar Suharjo understood it to be.

It was not until Umar later fully appreciated the strategy that he agreed that it was, in fact, brilliant. And it would not be difficult to achieve. It was just a pity that it would bring an end to the much needed information they enjoyed from those daily broadcasts. He prepared to move into Kupang.

As he had crossed the border so frequently, Umar scoffed at the ridiculous ease with which it could be achieved. There were few border gates and signposts to speak of and he selected almost any path he wished to take, just walking from one country into the other. It really was ridiculous, he felt. Maybe the island should be one country and not divided as it had been by the foreigners hundreds of years before, Umar thought.

He had read enough history to understand how the colonists worked. The *bulé* would occupy a country and then split it into two. As in Korea, Vietnam, Ireland and New Guinea. Even Malaya had been split away from its Motherland, Indonesia, by the British! He pondered these thoughts and, realizing that they achieved nothing, admonished himself for permitting his concentration to stray.

The experienced Javanese Major decided to do something constructive. He was restless and disliked not being occupied. It wasn't in his make-up to just sit around and wait. He would check on the FRETILIN troops latest movement activity to avoid contact with their guerrilla bands. Umar had no wish to bump into those Cuban animals. During his reconnaissance patrols he had come across their handiwork on more than one occasion.

They had left hundreds of bodies in varying states of dismemberment throughout the territory, and even he was disgusted with the way they had butchered the women and children. He had known of one incident when the Cubans had hidden the severed heads of their victims in jute bags, and rolled them into a village school yard, laughing at the screams of terror as children discovered that the mud caked objects they had run to recover, were not coconuts at all. The Cubans didn't really care who they slaughtered. They killed indiscriminately, whenever it pleased them to do so. Often they killed the Free Timorese just out of boredom.

This, and other grotesque mistakes almost cost FRETILIN the international support it so desperately needed. Seda was angry and demanded that Fidel's butchers be expelled by the separatist groups. The Timorese were scared. They did not want to incur the wrath of the Cubans by suggesting they were no longer welcome.

Seda was disgusted when he read the report which described one drunken spree when the Cubans had taken more than fifteen teenage girls from the surrounding towns and locked them in a makeshift bamboo cage on the beach. They had insisted that their FRETILIN comrades-in-arms join them in drinking rum, a commodity they seemed to have in abundance.

The day had progressed slowly into the early afternoon when one of Fidel's finest had opened the temporary cage and dragged the closest girl out onto the sand by her long black hair. He held her with one hand while unzipping his trousers.

"*No! No!*" the fifteen-year-old had cried, choking on her screams at the thought of being publicly raped.

He laughed and, holding himself with his other hand, urinated on the girl's face. She accepted the hot steaming and foul smelling fluid, fighting to keep her mouth closed as the soldier brutally kicked her in the stomach to force her to cry out. She fell to the sand, sobbing. Moments passed and the crowd of villagers stood silently under the coconut palms, transfixed with the spectacle. The young girl's body convulsed with the wracking sobs of fear as she remained face down not daring to look upon the bearded man.

He withdrew his revolver and placed it behind her head as the disbelieving child attempted to turn towards her attacker, and pulled the trigger once. Her body jerked forwards then backwards as the impact removed the full facial section of her head. Laughing loudly while brandishing the weapon threateningly, the soldier turned again to the other caged girls.

There was a hushed silence as he lurched drunkenly towards the bamboo prison. He opened the flimsy gate and pointed his finger at the smallest girl in the group. She stood there, shaking her head, unable to cry, the tears streaming down her face as the other girls behind pushed her forward hoping that this would distract his attention from them.

"*Mama!*" she screamed, as he pulled her by the shoulder, "*Mama!*"

A shot pierced the air and the girl's torso buckled violently, the bullet entering her chest with such tremendous velocity she died before hitting the sandy beach.

Immediately the other girls screamed, exploding with fear and terror as they tore at each other in desperation, while attempting to scramble over the makeshift bamboo fencing which enclosed them. The other soldiers, thinking that their *Komandant* had expressed his wish to eliminate these peasant women, withdrew their revolvers and started shooting into the confined space. The young girls fell executed by the drunken soldiers and the villagers numbly looked on as the slaughter continued. It was all over in less than a few minutes.

As the last shot rang out the air was heavy with the smell of gunfire. And death. The young bodies lay crumpled on the sand.

Several had managed to climb the bamboo fence only to be shot as they reached the top, ending their lives almost as quickly as the others. Some of the teenage women had clung desperately to one another, engulfed by their fear and the knowledge of sure death.

The majority of the dead teenagers were of mixed extraction and had been specifically selected by the Cuban *Komandant*. Although his original intention had been to use them as an ongoing pool of entertainment for his men, he was just as satisfied that they had fulfilled this purpose as he witnessed the drunken guerrillas laughing like children, staggering up to the dead bodies still firing aimlessly at the broken remains. By keeping them occupied and distracted he knew that his men would not be so homesick. There was always the possibility they might revolt in this desolate place so far from their own homeland.

He understood his men's capacity for bloody violence. They had been killing black Africans for more than two years when they were ordered to this remote and desolate country.

No longer amused the group moved away leaving the murdered girls' bodies bunched together in a grotesque pantomime of horror, their faces wide eyed in death, reflecting their last moments of terror. When the soldiers finally left and they then felt safe, the villagers slowly approached the carnage, the occasional cry of anguished relatives being the only sound evident as one by one they identified their children. Carefully, lovingly, the small bodies were lifted and carried to an area near a copse of palms, where they were washed then covered with cloth before being placed in a common grave.

Even before news of the massacre had reached the international press there had been mumblings amongst the Timorese that the Cubans must leave their land. Umar doubted if even the entire FRETILIN army could muster sufficient courage to disband the Cuban guerrillas. They didn't seem to care whom they killed, just as long as they were killing someone, or something.

* * * * * *

Upon arrival in Kupang Umar was disappointed to learn that the group he'd sought had already departed, causing him to lose track of them for several days. He then discovered they had hired a jeep and headed in the direction of Atambua. He followed.

And then he lost them again. Information concerning their movements was scarce and unreliable but finally he managed to re-establish the general direction they'd taken from some of the village men who had carried equipment for the foreigners with cameras. The group had taken guides and crossed the border this time heading for the small town of Memo. There were no others who matched the general description of these men and their equipment.

Umar Suharjo followed their trail. It hadn't been all that difficult in the end. These foreigners were obviously not professional soldiers as they had left a trail impossible to miss. Villagers had eagerly pointed out the direction the foreign men had taken. Umar felt positive that these men had to be the journalists and cameramen he'd been tracking. After Memo he followed them towards the village of Balibo.

Umar was concerned. During the night he had heard the heavy exchange of fire. He was surprised that the foreigners were heading towards the battle scene.

'*Bodoh semua!*' he'd thought, believing that the men would have no understanding whatsoever of the dangers and risks they were exposing themselves to in the search for their news stories.

It had become hot and very humid again as Umar stopped to talk to an old farmer living alone in an isolated hut. He confirmed that the men he was following were not too far away as they had passed by less than half an hour before. The previous village headman had insisted that the group was only two or three hours ahead. He increased his pace while consciously preparing himself for an ambush. So far there had been nothing to restrict his movements as he'd not seen nor heard any evidence of any hostile elements for hours.

He arrived at the clearing leading into the village, the track well worn, the soil turning from dusty brown gradually into a typical sandy colour as it meandered through the coconut palms and thatched roofed houses. He could hear shouts and harsh commands in the distance.

Finally, there they were! He could see that they still carried their cameras and were dressed in a mixture of military jungle greens and civilian wear.

Umar knew this assignment left no room for error. There might be only one window of opportunity and his training demanded that he wait patiently for that perfect moment, using the element of surprise and cover.

To his bewilderment they appeared to have met up with or were being escorted by soldiers. Suddenly, he could no longer see any of them. He was becoming annoyed with the wait but reminded himself to be patient. He had to be sure. The timing had to be perfect. He understood that he had to get them all. There could be no witnesses.

Loud voices drifted in his direction as the group moved back into view.

Umar concentrated on the team members waving their hands and arms angrily as he observed their reluctance to continue, for some reason not apparent to him. He continued to watch and wait, expecting that at any time an opportunity could present itself. They were finally all together, and he guessed that they were about to make camp or at least rest.

He moved quickly. The canvas strap now held the weapon firmly as his left elbow confirmed its position, providing the necessary support as he moved it across slowly from right to left. They were somewhere within the village amongst the mud-walled huts. Umar followed the noises the group made as they argued loudly.

Squatting just a short distance from the small village compound he glimpsed several of the men moving around. Suddenly one raised his hands while calling out loudly as a second foreigner attempted to constrain yet another figure holding a rifle.

Yelling and shouting continued for some minutes and Umar was surprised that he understood some of the muffled voices, identifying them as Indonesian. Umar assumed that a dispute had broken out between these foreigners and one of the Indonesian soldiers.

He could now see the angry soldier standing directly in front of the tall, fair foreigner, a rifle pointed directly at the *bulé's* chest as he screamed abuse at the unarmed man. He could not hear all of the exchange, but from the yelling it was apparent that someone was uncontrollably angry. There were more shouts, this time accompanied by the sound of blows. And cries for help.

Suddenly they all disappeared from view. Umar could hear the men moving away as the abuse continued, intermingled with an array of foreign words he could not understand.

It sounded as if someone was in severe pain. He decided to take advantage of the distraction, running quickly along the outside of the perimeter trees ahead of where he thought the voices were leading, his machine pistol ready to execute them all with one quick but deadly burst, should the opportunity arise.

He had to complete the task before these men were taken into custody. If necessary, he would also kill the soldiers, Umar decided, but was more than reluctant to engage the Indonesians alone.

If only he'd brought the grenades!

Puffing from the sudden exertion he hesitated, and was about to break into the clearing when suddenly there was gunfire from behind the adjacent hut. He froze, throwing himself to the ground. Umar waited. There were shots.

He counted. Two, three, four! Someone had fired four shots. He lay very still and listened. The shooting had ceased. A few minutes passed and, through the trees, he could see the man quite clearly, dressed in an assortment of military combat gear, re-holstering his pistol as he strutted back towards a small group of men. Probably an officer, Umar judged. Having heard the gunfire the other soldiers had suddenly appeared, their rifles carried at the ready to protect the man with the revolver. There were at least fifty, maybe more, he counted quickly, pleased he had wisely decided not to fire upon them. Then he heard more shouts from the foreigners.

The situation had become unclear and very dangerous. He knew he would have to postpone his move until the soldiers had moved away. It was obvious that there was some serious problem between the newsmen and this group he suspected were Indonesian soldiers. He thought it was idiotic for them not to be wearing their own distinguishing shoulder flashes and berets as it was just as likely that one of their own would shoot them by mistake if, in fact, they were Indonesian regulars. They certainly carried themselves and behaved like the soldiers he knew!

He was concerned that there was now very little noise coming from the men he'd followed. Umar decided that he had to get even closer to investigate. There were only a few more days left in which to complete this mission. He could wait a little longer if he missed this opportunity, which now seemed likely, as they appeared to have been locked inside one of the village huts. He guessed that they would be well guarded. That would make it very difficult as he surely wished to be able to escape after he'd completed the task.

Another twenty minutes elapsed and he could no longer hear their voices. He suppressed the urge to crawl closer. The foreigners did not reappear and this confused Umar Suharjo. Could they have slipped away? He was concerned that if they hadn't been detained then perhaps the journalists may have been ordered out of the village and left, parting company with the soldiers proceeding through the other side of the village while he had waited for them to emerge.

"*Sialan!*" he muttered.

Moving quickly, he retreated fifty metres then circled around behind the huts where they had disappeared from his view. As he approached slowly to the right of the shabby dwellings he could see one of the camera cases.

Clutching his weapon while edging towards the huts. Umar noted the sudden absence of soldiers and, taking advantage of the lack of security, he moved quietly around the second hut and prepared to fire as they came into view. His finger had all but squeezed the trigger when he stopped and gaped in astonishment. He could not believe his eyes. There were bodies strewn across the dirt leading into the shelter. The bodies of foreigners! There were three slumped outside in the small yard and the partly obscured body of another in the doorway. He counted. He shook his head in disbelief. That stupid Indonesian officer had executed them himself!

Completely bewildered and for the first time in many years, Umar Suharjo panicked. He just could not believe what had happened. And then he suddenly felt a cold chill pass down his spine. Did Seda send out a backup assassination team? Or did the young Indonesian officer just take matters into his own hands?

"*Sialan,*" he growled to himself again, cursing nobody in particular. Suddenly, he wasn't sure what to do. If the General had, in fact, sent out a second team then obviously his own days and usefulness had come to an end. He was suddenly shaken by the thought.

On the other hand, had the execution been carried out by the young officer on his own volition then he could claim responsibility and the General would still be pleased as the result was the same. In fact, better.

Umar considered this possibility and decided against it, coming to the conclusion that he should advise the General that the journalists were dead and leave it at that. Best not to lie to Seda. Not now. Not ever. Not if one wished to remain alive and healthy! He looked inside the hut quickly to check the remaining bodies, still counting. Three, four...

And then he discovered another, and potentially more serious problem. There were still two missing. Quickly searching the other huts he found nothing. Now he was very concerned. There was obviously a large number of Indonesian soldiers around the village area and he'd lost sight of the remaining foreigners. Umar scouted the perimeter of the area until he identified a number of men moving away to the west. There were, from what he could make out through the undergrowth, far more soldiers than he had originally thought. It was very confusing.

And then he saw them. They were flanked on either side by well armed escorts. The two men he'd been searching for, their hands tied behind their backs, moved forward with the column of soldiers. Umar cursed silently again, confounded by the new complication. He had no choice but to follow them.

* * * * * *

The column moved quickly, heading away from the hills. The vegetation changed. Coconut trees along the path indicated that they were heading towards the sea. The soldiers weren't wasting any time, he observed, as the line marched away quickly with the two prisoners positioned towards the centre of their captors' file. They moved well, obviously attempting to meet a deadline or some predetermined rendezvous down towards the ocean as Umar could now sense that they were not too far from the coastline.

Occasionally one of the two prisoners would fall only to be pulled up roughly onto his feet, forcing him back into the long line of men. They pushed on, maintaining their pace for several hours. He could see that the foreigners were exhausted, obviously not equipped for such strenuous physical exertion. After some time they rested briefly before continuing.

Umar was surprised at the pace these soldiers set. He cursed when they didn't slow as he desperately needed rest. His body ached as old wounds sent signals to his tired muscles that he was no longer the young soldier who could easily cope with the demands of a forced march such as this. He wanted to rest but knew that it was not possible. He had to follow.

They arrived on the coast before noon and rested. Towards mid-afternoon they started again returning to the gruelling pace they'd set before. Finally, as the rest of the afternoon wore away, they approached the fishing village of Babau. Exhausted and very hungry, Umar hoped that they had finally arrived. He remained hidden approximately a hundred metres off to their flank, observing the men prepare for the next stage of their journey. Where are they going? Umar worried.

Some two hundred metres down towards the village fishing jetty he could see a number of rubber dinghies tied together. Not far from his concealed position the Major could just make out the two foreign men being marched across the sand, hands tied, heading towards the boats. He moved in closer, just enough to get a better view, but not so close as to be discovered. Umar sat cross-legged and lifted the binoculars to his eyes, adjusting them quickly, worried that the foreigners would soon be removed from his reach. His hands shook as fatigue prevented him from maintaining a steady focus. He rested his elbows on the ground to steady his view.

'*Damn!*' he cursed under his breath, '*they're being taken back as prisoners!*'

He estimated that there were more than seventy Indonesian troops on the edge of the beach, some sitting with their legs dangling over the side of the short fishing jetty while others moved around slowly, almost aimlessly. They appeared to be resting. He squinted as he examined their condition, their gear and their faces. There had been a fire fight here, he knew.

The signs were all evident and he could clearly see that the young and inexperienced troops were still suffering from the shock of their first engagement as they moved slowly, listlessly, with the tell tale signs of fatigue. Although Umar could not hear what was being said, it was quite apparent that the soldier who had executed the first four foreigners was an officer, as several of his subordinates had saluted as he'd approached, leading the two prisoners.

Umar decided that the two groups of soldiers were from the same battalion and regiment from the reception the newcomers received from the others on the beach. He watched as the officer addressed his men. Standing to attention the captain suddenly barked an order. They jumped to their feet. Umar knew immediately what was going to happen and instantly recognized who these soldiers were. He knew, because he had been one of them, once. A long, long, time ago.

He looked on in disbelief. Slowly, Umar shook his head and then stared at the assembly of soldiers with their two prisoners. What were these soldiers doing here? And out of uniform? Suddenly, the two foreigners were pushed forward, their hands tied behind their backs, forced to bend to the ground onto their knees. Neither made a sound. Or if they did, Umar could not distinguish any from this distance.

Umar watched the Indonesian officer step forward and place his revolver behind the head of each of the men, and pull the trigger. Twice. The scene was reminiscent of the infamous front page photograph which shocked readers around the world when a South Vietnamese officer executed a Viet Cong suspect on the streets of Saigon.

The echo from the second shot left an empty silence. None of the soldiers had cheered. Some had turned away, not wishing to witness the executions. They knew that what had just taken place was terribly wrong. A few even turned their heads away, not from the bloody site but in shame, knowing that one of their own officers had executed unarmed men. Foreign men!

Minutes passed when the order was given to bury the bodies.

He'd seen enough. The job had been completed even though he personally could not claim responsibility. The General's plans had been carried out by another. But the result would be the same. International condemnation of Indonesian forces and their invasion of Timor-Timur. After all, he thought, that had been the intention all along.

Umar Suharjo fled the confusing scene, leaving the foreigners and their executioners to create their own history. And they did.

* * * * * *

This senseless killing became the turning point, not just in the military war, but also on the political front. The international press focused on the slaying of the unarmed journalists who had been executed arbitrarily by the Indonesian paratrooper, whose only justification was that he personally believed that these newsmen were

344

responsible for relaying vital military information by reporting what they had observed while in the active zone.

It was ironic. Some later called it fate. The officer who executed the journalists shared the same name as his President. Soeharto was a common enough name in Java, but one which was immediately buried along with the disgraceful act. Captain Soeharto also didn't make it back home to his family.

* * * * * *

Somewhere off the coast not far from the scene of the killings an order was given. Immediately, engines were started and as the powerful twin Cummings diesels came to life, the launch raised its anchors and moved out of the area, unnoticed.

On board, the man who was responsible for the collection and dissemination of the material that they had received on a regular basis from on-shore looked out across the sea towards the island's coastline. He wondered why transmissions had ceased so suddenly.

As their direct radio contacts had failed for five consecutive days, the mission, as agreed, was abandoned and the launch sailed directly back to Darwin, the captain concerned more for the safety of his media magnate passenger than the loss of communication contact with the journalists.

Chapter 16

Jakarta

The air-conditioning at Halim Perdanakusumah Airport was struggling to maintain some semblance of relief for the passengers. The terminal, recently converted from buildings originally used by the AURI Strategic Air Command, was quite inadequate to handle the increased numbers of businessmen and tourists now flooding into the vibrant economy. The former international airport, Kemayoran, had been retained as the domestic terminal.

Stephen used his pass to enter the restricted areas. The QANTAS Boeing 707 had arrived over an hour late. He stood patiently, observing the passengers disembarking slowly before struggling across the tarmac, heat rising up from the cement, increasing their discomfort. As they struggled across the searingly hot concrete, perspiration formed large ugly patterns on their clothes.

He scrutinized the disembarking passengers looking for Wanti. He couldn't believe the over-dressed tourists as they appeared from the long cigar-shaped airliner and were suddenly hit with the immense heat rising off the expanse of cement and reinforcing steel holding their aircraft in place. Obviously inexperienced passengers began the walk briskly then slowed to a lethargic stroll. Many of the one hundred and sixty had already entered the health and quarantine sections to complete their initial formalities when Coleman finally spotted them leaving the aircraft.

As they were near last off the plane this suggested to him that Wanti was still in need of attention and, perhaps, assistance in leaving her flight. Stephen discovered his error suddenly, recognizing them as the couple almost directly in front of him. He frowned.

They walked together, hand in hand and with that leisurely gait couples often develop together when moving as a single unit. Albert had aged a little less than he had expected. At his side, smiling and obviously relaxed, was the beautiful graceful woman he had loved so long ago, now physically more mature, her classic features even more prominent than he remembered.

She walked differently, he noticed. And her body had filled out, as graceful as before, now, if not more so, her shining long black hair as distracting as it had been when he'd first noticed her. She was everything he remembered. Stephen put his arm around her shoulders and kissed her lightly on the cheek.

"*Selamat datang, Manis,*" he welcomed his wife.

Turning to the older man, he extended his hand which Albert immediately grasped and pumped enthusiastically, a foreign habit obviously developed during his many years in Australia.

"*Selamat datang,* Albert."

Coleman escorted them through the immigration and customs procedures flashing his security pass. They completed their formalities in just twenty minutes. Most of the officials identified Coleman and waved him through with his guests as the porters fought over the large amount of luggage.

The driver had kept the Mercedes cool, and within minutes of leaving the terminal they were speeding down the new divided highway towards the Bogor-Tanjung Priok bypass. Stephen had placed them both in the rear of the red Mercedes 280, positioning himself alongside one of the drivers from the company pool. He normally elected to sit up front unless the occasion dictated otherwise. He talked excitedly as they drove back into the city along Jalan Gatot Subroto past the Air-Force Headquarters and down around the clover leaf roundabout into Jalan Jenderal Sudirman.

Jakarta had grown incredibly, and high-rise structures now dwarfed the remnants of red clay tiled roofed *kampung* houses scattered alongside the new hotels and office blocks. Wanti was engrossed in the apparent quantum leap the Capital had experienced since her last visit. She had forgotten the noise of this bustling city. And the scream of the thousands of motorcycles.

Stephen observed Wanti sitting serenely, almost unaware of the excitement around her. She appeared to be preoccupied, although there was a peacefulness about her that puzzled him. He smiled at his beautiful passenger and leaned back reaching for her hand as he spoke.

"Wanti, you will find the shopping here an improvement from the old days. I will take you down to the new plazas tomorrow after you have rested."

She withdrew her hand slowly and smiled.

"Albert will escort me, thank you Mas. We don't wish to be a burden during our visit."

Surprised, Stephen glanced at Albert who immediately looked away to avoid further eye contact. They continued to drive in silence. Coleman was puzzled. He decided to wait until the opportunity arose, as it appeared that his wife's rehabilitation process had not been as successful as he had at first been advised.

As their vehicle entered the driveway the office staff and servants were all outside to greet the new arrivals. The houseboys swarmed over the car grabbing the luggage in their excitement and wishing their *njonja* welcome home. Minutes later they sat quietly in the living area.

It was apparent that there was something amiss, and Coleman decided to take Albert aside to discuss the problem. He escorted his old friend into the business conference room which was maintained primarily for VIP discussions.

The room was furnished with Javanese carved tables and chairs, the walls covered with letters of appreciation and miniature banners from the many military commands which had benefited from his activities. Photographs of a slightly younger Coleman shaking hands with the President at an aviation day ceremony remained the centre piece, framed in a gold leaf frame. He indicated where his guest should sit and then placed himself directly opposite.

"Stephen," Albert commenced, his embarrassment now obvious. *"Stephen, we must talk about Wanti."*

"All right, Albert, we have been close friends, almost family for many years. I have learned to identify from the expression on your face when something is bothering you. What's the problem?" he asked, taking a clove cigarette from the opened packet lying on the table and lighting it without first offering one to his guest.

Stephen had that feeling. It was rarely wrong. His sixth sense had guided him into safe waters more than once in his business career and, he remembered, whenever he'd ignored the sensation it had cost him dearly. Stephen took a long draw on the *kretek* and then leaned back into the chair and observed his guest. He looked uncomfortable and Stephen wondered why.

Albert had acknowledged that the decor was expensive as soon as they had entered the premises. He didn't appreciate who the designers were or the artists' names whose works hung on the walls, he just knew that it looked expensive. His friend had come a long way. Looking at Stephen, he was suddenly at a loss for words. He didn't know where to start, but he did.

Slowly and precisely Albert explained the history of Wanti's recuperation process. The total blackouts. The inability to identify familiar faces of friends. Her complete loss of memory and the painful hours of therapy, month after month, eventually becoming years. Painful, Albert suggested, not just in the physical sense but distressful to those around her also who continuously cared and nursed her through the slow recovery process. He explained how dependent she had become on his friendship.

Albert then paused as if not knowing how to continue. Surprised, and a little confused, Coleman encouraged his friend to finish the discussion.

"*Come on, Albert,*" he encouraged, "*don't keep me in suspense!*"

"*Stephen,*" Albert hesitated. "*Stephen, I know that this will be difficult for you.*"

Again he hesitated, obviously ill at ease.

"*Stephen, Wanti has come to ask you for a divorce.*"

He heard the words but didn't identify their meaning. Not immediately. The words still hung in the air as Stephen looked down at the floor. There was nothing there. Some moments passed and he felt as if someone had delivered a severe blow to his chest. And yet, at the same time, he felt something else. What was it? Relief? He had anticipated that Albert had serious news concerning his wife and he'd assumed it related to her health. He lifted his head and stared directly at the Timorese.

"*Why?*"

Albert's eyes dropped and softly he said, "*Maafkan kami, Mas,*" clasping his hands together. *Forgive us.*

"*Us?*" Stephen asked, confused, as the import of the statement slowly dawned on him.

"*No one ever plans these things, Mas,*" the older man offered.

Coleman sat rigid in his chair, bewildered by the mixed emotions he now experienced simultaneously, trying to separate what had been said from what he felt as the shock took hold. Was it outrage? He felt both betrayed and dissappointed and yet, mixed with these feelings was a touch of guilt for the relief he now felt in the knowledge that he would no longer be responsible for her condition and that this man, his old friend, would now assume that moral responsibility. He stared at the man in front of him. He felt a wave of emotion. Was it an attack on his pride?

Stephen was suddenly very confused and needed to escape to regain his composure. For a few moments he stared at the opposite wall away from his old friend's eyes, not wanting to look at his face. He was disappointed with his own reactions, even surprised.

"Albert, you must give me a few minutes to collect my thoughts. I really don't know what to say and, to be honest, I am not entirely at ease with the way I feel towards you both at this moment."

"We will leave immediately."

"No!" Coleman demanded loudly, almost shouting. *"Just take the car and driver out for an hour or so while I think this thing through."*

"What is there to think through, Stephen?"

Immediately he hated this man. His old and trusted friend. A friend who had just walked into his house and announced that he was responsible for Wanti's request for the dissolution of their marriage.

'What the hell has been going on in Melbourne?' he asked himself bitterly.

He then looked directly at the Timorese, unable to contain his feelings. Stephen knew he had to be alone. To think!

"Probably nothing," he answered, controlling his anger, *"but do this Albert, as I would appreciate an hour or so to work this out in my head. Okay?"*

"Baiklah, Mas," he agreed and rose to leave the conference room in search of Wanti.

Coleman called his senior houseboy on the intercom and instructed him to arrange for the driver to take his wife and guest out around the city for a couple of hours sightseeing.

"When tuan?" he asked, surprised as the guests had only just arrived.

"Now!" his employer had answered tersely and in a tone unfamiliar to the old *jongus*.

The surprised servant obediently arranged the car to stand-by while he informed Wanti and Albert that their transport was ready. The couple left immediately.

Stephen stood looking down the road as his car disappeared from view. He was saddened by the events and was deep in thought when the houseboy knocked, apologized and informed him that the housemaid had completed the unpacking upstairs. Perplexed, he waved the *jongus* out without any acknowledgment and considered the immediate problem of the sleeping arrangements. There was no way that Wanti and Albert were going to share a bed in his house!

Suddenly he was angered by the delicate predicament in which he found himself. He thought the situation through and decided to instruct the staff to prepare a third room which he would occupy for himself. His domestic staff and, indeed, most of Jakarta was conversant with the state of his wife's mental health, or had been, before her miraculous recovery. The thought passed through his mind that Albert had deliberately not informed him that Wanti had recovered. How long had it really been, a month? Three months? Perhaps even a year? His pride was hurt but that did not diminish the feeling of betrayal.

Coleman spoke quietly to his trusted *djongus* and suggested that *njonja* was still not completely recovered and, acting under her doctor's instructions, she was to sleep alone during her visit. He further instructed the staff not to discuss this arrangement outside his household, knowing that the whispers would commence immediately the opportunity arose. They would think well of him for being so considerate to the beautiful woman he'd not seen in such a long time. The other ladies would applaud his behaviour as long as he could disguise the real situation. Certainly separate bedrooms would be appropriate. Considering the predicament he found himself in, Stephen had no great difficulty with the sleeping arrangements. If handled discreetly, he imagined that it could even work to his advantage. Later, when the couple had returned to Australia, he would fabricate a suitable story to account for the unusual relationship which, he surmised, would put the gossip-mongers to rest.

Convinced that he had handled the matter in a mature manner, Stephen waited for their return. They had been gone for almost two hours when Sukardi announced their arrival. Stephen waited inside as the couple entered. He spoke briefly to Wanti and then took Albert aside and advised him of his decision.

The older man was nervous and wasn't sure just how close he should stand to his former friend. He flinched as Stephen leaned forward quickly and put his hand on Albert's shoulder.

"*It's okay, Albert, nothing's going to happen,*" he assured the other man with a slight squeeze before releasing his grip. Suddenly he felt saddened and ashamed by his earlier reactions. Stephen could sense the fear and realized just how impossible their respective situations were.

"*Albert,*" he started slowly, looking directly into the eyes of the man whom he believed had betrayed him in the worst way, "*firstly, I wish to assure you that I have no ill feelings towards either of you.*" Stephen lied as he paused for the effect. "*I believe that I understand how the relationship evolved and, having considered how difficult it must have been for both of you then I must also accept some of the responsibility for what has happened. The neglect I showed during Wanti's illness....*"

"*No, Stephen,*" Albert interrupted.

"*Please, Albert! Let me to finish,*" he insisted, holding one hand up to indicate that he intended to do so anyway. "*It was not easy for any of us having her down there for such a long time without considering our own needs while she was away, if you understand what I mean.*"

Of course Albert knew exactly what Stephen was alluding to, but was embarrassed to say so considering his own behaviour and the question of Wanti's infidelity. The Timorese sighed and, cupping his hands under his chin, eyes downcast, listened to the younger man as he continued to explain his position. He wished he was back in Melbourne sitting with Wanti together and away from this confrontation. He could hear Stephen's voice rattling on.

He said nothing. After all, what could he really say?

They discussed the arrangements and, after an hour both settled on the plan Stephen had proposed. Albert really had little choice. As the moment provided the opportunity, Albert asked the final question. "*Mas, will you give her the divorce?*"

Coleman paused momentarily and nodded affirmatively.

"*But it's conditional, Albert. You must seek a dissolution only in Australia. Do not apply while you are here. Agreed?*"

Albert wanted to explain that divorce proceedings in Jakarta would be swift and permit them all to get on with their lives. He remembered that this man could be stubborn and all that had been achieved in the past few short hours could easily come undone if he persisted in obtaining the divorce in Indonesia. Wanti would not be pleased. Albert was not happy with this dilemma.

He hesitated and replied softly. *"Stephen, a divorce in Jakarta would be more convenient. However I will respect your wishes and finalize the necessary procedures only when we return to Melbourne."*

Satisfied, Coleman nodded his head in satisfaction.

"When will you return?" he asked.

"There is not much point in staying too long. Wanti should see her brother Bambang and then we could return when airline seats are available."

Coleman weighed the problem in his mind. It would be difficult enough for all three to remain under one roof too long, considering the circumstances; however he felt that they should spend at least a week there, for appearances.

"I will have my staff arrange your return bookings."

Relieved that their difficult discussion had finally come to an end, Albert extended his hand to his once close friend. *"Terima kasih, Mas."*

"Kembali kasih," he responded, surprised at how tired he felt from the emotional drain of the last few hours.

Saddened by the events, both men rose and shook hands, each realizing that their friendship could never be as before, while regretting the loss of the strong bond that had tied them together over the past ten years.

Stephen left the building providing Albert with the opportunity to explain to Wanti just what they had agreed. When he returned later in the evening, his houseboy informed him that both guests had apologized as they were tired and had each retired to their respective bedrooms. A trace of a smile passed his lips as he discovered that his faithful old servant had diplomatically placed a selection of his wardrobe in the middle of the three bedrooms thereby symbolically separating his *njonja* from the house guest. It was almost impossible to keep anything secret from the old houseboy.

* * * * * *

That night the household slept restlessly. Wanti lay awake, thinking of the two men who had played such a significant part in her life. She felt saddened understanding that now she was divorcing the very man who had picked her up and given her everything except the one thing she longed for most. And he didn't understand as he had no comprehension, she was sure, as to what had always seemed to be missing in their relationship.

Albert lay on his side listening to the occasional traffic as it passed by his bedroom window. Car lights flickered across the room, running up the wall from one side and over the ceiling until disappearing altogether down the other. He was pleased that the meeting had gone as well as it had. Wanti had scolded him for not insisting that the divorce proceedings be carried out quickly while they were there, and although he had argued against it, she was still unconvinced. For a moment he feared that she might insist on talking to Stephen alone but, thankfully, she hadn't.

Stephen lay on his back, his hands clasped behind his head as he lay quietly, thinking of the days ahead. Although the tension between them had all but disappeared, he understood that there is no such thing as a friendly parting of the ways when a couple dissolves their marital relationship. He was pleased that Wanti would not claim from him in any way as he'd agreed not to contest the divorce. The potential problem of a messy financial haggling match had been avoided.

He had been concerned as he knew that Seda would have been displeased with further attention being drawn to his already high profile partner. All in all, he thought, everyone got what they wanted. He tried to sleep but there were too many thoughts waiting to disrupt his attempts. He had many things on his mind.

Like Seda. And the incredible volume of shipments that had already been dispatched to assist the Indonesian military with the Timor problem.

The city became quieter and only the occasional bell could be heard as the *becaks* passed. Coleman finally fell into a fitful sleep, just hours before being woken again by Sukardi.

The following morning, on the eleventh of December, the Indonesian Armed Forces invaded East Timor.

* * * * * *

With incredible speed, the Indonesian military machine moved across the border into East Timor. The Indonesian losses remained excessively high. The guerrillas continued to resist the larger force and inflicted tremendous casualties. But not without their own terrible sacrifices. In spite of their losses, the Timorese were jubilant.

Central Command in Jakarta had predicted that the excursion, as one general had jokingly described the invasion, would be completed within one week and would possibly only require another fortnight of mopping-up operations to round up the terrorists. Their intelligence had been incredibly inaccurate. During the first three days Indonesian casualties reached three thousand and the communication lines between the field and command headquarters ran continuously hot. Each time the crack Indonesian troops mounted an attack, they were rebuffed almost easily.

The Siliwangi Division suffered severe losses as well. Never in the history of this elite division had its troops been routed. The soldiers were young and experienced primarily in riot control support and other training exercises aimed mainly at assisting the police during civil unrest. They had never had to face a real enemy before! One or two of the older soldiers had seen action during engagements in Sarawak during the *Konfrontasi* era, but their numbers were insufficient to withstand the surprisingly superior soldiers confronting them in the Timor jungles.

Air support had been practically useless due to the dense terrain. Ground fire had already accounted for six of their helicopters, and the AURI Commander had insisted on grounding his remaining squadron until the infantry could guarantee adequate support in the hostile areas. He also insisted that the intelligence at least attempt to be more accurate when determining targets and requested a few sorties with reduced risk to those they had already encountered, as morale amongst his crews was dangerously low.

One hundred KOPASGAT airborne had been dropped at the eastern ridge, leading to what had been identified as an Indonesian Siliwangi position. The severity of the ground fire reduced their number within seconds to but a few before any of the parachutists realized their predicament.

Many died in the air, their bullet riddled bodies floating aimlessly to the ground. Within twenty-seven minutes from the jump command all but six of the commandos had died. Five of the remaining men had been captured. And tortured. An uncaptured

soldier looked on in horror from his hiding place in the undergrowth as the guerrillas gouged out the eyes of his comrades, laughing as they worked their disgusting torture on the young soldiers.
He was overcome with paralysing fear.

The concealed corporal shook in terror praying that *Allah* would
guard over him in his moment of need. He struggled to keep the
bile from rising in his throat and discovered, much to his dismay,
he had fouled himself through fear. He wanted to rush out and
help his comrades but his legs were frozen and he couldn't breathe.
Holding his breath, the soldier willed the enemy to leave, too scared
to run and too frightened to fight. He waited, engulfed by the terror around him.

As he hid amidst the thick grass he closed his eyes, hoping this
would help disguise his presence as sounds of the enemy passed
ever so close to where he had hidden. Ants poured over his body
examining their potential meal, the bites painfully working their
way along his legs towards his groin. He prayed for the strength
not to cry out as the carnivorous insects covered his body.

It seemed as if hours had passed when the camouflaged NCO
tensed as he noticed one of the enemy turn and look directly in his
direction. The guerrilla's features were vastly different from those
of the other Timorese he had known. This man was heavily bearded
and his eyes were light steel blue! He barked an order and immediately the band ceased their ghoulish activities.

"Leave them!" he demanded. "Their condition may act as a
deterrent to their comrades." As he spoke, several others similar in
appearance moved to his side.

These men were obviously not indigenous Timorese, the astonished corporal concluded. It was apparent from their manner that
they were in command of the band which now commenced moving silently away from the tortured soldiers still screaming from
pain. One of the wounded managed to struggle to his feet, only to
fall down again. He rose once more, holding his hands to his head,
covering the gaping holes where his eyes had been minutes before, and screamed a curse at his captors.

"*Djahanam! Djahanam!*" he cried aloud with the pain, "*mampus
kamu kalian!*" and again fell to his knees, sobbing with distress at
having been deserted by *Allah*, the One and Only True God.

The Cuban turned and walked to the side of the young

Sundanese. His hand moved swiftly, extracting the self sharpening commando knife from its sheath, which he placed directly under the wounded man's left ear. The blinded soldier recognized the sound. He had heard it before. Immediately the brave young man ceased yelling his invective at the unseen enemy. He sat motionless, his body leaning forward slightly over his knees, the cold steel blade touching his skin lightly. He realized that the weapon would end his life.

This was his *ajal*, his predestined moment of death and, as with all faithful Moslem followers, he believed that this moment was determined at birth with the commencement of one's life. He lifted his head in a gesture of acceptance of his fate. The Cuban misinterpreted the gesture as one of defiance. The blade moved swiftly and the soldier felt the beginning of the stroke and the flow of blood simultaneously. He didn't scream.

His ear fell to the ground - but he was still alive! His bladder opened and he fell forward, sobbing with fear and shame. The Cubans laughed and, at the leader's command, the band of Timorese followed the foreign killers back into the dense jungle.

Corporal Budiman waited until he was certain that they had not left one of their number behind to lay *ranjau*, the dreaded antipersonnel mines. Convinced that he was safe to venture out from his concealment, the NCO cautiously approached the Sundanese, who now lay groaning softly in prayer. The wounded man stiffened as he heard the footsteps approach.

"*Sudahlah, dong! Bunuh sajalah aku!*" the commando pleaded, seeking a quick end to his agony. "*Diam, diam!*" the corporal whispered urgently, "*Aku Budiman. Diam dulu, dik!*" the soldier whispered hoarsely to his comrade, consoling the man while identifying himself.

Quickly he checked the others. Two would die, he could see from the wounds and he was not certain how to provide emergency care for the others. He located several of his fallen comrades and, tearing strips from their clothes, he commenced applying makeshift bandages to the disgusting head wounds the tortured men had suffered. Satisfied there was little else he could accomplish, Budiman went in search of the communications soldier to establish contact with his base Commander.

It was hopeless. There were bodies everywhere. But no radioman. He searched for half an hour and decided to use distress flares instead. These he fired and then settled down amongst the wounded to await assistance. Throughout the night he was terrified each time there was a sound. Any sound. He feared the return of the strange looking soldiers who had butchered his comrades. As the moon disappeared, only to be replaced by the morning sun, he sat alone, praying for forgiveness of his past sins.

The following afternoon two platoons of infantry arrived. They were accompanied by several officers from the ill-fated paratroops' regiment. By then, all but two of the original eighty-nine paratroopers had died from torture, shock or were unlucky enough to lose their lives even before their parachutes could lower them safely to the ground. Many of these remained hung in their harness, held aloft by the trees which had caught the unfortunate men, providing the enemy with easy targets.

Corporal Budiman helped the fearless Sundanese soldier to his feet and put his arms around the shorter man.

"You are a very brave soldier," he whispered, *"may Allah go with you and protect you."*

The wounded man groped at the corporal and, in his anguish cried, *"Where was Allah when we needed him?"* and broke into sobs, while his fists clenched in anger.

"We will take Allah's revenge on those animals, Mas. This I, Budiman, swear to you."

"Budi, Budi," the wounded man cried, *"they have taken my sight!"*

"I know, Mas, but they will pay for their atrocities, this is my promise to you."

"Kill them all, Budi, kill them all!" the man sobbed.

"We will. We will find them and kill them all!" he promised the now semi-conscious soldier as he slowly passed into a deeper state of shock and, finally, the soft world of oblivion.

Budiman sat for a while holding the dead man's hand until it was time to go. The young officer who headed the platoon ordered the bodies stacked side by side and advised his command centre of the final body count. There were too many to bury.

They merely collected the dog tags and placed these in one knapsack beside the body of the Siliwangi Colonel who had died in his parachute without having fired a shot. His magazine was still full. Acting *Kapten*, Bambang took the machine pistol and discharged

359

the weapon into the air. Surprised, the junior Lieutenant turned towards the Javanese with a quizzical expression on his baby face.

"*The Bapak Kolonel's weapon had jammed*," he lied, placing the light machine pistol beside the officer's body.

* * * * * *

When he first arrived at the scene of the massacre, Bambang could not believe his eyes. The company had virtually been wiped out to a man. As he walked around checking the bodies, the shock of what he was witnessing prevented him from feeling any other emotion but anger over the mutilated bodies left by the Timorese butchers. He had been ordered to hunt for the guerrillas responsible for the massacre.

Bambang told the terrified Budiman to accompany them on the search and destroy mission. Although the Corporal could not identify the strange and brutal foreigners he had observed, headquarters assumed that these were remnants of the Portuguese garrison now fighting alongside the FRETILIN guerrillas. They had been instructed to eradicate these killers. The members of Bambang's platoon, relatively inexperienced in any type of warfare, were nervous when informed of the objective of their mission.

The Cuban officer had indeed been clever. The tortured bodies of their comrades acted as a deterrent to the Indonesians, and already some were completely rattled by the demoralizing scene they had come upon just hours before.

The Captain was aware that many of his men had been intimidated by the mutilated bodies. Most were Moslem and their sect specifically forbade such disfigurement. Even the young Javanese officer had difficulty maintaining his composure when he discovered the eyeless corpses. Although a soldier, Bambang was disgusted by the torture his countrymen had suffered and undertook to deal harshly with the guerrillas when they eventually located them.

He was convinced that they would have a bloody fight when they met. However he was also confident that they would be successful, as his men were already on the ground and could not therefore suffer the same fate as the parachutists who hadn't been given the opportunity to fight. The initial problem the officer was faced with was to determine the whereabouts of the guerrilla band. It was unlikely that he would obtain any local support as the hill tribes disliked the lowlanders and feared the Indonesians from the other islands.

The Moslem faith had a scattered following. The Timorese had developed their own animist practices and ancestral and other spirits were worshipped by all. These people believed that life was a transferable spirit and, consequently, heads were taken in war. The Japanese had learnt that the hard way.

The young Captain shuddered uncomfortably. Warfare had been endemic amongst the various tribes throughout both the Portuguese and Dutch areas of Timor. Villagers built stockades around their houses, which were raised on piles providing additional protection from marauding bandits. He decided to avoid contact with the local hill people.

Unlike their fellow citizens in Irian, the majority of Indonesians knew nothing of the art of tracking. Bambang decided that the best course of action would be to head around the mountain, maintaining the same elevation as necessary then dropping quickly down the far side. He thought that this may offer them the opportunity to place themselves ahead of the guerrillas and perhaps the chance to ambush them for a change! Should they not encounter the enemy there, he would swing back and reconnoitre before formulating another plan. He wished the Colonel was there with them to advise. The other platoon was to remain where it was until contact had been established. They were then to move across the hillside as well, dropping down behind the enemy, and attack from the rear.

He could not have selected a more dangerous route as this had been the exact same path taken by the three hundred strong guerrilla force. Budiman had not been able to assist with any detail as to the enemy's strength. Their latest intelligence reports suggested that they were less than twenty. Bambang thought about the estimated enemy numbers. He knew it was unlikely that just twenty men would be able to eliminate so great a number of their airborne as they had the day before, although shooting men in harnesses wasn't difficult. His anger returned as he recalled the number of men dead, hanging in the trees.

He called his platoon together and explained his plan. They then set out, walking in single file, trying to remember what they had learned as the platoon climbed up one hill and across a small ridge, staying close together under the forest's dense cover.

As evening fell Bambang began to lose confidence. He had now lost radio contact and, as darkness enveloped his force, images of his fallen comrades began to play tricks in the jungle darkness. He became afraid. His men felt his fear and they too began to pray silently, for their safety and his leadership. The sergeant went from man to man checking their gear as they rested, offering them support when they needed it, and instant reprimand when they deserved to be reminded of their mistakes.

* * * * * *

Coleman had breakfast with Greg Hart in the Hotel Indonesia coffee shop. He didn't particularly enjoy eating there but he knew that his offsider would have been there anyway and it just seemed easier that day. He had arranged the meeting to avoid having to share his own table with the couple now occupying his home. He realized that his actions were childish and identified his feelings as more of pique than jealousy. It was of little compensation that the relationship had developed when Wanti's state of mind was questionable. Although his own behaviour had not been exactly chaste during their separation, he justified his sexual pursuits as necessary functions of his life which were not available, or could not be fulfilled, by his legitimate partner.

He could not have imagined himself sleeping with Wanti after her collapse. He felt it would have been totally incomprehensible that advances could be made when the woman was obviously not completely conscious of her own actions. Perhaps, he thought, this was the basic crux of the problem. He had imagined that Albert had taken advantage of her condition, as the Timorese was not exactly a younger or a more attractive man. Silently Stephen admonished himself for permitting his thoughts to follow this path. Albert had always been a kind close friend and what had happened had happened and that was that.

It was unlikely that with Albert's religious background, Stephen decided, Wanti had even slept together with the older man. 'Damn!' he muttered, continuing to stir the already cold coffee, what a mess! He observed his assistant, Hart, staring at him.

"Problems?" he asked.

"A few."

"You were supposed to take some time off. What happened?"

"HANKAM will undoubtedly be raising hell any time now. I decided to stick around for awhile and see if they needed to speak with me. Also, I hadn't anticipated having a wife around when I first made the arrangements. I was due out today and may still go. I'm of two minds at the moment although I could do with a break."

"How is the invasion going?" Hart asked, for if anyone in the city outside the Indonesian Military would know then it would certainly be his boss, Coleman.

"Too soon to tell. Shouldn't be too much for them to handle though, as they outnumber the separatists at least five to one. And the FRETILIN are a disorganized bunch of misfits with no more than a few disillusioned Portuguese followers."

"The Melbourne broadcasts were surprisingly specific with their reporting this morning," Hart suggested, watching Coleman for his reactions.

Surprised, Stephen suddenly realised that he had missed the program, one which he regularly heard with his breakfast. It usually offered an up-to-date coverage of world news with, he believed, very little Australian bias.

"That's impossible, Greg. How in the hell could they be reporting the action?"

"This morning's broadcaster claimed they were receiving information directly from Timor. I must admit though, it was eerie to hear the Australian news actually identifying combat groups, casualties and troop positions."

"My God, that's insane! The military will go berserk!"

"Maybe it's the station's revenge on the Indonesians for sending their representative home."

"Greg, listen chum. If I was a part of their High Command right now I would be looking for blood. Let's hope that this lunacy does not result in the Indonesians losing any of their troops; otherwise we may as well close up shop and disappear. Are you certain that it wasn't the Voice of America? Was it really one of ours?"

Christ!" he exploded, "What a bunch of arseholes!"

"Spot on, I'm afraid."

Coleman thought for a few moments and then decided.

"Greg, I have changed my mind again. You hold down the fort, I will be gone for a few days. Okay?"

"Sure, Stephen. Where are you going?"

Coleman ignored the question, signalled for the bill and when it came, paid in Rupiah and left Hart alone to finish his breakfast.

* * * * * *

He watched Stephen hurry away to yet another of his secret assignations. Hart was annoyed with the action. He was disappointed that, even after the now lengthy time he had worked for the man, there was an obvious lack of trust, as considerable secrecy surrounded most of the company's operations.

His access to whatever Stephen's activities were off-shore was strictly blocked as the man made most of his own arrangements when travelling and there was practically no company record of his movements when he disappeared, sometimes for almost a week at a time. He needed to have this information if he was to feel that Stephen really trusted him.

The general business of the company was quite easy for Hart to follow. It was the armament supply arrangements which were complex and jealously guarded by Coleman himself.

Hart had guessed that most of the company's financial success had originated from the secret deals Coleman had obviously struck with HANKAM, as he was very close to most of the military leaders and was practically the only foreigner who was regularly seen at the Saturday night *Ramayana* puppet shows the Presidential household held for special guests and close friends of the Indonesian hierarchy. It was also obvious that the man's wealth had grown immensely over the years.

He was practically a legend amongst the other foreigners his success story, although often distorted out of all proportion provided for them a sense of their own achievement, for one of their number had been able to beat the system and secure the helm of a substantial enterprise, not as an employee, but as its owner. And all of this before he was even thirty!

Hart had estimated the company's worth at around fifteen million dollars but he knew he could never be sure. Even the string of nominees holding most of the property in the mountain resort areas had been arranged without his knowledge. He had a fair indication of who these people were as their names appeared regularly in correspondence relating to other matters, mainly in the defence representation contracts which the company held with a number of shadowy Hong Kong and Macau suppliers. These were the names who, more often than not, appeared as some of the approved signatories at the Indonesian Department of Defence, HANKAM.

On occasion he had approached Coleman and suggested that the operation could benefit from a more open relationship, as he personally had now made a substantial commitment to the company and believed that if he was to make the association a career then, perhaps, Coleman might like to consider bringing him into the company on a different basis. His superior had treated the suggestion coolly and indicated that there would be no immediate change.

* * * * * *

Upon leaving the other man to finish his coffee, Stephen had driven directly to his house. He didn't spend much time thinking about the man he'd just left. He did his job well and that's all that was required. Hart had little personality, he felt, and could go nowhere in the commercial sector as his leadership qualities were also questionable.

The amount of energy required to administer the known activities of the company was huge and, Coleman knew, Hart dedicated himself well when it came to the paperwork and more mundane requirements of his operation.

He didn't underestimate his assistant. Stephen decided that it would be a mistake to sell the man short as he had seen him take what would have been an administrative nightmare for others and turn the mess into a coherent form suitably presented and clear enough for his office staff to understand. He just didn't like the man.

Stephen thought he had the personality of a mangy dog. He didn't understand why he felt that way about Hart. Maybe, he thought smiling to himself as the Mercedes pulled into his driveway, it was because the man was an accountant.

Arriving at what he considered his nerve centre, Stephen checked in with his personal secretary and sat down to prepare the message he believed should be sent urgently to his associate. He sent a telex to the Hong Kong office with the necessary codes and settled back awaiting a response. It would take less than an hour, he knew.

Sukardi interrupted his thoughts as he lay on the sofa.

"Tuan, is it all right for Njonja Wanti to use the car for awhile?" his *jongus* asked, having knocked first to alert his employer of his presence at the open doorway.

"Sure," he answered quickly, almost impatiently.

The houseboy disappeared, sensing the *tuan's* mood. It was always best to distance one's self as far as possible when he was like this. The last time the *tuan* had threatened to fire him again, and at last count that would make it almost thirty times in just this new period of the Moslem calendar, he appeared really serious!

The servants had discussed this together and all had agreed. The *tuan's* mood swings were directly related to the fact that his wife was in his home but not in his bed. Since she had arrived the laundry and chamber maids had all observed that nothing much had happened since she returned. Not that the *njonja* looked all that sick. They all hoped something would happen quickly. The *tuan* had never gone this long before without a woman's company in his bed.

After the houseboy had left Stephen rose impatiently and strolled over to the tall windows overlooking the well manicured garden driveway. Albert and Wanti could be seen standing outside the office alongside his Mercedes.

He continued to watch them together.

'God!' he thought, 'please don't let them hold hands!'

As he observed the two entering his car his thoughts were interrupted by the telex machine noisily coming to life. He waited impatiently until the lengthy signal had been received and, using the established references, decoded the deliberately ambiguous message. It was as he had anticipated. There was trouble and he was required in Hong Kong immediately.

Stephen instructed the servants to advise his wife and guest that he had to depart suddenly and ordered his secretary to phone Garuda and get him on the first flight to Singapore. Once at Changi Airport he would purchase the next leg of the ticket to avoid his office discovering his whereabouts and any other detail he felt it prudent to keep to himself. It had been burdensome maintaining this level of secrecy but it had paid off. Stephen was not about to destroy the years of hard work by ignoring the basic premise which had protected his secret operations throughout the past decade.

Seda had made it quite clear to him during the embryonic stages of their relationship that everything depended on their ability to keep their dealings strictly confidential. If their positions were compromised in any way, the result would be more than disastrous. For both of them.

His secretary knocked and entered. *"Your ticket will be waiting for you at Halim. It leaves in just over three hours, boss. Shall I inform Mister Hart?"* she asked, not particularly fond of the other man, who continuously needled her for more information than she thought he should have about Coleman's travel arrangements and other personal details. She had never discussed this annoyance with her employer, fearing that the foreigners always stuck together when it came to staff. He'd even asked her out but she'd refused.

Coleman's secretary knew that would be most unprofessional of her and simply illogical on his part, as she was conscious of her age and homely appearance. Hart could only want something that she wasn't prepared to or was unable to give him. Information, always information.

"Okay. Phone him now and let him know what flight I'm on. He's sitting down at the coffee shop and I guess you know where." Stephen smiled at her.

"Consider it done, boss."

Hart was a creature of habit and nearly always preferred to eat there. Coleman thanked the woman.

The time passed quickly and he was reminded by the staff that the car was standing by. His clothes already packed by the *jongus* and with tickets and passport in hand, he locked the private room after removing the tapes from the telex, then carried out one final check before leaving. He put his head into the office section and waved at his secretary.

"Bye," was all he said.

"Oh, boss!" she called as he closed the door, *"I managed to get through to Mister Hart. He said that he wouldn't be back here today as he needed to return to the Jalan Thamrin office. He said to wish you a good trip."*

CARTHAGE PUBLIC LIBRARY
CARTHAGE MISSOURI

Ten minutes later he left for the airport in one of the Nissan Cedrics that had been parked below, the air inside already cooled. Stephen was pleased to be leaving. He thought about his house guests. He expected that Albert and Wanti would assume that he had left because he was angry. This, under any other circumstances may have been so. The obvious discomfort they all experienced as a result of Albert's disclosure certainly supported this action. This suited his plans although he felt a twinge of remorse at not having spoken to Wanti at any real length.

The traffic moved quickly and Stephen arrived at the airport in less than half an hour and checked in, as his flight had already been called. He was pleased that it was on time. Stephen was looking forward to an evening in Hong Kong. 'Maybe I'll phone Mr Lim,' he thought.

******

As he boarded the wide-bodied jet, Coleman identified a familiar face sitting half forward in the first-class section. It was John Anderson. He was about to speak but decided just to smile and nod, acknowledging the man's presence. Coleman then permitted the stewardess to escort him to his seat.

Being naturally suspicious, Coleman could not help but feel a slight discomfort at bumping into this man and at this time. He immediately hoped that it was mere coincidence that they were to share the same flight. Stephen resisted the temptation to move out of his seat and speak to the man. The aircraft's first class section was practically empty and it would not have been too difficult to make the gesture.

As he accepted the Chivas and ice from the hostess, Stephen thanked the Garuda stewardess politely in her own language.

"*Tuan can speak Indonesian?*" she asked.

"*Of course,*" he answered.

"*Tuan is very fluent,*" she smiled warmly.

Coleman laughed. He needed the quick exchange, if for no other reason but than to distract him from the dark thoughts which immediately sprang to mind as he boarded the aircraft. He didn't like surprises and this chance meeting already had the ominous signs of ASIS stamped all over it. If Anderson's presence had been orchestrated, how could they possibly have known he was leaving when he himself only knew less than a few hours before the aircraft departed? He sipped the soft and soothing elixir, forcing the attack of paranoia back into the depths of his other thoughts.

The weather was good. He was already feeling a little more relaxed. The smiling stewardess stood beside his seat and inclined her head with a smile as she held the bottle firmly. Stephen accepted another Chivas, then settled back as the crew completed their final checks for departure.

The DC-10 lifted and banked to the east and the opposite side of the airfield across from the international terminal came into view. The military shared the airfield with the International Terminal. Funding for the upgrading had been arranged through non-military aid programs. HANKAM had willingly surrendered their control over the facility until the improvements had been completed, resulting in new runway surfaces which, in the future, could withstand the onslaught of fully laden Boeing 747s. According to international lending authorities, these futuristic aircraft would bring mega-dollars which would, in turn, repay loans provided for the development of the country's tourist industry. The airport's runway and other facilities had been completed, on time, and in accordance with United States Air Force specifications to enable B-52s an easy access with a full load, should their deployment become necessary in the future. Upon completion, the Indonesian Air Force reactivated most of its dormant facilities and recommenced Hercules and other military flights directly from the restructured airport.

Coleman stared out to where the hangers housed the military squadrons. There was considerable activity. He identified the recently refurbished C-130s which the Americans had refitted and supported with a generous supply of spare parts. He smiled and gave the aircraft a mock salute, for it had been a profitable contract for all concerned. American aircraft were always in demand. He considered the looming political issues and wondered if the pendulum would swing in Indonesia's favour, or would the Americans be obliged to bend under world opinion. The United States Congress would not permit the sale or gift of any of its military hardware to another nation should the intent be to use the equipment for expansionist purposes. They were quite clear on this point.

Stephen wondered how long it would take for the Americans to cease supporting the Indonesian military machine. After all, their newly acquired friends had invaded a neighbouring country and engaged in extreme military action. Along with everyone else, he was not quite sure just whose sovereignty had been violated as the former colony's status was still most unclear. The region would remain in a state of limbo until a clear signal had been sent by the United Nations, which he knew meant the United States, as to who should assume control over the desolate and insignificant piece of real estate called East Timor.

The Broncos would be a problem, Stephen mused. There was little doubt that the American Congress would put a hold on the delivery of the sophisticated aircraft as a result of the invasion. Originally, the deal appeared to have been struck as a direct result of the powerful Texas oil lobby.

The Americans had pulled out of Vietnam. Now they were investing heavily in Indonesia's oil and gas fields.

The Soviet-backed Vietnamese Air Force had suddenly acquired the strike capacity to threaten the rich gas fields of Natuna Island.

The Pentagon had quite cleverly decided to assist the Houston oil men. Congress required little persuasion to support the aviation package, not only because aircraft and defence sales were healthy for the United States economy, but also as this particular agreement provided for future protection of American interests while sending a clear message to Indonesia's more hostile neighbours that they were prepared to protect their trading partner's borders.

The American defence establishment had arranged the meeting which was attended by all the parties with vested interests in the future development of the field in question. As they sat around the table discussing the small island of Natuna which, according to satellite data and recent seismic interpretation, represented a massive oil and gas deposit, the Americans unanimously agreed that they must have control over the concession rights.

The parties were all aware that the island was in dispute as to who actually owned the potentially wealthy field. The Pentagon was adamant that it would not belong to the Vietnamese. The governments of Indonesia and the United States entered into a covert pact and, consequently, the aircraft were slated for delivery to the former pro-Communist country to protect itself from any possible intrusion by the newest Communist force in the region. Vietnam.

An airfield would have to be built quickly and quietly while funding needed to be diverted from other budgets to cover the construction costs. American engineers were consulted and the plan proceeded to the next stage. It was imperative that the ASEAN countries did not misinterpret the deployment of these aircraft as a hostile act nor speculate that Indonesia was positioning itself for an American re-entry into Vietnam.

The new airfield was not scheduled for completion until the Broncos had already been delivered to Indonesia and based at other airfields for at least one year. Indonesian pilots would require this time for training and logistical ordinance programs demanded strict scheduling procedures be implemented well before delivery. Neither country anticipated any real difficulty with the arrangements and within months of signing the joint defence memorandum, Indonesian pilots commenced their training in the United States.

The political storm started brewing when members of the Fourth Estate discovered the disappearance of some of their number in the Timor area. Accusations flew to and fro. However, as there was no clear evidence that the Indonesian forces were responsible in any way for the journalists' demise, Congress had little choice but to continue to support delivery of the sophisticated aircraft. Then came the Timor invasion. The Separatists had been powerless to prevent the action.

The Americans were immediately concerned that world opinion would turn against the Indonesians. They understood the complexity of Indonesia's position in relation to its regional partners and the separate commitments the United States had made with its neighbours, such as the Philippines and Thailand. However, the United States was still suffering the aftermath of their involvement in Vietnam and, consequently, pressure mounted on the politicians to veto delivery of any further military aid to the Soeharto regime.

There were many stories circulating at the time and both Seda and Coleman had heard them all. Rumours were, US satellite intelligence had proven the existence of considerable Eastern Bloc weaponry and had confirmed the presence of Cuban advisers in the former Portuguese colony. There were even fears that missiles had already been shipped to the area.

Coleman knew that under the ANZUS Treaty the United States was obliged to assist Australia and New Zealand in the event that hostile forces threatened their sovereignty. The Americans were not entirely convinced that the small Cuban presence in East Timor represented such a threat until their satellite photograph interpretation experts identified a substantial increase in Soviet arms already on ground in the disputed country and a disturbing array of large ominous containers. The United States Military Attaché in Canberra had reluctantly passed this information to his Australian counterpart. As a result of what appeared to be an aggressive Soviet move to support Cuba's adventurous incursion into areas outside its own sphere of influence in Latin America, satellite surveillance was stepped up to meet the new threat to regional stability, in the Far East.

Alarmed by these developments, the Pentagon believed that they had no choice but to circumvent their own congressional leaders and arrange for delivery of the aircraft as soon as was practical. The Americans were all too conscious of the dangers in permitting the Cubans to establish any form of missile capability on the strategically situated island. On the other hand, Congress would not permit support for the Indonesian violation of the newly created independent state, although FRETILIN's announcement had yet to be recognized formally by any of the world's leaders.

The Americans were confused with their friends Down Under. They had been closely monitoring the growing anti-American sentiment in both New Zealand and Australia ever since the 1973 withdrawal from Vietnam. The United States intelligence chiefs argued against informing the Australians of their intentions. Instead, they acted to cover their positions by insisting publicly that any country which enjoyed American military hardware, whether by gift or by purchase, could not use this equipment to assist or aid a third country involved in any expansionist military action.

Indonesia obviously fitted the description perfectly, and the defence apparatus moved successfully in keeping the meddling Aussies out of what was potentially a most dangerous game. Besides, just weeks before Gough Whitlam, the country's former Prime Minister had pledged total support to the Soeharto government and where was he now? They were still unsure of the new Prime Minister, Fraser, but they understood that at least his party's politics were somewhat similar to theirs.

An unhappy American Ambassador to Australia was therefore instructed to inform his country's allies of the U.S. position.

The Indonesians could use the OV-10Fs against the Timorese as the aircraft was perfect for such action. Equipped with a twenty millimetre cannon and up to four missiles AURI believed that, with experienced pilots, they could wrap up the invasion in days. It was decided in secret that American interests could best be served if delivery of the Broncos was not delayed any further. The military sales program would be accelerated enabling earlier delivery of the Skyhawks as well.

Coleman contemplated the seriousness of the conflict. He hoped that his meeting in Hong Kong would provide the information necessary to allay his concerns. If not, he would need to take whatever action was appropriate to avoid what were potentially serious political repercussions as a result of the company's armament activities. Australians had always enjoyed a close relationship with the Indonesians.

Suddenly that had all changed.

He had asked Seda about the killing of the foreign journalists but the General had claimed it had been an accident. There had been so many conflicting reports creating a great deal of confusion as to what actually happened.

* * * * * *

Recalling the breakfast meeting he still could not understand how the Australian Broadcasting authorities had permitted the news bulletins to go to air and divulge military and strategically sensitive information through its programs. The situation was extremely serious and volatile. He felt that the Indonesians would have every right to retaliate and, if this happened, being an Australian in Jakarta would be dangerous. Stephan hoped that the broadcasts would not be repeated. Still considering the ramifications of the potential political fallout, Stephen rose and headed for the toilet.

He glanced away as he passed the familiar figure sitting three rows behind his seat.

"Stephen?" Anderson called but Coleman ignored the man continuing to the bathroom. When he had completed his ablutions he returned to his seat only to discover John Anderson occupying the seat next to his.

"You're looking well, Stephen."

"You're sitting on my menu," the younger man snapped.

"Just a few words. I promise that you will be very interested in what I have to say. In fact, I would have phoned your office today as I have been in town since yesterday and planned to catch up. Had you not decided to leave unexpectedly we would probably already be sitting down somewhere having the same discussion. As it is, I've had to rearrange my entire itinerary just so we could have this private time together." Anderson could see the surprise on the other man's face as he alluded to the fact that he had actually orchestrated his travel to be on the same flight.

"We have to talk, Stephen," he said, almost staccato in emphasis. Anderson looked directly into Coleman's eyes as he emphasized the words by tapping the tray locked in front of his seat, one tap, one word as he'd said "we-have-to-talk, Stephen!"

Coleman, immediately infuriated at the master-pupil approach snapped back. "Stick it!"

"Come on, man, grow up!"

Coleman sighed. It was a difficult situation as there was really nowhere he could go. Not at thirty five thousand feet. Reluctantly he decided to hear him out.

"What do you want, John?"

The grey-haired distinguished Intelligence Chief leaned towards his former junior officer and lowered his voice.

"Are you going to Hong Kong?" he asked softly.

Startled, Coleman was caught off guard. He hesitated, looked Anderson directly in the eye and lied.

"No. Just to Singapore this trip."

"Too bad, I had hoped for a little company on the longer section."

"I doubt we would have too much to discuss."

"Oh, you never know, Stephen, we could talk about the arms shipments you have been handling and, if that is of no interest, we could move on to more personal matters."

Coleman felt the hot burning anger beginning as a flush, moving across his face. He remained silent, gathering his thoughts.

How did he know that I would be on this flight? Stephen asked himself. Then it dawned on him. The bastards, he thought, they have been keeping tabs on me and bugging my phones. And Albert's!

He glanced at the other passenger, controlling his rising anger. "What do you want, John?"

"Are you going to Hong Kong?" he asked again.

"Maybe," he answered, this time sullenly.

"Then I insist we talk. Now!"

The command was too much for him, the anger suddenly bursting forth.

"Where in the hell do you guys get off, John? I don't cash your cheques any more and certainly have no intention of participating in any of your clandestine activities."

Anderson's eyes narrowed as he leaned a little closer to the other man. "We know about Seda."

He had made the statement in his soft resonant voice and yet it seemed to Coleman as if it had been shouted at him in a thunderous roar.

"Are we discussing Albert?" he inquired hopefully, his throat suddenly dry. He swallowed a large mouthful of whisky.

"Yes, and that too," Anderson replied softly. "I'm sorry."

"Christ! Your bastards have been tapping my lines," he accused.

"It really doesn't matter now. The important thing is that we have the chance to correct a few problems and prevent at least one major catastrophe."

He was stunned by these revelations. His mind raced quickly. How much did they know?

"How did you know I'd be on this flight?"

"As I said. It doesn't matter how we knew. We needed to talk to you urgently and out of the country. It was a stroke of luck that you jumped when you did."

"Jumped?" Coleman asked, incredulous disbelief crossing his face. "Just an euphemism, don't over react."

"Are you trying to tell me that you orchestrated my departure today?" he asked disbelievingly, "That's just so much bullshit, and you know it!"

"Let's cool it," Anderson said as the stewardess moved past and checked the drinks. She continued on down the aisle as she could see that they weren't ready for another.

Stephen jabbed his thumb on the service button. The steward-ess went directly to his service.

"*Tuan mau minum lagi?*" she asked slightly startled, now an-ticipating his request for a further drink, as foreigners always drank heavily and on these short sectors.

"Chivas," he snapped.

The young hostess identified the tone. "*And would you also like something, sir?*" she asked the tall grey haired gentleman sitting alongside. Stephen looked up at the lovely smiling face and im-mediately felt guilty for his display of temper. Although he really didn't feel much like it, he returned her smile.

"*Sorry, sis, I'm not angry with you. It's just that the old man beside me is very annoying,*" Coleman explained.

The girl smiled at the handsome passenger and then looked at the other man who had obviously been the source of his rudeness.

"The lady wants to know if you require a drink." Coleman snapped.

"Thank you, yes. I will have a Chivas also," he replied, unruf-fled.

Stephen sat and sulked until his drink arrived. He sipped in silence, refusing to communicate with Anderson. He knew he was in trouble. They had information that was only supposed to be available to Nathan Seda and himself.

Half an hour passed and the plane began its descent into Singa-pore. The two men disembarked together and walked briskly to the transit ticketing counter. Coleman purchased his ticket and the older man stood by watching. An observer could easily have mis-taken them for father and son. Recognising that Anderson was not going to leave him alone, Stephan sighed, shrugged his shoulders and turned towards his former mentor.

"We have half an hour. Let's find somewhere to talk," he sug-gested.

Anderson nodded his agreement. They selected comfortable seats towards the rear section of the first class lounge. Anderson had taken a wine from the complimentary bar and offered a glass to Coleman who declined and prepared another Chivas with just one cube of ice. He stood facing the government man slowly swirl-ing the whisky around the cube and then he took a seat positioning himself so that they could not be overheard.

"Okay. Give it to me. What's happening, John?"

"Well, Stephen, the shit has hit the fan and you seem to be sitting right in the middle of the target area."

"Let's cut through it. We don't have much time. What is it I may or may not have involved myself in that is of interest to ASIS?"

"Firstly. You are still tied by the Official Secrets Act," he warned.

"Hold it!" Stephen snapped, "I won't sit here and permit you to threaten me, John. Knock it off!"

"It's no threat. You are in serious trouble. This mess is partly of your own doing and, to put it bluntly, had I not been the man in the chair, as they say, your number would be up. Half of ASIS wants you put away, Stephen, they think you're an arsehole!"

Stephen had never heard the Director speak in this tone. Not even when he was angry. He then realized that the man was deadly serious and maybe out of some previous loyalty had decided to give Stephan the opportunity to extricate himself from whatever mess they thought he was in.

"Okay. I'm listening."

"Good." Anderson smiled, weariness now apparent as he extended his hand.

Stephen accepted the gesture.

Anderson then began to speak slowly in a soft monotone which, had the content not been so dramatic, would have made the listener drift off to sleep. He spoke without interruption for twenty minutes and when he had completed his explanation Stephen sat quietly, his face ashen, shocked by the information he had been given.

Forty-five minutes later the Cathay Pacific Tristar Star departed for Hong Kong. Stephen Coleman sat alone, sipping yet another whisky with no effect, as he was stone cold sober. He felt numb, not from the alcohol but from the secret and shocking disclosures he'd just been provided with at risk, no doubt, to the courier himself. He knew just how indebted he now was to John Anderson. A cold sensation passed through his body and Coleman shuddered involuntarily.

Anderson's revelations may have just been in time. He would know, for sure, after his meeting with Nathan Seda in Hong Kong.

* * * * * *

Nevada — USA

The inconspicuous building lay well back from the main road and out of sight behind a small spur that ran parallel with the secondary road leading back towards the Californian border. The total acreage was near to a thousand and most was covered with timber stands protected by numerous signs, designating the area as a special reserve. The photo interpretation unit had been established during the years when Khruschev headed the Kremlin. There had been a rush of new data collection facilities built as a result of even more sophisticated satellites being launched. This unit was dedicated to the intelligence monitoring of product, sent back to earth by the United States Military's Series Four birds which flew across the heavens orbiting specific areas as designated by the powerful men in the Pentagon. The air-conditioned centre and surrounding forest was encircled by a perimeter fence carrying sufficient power to deter the curious from entering the secluded facility. Signs had been erected warning trespassers of the charged fence and ranger patrols. Strangely enough none had breached the unit's security since it was first commissioned.

Lieutenant Collins had been engrossed in his own work when he heard the soft whistle of surprise from across the other side of their compact room. He looked up and spotted Davidson, one of his senior photo analysis experts standing as he held the two photographic records in one hand and waving them as one would a hand fan.

Collins gestured the other man over to his work area, now covered with detail of the last two runs obtained by the satellite over the Philippines. They had been monitoring shipping in that area consistently for the past three months at the request of their Intelligence masters.

Davidson handed the Section Commander both of the enlarged photos taken from space and sent by electronic impulse back to the earth station which, in turn, had passed the garbled signals to the relevant agency for interpretation and dissemination.

"This is fantastic, Davy boy! Great clarity, although there's some degradation in this one," he said shaking the photograph in his left hand.

"Thanks boss," the experienced hand responded, pleased with

the Lieutenant's reaction. They worked well together and he didn't mind putting that little extra effort into the demanding and sometimes boring intelligence work. The monotonous routine was extremely intense in nature as, the longer one was obliged to stare down through the enhancement apparatus the more the details became difficult to differentiate, even with the assistance of the latest developments in their field of pseudoscopy.

Collins looked at the detailed views and the sections already highlighted by Davidson and went into the computer immediately. He then compared the results with the photo-imagery taken of the Russian freighters which had been seen and photographed heading for Cuba almost fifteen years before. As a senior analyst he was responsible for confirming his team's results before passing the information to his superior. Their work was demanding at the best of times and mistakes were easily made, for it was not always just a simple matter of identifying what had been caught by the satellite's lenses as it moved across the sky at incredible speed, but also the difficult task of suggesting what the objects were in the black and white scenes.

Ten minutes after receiving Davidson's interpretation, the Lieutenant stood across from the Colonel with the information. Believing that they had confirmation of the cargo, the report was immediately transmitted to the Pentagon's South East Asian hostiles' desk. Less than half an hour had passed from the time Davidson had first spotted the configuration which sent alarm bells ringing directly to the President's Defence Advisor.

There were a number of possibilities according to the intelligence report. The crate sizes and numbers were almost identical in every way with those in the earlier photographs and, should the contents be the same, then the *M.V. Setia Budi* could be carrying a Soviet Skean (SS-5) ballistic missile on board as deck cargo. The report went on to describe the deadly weapon.

The Pentagon had data showing that the intermediate range missile was another of the liquid-propelled series which could be fitted with nuclear or thermonuclear warheads. The Skean series had a range of some two thousand miles, or approximately three thousand two hundred kilometres, and was regarded as the ultimate in postwar development applied to the old German V-2 series rocket. According to other satellite intelligence reports it was confirmed that the Soviets had deployed approximately one hundred of the missiles each with a warhead capacity of up to one megaton yield. These were housed in underground silo-launchers scattered around Europe with a few along their borders with China.

Once the information had been absorbed and acting upon White House directives, the Pentagon issued the order and signals were flashed across the oceans. These were intercepted then confirmed by the Fleet's Admiral.

As the freighter approached the coastline of the former Portuguese colony, approximately one hundred nautical miles from its probable destination, the Captain and crew of the M.V. *Setia Budi* were startled by the incredible noise which ruptured the vessel. In those few brief seconds as the two conventional warheads struck the ship almost simultaneously, cutting its hull in two with the massive force of detonation, all the men on the bridge died.

The ship sank in less than eleven minutes. There were only two survivors and both claimed that their vessel had struck an old mine, taking the freighter, its master and most of its crew to the bottom before anything could be done.

Having confirmed the kill, the United States Lafayette Class nuclear submarine turned back once more on its track and headed for the deep waters of the Ombai Wetar Trench, where its presence was practically impossible to detect.

In the following weeks American SEALS posing as tourists sailing through to Singapore from Australia visited the site. They required only three dives before they were satisfied with their conclusions, supported by the sensitive sonar instruments on board their yacht. These had suggested the unexpected results even before they had even considered the physical sightings as being necessary.

The Presidential advisor read the report and advised the country's leader that the threat had been removed. The shipments, containers, and box identifications were deliberately meant to be misleading. The Soviets had just been playing at their old tricks to test the American's response. The deck cargo had been nothing more than a series of empty crates and containers.

It had all been another Russian hoax.

* * * * * *

Timor

Bambang had managed but a few hours sleep before the heavy downpour forced his platoon to break camp and continue their mission. The trail was slippery. The underbrush ripped at their uniforms, cutting through the camouflaged material supplied by some distant clothing factory in Hong Kong. At least they had reasonable fire-power when the time came for them to fight, as he knew it would. The enlisted men all carried the American M-16s with the exception of the Sergeant who struggled under the weight and additional rounds he carried for the heavy M-60.

Bambang knew that the weight of the ten kilo weapon would be taking its toll on his most experienced soldier, but someone had to carry the machine gun and it might as well be the man who would eventually be the one to fire it.

He looked across at the soldier who continuously slipped with every step. The M72 LAW didn't appear to be any the worse for wear from the constant beating it had received. Bambang considered taking the rocket launcher himself as he felt that it would be called upon early in the engagement and he preferred knowing that it was in responsible hands. With its three hundred metre range he expected to be able to keep the guerrillas well at bay. During their briefings they had been advised that the enemy was poorly equipped. Some, they had been told, carried antiquated weaponry, while only a few had the Soviet Ak-47s. They were practically guaranteed by the Major who carried out their Intelligence briefing that there would be no likelihood of their encountering any real resistance or, for that matter, any sophisticated weaponry.

Somebody should have told the enemy, Bambang thought, remembering the bodies hanging from the trees in their harnesses. The men were demoralized. They were tired. They were wet, and very, very hungry. Captain Bambang knew that he would have to achieve their object quickly before his men tired to exhaustion. The point reported a small compound not far around the next ridge, and he decided to seek temporary refuge and shelter, enabling his men to eat and get out of the weather for a short spell. The villagers would have prepared rice. The one thing you could count on in this world, the Javanese officer thought, was that regardless of location, someone, somewhere within spitting distance of wherever you were

 DISCARD

would have rice on the boil.

They scrutinized the perimeter fence before calling out to the villagers. There was no answer and the sergeant called out again.

"Tell them we will pay them for food. Tell them we will do them no harm. Tell the.." the Captains instructions were interrupted as a voice called out to them to go away.

"Pergi! Go!" the frightened voice demanded..

"We're not your enemies, we won't do you any harm!" the non-com called back hoping that the simple people there would not panic.

Minutes passed and the tall gate opened. At first, just a little, but sufficient for an ageing head to peer out and reassure itself that these soldiers really meant no harm.

"Why do you come here?" the old man demanded.

"We need food, Pak."

The withered body of the little man was now in full view.

"You eat, then you go, yes?" he asked.

"Ya, Pak, we will leave as soon as we have eaten," they promised.

Carefully, in single file, they entered the village compound.

They huddled below the huts which had been built on stilts, the ground was filthy and mud greeted them wherever they looked. It was a poor and desolate place to be, the men had thought, although thankful for the break to rest and eat. The village people fed the soldiers who in turn rewarded their hosts with warm smiles and a fistful of Rupiah. The old village headman shook his head sadly. He explained that they had little use for the paper money as it could only be used down along the coast and in the large towns.

They asked instead for one of the soldiers' watches. Captain Bambang sadly agreed and he, as platoon Commander, unhappily surrendered his Seiko to the headman. He knew it was extortion but felt saddened by the scene around him. These poor village people had given what was probably a large portion of their food stocks to his men. They didn't understand the conflict and were merely innocent bystanders to the fighting taking place all around them.

Bambang removed the wrist watch slowly. The old wrinkled face broke into a wide toothless smile as he accepted the piece. He examined the gift and noticed writing on the back cover. He asked the Javanese what the inscription meant as he was illiterate.

"Always be safe, Bambang, love Wanti," he read aloud, explaining to the village elder that it was a gift from his sister.

The old man nodded and looked up into the young officer's sad brown eyes. Then he returned the watch and walked away.

Their spirits lifted by the hot steamed rice and vegetables, the soldiers departed. They continued around the mountain and descended down its slopes, the trees and undergrowth, becoming much heavier as they advanced, impeded their movements. Bambang continued to monitor his men, as did his sergeant. They were already beginning to feel the effects of the constant downpours and inhospitable surrounds. They continued down another slope, the non-com cursing both his men and the slippery soil, saturated by incessant rain.

The men were nervous now, sensing that the enemy was near. They were able to increase their pace for awhile as the trail moved away from the thick growth and provided the men with the opportunity to move a little more freely. As the afternoon hours passed, Bambang decided that they would establish their camp earlier rather than later, permitting the men to rest well before any encounter.

They established camp observing their instructions not to start a fire. Bambang had wanted the men to refrain from smoking their *kretek* as he knew that a non-smoker could distinguish the easily identifiable aroma of the Indonesian cigarette, putting them at risk, but the sergeant indicated that it would be all right as the men were tired. And jumpy.

Conditions were not much better than the previous night. Bambang slept for a few hours, rose when awoken by his non-com and together they checked the perimeter before returning to take some fruit from their limited ration packs.

The corporal sat huddled against a coconut palm. He judged from its condition that they had come a considerable distance down from the mountain slopes as this tree was covered with full ripe clusters of the hard shelled fruit. Bambang nudged the soldier, indicating the coconuts hanging directly overhead. The corporal nodded accepting his mistake and moved away from the potential danger. The impact from the weight of a ripened coconut could be deadly and Bambang did not wish to lose any of his men so foolishly.

* * * * * *

As daybreak arrived the soldiers prepared themselves for the day's patrol. Those who were Moslem prayed, facing the west, in the direction of Mecca, while the two who were not just went about their ablutions silently praying to their own gods that they would see this day through. The platoon set out and within a few hours made their first contact with the enemy, when they heard the sound of weapons being fired.

Bambang wisely ordered one of his men to reconnoiter the area, and waited for his report.

An hour passed and when the point man did not return the Captain assumed the worst and ordered the men to prepare their weapons for he knew that the enemy were close. They proceeded cautiously, listening for any tell tale sign of the enemy's position, nervously anticipating the encounter. Ahead lay a clearing but the missing soldier was nowhere to be seen.

Last night's campsite, Bambang concluded, as he identified the tell tale signs. He barked an order and the men obeyed.

They encircled the area, but there was nothing.

Bambang considered the possibility that the man he'd placed on point had deserted. It was unfortunately common with some of the first timers. It was just so simple to do and he'd wondered why many more had not deserted the same way. Once away from their units all they had to do was throw their military gear away and slip back into any village then hide.

Bambang instructed his men to spread out and remain alert. The minutes dragged by and still there was nothing. He was worried that the guerrillas may have doubled back behind them somehow. He discussed this with his senior NCO, a veteran of the early Sixties invasion of Irian and the *Ganyang Malaysia Konfrontasi* era. Many of the veterans had left the military, disillusioned after the entire exercise became a totally useless effort on the government's part to not really wage war, but merely distract the people at home from their economic problems.

The sergeant suggested that it was unlikely that the guerrillas would remain down in the lower areas as they risked observation by aerial reconnaissance flights. *"Maybe they have a supply base back up in the mountain,"* he advised his officer.

"They would expect to be followed," Bambang had replied, anxious that they might have missed the enemy.

The sergeant thought about this for a moment and replied.

"They must be poorly equipped. If they were expecting us then why haven't they attacked?"

As Bambang listened to the experienced veteran he suddenly realized his mistake. They had entered a trap!

It took all his strength to control the sudden flood of fear that gripped his stomach. He crouched low and called out to his men, warning them to hold fast, where they were and not to advance any further. He hissed at the soldier next to him to keep low and, as the man crouched forward, his body suddenly jerked up and was flung over backwards as the crashing sound of the bullet ripped through the morning air. Crack!

Immediately his men panicked. Lacking in experience and caught by fear, they fired wildly as they could not see their targets in the thick undergrowth. The air was suddenly filled with the screaming cacophony only a fire-fight could produce. Explosions ripped through the trees and automatic fire produced the most incredible shock waves on all sides of the action.

Men screamed with pain. Others screamed just from the fear of dying. Bambang turned in time to see his sergeant's face twist and contort as a bullet passed through one side and then out the other, throwing him with such force his body spun through the air as if it were some rag doll. He grabbed clumsily for the M-60 but it was pinned under the dead man's body. He screamed for his men to hold their fire but they ignored his command.

Fear had taken control and they emptied their magazines shooting blindly through the trees, as they panicked and died. As the deadly fire continued Bambang responded shooting in the direction of the enemy's position without seeing any of their soldiers. He screamed at his men to retreat but he couldn't be heard over the fierce noise of the battle.

Suddenly the shooting stopped. The Javanese officer called out softly for his men to report but there was no response. Someone groaned aloud nearby. He crawled over and found the corporal doubled up in pain. He had been shot in the stomach.

Bambang assessed the situation quickly. He was not sure just how many of his thirty soldiers had survived. He crawled through the muddy grass and discovered another body. The radio operator lay face down half his torso blown away where he had been hit by automatic fire.

He called out again, softly. There was still no response. He heard movement on his flank and immediately froze.

A voice called out. Someone screamed and was quickly silenced by small arms fire. Bambang waited. He counted off the seconds as he had learned during basic training. He could practically visualize his instructor standing over him during that day when he had lifted his head far too soon, only to have the angry Sergeant-Major yell abuse for him to get his head back down and to count. He crawled forward and could now see directly across the clearing and his heart skipped a beat. There were hundreds of them!

He froze instantly, holding his breath for as long as his lungs would permit. Slowly he eased his body back down a small slope and lay perfectly still in the mud, half hidden by the long grass.

Suddenly he could hear the voice of a man in extreme pain. He dared not lift his head. The soldier cried out loudly, his screams piercing the almost otherwise silent air.

"*Help!*" he cried. "*Please help me!*"

The screams continued until suddenly these too ceased simultaneously with the report of a gun being fired. Bambang understood. There would be no prisoners! Fear now gripped his very being and he felt ashamed. He couldn't will his body to move. His fear of death was too great. His limbs would not obey.

Bambang remained where he was hidden from the enemy. He had heard more screams and more shots silencing the soldiers under his command. Until there was no one left. And then there was the terrifying empty sound of silence.

He lay on the ground for what seemed to be an eternity, listening for sounds, the sounds of the enemy moving through the long grass, slowly, carefully, knowing that they had not yet discovered the body of the platoon's Commander. He lay still, willing his heart to slow, praying that they would not find him. He sobbed, his face smothered in his arms as he lay in the muddy undergrowth, silently weeping with shame. He cried, for he was weak and now all of his men had been killed. He knew that he too should be dead, as they were, accepting that only his cowardice had saved his life.

* * * * * *

As the darkness descended he forced himself to his feet. Like a man in a daze he wandered slowly around the battle scene, staring numbly at the carnage which lay before him. His platoon. Shattered. He moved slowly, checking the bodies, startled with every noise the trees and wind made. He started to shake as the fear once again took charge of his body abd he fell down to his knees and held his chest tightly, the racking sobs of despair choking in his throat. Finally, exhausted, he crawled back into the thick grass and slept, only to awaken by the cold soggy clothing stuck to his filthy body.

He remained crouched, his arms locked under his knees, shivering with the biting rain and fierce wind until morning finally came, bringing with it the horrors of the day before.

The bodies lay as they had fallen. Except for those who had only been wounded. Soldiers who had not died during the engagement had eventually paid the price of capture. Some had their faces mutilated similarly to the victims of the previous massacre. Hollow skeleton-like eyeless heads made even more terrifying with the wide open mouths holding frozen screams, evidenced the extreme cruelty of the guerrilla band. Others had their testicles severed and their organs stuffed into their mouths.

Bambang retched, but there was nothing in his empty stomach to help him. He ran his hands over his face and screamed out loudly in anguish. He called for *Allah* to save him from the hell in which he now found himself. He cried out again and again but none listened. He panicked and ran. He ran wildly through the jungle until exhaustion overcame him, collapsing beside a small stream.

He woke to the silence of the early morning and discovered that he had slept for almost an entire day.

Bambang realized that he had no choice. He had to go back to his men. He would collect their dog tags and search for the radio. He experienced the sudden return of his shame and knew that it would almost be impossible for him to face the other men in his regiment as the only survivor of the ambush.

They would think he was a coward, he knew.

And so he returned to the battle scene. There, slowly but carefully, he dragged his fallen comrades bodies to a small clearing. He had located all but one, the wounded corporal.

He placed the dead in a row. Bambang then removed their identification tags and tied them together placing these in the top of his battle tunic. All the weapons had been collected by the guerrillas. There was no radio. He was completely alone but he knew what he must do. He was still a soldier and he would follow the large band until he discovered their base camp. Then he would return to his own unit and bring adequate reinforcements.

Bambang peered back up in the general direction of the trail which had led them into peril. He looked back over his shoulder at the dead, then turned and addressed the task before him. Slowly he commenced his climb, forcing his aching body to obey his mind's commands. Within moments the clearing covered in mutilated bodies was hidden from view and he marched on.

Less than two hundred metres from where he had remembered the wounded corporal had fallen he was astonished to discover the man sitting up against a coconut tree.

Caught by surprise, Bambang hurried forward to ascertain whether he was still alive. The soldier's eyes were closed and the blood had dried. The young Javanese Captain bent down and placed his hand gently on the still body, gently prodding, to waken the soldier.

Bambang heard the noise and admitted to himself that he really hadn't deserved the second chance to live. In the passing of one brief moment and as his hands moved slowly over the fallen soldier Bambang understood that the corporal was dead. And in that instant, as he heard the thunderous click of the trigger mechanism activated when he tried to remove the man's dog tag, Bambang knew that he too was a dead man. The moment created between life and death was infinitesimal in time as his body was separated from his soul.

The blast hurled both soldiers through the air, ripping the uniforms from their shattered remains. The broken Seiko lay smashed, the inscription still clear. "Selamat selalu, Bambang, dari Wanti."

Days later the watch was exchanged by the old headman for a carton of kretek cigarettes. The hill people had collected whatever remained on the bodies of the unfortunate platoon and returned to the security of their enclosed compound. There they would remain until yet another Indonesian group of soldiers came by.

When a further detachment of the unwanted soldiers came in search of their fallen comrades the headman watched them also slowly disappear down the same trail which had led Bambang's soldiers to their deaths. The wise old man just shook his head. When these intruders were finally out of sight he dispatched a runner to report the presence of these soldiers to the FRETILIN post.

* * * * * *

"I'm really sorry about the reports. Have you been in contact lately with your family?"

Hart sympathized with Albert. The Timorese was heartbroken, having heard the morning report on the international news bulletin. It seemed that everyone in Indonesia these days now listened to the foreign broadcasts on a regular basis as there was little information filtering down from the government. The news had indicated that fighting had been stepped up with considerable casualties on both sides. Even the villages were being burned.

"Only by letter," he replied, "and that was some months ago."

"I'm sure they're okay. Just wait. Probably find some news waiting when you return home to Melbourne."

It felt strange to both of them that he had referred to that city as his home when, in fact, he'd been born in this country he now visited.

They discussed the broadcasts and both agreed that it was quite incredible how the Australian broadcasting station was disclosing Indonesian troop positions in such a blatant fashion. The Indonesians had no choice but to assume that it was a deliberate attempt by the Australian Government to prevent the success of the annexation. The Indonesian hierarchy was completely confused.

On one hand, the Australians had virtually given them *carte blanche* to assume control over the former Portuguese colony while on the other, the country's deliberate disclosure of Indonesian troop positions and other relevant military information, via their official radio station, had them totally bewildered. In Indonesia, such action would not be tolerated. The offenders would be dealt with quickly and the matter resolved within hours. Why was the Australian Government so weak, even timid, when it came to dealing with its media? They just couldn't understand why their old friends had let them down so badly.

Thousands of Indonesian troops had died by simply walking into traps laid easily by the FRETILIN as they too had listened to the broadcasts. At first the separatists had been highly suspicious of the information but, when they discovered the accuracy of the reports, they laughed at the relative ease with which they had dispatched so many of Indonesia's finest soldiers.

The windfall didn't continue, of course. It seemed that the flow of information ceased almost as quickly as it had started. All sides involved in the conflict had suddenly made a point of listening to the foreign radio broadcasts. Reportedly these had become unreliable over the previous days and appeared to contain more misinformation than real substance.

"Have you heard from Stephen?" Albert was disappointed that Stephen had left so suddenly without further discussing their future arrangements. He had difficulty obtaining return bookings and speculated that Coleman's secretary wasn't really trying as hard as he suspected she could.

"Nothing for a few days I'm afraid, perhaps we'll get something today." Greg Hart had taken breakfast with Albert. He didn't believe for one moment that Coleman would be in contact until he suddenly reappeared without notice in his office-cum-home. Hart had not entirely been happy when the company's other offices started appearing all over the city and neither was he pleased with Stephen's insistence that the bulk of the administration be moved out of his personal office to the company's main location down on Jalan Thamrin.

They discussed the events in Timor and Hart had assured the soft-spoken man he was certain that fighting was only occurring on the eastern side of the island. This was a complete off-the-cuff fabrication as he had no more knowledge of the real circumstances than the man sitting opposite him but felt that it wouldn't hurt to offer Albert some reassurance. Albert was not convinced. He was tempted to make contact with his step-brother and ask for his assistance but he knew this effort would be fruitless, if not dangerous.

General Nathan Seda had been adamant concerning this point. He did not want Albert to make direct contact under any circumstances and, as he had insisted, Albert would obey the General's wishes. Thinking about the man made him nervous. He swallowed too quickly, causing himself to cough. Embarrassed, he reached for a glass of water.

"What's Wanti doing today then?" Hart asked, changing the

subject as he could see that the other man was uncomfortable discussing the hostilities in his former home country. Albert replied briefly, his thoughts still clouded with the prospect of further delays due to Stephen's untimely absence. The conversation then drifted to more mundane matters.

Wanti had enjoyed the shopping as clothing was considerably cheaper in Jakarta than Melbourne. Already she had selected an array of fine lengths of material and these were being tailored for her in a shop off Blok M. All three had dined together at the beautiful Oasis restaurant in Cikini.

It was strange at the time that both men recognized the change in her mood. During the course of the evening Wanti continuously looked out through the magnificent gardens, admiring the landscape and yet, from time to time, a sadness became evident, just a shadow in her eyes; she seemed uncertain, and lost. Albert could detect that there was something different about her demeanour that evening but decided that she was just tired. As they sat together in the second and larger of the dining sections, the Batak singers entertained singing their melodious traditional songs from Sumatra.

The majority of the guests were from Embassies, the business sector and the Indonesian Government. Rumour had it that one of the Vice President had actually purchased the magnificent premises which was once the residence of the United States Marine Attaché.

Wanti wasn't sure for certain but she felt that Stephen had brought her here, once before, when they had first met. There was just something about the magnificent gardens that sparked a faint recollection from her past. In fact, it was in this very mansion that they had met and fallen in love. Wanti could no longer recognize her surroundings as they had been altered considerably to accommodate the new restaurant's requirements.

The following day, feeling obliged to entertain Stephen's wife and friend once again, Hart had introduced them to one of the expatriate drinking spots. This English-style pub and restaurant was located across the canal from the Hotel Indonesia and adjacent to the Kartika Plaza hotel. He'd told them both that it was one of Stephen's favourite haunts where he would spend considerable time with his friends and business associates. Hart didn't mention that his boss often entertained the ladies here as well for the atmosphere and cuisine were, at that time, perhaps the best the city could offer.

They had been welcomed by the pub's owner who often stood propped at the small corner section of the bar with his 'drinking team', as they were known, for the group of six or seven were rarely seen drinking elsewhere and virtually claimed that area of the bar for themselves. They would arrive around midday and take up the exact positions they had occupied the day before. Rarely did the group break up before evening and their presence helped develop most of the character, the ambiance, and the popularity that The George and Dragon enjoyed over the years.

The colourful manager, a short Cockney with considerable culinary flair, added to the pub's atmosphere, as his repartee often lifted the level of conversation and stories to new highs, pleasing the hard core drinking clientele who kept the till happily ringing away.

Although Hart enjoyed himself at the bar surrounded by a variety of foreigners throwing back drinks faster than Albert imagined possible, neither of his two guests appeared to particularly enjoy the venue. Unbeknown to the visitors and the public in general, this establishment had, in fact, been used for more than one covert rendezvous until articles appeared in the Hong Kong press suggesting that the popular pub had more than one purpose for its existence. The Russian and British Embassies were situated directly across the street and, as The George's reputation grew, so did the mystique surrounding it.

Journalists frequented its bar along with tough sounding riggers off the oil platforms. All in all the place was basically a communications centre as it was more convenient and, in most cases, more productive to arrange to meet downtown in this bar than spend hours dialling hopelessly through the local telephone exchange.

Having finished their lunch Hart excused himself. "Take the car, I have only a short walk from here," he'd offered.

The pair disappeared quickly, not content to sit around in the now noisy place, as they had friends to contact and more shopping to complete. Wanti had also made arrangements to meet with Bambang's former base Commander in Jakarta later in the afternoon as she was anxious to learn where he had been billeted at his new station. Phones were never connected to the men's single quarters and she wished desperately to contact him to see if he could get away and visit before they returned to Australia. Wanti intended using her Javanese charm to seek a special favour and ask the Colonel if there was some way her brother could be called to the officer's mess phone to speak with her. Bambang had written to her in Melbourne but she was unable to contact him prior to her departure.

They drove out to the military station and Wanti entered the building alone. Unfortunately the Garrison Commander was not available. Wanti had noticed the unusually active scene around her when shown into the officer's protocol liaison centre.

"*Sis, you indicated that you wished to see the Colonel,*" the liaison officer had asked. "*I'm sorry, but the command is very busy and it would be impossible for you to meet with him. Can I be of assistance?*"

Wanti smiled at the soldier.

She turned on the charm and the helpless little girl act that she'd found worked so well with others.

"*I really need your help, 'bang, to contact my brother in the Surabaya barracks. I haven't seen him in years and I must return to Australia in a few days. I would be very sad if I missed him during this visit.*" With which she looked up at the young officer who had now leaned across the service counter separating the staff from visitors.

"*Give me his name and rank, and I'll do what I can,*" he offered.

Wanti had quickly written the information down and passed it across the counter. Without speaking, the protocol officer took the piece of paper and disappeared through a rear door, leaving her to sit on the rotan chair staring at the photographs of the Army Chief of Staff and those of the country's leadership. A large Garuda hung on one wall directly above a number of flags which had been placed on either side of the office entrance. She waited patiently for an hour.

Wanti was aware that her brother had been posted to his regiment in Surabaya a few months before and clearly understood the difficulty she would have had in attempting to arrange such a call herself through non-military communications, as the government's telephones were impossible enough for just city calls, let alone inter province. Expecting to make such a connection for a long distance call in less than three or four hours would be naive, she knew.

Another thirty minutes had passed when the Lieutenant returned.

"Sorry, sis. All communications to the Surabaya command have been blocked for military traffic only. I've been trying to call one of my own friends down there to assist but everything seems to be very busy. I couldn't get any priority."

He observed the disappointed look on the girl's face. *"The traffic should die down a little before five if you want to wait and let me try again. Or, if you wish, I'll write down the officers mess number and you can try from the post office or from wherever you're staying."*

"Terima kasih," Wanti replied indicating that she would take the number and leave.

Albert had waited in the car. He was nervous enough just being in the military compound without having to enter one of their buildings. He didn't require any reminders of his last visit to an army establishment, the memories of which had haunted him for years before he could put the whole thing behind him. When Wanti returned to the vehicle she found him sitting in a pool of perspiration, his face quite pale. She didn't understand why he hadn't turned the air-conditioning back on if he'd been that uncomfortably hot.

She explained what had occurred inside. Understanding her disappointment at not being able to contact him directly, Albert offered to fly down with her to meet with Bambang, before returning to Australia. They discussed this alternative.

"Of course, there is still the possibility that we can make the call direct to the Surabaya station and arrange for Bambang to be called to the phone, now you have his mess number," Albert suggested.

She had agreed. They returned to the house, tired but determined and immediately started dialling the long distance number themselves. After some hours they gave up any further attempts for the day as it was then probable that the mess would have closed, having finished with the evening meal some time before.

The next morning they asked for Hart's assistance in arranging for the change in tickets and bookings. He came over from the other office and, having been told about the connection difficulties they'd experienced, instructed Stephen's secretary to keep on trying until the operators were successful.

"Mr Hart," the woman had started, entering the guest lounge

area without knocking, "the lines are going to be congested to Surabaya for some time. Especially all military installations."

"Just keep trying," he had ordered, dismissing the personal secretary brusquely.

"I don't expect we will have much luck," Hart said turning to his guest, "the military will have everything tied up what with the action in Timor right now. Even flights will be difficult if you really wish to go down that way."

The conversation then centred on the Indonesian invasion of Timor-Timur.

"The losses are outrageously high.

"According to the Indonesian Sinar Harapan paper the Armed Forces information bureau has released data suggesting that Radio Australia has deliberately exaggerated the Indonesian casualty figures to create doom and gloom in retaliation over the expulsion of one of their reporters some time before. They also challenged the Radio Australia broadcasters to identify their sources as, according to the Indonesian Minister for Information, no permits have been issued for any foreign journalists to enter the region," Albert advised, having read the *Bahasa Indonesia* language newspaper.

"That's a good point," Hart agreed, "but I doubt that their sources would be exposed. Still, it is quite amazing that they are able to report what the diplomatic community here suggest is reasonably accurate information."

"Well, one thing is for certain. This will certainly test relationships between the two countries. Australia and Indonesia will require some time to repair the considerable political damage sustained as a result of the broadcasts."

Hart considered Albert's last remark. Public reaction in Jakarta to the broadcast would, undoubtedly, affect the warm relationships Australia had enjoyed over the years with its giant neighbour. It was not inconceivable to expect student unrest and even demonstrations against the Australian Embassy. Hart felt uncomfortable with the thought of rioting students as he recalled the anti-Japanese demonstrations of some years before.

"Perhaps it would be wise for you to skip Surabaya and return to Melbourne, just in case things take a turn for the worse here?"

Albert laughed. "It is unlikely that the inhabitants of even this city would throw stones at a Timorese, Greg!"

"And besides," he continued, "Wanti would never forgive me if she missed the chance to see her brother."

"Albert, we will push the operator again for the Surabaya connection. If that is successful and you don't need to visit him or if he can't get leave to come here then, why not just return via Singapore? Chances are that you will have considerably less difficulty arranging seating from there."

Albert didn't respond.

The offended secretary returned and suggested that Hart attempt to speak to the operator himself as often a foreign voice would be enough to swing their attention and assistance in the caller's favour. He agreed. It was a good idea and he understood the reasoning. Many of the operators were looking for better paying positions with the foreign companies as most were reasonably fluent in the English language.

Hart settled beside the lounge room extension and commenced dialling. The lines to Surabaya were very busy the operator had complained, but should the *tuan* care to hold maybe she could connect as the opportunity arose. Hart had agreed, struggling to find the correct words to facilitate the conversation from his limited vocabulary, as he had the misfortune to strike one of the non-English speaking operators.

The minutes dragged on and suddenly Hart motioned Albert urgently to come to the phone.

"Contact!" he announced excitedly. "I'll call Wanti while you keep him on the line." he instructed, moving quickly to the rear of the building to alert the servants to call their *njonja* to the phone.

Wanti appeared within what seemed to be seconds, flushed with the news that they finally had Bambang on the phone. She took the receiver from Albert who also was smiling, for Wanti was obviously in high spirits. He stood beside the other man and together they watched the attractive woman as she spoke.

Hart noticed a look of concern begin to grow on Albert's face as Wanti continued to speak to the Surabaya party. Suddenly the call was finished and she replaced the receiver. Surprised, Hart looked questioningly at the two as Albert stepped forward towards the young woman. They spoke quickly and the Australian was unable to understand all that they said.

"What is it, Albert, is everything okay?" he asked.

"Maybe," he replied, "maybe."

"Wanti?" Hart questioned.

As she spoke he noticed that Albert had moved up alongside her and had taken her hand. He did not interpret the gesture for anything but for what it was, the hand of comfort for a friend in distress.

"My brother is not available as he was sent along with his division to Timor. They have no further news as all communication with Kupang must be requested through HANKAM in Jakarta."

"I am sure he will be all right, Wanti."

Hart thought quickly. Who could he call in HANKAM in Stephen's absence to assist with an inquiry?

"Look. Stephen will probably return today or, at the latest, tomorrow. I appreciate that it's difficult but if you try not to anticipate the worst and just believe that your brother is okay, then your husband will be able to use his contacts in HANKAM to reach Bambang," Hart suggested. "Stephen has many senior contacts within the military and I'm sure he could put your mind at ease as soon as he returns."

Albert continued quietly squeezing her hand reassuringly.

Wanti examined their faces as if attempting to determine the substance of what they proposed. She nodded her head slowly in acceptance. She closed her eyes and lifted her chin slightly.

"*Oh Allah!*" she whispered softly, praying for her brother's safety, "*Please watch over my Bambang!*"

Albert escorted her back to her room and instructed the houseboy to have one of the female servants stay with her.

Hart watched them leave the room. The company had the capacity to provide for its own but at this moment was powerless to do what was necessary without Stephen's presence. He knew that had Coleman been there his wife's fears could so easily be put to rest with just a few calls through his confidential military conduits. He didn't even know how to contact the man! Other than leaving messages with Coleman's private secretary should he phone, there was never any other avenue of communicating with him when he disappeared on these mysterious trips. Considering Stephen's strong contacts in the Indonesian defence establishment even these were useless without him being present to make the necessary personal calls.

Where in the hell was he?

* * * * * *

Coleman sat across the table from the General. It was difficult for him to maintain the required level of conversation as Anderson's revelations continued to remain foremost in his mind, clouding his thinking.

He let his thoughts drift watching the ferries on the other side of the harbour prepare for departure. The Kowloon side appeared busier than usual. The mid channel chop had already grown, sending spray up over the bow and back down the sides of passing vessels as they made their way through the congested sea lanes.

Seda was dressed casually in comfortable slacks and a long-sleeve beige coloured shirt, the neck open down to the third button. He sat cross-legged, holding his left ankle with both hands as he continued his discourse, only occasionally moving his right hand through the air when emphasizing a point, speaking with authority as a lecturer would to an assembly of students.

Coleman sat there and listened to the man drone on describing events as he claimed to understand them and offering his opinions as to how these evolved. He attempted to appear his old relaxed self, knowing that the man sitting in front of him was blatantly lying to him, again. And with the ease and skill of a practiced master.

Anderson had provided the most incredible insight into the powerful man he'd known all these years. Only now, Stephen realized, he hadn't really known him at all.

He continued to listen to Seda's monologue wishing he'd not come to the meeting. He should have taken more time to prepare himself. It was as if he was now swimming in one of those gas riddled oceans he'd read about when the undersea deposits suddenly aerate the surrounding waters, reducing the ocean to a wet bubble in which everything sinks and everybody drowns.

Anderson had said that the man sitting in front of him was personally responsible for the military information leaks made to the Australian media and the constant supply of military hardware to the separatists and other guerrilla groups. He had said that, without Nathan Seda, there would be no resistance of any substance within the former colony and the lives of tens of thousands of ignorant villagers would not have been wasted supporting his dreams of an independent state.

Coleman immediately scoffed. The accusations were outrageous!

"But why would he do something that stupidly dangerous?" he'd asked.

"Because he's ambitious. Because he is greedy. And because he is dangerous!" had been the reply.

"What would he stand to gain?" Coleman had probed.

"For God's sake, Stephen! Didn't we teach you anything?"

"Again," he'd insisted, "tell me again!"

"If you still have the capacity to be objective now is the time to do so. Ask yourself the question, why? The answers are clear. Wake up, man, listen to your brain and not the sound of the endless stream of dollars hitting those hidden bank accounts!"

Stephen remembered how he'd felt when that particular comment had been thrown in to shake him just that little bit more. They had really done their homework, he decided.

"Let's cut to it, John. Just explain to me. Why?"

"It's not simple. People like Seda rarely embark on anything that is so bloody complicated to start with that even they lose sight of the initial objectives as their scheming continues. Seda has followed his course with total devotion. It has taken him years of patience and dedication to achieve what he has, and right under our noses. And yours."

"You would know only too well, Stephen, just how much power he has acquired from the proceeds generated by the military contracts the two of you have enjoyed, awarded to your company year after year with his backing, the staggering amounts of commissions remaining offshore to fund his covert activities. In your case, your greed and ego sent you on a property hunt and the quest for the good life of the high-flyers. You were, sorry are, successful but nowhere near as competent as Seda. For the General, every penny he squirreled away was directed towards achieving his ultimate goal. Rebellion. Rebellion in East Timor and, hopefully, an amalgamation of both Timors under one flag. And quite possibly, one leader."

"From your tone it sounds as if you're actually proud of him," Coleman accused.

The older man had smiled as he responded. "Admire, Stephen, admire. When you consider that when he inherited the mantle from Sudomo the Indonesian Intelligence Services were practically a joke by our standards. Within just a few years he built an enormous network of agents and information sources even we would be pleased to have access to, today."

"Remember, Stephen," he had continued, now enjoying his description of the Timorese's dark activities, "He had to develop a secure Intelligence section while consolidating his own position within the country's powerful hierarchy. It wasn't easy, being outside the Javanese clique and all that, but he did it."

Coleman was surprised at Anderson's obvious admiration for the subject of their meeting.

"When the Apodeti first became a political force in East Timor very few knew that it was, in fact, an operational arm of the Indonesian military, under the direct control of BAKIN. We all know who controls that august body, don't we?" Anderson continued, rhetorically.

"This provided the man with a direct source of information from the colony. As the Senior Intelligence Director he also had the authority to censor information, question its reliability, control its entire flow in the dissemination process to other ABRI arms and, in short, become its puppeteer."

"What makes him such an outstanding and manipulative bugger is the fact that while he was providing his own Armed Forces with information gleaned from the *Operasi Komodo, Apodeti* and other sources, he also briefed the FRETILIN providing them with a continuous flow of intelligence of such import they were able to ensconce themselves extremely quickly as a power base within the disputed territory."

"Then, of course, we come to the arms shipments to which you were a party. I am still not convinced that you are so naive, Stephen, that you failed to identify what was really happening but elected to go along because of the enormous amount of wealth it was producing for you. For the time being let's just say that you have the benefit of the doubt and we'll reserve judgment until later."

Anderson went in harder. "You have compromised almost every ideal I believed you had. You are responsible for permitting the flow of not only substantial shipments of arms to what is potentially an enemy of the Commonwealth of Australia and its allies, but also you should consider the number of dead and wounded who represent the harvest of those weapons."

Stephen had sat quietly. Numbed by the revelations being made to him. If, in fact, what Anderson had said could be substantiated then he recognized that the ramifications of his involvement with the shipments would, undoubtedly, result in hostile action being taken against him. And at any time.

Stephen's first reactions had been to immediately discount everything that the Australian Intelligence Chief had said. Not only did it border on the absurd and ridiculous but it offended his own intellect. Anderson was expecting him to accept whatever he was told, he thought, without question, as the Director was not accustomed to having others challenge the authenticity of his statements. And his lies!

When Stephen had scoffed at the suggestions, Anderson had produced irrefutable evidence of the General's role in providing the journalists with sensitive military information, copies of communications between BAKIN and East Timor agents (Coleman didn't need to guess how he'd obtained those!) and copies also of bills-of-lading which he knew were related to consignments that he himself had arranged through Hong Kong. Only the annotated destinations were questionable. Stephen knew that the latter could have been falsified by anyone but, somehow, he just sensed that there was more to the documents than what could be assumed from a casual glance.

It was still difficult to accept. Tens of thousands of Indonesians and Timorese now lay dead, their corpses rotting in the fields of Timor partly as a result of his ignorance and, as they sat calmly discussing his position in terms of his own involvement, Coleman realized, for the first time, just how dangerous both Anderson and Seda had become to his own well being. And to each other.

It was complicated. Had the Australians accepted the military information and permitted its deliberate release? In so doing they would have not only condoned the slaughter of the Indonesians but actually assisted in the execution of the General's plan purely for his substantial monetary gain! Did Anderson and others in similar positions of power set a trap for the General in order to hook him for the future, just keeping him on line until they could see which way events would develop?

Or was it the other way around? Had Seda deliberately provided the separatist forces in Timor the opportunity as Anderson
had suggested in order to orchestrate his own rise to power in the
former colony?

Why hadn't the Australians gone to the Indonesians with this
information and immediately ingratiated themselves by exposing
the General?

God! he thought, rubbing his throbbing temples to ease a split-
ting ache, it was either all a load or crap or really was down in the
hole so fucking deep they would need a crane to drag him out of
the shit he was in!

"Where do we go from here then?" his voice betrayed fatigue.

"That's up to you now Stephen."

The brief and enigmatic answer didn't help. He wanted to stand
up and shout at the man in front of him, the other jet-lagged passengers, Seda, the world, everyone, for being unfair, for trying to
destroy him and undo everything he'd built.

At that moment he hated Anderson more than even he thought
possible. The man had enjoyed bringing him the news. And the
ultimatum. Ah, yes, he remembered. The ultimatum.

And, as he now sat in the room with the man who had created
this incredible quagmire of international intrigue involving gun-
running, terrorism and subversive support for revolution against
his own country, he knew that he would never survive to enjoy the
fruits of his involvement in these activities should the General became aware of his partner's recently acquired knowledge as to the
real purpose of the company's operations.

On the other hand his former intelligence associates could just
as easily place his name on the *'unfriendlies list'* and it would only
be a matter of time before he, too, would need to go into hiding or
cooperate with them.

He turned his head slightly, looking at the General.

How did you manage to source all of that additional equipment?
he wondered. Who has been assisting this man with the enormous
amount of detail required to transfer shipments, re-box the supplies, change documentation and maintain the liaison necessary
for such covert activities?'

The task was so unbelievably enormous Stephen had considerable difficulty in accepting that the information was indeed accurate.

He continued to rerun the details through his mind. It was clear that Anderson, and therefore others, had information — no, he corrected, proof — of his relationship with the General and their activities relating to the supply of weapons to the Indonesian Armed Forces. So far, he had not committed any offence except, perhaps, from the social aspects of being an arms supplier.

That Seda was responsible for the diversion of these shipments to the separatist forces in Timor played heavily on his mind. The accusations of Seda's involvement in the deliberate release of classified information relating to his own defence forces' troop movements had him baffled. Why would they fabricate such a story if it was not their intention to expose his activities, sending him into immediate disgrace and, most likely, prison?

Anderson had revealed what the intelligence services had discovered regarding Nathan Seda's true allegiances, or so they said. The chances were, he thought, that they had it all arse up again, as they had often misread what was happening in the past. And this might just be a simple case of the Intelligence Agencies screwing up again. Or overreacting.

Maybe Seda believed that the information leaks would make it appear as if the FRETILIN forces had the upper hand in the war? This would justify the Indonesian invasion and a more concentrated involvement by the Indonesian Military. If that had been his motive then, according to the latest casualty statistics, his strategy was successful.

Coleman had questioned the Australian Government's motives in permitting the broadcasts. The Intelligence Chief had smiled thinly and slowly outlined the government's political position. Australia was faced with the possibility of the creation of a hostile nation sitting on its doorstep. The Americans and Australians anticipated the probability of United Nations support for the fledgling nation which would permit Communist forces to gain control. There was no doubt that the United Nations would also condemn the Indonesian invasion.

The Americans and Australians believed that the Indonesian annexation was, in fact, the more acceptable solution but could not openly support the expansionist move. Should the FRETILIN forces win several decisive battles against the superior number of Indonesian troops then there was a distinct possibility that they would be carried away with their successes and reverse the role in Timor by crossing into the Indonesian territory threatening regional security.

As satellite intelligence proved beyond doubt that FRETILIN had support of the Eastern Bloc and there was proof of Cuban involvement then, it was suggested, Indonesia should have the right to defend itself from the aggressor. Under these circumstances, Australia could play an immediate role, the Americans could recommence military support and, more importantly, the Indonesians could legitimately claim the necessity to re-invade the former colony to secure its own borders. International support would follow.

The FRETILIN movement would be crushed and the threat of medium range missiles threatening Australia's security would disappear. And more importantly, the Americans would maintain their use of the Ombai-Wetar Straits.

"What the hell do they have to do with all of this?" he'd asked.

"You've been out of the mainstream of intelligence flow for some years and would have no current idea of what really is happening in the real world Stephen," Anderson had replied, not insultingly, "but basically the Yanks desperately need to maintain their use of the straits. This is why the American navy had insisted that the Pentagon concoct some red herring to distract others from the identifying their operational use of the waters there.

The Pentagon had used the threat of the newly occupied and former South Vietnam in relation to its potential capacity to assist the Soviets expand their sphere of influence in the immediate region. The red herring was the threat of Russian built IL-28s which they'd given to the Communist Vietnamese well before the fall of Saigon but had eventually found their way down to the south and within striking distance of the gas deposits off Natuna Island.

The story worked because the oil-hungry cartels soon used their powerful lobby to ensure that not just Natuna but all future and existing concessions under production sharing contracts within Indonesia would enjoy the protection of American military equipment. This would give Australia a de facto first line of defence without the crippling cost of supporting such a strategy.

East Timor's real significance to America's global strategy lies to the north of the island in the Ombai-Wetar Straits, which are exceptionally deep and through which nuclear submarines can travel undetected in their passage from the Pacific to the Indian Ocean. These straits remain crucial to the United States Navy as should this route be denied to them as the result of Timor's becoming Communist or fall under the expanding influence of the Soviets, the cost in terms of strategic positioning would be disastrous. An additional eight days steaming would be required for a concealed submarine journey between the two oceans via the alternative Lombok or Sunda Straits.

"Now perhaps you will understand their reluctance to accept any Marxist authority over the former colony as the American administration requires an acceptable conclusion to the hostilities in East Timor to protect their own strategic interests."

The concept was Machiavellian and Coleman understood how it would appeal to the politicians and military chiefs. He wondered just how many more Indonesians would die in the poverty stricken island before a halt would be called to the senseless killing.

Seda was still talking. Coleman listened, occasionally murmuring a response. The meeting concluded.

"*I will be returning directly to Jakarta, Stephen. Is there anything else you wish to go over now while we have the opportunity?*" the General had asked.

"*No. I don't believe so, Pak. Not at this time,*" he replied, while thinking, '*and perhaps not later, either.*'

"*Have you been to the bank yet?*" he asked, grinning at the suggestion. He knew that Stephen always went to the bank to check his deposits as soon as soon as he arrived in Hong Kong.

Umar had told him.

"*Yes,*" he answered, "*all is in order there.*" He remembered that he had already decided to change most of his accounts quickly due to the potential change in circumstances. He'd do it first thing tomorrow, he thought.

But not before sitting down and working out his future and evaluating the damage that was imminent to his company operations. Stephen needed time to get his head straight. He decided to slip across on the ferry to Macau. So much was suddenly happening in his life he needed to release some of the pressure and consider his options. Obviously, his future with the General looked nebulous and, for the first time since meeting with Anderson on the flight, Stephen Coleman was concerned for his life. Once he'd returned to his own room in the hotel Stephen phoned Mister Lim and asked if Angelique was available.

He needed to clear his mind. And think.

* * * * * *

Greg Hart was not impressed with the call from Stephen. He had been awakened at some ungodly hour and Coleman, true to his past behaviour, had imparted little information and yet had managed to issue instructions ranging across his own personal spectrum from financial matters to reminding his assistant to send his personal secretary's birthday gift. Everything, in fact, except how to resolve his wife's dilemma.

During the early morning telephone conversation Hart had raised the problem. Wanti's brother was part of the contingent that had been sent to Timor and she was desperate to contact him. Latest reports relating to the invasion were not looking good and she looked very worried, he'd told Coleman.

"She needs to speak to him, Stephen," he'd said, still groggy from the two hours sleep. "Why don't you give me some numbers and I'll phone HANKAM early in the morning. You know they'll bend over backwards when I tell them it's for you."

Coleman had been sharp and uncharacteristically blunt. "Do nothing until I return," he ordered.

"But Stephen, I know this may be a little out of my jurisdiction but your wife is frantic. Couldn't you make a few calls from wherever you are and then let her know?"

"Butt out, Greg!" Coleman snapped. "I'll do what is necessary, just leave it alone. Okay?"

"Okay," Hart acquiesced. He thought Coleman sounded a little drunk.

"Fine. I will be back in a day or so. Just hold the fort."

Hart had replaced the receiver and cursed the caller for his attitude. He lay in bed thinking about the problem and his own complicated life, and how he was neither one nor the other, referring to his current employment and his other masters. They would leave him alone for months on end and then, suddenly, out of the blue they would contact him with what were mostly menial tasks. He'd been debriefed several times regarding the company operations and had passed whatever information he managed to access from the records but this was not what they were looking for, he could tell, from their bored expressions each time he'd made his report.

Coleman played his game close to the chest, Hart knew. It was impossible to follow his trail as the overseas trips severed all connection to his movements and dealings, making Hart's task irritatingly counter productive, as he dedicated so much of his time endeavouring to resolve the enigma surrounding these trips, without any real results.

Several more hours passed. He looked at the bedside clock. It was almost five o'clock. Unable to sleep he showered and decided to take Albert and Wanti out for a Dim Sum breakfast at the Blue Ocean which operated as a non stop cabaret night club and restaurant, catering to the players who lived for the late nights, often carrying on until the sun demanded that others attend their offices while this small section of the community disobeyed the clock.

The steamed breakfasts were renowned for their flavour, the dishes carried on small trays by waiters from table to table as the round bamboo baskets containing the delicacies were snatched off the trays by the hungry guests.

Hart had to steer himself from his house to Jalan Cik Ditiro where Wanti and Albert stayed as his own driver wasn't due to start work for another hour. He arrived at the premises still too early to awaken anyone. The security personnel recognized Hart and opened the outside security gate permitting the car to enter before locking the sliding steel barrier again from behind.

He entered the office through the servants' access and went about checking the main office for incoming telex communications. There was one for Stephen to contact a supplier in Germany and several other mundane messages providing lists of available military equipment in France. And one incongruous request which surprised and baffled Hart.

The three lined message was so short and innocuous in content that, at first, Hart had missed the message completely as the telex pages had run together, causing the type to slip.

He reread the text. In spite of the hour he lifted the telephone receiver and dialled the number designated in the return confirmation advice. The number rang for several minutes before a tired and irritable voice barked into the instrument. Startled, Hart replaced the phone immediately. Then he reread the message for a third time.

Why, he thought, would Stephen Coleman be receiving communications from them? Hart stared at the page. He was not to know that the message in his hands should, in fact, have been sent to the direct number on the machine still locked upstairs in the private rooms.

There was no doubt that it was addressed to Coleman. The question was, what was Stephen Coleman doing arranging meetings with the *Badan Koordinasi Intelijen Indonesia*, Indonesia's Central Intelligence Agency?

He decided to forgo the breakfast and instead, placing the telex in his wallet, Hart left the office advising the houseboy that he would return later in the morning.

The old servant mumbled and went about his mundane chores. The *tuans* would come and go as they pleased. He didn't mind. He never pried into other's affairs. Life was difficult enough without the burden of responsibility which often came with the knowledge of someone else's problems.

* * * * * *

Far away, or at least what Sukardi, the ageing houseboy, might have considered to be far away, casualty lists were on the wire and being registered in the Ministry of Defence's Jalan Merdeka offices as the names spewed forth from the archaic communications machine. Seventh on the list on the first page of KIA's was the name, rank and serial number of the young Javanese Acting Captain who, in what was another lifetime, once laughed and played with a little girl in the distant village of Kampung Semawi. A little girl who had grown up to finally escape the horrors of their past and who now slept quietly in the bedroom above Coleman's office.

A simple and unassuming servant, unaware of the enormity of events unfolding around him, Sukardi cleaned and prepared Stephen's household for the coming day.

As there was no address registered on file for the dead Captain's next-of-kin, details as to his demise were passed to his regimental headquarters in Surabaya. There the information remained until later in the day when, having read the lists posted on the information board for all to read, the officer of the day who had spoken to the dead Captain's sister just a few days before, remembered that she was in Jakarta. He returned to his office and went in search of the telephone number he'd noted when Wanti had called.

Coleman's personal secretary had received the call and informed Hart. She also asked to speak privately with Albert, who accepted the news calmly, thanking the embarrassed worker for her consideration in passing the unfortunate news to him rather than directly to the dead officer's sister.

He discussed Wanti's condition with Hart. They agreed to call a doctor to sedate her, if possible before breaking the news, considering her previous reactions to shock. Albert agreed and Hart sent the secretary out to request assistance from one of the consulting doctors in the Cikini hospital.

An hour later she returned with the doctor who, by that time, had been briefed as to Wanti's condition, her previous attacks and the long periods of convalescence required as a result of her trauma suffered during the anti-Japanese riots. Albert had asked Wanti to go upstairs to her room as he wished to speak privately with her. Sensing that something was wrong, Wanti searched Albert's eyes for some indication of what was worrying him.

When the doctor entered the bedroom she knew immediately that Bambang was dead. She had sensed it the moment she had heard that he had gone to Timor to fight.

"*No, Tuhan, no!*" Wanti called, struggling as she resisted the needle being inserted into her arm. As she froze, her features contorted with shock, the grotesque ugliness of her expression reflected the trauma her brain endured while fighting to cope with the realization of her brother's death.

The doctor immediately administered a second sedative but the shock was too severe. There was nothing they could do for her. Her body remained locked in a catatonic seizure. Her reaction to the news of Bambang's death had blasted her away.

Throughout the night, Albert sat holding her hand, crying softly until tears ceased to flow. He talked to her, sang soft chants which suddenly, blessedly, returned to him for the first time since his childhood as he stroked her arms and offered God his own life in exchange for hers. He rocked gently backwards and forwards humming a distant melody which had haunted his soul from a time he could barely remember, a time when a warm and loving father had taken him by the hand down to the fishing village and held him close and kept him safe.

He spoke to Wanti as she lay there, telling her of the warmth of the sun, the cool winds of the early evening and the soft sweet fragrances of the flowers in the mountains. He kissed her cheeks and, as he did so, his tears fell onto her face as evidence of his love for the beautiful woman whose heart and mind had been taken by some unseen spirit and dashed against the walls of despair.

Wanti breathed slowly, peacefully, unaware of the words being softly whispered as her brain had now severed all links with the real world. Albert Seda stroked her hair, her hand and gently touched the soft colourless cheeks, refusing to acknowledge the distorted features that stared straight back up at him. The servants attempted to have him leave her side, to rest, but he ignored their efforts.

Now, for the first time, they understood. Albert refused to leave her. He had to stay with Wanti, she needed him now, more than ever.

Throughout the following day he remained by her side. He could see from the cruel and twisted ugliness that the muscle spasms had produced where before there had been a beautiful smile, that she was lost. There would be little hope, he knew, that she would recover. As she lay calmly Albert decided that he had no choice but to return immediately to Australia. Arrangements had been made. Hart had helped.

The following day Coleman unexpectedly returned, surprised at the cool reception he received upon arrival at his home.

Hart, angered by the events of the previous day, marched unannounced into his Coleman's office and slammed a letter down in front of the surprised man. "That's my resignation, you bastard!"

Staggered by the vitriolic attack, Stephen looked up at the man and, stunned by the outburst, merely said, "What the hell? A simple good morning or hello would have been sufficient!"

"What you did is unforgivable, Coleman," he started, using Stephen's surname to emphasize his contempt, "and the whole bloody community will know about it if I have my way. You're a fucking arsehole!"

"Greg, wh.? " he started.

"All you had to do was phone your own bloody wife once and maybe you could have prevented all of this!" he yelled unreasonably, half believing his own outburst, knowing also that he'd been given the perfect excuse to pull out, as instructed and withdraw from the company's activities before it sucked him down also into the incredible mess only his superiors understood.

He slammed the desk with his hand confirming to all who had heard the outburst within the office that the *tuans* were deep in argument.

The embarrassed staff lowered their heads quickly, suddenly engrossed in whatever they were doing when the argument had broken out between the two. They had no training in how to handle these predicaments and, identifying the delicacy of the situation, the secretary put her finger to her lips and gestured with her other hand for them to depart silently, as it was already close to the end of office hours anyway.

"Hold it!" Coleman yelled. "What the hell are you talking about?"

"Jesus, mate, you're good!"

"Again, Greg, what the hell are you carrying on about?"

"You know bloody goddamn well what I'm talking about!"

"What?" Coleman yelled, so loud that the servants heard the demand right through the office and through to their quarters. "Tell me for Chrissakes, man, fucking what?"

"Your wife, damn it man, your wife!"

Suddenly Stephen realized that he had no idea what was going on even in his own home.

Ignoring Hart, he ran quickly through the building and up the steps to his room, now for the first time, occupied by Wanti.

There he found Albert, sitting alongside the woman whom he knew was his wife, but now wore the mask of a stranger.

"What happened?" he demanded, shocked to see her condition.

Albert rose and escorted Stephen from the room.

"*Bambang's dead, Mas!*" and immediately Stephen understood.

He stood silently with the other man not knowing what to do. He had no power of healing and knew, more than everyone else, just how much pain this man would now have to suffer as Wanti lay in her own world, protected by some intricate trigger mechanism inside her head, distancing her from reality and the pain of living.

The following day Albert asked his permission to take her home. Sadly, Stephen agreed. He asked his staff to make the arrangements and seats were booked for the following day. It seemed that everyone in Jakarta suddenly knew of her demise. And was sympathetic to her condition. The two men only spoke when necessary and it was clear to Stephen that he was to carry the blame for the tragic events surrounding his wife's collapse. The subject of the divorce was not raised again.

* * * * * *

On the day of Albert and Wanti's departure Hart left the company. Stephen didn't really mind. But then again, Stephen didn't know that Hart had been instructed to do so as the company appeared to be heading for a confrontation with the military and his other masters wanted him well out of the way when this happened.

Stephen couldn't understand why he was being blamed for Wanti's condition. Bambang's death certainly had nothing whatsoever to do with him. He knew that even had he called at the time there was no guarantee that this could have resulted in the soldier not being killed. Hart never did advise Stephen of the telex.

Suddenly everything started to change drastically for Coleman. His world was turning inside-out and he did not know what he could do to prevent or correct what was happening to him. Of one thing he was certain. Timor was a much greater problem for him than Anderson had suggested. He could lose everything. Even his life! He still wondered why the Australians had not just exposed the General.

There had to be another agenda. One in which he was to play a role without knowing who all the other participants were to be. A dangerous game no doubt, he guessed, considering he was now sitting squeezed between two highly skilled professionals, neither of whom would have any compunction in ordering his permanent removal should they deem such action necessary to their respective causes.

The General had access to considerable funds and no doubt had successfully compromised more than one of his peers throughout his years climbing to the powerful position he now held. Stephen remembered the veiled threat made when they first embarked on their journey together, forming the alliance which had built an empire for each of them. An empire that would soon come crashing down if he did not now proceed with extreme caution with every move he made.

Maybe a few months away in Europe or Canada would be a wise decision at this time, he thought.

He needed time to rearrange his activities but he knew that time was running out and there was a distinct possibility that he would be unable to extricate himself from the mess in which he was slowly drowning, and had been for some considerable time, without even being aware of it.

He considered what the outcome would be should the General and FRETILIN react as predicted and retaliate, crossing over into the Indonesian half of Timor, creating the opportunity everyone appeared to support. This would be most unlikely, Stephen decided, as it would result in yet a further invasion of such a scale that all separatist forces would be totally destroyed once and for all! Alternatively, should Seda successfully secure an independent state for FRETILIN, did he see himself as the country's first leader? Its first President? And would the Indonesians sanction a man who had betrayed them to sit as the head of state in the neighbouring country? Coleman thought this through. Actually, knowing the General as well as he did, he knew it was unlikely that he would permit Cubans or any other alien group to control his military if he were to gain power. Should this be the case then it would surely follow that Timor could, in fact, become a reasonable, albeit poor, democracy in its own right. And Coleman would benefit from the relationship.

It dawned on him that such a scenario would also benefit the Australians and perhaps the other and smaller neighbouring states who were edgy about the powerful Moslem country dictating regional foreign policies. The Americans would rest easy knowing that their nuclear submarines could pass unhindered by the Soviets.

Was this is the strategy Anderson wanted to see in place?

Stephen concluded that this made a whole lot more sense than the other possibilities and would explain why ASIS had not exposed the General and perhaps even why they had moved back into his life to manipulate events even more from the sidelines.

He decided he should just wait for a few more weeks to see how it all developed. After all, according to the press, the fighting could continue for some time and that could only be good for their business. He would stay around for a few more weeks and monitor his relationship with Seda. Should the signs be positive he would maintain the status quo and work his way through the problems.

Feeling once again in reasonable control of the situation he decided to delay acting on Anderson's demands until he'd had enough time to further review the complicated mess. Coleman concluded that, short of nuclear weapons being introduced into the conflict, little else could change the current position of the warring parties. High casualty figures would mean support for Indonesia's invasion would deteriorate both domestically and internationally.

General Nathan Seda appeared to be heading towards the successful realization of his dream. An independent Timor.

Or, at least, an independent East Timor!

THE TIMOR MAN

Chapter 17

Jakarta — Timor-Timur

Seda arrived early for this vital meeting. He noticed that the priority files he had ordered to be circulated to the heads of each contributing department in preparation for this discussion were in place. They were set out ready for the head of OPSUS at his place opposite Seda. There were seven seats prepared, he counted, all with the customary blotting pads nobody ever used as they only carried ballpens. He made a mental note. No more blotting pads.

Only three of the powerful generals had arrived as Seda entered the well-guarded room. Military police armed with carbines stood watch at the door. He knew that they wouldn't be enough should someone really want to get in and blow them all away. Window dressing. Just window dressing, he thought.

The session had been called by the army's Chief of Staff. He was angry. His men were being annihilated and he found this to be personally humiliating. He was looking for a scapegoat and expected to have one.

Seda was ready. The meeting commenced, not with all present sitting down and formally being addressed as one would expect of such powerful men called to discuss the nation's security, but more on an unhurried and familiar basis, and one with which they were more accustomed. As the generals waddled into the chamber and casually took their chairs while already discussing the sensitive problems with each other Seda noticed that the Airforce Chief of Staff had moved his position up next to the Lieutenant General. He was surprised.

"Ready, gentlemen?" the army Chief commenced, not really caring whether they were or not. He did not enjoy having to brief the other services and particularly disliked the intelligence heads being

present. They always kept something back, in reserve for themselves, he believed.

"*The President has asked me to consider withdrawing our forces from Tim-Tim,*" he started, observing the startled faces of the most powerful men in the country outside the presidential household. "*Bapak has been emphatic in his request that as he did not wish to have the invasion bring the new Five Year Development Program's overseas funding into contention then, as international opinion seems to be shifting, he has directed me, us, to consider the ramifications of a withdrawal from the province.*"

Seda listened, transfixed on the tubby little General's mouth, not believing what he was hearing. A withdrawal!

Immediately there were cries of *tidak! tidak! no!* from the other generals, as that was what was expected of them. In reality most didn't care too much one way or another as none had been successful in enjoying any financial gain to date, from the buildup and then the invasion, causing considerable discussion and concern with their Chinese financiers.

All those present were aware that the President really wanted to have East Timor annexed and over with as quickly as possible while his team of civilian technocrats wooed the World Bank and International Monetary Fund in their ongoing attempts to source the much needed capital required to meet the development programs already in place.

It was an incredible juggling act and a new exercise in international diplomacy. They knew, of course, that the Americans would support them due to the fall of Saigon the year before, and the presence of Leftist guerrillas always generated sufficient congressional support when lobbying for additional military hardware. Only now they had failed to produce any real results, placing the President in a difficult and indecisive mood. He needed time to consider all his options. There were none present who would object, since the President enjoyed the popular support of the people and of rank and file members of the infant political parties.

The President wanted the military to go in quickly, fix the problem and then hold the annexed country until such time as the United States gave them the nod to hold yet another plebiscite, such as they had carried out in 1969 in West New Guinea.

But for some reason, this time it wasn't as easy as they had expected. The Indonesians could not understand why the Americans were really so interested given that they already held the majority of the oil and gas concessions and even they knew that Vietnam was no real threat to their northern islands. There just had to be something else. And then there was these Australians who always seemed to run hot and cold. Their own Prime Minister made the effort to visit informally with the Soeharto in Central Java, even spending quiet time together in the mystical cave while they discussed the Timor issue. The Australian Head of State had emphatically given his country's undertaking to support a united Timor, even suggesting that it should be under Indonesian control. Then, suddenly, while their troops were preparing to cross the border *en masse*, the man was replaced by his opponent! It was really very difficult to understand how these Western nations managed to survive with no frequent leadership changes, they all agreed.

The threat of an independent hostile state strategically positioned such as Timor remained a major issue throughout the region. The Indonesians sensed that they had international support but didn't know how to go about securing it publicly.

"*Pak General*," Seda said, as all eyes concentrated on the Timorese. Apart from the Sumatran, all of the others were Javanese. "*Pak General, I believe that we can win this action quickly now that we have the new American Bronco aircraft arriving next month. These machines were designed specifically for counter insurgency attacks and I am convinced,*" he said, *emphasizing the point and looking directly at the Airforce Chief,* "*that once these aircraft and their support teams have been deployed then resistance will diminish dramatically!*"

"*That still won't finish the problem on the ground, General.*" The Admiral felt he had to offer an opinion as only too often the Navy was left out of these discussions. Hadn't his ships already proven themselves in the first instance by bombarding the target areas in preparation for the assaults?

He watched the others. The Navy had done poorly with recent budgetary considerations and knew that he must guard against the army and airforce gobbling up all of the funds. After all, without any supply or maintenance contracts, how would he live?

The Army Chief of Staff looked smugly towards the Admiral, thinking *What would he know?*

The piggy-faced man had the education of a peasant farmer and only enjoyed his position because almost all of his superiors had either died of old age or had disappeared due to their involvement in the communist push to take over the country. The Army General ignored the statement.

The discussion continued for no more than fifteen minutes and, as it was approaching the mid-morning prayer period which the majority of them would often use as an excuse to leave whatever meeting they may be uncomfortably locked into, the Army Chief procrastinated no further.

"*I believe what the President is looking for is a firm commitment from us that we will finish the job quickly and without any further embarrassment.*" He looked around the table knowing that, whatever he said, they would agree. It was called consensus. He knew that.

"*I agree with you Pak,*" the OPSUS General said, quite loudly.

"*So do I,*" called another. Then another, until each and every member in the room had confirmed what he had known all along, that they would react like sheep.

The four-star General observed them all. Placing his arms on the table as he clenched his fists together, he played the role of the second most powerful man in the country.

"*This will not be like before. The Bapak has insisted that we use all of our numbers and weaponry. Should we disgrace the country it would be unlikely that the President would be at all forgiving. We must not fail!*" And, as he let the words hang threateningly in the air, the General rose leaving his file for others to collect and left before any further discussion could take place.

The Intelligence Chief stayed long enough to be seen to be a cohesive part of what had just occurred in the briefing, then left with the others, ensuring that none of the sensitive files had been left for the inquisitive and talkative clerks or aides to read.

Seda considered the commitment he'd made. The Bronco aircraft would be ready providing they could take delivery before too much more pressure was placed on the Armed Forces Standing Committee in Washington to cancel the dead. He now wanted the Indonesian Airforce to have the sophisticated aircraft as it would make the FRETILIN resistance that much more admirable in the eyes of the world, knowing that the simple people of such a small island fought bravely against such tremendous odds. Their resources were extremely limited against the American-manufactured weaponry. Seda was excited when the army suppliers had offered the new ground-to-air missiles suitable for individual soldiers to carry. The problem was that the product was American and difficult to source but he knew he had to have these deadly weapons for his separist fighters.

Also, he knew, delivery and repositioning were entirely different considerations. He estimated that it would require at least six more months before the AURI pilots were able to demonstrate the incredible capacity of the aerial killing machines soon to be placed in their hands.

The Rockwell Broncos were a mass-produced aircraft which the Americans had tested for some years and used successfully in their marine forces. It was a superb lightly armed reconnaissance airplane designed specifically for counter-insurgency missions and suited the Indonesian Airforce's requirements perfectly in targeting the FRETILIN forces. With the additional modifications these sixteen aircraft would undergo, they could be utilized at night for forward air control and strike designation purposes.

Seda had also orchestrated to have the manufacturers add further modifications at tremendous expense to AURI. These would permit the aircraft's stabilized night periscopic sights, which were coupled with a laser rangefinder and target illuminator, to act in tandem with another Bronco permitting direct attack or illumination of a target. He also believed it would be too sophisticated for the pilots' missions in Timor. And even if they did finally master the aircraft successfully over Timor's rugged terrain they would always be given sufficient advance warning of flight missions. With a little luck the ground forces would be given the opportunity to destroy two aircraft with just one missile.

Seda knew that there would be a price to pay. He also knew that had not his *kongsi* with Stephen become directly involved in the aircraft sales then others would have, costing their company millions of dollars in lost commissions and influence over sourcing the country's armaments acquisition program. Seda was pragmatic enough to accept that Indonesia would purchase these aircraft from someone as being inevitable and, why not ensure that he personally benefited financially from the squadron acquisition? At least he could continue to monitor what was really taking place offshore whenever deals were being struck with the suppliers and manufacturers' agents. He would often arrange for senior officers in the other services to be invited overseas where they would receive substantial remuneration for their support in recommending the equipment Stephen's company represented.

Seda thought about the numerous trips made by some of those present at the morning's meeting. It had really been so simple as they had been so greedy. Agent's commissions on aircraft sales rarely ran over five per cent of the purchase price. The real money lay in the spare parts which were loaded by over thirty and up to forty percent of the contract value and would apply to all ongoing spare parts purchases made by the client which, in this case, was the government's military. Even he had not realized the incredible flow of funds these contracts would generate until the company had entered its third year of operation and he'd spent three days in Seoul with Stephen going over the records together.

He had to admit, his partner had done well. By securing the agencies for the armaments and other weaponry required by not just the armed forces but also the police, they had cornered the majority of the HANKAM supply contracts.

They had been careful to permit a number of the less lucrative deals go to influential parties. Seda had discussed ways and means of spreading the large number of contracts over a range of acceptable suppliers to avoid suspicion and so Stephen had cleverly organized a number of separate corporate entities registered in what he'd explained were tax havens, to overcome the frequency of their own company's name appearing as the successful bidder for the lucrative deals. At first he was unwilling to agree with the procedures initiated by his partner. The complicated arrangements were bewildering to him and he believed that he would lose control of his own funds, giving Stephen far too much information and power over his activities.

They had taken a week away from Jakarta and met in Hong Kong first where it was all explained to his satisfaction. Then it had been necessary for them to continue on to Luxembourg where they established individual numbered accounts and then London from where they had purchased several already established shelf companies registered in the Channel Islands. By the time they had visited Panama, Seda's head was swimming with detail, but at least he felt secure and confident with the complicated arrangements made with the respective agents and nominee directors who were to act for them in the future.

Since that time Seda had changed most of his offshore structures, having developed considerable knowledge of how the system worked, as he felt that the time would come when it would be better that even his partner not know where he held his accounts. His golden hoard.

The General pondered the Indonesian military buildup. He wasn't too sure about the French. They had become close to the Airforce Chief and he believed that they would offer to build, or at least assemble their Puma helicopters under license in Bandung. He could see no way of benefiting from that exercise. The choppers would be far more dangerous to the FRETILIN forces as these would no doubt be utilized by Indonesian forces for rapid troop movements across the mountainous terrain.

Next would be the purchase of the Skyhawks. These contracts would be lucrative while the aircraft themselves would be very demanding of their newly trained pilots. Both squadrons had been approved by the Americans under the US Department of Defence Military Sales Program, as were the Broncos. These were state of the art aircraft and he knew that it would be best for the separatist forces that the question of Independence be resolved before the A-4 Skyhawks were delivered as these attack bombers were to be armed with air-to-surface Sidewinder missiles, Bullpups and an array of ground attack guns which could destroy all of his ground support in a very limited time. It would all be too much for his poorly equipped allies.

Day by day, even against the tremendous odds with which they were faced, FRETILIN's political and military strength had continued to improve. The majority of East Timorese now fell in behind the party's village programs where they had won considerable support away from the UDT. Their brave resistance against superior numbers of well-armed Indonesian combat troops had increased their following threefold in less than a few months swelling their ranks beyond expectation.

The General knew that it was imperative that the East Timorese become one united force and under one leader if they were to succeed. The fractured policies of the fledgling political parties confused more than united his people. He hoped that as FRETILIN had put its former ASDT mantle aside and was winning so much support, that there would soon be only one major political and military force to lead his country to its rightful destiny.

Seda considered Indonesia's unofficial political arm in East Timor, Apodeti and felt reasonably confident that whatever these sympathizers and agents had actually been able to achieve had not resulted in any real threat to his people. Whatever military information had been disseminated to the Indonesian commands he had also given to FRETILIN intelligence. Apodeti's following was restricted to a few hundred as everyone knew that they supported Indonesia's annexation only because of their close financial ties to prominent Jakarta businessmen. At worst, he believed, they would continue to act as a fifth column although, from the reports he'd examined which had passed over his desk, they were beginning to acquire some small arms supplies from across the border. He would put an end to that!

Taking the files and placing them in his briefcase, a recent present from his mistress in Tebet, Seda left the Ministry of Defence building and headed directly to his own. This was going to be one hell of a year, he thought, as the driver pushed through the heavy traffic flow along Jalan Thamrin and into Jenderal Sudirman. He reflected on the recent visit to Hong Kong, where he and Stephen had discussed the invasion and what it would mean to their *kongsi* arrangement.

"*Shall we close it down?*" the Australian had asked.

"*Why?*" Seda had replied, surprised at the suggestion. "*This could only mean further opportunities!*"

"*But the ABRI forces will have it all wound up very quickly and then they will find themselves with an oversupply of just about everything they have in the field, in their warehouses everywhere, not to mention orders not yet filled.*"

The General had spoken convincingly of future projects, the Skyhawk and other orders, and the non-military supplies which would be required once full annexation had taken place in East Timor.

Coleman had sat there quietly, listening, even appearing almost disinterested, Seda had thought at the time. Maybe his partner was becoming bored with the company now he was wealthy? As his Mercedes moved slowly around the Prapantja area Seda decided to have Umar pay more attention to the Australian's other activities. Just in case.

* * * * * *

Stephen sat at his desk going over the mountain of information that had piled up over the past year. He couldn't believe that the time had passed so quickly. As he started to recollect the year's highlights, he had to agree that it did, in fact, feel more like two years had passed and not just one, trying to understand just how far behind they'd slipped since Hart had left the company.

They had advertised, of course, but after a number of interviews none of the applicants really had what he needed in an administrative assistant. His local staff couldn't even understand the systems put into place by Hart. The filing and accounting had become so intertwined; nobody could understand where it started and where it finished due to the complexity of the methods the man had initiated for the company's records.

"Stuff it!" he said, leaning back into the chair and rubbing his forehead.

He rested from the laborious task for a few moments and then rose, leaving the pile of documents all over his teak desk as he stepped over two more cartons of similar records which had been delivered from his Thamrin office several days before. Coleman had promised himself that he would attack the paperwork and simplify the system so that he and the others could understand and operate the records more easily.

After twelve hours straight examining the illogical sequences that had been put in place by his former employee he'd decided that it may just be easier if the whole mess was just burned! He went upstairs and showered. An hour later Coleman stood comfortably at the Captains' Bar and observed that he was alone. Not that he minded the privacy, acknowledging that he was early and at any moment the bar would begin to fill with the regulars who frequented the Mandarin Hotel's main lobby drinking hole. Out in the main hotel foyer he could see some of the embassy crowd gathering before proceeding upstairs to the *cordon bleu* restaurant where a trade delegation was holding one of their many functions. It had been some time since he'd had an invitation to one of these luncheons, he recalled, watching one or two familiar faces pass through the marbled space.

Stephen thought he identified one of the men who waved to him and so he returned the gesture, only to discover that there had been someone else on the other side of the glass partition who'd been the object of the man's attention. It'd been like this ever since he'd returned from Hong Kong and found Wanti collapsed.

Any expatriate community feeds off itself and there was nothing more than an ugly rumour to throw them into a feeding frenzy, he acknowledged. Invitations to embassy functions dwindled away in frequency and even some of his Indonesian friends' wives had put him socially off limits as they too sympathized with his wife's condition.

Stephen could understand their negative attitudes. He just didn't enjoy being held responsible for what had happened and being treated like a pariah. He hadn't even heard any more from Anderson and this really surprised him considering the *kongsi* association with Seda continued without any real hiccups. Stephen had almost convinced himself that they had decided to leave him alone as now the tide had turned considerably in Timor. The separatist forces continued to successfully resist the greater forces of the Indonesian military even after annexation was officially passed through the Indonesian Parliament.

Stephen had spent numerous sleepless nights justifying his decision to stay on with the General and risk the wrath of the men in Canberra. He now believed that one of his assumptions had been correct. The Australians were fence sitting, waiting to see if Seda could pull it off.

As the FRETILIN forces had grown from strength to strength, the international community had seen world opinion move behind the separatists who had now declared their own independence and continued to amaze the foreign press with their displays of courage and resilience faced with such a formidable enemy.

Even the punishing devastation inflicted by the Broncos couldn't stop the movement from strengthening its position in the villages where the party members threw down their weapons to help work the fields whenever there was a lull in the aerial attacks.

Now that the American Government had put a temporary halt to the supply of the two squadrons of Skyhawks, knowing that the independence movement could not survive such punishing aerial bombardment these aircraft were built to deliver, there appeared to be a growing possibility that the Indonesians would be obliged to withdraw to their own side of the border. Even the United Nations was heading for a vote in favour of an Indonesian withdrawal.

Stephen didn't mind forgoing the commissions he and Seda would have earned from the aircraft contracts should they be cancelled. He imagined that the General was relieved when the news had been broken to him although outwardly he would have to appear displeased.

He was no longer puzzled by Seda's incredible ability to display such obvious loyalty to the Indonesians whilst plotting the resistance by the very groups he had publicly sworn to assist defeat. Stephen knew that he would be inviting his own demise should he ever infer that he knew what the General had done and who had informed him!

A New Zealander he'd met and shared a few drinks with while out in the islands entered the bar and Stephen put these things momentarily out of his mind to greet the man. Stephen needed to look after whatever friends he still had as their number was rapidly dwindling.

Chapter 18

Timor-Timur

Refugees flooded into Australia and the newspapers had a field day printing their reports describing atrocities carried out by the Indonesian troops on the poor villagers and hill tribes.

The Cubans had all but disappeared from the fighting arena as, without Fidel's financial support, they could not remain any longer. Things were bad enough back home in Havana and by the end of 1978 their violent incursion into Timor was but a memory, some thought a myth.

Nathan had been pleased, knowing that their continued presence would provoke the Australians into supporting the invasion and, in consequence, when the butchers were all repatriated during the first months of that year, he breathed a sigh of relief.

He needed something to go right for a change, the struggle was not proceeding with the support he'd envisaged and he now felt betrayed by both the Americans and Australians. Even the British had now decided to enter the debate insisting that the Indonesian annexation was to be considered beneficial not only to the long term welfare of the Timorese but also in its regional context.

Having made the statement the British Ambassador had stood back and witnessed the British Aerospace Company sign contracts to provide eight Hawk ground attack aircraft for the Indonesian air force. He had hoped when the UN vote had taken place that world opinion would force the Indonesian troops out.

It hadn't. The UN General Assembly rejected the integration and instead called for an act of self-determination to be held in East Timor. The voting record, he'd read, was sixty-seven in favour, twenty-six against with forty-seven abstentions.

He knew that, if only they could hold on, the dream would be theirs!

Although FRETILIN had been relatively successful the sheer weight of numbers now entering the area from Indonesia's base camps started to change the course of the war. The Americans had cleverly devised a scheme to circumvent their own Congress again and now the sixteen Indonesian pilots were flying sorties in their new Skyhawks with devastating results.

The guerrilla bands hid in the mountainous regions but their numbers were severely reduced by the pounding inflicted on their camps as the new aircraft located their targets and destroyed the FRETILIN supply centres with ease.

The General had been outraged when he discovered that the AURI Chief of Air Staff had received his orders directly from the President, to arrange for his pilots to proceed secretly, from where they had been trained in the United States, to a location in a friendly Moslem country on the Mediterranean. At first, Seda had not believed their cunning, and their ability to put aside religious dogma, when the need arose.

The Indonesian pilots took delivery of their first squadron of fighters directly from Israel which, in turn, received replacement aircraft from the Americans. The Israeli pilots were amused at the irony of it all, but understood the necessity of maintaining their solid relationships with their US supporters. They volunteered to fly the aircraft on their first leg directly into the hostile Arab neighbouring state, where a quick hand-over was conducted before the grinning pilots returned home under instruction to maintain the utmost secrecy regarding their mission. They had not been informed, of course, as to the final destination of their Skyhawks but they soon understood when they read press reports of the aircraft's use against the poorly armed resistance fighters in Timor.

Surprisingly, the aircraft were then flown halfway across the globe virtually undetected; as all refuelling stops were located in Arab and Moslem nations until finally, the squadron arrived safely in Indonesia. He couldn't believe his eyes when they gathered at the aircraft hanger to witness the squadron's arrival.

They had landed in tandem, the aircrafts' magnificent lines displaying the latest technology in aircraft engineering, bringing tears to the eyes of the Deputy Chief of Air Staff as he observed his son in one of the two lead jets.

There was considerable mirth as the aircraft came to rest, in line, and the pilots had stood proudly beside the new machines, for the aircraft identification marks still bore their country of origin's insignia. The group had shaken their heads in awe that such a mission could have been so successful and secret. Each and every one of the sixteen attack aircraft sill bore the Israeli Star of David emblazoned on the fuselage!

Nathan had applauded the feat in his weekly discussions with other military chiefs but secretly he was most concerned at having been bypassed in the information chain. This fear was soon allayed as he discovered that all but the Airforce Chief and the President were aware of the arrangements until just hours prior to the jubilant arrival at Halim Perdanakusumah. The Americans had insisted that it be so! And now his freedom fighters were also losing press support as well.

The Indonesian Government placed a blanket on all information relating to the war and, within weeks, the Timor conflict moved off the front pages. He noted that the number of media reports in the international press had also decreased considerably. What he didn't know was that this policy had been put into place deliberately by the Americans who then advised the Australians that they now favoured the annexation in a de facto sense. Sensing an international political *coup* the Australians jumped the gun and announced their own *de jure* recognition before the Yanks could steal the limelight.

Australia had been preoccupied with the former mandated territory of Papua New Guinea, which had achieved full independence just three months prior to the Indonesian invasion of Timor. Demands were already being pressed for the political separation of Papua from New Guinea and there was a strong secessionist movement developing on the copper rich Bougainville Island. Australian interest in the Timor conflict waned.

Indonesia, detecting the decline in support for the opposing forces, decided to formalize their position in the island. And there were other problems. After Indonesia had formally annexed Portuguese Timor, to Seda's and the world's amazement, the act was promptly recognized by the former colonial masters. The FRETILIN death toll grew beyond belief and the party's President, Xavier do Amaral, was arrested by his own Central Committee once they had received Seda's secret reports that he was alleged to have opened negotiations directly with the Indonesian military. The General had listened intently as the information had been delivered verbally by one of the KOSTRAD Generals during a debriefing exercise.

Seda had been livid. Hadn't they all agreed never to surrender and definitely not negotiate under any circumstances with anybody but the United Nations? He'd felt betrayed.

In spite of the considerable international reaction, neighbouring countries protested little, if at all. The general consensus was that the conflict would soon be resolved, and regional stability would be ensured, a political position supported by the simple justification that it would be foolhardy to invite the animosity of their powerful neighbour by not standing up and being counted as a friendly supporter of the oil rich Moslem country.

Timor-Timur officially became known as Indonesia's newest and twenty-seventh province, the province of East Timor, and within a very short period of time the annexed state was only referred to by its new acronym.

It became known simply as Tim-Tim.

* * * * * *

He disliked being faced with this conundrum, especially as it related to a situation over which he was not entirely convinced he had any real influence or control. Invariably, whenever this happened he would let whatever the problem might be run its natural course before deciding on any remedial action.

It was Stephen Coleman. He was the problem.

The time had come to dissolve their relationship and, although Seda believed that the Australian would not overly object as he had appeared to have lost interest anyway, his generous bank balances obviously in excess of his future wants and needs, there would always be the uncertainty of his disclosing details of their commercial arrangements.

The General refused to underestimate the man. It was he who had established the intricate network of their corporate structure and handled all of the offshore arrangements. Most, that is, before he had become personally involved. Seda imagined himself being Coleman and attempted to evaluate how he would have behaved in a similar situation.

Seda concluded that he would have put some mechanism in place to protect himselfagainst threat.

The question was, what and how?

The problem would not just go away and he knew that as long as Coleman lived he would be a danger, a threat. And yet, should Stephen suddenly disappear would he have left something behind to alert others to his activities and his relationship with the General?

The powerful man drummed his fingers on the teak arm rests. He remained seated for some hours before making the decision. It was worth a try and, if it failed, he could still distance himself from the outcome. He went into his private study, picked up the phone and dialled. A voice answered and listened to the instructions to meet later in the evening. He didn't need to write the information down. He had been there many times before. The General then prepared himself for his dinner.

Some hours later and across the roundabout facing the block of three story walk up apartments built for senior employees of the Ministry of Foreign Affairs, a man exited the BAKIN building and walked slowly to his unmarked vehicle. As he turned out into the mainstream of traffic the unsmiling soldier cursed softly at the thought of yet another late night. One day, soon, he thought, one day soon I'll take a rest from them all, perhaps even the General!

He observed his rear vision mirror and then drove out through the outer suburbs towards an old village building which the Timorese had retained as one of his safe houses. He could remember when the trip could be completed within thirty minutes but now, with all of the new housing estates springing up everywhere and the enormous amount of congestion that had occurred over the past few years, he had to allow an hour to reach the same destination.

Checking his Rolex as he approached the dilapidated house he knew that he was still early for the meeting.

'What could be so important this time that couldn't be discussed back in the privacy of the General's own and very secure office in the building?' Umar asked himself as he lit a cigarette and opened the window to wait.

* * * * * *

Stephen had really enjoyed the party. Comfortably drunk, he laughed to himself, relishing a joke he had just remembered. As he drove the red Mercedes towards his house weaving dangerously enough so that the following car elected not to overtake, he looked across at the girl sitting beside him and realized that he was still in a party mood. He reached out and placed his hands between her thighs. She giggled and he had to retrieve his hand momentarily to swerve away from the traffic island as the off-side tyres screamed their annoyance at his alarmingly close encounter.

They rounded the corner and he could see his house. Stephen nudged the car into the driveway and the engine died suddenly as he braked, barely stopping before touching the huge sliding steel security gate. He tapped the horn, once and waited as he looked at the girl and smiled through the alcoholic haze.

He hit the horn again, annoyed that his security had not immediately opened the gate.

"Bloody hell!" he muttered, opening the door, "the bugger's probably out having a pee, saying prayers or doing something or other to the bloody cook!"

The headlights permitted Stephen to see some of the yard beyond the gate and, noticing that it had been left open a fraction, he got out and pulled the heavy structure across the closed driveway as the small un-oiled wheels groaned fiercely. Puffing from the exertion he then returned to the car and restarted the engine, moving the expensive sedan, jerkingly, into the double garage area.

He noticed that his security had fallen asleep right in the middle of the entrance and, turning to the girl who was to be his companion for the night winked and said, "Watch this," he said, "I'll frighten the shit out of him."

Stephen exaggerated his drunken movements, lifting his arms high in the air moving into the glare thrown out in front as the powerful headlights caught his figure and cast a dark shadow behind. He approached the sleeping servant and was about to yell loudly for him to wake up when he became confused with what he actually saw on the ground. There was blood everywhere!

Shocked and confused, he bent down to touch the body and, as he rolled it over he could see, even in his inebriated state that it certainly was his servant. Only he was dead!

A shrill scream pierced his ears. Startled, Stephan fell forwards onto the slain security guard. His female companion stood in front of the sealed beam lights screaming in terror at the huge amount of blood and, of course, the servant's body.

Stephen scrambled to his feet and stumbled towards the night entrance door only to find that it was open. He continued quickly, bumping into furniture and columns without feeling the pain as he hurried forward towards the servants' quarters.

There were two rooms. Both had their single doors wide open and he could see through the dim light that there was no movement. His hand reached for the switch. As the room turned to brilliant light his eyes opened wide at the bloody mess that had been left. There were two more bodies here, the houseboy's wife and teenage son who occasionally helped his father around the house.

Stephen backed away from the scene, turning slowly to check the other room, fearing the worst. There he found another body, this one the inside maid. He was confused and disorientated by the bloody scene.

And then he remembered Kardi. Where was he? His brain now screamed as the import of what had occurred pumped more adrenaline through his body.

"*Kardi,*" he called out loudly. "*Kardi, where the hell are you?*"

There was no answer, the deafening silence sending a chill through his spine. He crouched forward prepared to defend himself and moved deeper into the large rambling house, past the kitchen and store areas, past the preparation room where he checked the rooms downstairs.

There was nothing there. Not even signs of a break in or theft as everything appeared to be in order. He was completely mystified. Stephen returned to the stairway and cautiously climbed the flight of marble steps, listening for any sound which might alert him to another's presence on the next level. There was nothing which signalled evidence of danger.

At the top of the stairs he turned the remaining lights on, the wide verandah instantly illuminated before him.

Stephen approached the master bedroom slowly, his heart pumping furiously and pulled the sliding glass French doors open quickly revealing a room filled with fearful darkness. Long drapes

brushed against his face and he flung these aside then groped
through the dark towards his bedside lamp. He knew that this
should be on, because the servants always prepared his room before retiring themselves and this light was left blazing to enable
their *tuan* to cross the otherwise darkened room, as there was no
place for a switch to be affixed to the glass panelled doors.

He stumbled and fell, cursing himself as he scrambled back up,
holding the side of his double bed, finally finding the switch for
the lamp. He pressed the small button and immediately the room
was flooded with light.

Stephen froze. His rigid body choked the scream before it could
escape from his lips.

Spread out across the top of his bed lay Sukardi, the man who
had dedicated so much of his life to his *tuan's* well being. He lay
spread-eagled, a distorted grin across his face, his eyes open wide
as if he had been about to shout when the blade had been pulled
quickly across his throat ending his life before any cry could emerge.

Staggered by the bloodied appearance of the *jongus'* body he
turned quickly and fled, running from his bedroom down the steps
until he reached his car and ripped the door open violently, yelling
loudly for the girl to climb in quickly as he fumbled with the igni-
tion keys, trying desperately to restart the car so that they could
escape from the violence that had permeated his home.

As the effects of the alcoholic curtain rapidly lifted permitting
his brain to function with some semblance of logic, Stephen
Coleman experienced the chilling realization that, had he been
home that evening, then it may easily have been his body now
lying on the huge bed in the upstairs bedroom and not that of his
dear and trusted old friend, Sukardi.

As the engine responded to its driver's desire for speed the car
raced away into the darkness of the night, leaving behind the bodies of all of Stephan Coleman's servants and a grim message of
what now lurked in the shadows waiting. Just for him.

******

In a distant village school thousands of kilometres from the killing fields of East Timor, the young children sat happily singing the
chant which assisted them to remember their lessons. The children's

eyes followed their teacher's arm as she conducted them.

One by one, they would shouted in unison as the individual province's names and numbers were called out for them to remember and, one by one they repeated the corresponding phrase in consequential order as they passed from the special areas of Jakarta and Jogjakarta, "*One, two*" they chorused as the teacher continued through the many provinces of Sumatra and Java, "*ten, eleven*" and Bali, across the wide expanse of sea to Kalimantan, "*fifteen, sixteen*" and Sulawesi, "*twenty-three, twenty-four*" and then down through the Eastern Tenggara states to Irian, West New Guinea, "*twenty-six*."

The children were pleased when they reached the last and twenty-seventh province in the sequence.

But the children were also happy because their teacher had explained to them they had new brothers and sisters in the new province and they should be proud that these people had become one under the Indonesian flag to strengthen their *Republik*.

The children all shouted in rehearsed chorus the name of the distant province which had become Indonesia's latest acquisition, the twenty-seventh province. And the sound of their voices could be heard drifting across the valleys, echoing though the hills, beyond the mountains and in every corner of the archipelago as Indonesian children everywhere chanted the new province's name for the world to remember.

'Timor-Timur, Tim-Tim!'
'Timor-Timur, Tim-Tim!'

Book Three

The Present

Chapter 19

Saigon

Jack Brindley leaned his thin frame against the bar and sipped the cold Tiger beer. Things had certainly changed in Saigon, or Ho Chi Minh City as the world now knew the vibrant river port. Communism had all but died and the collapse of the USSR had ushered in a new era of hope as, one by one, even the former communist satellite countries opened their borders to Capitalism.

Vietnam had been no different from the others. The country had been at war for most of the millennium fighting Kublai Khan, the Chinese in the north, the French Colonialists, the Americans and their Allies. Not to mention their incursion into Cambodia, or Kampuchea, as it was more commonly known. Vietnam's market economy had leapfrogged, not unlike Indonesia's in the late Sixties and early Seventies. Foreign investment had pumped much needed millions into the war-torn economy, developing infrastructure, paving the way for domestic growth.

Jack Brindley had seen this all before. He had been a merchant banker in Jakarta during Indonesia's heady years and now resided in Saigon as a financial consultant to one of the major investment houses. Today, as usual, he was holding court in The Shakes Pub, a pseudo English bar overlooking Me Linh Square across from where the old Bank of America building had stood near the roundabout on Phan Van Dat Street.

Vietnam's revamped investment philosophy, Doi Moi, had been introduced by Vo Van Kiet during the preceding years. Consequently, demolition teams had moved in and destroyed large sections of this part of the city making way for hotels and offices to cater for the rapid increase in demand.

Jack watched the freighters pass along the congested Saigon

river. These huge ships, with tonnages of up to twenty thousand, sailed up the river more than thirty nautical miles before berthing in the crowded river port. As they sailed past, majestically, they created a strange illusion that it was possible for one to reach out and touch the huge structures.

Several of Saigon's hard-core expatriate drinkers stood alongside the financier, only too pleased to be seen in his company.

Vietnam's sudden change to a market economy attracted entrepreneurial types from all corners of the globe. The last recession in the West had encouraged opportunists to depart their own shores and investigate South East Asia. Vietnam's potential attracted a wide variety of these dubious characters, including a few former politicians from Western Australia who, after completing their brief period of incarceration in the Fremantle Prison, had fled their native country.

Vietnam's overseas image was that of a last frontier and this, coupled with its recent violent history, caused tourists to flood into the country. They had came to visit the land made famous in so many Hollywood movies over the last twenty-five years.

The contrast between Hollywood fantasy and the grim reality of everyday life in Vietnam shocked the naive visitor. Filth and misery were everywhere. Blocked gutters, broken footpaths, beggars lining the streets and pickpockets on all the main thoroughfares. Saigon presented an entirely different picture than they had anticipated. Even Dhong Khoi, with its string of boutique coffee shops, bars and Vietnamese restaurants, was not spared.

Violence was endemic. Mutilated bodies were often left lying on the footpaths until the early hours of the morning when they were removed by some passing truck.

Robbery was rife. Life was cheap.

Outside the hospital's dirty walls, groups of people gathered in silence. To the uninitiated, they might appear to be anxious friends or family waiting for news of some loved one. In fact, these people were Saigon City's mobile blood bank. The group would congregate and wait until approached by a distressed soul, desperate for a blood type for their child or relative and then the donor would haggle over the price. The price of blood depended not only on rarity of type, but the gravity of need.

Expatriate numbers had grown to several thousand boosted by

the recent influx of oil and gas companies anxious to develop the offshore fields of Vung Tau and Da Nang. Many had come and gone, discouraged by the difficulties in dealing with a socialist government still suffering extreme xenophobia. Most of the foreigners who pioneered Vietnam's emergence from the dark corridors of a mismanaged Communist bureaucracy were well-versed in the Orient's confusing ways before venturing into the now vibrant economy. Not that Vietnam didn't still suffer from the long period of stagnation caused by the crippling embargo placed on it by the American Government.

Deep warning blasts sounded downstream as one of the large freighters approached the port. A flotilla of small canoe-style ferry boats scurried quickly away from the oncoming giant's threatening bow wash.

Brindley ordered another round of drinks for everyone and the fat, ebullient bartender waddled over to pour a beer into his glass before the others. Quickly and efficiently, the waitress replaced the used glasses with clean chilled ones. All, that is, with the exception of Brindley who liked to hang onto his seasoned glass. He had a theory that glasses too chilled or washed in the wrong detergent would make the beer flat. It suited him to be the odd man out. He enjoyed the additional attention. Brindley was about to raise his hand to call for a packet of cigarettes when he sighted the tall pale foreigner at the other end of the bar.

Brindley observed the other man. "And a drink for my friend over there too George," he said, indicating the man sitting at the end of the bar.

The affable barman served the beers and delivered a generous measure of whisky to Stephen Coleman, merely indicating with his finger that the order had come from "Mr John", the tall thin gentleman standing in the group next to the darts area.

Coleman raised his glass in salute and drank. He could not remember the man's name but he dimly recollected the face and build. 'Dimly' was very appropriate, he thought wryly. He was not altogether clear just how many drinks he had consumed already in the course of that day. He no longer bothered to count. Not that he was an alcoholic, he easily deluded himself, it was just that he had not been able to get it all together again and, he worried, time was running out.

How old was he now, forty-nine? No. That was last March! And now it was March again. So, he decided, confused by the mental haze, he would now be forty-eight! He laughed privately at his own joke. He checked his whisky and observed that it already needed replenishing. Pleased with himself at not yet having broken through the magic 'fifty,' Coleman gestured to George to bring him another drink and, waving his hand in a circle, indicated that he wished to buy a round for everyone present.

The bartender wobbled back down to the other end of the bar and organized drinks for the group.

"I tell you, he had millions!" the fat bearded New Zealander whispered.

"Bullshit!" the Australian challenged.

"Actually," the British born financier offered, "no one really knows just how much he did have, but I will say this," he paused for added emphasis, "it was considerably more than reports would have it."

The group absorbed the information occasionally glancing over in the direction of the man sitting alone at the long bar. The conversation was typical banking fraternity gossip, each attempting one-upmanship over the others present. By offering opinions and observations without substance, they often irretrievably damaged the reputation of the unfortunate subject.

"What did he do with it then?" the Australian inquired, probably keen to discover a potential investor in his new project.

Brindley raised his glass and sipped slowly before replying. "No one really knows."

"Is that the guy that was deported from Indonesia about ten years back?" the Australian persisted.

Brindley considered this before replying.

"A little longer than that, if my memory serves me correctly, and I don't believe he was actually deported. Stories regarding situations such as the one in which he became embroiled obviously become distorted with time."

Brindley paused to drink then continued. "Stephen Coleman carried a very big stick, as they say, before he stumbled. There were many who were pleased when he finally fell out of favour and lost, or appeared to lose, the lot."

"What happened?" Bruce Point the New Zealander eagerly

asked.

"He was involved very deeply, or so the story goes, in an arms scandal revolving around the Timor fiasco back in the late seventies, or it could even have been the early eighties. At the time he went into hiding, and disappeared from Indonesia when it became a little too hot. Now he pops up from time to time in the most surprising places."

"Bloody hell!" the fat Kiwi announced, "A gun-runner!"

"Keep it down a little, Bruce." Brindley admonished.

The men turned their heads to see if Coleman had noticed, but he appeared to be lost in thought.

"When his group started to crumble," the well informed Brindley continued, "there was also some unsavoury gossip concerning his wife."

"And?" prodded one of the men.

"Well, I am not sure. It has been a long time and quite frankly, I believe that his private life should remain just that. The long and the short of it all is that he disappeared about that time. Although the stories have been embellished over the years, I never found the man to be anything but hard-working and reasonably friendly when I knew him back in those times."

All heads had once again turned in the direction of the Australian sitting alone. Stephen looked up and caught their glances. He just smiled thinly, ignoring their obvious stares. It had happened before.

* * * * * *

During his years of relative seclusion he had often encountered knowing glances and whispering voices when he ventured into the drinking dens frequented by expatriates. He remembered how in Mandalay, one afternoon, a complete stranger had walked up to him and accused him of unspeakable acts, abusing him so savagely that he had been totally bewildered and at a loss to defend himself. And now, here in old Saigon his past had followed him again, judging from the inquisitive stares from the group off to his right.

Stephen Coleman had dragged himself up the steps into the bar. He couldn't remember what time that had been. The hotel lifts stopped two floors short of the top, obliging the clientele to struggle up a series of steps before arriving at the roof-top oasis with its magnificent view across the Saigon River. He had seen the group at the bar on arrival but the painful effort of climbing, together with the fact that he was in no mood for company, made him decide that he wanted to be alone.

Fifteen years of self-abuse had produced the red, telltale blotches and dark bags under his eyes. He didn't care. At least it helped disguise his identity, most of the time. Today, however, he suspected that his cover was blown, but he didn't particularly mind. He was concentrating on getting drunk.

He had not been on a binge of this magnitude for at least a year, and it had started with the Cathay Pacific flight from Hong Kong a week ago. Of course, he could blame the attractive Japanese flight stewardess. It was she who had offered him the newspaper that had triggered his present bender.

He thought back over that flight. As a rule, Coleman disliked reading on flight. He always found that the overhead light didn't quite match the position of the seat, and he didn't enjoy holding the reading material close to his eyes as the Chinese seemed to do. And then there was the problem of the black smudges he'd find from the poor print quality.

It never failed. Whenever he was given a newspaper he found that the print always seemed to come off on his hands and then, inevitably, smear over his shirt. And for some reason he could never understand, the moment he'd manage to fold the cumbersome oversized paper into some more manageable form, the cabin staff would commence serving meals! So he had taken the newspaper more to appease the smiling attendant than to provide himself with an update on world events.

He had refused the overly sweet pre-flight concoction served while the aircraft waited for the remaining passengers to board. Instead, he had requested a Chivas. The girl had smiled sweetly and apologized, citing the IATA regulations, or was it the Customs regulations, which prevented the consumption of alcoholic beverages before takeoff.

He had already been drinking prior to boarding and wasn't in a particularly good mood. He knew all too well that up forward in the first class section they would be pouring Bollinger or some other fascinating drinks down their throats while he sat crammed between the two Indian gentlemen in economy.

It was not that he did not have the means to fly first class. It just seemed more prudent to sit down the back with the tourists where he could maintain a low profile. Although he no longer needed to take such security precautions, it helped him to avoid bumping into old associates who might stir up the bitter memories which continued to haunt him. The skeletons of his past. There were more of these than he cared to remember.

Stephen drained the last dregs of his whisky then looked up blearily at the growing crowd in The Shakes Pub. He was pleased that the memories were becoming more vague with each year that passed, buried, as they were, under a deluge of alcohol and self-pity. What the hell! He didn't care too much any more.

His thoughts strayed back to the Cathay Pacific flight. The sector was only two hours so he hadn't taken too much notice of his seat allocation. Consequently, he found himself stuck between two overweight men whose bodies spilled over into his limited space. He remembered deliberately exaggerating his arm movements as he opened the pages of the large Sydney Morning Herald so as to annoy his neighbours. He had skimmed through the first few pages without particular interest in the happenings back in the land of his birth when suddenly he saw it, on page three.

He stared at the image before dropping his eyes to read the underlying caption. The lines blurred as the words meshed together. He stared at the photograph again and General Nathan Seda smiled back at him, almost mockingly.

Coleman had not wanted to read on but his attention was dragged like a magnet to the story accompanying the photograph. He read the article again, in disbelief.

His eyes remained transfixed to the photograph. Having finished the article, he unbuckled his safety belt and went in search of the flight attendant. The stewardess permitted Coleman to stand next to the galley only after he had complained about the other passenger's body odour. The male flight attendant, a Filipino, had smiled knowingly and presented Stephen with a full tumbler of Chivas with barely enough space for the single ice cube. For the remaining one-and-a-half hours of the flight his demeanour deteriorated to the point just short of being obnoxiously drunk.

And he had remained in that condition until he awoke some

CARTHAGE PUBLIC LIBRARY
CARTHAGE MISSOURI

time later in his hotel room in the early hours of the morning with a raging thirst. Stumbling around the room, searching unsuccessfully for a light switch, he discovered the washbasin and drank copiously from the antiquated water system. Then he crawled back into bed.

Stephen grimaced with the memory. How could he have done such a reprehensible thing? He'd been living in the tropics long enough to know that drinking local water was tantamount to suicide! His judgement had been clouded by the tremendous infusion of alcohol. When he awoke for the second time, he had been completely disoriented. He tried to make some sense of his surroundings but there was nothing familiar about the room to indicate where he was. After some minutes, he gradually allowed himself an attempt to rise from the bed. A gigantic wave of nausea flowed from his stomach, forcing the bile upwards as he lurched forward in search of the bathroom.

He retched. The heaving attack continued until he was totally exhausted. The combination of alcohol and whatever filthy parasite that had infiltrated his body produced wracking spasms and extreme stomach cramp, causing the already exhausted Coleman to fall forward weakly, until the next wave forced him to produce the physical strength to raise his body back up to the toilet bowl.

The attacks continued. At last, totally debilitated by the spasms, he fell insensible to the bathroom floor where the room maids discovered him and raised the alarm.

After administering medication, the doctor had issued instructions to have him bathed and instructed the staff not to disturb the man until he had slept for at least a further ten hours. In the early evening he was given soup, after which he again fell into a deep sleep. As he'd slept, a constant flow of staff had passed through his room, concerned that he might die in their hotel, especially during their shift. It was a further twelve hours before he awoke and looked around the still unfamiliar room to see a serious faced short man watching him, obviously worried.

Stephen shifted his position on the bar stool and lit another cigarette. He could recall the conversation he had as if it had happened just five minutes ago.

"Good morning, Mr Stephen Coleman," the small wiry person had called clearly, "we were about to waken you."

CARTHAGE PUBLIC LIBRARY
CARTHAGE MISSOURI

Stephen remembered watching the man for several moments before responding. He had assumed he was in some sort of hospital.

"Good morning," he said, struggling to make a sound.

"The dryness in your throat is from the vomiting. Also, I would assume, the soreness surrounding your chest and rib cage. Your lower abdomen will be tender from the cramps at least until tomorrow. " The doctor waited for some indication from Coleman that these symptoms were correct and, receiving no response, continued. "Is this your first time in Vietnam, Mr Coleman?"

Stephen eyed the man suspiciously.

"Do you mean that no one has checked my passport?"

"It is not usually part of our medical procedures," the doctor answered caustically. He was a Southerner.

"Then maybe it should be," Coleman ungraciously suggested.

"I see that not only do you show bad judgement but bad manners as well."

Stephen studied the man and decided that he had gone too far.

"Sorry, Doc." Stephen apologized. "Where am I?"

"Room 507, Rex Hotel, Ho Chi Minh City."

He absorbed this information and decided there were other questions he should be asking but tiredness prevented him from pursuing these.

"Saigon? How long have I been here?" he asked.

"Just a day or so. You should rest now. We can talk when you have slept."

"What is the medication, Doctor..?"

"My name is Thuan. The medication I have given you is a simple sedative to make you relax, together with pain killers and Geomyacin which would have reduced the cramps."

"Thank you, Doctor Thuan. Again, I apologize for my rude behaviour."

"You should rest as long as the cramps and nausea continue." He hesitated and then added, "Avoid alcohol."

Stephen nodded. The mere thought of whisky induced a warning twinge in his stomach. Satisfied that he would recover, Coleman had thanked the doctor and, following his advice, rested in the room for the remainder of the day.

By evening, Stephen remembered he was well enough to wander along the passageway and out onto the magnificent beer garden, where he sat, relaxing under the stars. He couldn't believe the sudden change in temperature. There were a number of stuffed animals placed around in frozen postures together with some rather fine sculptures of elephants in different artistic poses. A large dome-like crown sat majestically on the centre roof structure, covered by hundreds of lights so that the hotel's popular garden setting could be easily identified from most parts of the city.

Occasionally he would catch a glimpse of the river's floating restaurants, brilliantly lit with thousands of lights strung in the shape of an enormous fish. The colourful lights and electrical display brought it alive.

He enjoyed the sense of history as he sat quietly on the iron garden chairs amidst the orchids and other pot plants, listening to the street noises five stories below. Taxis and buses fought for position in the traffic, moving perilously close to brave pedestrians who attempted to cross on the complicated pedestrian markings. The constant flow of motorbikes, cars and minibuses chased each other around the square and then into the dangerous roundabout.

* * * * * *

Stephen knew something about the Rex. He recalled that when Saigon fell in April of 1975, some eighteen months after the Americans, Australians and Koreans pulled out of the country, choppers could be seen hovering over the American Embassy compound just a few hundred metres away from this hotel. The noisy mechanical birds also swooped down to rescue the few remaining advisers caught unawares in this hotel, winching them straight out of the beer garden before whisking them away to the waiting transports at Tan Son Nhat. The Rex Hotel had been basically an officers billet where many of their number remained in the comfort none of the other addresses could offer.

Not two hundred metres to his left, as Coleman faced the river, he could see the newly renovated Caravelle which housed the Australian Embassy during the years of conflict that had claimed the lives of some five hundred young men from Down Under. He had been told that, immediately after hostilities had ceased, the new regime had turned the two upper levels, formerly occupied by his countrymen, into a dance hall and night club. This was used mainly for the elite Communist Party officials who then plagued the city.

Stephen was surprised to see that so much of the old Saigon had already disappeared. High rise monsters now dominated the skyline, changing the city into a mini metropolis not unlike other South East Asian capitals. It was quite depressing to see how the character of the city had changed. Forty years before it had been a city which had prided itself as being the most advanced of any other capital in the region with an infrastructure well ahead of Singapore and Hong Kong.

The Communists had changed all that. Mismanagement, graft and corruption were mixed together in a melting pot of confusing politics and religious dogma. These were stirred with the fear of reprisals which turned the former capital of South Vietnam into a cesspool of humanity, most of whom had only one wish in life — to flee.

And many did.

Now they were returning, carrying their new passports for the security these offered, visiting family and friends and cautiously checking around for investment opportunities. Their familiarity with the language and culture gave them a real edge over other foreign investors. The government welcomed them back with open arms and did not differentiate too much between these overseas Vietnamese which they called Viet Kieu and others, unless they became embroiled in anything remotely resembling political or religious activities.

Stephen recalled how he had observed a number of foreigners arguing with the white uniformed security guard near the beer garden's entrance. The Lilliputian-sized lifts stopped there as the building reached only to the fifth level, which accommodated the beer garden, a swimming pool and sauna area, the main restaurant and a small number of suite rooms, one of which he now occupied as a guest.

The men were accompanied by two Vietnamese girls dressed in *au zais*, the long white traditional dress and slacks. The security officer was adamant. The girls were not permitted into this section of the hotel unless they were guests. The police were severe when they caught local girls in areas of hotels where they were not permitted. Stephen had heard many tales of tourists who had slipped a girl into their room only to discover that the receptionist they had tipped to turn a blind eye had immediately betrayed them and phoned the police. The Vietnamese gendarmes would arrive immediately and take the girl down to the station and throw her into the prostitutes cells where, more often than not, they would be raped by the very men who had carried out the arrest.

Vietnam was still a cruel country, he knew. He had been there briefly before. In Nha Trang he had been terribly disappointed with what could have been one of the finest destinations in Asia. The scenic mountains rolled down to the white sandy beach and the offshore islands were almost within swimming distance. The beautiful ocean colours were magnificent except where the filth suddenly poured down from the city's river, polluting the coastline with ugly brown substances, plastic bags and other unmentionable effluent. He remembered being able to see a distinct line separating the brown polluted water from the ocean's blue as the filth encroached upon the beach.

Coleman remembered how he had left Nha Trang the following day after being revolted at an altercation he had seen near the beach when a policeman had shot a young boy dead for no apparent reason.

A police officer had been with his friends amongst the coconut trees drinking hot beer. Two cans had been enough and the red faced official grabbed at a young fourteen-year-old street urchin, who had gone to the beach to bathe under the watchful eyes of her brother. The policeman knocked the girl to the ground.

The others crowded around and urged him on. He ripped at her dress and tore the worn clothing to her waist. His friends had laughed at the girl's brother who had tried desperately to pull the attacker off his sister. Drunk and angry, the young policeman had pulled his revolver and shot the boy dead.

Then they all raped the girl.

It had all happened so suddenly. Coleman didn't understand the language and before he could do anything, the girl too was dead.

* * * * * *

Yes, it was a cruel country all right. Coleman reflectively sipped a fresh whisky which George had obligingly just supplied. His thoughts returned to the incident he had witnessed on his second night at the Rex.

Voices had become raised as an argument developed. One of the foreigners was obviously showing the effects of an earlier session in one of the many bars in this quarter of the city. Suddenly there was a scuffle and both the men were thrown to the ground. The two girls panicked and hit the 'down' button on the lift indicator panel in a desperate attempt to leave the scene before they too became embroiled in the dispute.

Moments later the lift doors closed and both the young women quickly disappeared, leaving their dates lying on the hard concrete floor with looks of disbelief that the relatively small security man had downed both of them with just one swift movement of his arms and legs.

The manager appeared and the guests, whose only injury was their pride, moved towards the bar as the security officer simply crossed his arms and waited for the next altercation to occur.

Drinks were poured while one of the men rubbed his now bruised hip and elbow still glaring at the person responsible for their losing the women. Stephen could see now that the man was quite intoxicated, almost belligerently so. He appeared to ignore the dangers of carrying on the dispute with the well-trained and disciplined Vietnamese who simply ignored the angry stares.

Stephen recalled he had observed the men for a few more minutes. It was then that he admitted that he, too, had behaved just as badly when on an alcoholic binge. He'd made a resolve at the time, he remembered with a self-mocking smile, to stop drinking - or at least slow consumption to an acceptable level. He knew that his heart, liver and kidneys would soon succumb if he did not adjust his habits. He'd retired, that day, pleased with himself that this had been his first alcohol-free day for some time.

Stephen had managed to repeat his success the following day. Feeling somewhat recovered he ventured out of the Rex and down to the Saigon River's edge.

The beggars had irritated him. Although the temptation to give them a few dollars to be left in peace was great, his experience dictated that he shouldn't as once you gave to one, others would immediately appear. The street urchins followed, tapping their target's legs with an empty can, following the distinct whistled instructions of their team leader, who positioned himself at one of the main intersections directing the dozen or so poorly clad youngsters towards likely marks among the tourists. Shades of early days in Jakarta, he'd thought, remembering similar problems that city had suffered when thousands of beggars, mainly lepers, lay across the footpaths, desperate for food.

Stephen swirled the ice around the bottom of the glass and stared moodily into the dregs of his drink. It was on his fourth day in Saigon that he had an unwelcome encounter with his past. A man had almost knocked him over in his haste, hurrying out of the Bong Sen Hotel.

It was Greg Hart.

Startled, Coleman attempted to follow the man but was unable to catch him before he jumped into a *cyclo* and disappeared into the congested traffic. Similar to the *becak* in speed the *cyclo* was peddled away quickly by the wiry legged driver and he soon lost sight of it. Stephen looked around for another cyclo but by the time one had managed to venture across the busy intersection it was too late. Twenty or thirty other similar drivers moved in the same direction with the traffic flow, making it almost impossible to distinguish one from the other.

Furious at not having identified Hart immediately outside the hotel lobby, Stephen rode the three-wheeled machine around for two hours on the off chance that he would sight Hart again. He returned to the Bong Sen and checked with the reception to see if he had registered at that hotel only to discover that Hart wasn't known to them.

He wandered around District One, checking the bars on the chance that he could locate the man whom he believed had been partly responsible for his downfall. Stephen really wanted to sit down with Hart and find out why the man had created so many stories about his business activities and spread so many filthy lies concerning Stephen's relationship with his Wanti.

* * * * * *

It was during his quest to find Hart that Stephen came to be in The Shakes Pub at the same time as Brindley and company. Having broken his pledge already once that day he commenced with beer to quench his thirst, then went on to whisky when his still-tender stomach had started to rebel against the gaseous liquid.

John Brindley had, by this time, also consumed a considerable number of drinks although, unlike the man at the end of the bar, he was not feeling the effects; he was accustomed to drinking for hours on end, without the benefit of food, each and every day of the year.

Casually he approached Stephen and extended his hand.

"Don't know if you remember me or not. Stephen Coleman, are you not?"

"Correct. Do I know you?"

"John Brindley. Jakarta."

Stephen thought for a moment and slowly his memory produced a vague recollection of the man.

"Sorry. Not thinking too clearly today. A severe case of the trots, too many pills, some foul tasting medicine and the walk up those bloody stairs have succeeded in impairing my ability to think straight."

"Well, I wouldn't have expected you to remember. It's been a few years and we didn't have a great deal of business together." Stephen felt Brindley's gaze take in the ravages of his countenance. "Would you care to join us?"

Coleman hesitated. It was no longer his form to drink in company but obviously these men had been around the scene long enough to assist him with a little information.

"Yes. Thanks. I'd enjoy that," he lied.

John Brindley took Coleman back to introduce him to the others.

The conversation was a little stiff to begin with so Stephen attempted to lessen the tension. He encouraged the tubby New Zealander to discuss the timber industry in Vietnam, the man's obvious area of expertise, and after exchanging views on other relatively unimportant subjects, Coleman popped his question.

"Thought I recognized someone I used to know bouncing around in one of those bloody *cyclos*. I don't suppose any of you know a Greg Hart by chance?"

The response was immediate.

"Shit yes!" one of the group answered. "He's been in and out of the city like a bloody yo-yo doing some promotional work for the Australian Government's Communication's Program."

"Not that it's done much to improve the phones around here," the tubby drinker added.

He was pleased. Stephen encouraged them to talk on and within a few minutes he'd been able to drag out enough information from them all to satisfy his needs.

So, he thought, half listening to the men discuss the day's exchange rate, Hart had been in Saigon for some time working with the Australian communications group which had established itself in Vietnam several years earlier. That was interesting. As it appeared that they had been relatively successful, he wondered just what role Hart had played or still played with the company which now employed him.

An hour later Coleman left the bar, in his pocket he carried his former assistant's address and telephone number. He would visit the man. But not until he was stone cold sober. At least he would have the satisfaction of telling him where to get off about the filth that he had been spreading. He could just about forgive the rumours Hart had started about Coleman's business activities, although even those were damaging enough. But he would not be satisfied until he made the bastard apologize for the lies he'd told which, in turn, had become the substance of the stories that had been repeated back to him from time to time by some of his dwindling group of friends. He had to confront Hart about the provocative statements he had made regarding Wanti's collapse which had indeed made him a pariah in Jakarta circles. Although the years had lessened the pain Coleman was determined to at least rid himself of that slander and now he had the opportunity. He returned to the Rex and ceased drinking for the rest of the day.

That evening, after bathing and resting for a few hours, Stephen felt refreshed and elected to dine in the hotel dining room located on the same level as his room. The atmosphere was excellent. A pianist softly accompanied the female violinist. The cuisine was an assortment of French and Vietnamese. He ate sparingly, still sensitive to his condition. He knew that the spicy rolls and seafood dishes could be too much of a challenge to his stomach as yet.

Relaxed, Coleman gazed around at the decor, the artefacts which were positioned around the hall, and the various foreign groups dining quietly. The staff glided from table to table efficiently and effectively serving and removing dishes as the soft dinner chatter continued. He was pleased to see that the majority were dressed for the occasion in an almost old worldly, colonial style. The women wore elegant dresses while some of the older men sported white dinner jackets and black tie.

The *maitre d'hotel* offered Stephen coffee which he asked to have served on the terraced garden. He sat at the glass-topped wire garden table alongside the well manicured hedge. This partly enclosed section had been raised slightly, permitting guests to remain comfortably seated while overlooking the avenue with its uninterrupted view down to the river. The strong Vietnamese coffee was not unlike the old familiar Javanese brew he had consumed in great quantities during happier times.

As he sat, unwinding, Coleman permitted his thoughts to float as he had so many times before during these long, lonely years. His thoughts drifted aimlessly, taking him back through his past and the deep rooted memories of lost love and disillusionment; to times when he was content with his life, even happy; to times when he enjoyed the success and accolades which accompanied his achievements; to times when he had the satisfaction of the company of many, and to the times and events which finally precipitated his hasty departure from the Republic of Indonesia.

And from General Seda.

Chapter 20

Jakarta — Macau

The General had been difficult to contact. Conditions had deteriorated dramatically for the separatist forces and FRETILIN had suffered tremendous losses. The war between Indonesia's invasion army and the defending East Timorese groups, often overwhelmed by the superior forces, had resulted in the deaths of more than two hundred thousand Timorese men, women and children.

As the territory had now been annexed by the Indonesians, those who resisted were now considered subversives and any captured separatist sympathizers were summarily executed without the benefit of trial. The Indonesians knew that they would be unable to prove in any court of law the legality of their brutal occupation of the small nation they had annexed. The list proclaimed by the new masters as to what constituted subversion was long. The charge carried the death penalty.

FRETILIN continued to fight, taking their resistance into the hills and away from the villages, where the mud walled shacks were burned, the young women raped and the children forced into camps to die from malnutrition and disease. FRETILIN was now severely outnumbered and out-gunned. The sky was consistently covered in strings of vapour trails as the efficient Broncos and Northrop fighter bombers ripped across the country, bringing devastation to even the most remote mountain tribes. Everyone had become a target for these aerial attacks, whether they were part of the resistance or just an appropriate and opportune target. Pilots killed indiscriminately, urged on by an incredible adrenaline rush to strafe the screaming villagers time and time again.

The guerrilla movement dissipated, unable to withstand the superior enemy numbers, breaking up into small bands which the

Indonesians then had little difficulty crushing. Those who believed, carried on the fight from their mountain hideaways. Even these insignificant bands were sufficient to drive the Indonesians into a frenzy at being unable to completely wipe out all resistance without annihilating the entire population. They came close. Almost one third of the population was killed in those very short years of resistance.

Although the United Nations called for Indonesia's withdrawal of its troops the country simply ignored the UN vote, which recorded fifty-nine in favour of withdrawal with only thirty-nine countries against such recommendations.

The Australians had done a complete turn-around, and now supported the annexation even though their own country had become inundated with refugees flooding into the northern city of Darwin. The Australian banks froze their funds, which had been deposited from the sale of coffee and other produce, reducing the overseas supporters' capacity to provide any form of assistance to their brothers in Timor.

Nathan Seda's dream seemed to collapse along with the partial defeat of the resistance and separatist groups. The General had moved swiftly to protect his position, eliminating those who could directly connect him to the movement in Timor. Umar Suharjo had been kept very busy indeed. FRETILIN's President, Nicolau Lobato, was shot and killed in a surprise attack by Indonesian troops.

* * * * * *

The first indication that Coleman had of any difficulties was when his conduit to the powerful man was disrupted, finally cutting him off completely from the Hong Kong apartment specifically maintained for their communication purposes. He had needed desperately to speak to his benefactor. He was scared and wanted the General's reassurance that his own personal security could be guaranteed after what had happened at his house and office.

He remembered driving for almost two hours that night, leaving for the mountains as soon as he had dropped the hysterical young girl back at the party where he'd found her earlier in the evening. That had been a mistake. He should have taken her with him and only returned after she'd spent a few days with him in the mountain villa, recovering from the shock of what she had witnessed in Coleman's driveway. At least she hadn't ventured inside!

His second mistake was not returning immediately after escorting the girl back to her friends. When he did return the next morning, the area was cordoned off by the police and even he had difficulty in entering his own office and home.

His office staff had all gathered outside in shock. He spoke to his personal secretary and briefly explained what had happened but she just stared at the dead as they were carried out to a waiting van, uncovered, for all to see. As the mutilated bodies were driven away, and after he had been briefly questioned by the police, Coleman asked one of the staff to find someone who could enter the house and clean it so that they could go about their business.

His secretary had looked at him in disbelief. 'You must be mad!' she thought. 'Go back in there?' She mumbled something quickly to her boss and left hurriedly, only to be followed by almost all of the other staff within minutes. Only one remained and Coleman instructed him to find the necessary cleaners. Promising those whom he was able to solicit a special bonus payment, the clerk returned within the hour with a team of ten men and women who commenced washing down the bloody walls and removing all signs of the brutal attack.

Over the next weeks Coleman's telephone lines were cut off from the exchange and, although he spent considerable time and a huge amount of sugar money, his phone remained dead. Then Stephen had a visit from a number of government department officials whom he had met regularly over the years, mostly when their annual 'consultancy' fees were due.

But it was different this time. His old friend, Hasnul, from the Taxation Department arrived with four others and seized all of the office records. Stephen was flabbergasted when they started ripping files from the office cabinets.

"What the hell's going on, Hasnul?" he had asked, disbelievingly.

"Orders, Mas. Sorry," was all he said.

The following day he had a visit from the immigration officers who wanted to examine his documents. While they were there, they asked about his former employee, Hart. They had left after only twenty minutes, their briefcases filled with cash, only to return late in the day to ask for his passport as it required endorsement.

"What endorsement? My documents are all in order!" he had yelled, calling them thieving little bastards, his temper flaring. He received no explanation as he reluctantly surrendered his passport.

The following morning his credentials and other documents were returned. By the police. Next, the Macau clearing house was closed.

Stephen had attempted to contact the General directly in Jakarta without success. He had broken with established procedure and phoned Seda's house and was surprised when even the servants treated him coldly.

Then there were rumours that an attempt had been made on the lives of several of the high ranking military, including Nathan Seda, which, he assumed, explained the difficulty in being able to contact the powerful man. Even his HANKAM access dried up, leaving him feeling desperate and politically powerless. And then, for reasons he could not understand, it was as if nothing had ever happened! Within two weeks his business appeared to return to normal and, enormously relieved, he set about restoring the company by employing new staff and re-establishing communication links with all of the foreign callers who were, by then, more than curious with his lack of response to their many inquiries.

He had tremendous difficulty in getting everything back on track. It wasn't just inexperienced staff that were to blame. There were constant visits from government departments he'd never dealt with before; these continued to eat into his time, creating even more credibility problems with his international business relationships.

And then it all crumbled into shit again. The mountain resort development suddenly had more problems than he considered possible. Almost all of his nominees had refused to return his calls and the Provincial Governor had sent an urgent letter demanding to see the original licenses for each and every dwelling that had been constructed on the extensive project. Days later this was followed by calls from the construction department to send original copies of all engineering documents for their perusal.

Coleman started to panic. He had most of his wealth tied up in these land developments! Whoever was after him had created sufficient momentum to cause his world to collapse and he couldn't understand why.

He had asked himself a hundred times each day, who might be responsible for his predicament, but was uncertain as to who had either the power or resources to destroy his commercial empire that Seda had helped him build.

The possibility that this had all been the work of ASIS had crossed his mind but even John Anderson, Stephan decided did not have the access that Coleman had built over the years with senior Indonesians. It had to be Seda!

But why? He considered the question, going over and over in his mind why the General would do such a thing to him after all of these years. He'd done nothing to warrant this action, he was sure.

Time passed and his business activities turned into a nightmare of demands from overseas suppliers and an horrific claim from the Indonesian Taxation Department which, he believed, could be amicably settled as had been done in the years before.

When he tried to resolve this amicably they refused. He was asked to pay more than three million dollars in back taxes and fines! He just couldn't believe it. His whole world was collapsing and he didn't understand why.

Suddenly, none of his old friends or contacts wanted anything more to do with him. Somebody had closed the doors on him, the realization driving him into despair. He drank heavily, often alone, for even his once close drinking buddies had now identified that having Stephen Coleman as a friend was tantamount to asking for a quick and negative endorsement on one's work permit or visa extension.

His launch was impounded by the customs authorities as they claimed that it had been used for smuggling treasures out of the country from the recent black ship discoveries thereby depriving the nation of its valuable heritage. Stephen was aware that there had been a discovery, but this was part of a major haul which had been recovered by a British salvage expert and auctioned by Christies in Amsterdam, achieving seventeen million pounds in revenue from the illegal operation. He had not been a party to that.

And there was more. Having checked the original import declarations for his Grand Banks launch they claimed to have discovered errors in the shipping manifests, which reflected an underpayment on applicable sales tax. The penalty would have to be paid before he would be permitted use of the vessel again. He was devastated. The small ship was his pride and joy.

When an enigmatic message suggesting a rendezvous at an address in Macau arrived, he assumed it was from the General and felt a flood of relief. Now perhaps he would know why he had been deliberately targeted by the Government, his life turned inside out, his launch confiscated and the HANKAM doors suddenly closed. These were but a few of the many questions which raced through his mind as he prepared a simple carry-all for the trip. He had departed immediately and connected with a ferry within an hour of arriving at Kai Tak airport. The taxi to the Kowloon terminal had taken only twenty minutes.

The weather was foul. Even the flight had caused some concern as they hit the second hurricane warning that Hong Kong had seen in the course of the past few days. The aircraft had bounced around, forcing the captain to insist that the cabin staff secure the galley equipment and take their positions due to the turbulent conditions.

The seas were exceptionally rough. After boarding the ferry, the passengers were instructed to wait for an hour to see if the next weather signal would be hoisted to warn ships at sea and, when the winds had abated enough for the Captain to get under way, they departed. Even in the more protected area of the harbour waves smashed into the vessel. As the first of many spine-jarring jolts caused the passengers to hold firmly onto the head rests of the seats in front, most cursed themselves for not remaining ashore until the violent weather had passed.

When they berthed, Stephen waited patiently until the all clear signal had been given by the crew. The overpowering smell of vomit permeated everything aboard the vessel, threatening even those who had been stoic enough to endure the crossing without succumbing to the motion sickness.

He scrambled ashore with the others and went directly to one of the small tourist hotels. He slipped the receptionist an additional one hundred Hong Kong dollars to avoid producing his passport for registration.

Coleman knew that it would be foolish to risk exposing his whereabouts to anyone. He still wasn't entirely sure that the trip had been a wise decision, one that he'd taken in haste due to the turmoil that had inexplicably beset him.

The ageing porter had insisted on carrying his one light piece of baggage up to the room on the second floor. He tipped the man, not too generously and asked him to find him a girl. The porter had understood the request immediately and smiled.

An hour passed and then a loud knock announced the old man's return. Coleman was surprised to see that the porter had brought two women. When he looked inquiringly at the stooped Chinese porter he was met with a wave of the hand and the two girls settled down on the side of his bed ready for the negotiations.

He didn't really need the hookers. It was just another precaution he'd considered necessary to complete the picture of what the locals perceived to be natural behaviour for a tourist. None of the three could speak any English. The old man gave the shorter of the women a ballpen and disappeared into the bathroom, returning within moments with a section of toilet paper which he then passed to the prostitute. She wrote a figure down and passed it over to Coleman.

"No," he said immediately, even though the figure was not too astronomical. He was tired enough to accept anything but he felt that it was necessary to continue playing the role by refusing the offered amount.

The pair broke into animated discussion. He wished he could explain that one of them could go home if she wanted but the language barrier was too great and he really didn't feel up to a prolonged haggling session with the two.

"Mister?" the one with the ballpen asked, having scratched out the original figure and halved it, showing just how generous they could be as the other woman commenced removing her clothing.

"Okay," he accepted knowing that he'd still paid well over market for the service.

Before the porter could escape to wait for his commission back down in the small reception, Coleman gesticulated with imaginary chopsticks to indicate that he was hungry. One of the women immediately smiled and put out her hand. He gave her one hundred Hong Kong dollars and she pouted. He laughed, they both then smiled and so he added another hundred knowing that whatever she returned with would not exceed his first offer.

She was gone for only twenty minutes by which time Coleman had been stripped and almost raped by the small tiger who had stayed behind. Obviously, he thought, the two had discussed their timing and this one was determined to have him laid and out well before their dinner arrived.

An hour later the three sat cross-legged on the bed having eaten the combination of noodles, vegetables and steamed fish.

He smiled to himself, wondering what his old friends would have said if they could see him now, sitting with two Chinese prostitutes probably well past their prime judging from the neighbourhood they were working, drinking the local sweet beer while being hand fed roadside food. If it hadn't been for the lingering doubts he still carried as to the purpose for his summons to Macau he might have even enjoyed the moment. But he couldn't.

There was no way that the three of them were going to squeeze into the bed comfortably together, no matter how vivid the imagination and regardless of how he tried, neither understood that he then wanted at least one of them to go home. They either didn't understand, or had elected to stay together as they were quite happy. It wasn't often they were paid so handsomely and fed for their efforts.

When he awoke they had both gone. He was still tired, stressed out completely from lack of sleep, and from the strenuous efforts to satisfy the rapacious desire of two women.

Then suddenly he remembered his wallet.

"Bloody whores!" he called. Jumping out of the bed too quickly he hit his leg on the bedside table in the cramped room. The pain forced him back onto the bed, holding his knee until the cruel ache subsided. He then limped across the room to check his pockets.

Nothing had been removed. Quietly relieved, he showered and paid for the room, leaving his soft leather carry-all with the old porter, who kept on grinning and giving him the thumbs up whenever he attempted to speak to the man.

He slipped another twenty dollars into the man's white jacket, borrowed his black umbrella and left for his rendezvous. He walked slowly, the humidity had already climbed well towards saturation point. Coleman found that it was easier to lean forward as he struggled against the strong wind.

It wasn't all that far. In less than half an hour he had passed through the small narrow cobblestone side streets down through the casino area and then back across to the small commercial harbour district in time for the prearranged assignation.

The sky was ominously dark as sheets of rain cut across the harbour. He held one hand over his eyes to protect them from the stinging pellets of water which forced in under his umbrella and quickened his steps. Running was inadvisable as the road was now covered with large puddles which were difficult to detect. Rain poured down furiously. Fierce gusts struggled with the umbrella. He considered folding it as his clothes were already wet but before he could do so, another blast of wind ripped the nylon up and back over the shaft, rendering the umbrella useless. He discarded it immediately.

Coleman had been advised that the meeting was to take place in the old warehouse which he had often visited and where, unbeknown to him, the armament shipments for Timor had been split. He was convinced that Seda had to be behind the meeting as, apart from the General's strange and hostile assistant, there were no others who would have been aware of their previous meetings in that place. Consequently, Coleman considered the warehouse an obvious choice for the deliberately vague arrangements.

Strong gusts continued to blow as he approached the large sliding doors. The wind rocked the steel structure and it creaked and moaned under the onslaught. He'd remained outside for a few minutes trying to detect whether it was safe to enter and finally accepted that it was impossible to know. The old building hadn't really changed. A warehouse is a warehouse, he thought, taking one last deep breath before stepping through the Judas gate. As he entered, Coleman thought he'd felt a cobweb clinging to his face and shoulder and quickly brushed the imaginary spider away.

The building was dark in the late hours of the overcast morning. Apprehensive, Coleman moved through the building cautiously, concerned now that he had committed a grave error attending the meeting unarmed. He regretted throwing the broken umbrella away. It would have given him some comfort, he thought, even if only psychological.

A light hung dimly in the far corner. He experienced a sense of *déja vu*.

Nothing had changed since his last visit. Except the pattern of his whole life. Pausing for a moment to allow his vision to adjust to the poor light, Coleman squinted across at the shape he could just make out in the far corner. The solitary figure sitting at the small desk waved impatiently for him to advance.

Coleman obeyed, moving cautiously in the man's direction. It was Nathan Seda. Coleman could sense that there were others close by but could not detect their presence in the sparsely lighted building.

"*Come, Stephen, we don't have much time,*" Seda ordered.

They sat facing each other. It was as if the General represented the master and Coleman the errant child awaiting punishment. He suddenly felt cold, his saturated clothes causing him to shiver involuntarily. He stared at Seda.

The Timorese was dressed like any other would around the docks. His voice sounded tired, almost old, and Stephen wondered if he'd come directly though from Jakarta or, as he himself had done, arrived the day before during the rough weather.

Maybe that's his problem, Stephen thought. If the rumours were true and an attempt really had been made against the General's life then, in all probability, Seda would perhaps expect his assassins to try again and this would account for the months of silence and subterfuge surrounding their relationship.

A length of iron sheeting shrieked as a strong gust of wind picked it up, violently slamming the metal roofing back into place, startling both the men.

Coleman was tense, waiting for his partner to commence. The light swayed slowly from side to side, pushed by an occasional puff of air forced through one of the many cracks in the damaged asbestos walls. Shadows danced, almost in slow motion, following the bulb's casual movements, creating an almost mesmerizing effect which he tried to ignore, concentrating on the other sounds he could hear behind the crates stacked to one side of the small desk. The palms of his hands were moist. He hoped the nervousness was not evident, and looked closely at the General to see if he could read anything from his expression, but couldn't.

"*It's finished, Mas,*" the Timorese suddenly announced.

Stephen paled. '*What do you mean, finished?*'

"*It's time to clean our house and put things in order,*" Seda said, cocking his head to one side, causing his features to appear almost sinister in the half shadow.

"*What do y....*" Coleman was cut off by a sudden gesture as the General raised his hand impatiently to indicate that he had not finished.

"The company is closed. Our kongsi is finished and, sadly, our relationship must now come to an end."

"Pak Seda, I don't understand what's happening here! What is going on? Why must we terminate the company's activities?" Stephen asked, as he felt the panic rising, events overtaking him at a speed he could not comprehend.

"Because we must now eliminate all traces of our involvement in the weapons supply companies. Because some of these weapons have fallen into the hands of the Timorese rebels and we will be blamed!"

We? he thought quickly. How could we be blamed when the whole goddamn operation has your personal stamp all over it? His mind raced. What was coming next? Was there someone lurking behind those crates waiting to tidy up after the General departed?

Stephen recognized the strange glint in the General's eyes and instantly realized that his life was in grave danger. This man, his partner, obviously intended to have him removed as one of the traces he had just mentioned.

But not right away, he could tell. Seda would not have risked exposure if the sole purpose of this meeting was simply to bid his partner goodbye. There was something else missing here, he knew, something more that the General wanted.

His mind raced silently. If Seda was aware that Stephen had known about his activities in supporting the separatists then that would certainly explain a great deal. But how could he know? Who would have told him? Only Anderson would be in a position to do so and he hadn't been in contact for ages.

Slowly it dawned on him. Of course. Anderson! Anderson and Seda. Together! But why go to the trouble of bringing him to Macau? Why didn't they just have him eliminated in Jakarta? Coleman searched desperately for a solution to his precarious situation.

Suddenly he knew. The General first needed to know if Stephen had kept any records which might come to light in the event of his death.

"What should we do, Pak Seda?" he asked, holding his voice even, determined not to display any sign of fear.

"Destroy all evidence and cease all activities immediately!" he demanded.

So, that was it! The General was obviously very concerned that evidence existed which would incriminate him and, should Stephen suddenly disappear, the General feared that this information could be revealed! Was what had happened to his servants some of Seda's handiwork? Had it merely been a message to warn him of what could have happened if they'd so wished?

He hesitated. Whatever he said or did next would undoubtedly determine whether or not he walked away from this meeting.

His hands were shaking. "*Pak Seda,*" he commenced, "*This will not be a simple task.*"

The General scowled at the Australian.

"*Why?*" he snapped.

"*Why?*" he countered, "*because there are companies incorporated in at least five different countries all requiring my seal. These would have to be dissolved, agreements with nominee directors terminated, bank accounts closed and,*" he added, his mind moving quickly, "*there is a mountain of administrative work which would be necessary in order to completely bury the trail of all of our activities.*"

Seda recognized the emphasis that had been placed on the 'we' as he spoke.

There was a long silence before the impatient general snapped again. "*How long?*"

Stephen hesitated. He had to play for time. It was obvious that once he had completed these tasks to his associate's satisfaction, his life would be worthless!

"*Six months,*" he suggested.

Nathan Seda's eyes flickered once, then he nodded slowly. "*You must do it faster if you can, Stephen!*"

"*We have known each other for a long time, Pak Seda. You must trust me. I will do whatever is necessary as you have instructed,*" he said, relieved at the General's reaction.

Seda remained silent for several long minutes before continuing the discussion.

"*You are not to return to Indonesia, Mas, under any circumstances. Do you understand?*"

For a moment, Coleman was staggered by the unexpected command, and remained speechless waiting for the explanation.

The Timorese remained silent.

"*That's crazy, Pak General, why would I not want to return to Jakarta?*" he asked, anger suddenly taking the place of fear.

Seda's eyes narrowed immediately.

"Crazy?" he hissed.

"A poor choice of words, Pak, but the question remains the same. Why am I not to return to Indonesia?" he demanded, feeling more confident that his assumptions were correct.

Seda smiled.

"Simply because you would now be arrested and tried for subversive activities, Mas!" He hissed again, venomously.

"What?" Coleman cried incredulously.

"Subversion. That's right. And it carries a death penalty, even for a foreigner!" he snapped.

"On what grounds?" the amazed Coleman asked.

"It has been suggested that your activities have not been restricted to the business sector. There is quite an anti-Coleman lobby developing back in Indonesia." You have messed up your private life making public those things we Indonesians prefer to keep private in our own homes and bedrooms. And there has been suggestion that you have been engaged in political activities on behalf of your own government. Confidential discussions have already been held with your embassy officials. You could easily confirm their concerns for your behaviour. Just call them! In short, you have become an embarrassment to them as well."

Stephen was stunned. A feeling of helplessness washed over him. He had been a complete fool. This had to be Anderson's work.

"What if I ignore the advice, General, and return anyway? Surely I can count on your ongoing support considering our past relationship?"

Seda identified the implied threat and jumped to his feet, kicking the chair noisily as he did so. Startled, Coleman reacted also, rising quickly, anticipating violence. Immediately a figure darted out from behind the darkness and pointed the semi-automatic pistol at Coleman's head.

Umar Suharjo's eyes were blank. He maintained his threatening stance waiting for the command to kill.

"No, you fool!" the General yelled.

Slowly Umar backed away into the darkness from where he had come, the weapon still aimed at what he perceived to be a threat to his master. Coleman's legs turned to jelly. He knew that the man had been present to execute him in the event that Seda had felt comfortable in doing so after determining whether he represented any real threat. His only protection now would be their concern that in destroying him, they may also destroy themselves.

"*You were responsible for everything that's happened to me and the company in Jakarta!*" Coleman accused, his voice now rising. "*Why?*"

"*That will be enough!*" Seda snapped back, "*Don't say any more!*" he commanded, "*or you will live to regret it!*"

The General paused to regain his composure.

"*You still have plenty. You have always been a greedy man without principles. You did nothing for my country and now you have lined your pockets. You demand more than you deserve.*"

He sensed that the powerful man standing facing him had almost lost control. Stephen realized he was still close to death. He remained still. And quiet.

Moments elapsed before the General spat the words at him.

"*Do not attempt to be too clever. Everyone has a limit to their patience. You must do as you have been instructed otherwise, next time...*" he paused, looking over his shoulder in the killer's direction, "*I think you are smart enough to understand?*" Again he paused as if reconsidering what he should do. "*Go now! Do those things which you must and remain in contact via these numbers,*" he ordered, handing a slip of paper to Coleman.

"*And Mas,*" he paused adding to the effect, "*Ring every week. Or perhaps we will believe that you really have become expendable. Now go!*" he hissed menacingly.

Stephen obeyed, drawing himself slowly to his feet and, with a slight shake of the head to show his disgust, walked towards the exit.

He had to lean hard against the Judas gate to force it open as the wind continued to blow fiercely outside. As he stepped through the small hole, the sheet metal door banged hard against his shoulder but he didn't feel the pain. He just wanted to get out of there.

Stephen fled the building, willing his legs to hold. He wanted to turn and check if he was being followed, but didn't.

Somewhere behind him in the overcast morning he knew the killer Umar was watching him. He refused to look back and continued along the wharf area until comfortable with the distance he had put between himself and the warehouse. His heart pounding, Coleman turned down a small street and then ducked behind another building until he was satisfied that he was not being followed.

The tall structures on both sides of the narrow alley offered some protection from the wind and rain. He knew there would now always be someone following his every move, watching and waiting until they could be sure that by dispensing with him permanently, there would be no lingering problems to concern them.

Coleman pushed himself hard up against the old stone wall and tried to breathe slowly. His heart was pounding with the rising panic. The sound of someone running in his direction caused him to tense. He waited. There was a loud thump followed by a man's voice cursing angrily. Still he waited. He could hear the undersoles of the man's shoes hit the cobblestones clearly with each step, even above the drizzling rain. Coleman tensed again, preparing to defend himself, sensing the danger. Clenching both fists into a tight ball he drew a deep breath as the man turned into the small alleyway where he stood. His hands came up immediately to strike, to defend, to kill, if necessary.

"*Aiiee ah!*" the startled Chinese cried out loudly as he almost bumped into Coleman, one hand already holding his appendage, as he'd prepared to piss against the wall, out of sight of other pedestrians.

"*It's okay, it's okay,*" Stephen had called after the man who continued to run from his attacker, tripping as he tried desperately to re-zip his trousers.

Stephen leaned back against the wall, head lowered, his energy gone. He'd been just as startled and, looking at his hands discovered that they were shaking violently. He crouched down, knees bent. Some distant voice in the back of his head yelled at him to breathe deeply. He obeyed and slowly his breathing became less erratic. He then managed to drag himself upright. Now move! the voice ordered. Move it! Move it! Move it! And he did, unsteadily at first, but then moving faster and faster until his feet were splashing down hard on the cobblestones.

A voice from his past kept yelling at him to run, and he obeyed, remembering his punishing training. He ran until his lungs screamed out for his limbs to stop and rest. Coming suddenly to a halt, Stephen realized that he was lost. He wanted to laugh, but couldn't. How could you be lost in Macau?

A couple huddled under one umbrella moved away from him,

possibly because they thought the *gwailo* was drunk. He looked around and spotted a familiar advertising hoarding. Now he had his bearings back. The small hotel wasn't far and he stumbled off in that direction, not even caring if he was being followed.

The porter saw him first, calling to the receptionist to look at the soaking wet *gwailo* stumbling down the street in the rain. An exhausted Coleman stepped gratefully inside then leaned against the polished rosewood reception desk, dripping copiously onto the worn carpet. After he'd rested for a few minutes, Stephen retrieved his carry-all and headed down to the ferry terminal to see if he could jump on the next boat leaving for Hong Kong. He'd given the old man twenty Hong Kong dollars for the lost umbrella.

The overhead signs indicated that the next departure would take place in an hour and so Coleman produced the return half of his ticket and then found himself a seat in the terminal from where he could observe the other passengers. He knew that he must now be extremely cautious. Seda knew that Umar was known to Stephen so it wouldn't necessarily be him that the General sent after his former partner.

* * * * * *

The return voyage was not much better than the previous day's. For the first time since he could remember, seeing the Hong Kong skyline didn't raise his spirits. There didn't seem to be anyone among the passengers who showed any special interest in him. He had watched them all closely as they boarded before taking his own place on board.

He needed clothes. He went directly from the Kowloon arrival terminal into the massive complex of shops overlooking the ferries and harbour across to the Connaught Building.

An hour later Stephen had purchased enough clothes to carry him through the next two or three days while he considered what to do next. He decided against checking into his old haunt, The Peninsula in Kowloon, as he was too well known there. He remembered the Hyatt around the corner but also decided against this or any of the other four-star hotels, as now he needed to be inconspicuous, to disappear.

He walked around the Holiday Inn, crossed the road and walked briskly down the steps into the efficient underground train system. Minutes later the Mass Transit Railway had him standing on the other side of the harbour where he easily slipped unnoticed into the swarming crowds moving hurriedly through the central business district. It would be safer for him here, he thought. At least fifty-thousand *gwailos* were permanently based in this area, employed as accountants and engineers to fill the void created before Hong Kong was officially passed back to mainland China. He knew that there were more than fifteen thousand Australians employed in the city, ironically filling positions created by departing professional Chinese who now lived in Sydney, Perth, Vancouver and many other cities far from Beijing's control.

Stephen visited one of the business bars off Central for a few hours. He ate simply and then caught a taxi away from the upmarket business district across to Queens Road East where he rented a room in a cheap Chinese hotel that also demanded no identification when he signed the register. He was tempted to phone Mister Lim but decided to keep his head down until completing the tasks he had now set for himself.

The next morning Stephen visited the Hong Kong and Shanghai Bank in Central. He closed all of his accounts and concealed most of his cash in a safety deposit box. Then he went to the Standard Chartered Bank and closed the company accounts. The staff were not at all curious. Transactions such as these were common and rarely warranted any query as to why such a long standing account had suddenly been closed. When it came to money, there was no race in the world that could be as discreet as the Chinese!

After this, Coleman went directly to the First National City Bank and closed both his private account and several of the existing company accounts there, removing any cash that was there. He sat for two hours signing applications and proof signatures for the travellers cheques he'd requested. By the close of business that day Stephen had deposited more than half a million American dollars in safe deposit boxes that he could access at any time, and converted the balance to traveller's cheques.

He had just under one million dollars.

Stephen had kept twenty thousand in traveller's cheques on his person and another five thousand Hong Kong dollars cash in his wallet. He was now ready. Six months before, at least on paper, Stephen Coleman had estimated his worth at nearly twelve million dollars. It had all gone. Disappeared. Taken by others. Stolen. Now he would go away and hide. Away from the pressures of the world which had become so full of uncertainties and danger. He would disappear.

Slowly and carefully, Stephen planned his exit from the city, the one remaining place he really enjoyed. He accepted that from the moment he had left the General back in Macau he had committed himself to a lifestyle which would require a complete change in his habits and a discipline he wasn't sure he could still maintain. Just having to forgo everything he'd either left behind or had been misappropriated in Indonesia was the hardest part. Still, he acknowledged, he had a nest-egg that most people only get to dream about.

* * * * * *

The following week Stephen left Hong Kong taking along sufficient funds to keep him in a modest lifestyle in the islands. The remaining cash he left locked away in the security of the Hong Kong and Shanghai Bank. He had planned only to return whenever he needed to draw upon the reserves and didn't expect that this would happen for some time to come.

He had set out, initially, for the Marshall Islands and the Philippines, spending almost a year in both areas. He moved around regularly, concerned that by staying too long in one spot he would increase the chances of recognition. And he knew also that somewhere Umar would be watching him. Whenever he moved into a new location Stephen would first stay at a modest hotel and then, once he familiarized himself, find a beach house suitable for his needs. His days were spent walking, eating, sleeping, and at first, thinking about his life and what he had to do. Eventually this deteriorated into an existence which consisted of nothing spectacular, the days seemed to roll into one. Weeks and months passed without incident.

He'd had the occasional affair or two but these never amounted to anything. He had no wish to make commitments. During his first year in the Philippines there had been one girl, but when she discovered that he'd never divorced his first wife, she had left him and taken up with an Italian. He had not been bothered by the strange behaviour, or at least he thought it was strange, considering the Catholic morality that existed in a country which did not even permit divorce.

He'd moved on then to Palau where he was pleased to discover that the people knew little of Indonesia and kept mainly to themselves. He remained happily ensconced in the small community for almost two years.

Stephen always attempted to position himself close to a beach and not too far from a bar. Mostly he was successful. He would sit in a canvas sun-deck chair around a pool or spend the afternoon lying in a hammock permitting the sea-breeze to rock him gently.

He really didn't want to think about the past. He knew he should try to sort out in his mind what had happened to him but he preferred to try to forget the past, with its painful memories.

Ignoring Seda's instructions Coleman never did make contact with the Macau number. He was convinced that it would only be a matter of time before the Javanese killer called on him. Umar could decide that Stephen's time had come and take matters into his own hands despite his master's concerns over repercussions.

He refused to return to Australia, but sent postcards with scribbled messages to his mother. For some time he hadn't known that she had passed away, and now couldn't remember how he had discovered that she was gone.

Sometimes he was annoyed with himself for doing nothing constructive with his life, but this feeling of regret would last no more than a day, or at most two.

He had no feelings of guilt. When he considered what had happened in Timor he reasoned that, as he had not known what the General's real agenda had been from the outset, how could he be responsible for what had happened? And the hundreds of thousands who died were almost forgotten, who really cared? The passing years and historical fact had treated them all so very badly.

He recognized that somewhere there was a woman to whom he was still married and that he had neglected her out of lack of compassion and understanding. Because most of his life he had acted in a most self-serving manner his present demise was a direct result of that selfishness, and he was now paying the price for his selfishness and the selfishness of others.

Sometimes he would wonder about Anderson. But not for long. When he reached his fortieth birthday he had celebrated alone, privately, sitting on the raised wooden veranda of a beachside bungalow consuming the bottle of Dom Perignon he'd saved for the occasion.

On that one day, as he sipped the long cool mixture of rum and coke, he realized that he had no ties, no friends and virtually no family. His life had no real value. He was nothing.

He made an annual visit to Hong Kong to replenish his money supply, and even that city had slowly lost its character and become sad. Most of the intelligentsia had fled for greener and safer fields as time began to run out for the former British colony. He felt that it was as if suddenly, one day, some monstrous world clock somewhere had suddenly chimed, passing ownership of the land and its islands to the undeserving mass of humanity across the hills, leaving the struggling few to cope with their new masters.

It would be a sad day for all, he knew.

* * * * * *

From time to time in his wanderings Coleman bumped into vaguely familiar faces. He always left when the whispers started, but as the years progressed this happened less frequently. It had to be expected, his having been such a prominent, even notorious figure. Stephen had at first grown a beard but then considered it ridiculous and had it removed, explaining to his bed partner of the time that he was only doing so to please her.

Funds were never a problem. He continued to live off his capital, living modestly without being overly frugal. Stephen felt that there was just a limit to how much one could spend without making a career of it.

There was no necessity for him to place his funds on deposit. Besides, that would leave trace records and, although he was a staunch convert when it came to believing in the sanctity of the specialized numbered deposit system most of the Asian capitals had developed, he had never really believed that these could not be compromised under pressure should the situation arise.

Switzerland was a good example, he thought. Recent years had seen an exodus of capital from that country as it assisted other governments recover funds secreted away by former dictators, drug lords and even the more ordinary criminals.

He no longer cared about all of that. He was now totally devoid of ambition. His life had drifted along and Stephen Coleman became accustomed to, and even accepted, the emptiness and lack of commitment that filled his days.

* * * * * *

How quickly the years seemed to have passed, he reflected, dragging his thoughts back from this self-indulgent reverie. Reminiscence was not necessarily good for the soul.

A car horn sounded down below. He smiled as the waiter brought him another coffee and addressed him in French. Stephen sat for a while longer enjoying the evening air. A sense of drowsiness enveloped his body. He pushed the remaining coffee aside and called for his cheque. The relaxing atmosphere had almost caused him to become philosophical about his self, his life and his future.

He'd travelled the region for years and expected to do so for many more. He had been to Kathmandu and Shanghai, to Yangon and Mandalay, crossed the Thai countryside until he knew it almost as well as the inhabitants themselves, smoked grass on the beaches of Phuket and Pattaya, and fornicated in almost every resort on the tourist map.

And now he was in Saigon. And so was Greg Hart.

Chapter 21

Canberra — Ho Chi Minh City —
Jakarta — Hong Kong

The Prime Minister disliked immensely being referred to as that silver-haired politician. But as he ran the comb vigorously through his ample grey waves it wasn't his appearance that occupied his thoughts. It was those fucking files! He wished he could burn the documents.

Prime Ministers might come and go, but you still had to deal with the bloody political garbage they left behind hidden like some stinking skeleton, waiting for the new and unsuspecting tenant to take the leader's chair. It was just not possible that even his predecessor has been this capable a liar, he thought angrily, pulling at the knot in his tie one more time. He checked the handkerchief — it didn't match.

"Shit," he muttered, throwing it away then digging like some feral animal amongst the harmoniously laid out clothes accessories in the second drawer of the Victorian dresser.

"Gloria, where the hell is the other half of this combination?" he called, turning to his wife, pointing to the tie he had so laboriously worked on for almost ten minutes before discovering that it clashed.

"I don't know, dear. Have you left it somewhere?" she responded distantly. He guessed she was still annoyed with the magazine article featuring his latest indiscretions.

"Hey!" he snapped, knowing where this was leading. He'd read the bloody article himself.

The Prime Minister scrimmaged around for a few more minutes before deciding that it would be easier to change the tie.

The press were going to have a field day. Today, he thought, they were either going to harass him about the intimate article or, some smart-arsed little bastard would pick away at the Australian

Indonesian Defence Accord that had been signed by his predecessor without even consulting the other representative parties in either House. And as if that wasn't bad enough, the Prime Minister thought, the silly prick had waited until the twentieth anniversary of the Indonesian invasion of East Timor to make the announcement!

The press hadn't appreciated the lack of sensitivity. It had been precisely twenty years also since six of their number had been murdered in the area. At the time, most of the world's leaders had fallen over laughing at the naiveté of the man from 'Down Under'.

The only country which could qualify as being a potential danger was, they chortled, the counter-signatory to the agreement. It was almost another case of history repeating itself, like another agreement signed many years before in Europe, he cited.

'It will be just like Chamberlain and Hitler!' he had argued in the House at the time, leading the Opposition ranks to rally against the legislation which would legalize the document. As a member of the Shadow Ministry he had the numbers to have his voice heard, and heard he was, at the time, albeit unsuccessfully.

When the government had initiated the ridiculous agreement, the intellectual lobby screamed foul and endeavoured to defeat the government by working against this cosy arrangement. It had the potential to emasculate the Australian Defence Forces. Australia's military strength was only a fraction of its giant neighbour's and would remain so, he believed, as long as the country's defence strategists insisted on competing on a weapon for weapon basis.

The new Prime Minister was a realist. Although he knew that it would probably not happen in his life time, he had always expounded the premise that the country was too large to defend in terms of conventional defence policies. The country's coastline was difficult to maintain in terms of national integrity.

The long term solution would be to change the very nature of the armed forces by following the principle of dualism. In short, he had argued, when the servicemen were not occupied fighting wars or protecting their country elsewhere he believed that they should be gainfully employed in a civic capacity, similar to Third World countries whose maximum utilization of such military manpower had proven successful.

"Stuff the airforce!" he would say when the military budgets were discussed. "Why waste hundreds of millions of dollars on aircraft that can't even fly across the bloody country?"

The Prime Minister's position was simplistic, but he considered it appropriate for his under-populated country.

He envisaged an Australia protected by a massive fleet of gun boats which could double up during peace time as immigration and customs patrol vessels. These would operate in concert with a number of rotary and fixed wing aircraft squadrons consisting of the more conventional type of aircraft.

This would cut out the need for expensive jet fighters that defence departments always scrambled to acquire for their air forces. The savings in terms of the number of refugees who would be turned back alone could pay for a considerable portion of the budget, not to mention the positive counter-smuggling effects on the national economy.

When he had been Shadow Minister for Defence, well before he became the country's leader, he'd been asked how the Defence Forces would protect Australia in the event of attack. He remembered with some satisfaction, his response. "Well, we don't really have the resources to protect all of our coastline. It would be ridiculous to even attempt to do so. As I have maintained in the past, providing we have the ability to secure our coast with patrol vessels and air reconnaissance, then all we would need would be three of our own ICBMs." There had been a hushed silence after that particular reply. He wished the interview had never taken place, not least because of the copious amounts of wine he'd consumed prior to what should have been an informal discussion.

"How would we maintain the integrity of our own missiles?" he'd been asked by one of the more experienced Canberra reporters. The wine and the attention of the media had provoked an incautious reply.

"Simply, David, if we came under attack, we would send the first one off to one of their larger cities and then phone the bastards and ask them where they wanted the second!"

This had been met with a burst of laughter from the press and the following day's headlines had not done him any harm. Australians had always been concerned about their Asian neighbours' real intentions. It was odd but that off-the-cuff remark had probably been responsible for gaining him the Prime Ministership. Cartoon caricatures of him had appeared for weeks, depicting him walking around the countryside with the third missile hanging out of his back pocket stamped 'wherdoyawantit?' Overnight his popularity doubled and shortly thereafter he challenged the party's leadership, winning easily.

He had been successful, although the growing debate had not been easy. Dealing with a complacent public which had not been obliged to fight for their country in almost a quarter of a century had, at times, been tough going.

He understood that memories were short. He was a Vietnam veteran. He remembered how they had been treated like the enemy themselves after they had returned. If only the public had understood! The greatest loss the Viet Cong ever experienced was when they flooded into the province of Baria, south of Saigon, and overran the area, then held by the Australians and New Zealanders. More than two thousand seasoned Viet Cong and North Vietnamese regulars were repulsed at Long Tan by a handful of brave Australians who, when outnumbered by more than fifty to one, managed to lose only eighteen soldiers against tremendous odds, accounting for more than four hundred of the enemy.

'I wonder how many of my constituents would know that Hanoi then ordered the Viet Cong regiment to be disbanded out of sheer embarrassment?' he asked himself, knowing that the answer would probably be, none! People just don't care, he realized, especially when you encouraged them to become involved in their own politics.

The press still controlled the public. Whoever owned the newspapers and electronic media had become the de facto government of the people. The cross-ownership rules relating to the media in general needed to be further revised, he knew, so that the powerful few did not further tighten their stranglehold as they had during his predecessor's term in office.

He had read somewhere that the American President elect, once permitted access to the secret horror files that the public would never be permitted to read, was virtually given the choice to continue to maintain the recorded history of his predecessors' follies, or magnanimously destroy the evidence maintaining the public's perception that the man in the White House actually rode a White Horse and was guided by the purest of motives in the execution of his duties in the office of the most powerful nation in the world.

The PM shook his head at the thought of his inevitable battle with the media giants. Most Australian Prime Ministers had been faced with a similar problem when they took office.

He turned his head as his wife approached to check his tie.

"You'll be late, dear," she said.

"Tell Peterson to ring ahead. I'm on my way now," he ordered, examining himself in the long wall mirror again and, satisfied that he looked his best, he left the room, forgetting to remind his wife that he would not be able to attend the charity function with her again.

The drive from the Lodge, the Prime Ministerial official residence, never lasted much more than a few minutes and often he'd wished that his country operated on a similar basis as the Americans so that he could work from home, so to speak. He thought it absurd how most of the day he and his colleagues were forever running around the billion dollar Houses of Parliament when they could be just as effective plotting and planning the nation's course from the den of his temporary home.

The political system of the United States did not require that the nation's leaders necessarily be members of their Congress and the President, unlike his Australian counterpart, was certainly not required to stand and argue with the Opposition each day for hours on end, often as the object of considerable verbal abuse.

It was almost counter-productive, he believed, to elect a person to lead the country and then expect him to perform, when the majority of the time was dedicated to political infighting or slanging matches on the floor of the House each day.

"I wonder what the bastards are up to today?"

His Minister for Foreign Affairs, sitting opposite him in the limousine was caught off guard by the Prime Minister's question, as his thoughts were still concentrated on the sausages and bacon he'd been unable to finish.

They were running late for the meeting, again.

"Say again?" he asked, his mind still on the tantalizing aromas left behind.

"I asked, what do you think the Indons will get up to today?"

The head of Foreign Affairs shrugged, then shook his head and

KERRY B.COLLISON

immediately placed his left thumb nail between his teeth, a habit he had perfected over the years.

"Probably another demonstration, I'd expect," he answered.

"You'd think they'd cut us some slack considering the fifty million dollars in aid support we gave the ungrateful pricks just in this year alone! For Chrissakes! They should be giving us bloody aid! Look how well their economy has shaped up, and look at our unemployment figures. We could buy one hell of a lot of voter support if we used the aid budget allocation for domestic purposes, you know!"

The Foreign Affairs Minister silently took one of his long deep breaths as his leader commenced on one of his tirades. He hated these early morning sessions, and today's rhetoric was shaping up to be no better than any other he had been forced to listen to in the rear seat of the PM's limo. He really disliked accompanying the man when he went on and on like this. Especially when he hadn't eaten!

The one-sided conversation continued until the black Limousine glided into the area leading up to the steps of the House. Australian politicians considered themselves relatively safe. Only one real attempt had been made against a senior federal politician since Federation and even he had not been the Head of State. He'd suffered only minor scratches as broken glass had been scattered around inside the Leader of the Opposition's vehicle.

The men walked together, smiling at the television crews that had already lined the steps hoping to catch them for an interview.

"Prime Minister, what's happening in Jakarta?" one called out above the head of the man in front of him. "Will you be speaking to their President?" asked another as his cameraman followed the pair up the steps.

They didn't stop but merely smiled and waved, offering a nod of recognition to some of the more senior crew members as they passed through the throng and headed directly to the PM's offices. As they entered, his personal secretary was standing with her hands clasped in front, unsmiling as always.

"Good morning, sir," she said, coolly.

"Now, now, Shirley, don't be like that. It's his fault," the PM said, pointing over his shoulder at the surprised Minister. "He in-

486

sisted on having breakfast."

"We're late," was all she said, handing him the newspaper cut-outs and other press clippings.

"Ring them. Anything here?" he asked, running through the thick selection of articles.

"One or two I think you should read before the meeting. I have highlighted those in red."

He turned to his Minister for Foreign Affairs who knew that he would now be obliged to wait until the PM had finished reading the articles. They both detested the media but were astute enough to appreciate the power that they wielded and consequently the attention they demanded at all times. He sat in one of the leather chairs as the nation's leader walked into his office leaving the door ajar for his secretary to follow.

This was the PM's routine. He would read the articles, and they were usually damaging due to his position on the cross-ownership question. His secretary took notes of his comments for the PM's personal records.

This morning's editorial on page two was scathing on the government's inaction over the widening gulf between Australia and Indonesia, which were now experiencing a cooling off in their relations. The article felt that both countries' national interests could best be served if their leaders resisted calling each other names, such as 'recalcitrant' and 'racist', and got on with the job of repairing the damage that had been done over the past year.

"What a bunch of lying bloody..." the Prime Minister's invective flowed unrestrained.

His secretary listened for the umpteenth time to the new leader making his characteristic Monday morning outburst prior to the cabinet session.

His colleagues had publicly praised his abilities as if he was some new economic Messiah, ordained by the voters to cure their financial woes. Voters being what they are, especially in an environment controlled through an antiquated political system, cast their votes without understanding the simple principles of government and what was really required of their elected representatives during their term in parliament. The complicated procedures were bequeathed in a manner which virtually precluded any remedy. He was resigned to the fact that the public were prisoners of the Westminster System and its inherent problems, which would continue to dominate their lives and the former colony for years to come. He had supported the move towards a Republic, but common sense dictated that the transition from one political system to another should not be rushed as the opposition would have it. Instead, he advised less haste in changing all of the statutes, as that alone would burden his government with years of effort untangling the complicated laws of the land already based on there being a Monarchy at the head of the country and its Commonwealth.

"Anything else?" he asked, throwing the clippings onto the desk.

"Just this," she answered, passing the red file cover stamped 'Most Secret' and 'Prime Minister's Eyes Only'. She had not broken the seal.

The PM took the file and read on through the report.

"Have the director r eport to me immediately after the morning prayers session," he instructed.

The new Prime Minister had appropriately coined the expression describing the weekly gathering of his Cabinet when he had read in the press, not long after taking up office, that the lack-luster team now sitting on the front benches had been described as a gathering of lay-preachers who thought they understood but were not quite ready for the heavy responsibilities of their new positions.

"Yes sir," the woman had responded.

"And you had better remind the Attorney-General of the meeting."

He continued to read the highly classified report, grunting from time to time as specific points met with his disapproval.

Glancing at his watch he realized that time would not permit him to complete his examination of the secret contents.

"Open my safe, please," he requested.

His secretary immediately checked the single tumbler's position and, using his key to unlock the door the tall man bent down and placed the folder safely inside the heavy duty steel Chubbs cabinet. He'd wished it had been a shredding machine.

The Prime Minister then went about preparing for the Monday prayers session with his colleagues.

* * * * * *

The Attorney-General was uneasy as he waited quietly with the

Chief of Intelligence, John Anderson. They had both been called to the PM's office for a special briefing.

Privately, he considered that the Intelligence Chief was well past his prime and should be put out to pasture. The AG resented the man's power. Even though the Director should, in fact, report first to the Attorney-General before taking any direct action, this had proven to be impractical. As a result, Anderson only dealt with the PM and this infuriated the AG. He took heart, however from the certainty that the Director would soon reach the end of the service extension granted personally by the PM and this would put him well over the mandatory retirement age. It was unlikely that he would be around too much longer with his direct access to their leader. Then the AG could go about selecting a suitable replacement.

Had the AG known John Anderson a little better, he would not have been so complacent. Anderson had no intention of letting any politician appoint his replacement. When the time came, he would orchestrate this with the Prime Minister himself.

The Prime Minister had called them both in for this meeting so that the Director could explain the conclusions he had made in the documents now locked in the PM's personal cabinet. Anderson was obviously uneasy with this request. Due to the sensitivity of the contents he would have preferred the discussion to remain one-on-one with the Prime Minister. The fewer politicians aware of the details, the better, he had wisely thought.

"Well?" the country's leader waited.

"We've seen it all before."

"It is almost a repeat of an earlier era. The situation has failed to resolve itself and it is my opinion that we are heading for an extremely dangerous confrontation." He paused, glancing in the direction of the Attorney-General.

"Your predecessor, sir, was very concerned at the rapid deterioration of Indonesian-Australian relations brought on generally by the emergence of the former General, Nathan Seda, whose influence over their President has grown incredibly strong in recent years."

"Our reports indicate that not only is he a frequent visitor to *Jalan Cendana*," he paused, turning slightly to the AG and adding, "that's the unofficial name of the President's home," he went on "strong rumour has it that he is being groomed as the next Vice President."

"Obviously not being of Javanese stock would prevent him from the leadership's top position; we should however be conscious of the facts. Politically, it would be a clever move for their President to appoint him to the position, not just because he is such a prominent and powerful figure, but also we should remember that the country's more than ten million Catholics would support such a move. There are also more than one hundred million Indonesians who are not Javanese and the majority of these would also, we believe, strongly support any such appointment."

"In theory, gentlemen, he would have as much voter support as the President himself without, obviously, the backing of the military. The escalating political and social unrest we have observed has not been entirely a result of falling oil prices. Corruption has reached levels where these practices have created billionaires. Family members of high ranking officials actually own or control whole sections of the non-oil and gas economy." He paused, taking the glass of Perrier and drinking before continuing.

"Singapore's banks are overflowing with most of the hidden proceeds and, generally speaking, infrastructure is suffering throughout the country because so much capital has been siphoned off and left to idle in secret numbered accounts throughout Asia. The emergence of right-wing extremist elements now influences their foreign policies. Many of these supporters have considerable disdain for Australia and the day has come for the Asians to no longer consider our country either economically, or militarily, a threat to any of their expansionist movements. Our agreements covering the use of sea lanes for both merchant and military shipping are being challenged. The Ombai-Wetar Straits may be closed in the near future to both our and United States' submarines. Australia's entire export programme to Asia is at serious risk. In short, gentlemen, we should batten down the hatches, so to speak, and prepare for an extended period of tension with Jakarta unless we take the necessary steps to prevent any future escalation."

"I have read your recommendations John, I can't say I entirely agree with your suggestions. They seem a bit extreme to me."

The Prime Minister pursed his lips and leaned back in his chair.

"Sir," Anderson began, "you have had access today, perhaps

for the first time to your predecessor's 'Eyes Only' file."

At the mention of this the new Attorney-General immediately interrupted.

"Do I also have access to this information?" he asked.

The Intelligence Chief smiled courteously and shook his head silently.

The AG bristled. "Prime Minister, I must insist! After all, as Attorney-General I should be conversant with what is happening in Anderson's department."

The PM shook his head.

" 'Eyes Only ' means just that! It is not a consideration of whether the Attorney-General's office can be trusted with the contents of the document. It is a question of procedures."

He looked at Anderson, who appeared pleased with the PM's support.

"I certainly would not rest easily with the knowledge that others will access information relating to my period of service in this office subsequent to my departure which, I trust we all hope, will not be for some considerable time to come." He had attempted a smile. "It's worrying enough that when I do leave my successor will, however, acquire that right."

Question Time in the House prevented the meeting from continuing. Anderson rose to depart with the Attorney-General and, observing the Prime Minister's sombre expression, he knew there would be another summons to this office. Alone. The country's leader would certainly not wish others to be present when he authorized the steps which both he and the Intelligence Head would come to accept as imperative action.

As John Anderson was driven down Commonwealth Avenue, he considered the data contained in the secret file now in the possession of the new Prime Minister. He understood the sense of despair experienced by a new PM who, having accepted the mantle of the office, was immediately burdened with the information contained in the complex record of Prime Ministerial covert directives. And even with the most secret accounting Anderson knew that the records were far from complete. Information was the tool of his clandestine trade and he believed, as had his predecessor, the agency's first Director, that politicians were never to be trusted and that it was essential to the service's survival that some secrets continue as such. Even if it meant keeping these from the national leader.

His thoughts turned to the report dispatched by Hart.

* * * * * *

Director John Anderson rarely sat behind his desk. Most of the time he would walk the room as he thought through whatever had been troubling his mind. This day was no different from all of the rest. There was a major problem to be considered and resolved with as little fuss as possible. As soon as the first signs had begun to appear, his years of expertise flashed warning signals immediately telling him to extinguish this fire before it became impossible to control.

He read through the report again.

"Silly bugger," he said to the empty room. He continued to pace over and around the Tai Ping carpet which he had received as a gift from one of the graduating classes. He smiled. 'Classes' was not exactly the appropriate nomenclature for the graduating group of three. The year before it had been five. Before that, only two.

He looked at the facsimile in his hand and shook his head again. Sometimes, he reminded himself, some of the graduates just don't show their weaknesses until they are out in the field. And often, not even then, he remembered, thinking of Stephen Coleman. It seemed that fate had decided to play him a difficult hand for the day. Now he was faced with the problem of sorting out two of his former graduates and, as luck would have it, they had come into direct conflict with each other quite unexpectedly.

The Director thought about Hart. Then he remembered his holidays with Coleman on the slopes and smiled. Actually, he was quite pleased that Stephen had bloodied the cocky Hart. He wished he had been present to see it. Not bad, he thought, considering his age and the sedentary life style the man had lived over the last, how many was it, fifteen or sixteen years?

Anderson accepted that he had lost one of his most promising men when Stephen had decided to resign. He also admitted that he had not been pleased and had, at that moment, wished the young man an injury. Had it not been for the young man's mother, Stephen would not have been considered for the training. They had always been close friends and he was saddened by the way her husband had decided to pick up his belongings and just leave. He had offered her comfort. And she had accepted.

Now he was faced with the dilemma of her son, once again. Stephen had not been a particularly opportunistic soul and would not have made it to the top in his profession had he stayed on with the Service. He lacked that one instinct that was vital to operatives world wide. Self preservation.

Somehow he had known, even in the early days of basic training that, although his friend's son had ability, he had no real killer instinct! Now Stephen had become an alcoholic wanderer. A bum! And as Anderson always knew he would, Coleman had re-emerged to become a thorn in his side. He had to use this information and work the man who had become the thorn.

He looked at the photographs. Coleman certainly looked his age. Anderson knew that it had to have been the alcohol. The effects of liquor and a dissolute lifestyle were evident in the puffy features. He had seen many a good man destroy themselves, at first gradually, and then in a blind rush to reach whatever end they visualized for themselves through the bottom of a bottle.

He looked back at the photographs again, recalling with some sadness the vibrant young operative whom he had sent overseas, destined to enjoy a promising career with his Department. He also remembered seeing the same man in a hospital bed, hovering between life and death from his horrific injuries. He saw again the bleak, distant look Stephen had given him when he had told him of the death of Louise. That had been the turning point, Anderson reflected. At the time he had been perplexed and somewhat disappointed with Coleman's over-reaction to the loss. After all, Stephen had hardly known the young woman and certainly not long enough to warrant such a magnitude of grief. It was so prolonged that Anderson had been prompted to suggest a period of further training and a holiday.

The extended holiday had been a mistake, he now realized. Often he'd thought about the decision to permit the young man a few extra months as part of his psychological recovery process. Anderson misjudged his agent, believing that Coleman had purged the past from his system and was particularly annoyed when the young and promising operative had resigned. Now he was back.

The Director was conscious that this time he was dealing with a man who had already experienced life's peaks and troughs and would require delicate handling if he was to be of any real use. The Intelligence Chief was also aware of the limited power he would have over the man. He would need to develop a strategy suited for a man of Coleman's intelligence. He must be very careful. The man was no fool.

The ageing bureaucrat called his secretary and gave her the name. He would go over Stephen Coleman's file again and see just where he was most vulnerable and where his weaknesses exposed the man most to compromise.

******

Most would consider it unusual for one to retire to a city populated primarily by public servants. Albert had gratefully accepted the adequate pension and moved from Melbourne to the small unit. It suited his needs. And there was considerably less violence on the streets of this well designed city. In fact, he thought, when comparing it with Saturday nights in Melbourne, the Capital was a dream. There had been already too much violence in his life.

It had been more than a year since the government troops had opened fire on mourners at the funeral of pro-independence sympathizers in the in town of Maliana. The people had been devastated by the unwarranted and violent attack. At least two hundred had been killed. Many others had never been accounted for, including his sister's grandchildren. He'd had no idea that many of his relatives had moved back into the area where the slaughter had taken place.

'Would they never learn?' he had asked upon hearing the news. Not so many years had passed since the Indonesian military had opened fire also on a group of mourners in Dili, killing sixty to seventy Timorese as they paid their last tribute to yet another separatist leader.

Albert could not understand why the world refused to acknowledge the cruel impact suffered by the East Timorese at the hands of the invading forces. Documents had been tabled in the United Nations evidencing the first campaigns of enforced sterilization organized by the Indonesian military, and clear proof that these actions had continued since earlier documents had been submitted to the authorities in Lisbon.

Again there had been no world outcry. He was devastated by the inaction and feelings of helplessness. The Timorese had pleaded for the international community to acknowledge their plight but none came forward to help. It was if they were to be ignored forever and the simple people, whose only fault was to seek their own independence from an outside power, suffered the indignity of being forgotten.

Even during the three years of killing in war torn Bosnia the people there had not suffered the losses the East Timorese had during their twenty years of struggle. Why then, the Timorese refugees in Darwin often asked, does one country deserve more consideration over another? Why doesn't the United Nations position a peace keeping force in their country, as they had in Bosnia?

Why had they been left to the mercy of their giant neighbour? They asked those questions, and many others, knowing there would be no response. The Timorese sadly recognized that their plight would continue to be ignored as the superpowers arbitrarily accepted Indonesia's dominance over the Tim-Tim. *Republik Indonesia* had become a world force in her own right and vested interests now controlled policy. Economic criteria had a greater priority than humanitarian considerations.

These questions had also haunted Albert. He just couldn't understand how it could be that the United Nations had called for Indonesia's withdrawal so many times, and supported a supervised vote on the right for self-determination in the ravaged country, only to be ignored. Albert believed that had the same set of circumstances existed in a country of greater significance to the superpowers then their cries for help would have been heeded well before this.

It seemed that it just wasn't to be. After the most recent slaughter the Indonesian central government attempted a cover-up but the Australian media managed to keep the massacre in the news, again opening old wounds between the Indonesian muscle men and the international free press. Unfortunately this had the disadvantage of providing the Timor separatists an exaggerated view of international support for their call for independence resulting in even more arrests as they continued with their struggle.

On the other hand, the Indonesian people could not understand Australia's persistent interest in supporting the terrorists, as that

KERRY B.COLLISON

is how they had come to identify the separatists in Tim-Tim. *'Why do the Australians pose as our friends,'* they would ask first time visitors to their country, *'when the separatists support the destabilisation of one of our provinces?'*

Albert knew all about this. He still read the foreign language newspapers regularly. And in those pages he would often see the familiar face of his stepbrother Nathan Seda. The General's rise to political prominence was seldom out of the news.

He had not maintained any further contact. In fact, he had deliberately avoided contact with those who had remained in Indonesia, receiving only scant news, usually of accidents or deaths of a family member which would immediately be followed by requests for money. He didn't mind. They were far less fortunate than he and it was an obligation he could not refuse when asked.

And then there had been the occasional news of Stephen, but this too had ceased some years before. He felt extremely sad for his old friend. Bad news travels fast, so they say, and Stephen's fall from grace had been swift and severe, according to the gossip he had heard from other members of the Indonesian community in Melbourne. Perhaps it was for the best that they no longer communicated.

Maybe he was dead, although he thought that unlikely as this news would also have slowly filtered through the system. They had not spoken since Wanti's collapse and their departure from Jakarta. Albert had not returned to Indonesia nor made any attempt to contact her husband since those times. He still felt bitter at Stephen's treatment of Wanti.

If only they had known Wanti's secret then, perhaps their lives would not have resulted in so much despair, tragedy and disgrace. All Stephen had to do was agree to the divorce. It could have been handled in Jakarta within days and may have prevented, or at least softened the shock of her brother's death. He knew that the final decree would have been automatic and issued within the month even considering her condition at the time. The authorities in Indonesia would have been far more sympathetic to their needs than the bureaucrats in Melbourne. Now it was all too late.

Albert contemplated his past, reminiscing while strolling slowly along the cycle track, in the cool clear winter's day. He had long given up smoking cigarettes. His pipe was now one of the few remaining luxuries left in his life, and he puffed away furiously as he moved around the park opposite the apartment block.

Albert did not light his pipe when inside. His daughter, Seruni, would usher him outside immediately she detected the powerful odour.

"Please, father," she would scold in textbook Indonesian, *"you promised!"* and he would smile contentedly.

He had accepted her polite demands for, although barely out of her teens, he adored her bossy childlike tone. She had effectively become the lady of their household.

When her mother had passed away Albert did not feel that he had the strength to go on with his life. But as one soul had passed on to be replaced by another, he had found that it was possible for him to continue. He cherished the child who had been given to him to love, as he had loved her mother.

Wanti had meant everything to him and, even during her last months, Albert had tried in vain to persuade the authorities to let them marry before the birth of the child.

He thought back over those painful last months of Wanti's life. Her doctor had expressed surprise that the shock she had experienced while in Jakarta, let alone the return travel, had not induced a miscarriage spontaneously. As Wanti had remained silent regarding her condition during her early pregnancy it was not until she had advanced well into the fifth month that her startling diagnosis had been determined. An abortion was totally unacceptable to Albert and medical opinion merely confirmed that even under more favourable conditions such an operation would be ill-advised.

He had attempted to locate Stephen to seek his assistance in arranging an immediate divorce in Jakarta. Albert knew that Stephen had the influence and money to facilitate such matters. He had spent considerable time planning how to approach him. It was obvious that he would agree but it really came down to how well he could present the situation without having Stephen fly into one of his memorable temper tantrums.

Albert decided to gauge Stephen's reactions before proceeding with the request. Should his former friend be receptive, and not still carry a grudge over what had transpired, then it was his intention to ask that Stephen give consideration also to providing assistance in producing documentation evidencing the marriage of

Wanti to Albert, backdated to when they had visited. He believed that this was imperative for his child's future.

Due to her mental condition no one, of course, would entertain their marrying in Australia even had she already been divorced. Divorce proceedings could no longer be initiated by Wanti due to her condition, this course of action only then being open to Stephen.

'It isn't fair!' he wanted to yell at the bureaucrats who had explained the legalities of their problem and the limited options available to him. They couldn't even claim a de facto relationship due to her mental status.

He had phoned for days on end, attempting to locate Stephen, without success. Finally, having left messages everywhere regarding the seriousness of Wanti's condition, and the importance of his returning their calls, Albert decided that Coleman had deliberately ignored their requests out of spite. His disappointment became frustration and, eventually, totally disillusioned with the one time friend, he ceased further attempts and accepted the inevitable.

The pregnancy continued, the foetus alive in its own world slowly developing, oblivious to the fact that its life support systems were far more fragile than nature had ordained.

It was then that he grew to despise his former friend. And as the child inside approached term, preparing for its chance to enter the world, Albert sat and wondered what it would be. The nurse who now visited, out of a deep affection she had developed for the stricken woman, had volunteered her services regularly and Albert was extremely grateful for her kindness.

There had been little or few complications with the pregnancy. It was Wanti's mental condition that had induced her demise.

He had been at her side continuously. Within the minutes following his daughter's birth the baby was held to Wanti's breast, and suddenly, as the tiny child cried, the once beautiful woman squeezed Albert's hand, then called his name and smiled. Her twisted face even more grotesque with the effort of the labour, she had called out, *"Albert! Albert, the baby's beautiful!"* and he then believed, and always would, that God had blessed her with that one brief moment of consciousness to understand she had given birth. And then Wanti had died.

As she had closed her eyes Albert was certain that she had merely surrendered to exhaustion. He called her name, softly, and then urgently, still holding her hand, his heart tearing apart. The nurse had taken her hand away gently parting the couple. Suddenly the realization that she had really gone struck him with such force that he cried out loudly, his grief then taking charge.

The nursing staff had been efficient. He was sent away while they cleaned the body and prepared it for its next journey.

He had left the hospital complex, not knowing whether he wanted to live or die. The thought of the newborn child had not really registered as the pain of his loss was far greater in his mind than anything he had ever experienced, even as a child in that faraway place.

Days had passed before he could bring himself to visit the hospital again. As the nurse held his daughter for him to see through the plate glass partition, Albert's heart had skipped a beat and he felt awash with the proof of Wanti's love for him.

He had the child registered with his surname. That, he knew, was his right as the natural father. He even waited to be challenged as he submitted the forms, eager for some form of confrontation to question his rights over the infant, but none occurred.

The first time he held her in his arms he cried softly, the hardened nurses around him turning away, holding back their own tears and as Albert proudly walked out of the hospital with a new life in his care, he swore that he would always watch over her and that nothing would ever harm his daughter as long as he lived. She was later christened Seruni and Albert dedicated his life to her.

As her features took shape Albert became more and more pleased with her appearance. Her hair was a little wiry and perhaps she was not quite as pretty as her mother had been. But she was his daughter and he loved her dearly. Albert remembered her early days and smiled to himself. Scenes of their lives together flashed through his mind as he continued to walk around the tree-lined pathway, not really uncomfortable with the cold morning air. He remembered her as a tall slender teenager, intelligent and slightly over-demanding.

Now she was a young adult. Almost a woman.

'Ni, as her friends took to calling her was, he thought, most unlike her mother. Albert was pleased that she had become so independent, so strong and yet there was still a softness which he knew came from the magic of her mother's soul. As she had left her teens he tried not to be overly protective even though he was concerned that she would be hurt, or that soon he would lose her.

As the years progressed Albert had buried the sorrows of the past and now, as his child grew into a young adult, she would soon discover their secrets. He prayed that when the time came 'Ni would understand that her parents had been given no other choice.

Albert, however, would never forgive the man whom he held responsible for all of the suffering he and his family had born. He resented the intrusion of the man's memory in his thoughts.

As the ageing man climbed the few stairs leading to the apartment lift, he attempted to erase the face of Stephen Coleman from his mind.

* * * * * *

Saigon

Hart knew there would be a confrontation. There was no point in avoiding it. He accepted the call from Coleman and had consented to the meeting.

Greg Hart had agreed to his suggestion of midday in the beer garden behind the lobby of the Continental Hotel. The setting was normally quiet and not overly frequented by foreigners other than tourists. Hart walked through the lobby just minutes after the other Australian had seated himself on the far side of the terraced area which, he observed, permitted Coleman the opportunity to scrutinize arriving guests.

He'd seen his former employer a few days before when he almost knocked him down in his haste to get to his next appointment. He recognized the man instantly even with the additional weight and greying hair. It was the second time in less than four days that he had come that close to Stephen.

Hart had known of his presence in the city the very same day the man had been confined to his hotel room recovering from an obvious state of alcoholic poisoning. Identifying new arrivals was one of his tasks in Ho Chi Minh City and Coleman's presence had not exactly been low profile. He had reported immediately to Canberra and was instructed to maintain quiet surveillance, and in the event that he was seen, contact was approved conditional on his carrying the Berretta issued through the Hanoi Station Chief.

Coleman had also selected the Continental's rear terrace because it was on the ground floor with three separate exits should a discreet departure suddenly become necessary.

Coleman spotted Hart and raised his hand in recognition. Hart approached feeling wary and aggressive.

This was Hart's first opportunity to observe the other man closely and he was now startled by the change.

Stephen Coleman had aged considerably.

As he approached, Coleman rose but did not extend his hand.

"Hello Hart."

"Stephen," the younger man responded and slipped into one of the heavy chairs, unbuttoning his jacket.

The silence was broken by one of the staff who had approached their table to take orders. They both accepted coffee.

Hart was the first to begin. "I trust we won't have any unpleasantness?"

"Why?" Coleman replied. "It would certainly be in character!"

"Shit, Stephen, I wouldn't have agreed to see you if I'd known that you were going to cause a scene."

"Mate," Coleman started, years of bitterness welling up as he now sat faced with the man he believed had caused so many of his problems with the authorities back in Indonesia, not to mention the expatriate community, "Why else would I bother to look you up? You don't really expect me to believe that you honestly think there is no bad blood between us? For Chrissakes, what you did to me in Jakarta would have earned you a box in most countries!"

"You don't understand, and probably never will. I did only what I thought was best."

"What a crock of shit! How could you possibly sit there and make that statement when I know, for a fact, that you spread so much shit around the market place regarding what had happened between Wanti and me that the gossip mongers had a field day!" Coleman was trying desperately to keep his cool. "And the bullshit you also started about my company and its activities. I hold you personally responsible for that, as well!"

"I think that this meeting was a mistake," Hart said, beginning to rise out of his seat.

"Sit down, you arsehole!" Coleman yelled, losing control of his temper.

"Go fuck yourself, Coleman," the other said, now on his feet and buttoning his light weight jacket.

Coleman caught a glimpse of the weapon as Hart hurriedly buttoned the coat.

"What the..!" he started to say, leaning across to rip the jacket open.

Hart resisted and suddenly they started yelling at each other, not loudly, but enough to cause considerable anxiety over at the waiter's station. They were watched carefully by the hotel employee as they argued. The concerned waiter decided it would be inappropriate for him to interrupt and stood discreetly away from the two foreigners as their voices rose.

Suddenly there was a shout and the Vietnamese was startled when the older man jumped to his feet and delivered several blows to his companion. The waiter fled in search of the hotel security.

Coleman stood over the prostrate figure, watching the blood ooze from the man's nose and mouth. He had hit Hart with all the force he could muster, the first blow releasing years of pent up hostility as his fist smashed teeth and bone. Hart had not anticipated the sudden blow and, stunned, did not even see the second nor the third punches which were expertly delivered with extreme force, smashing teeth through his cheek and ripping his lips.

The injured man lay still but not unconscious. His assailant remained standing, poised to strike again, arms raised, muscles tense and fists white with the skin broken around the bone. Moments passed and slowly Coleman lowered his hands. Someone called and he turned in time to see the waiter returning with what appeared to be security. Extracting a fist full of dong from his pocket Coleman waved the large bundle of notes at the approaching men. He convinced them that the altercation had ended and that his companion had not been seriously hurt, just his pride.

Stephen explained that they had argued over a woman and immediately the men departed, accepting the fabrication, amused that the older of the two had beaten the other to the ground with apparent ease. The Vietnamese enjoyed a good fight and so why not the foreigners?

"Must have Vietnamese blood," joked the security officer as he looked back over his shoulder just a moment too late to witness the man still standing bend down and remove the automatic from the other foreigner's body.

Stephen waited several minutes for the bleeding man to recover. As Hart slowly regained his composure Coleman turned to see if he was still being watched by the waiter and, as he was not, bent down to position himself even closer to the half prone figure. Glancing quickly once more to ensure that he wasn't seen, he punched the prostrate body hard with severe blows to the stomach and ribs.

Coleman thought he heard a cracking sound and stopped his assault, breathing heavily. He then checked the coat and trouser pockets but found nothing of any real interest. He looked down at Hart dispassionately, he was groaning painfully.

Satisfied that Hart would survive, Coleman rose to his feet, straightened his clothing and left, the injured man still lying on the ground. The bitterness he had harboured through the years seemed to dissipate and, for the moment, he sensed a feeling of exhilaration he had not known in a long, long time.

As he stepped back into the hotel reception he heard the steel gates being pulled aside and, turning his head, he noticed that the lift had just descended. It was one of those noisy concertina shaped lifts, a restored version of the old cage models used widely during the French Occupation. Stephen waved to the security officer who had opened the exterior door to assist the guests inside.

The Vietnamese smiled warmly and lifted his fists in the boxer's stance followed by which he gave the Australian the thumbs-up sign indicating his approval.

Adrenaline still flowing quickly, Stephen Coleman walked briskly back to the Rex, caught the lift to the fifth floor and settled down at the bar to plan his future. The confrontation had triggered a response which had not displeased him. He had reacted positively to a basic human emotion and now realized that he could no longer avoid the ghosts which had haunted him for more than fifteen years.

It was time to settle with the General.

* * * * * *

Later that afternoon, nose bandaged and his face puffed terribly the bitter and badly beaten Hart sent a further communiqué to

Canberra. He advised Anderson that Coleman had attacked him and was, in his opinion, a threat to their network in the region.

The Deputy Director had responded immediately as the Intelligence Chief was away, advising their man in Ho Chi Minh City that they had initiated action and his instructions were now to avoid any further contact with Coleman.

Greg Hart attempted a smile when he received the message. Wincing with pain, he gingerly touched his swollen lips. They had required eleven stitches.

He hoped that the action his superiors had initiated would compensate for the thrashing he had received at the older man's hands. Hart knew he had never really been considered as having the right material to rise much further beyond his current position in the Service. This was only his second field posting since leaving Indonesia. The last had been seven years before and had not been entirely successful when they had to pull him out of the Philippines when he had been mistaken for another Australian engaged in one of the paedophile rings there. Still considered relatively junior in the Intelligence Organization, due to his limited abilities, he felt he really had no appreciation of what steps would be taken against his antagonist.

He leaned back in the swivel chair carefully considering this point. His pride had been seriously wounded. It would be obvious to all who witnessed his condition that he had been on the receiving end of a bloody good hiding!

'What if the staff at the Continental talked?' Coleman's beating enraged him. He fantasized wildly about being the one selected by his superiors to deliver the appropriate punishment to his adversary.

"Bastard!" he cursed, then wishing he hadn't as the pain shot through his broken face.

* * * * * *

Jakarta

Seda had never become disillusioned with the cause. He had committed his life, his being and his very existence on this earth to achieve his ambition for an independent Timor and would continue to do so until he had given his last breath. His resolve became even firmer, if that was possible, as the slow annihilation of his people continued, unwillingly conceding that the time had not yet arrived when his people could enjoy their freedom.

But he continued with his plans, adapting them to suit and rearranging them, whenever required, patiently yet impatiently reworking his strategies until he was satisfied that he had exhausted all possible scenarios available, eventually settling on one final and, what he believed, brilliant concept. Although it appeared that all was lost after the FRETILIN defeat, there was still considerable resistance to Indonesia's occupation of the territory.

Another generation had appeared. The new youth had again taken up the cry for independence from the Indonesian invaders, and they too were prepared to sacrifice their lives, if necessary, as many parents had before them.

The separatist problem just refused to go away. Support had increased after the indiscriminate shootings in Dili in 1991, and again as a result of the slaughter in Maliana in 1996. Children were taught secretly in their homes about the sacrifice their elders had made, and were encouraged not to forget the historic clashes in which their own people had won decisive battles against the much stronger adversary.

Names and dates were not forgotten. The death of Nicolau Lobato, the FRETILIN President who had been so treacherously betrayed on the last day of December in 1978, was remembered with sadness. And so too were the others, the painfully long list of their heroes who had given their lives in support of their freedom. Songs were sung softly in the mountain villages far from the ears of their enemy; songs of their heroes, and of the battles fought in places such as Bobonaro and Quelica, and of despair for the thousands of children who had died in the fierce aerial strafing attacks. The sterilization programs had continued unchecked by the international community.

The United Nations had all but given up voting on the issues relating to the enslaved state. It just wasn't in the interests of the major powers to intercede on their behalf. They had no money, no resources and now, very few weapons as, one by one their armories had been destroyed in the mountain depots. It was becoming clear that the status quo might never change as the Australians had not only signed defence agreements with the new colonial power but also entered into contracts to share the substantial reserves of oil and gas discovered within the former colony's territorial waters. The issues had become far more intricate in nature and complicated by the ever changing regional politics.

It was the hypocrisy of business, they sadly acknowledged, and their one time ally had now completely deserted them. It seemed that everyone was to prosper except the rightful owners of the land.

Even Seda's substantial wealth had grown, and with it, his power. He had discussed the offer of the Vice Presidency on a number of occasions with the President.

At first he declined. After a time, when the national mood swing supported such a decision, Seda accepted. It fitted into his general strategy, and his international standing would be greatly enhanced with the appointment. It would also permit the final touches to the strategy which could easily be his last attempt to achieve his dreams, and his destiny.

The incumbent would step down in one more year as agreed. Nathan Seda had suggested to the President that relationships with Indonesia's neighbours could be improved if, while waiting for the Vice Presidency to become vacant, he helped their Foreign Affairs Department to settle some of the main issues. Would it not be beneficial for him to spend some time visiting these countries in a gesture of rapprochement? The President was supportive of the idea.

Seda's enemies within the small powerful group of advisors, albeit few, threw their support behind the suggestion as they wanted him out of the mainstream of power and saw it as an opportunity to remove him from the political scene. This was the second time in the nation's history that the military hierarchy had become uneasy with the meteoric rise of one of the country's sons of non-Javanese stock. General Benny Murdani had caused them considerable concern when he almost clinched the post only to lose the opportunity due to his religious affiliations. National ideologies had changed considerably since the days of strict military control, producing a new generation of young men and women who were well educated, and less tolerant of the armed forces than their parents had been.

It was becoming more and more difficult to intimidate the

masses. Support for non-military figures had grown alarmingly, reflected in the number of seats now held in the Parliament. Student demonstrations were not always aimed at foreign issues as they had been twenty years before. Now the youngsters had the audacity to even confront their elder statesmen with placards calling for inquiries into corruption and nepotism within the government.

The new generation of Chinese had all but forgotten the frightening tales of slaughter that occurred throughout the archipelago thirty years before. They ignored the re-emerging signs which reflected the deep rooted animosities that had predicated the deaths of many of their ethnic minority during the abortive coup d'etat, under the Soekarno regime.

The powerful military lobby was painfully conscious of Seda's evergrowing popularity with the other ethnic groups and non-Moslem Javanese.

With half the country now no longer easily intimidated by the army, their concern was real, for Seda represented a role model which many wished to emulate. He had risen from humble beginnings and had never lost the common touch. He had served his country well both as a senior military officer and as one of the custodians of their country's economic growth, throughout the term of his service. The General had become statesman-like in his demeanour and didn't kow tow to the Palace over issues that were important to the *rakyat*, the people. When the Australians demonstrated in their cities against Indonesia's position over the ongoing oil and gas shelf territorial dispute it was their Seda who had spoken out publicly threatening to support a military blockade of the drilling areas. He was different from all the others, they knew. The people could sense it. And he was a Christian.

The former General's enemies were ecstatic at the suggestion that he be appointed as the country's Ambassador as they believed that once he had left their shores his popularity would soon decline, his name would then be quickly forgotten by his following. They had all seen it happen before and believed that Seda would be no exception.

Letters containing diplomatic necessities were exchanged regarding the appointment. The Australian people, once pumped into action by the opposition, would normally not have been receptive to such an appointment as the General had been identified as one of the principle movers behind the invasion of East Timor, and also a member of the elite military establishment which had been responsible for the slayings in both Dili and Maliana.

Had it not been for the direct and covert intervention by John Anderson, the Australian Government may have been submitted to considerable editorial pressure not to approve the appointment. As it happened, two of the larger circulation newspapers supported the selection of such a prominent Indonesian, once again reflecting, they wrote in their columns, the high regard the Indonesian Government had for the Australian people by nominating General (retired) Nathan Seda. The appointment was accepted, in principle, subject to the normal diplomatic procedures being respected.

The press had printed the story and suggestions were made that his appointment was appropriate, not only because Nathan Seda had served his country in a military capacity and then had continued on to become a successful entrepreneur in his own right but, primarily, because he was of Timorese extraction. The editorial in the Sinar Harapan suggested that his ethnic origins may even assist strengthen Indonesia's negotiating position during the forthcoming bilateral talks scheduled to be held in Canberra, Australia. It was hoped that the Australians would be reasonable in their demands and assist to diffuse the current tension over the Timor shelf oil contract concession areas.

The Armed Forces' sponsored daily newspaper, *Berita ABRI*, strongly supported their former General's selection citing not only his impressive service record but also the need for someone of his calibre, whom they believed was needed now at these difficult times when Australia and Indonesia were experiencing a major breakdown in their traditional support for each other; and although Indonesia's military believed that these reflected domestic issues in both countries, the Armed Forces were one hundred percent behind any efforts that General (retired) Nathan Seda saw necessary in restoring the good bonds that had existed until just a few years before.

* * * * * *

The day Seda departed on the Garuda 747 flight, almost ten thousand students and other supporters gathered along the route to the Sukarno-Hatta international airport to bid him farewell. As he climbed the steps of the huge aircraft which had been parked away from the terminal building due to traffic congestion, the crowd waved furiously from the observation level at the man they had come to admire so much.

He could just hear their chant above the roar of the other aircraft's Rolls Royce engines as it had taxied past, their voices drifting across the large expanse of concrete as they chanted, *"Se-da! Se-da! Se-da!"*

It was then, for the first time throughout his years of struggling to achieve the position of power that was almost in his grasp, he knew that his dream was imminently achievable and that he was almost there. He had stood majestically for a moment on the steps and waved back to the young people who had called to him, knowing that one day they would probably learn to hate the very sound of his name. This thought did not concern him. He could not permit such sentiment to cloud his judgement, as he understood that whatever they may feel in the future, regarding his actions, would depend entirely on just how successful his efforts were in achieving his goals. As the aircraft drew away from the terminal building Seda realized that he was actually entering the final phase of his plan. And should it be unsuccessful, he doubted that there would be another opportunity as his time had all but run out. This time he could not fail.

* * * * * *

The diplomat had orchestrated the travel itinerary so that his arrival would precede the international forum on regional stability. As a guest speaker, Seda would have an opportunity to achieve even greater exposure, consolidating his position as an international leader. The man who would become the next Vice President of Indonesia, and then even the President of his own country, Timor Timur. The small group of people who continued to support their dream of sovereignty would reclaim their country, silently, this time without bloodshed, while the two neighbouring countries of Indonesia and Australia concentrated on settling their own disputes as each fought the other to protect their territorial rights. His dream continued and Seda believed that it would soon be realized. One way or another.

KERRY B. COLLISON

The central government would never surrender the annexed territory, now just another of the industrial giant's many provinces. It would become part of the overall settlement when the bloodshed had finished and the two countries were obliged to sit down together and resolve their regional differences. He would ensure that this was so. As the country's Vice President.

His people had not benefited from the amalgamation of the two halves of the island: only suffering and extreme cruelty had come with the annexation. Amnesty groups had estimated that the death toll had risen to above three hundred thousand Timorese during the prolonged resistance against the Indonesians.

Seda considered that, as New Guinea was now also a serious regional trouble spot and, with tempers running high between Australia and Indonesia, there was still the very strong possibility that the people of New Guinea could also be dragged into the conflict, as even they no longer enjoyed the special relationship that had once existed between the two nations. The country was now considered unsafe for Australians and their investment houses. Violence was common between the two races and environmental issues and claims had all but brought many mining projects to a grinding halt.

Freedom fighters continued to cross the border into Irian Jaya causing havoc, and the Australians had accused the New Guinea Government of deliberately destabilising the area.

That self-determination could be achieved for the eastern half of Timor no longer seemed feasible as even political radicals agreed that it was highly improbable after so many years of Indonesian rule. The UN had become fragmented over the past twenty years and strong protest at the increasing volatility within the region had begun to cause some concerned nations to react unilaterally. They no longer believed that the UN had the power to resolve such issues unless the countries with vested interests, such as the United States, put their own priorities aside to bring about a peaceful resolution to the regional problems.

Now that the first steps of his project had been initiated there would be no turning back from this final commitment. It was a daring scheme but he knew it would be successful.

Seda had spent millions disrupting the fragile relationships between the two countries and, with his presence in Canberra, he believed that he could ensure an end to the Australian support for

510

Indonesia's control over East Tmor by committing all of his resources into this one final effort.

He was counting on the support of his own *Fifth Column* who, as refugees, had quietly ensconced themselves within the Australian community. In particular, he could rely on the large number of men he had assisted to cross the few hundred kilometres into Darwin and down to Port Hedland. Almost all had now been given political asylum over the years and the majority, at his request, lived in the northern Australian city of Darwin. Many now worked as tool-pushers or mud men on the offshore rigs operating in the areas now in dispute. When the time arrived they would sabotage the Australian operations and take control of those sites. This was essential to his strategy.

It would be extremely difficult, he knew, to establish a beachhead even for the few short days required, without the total support of the refugees and his own men who had successfully infiltrated most of the other political movements in Darwin and Port Hedland. They were all crucial to the successful implementation of his plan.

It hadn't been easy maintaining control of the separatist forces through his intermediary, Umar Suharjo. The FRETELIN rank and file were still not aware of his identity and he continued to use the former major as his only direct contact with all of the parties involved. They rarely asked questions. When they did, Umar's cold stare would be their only response and normally sufficient to curtail their curiosity as they were aware of his reputation. Most were satisfied with just the strength and sincerity of their secret supporter, as the constant flow of funds and weapons had never ceased. They accepted that this powerful entity needed to maintain a cloud of secrecy as to his identity, and understood also that his support was dependent on that secrecy being preserved. Whoever he was, they believed they could count on him and he on them.

Many of these former guerrillas had already been enlisted as part of a special task force which he planned to mobilize towards the third quarter of that year.

Seda's time was running out. Each morning as he observed himself in the privacy of the bathroom mirror he could see that his age would now be his major handicap should this final attempt fail them all. There had just been too many battles and far too many sleepless nights worrying about whether he had covered his involvement successfully.

The subterfuge had continued. Would there be a knock on his door late one night to relieve him of his power and all hope for his dreams?

There had been a time not so long ago, he remembered, when he sensed that his secret would become public and all would be lost. Seda had never understood how Coleman had successfully managed to evade Umar's search. He had worried that Coleman would suddenly reappear and accuse him of involvement with the arms company although the paper trail had long since been destroyed. As the years passed, and Stephen Coleman didn't appear, it seemed that his secret was to remain intact. Not that the Australian could really do him any harm now, after so much time had elapsed.

Anyway, Seda thought, it would be unlikely that anyone would believe the man. Coleman would be accused of deliberately agitating to further exacerbate the problems between their two countries at a time when even minor incidents caused social unrest and public reaction. No, he thought, he was no longer a threat to Seda nor the intricate plans that had taken years to put into place.

The retired General's rationale was a brilliantly conceived strategy with a simplicity in its application that virtually guaranteed success. He understood the phobia Australians had regarding their Asian neighbours. There was almost an inherent fear that, one day, hordes of yellow skinned devils would pour into their country and take their women, their land and eventually become their new masters. This myth had, he knew, been perpetuated by the Australian leaders themselves as a means of maintaining power, increasing defence spending and generally using the Asian population as a prop for whatever excuse required as the country slowly deteriorated economically during the latter half of the century.

He would attack their isolated towns, creating a moment of terror that they had not experienced since the Japanese destroyed Darwin with their air-raids and the mini-submarines attacked Sydney Harbour, executed as part of their desperate attempts to invade mainland Australia during the Second World War.

There would be other and simultaneous breaches of Australian security, but none as deadly as the bomb he had planned to deliver into the basement section of the nation's Parliament.

He sneered at the Australian's informal ways. Seda despised them for their lack of loyalty. His people had fought side by side with the soldiers and their funny shaped hats against the common enemy when the Japanese threatened to rule the Far East. Soldiers from both nations had died side by side. When the Timorese had sought the support of their old friends, at the time their impoverished land was invaded by Indonesians, they had received nothing more than a cursory commitment that the Australians would ensure the sovereignty of the fledgling nation which, in spite of those casual promises, never did have the opportunity to enjoy its own state-hood.

His armed groups would raid one of the small Australian coastal towns killing many of its inhabitants. When the sleepy southern nation retaliated, which he expected would be relatively slow in terms of response as they were so poorly equipped, Seda would have the opportunity to drag them even further into the conflict; this would, he anticipated, result in not just a regional swing against Indonesia, but also provide him with the opportunity to widen the split between the two countries until international pressure forced the warring nations to the negotiating table.

It was imperative to his plan that the United Nations finally be pressured by the other powers to intercede in the conflict, creating the opportunity for Timor to be used as a bargaining instrument in the final settlement. The rich Timor oil fields and the strategic military importance of the Ombai-Wetar Straits virtually guaranteed vested interest support from the Americans in achieving stability once again over the area. The United States was desperate to maintain their secret nuclear submarine presence in those deep ocean depths. The Australians would not wish to see their access through Indonesian waters blocked, cutting off their most important trade routes, and would have no choice but to also support an independent Timor. This would guarantee ongoing access to the deeper sea lanes, essential for the huge ships carrying iron ore and other shipments into Asia. Under the terms of the Law of Sea Convention, which Australia and Indonesia signed back in 1994, disputes over sea lanes were to be settled before the International Marine Organization. The President had agreed to withdraw Indonesia from that convention if other countries would not accept the routes revised by his generals. It would not be long before Indonesia could block all sea traffic through its territorial waters. Australian trade would suffer immediately, bringing about the loss of established markets. The Australian Collins class nuclear submarines would no longer be permitted to pass through the deep straits off Timor. Under the Law of the Sea, Indonesia was declared an archipelago state which gave it special rights over its waterways in exchange for providing an appropriate number of international sea lanes. The Indonesian military, as a result of Seda's influence, developed a different interpretation of the Law as they had become extremely suspicious about international shipping. Seda had a joint venture shipping *kongsi* with those close to the President and wished to develop a monopoly over the use of Indonesia's sea lanes.

Seda believed that all of these factors would contribute to the success of his plans. As hostilities increased between Australia and Indonesia he would step forward and offer to prevent further escalation and invite the United Nations to intervene. Seda knew he had substantial support from the Indonesian people. He would use this strength to force the Javanese to accept the terms negotiated with its neighbours.

As one of the country's senior leaders, Seda could ensure that Indonesia would bend to international pressure and grant Tim-Tim its independence. As a gesture, he would suggest that Timor be placed under the protection of the United Nations until such time as elections could be held. He didn't want to see a recurrence of the blood-letting that his people had already suffered. But, if necessary, he had promised they would once again fight, creating three fronts for the Indonesian military to consider. As almost half of the country's population were Christian, Seda was confident that he would have the necessary strength to achieve his aims.

The OPM freedom fighters would cross from New Guinea as they had done before, raiding the transmigration villages established by the Javanese in Irian Jaya, killing and terrorizing until the migrants fled and they themselves returned across to the safety of their own borders. They would burn the freeport copper town of Tembagapura and destroy the mountainous mining facility which continued to fatten Jakarta's coffers.

Australia would immediately go on the defensive once their coastal areas had been threatened and their cities attacked. The Timorese would press for yet another UN-sponsored resolution supporting their independence and, should this also fail, insurrection would occur immediately. Teams would take over the drilling rigs and those which could not be secured would be destroyed, with their crews.

His strategy was to activate the groups simultaneously. The first group, numbering twenty and armed with the weapons to be distributed by Umar, would strike the small town of Broome on the northern coast of Western Australia.

Their instructions would be to shoot and kill as many of the inhabitants as possible in one hour and then retreat. They were not to differentiate in their random selection of targets. Distasteful as it may be for the guerrillas, they were told that maximum effect could be attained if a reasonable number of women and children died in the attack.

The strike team would enter the area in vehicles which would be transported to within a few kilometres of the small town along with the weapons. This equipment would be in place three days prior to the attack, stored in two semi-trailers along with other essential items. The large trucks would be driven from the interstate storage company in Perth, an outfit Seda had arranged to purchase, along with the vehicles, the previous year. These would then meet up with the team at an abandoned cattle station airstrip.

Their escape would be by air. Two Nomads that had been acquired were currently housed in their hanger in Port Moresby. When the time came, both would be flown down through Queensland and across towards the target area where they would wait until after the raid, and then ferry the group back to Darwin, from where the aircraft would then return to their original departure point. The aircraft would fly low on the sectors in and out of the strike zone area. Flight plans would be submitted excluding these sectors, nominating other unmanned private airstrips, any number of which could be found throughout the enormous expanse of the great Australian outback. The Nomads would not be detected and, even if they were to show up on the traffic controllers' screens, they would probably be mistaken for another couple of foolish country flyers building up extra hours on their private licenses.

Seda had first developed the concept when reading how so many small aircraft continued to enter Australian airspace undetected. Many of the flights were drug-related shipments and he could never understand why the Australian air force was so complacent when it came to light aircraft landing at their military strips.

As the attack was to take place during the early evening, the raiding party would have sufficient time to complete their task and disappear before the shocked Australians could even begin to understand what had happened to their town. He estimated that, as the killing would occur during the school holiday period, the dead could number as many as three or four hundred.

His men would wear Indonesian uniforms, complete with their colourful berets and shoulder flashes. They had to be seen to be an elite Indonesian military corp responsible for the attack. Seda smiled at the reverse role some of the older men would play, former FRETILIN soldiers who would finally have the opportunity to take their revenge and have the Indonesians taste a little of their own for a change, once the Australians retaliated! The town would be in shock and relatively defenceless.

The men were to move in quickly, driving the jeeps through the main street and into the police station where they were to kill those present and set fire to the building. The post office would be closed, but the Telstra communications were a first priority target and had to be destroyed quickly. It was unlikely there would be many cellular telephones operating although, if there were, there was little they could do about this problem. Next, the team was to drive to the hotels and bars, strafing the windows and doors, and randomly shoot all pedestrians within sight. In the event some of the local inhabitants were able to take up arms and return their fire, bodies of any of their dead or wounded were not to be left behind.

The second group of seventy-five men, similarly dressed, would hit three or more of the small fishing villages across the Torres Strait killing as many of the islanders as time permitted. These raiders would escape, also through the night, by small high performance boats returning to one of Seda's offshore crew vessels, their point of embarkation. The smaller craft would then be scuttled.

They would remain on board until receiving further instructions from Umar. A specialist team of three would work from his residence. A catering truck would depart from the embassy compound where it would have been positioned away from the inquisitive eyes of the police until the time was right for its special delivery to the people of Australia. The vehicle had already been purchased and was being prepared by his Security Attaché. Seda smiled. Umar with a diplomatic passport! He wanted to laugh, and would have, had not the thought been so serious.

The small truck had already been repainted leaving only the appropriate company logo and colours to be affixed. They had done their homework with relative ease; security in the capital was quite deplorable, as he'd discovered during first investigations as to the viability of his plan.

It would really be so incredibly simple! Umar had come up with the idea and he had approved of it almost immediately. It was brilliant! The small truck had double lock doors at the back and a sliding access hole on the roof of the aluminium housing which rested lightly on the extended tray. Inside the container and immediately in the centre, Umar would place a drum of diesel oil and then steadily pack the metal bin with ammonium nitrate until the relative proportions had been achieved. When he had finished there would be approximately seven percent of the total contents in fuel oil sitting silently in the compacted mass of fertilizer, which they would purchase through the same trucking firm Seda had acquired for the Western Australian operation. As ammonium nitrate absorbs humidity from the air, making it much more difficult to ignite, the diesel oil was necessary to keep the chemical from absorbing the humidity, making it more combustible and compatible with the detonators they had planned for their surprise delivery.

Then it was just a matter of using the simple technique that Umar had observed so many of the registered suppliers were instructed to follow when on a run into the service areas of the Houses of Parliament.

The truck would be left parked below in one of the appropriate bays designated for light deliveries, and Umar would simply take one of the service lifts, walk through into the building and follow the staff until accessing the public passageways in the uncomplicated structure, leaving through the front entrance. Umar had already visited the buildings and had conceived the idea after discovering the incredibly lax security. He had been amazed when first entering the building that they had even given him a brochure complete with plans of the overall layout. He had tested his idea at least a dozen times, casually walking through the entrance which leads into the Great Hall, turning to the left as if he'd intended using the toilet before taking the lift down to the underground carpark. Umar had discovered that there was an alternative choice available. Should any difficulties occur on the day, he would park the van on the common carpark instead as the lifts permitted visitors to exit directly outside the main structure.

The truck and its contents would remain in place until news broke of the successful attack on Broome. This would, no doubt, result in an emergency meeting of both Houses of Parliament. The building would be packed full of the nation's representatives!

Umar had estimated that the force of detonation would be similar to the Oklahoma City disaster or even the IRA bombing of London's East End. The explosion would almost certainly destroy the main building, killing most of the politicians present at that time.

Perhaps the Australian public would give him a medal! He laughed silently to himself, relishing the thought of removing the majority of the so called policy makers in just milliseconds! He expected that the military would act in the absence of any political leadership. The ageing General believed that the plan was almost flawless. The unpredictable Australian cyclone season may present a problem but apart from this consideration, he felt that the operation would be successful.

Umar had already taken up his post as Head of Security in the Embassy, acting as his co-ordinator and making preparations for his own arrival to take up the position as the new Ambassador.

The first team which was to be designated the task of attacking Broome all resided in Australia. These were loyal FRETILIN soldiers, Timorese whose sympathies still supported the use of force to liberate their homeland.

Almost everything was now in place. All that remained was his presence in Canberra, where he would present the new Australian Head of State his credentials, appointing him as the Indonesian Ambassador Plenipotentiary and Extraordinary to the Government of the Commonwealth of Australia.

Seda could hardly wait.

THE TIMOR MAN

* * * * *

Canberra

The Prime Minister had, by now, developed a distaste for the all too frequent meetings with the tall grey-headed Intelligence Chief. Having listened to the arguments proposed by Anderson the politician reluctantly admitted that it did, in fact, make a great deal of sense to go along with the appointment.

His first reaction was to instruct the Foreign Affairs Minister to refuse to accept the notorious Seda as the proposed Indonesian Ambassador however, as Anderson had quite rightly suggested, although it would not be exactly palatable having him sitting in Canberra, the general public in both countries had no inkling whatsoever of the powerful man's covert activities and, away from the central power base of Jakarta, he would lose considerable strength and influence in that city. In consequence, the Prime Minister had, with reservations, agreed to the appointment. Normally he would not interfere in such matters; however, when the former General's name was mentioned during a prayer meeting the Prime Minister remembered having seen something about him in the 'Eyes Only' classified documents.

Later, in the privacy of his inner sanctum, he was disgusted to discover that he had been correct and that his government was being asked to accept this evil man at Ambassadorial level.

The afternoon following the ceremony accepting the former General's credentials in Canberra, John Anderson visited a two-room apartment in Braddon, one of the capital's older suburbs. It was the home of Albert Seda.

Chapter 22

Hong Kong

Stephen had stayed on the island of Koror in the Palau group for four weeks, swimming and snorkelling around the beautiful islands almost untouched by the tourist industry. The pristine beaches remained one of Palau's attractions, pulling him back regularly, like some gigantic magnet, whenever he felt the need to disappear and collect his thoughts.

He had lazed around on the main island for the first week, doing nothing more than walk around the small capital, eat, drink and generally play the tourist in what he considered to be one of the most beautiful islands in Micronesia. It was the combination of the overweight locals, content with their lives and always happy to sit down and talk to a newcomer as they were a naturally hospitable people, and the lazy tropical days, that made one feel completely relaxed. The sun's rays were not overly aggressive and the flat calm lagoon effect of the ocean as it barely moved upon the sands, the faint sound of the ripples licking at the minute granules of coral sand, could guarantee sleep at any time.

Each time he revisited, Coleman had difficulty believing that the tiny paradise, although it still enjoyed the protection of the United States, was in itself not subject to any external threat; nor was the minute republic exploited, even though it was truly one of nature's tropical wonders that had to be visited by all. Even the domestic political disputes were, by very nature, almost tribal, and the casual visitor soon became familiar with the more prominent personalities in the isolated and relaxed capital.

Stephen primarily dedicated his time to exercise aimed at reducing his weight. He ate sparingly, enjoying salads and the popular steamed fish dishes the islanders prepared so well. He drank only in moderation and was quite pleased with himself at being able to abstain until the late afternoon sun had disappeared below the horizon, providing him with the motivation to continue with these efforts to restore his health and get his life back into order. When he remembered the copious amounts of alcohol that he'd consumed every day over the past years, even he was surprised that his body functions had not given up well before, leaving him to die in some stinking hospital in Vietnam or China.

He read the American newspapers when they were available. Inevitably, the tabloids emphasised news from the States and hardly mentioned his area of the planet. There was still plenty of time to catch up, he thought, and once he had restored his energy level to where he felt confident of being able to withstand the demands he planned to place on his mind and body, then he would make the effort to find out what exactly had been happening in the rest of the world that may be of any real consequence to him.

Towards the end of the fourth week Coleman felt totally revitalized. He had lost eight kilos, almost eighteen pounds of fat, due to his healthy diet and exercise program. His skin had lost its jaundiced tinge, replaced by a healthy tan. He looked at himself in the beachside bungalow's long dressing mirror and decided that he should have embarked on this road of self care years before.

Admiring his improved shape and tan, he decided it was time to move on.

That evening he arranged his onwards travel a little saddened that he would be leaving the magic of these islands behind. The airstrip severely limited the size of the aircraft that could land in the scattered island group and he decided to follow the path established by many of the American servicemen still stationed on Guam, making his way south across the myriad of small islands down to Port Moresby, where he intended then sailing on to the northern tip of Queensland, via Cooktown and the other small coastal towns.

The typhoon changed his plans to island hop across the region as the sky turned ominously dark and the wind howled threateningly through the coconut palms and rooftops.

The power of nature's forceful winds alarmed Coleman. He had no wish to fly around the islands in a light aircraft being tossed around in the turbulence. The typhoon kept him indoors for almost three days and, sensing a bout of depression, he cancelled his immediate plans, electing to remain on the island for a few more weeks. Stephen scrapped the original itinerary and decided to replace his wardrobe and replenish the dwindling contents of his tattered money belt. He returned to Hong Kong.

No longer concerned with anonymity, Stephen checked into the Hyatt on Hong Kong Island, as the Kowloon side had suddenly been inundated with another flood of Chinese investors intent on purchasing whatever property they could now that the gates had been opened.

He visited some of the old familiar haunts but found that many had given way to even more high rise development on the already over-saturated land. The city's character had changed to such extent in just a few months he had difficulty identifying the real 'Hongkies'. The new tenants had flooded into the world's largest marketplace, placing unprecedented pressures on everything from public utilities to exotic and previously outlawed forms of Chinese cuisine. This new breed, descendants of Shanghai coolies and street traders who had become China's *nouveau riche*, had brought with them many of the old habits and ways which had been prohibited under the British.

Restaurants blatantly advertised animal organs from protected species as main fare for the day. Stephen noticed that one restaurant he'd passed had no compunction preparing the rhesus monkeys from India, locked in their cages, screaming at their temporary masters, almost knowing that they were doomed to a tormented living death when the expensive meal was taken by the discerning Chinese connoisseurs, scooping pulsating brain through a hole made in the table's centre section so that all of those present could participate simultaneously, believing that eating the live monkey's brain would give them tremendous sexual vitality.

He wasn't disgusted that the city's inhabitants had seemed to have taken a major step backwards and forgotten whatever the one hundred years of colony rule had taught them. Western civilization's perception of how human behaviour should be as the world approached the twenty-first century meant very little here.

Stephen understood that. Instead, he merely reserved judgement even though the thought of the monkey's brain appetizer would spoil his appetite. He remembered where he was, and how the people in the real world of Asia actually lived, and would probably continue to do so millenniums after Western civilization had been put well to rest.

Mister Lim's operation had quietly closed after he had fled to Canada prior to the Chinese takeover of the former colony. The hotel's concierge soon put him into contact with an up-market service, which he had dialled and made arrangements for the following evening.

He had ordered a selection of new clothes to be tailored and, although the fashions had changed to a combination of baggy shirts and semi-stovepipe trousers, with button-less coats left open, he'd insisted on the older and more traditional cut for his single-breasted suit. He intended at least to look the part of the role that he knew he must play.

When these were ready, Coleman phoned the Australian Consulate General and arranged an appointment with the passport control officer as his travel document once again required renewal.

Then he visited his safety deposit boxes and confirmed his assets, smiling to himself at the wise decision he had made all those years back when the pressures of the moment could have caused him to panic and lose it all. As he sat in the private cubicle prepared by the bank's clerk, viewing the first of the two boxes, a flood of memories returned as it always did each time he opened what he jokingly thought of as being his own private bank. He picked up the faded photograph and smiled before placing it back inside the box. Then he checked the cash.

Stephen counted. There was still more than four hundred thousand dollars left in the steel boxes. Even when he'd been in a permanent alcoholic haze in the past, he'd kept track of his cash.

There were also three envelopes.

He had not considered it necessary to take precautions before the threats against his life. When making the notarised declarations at the time, Coleman had thought that the ignominious material contained in the letters wasn't much of a testimony to his life. He understood clearly that, should the letters become public or actually be read by the addressees as annotated on each of the revealing envelopes then, of course, he would be dead.

His instructions to the bank management had been simple and explicit. At least once in every year he required that his signature be presented when either transferring funds or just inspecting his own safety deposit. In the event that a year had passed and he had not appeared in person then the bank was to open his security boxes and forward all of the contents to one Albert Xavier Seda as per the address he had given. Coleman had attached a will leaving the cash contents to his wife, Wanti.

The three brown envelopes were addressed to each of the editors of The Jakarta Times, The Sydney Morning Herald and The Mirror with copies of details of Seda's involvement in their *kongsi*, attaching invoiced proof of funds with the relevant banking authorizations nominating the General's own accounts as the recipient of huge commissions. Each also contained a statement regarding his earlier role working for the Directorate headed by John Anderson — sufficient information, he had thought at the time, to severely curtail their activities for some time to come.

Before closing the lid of the second container, he considered the contents of these damaging envelopes and smiled. Stephen sat quietly for a few moments before passing the cream-coloured steel boxes containing his whole life's possessions over to the clerk for double locking. He then left the bank's cellars and returned to the hotel, already bored and exhausted by the bustling city.

Stephen phoned the escort service and advanced his booking.

* * * * * *

The officious immigration officer had insisted Coleman return for his passport after two full working days, looking up at the applicant as if he were some dirty piece of dog's excrement, carried into the consulate stuck to the underside of his public service shoes by mistake.

At the time Stephen had bristled. He knew that this type of petty bureaucrat entertained themselves at the expense of the public and willed himself not to over react. Stephen knew how Australians were perceived by their Asian counterparts, although they were normally too polite or embarrassed to say. Often, when confronted with these minor officials whose supercilious behaviour resulted in adverse first impressions, the Oriental would accept the insulting conduct as normal and in line with what they had learned to expect of all European races.

As it was now already Thursday, Stephen had little choice but to wait until the Monday morning when the Consulate would have his new passport ready. They agreed that he could retain his old passport, reluctantly, until he had insisted that it would be required for banking purposes.

"You must surrender your old passport on Monday when we give you your new one." he was told.

He had thanked the obnoxious consular officer and left before his temper got the better of him. Coleman knew that he had to remember to keep his cool. It would be important in the weeks ahead. He had time to kill and decided to spend the next two days visiting Guang Zhou as he had not been there for some years. Disappointed with the industrial pollution, he returned late in the afternoon in time to confirm the arrangements for his Saturday night's entertainment.

She was exceptionally attractive, but not in Angelique's class, he thought, watching her undress hurriedly. Their lovemaking had been mechanical at first, and Stephen was tempted to pay her then and there spending the remainder of the weekend alone. She had showered and was sitting silently as if waiting for further instructions.

"You can go home now if you want," he said.

"Why?" she asked, surprised.

"Well, I thought maybe I'd take a rest and just watch a show on television."

"You no send me home, okay!" she had pouted, obviously thinking that an early departure had meant her client was dissatisfied with her.

Stephen had laughed at the serious expression and the accompanying act, fully aware of the reason behind the reaction. "Okay, you stay," he said, with which the towel around her breasts was immediately flung aside as she jumped onto the bed pulling him down playfully.

They left the room only to dine in the hotel's well-appointed restaurants and, as he was not drinking anywhere near as heavily as before, he found that his old stamina was slowly returning to form.

It had been a long time since he had really enjoyed the company of a woman for more than just a few hours. Her name was Kwai Fong. She was expensive. Coleman didn't complain as her attitude had changed when they returned to the suite, this time undressing slowly in well rehearsed and tantalizing movements, before engaging him in a long slow fantasy showing the sexual finesse of a practiced artisan.

Stephen was content to remain in the hotel room, eating, being spoiled and occasionally running the remote control through the multitude of channels offered through the hotel's satellite television service. He had arranged a final fitting for the rest of his new wardrobe and, satisfied that there was little else to do but wait, spent the remainder of the weekend being entertained by the beautiful woman.

* * * * * *

It was a short taxi ride to the Consulate's offices. The mass of humanity gathered around the ground floor lift access spilled out through the building's foyer onto the footpath. Visa applications for Australia, he assumed. Thousands of the old Hong Kong citizens waited for their families overseas to process their applications to join their children who had the right to sponsor parents and other immediate relatives under the revised immigration scheme. Too impatient to join a queue, he pushed through the crowd and found that it wasn't all that difficult. The others thought he was a member of the staff and quickly stood aside as he asked them to move.

The lift doors opened at the appropriate level and immediately Stephen had to fight his way through yet another large number of Chinese pushing to reach the numbered roll of tape allocating a position to those who wished to make an inquiry from the Consulate.

Again he pushed through and was relieved to see that one of the consulate staff had identified him. He signalled for Stephen to pass through the side security door and into another holding area. Stephen was impressed by the thick heavy door clicking firmly shut behind him.

He was ushered into an office where the almost effeminate creature, the man who had caused his blood pressure to rise when he'd last visited, was seated. The consulate officer smiled sweetly and advised him that his passport had been endorsed by the Consulate, but not renewed.

"What do you mean endorsed? What sort of crap is this?" he

had asked immediately, standing over the now agitated official.

"I am not the Consul, Mr Coleman, you will have to speak directly to him. He has asked that you meet upstairs and he will explain."

Coleman was then ushered upstairs and through another series of security doors, similar to the first, to another section where he was instructed to wait. He became impatient to get out of the building with its overhead fluorescent lights and sterile atmosphere.

Twenty minutes had dragged by when finally Stephen was asked to follow the security officer. The man was dressed smartly in his new Federal Police uniform, one of the first issued under the restructured department's new image edicts. Stephen became uneasy when he noticed, with some surprise, the Smith and Wesson Thirty-Eight police special strapped to the officer's hip.

Immediately Coleman sensed that he had made an error in judgement. He should have had his documents renewed in Manila, he thought, as the journey from Palau took him through that city, where he had spent two days and would have had ample time to complete the necessary formalities without this inconvenience.

He turned suddenly to the consulate officer, unhappy with the way things were developing and concerned that he might now be under armed escort. Stephen hoped he was overreacting.

"What's the problem? Look, if there's a problem, just give me my old passport and I'll proceed on to Shanghai and have it done there. It won't be a hassle for me as I have business there and my passport still has enough space for limited travel," he lied.

"I'm sorry, but you'll just have to wait."

"Okay, ten minutes then I'm out of here, passport or no passport," he warned.

"All right, follow the officer then," he was instructed, "you can sit in the other office."

Tense and convinced that he was justified in feeling hostile, Stephen followed silently as he was escorted into yet another room and again left to wait, impatiently, for what seemed an excessively long time. It was impossible to know, but he felt sure that the armed security who had not spoken during his exchange with the consulate official, had taken up post directly outside the room in which he now found himself. He was angry and was about to leave without his documents, deciding to return later or arrange to have someone else pick the passport up on his behalf, when the he heard voices approaching.

The door opened and Coleman stared at the visitor in disbelief.

"Good morning, arsehole!" the man snarled at him.

Coleman still couldn't believe his eyes. Standing across the room at a safe distance was the man he had left lying on the ground in Ho Chi Minh City. Greg Hart.

As he rose to his feet cautiously the doorway was suddenly filled with several other men who pushed in quickly and stood still, saying nothing, just glaring at him. These were unfamiliar faces but Coleman guessed from their size they were there to restrain him, should the necessity arise.

Hart smirked. Or was this his new natural smile acquired as a result of their last confrontation and the beating he'd given him?

"I won't give you any crap about the good news and the bad news Coleman," he spat sarcastically. "For you it's just all bloody bad!"

Stephen looked at the man silently, refusing to be baited in case he was being set-up. The heavy-set pair looked like they were just waiting for an opportunity to use their muscle on him.

What the hell was Hart doing here?

"You are being placed under arrest," Hart began, "and you are being charged under the Official Secrets Act."

The other government men in the room could see from the cocky manner that Hart was enjoying himself. The sarcastic tone and method of delivery wasn't lost on them. This was the first time either of the security men had been party to an arrest under The Act and they were nervous, understanding the gravity of such charges.

Had they been privy to the thoughts of the man now detained their concerns would have been justified. At that very moment, more than anything he'd ever wanted before, Coleman wished they would leave the room, if only for just a few minutes, so he could kill the smiling Hart. He knew he would do it, without hesitation. Coleman sat stunned with the incredible realization that it was Hart who was making the statement for his arrest. He must have been involved somehow with Coleman's former government associates and had been, even way back in Jakarta when his now apparent treachery had resulted in the collapse of Stephen's world.

He wanted to kill. More than anything he had wanted ever in his life before, he wanted to kill this man who had betrayed him. He cursed himself for leaving Hart's automatic behind in Ho Chi Minh City. Even without a weapon he knew he could do it. He stood rigidly still willing the guards to leave them alone as he half heard Hart's voice continue with the official statement.

"At this time you will not be given the opportunity to call or communicate with any legal representation." Hart paused, placing his hands on his hips before continuing. "I am advised that you will, however, be provided with such an opportunity when you arrive in Australia."

Coleman stood very still, only his fists moving as he clenched them tightly, almost cutting off the flow of blood to his fingers.

"Furthermore," the sarcasm evident in voice, "you will be escorted back to Canberra by these two gentlemen standing beside me."

Hart then turned to the men.

"Be careful of this piece of shit! You can see what I copped when I wasn't looking!" he lied, gesturing with one hand towards the fresh scars on his face.

"Well, he's welcome to bloody well try," said the thick-set ex-rugby footballer. Stephen's eyes darted to the man and knew that there would be no chance of escape.

"Well, that's it then," Hart said, his voice now slightly pitched as he was enjoying Coleman's dilemma. "Guess we won't be seeing you for awhile, eh Stephen?"

"My guess is about thirty years," stated the other Service escort, not really knowing what the exact charges were against this man but wishing to be considered knowledgeable on the subject of the arrest.

Coleman remained very still.

He wanted to scream. But even more, he wanted to spring across and pound away again at the sneering face as one of the men stepped forward and, to Stephen's chagrin, handcuffed his wrists tightly and deliberately heeled his right ankle, sending a searing spear of pain up through his leg.

They kept him there for five hours. Nobody was permitted into the room with the exception of his guards and the arresting officer. He was not given anything to eat or drink and he didn't want them to have the satisfaction of his asking. Coleman's mind was racing.

He knew that this had to be Anderson's handiwork but somehow it just didn't make any sense to him. Surely he wasn't being detained just because he bruised one of their men? And how could they have possibly made the mistake of employing such an incompetent in the ASIS?

No. There had to be something else. Surely after all these years there was no reason for them to harass him, as he had not been involved with anything of any interest to them for over fifteen years? He thought quickly and decided that Anderson would now be too old to still have any involvement in the intelligence network.

Then he remembered seeing the photograph some months before as he flew from Hong Kong to Vietnam. And suddenly he thought he understood. It had to do with Seda!

He didn't offer any resistance to the two huge men as they moved him out of the room and down to the basement carpark where a consulate vehicle was waiting, engine running and driven by yet another Australian. They had been to the hotel and packed his belongings. No doubt, he thought, they would have flashed their Interpol identification cards issued to Federal Police stationed overseas, and easily accessed his room.

There was nothing there of any interest except for his new clothes and other baggage. He still had the safety deposit key and the cash he'd withdrawn in his back pocket. There would have been no evidence of his banking anywhere in the room. He always destroyed these as his arrangements were simple enough to remember and really only required his personal attendance and passport when withdrawing funds from the security boxes.

He tried to concentrate, checking in his mind whether there was anything at all in his baggage that could be of interest to these people. Deciding that there wasn't, apart from maybe three or four hundred American dollars he'd made a habit of secreting away inside his toilet bag for emergencies then, he felt certain his safety deposit would remain intact. As for the small cash reserves, he wasn't concerned, knowing that these men would slip the few hundred dollars into their own pockets when they discovered its whereabouts.

Six hours later a completely shocked and confused Stephen Coleman sat, still handcuffed, on one of the RAAFs ageing Mystere jet aircraft en-route to Canberra. His exit from the former colony had been expedited swiftly without fuss as the Federal Police Officers rushed him through the private diplomatic counter at immigration as one of the pair spoke fluently in Mandarin.

Coleman could see from the expression on the Chinese immigration officer's face that the story they had concocted was obviously believable; he saw the official shake his head from side to side in disbelief at whatever he was being told in his own animated tongue. They checked his baggage only in a cursory manner, eager for the evil man to leave quickly. They knew that sometimes these sort of people brought bad *joss* and there was already enough of that around!

He was then taken directly to the aircraft and, when he recognized the markings, knew that whatever was happening was in fact, serious. The aircraft's engines were already idling as their diplomatic vehicle, escorted by a jeep flashing warning lights, crossed the tarmac and quickly deposited Coleman and his escort officers before disappearing again.

They had been given immediate clearance and, within five minutes, Coleman looked through the small round aircraft windows to see the terminal lights of Chek Lap Kok flashing by as the engine's thrust hurled them along the busy runway.

An hour later he was given a cardboard box containing sandwiches. No weapon there, he observed, picking at the small tuna fish and lettuce sandwich. He remained cuffed for most of the flight. When he needed to use the toilet Coleman was obliged to leave the small cramped toilet's door open each of the three times he visited the heads.

He didn't attempt to sleep. The speed of the events resulting from his arrest still had his head spinning. As the aircraft continued through the night, passing over many of the idyllic beaches where he'd lived an uninterrupted life without the cares of his peers, Coleman thought long and hard concerning his predicament and what it may really mean to his future. He believed then that his assumptions were correct. It was all somehow connected with his former activities with the General, that much was becoming clear as he thought it all through. But why would the Service go to such elaborate lengths to force him back to Australia? He was annoyed with himself at having being so easily tricked with the charade back in Hong Kong. It was just that so many years had passed since he had to be so alert he'd not identified the signs in time.

Coleman remember reading in the Hong Kong papers a few years before that the Intelligence Service had finally been compromised. Its existence was shouted out across the nation by a former agent who fed the classified information to several journalists. These in turn promptly printed their exposé and released the incredibly embarrassing disclosures for the world to read. The report was, in essence truthful, but surprisingly had not been of real consequence to those involved as the Australian public just sighed at the revelations as if they had expected as much from their leaders and promptly forgot about the matter. It was as if the existence of a clandestine government department had little consequence in their lives. The offending agent had been given a slap on the wrist for his offence and asked to find other employment.

Knowing all this, Coleman was sure that his previous involvement with the covert group had little or nothing to do with this current action against his person.

Realizing that it was rather pointless exhausting himself further worrying about the reasons for his predicament he decided to wait for their explanation. He knew there would be one.

* * * * * *

The small sleek-lined jet refuelled twice and then, eighteen hours from the time he had entered the Australian territory of the Consulate General off Wan Chai, Stephen Coleman was surrendered to another team of Federal guards. They were waiting for his flight, standing patiently beside their unmarked van parked on the military side of the Fairbairn airport in Canberra. Moments later he was again whisked away with considerable speed into the city, where he was taken through the heavy steel restricted access gates leading down into the bowels of the huge gray complex on Russell Hill. There he was immediately locked in the special security wing in a military holding cell.

Sitting inside the dark van as they journeyed from the airport, Stephen had been unable to see where they had taken him. He had no idea whatsoever that he now was imprisoned directly below the very building in which he had first obtained his basic administrative training some thirty years before, that he was locked in the basement below the offices of the Department of Defence in the nation's Capital. There he was detained incommunicado for three weeks.

The guards could not be seen as they slipped his food and drink through the small steel hatch and, although he had managed to remain in reasonable spirits during the first few days, eventually he surrendered to the silent treatment, the isolation and rising fear, yelling abuse at this unseen jailers as they arrived from time to time to deliver his meals and other basic necessities.

The detention cells had been, unfortunately for the very few who had ended up incarcered there, one of the better kept secrets of the Service. These had originally been designed many years before as an interrogation centre for political radicals but had not been put to use for these purposes.

Towards the end of the Korean War, the country's xenophobic masters, believing with incredible zeal in the subversive intentions of the Communist nations, had sanctioned the secret construction of the facility. Originally it was designed as an atomic bomb shelter, or at least that's what the architects, engineers and construction teams believed. Once the civilian workers had completed the buildings another small team of skilled technicians moved in and went about installing their own equipment and modifications to the original design.

The access codes were so intricate and carefully monitored only a select few had ever been approved for the sensitive positions occupied by these highly paid officers.

The design was such it also prevented visual contact between the prisoners and the hand-picked security personnel. The spartan facilities contained only the basics, although these were adequate for their purposes. There were three sections, all identical in design and purpose. The planners had not thought that more than this number would be required and, as it happened, they had been correct.

A single bed had been pushed up against one wall tiled with small cream coloured ceramic squares. The cement used had faded in colour with the years and now created the impression that the many thousands of tiles would soon break away and fall. The secret installations were ten metres below the surface and the thickness of the walls at this depth was more than one metre. All concrete and steel. There would be no successful tunnel rats in this detention centre!

In the corner a compact shower and toilet had been installed, and two extractor fans activated whenever any of the plumbing functions were used. Fresh air was pumped through an uncomplicated series of ducts which seemed to hang, almost precariously, from the low concrete ceiling. He had one light but they had not provided him with any reading material.

They had permitted him to retain his watch, and Coleman managed to keep count of the days and nights as he remained locked away, completely cut off from the outside world. Until one day, when he knew he had already been incarcerated for precisely three weeks, along with his breakfast he was given a copy of the Canberra Times.

He grabbed at the paper and immediately commenced reading, convinced that the guards had committed an error and would soon retrieve the newspaper before he'd a chance to read it. Like a greedy man devouring food, Coleman's eyes quickly skimmed through the headlines before returning to the main news item.

Then he understood why he had been given the daily. At first, he completely missed the familiar face and article, on the third page. The photograph was captioned 'General Nathan Seda Arrives' and below was the story of Indonesia's new Ambassador to Australia.

Coleman read on. When he'd finished the article he sat back, deep in thought, before reading the article once more to ensure that he'd missed nothing. It was quite a build up for the man who had once been his partner. He tried to recall his conversation with Anderson years before when the Intelligence Chief had tried to warn him of the dangers of the *kongsi* Coleman had shared with Seda, his trusted partner in a multi-million dollar armament supply organization that ended up achieving two goals for the Timorese. Capital from the healthy and regular commissions made during the years the company continued to arrange weapons and other armament contracts with the Indonesian Armed Forces being the first, and secondly, cash and supplies for the separatists who had died by their tens of thousands in their struggle for independence.

It was clear to him now that somehow the former General's appointment had something to do with his incarceration. What was the connection? Why had he been detained? Where the hell had they buried him?

Frustrated by not knowing the answers, Coleman kicked at the solitary chair beside his steel framed bed, knocking it over loudly.

"Shit!" he cursed, knowing that the outburst was counter productive and that he had to continue to keep his temper from erupting again. He read the article again, for the third time.

Then slowly it came to him. They'd had him removed as he was considered a threat to the ageing Timorese!

But why? he thought, confused even more by his own questions. Why bother? Surely there would have been a much simpler solution? They already had him in Hong Kong where an accident would have been so easily arranged!

And where was Anderson? Was he still the Director? Or worse! Had John Anderson passed away, leaving the powerful post to another who could not vouch for him? Who had so much authority that they were able to authorize an airforce jet to have him delivered back to Australia, and why then lock him away, without any communication whatsoever?

All these questions continued to clutter his mind and Stephen became seriously conserned as to the length of his incarceration.

He heard the metalic click as the door to the prison suddenly opened and immediately he realized what a complete and bloody fool he had been. Of course! It had to have been him, all along. Who else could have manipulated so many and remained so obscure, while skilfully orchestrating all the players to carry out his commands?

He rose to his feet and stood to face the elderly man.

"Hello, Stephen," was all Director Anderson said.

THE TIMOR MAN

Chapter 23

Canberra

Coleman sighed. He and Anderson had talked throughout the day, breaking only for a light meal.

Anderson had produced convincing evidence proving that Seda was involved in a most dangerous game which he had played successfully for almost three decades. He had never been detected by his fellow generals or any of the others who had worked side by side with him. Slowly, step by step, the Intelligence Chief laid the whole picture out before the disbelieving Coleman. Much of the earlier information he already knew, as this had been the core of their discussions some years before when Anderson had provided the most amazing detail of the General's hidden agenda for East Timor.

Coleman also remembered that he had been given an ultimatum at that time which he had unwisely ignored. In retrospect, had he listened and cooperated when the demand had been made then maybe, just maybe, he would have come out of the whole mess in much better financial shape. Still, he thought, as he listened to the detailed exposition from the well informed bureaucrat, he hadn't done too badly. At least, up to now.

He watched the Director as his hands punched at invisible points in the air, emphasizing his facts, changing the pitch of his voice when he wished the story to take a more visual form in the listener's mind, and it was then that Coleman decided that the powerful man sitting on the edge of his bed was indeed an incredibly dangerous person to be around.

Twice he had made the point that Coleman was fortunate to have left Indonesia when he had as it was most likely that he would have come to grief had he stayed for the long haul. He cited the attack on the house and office which resulted in all of the domestic staff being slain.

"That was just a warning, Stephen," the Director said, "and a test."

"Test?" he had asked.

"Seda couldn't afford to have you eliminated until he was certain that you had not left incriminating evidence behind somewhere. He was reasonably confident that you hadn't but he was not quite ready to take that risk. Instead, he managed to send you a rather blunt message which, fortunately, you eventually heeded."

He looked directly at Coleman. "Have you kept any evidence that can compromise Seda?" he asked, examining the other man's face to detect whether or not he could identify anything in his manner which would help him determine the truthfulness of Coleman's response.

"No," he lied, knowing that he was again on very dangerous ground.

"Then the General could have saved us all a great deal of trouble years ago, eh?" he half joked, knowing that the remark would unsettle the other man.

Anderson went on to explain that Coleman's name had, on a number of occasions, been suggested for Executive Action by his department. This news sent a chill along his spine. He understood very clearly what the term meant in Service vocabulary and he looked quizzically at the Director.

"Why?" he asked, "what did I do that warranted such severe steps? Surely the armament company did nothing to jeopardize relationships between the two countries and I had certainly never disclosed any of my former activities."

"It wasn't so much you by yourself. We had considered taking you both out together. It would have been cleaner and tidier for us."

"Shit!" he exclaimed, "easier for you! What about me, for Chrissakes!"

"Take it easy. It never happened, or at least, not that way. I will tell you this much though, we made two runs against Seda and missed him both times!"

Coleman was very surprised. Not just at the secrets Anderson had revealed but also that they had failed in their attempts. He sat silently for a few minutes, absorbing this new data. Now he was worried that he would not easily leave this place armed with the information he had just been given! Why was he being told all of this? The information was most sensitive and probably only known to a select few. He realized that he was being slowly prepared by this master of control.

Towards the late afternoon he could see that Anderson was tiring. And fast. Even so, he continued to explain how precarious Coleman's position remained as he could no longer return to Indonesia; the government there, courtesy of his former partner, had placed his name on the list of approximately two hundred souls who had been identified as either politically dangerous, or had caused considerable economic harm to the people of the Republic.

"Bullshit!" Stephen had said, and then wished he hadn't as the other man withdrew several more sheets of paper from his coat pockets and placed them on the bed for him to read.

His name was half-way down the second page as being wanted by the government for taxation fraud and failure to pay the correct sales tax on a considerable number of shipments of non-military materials imported into Indonesia.

Coleman had just shaken his head. "Okay, so it's not bullshit. Why did they do this?" he asked, already guessing that it had something to do with Seda's powerful control over so many in the military machine's administration throughout their Defence Department.

"The penalty for what they claim you did carries the charge of subversion, Stephen," he said, reasonably softly so that the required effect was achieved.

Coleman knew that this was another method used by the Indonesian authorities to either silence opposition or prohibit its spread. Subversion carried the death penalty.

Anderson had then produced considerable evidence citing him as one of the co-conspirators behind the armaments supply lines to the FRETILIN guerrillas which, whether he was directly involved or not, had resulted in the loss of many thousands of lives.

"Bloody hell!" he had exploded, "how could they concoct such a load of crap?"

"Come on Stephen, don't pretend to be so damn naive!" he was answered in an admonishing tone. "Seda could do just about anything. Try and imagine just how much power the man had — has," he corrected. "Sitting on the military boards, controlling their intelligence apparatus, funding covert operations for both the Indonesians against the Freedom Movements of New Guinea while still maintaining a serious resistance movement in *Tim-Tim*."

There! Hearing the words *Tim-Tim*, used by an Australian official for the first time shook Coleman. Was it possible that his own country's leadership had always intended the disputed territory to fall under Indonesian control?

"Was it all just a sham?" he asked, knowing that whatever answer he was given there would be another lie buried somewhere behind, and perhaps another behind that as well, waiting to be brought forward whenever the argument demanded.

"Without being overly philosophical, Stephen, you, more than any of us, should understand that we are not masters of our own destiny."

He looked at Coleman for a while before continuing, as if gauging his mood, and also measuring just how far he could go in convincing his former agent that whatever they had done, the Service had provided nothing but the best for its members and, of course, its country.

"It was never a sham, Stephen. We couldn't just jump in, even when the threat was more real than even we indicated to the world. It is a fact that this country was threatened with the very real possibility of East Timor becoming a Soviet satellite. It is also true that the Americans were concerned with the Soviet's ever increasing influence in the region. But, at the end of the day, what it was really all about was Australia's final emergence as a regional power competing both economically and politically against the enormous changes that were taking place in our own hemisphere."

"The people of this country have never really been able to understand what would happen to Australia once Japan had proven its vulnerability - not by military power but by economic warfare."

"Our nation has retreated from being one of the most advanced societies with a living standard almost second to none, to become what one of our erstwhile leaders proclaimed as a Banana Republic. The sad fact is, he was correct."

"You will probably remember when you could visit say, Singapore, and change your Australian dollars into ringgits or straits' dollars and receive almost four of theirs for each of ours. Or, in Tokyo at about the same time, again one of our dollars could be changed for about four hundred of their yen."

"I don't need to give you a lecture on what has happened to our exchange rates; it's just that even our currency's deflated value is indicative of the country's inability to motivate the young, the business sector, or even the government."

"The country has always been an agrarian state, or was, up until our resources were finally exploited by the thousands of mining and oil companies which flooded into this land to develop whatever they found. But it wasn't and won't be enough for Australia to survive in the long term. We need to maintain our position along with every other developed nation in terms of accessing, then controlling the vital resources so desperately needed by industry, and much more so, as we move into the next economic cycle. We do not have sufficient reserves to guarantee this country's economic independence when it comes to fossil fuels, Stephen."

"In short, we need control over the Timor Basin."

For the second time that day, Stephen was speechless.

Anderson had ceased talking and Coleman knew he was expected to respond. He had no idea that the Intelligence Chief would drop such a bombshell. He was suddenly very concerned and almost afraid of the man who sat there with him, quietly discussing these most delicate and sensitive political issues that had obviously been the subject of extensive debate at the highest levels.

"This is why we need you."

The words hung in the air, and Coleman suddenly imagined himself standing in front of one of those recruitment posters that had flooded the United States during the first Great War. The one with the moustachioed soldier pointing directly at the observer with the slogan *Uncle Sam Needs You!* blazoned all over the lower section. He looked sideways, quickly, to see if Anderson had really lost his marbles or was just testing him. Like Seda had.

He could see from the other man's countenance that he had been deadly serious and earnest in his display of nationalism. Was it really just that? Stephen wondered, thinking that the Director may just be a little senile. He shuddered involuntarily. Whatever the truth may be, he knew that somehow he was not going to enjoy the rest of these discussions.

Only moments had elapsed but they felt like minutes. He knew he must say something, respond, or he would appear to not be in concert with the older man.

"The Timor Basin?" he asked, almost lamely.

The elderly Director paused before responding.

"The country's majors, or multinationals, have already moved to secure their positions through negotiation. Most of the fields have been assigned under agreements which the Indonesians are fond of referring to as production sharing agreements."

"These have been finalized after some considerable effort and many years of determining exactly where their territory begins and ours finishes. One of their arguments has always been that inter-national territorial limits should apply. Their whole goddamn coun-try is just a mass of piss-fart little coral atolls which they have the audacity to use to enforce their extended territorial claims over the shelf which, geologically speaking, really belong to us!"

"No sooner had our companies spent the many millions neces-sary to prove up the fields when suddenly our neighbours decided that the formal agreements already in place delineating bounda-ries, and crossover areas determined under the accord, to be no longer valid. Even the joint production contracts which specify bonus payments to the Indonesians based on volume extracted are in contention."

Coleman had no real idea where the harangue was heading.

"But that's not all. In fact, its just the tip of the iceberg," Anderson continued, having taken a small sip of the mineral water. "They have deliberately caused tremendous anti-Australian feelings to erupt in their major cities as part of their typical bullying tactics. Australian investment has reached an all time high in the country and, apart from the long-term considerations in the event we lose these substantial oil and gas fields, the immediate future for al-most eighty thousand of our citizens is, to say the least, bleak."

"We believe that the fields which extend from Timor across to-wards Darwin will produce more than this country requires for the next fifty years in terms of oil, not to mention the gas reserves."

His throat dry, Anderson then paused to take another mouthful of mineral water. He coughed lightly and then finished the remain-der of the contents before continuing.

Coleman was now impressed with Anderson's argument about

resources. He had not really paid much attention to what had been happening in those fields and was surprised that the area had attracted so much interest. Volatile interest, too, so it seemed.

"When the Soviet Empire fell apart you may have read that Russia and some of the other larger former states went on a selling spree, off-loading military equipment on a scale not seen since the Americans financed the British against the Germans earlier in this century. Most of the Black Sea fleet was sold, intact, to the Indonesians. Stephen, we're talking about some thirty five to forty naval vessels that were fully operational at the time."

Coleman sat quietly, listening attentively, still not sure where the conversation was going. When the other man had mentioned the ships he thought he had read somewhere about the sale but paid little attention to this also at the time as he was no longer interested in the world of armaments.

"They needed it, John. Their navy never really regained the strength it enjoyed before the attempted takeover in Sixty-five," he said.

"These ships were supposed to travel via India for their refit but the contract was slipped off to another group where major modifications were undertaken. It was quite a surprise to all of us that the Indonesians suddenly acquired such a massive fleet of ships. Sort of an instant navy, so to speak.

"I want you to think about the following. Without the total production of the areas now under dispute, the Republic will be obliged to start importing oil again in less than ten years. Maybe even five. They know that they can hold onto the areas now in contention and perhaps even broaden the scope of their claims to include some of the other disputed properties between Vietnam and the Philippines. The Chinese and Malaysians also consider these island groups to belong to them and have positioned gun boats to support their intentions.

"Indonesia's economy has grown dramatically as you are, no doubt, aware. This boom has created an enormous appetite and the consumers have pushed their country at incredible speed to fill their demands. Although they are the world's largest exporter of natural gas and have access to thermal power as well, all of this will not be sufficient for the giant economy to survive should it become dependent on imported fuels. It is a very complicated scenario Stephen. I am not trying to patronize you but I don't think you have paid too much interest over the last few years and I am only now trying to present you with the problem as an overview to help you understand where we are at. Okay?"

"Sure. It's okay. Under different circumstances I would probably even be enjoying it." Coleman couldn't resist the inference at his cramped accommodations, moving his head from side to side as he looked around the small quarters.

"None of us are able to look into a crystal ball and just come up with an accurate scenario of what will occur in the future but we do have the ability to predict with a certain amount of accuracy what might happen given the right set of circumstances. And that is what this government has had to do to protect its own national interests. You can safely assume that the Americans, Japanese and other nations involved directly in the region will be doing precisely the same and, in fact, we believe that the United States considers what we have forecast to be reasonably accurate.

"There are many regional issues which can affect these long term projections. For instance, India has the second largest navy in the world! The average man on the street has no perception of what that means to us but I can assure you Stephen, they could be a threat to our regional stability. Their country's population explosion has put their numbers ahead of China's. Did you know that they are faced with an even more serious problem with imports than the Indonesians?"

Coleman did not answer, assuming that the question was merely rhetorical.

"Do you?" he was asked again.

"No, John. Sorry," he answered tersely.

"Difficult as it may be to believe, India with its more than one billion people, will become a net importer of food within the same period as the Indonesians may be forced into a similar position with fuel. Interesting, eh?"

"John. Please. What does any of this have to do with my being here?"

Anderson sat quietly, thinking, before he responded.

"It all has something to do with the reason for your being here, Stephen, directly and indirectly, just about all of it!

"The Indonesians are becoming militant and appear to be preparing themselves for the possibility of regional instability. That they are responsible themselves for this instability doesn't seem to enter into their thinking as many of their leaders are old and have become irrational over the issues which directly affect Australia. They are not very generous when you consider that we have supported their annexation of Timor and, even as far back as the annexation of Irian we also supported them. Now they seem hell bent on challenging us over our oil and gas reserves and other issues most of which are just a smoke screen to disrupt negotiations to settle the issues peacefully.

"Our intelligence sources, supported by the Americans confirm that there have been covert activities aimed at a possible preemptive move against us somewhere, even, perhaps in New Guinea. In short, it appears that Indonesia wishes to expand its territorial sovereignty to include other potential resource areas to eliminate the future possibility of domestic fuel shortages. We didn't object when they just took East Timor, neither did we block their move when they took half of the island of New Guinea, which is also one of their more lucrative provinces. There are those who are foolish enough to believe that we would also acquiesce should they push across into New Guinea because Australia doesn't have the military resources to prevent such military action.

"The bottom line is, Stephen, we can't defend ourselves and can no longer count on the Americans to run to our assistance as they have done in the past because they too need allies like the Indonesians. I wouldn't like to put money on Australia if the Yanks were forced to take sides in any conflict. Ever since the ANZUS Treaty was virtually compromised by the Kiwis refusing American nuclear ships access to their harbours there has been a significant shift in how the Americans now perceive the old alliances. It's probably because were just too bloody British and expect too much from the old relationships."

Coleman listened intently, feeling that the punchline to this one-sided conversation was about to be revealed. Anderson's next statement rocked him.

"Your old friend Seda will, within the following year, become the next Vice President of Indonesia."

He let the statement sink in while watching the other man slowly shake his head, smiling, and then finally holding the palms of his hands up as if in surrender.

"Now I know it's bullshit!" he said.

Coleman was suddenly relieved. He had expected the Director to arrive at the end of his discourse with a more subtle conclusion, not something this melodramatic.

Anderson's shoulders suddenly fell, as if his lungs had expelled all of the air contained in the ageing organs, almost as if in despair. Coleman noticed the reaction with surprise. He remained still, saying nothing more. The tall, thin and now very tired Chief slipped slowly off the bed, and walked towards the security door.

He said nothing, not even turning as he approached the exit and pressed the buzzer indicating he wished to speak to the man on the other side. When the observation hole had been opened and the guard identified Anderson, the door opened then closed quickly leaving Coleman suddenly alone. He remained alone without further contact for another three days.

When the Intelligence Chief returned it was if nothing had happened. He had just marched into the small detention area and dropped another newspaper on the bed. Coleman knew he was expected to read it immediately and did so, looking up from time to time to ensure that he was reading the appropriate story as intended by his visitor. He commenced with page one which displayed the aerial photographs with the supporting story and followed the article through the following pages. It was an incredible display of photographic journalism. The headline read, *Terrorists Attack Australian Oil Rigs.*

The two oil rigs were caught perfectly by the photographer's equipment, as they burned furiously, spewing columns of black smoke and flames high into the atmosphere.

"Well, what do you think now?" Anderson had asked.

"More than provocative, I'd say," he replied, attempting to be slightly nonchalant, when his true sentiment was of one indifference. He was still annoyed at having been left alone so suddenly and treated like some errant child who needed to be punished for his ways. "What happened?" he asked.

"Seda," was all he said.

"How do you know?"

"It's got his mark all over it!"

"That's not good enough. How do you really know?"

"It fits with what he wants from all of us."

"Come on!" he said, determined not to permit Anderson to just expect him to roll over and accept everything he said as gospel. "That's a fairly broad statement. Fits in with what, specifically?"

"It fits in with his plan to create anarchy, Stephen, that's what it fits in with," Anderson replied, his voice still even but with an obvious edge to it.

"Is he really going to be the next Vice President or were you just winding me up?"

"I wish it weren't true either but it has all but been confirmed publicly by the Indonesian President. Seda arranged to be appointed as their Ambassador to Australia for approximately a year or so before taking up the new position. The fact that he selected this specific post when he could have had Washington or even Paris leads us to believe that he is right in the middle of something which has great importance to him. He has achieved tremendous power, Stephen, since the two of you parted company. I know you will have difficulty understanding this, but almost half of the entire country now supports him. It is even possible that he has just about enough strength in numbers outside Java to even succeed as President, although we still consider that most improbable due to the grip the Javanese Islamic groups have on the military.

"We feel certain that he is behind most of the sabre-rattling taking place in Indonesia, and definitely involved somehow with the intelligence reports we have of possible terrorist attacks. We just can't get enough information to support our assumptions of possible targets. Hopefully, this is all it was going to be," Anderson said, pointing at the sabotaged rigs in the newspaper. "But we can't afford to take that gamble."

Coleman waited as Anderson rose, and stretched, then rubbed his long legs to assist with the circulation.

"Stephen," he said sitting back down on the bed, "we are going to eliminate the problem with Executive Action."

* * * * * *

Stephen sighed. They had been at it now for just a few hours yet already his head ached.

Since their last session together, when Anderson had finally come to the conclusion of his Department's observations regarding the new Ambassador, Coleman had not been able to sleep more than a few hours at a time. The magnitude of what he had been told kept him awake right through the first night as he went over and over in his mind what his involvement might be in the covert action. He knew from his past association with the Service that whatever course was decided, it would be extremely dangerous for Stephen Coleman.

"I guess it's time we discussed your role in all of this," Anderson had said.

Coleman sat anxiously waiting for him to continue and yet, somewhere in the back of his mind, a voice was urging him to ignore what he was about to hear from the Intelligence Chief.

"You will be responsible for the final stage in the operation." By operation, he knew that this was to mean execution and immediately shook his head.

"No."

"You don't have any choice," he was told.

"That's crap and you know it, John. Apart from detaining me here you have no power over my life any more. That's all in the past. The answer is most definitely no, I won't do it!"

"You don't have a choice," Anderson repeated. He then went on to recite the possible charges that could be laid against Stephen.

"You're not really serious? How could you possibly sit there and expect me to believe that you could actually consider making any of those charges stick?"

"Stephen," he started, "you seem to have forgotten the wide range of powers that the department has in cases like these. Should we be obliged to bring charges against you then the hearing would be held in camera due to the nature and sensitivity of the Service's activities. We are well protected under The Act and, quite frankly, should I deem it necessary in the interests of our national security, all I have to do is speak privately with the PM and he will sanction whatever action I consider necessary with regards to your future.

"Do I make myself quite clear, Stephen?"

Coleman thought about what Anderson had just said. He knew that it was true. The man had incredible powers that could be applied against him if he refused to co-operate. He could just disappear and nobody would ever know. Suddenly this thought passed through his mind and he realized that he had already disappeared. He didn't even know where he was being detained!

His mind raced as he thought quickly about his predicament. Coleman knew that he was caught and they had a gun to his head. Thirty years would be more like a life sentence.

"And then, of course, there's the Indonesian problem, which still hangs over your head because Seda has kept it there, on the front burner, so to speak. I just never understood why he never really made any serious attempt to have you out of his life permanently."

Coleman understood that once proven, his involvement in the arms shipments would attract the maximum penalty in Indonesia, as subversive activities are considered to be a capital offence. And, should he be charged and tried in Australia, he was cognizant with the standard thirty-year sentences which, inevitably, were spent in solitary confinement. All in all, he really had no choice.

He continued to listen to Anderson outline what was required of him. The man had already assumed that he would agree, Coleman thought angrily, frustrated with his impotence, and the feeling of total helplessness for the situation in which he now found himself.

It had taken considerable time to convince Coleman that Seda's death was the only realistic solution. He had offered many arguments and suggested alternatives to the extreme measures being considered, knowing before he had even mentioned these, that ASIS would have made its own evaluation as to their effectiveness.

He was shown further evidence of the former General's ongoing role in supporting the FRETILIN separatist movement and, to his dismay, the full report of Stephen's own shooting intelligence suggesting that Seda may have been behind the attempt. Even if this were true, revenge was not in his nature, Stephen had argued. The Intelligence Chief had merely smiled and cited the violent attack on Hart, to contradict the other man's almost righteous position.

They had, however, agreed that any attempt to expose the powerful Ambassador could now be counter-productive, as the Indonesians would be compelled to deny any such accusations and any such claim could even result in cancellation of the forthcoming bilateral talks.

"What about these talks. Won't they assist in resolving the question of sovereignty over the oil areas? Shouldn't you wait until there is a result from these discussions?" he had asked.

"There won't be any resolution. Seda doesn't want one. Time is crucial, Stephen, we know there's some serious military activity afoot and everything points to Seda as the power behind the threat. Even if it comes about that they attack say, New Guinea, we are virtually sucked into the fracas anyway, as both our countries are tied together under the defence agreements which date back to the time of their independence, over twenty years ago."

"What about the defence pact we signed with Indonesia?" he asked.

"That's the greatest joke ever played on the Australians. Can you imagine signing an agreement which stipulates that both countries agree that they would come to the aid of the other in the event of attack, considering that the only country likely to do so in Australia's case was the other signatory to the agreement?"

They talked on. Coleman was depressed with what was expected of him. He wasn't even sure if he could still do such things any more. Even for his country.

"Why me?" he had asked early in the discussions.

"It is imperative that we have someone who can identify him perfectly, Stephen, specifically his voice over the phone. We want this to be a clean operation. We don't want innocent bystanders taken out as well."

"There must be a number of agents who could do the job for you without the necessity for all of this," he had said, indicating the concrete surrounds.

"Not any more. Operatives today just don't seem to have the same commitment any more. Not that you were particular outstanding in that area yourself," Anderson had said, referring to Coleman's sudden exit from the Service years before.

"Also, we would never be sure that we could guarantee their silence."

When Anderson noticed the sudden change on the other man's face he moved quickly to calm his fears.

"Obviously, Stephen, you'll be taken care of in the appropriate manner. You will need to disappear as you have done before, except this time we will provide you with reasonable cover. That would be another identity and travel documents should it become necessary. I personally believe that it won't," he added, almost as an afterthought. "You don't need funds from what I hear, so you will just have to be satisfied that we will consider your slate as being clean, thank you quietly for your participation, and ask that you go back to whatever you were doing before this bloody mess required our intervention. Okay?"

It required another two meetings before Coleman finally accepted the assignment. Until then he had remained adamant that he would not be Seda's executioner. Not until the last thirty minutes of their discussion.

"I had hoped that it would not come to this, Stephen."

"Let's get on with it John. I've been here long enough, and you know that I just can't do it any more."

It was then that Anderson embarked on an elaborate deception, one which he had concocted over the previous weeks once he had observed Coleman's determination not to participate, regardless of the possible consequences. He had tried threats, loyalty to his country, and that even referred to the old friendship they'd once enjoyed. None of these had worked.

"I just don't believe it!" Coleman had yelled.

"It's true, Stephen. I didn't want to raise the past unless I found it necessary. We all felt for you at the time. Your mother was very sad when she discovered how you felt for Louise. Of course, she was never aware of the circumstances. And, if revealing this information to you will result in the elimination of the very man who was responsible for what happened then I would call it sweet justice. Wouldn't you?"

That final discussion had clinched it. He had agreed.

The memories of Louise came flooding back as he remembered the brief time they'd had together. Brief only, as he had now discovered, as her life had been cut short deliberately by another.

* * * * * *

That night, as he lay alone, he tried to conjure up her face in his mind; he found that his eyes were moist from the tears of sadness and despair he felt for the one woman he had really loved, knowing that she had died such a tragic death as a result of political opportunism. Remembering his own early fears of flying, Coleman was bitterly saddened to discover that Louise's life had to end in that way. She hadn't needed to die at all but Seda's interference

KERRY B. COLLISON

had seen to that, or so he now believed. Anderson explained the
conclusions, albeit speculative, which had been derived from intelligence, as to what had actually occurred during that fateful journey. He was reluctant to disclose the source of the information,
even when Stephen had insisted that he would need to feel absolutely certain that the story was accurate, before he could even begin to accept it as truth.

Anderson had shown bits and pieces of United States intelligence and other exchanges which had taken place after her disappearance. It was convincing evidence, and he had believed the
elaborate story woven around the tragedy.

He had no way of knowing that this fabrication was in every
way false. All lies! Stephen wanted to know why she died and this
man had given him an answer.

Anderson's claim, supported by a reasonable amount of documentation, stated simply that Louise was most probably going to
be murdered along with him during their on site inspection of conditions in Irian. At the time the United Nations' sponsored resolution for the West Irian plebiscite, which the Indonesians referred to
as the Act of Free Choice, was criticized by the international press
as being partial and dominated by force through the Indonesian
military.

He was told that evidence had come to light, in the years
following the successful acquisition of the new province, which
proved beyond doubt that there were three separate factions involved in the many acts of terrorism and slaughter which had taken
place at that time. The Indonesians were already well ensconced in
the area and had been since the Dutch left in the early fifties.

Then, he was informed, there was the OPM, a raggedy and disorganized group which represented most of the freedom fighters.
They offered little resistance and were poorly equipped. Often they
operated from across the border, carrying out relatively minor raids
in their amateurish way before retreating back in to the relative
safety of New Guinea, relative being the key word as often the
Indonesians followed them well into the neighbouring country in
search of the rebels.

Coleman had listened as the Intelligence Director had continued. He claimed that the Australian Intelligence Services believed
that another group had been deliberately manipulating the primi-

554

tive mountain tribes into direct confrontation with Indonesian troops. It appeared that their earlier attempts to thwart the plebiscite had been poorly organized, resulting in only token resistance from the primitive mountain tribes.

However, as the Indonesian's interest turned towards East Timor, their subversive activities recommenced in the Irian area. They were not sure at the time and, in fact, not even until recent information became available were they certain that the person behind these efforts was Seda. His aim had always been to secure the autonomy for *Tim-Tim*. Prior to the Portuguese withdrawal his plans were embryonic, to say the least. The *coup* in Lisbon had been a windfall providing, for the first time, an opportunity for the General to formulate a strategy which could be successful. Anderson said there was little doubt that, had the Portuguese remained in the colony then, eventually, the world would have seen violence directed at them and most probably supported by the Indonesians. Either way, Seda would have, at one time or another, been given the opportunity to commence his plans for a free state.

Once the separatist movement got well under way, he needed to distract the Jakarta General's attention away from Timor. By forcing the Indonesian military to concentrate their efforts more in Irian than towards the confused former Portuguese colony, it provided the fledgling political party of FRETILIN the opportunity to build support before the Indonesians turned their full attention to acquiring their land as well.

His original plans for his homeland hadn't changed all that dramatically once he realized that with the Portuguese withdrawal the Indonesians merely took their place as the new masters. He had needed world opinion to turn against the Indonesians and what they were doing in Irian. It was almost like a trial run, Anderson had said, "And what better way than to attract the wrath of the international press?" he had asked. "Why, of course, have one or two of their journalists killed violently and lay the blame at the feet of others."

"This was just one of his early day strategies to build international concern for the future," Anderson had said. "We now believe that he was going to have her executed before your eyes, although we don't have enough information to tell us how the final plan was to be implemented.

"What is important, Stephen, is that she was to be killed and you were to witness the event. Ask yourself, what would you have done, full of rage and hate wanting to lash out at those who had harmed her? In terms of international press coverage alone, had you been a real journalist at the time, wouldn't you have pulled every string available to ensure that your woman's death didn't go unpunished? And if you personally witnessed men dressed as Indonesian soldiers actually take her life would you not be a major source of embarrassment to the Indonesian presence in Irian and their aggressive takeover of that country? Think, Stephen, think!" he was urged.

"Then how can we now blame Seda for her death?" he'd asked, confused and angry with these revelations. "And why then did he go to such extreme efforts later to assist build the armaments supply organization?"

"One thing at a time, Stephen, one thing at a time." Anderson talked slowly as he recalled the rehearsed lines prepared for such questions.

"Seda was definitely responsible although we can not prove this, beyond all doubt, as the aircraft has never been found. We believe that you had both been followed by one of the General's henchmen I believe you know reasonably well, one Umar Suharjo. When he recognized there was a problem between the two of you he acted quickly to prevent Louise from leaving. Obviously it was not difficult for a man of his skills to obtain the information he required such as to how she was to leave Bali. We gather that he somehow had one of the ground mechanics play with the aircraft's electronics hoping that it would be grounded, providing you with the opportunity to convince her to go with you. All of the staff at the hotel were abuzz with your predicament. You told me so yourself, if you can still recall our discussions during your convalescence."

"Do you mean he tampered with the aircraft and that's why it crashed?" he asked incredulously.

"Sorry, Stephen but yes, we do."

"And she would have probably died even had she not taken that flight. Is that what your suggesting?"

"Yes," the older man had replied softly.

"Shit!" he had yelled, "I don't believe it!"

They had sat in silence for almost half an hour, he remembered, as the realization of what had happened slowly sank in driving all other thoughts from his mind.

He was filled with rage. All those years of not knowing and now, only when they needed him, was he to know. Coleman hated them all. Even Anderson!

Stephen remembered that his life had lost all direction when she died. He hadn't cared about his own injuries at the time once they had finally disclosed the loss to him in hospital. He was receiving treatment and still recovering from the bullet wound he'd received during the disastrous tour. She had been missing for weeks before anyone had informed him of the tragedy. Prior to that, Stephen had thought that Louise either didn't know of his injury, which he found difficult to accept, or she had elected not to have any further contact with him at all. She had disappeared even before he had been shot.

'And all the time it had been Seda's doing,' he thought, his head filled with hate for the General who had insisted that they take the journey together.

'The scheming, conniving bastard!' he had muttered over and over to himself as the venom built quickly, his mind tortured with the face of the man who had sat together with him so many times throughout the years, knowing what he had done, perhaps even smiling silently at his partner's ignorance. It was then that he had agreed to kill the man responsible for Louise's death.

And that man was Ambassador Nathan Seda.

* * * * * *

During the weeks he had been detained, the situation between the two countries had deteriorated dramatically. Student demonstrations in both had erupted into violence, and Australians were being discouraged from travelling to Indonesia, even to the almost apolitical tourist destinations such as Bali.

Pressure increased on the Intelligence Service which sensed that Seda was moving closer to the first phase of his plans, as communication activity increased dramatically between the Embassy and unidentified posts in the far east of the Indonesian islands. Anderson was perplexed by the lack of recent intelligence to assist identify the former General's intentions but, of one thing he was certain, what ever these plans were, the department's head knew without doubt that the outcome could only be to the detriment of the peoples of both countries.

Coleman now appreciated why Anderson had coerced him into accepting the assignment. He was familiar with the diplomat's voice and understood the language. He would never disclose the Executive Action as he had too much to lose himself. And he had a reason for wanting to complete the assignment.

And then, of course, there was the alternative, but Stephen did not relish the thought of spending his remaining days incarcerated under the Laws of the Land, if that was the course the powerful and devious Intelligence Chief elected to take.

John Anderson had given his undertaking that, subject to the elimination of the target, Coleman would then be free to come and go as he pleased, enjoying the remaining fruits of the years he had spent working together with the Timorese living under the alias that they had agreed upon. This did not bother him at all. He had no surviving family and doubted if the necessity to live a lie would really bother him any more. Suddenly he was looking forward to completing the assignment and returning to the islands.

Their final meeting had lasted throughout the day. Anderson then offered Coleman the opportunity to leave the detention centre.

Stephen would have accepted had the Director not also shown him evidence that the new Ambassador had positioned his own Security Chief there in Canberra. He even enjoyed a room in the Embassy's residence, he'd read in the report. Stephen shuddered. He knew his life would be in danger once his presence became known to this man.

He studied the photograph taken of the Javanese as he had exited the international airport some months before, carrying an Indonesian diplomatic passport which stated that he was accredited to their Embassy as a First Secretary liaison officer.

Coleman recognized the man as a much older, but obviously still active, Umar Suharjo. Although he was already committed, it was then Stephen was convinced that he really did not have any other choice. He would participate in the execution of the General.

Retired national hero, entrepreneur, diplomat and would-be Timorese President, General Nathan Seda, would die on the seventeenth of August, the Indonesian Republic's national Independence Day.

* * * * * *

There had been very little left to prepare. Anderson had seen to most of the arrangements.

They had agreed that the man had to be isolated in such a manner as to avoid wounding or killing innocent bystanders, or at least they were to attempt to keep the number down to an acceptable level. Coleman had smiled when he heard this. Only Anderson would have the audacity to convince himself as to what was, and what was not, to be considered acceptable, when it came to counting the cost in real terms.

Other people's lives.

Anderson had easily arranged to have the Ambassador's private office compromised by depositing a substantial amount of dollars in the Indonesian Air Attaché's hands one evening. The man had been taking funds from just about every Military Attaché in Canberra. Coleman knew what would happen to the *Kolonel* once he was discovered. And discovered he would be, he knew, as they were all caught in the end, pushed by greed or the insatiable appetite for power until finally making that one mistake which would destroy their lives forever.

It was now possible to eavesdrop, as the simple but powerful listening device broadcast the Ambassador's conversations back to one of the discreet locations controlled by the Service. It had been used as a safe house in the early years during the Vietnam war but not by the Australians. This was one of the Soviet addresses which had been monitored by ASIO, the Australian Security Intelligence Organization. Once the building had been compromised, the address had been purchased. Control was then assumed by the Service as an occasional address for some of their agents' contacts in the numerous Embassies located around Canberra. They knew that the Eastern Bloc agents would avoid the premises.

The assassination called for a bomb blast contained in the Ambassador's immediate office. As his security was too tight to penetrate, and considering the current tension between the two countries, Anderson had planned the execution so that it would appear to be the work of some of the members of the retired General's own ethnic group, now living in substantial numbers as refugees in Australia. The newspapers would report the bombing as the work of the remnants of the FRETILIN who believed that the important statesman being of their extraction should have done more to help his own people.

Coleman had smiled at the irony of the plan. Now that he had come to terms with what he must do, he was even prepared to take a gun and shoot the man himself, if that became necessary. He became impatient to have it all done and finished. He could identify the signs in his mood and knew that he must control his anger. He thought about the briefcase again.

A small but effective explosive device would be delivered to the diplomat's office. When they were absolutely certain that the former General was alone, Coleman would detonate the plastique. Anderson had informed him that he had arranged for a courier to deliver the explosives.

Stephen had considered this aspect as being the one real weakness in Anderson's plan. Accessing the Embassy and ensuring that only the General would receive the deadly consignment would be extremely difficult to accomplish, requiring the services of someone whom the Ambassador could not only trust but also permit into his inner sanctum. It wasn't until all aspects of the plan were ready for execution that he finally understood.

Anderson had been very clever indeed as he continued to manipulate all the players in his game with the skill he had developed as an intelligence master.

The deadly briefcase would be delivered by none other than Albert Seda.

* * * * * *

Albert had been given an assignment he could not refuse. It had taken very little to coerce Seruni's father. The suggestion of his being repatriated to Indonesia was sufficient for the badly shaken man to accept the task. They had never approved his application to become a citizen and he had given up submitting the forms further back in time than he cared to remember.

There was even the suggestion that they would, if necessary, look into the legality of his daughter's citizenship as her father was not a citizen at the time of her birth. Also, the girl's mother had been an alien living in Australia as the wife of an Australian citizen but was, in fact, the de facto wife of another foreigner. It was all very confusing. Although he believed that it was most unlikely that she could be deported, having been born in the country, Albert also considered the more personal issues involved, which would become very public in the event of any inquiry. He just didn't want Seruni to be harmed in any way.

At first Anderson had merely implied that perhaps Albert had erred when registering his daughter's birth as her mother was still, at that time, Stephen Coleman's legal wife and had been staying with her husband prior to her collapse. Hospital records indicated that there was every possibility of this being so. Should they inform Coleman?

He never questioned the absurd innuendo. He was frightened of the government man and even more terrified of having to return to his former country which, in his mind, no longer represented his home. He had given all of that up many years before. He was terrified that they could separate him from his daughter. She was all he had left in this world. And besides, what he had been asked to do was not such a difficult task.

And he would be paid! Heavens knows, he thought when the offer had been made, he lived frugally on the pension and still there never seemed to be enough. When he had first retired it had not been too difficult but now everything was just so expensive! And Seruni. She was at college now and although his daughter never demanded anything of him, there were always costs to be met, fees to be paid. He had agreed. What other choice did he have? Albert thought.

Anderson had been concerned that this man would refuse his request and decided to go in tough from the outset. Albert Seda's file was complete with detail of his interviews over the years when he worked part time for the government agency without knowing to whom he was really reporting. There were many like Albert living in Australia who had been tapped by the Intelligence Services as an easy access into their respective ethnic communities. He had never known of one to refuse to assist maintain a listening brief over their own former countrymen. Most did it out of fear of officialdom while others merely wanted to ingratiate themselves hoping for future favours. Having established that the Timorese was definitely under his control, Anderson then put the man at relative ease by explaining the nature of his errand.

The Intelligence Chief had concocted a simple story and one which Albert easily accepted considering the principles involved. Anderson had explained that Albert was to deliver a large sum of cash to the Ambassador. He had not elaborated to any great extent, merely intimating that the new Ambassador was no different than most, and that the Australian Government wished to convince him of its good intentions. They needed to send someone the Ambassador would trust.

Albert understood. The two countries were locked in dispute and he believed that the gesture would be appreciated. But would Nathan receive him after all of these years? Anderson went on to explain that they had considered various means whereby the delivery could be effected and had come to the conclusion that the senior foreign dignitary would be unlikely to accept such a gift unless he knew the courier personally. Albert had considered these premises and was obliged to accept Anderson's logic.

He had been advised that delivery was to be made at precisely six o'clock in the evening on the seventeenth of August. Albert expressed surprise as to the timing of the hand over. Anderson had merely smiled and suggested that the delivery was to be his stepbrother's Independence Day gift.

* * * * * *

Anderson had easily arranged for the invitation. The Air Attaché had sent this out almost immediately only too eager to assist knowing that his services would warrant another fat envelope at some later date.

Albert was to arrive half-an-hour earlier than the other guests and insist on meeting directly with the Ambassador, who would be expecting him. Anderson would arrange that.

His instructions were to then proceed with the Ambassador who would, undoubtedly, have his step-brother escorted to a place of privacy. They knew from their sources that this could be the Ambassador's private office. There he was to surrender the briefcase personally and then take his leave.

It was relatively simple. Albert accepted the role of courier. He would deliver the gift for Nathan. And then they would leave him alone.

Chapter 24

Canberra

The Indonesian Embassy had provided the sombre-faced Java-nese Security Attaché with the means to move equipment into the country without question. He had arrived almost four months before the retired General, and soon demonstrated his ability by establishing the new security systems. The staff had been impressed with the quiet and dedicated officer. Several had commented, however, that they found him rather impersonal and uncommunicative. Others were surprised that he never attended functions or private parties, electing instead to remain on duty for more hours than the position demanded, arriving very early each morning and returning to his quarters late into the evening after the other staff had departed.

He must be very competent, they had thought, as this was the first occasion any of them could remember, even from their other postings, that the head of security held a diplomatic position and was accommodated in the official residence along with their Ambassador. Even though his quarters were out to the side from the main house, they still found the arrangement unusual.

After two months in the country they had become accustomed to his brusque responses and demands. Soon the other members of the legation accepted his manner as normal and practically ignored his presence within their circle without further comment. They no longer offered the new Attaché invitations knowing that he would refuse or ignore any of these courtesies extended to him.

Often he would just vanish for days on end, only to return as if there was nothing unusual with these sudden disappearances. They didn't ask and he never offered to explain. Someone in the secretarial pool started the rumour that the reason for the secret break away from them all was perhaps a woman, hidden outside somewhere and he was too embarrassed to be seen with her. After all, she couldn't be much to look at, the young girl had suggested, just look at him!

The new Ambassador had signed the instruction, to the surprise of the Consul, demanding that the maintenance section rearrange the lobby access rooms as an additional security measure. They obeyed and within two weeks the rooms internal layout had been changed to the specifications given to them, with only two exterior doors having to be relocated as part of the renovations. One of these now opened in a sliding action from the inside, permitting delivery vans and small trucks to back up to the building immediately in front, almost hard up against the door. The vehicles' rear doors could then be opened directly from the security room and the contents moved in and out undetected by inquisitive eyes.

Umar had decided that his very special stores should remain below on the Embassy's ground floor to avoid compromise. The lifts were impractical due to their size, designed to accommodate only four passengers, and even that was a squeeze.

Lugging the secret consignments up and down steps, could easily lead to discovery. His arsenal now contained the remainder of the stores required for dispersal to the strike teams. These special consignments would pass through Australian Customs unopened, as the lead-lined cases were endorsed as diplomatic cargo and protocol demanded that such luggage could not be checked by the authorities.

Umar's armoury had been constructed immediately adjacent to the main lobby reception area. The second set of external doors was also re-enforced with steel bars welded vertically and horizontally at twenty-centimetre intervals. These opened to permit access into the embassy gardens, which were pleasantly landscaped up to the dividing wall separating the delivery and storage areas from the colourful view. Usually, Umar would enter his stronghold via the embassy mail and registry room, which was located alongside the common interior wall.

Only he was permitted access to this area. Other embassy officers had correctly speculated that it contained weapons to be used if their building came under siege. They were not uncomfortable with these thoughts, as many had seen other legations destroyed over the years when demonstrators could not be prevented from entering the main buildings, burning, looting and on occasion, injuring the staff. Many even looked on Umar as their protector in the event their Embassy came under attack and, considering the current political climate, anything was possible. The mood in Australia was becoming tense.

The specially selected van had been repainted with the appropriate colours to comply with their needs. Umar had decided to wait before adding the delivery company's logos and other identification markings, as moving the van between the Embassy and its locked parking bay behind the Ambassador's residence increased the risk of discovery with each journey. He planned to complete the installations and leave the van locked where it was until two or three days prior to the target date. Umar felt safer knowing that it was within the compound where he could keep his eyes on it during the day. The rear of the van had been left hard up against the sliding door now for two weeks and the Embassy personnel had become accustomed to its almost permanent presence.

Inside the delivery van he had stacked layer upon layer of plastic lined bags around the open drum of diesel oil. Whenever the van was moved, he would re-attach the container's lid for these short journeys, removing the cover again once the vehicle was parked. He had finished storing the ammonium nitrate bags and had completed the finishing touches to the hydrogen canisters which would act as a 'kicker' to increase the impact of the huge bomb. The extra ingredient would give the explosives far more cutting power, allowing it to slice through the structure of the building.

Umar had checked the detonators behind the sliding doors. He had a choice of using the powerful industrial detonators or the PETN explosive sitting in the corner, separated from the rest of his volatile hoard. He considered the latter and agreed that the pentaerythoritol tetranitrate would probably be better, knowing that this explosive could generate a very powerful shockwave. Having made his final decision Umar completed his checks then locked and sealed the van's doors first, checking them once again to be absolutely certain that he had not missed anything before locking the sliding door securely. Satisfied that the important tasks had been completed, he returned to his rounds of the chancery and other areas frequented by the public.

As he passed through the registry room, he heard one of the typists whisper something to her friend. He couldn't hear what was said but knew they would be curious as to what kept him for so many hours each day inside the adjacent room. Umar Suharjo enjoyed the intrigue. He smiled to himself. Wouldn't they be surprised if they knew just what he had stored under their lazy little bottoms!

He was not overly concerned that one of the staff might accidentally discover what it was that remained such a secret within the four walls of his private domain. Anyway, he mused, considering the non-military staff with contempt, most of them wouldn't even know the difference between their hands and what was between their legs let alone have the capacity to identify any of the items in his store! The majority of these foreign affairs types hadn't even undergone national service training, Umar thought, annoyed with the civilians, and wouldn't be able to defend themselves if called upon to do so. He knew they would be useless if the Embassy came under attack.

He strutted around playing the role of the senior security officer. In all the years he had worked for the General this was about as close as he'd ever come to really enjoying his duties. He experienced a sense of elation, knowing that he alone would be responsible for the destruction of the Australian leadership when the massive explosion took place within the confines of their Parliament.

If only they knew, he thought, if only they knew!

* * * * * *

Nathan Seda enjoyed the exhilaration which resulted from the satisfaction of knowing that his dreams were almost within his grasp. This time it would be successful. He could feel it! The Ambassador had just returned from the function and met briefly with Umar before settling down to concentrate on the enormous number of unfinished tasks which need to be addressed. He had enjoyed the late luncheon.

When the approach had first been made, he was advised by the Embassy information officers that the invitation was considered to be quite prestigious, and would provide the Ambassador with an acceptable forum to raise issues not yet settled between the two countries.

Seda accepted the invitation to be the guest speaker at the Press Club luncheon. All in all, he thought, it had gone well, with the exception of the pedantic journalist who repeatedly interrupted his answers during the open question period. He had been asked if there would be any objections to an informal question opportunity for the other guests and, confident that there would be no difficulty in addressing whatever he was asked, Seda had agreed.

The man had insisted that the General be more specific in his answer.

"Why didn't the Indonesian Government provide adequate protection for the drilling crews against the attacks that had already closed down five drilling platforms in the disputed area?" he was asked. "Surely as these platforms and rigs are within what the Indonesian Government claims as their territorial waters the responsibility for the safety of the crews and multi-million dollar rigs rests with your government?" he was challenged.

"The Indonesian military does not wish to be seen by the international community as being overly aggressive in this matter. We sympathize with the families who have lost loved ones in these terrorist attacks and have asked your government to consider a joint military action to prevent any further recurrences of these disastrous assaults against not just Australian but also Indonesian workers in the Timor fields."

"Mr Ambassador. Is it not true that your navy already has a considerable presence in the area, and is it not also true that your country has the capacity to virtually guarantee the safety of these operations due to the very number of vessels that you are able to deploy in the concession zone?"

"Although it is correct to state that we have the capacity to provide such guarantees, our country does not consider that it should shoulder the entire burden of responsibility. Again, I remind you that we have offered your own navy the opportunity to work together with us on joint exercises to avoid misunderstandings as to our good intent, when our vessels entered the disputed territorial areas. Disputed only, I might add, by your government. We, in Indonesia, do not see that there is any argument. The area has always belonged to our Republic."

"Yes, sir, so we have observed. And what else do you want?" a voice from the back of the room had called, causing the assembly to laugh nervously while someone whistled his support for the question.

He had anticipated the response to his remark and, minutes later when he had finished replying to the faceless member, the assembly laughed politely while some even applauded his statesman-like wit and behaviour.

"Ambassador Seda. Would you tell us your own personal views as to where the United Nations will go on the latest call for the right of self-determination for *Tim-Tim*?"

He looked down from the podium to check the man who had asked the question. Seda didn't recognize the journalist but was pleased as he had hoped that someone would raise the sensitive issue. The room became quiet as he deliberately waited for the table banter among the members to discontinue to ensure their complete attention. He looked straight at the man who had raised the question.

"The people of *Tim-Tim* are Indonesian citizens by choice."

"Yeah, we all know that, but by whose choice?" shouted the man who had interrupted earlier.

"Knock it off, please, gentlemen," one of the committee called, embarrassed by the break in etiquette. "Let's remember who we are!"

"Thank you," Seda said, before continuing. "If you kindly permit me to finish. I said, the people of *Tim-Tim* are Indonesian citizens by choice. The reality is, they are. The choice was theirs, it became ours, and even you in Australia supported our declaration of sovereignty over the former colony. Show me one voice on the United Nations Security Council which condemns the current status quo in the province. Show me evidence that your own people don't support my country's annexation of the troubled state. And, if you can, please before you even consider asking the question, show me proof of the ridiculous claims that our Indonesian troops took the lives of your fellow journalists more than twenty years ago!"

"You can't" he continued, "because there is no such evidence which can irrefutably demonstrate the incredible claims made over the years concerning the loss of your some of your number."

"The Republic of Indonesia has demonstrated that it is a nation intent on peaceful co-existence with its neighbours. The Timor question remains no more as such because it has been answered by our country's actions, actions taken in the interests of all, including your own."

The questions had become heated. Seda had continued responding in the same vein and, at the close of the luncheon, he was confident that he had caused more questions to be asked than he had answered. But, more importantly, he had them all thinking seriously again concerning their own country's role in the sad demise of the East Timorese people. He was pleased with the day's events.

The Ambassador turned his thoughts to his discussion with Umar. The man was a genius with no sense of morality, he thought. It was a good thing he continued to command the man's loyalty, as the former Major had become totally indispensable in every respect, as there was just nobody else he trusted whom he could call upon with this man's skills.

The attacks would take place within the following week. Everything was now ready. The aircraft and vessels would take their positions within days and the combat teams had already been mobilized ready to move when Umar sent the command. The trucks and other support equipment had been ready for almost two weeks, the men standing by impatiently waiting for their next instructions. Umar had flown across and then driven out to speak to them. They had understood the necessity to be patient. He had told them, it wouldn't be too much longer, just wait!

Seda smiled again as he read his secretary's note confirming the number of invitations that had been acknowledged and accepted to attend the formal celebrations. Almost one thousand guests! This would be a function to remember, he thought, knowing that the whispers had already spread throughout the diplomatic community of his possible appointment as the next Vice President. All appeared to be on track and running according to plan, he thought.

Only the devastating consignment below remained as unfinished business, and this would be moved at the appropriate time. Umar had assured him that the final checks and paintwork could be completed in just hours once the van had been positioned at his residence's garage.

Seda had asked for it to be moved immediately but Umar had argued that it would not be safe out of his sight.

"What if there was a fire at the premises?" he'd asked, "or what if one of those bungling idiot servants from Semarang became a little too inquisitive while their masters were out and decided to fool around with the volatile cargo?"

In the end Seda had just walked away from the man. If it was safe enough for Umar, he decided, it was also safe enough for him!

Umar enjoyed the exchange. Even if he had moved the van to the residence there was just no way that the servants could even get a smell at the inside of the garage as he had always double locked everything. Umar expected the area would be safe. He had left small booby traps that were relatively harmless but enough, he knew, to scare the shit out of the domestic staff if they wandered off limits! He hoped that they feared him and wouldn't dare consider venturing into his domain without specific instructions to do so.

From time to time he had wandered through the kitchens as they were preparing meals. He could smell their fear as he stopped and looked casually around, picking up utensils and then replacing them without comment. Sometimes he would hold one of the carving knives up to the light as if he was inspecting the blade for cleanliness, but the staff understood the not-so-subtle message.

Even so, he preferred to keep his hands on the vehicle containing the explosives. It was just more convenient to keep the van where it was until the time came to move it out. He could see no problem. It was totally safe, although he knew that the General wouldn't understand this point. Like so many other intelligent people Seda had no idea how explosives were triggered. This one had not been activated. All of the components were in place but Umar had not connected the PETN charge directly to its detonation device. He would move that from the armoury and complete the complicated trigger only when he knew the exact timing for detonation.

Seda didn't understand the intricate workings of the bomb designated for the destruction of Parliament House and wasn't entirely comfortable knowing that the van was still sitting alongside the embassy building. Even if he had it moved to the residence's garage it would still be dangerously close to his person.

* * * * * *

The newspapers had reported his statements in the following day's papers. Seda was not entirely displeased with the biased reporting, having become familiar with the so-called objective media very early in his career.

He sat drinking his coffee while skimming through the pages, stopping to read only those articles which referred to the luncheon and reported on his comments. Some of the stories were inaccurate and slightly derogatory. Several also exaggerated the answers given in response to the question of Timor, even suggesting that the Ambassador had responded with an air of arrogance. Seda thought about this comment and was not irritated by the remark, as he had deliberately answered in an almost provocative fashion, hoping to ruffle the member's feathers. As it turned out, the result was positive and in no way did he consider any of the articles to be detrimental to his real cause.

The majority of the stories, including two editorials, came out strongly in support of a United Nations resolution to provide the people of *Tim-Tim* with the opportunity to vote on the question of Indonesia's annexation and their right to self-determination, and challenged the Australian people to push their elected leaders into action over the ongoing abuse of these simple people's humanitarian rights. They also demanded a further government inquiry into the deaths of the journalists years before in Timor. They expressed disappointment that the questions relating to these murders have never been properly addressed.

This is the result he had really wanted. It was time to prime the Australian public and prepare them mentally for the next frightening events so that their response would lead to more than just feelings of indignation towards the Indonesian people.

Seda's plan called for a much stronger response. One which would drag both countries to the brink of an outright war.

Chapter 25

Independence Day —
Canberra

The Embassy had been decorated quite spectacularly. Nathan Seda had strolled around the building and grounds admiring the preparations as they neared completion. They had invited more than one thousand guests.

This would be the social event of the year, he thought, anticipating the favourable press coverage the public relations group had planned. He expected that the increased exposure would assist considerably when he called upon the United Nations to intervene directly once fighting erupted between the neighbouring countries. They would listen to Seda, as he had the necessary influence to bring about a cessation in hostilities and was not considered by the international media to be overly militant, as some were, within the Indonesian leadership. He hoped that they would call upon him to intervene in negotiating a peace settlement, and he would, but only when the timing suited his purpose.

This time he would succeed. He could feel it. All the ingredients were in place and soon he would achieve his dream.

As the Ambassador continued his survey of the grounds, catering staff busied themselves arranging the white and red combinations around the buffet tables. The national flag was designed to represent the blood of earlier revolutionaries spread across their white *sarongs* as the brave peasant soldiers lay dead or dying from wounds inflicted by the former colonists. They had fought with sharp bamboo sticks against rifles and cannon.He would fight with terror.

They were almost ready. Nathan Seda could feel the excitement building.If he maintained his course and continued to be patient, the General knew it would all then fall into his hands. Understanding his own weaknesses and strengths had been crucial to preserving the plan and his own position within the community at large. Often he had wanted to move much faster but had reasoned with himself knowing that impatience could result in failure. It had been such a long wait.

But it was nearly over. He continued his slow stroll, nodding occasionally to senior staff as they rushed by, arranging the finishing touches to the preparations. The guests would begin arriving in less than two hours. The Ambassador was pleased.

Floral arrangements adorned the long tables covered with white Indian cotton tablecloths. As these stretched out through the full length of the extensive garden overhead lights provided a colourful display as the soft breeze rocked them gently in the chilly evening air. Large marquees had been erected to protect the guests from the elements. August could be bitterly cold in Canberra and the caterers had suggested that they place a number of mobile pot belly burners around to take the bite out of the cool evening. These had already been lighted and placed around the perimeter of the setting.

The Ambassador's table was positioned on a slightly raised podium. Directly behind, the organizers had placed a huge Garuda against the painted plywood wall, built as a temporary backdrop. Flags hung from poles positioned with care at regular intervals between the tables and bunting was strung along the large tent posts creating a festive atmosphere.

As a centre piece, the Embassy had instructed the caterers to prepare an ice carving of the mythical Garuda bird and this two metre high ice sculpture had just been completed before Seda arrived and observed the men packing their tools and chain saws.

He viewed the scene and nodded his approval. At the far end of the garden he could see the table where, in just a few hours, he would host his own Chief-of-Army-Staff Lieutenant General Suprapto, the Indonesian Foreign Minister and many other prominent guests from Australia and abroad. His wife had not accompanied him to Canberra as she wished to wait for the warmer weather to arrive before joining her husband in the Capital.

Seda walked slowly through the setting, glancing from time to time at the neatly placed guest name cards inscribed in bold italic script. Towards the centre where the large ice bird perched regally, scowling at the surroundings, he noticed that two tables of twelve settings each had been allocated to the press. Seda was slightly amused by this as the band occupied the position opposite, not ten metres from where the journalists and their wives would later struggle to make themselves heard above the amplified sounds. He imagined the loud music blaring across the short distance, swamping the evening's polite dinner conversations showing contempt for them all.

Everything was in place. Satisfied with the magnificent garden arrangements he turned to leave for his residence to change and, as he was about to enter the main building, his personal secretary, Nona Kartini, hurried towards him.

"*Pak Seda*," she called then hesitated, apologizing to her Ambassador as he looked over in her direction, "*I'm sorry to disturb you.*"

"What is it?" he demanded, surprised at her obvious concern. Normally his secretary was very composed and not given to any display of emotion.

"*Ambassador*," the agitated secretary began, "*I have received a call of the most confidential nature! May we speak in private?*"

Seda nodded and walked briskly to the lift followed by his confidential assistant.

They entered the Ambassador's private chambers. Seda strode directly across the heavily carpeted room and dropped, almost impatiently, into the leather swivel chair. As he sat behind the carved teak desk the General looked at the woman and nodded for her to begin.

Seda frowned as he listened to his efficient secretary report the telephone conversation which was, he discovered, the cause for her agitated manner. He watched the career woman refer to her notes, taken during the strange discussion with the caller and, when she had finished, he asked her to go over it again.

She obeyed and read the message once more. He then excused his assistant and sat quietly considering the message he had just been given.

Suddenly he felt very uneasy. Naturally suspicious of any coincidence, Seda ran the information through his mind trying to unravel its secrets. Although agitated by the telephone call he could see nothing sinister in the request. The General recognized that as pressure built over the next few days he would need to ensure that he remained composed at all times and not permit these minor disturbances to distract him from the real objectives. Especially now!

Seda frowned.

Why had the man come out of the woodwork precisely at this time? Had it something to do with that evening's function?

There was really nothing to discuss with the man, he thought. They were not even real brothers.

Why did Albert feel the necessity to leave such an enigmatic message?

What did Albert know that was of such significance that he had insisted on meeting so urgently?

And how did he manage to acquire an invitation?

Why hadn't he made the call himself?

There were too many questions to which there were no immediate answers. Suddenly Nathan Seda rose to his feet and headed for the armoury. He was annoyed. The Ambassador disliked puzzles and was surprised to see that he was, in fact, preoccupied with the nuisance call. Suspicious of the unexpected message, Seda decided to ensure that the surprise visit did not interfere with the evening's celebrations.

He would instruct Umar to wait for Albert.

* * * * * *

Coleman had replaced the receiver and immediately informed Anderson that the call had been completed. The woman hadn't recognized that he was not a native speaker. He was pleased that he had not lost his touch!

Stephen checked his watch. Five o'clock! Anderson would already be on his way to rendezvous with Albert.

Coleman felt the tension and was conscious of a burning sensation in the pit of his stomach, which he knew was not a result of the second packet of cigarettes he had already consumed that day, but more likely the knowledge that within the next few hours he was going to kill.

Several times during the days leading up to this moment he had almost declared the assassination off, unable to sleep with fear of the consequences and the complicated reasoning for his actions. He had accepted that Seda was evil and should be removed completely from the political arena. His own personal justification for killing the man was more difficult to come to terms with now that he had examined his motives for the umpteenth time. Sure, he hated the man for what he'd done to so many others without remorse. The death of his servants had plagued his thoughts for years and that act alone was enough for Stephen to want to kill the man responsible. But wanting and doing were two very separate processes.

It was the memory of Louise that now played with his mind. Somehow he knew in his heart that the woman he had so deeply cared for would disapprove of what he was about to do had she been alive. But she wasn't, and because of that fact, he was still going to do it! This was his justification.

He wanted to avenge her death.

Coleman had dreamed ugly visions of her last moments. He knew that it would be impossible now or ever to come to terms with how she died. No one would ever know. Not he, not her family and certainly not Seda, even if the man really did have a soul.

The man was manipulative, ambitious and cruel and threatened the lives of millions in his quest for power. In those few days subsequent to Anderson's revelations, as his anger turned to a deep burning hate, Stephen no longer required any further self examination or justification of his motives to execute Seda. He was going to do it!

Coleman checked his watch yet again. His stomach erupted with another twist forcing him to belch. He drummed his fingers nervously, waiting for the minutes to tick away, as they did, slowly. Then he rubbed his face, pressing both temples with his fingers before readjusting the headphones. Strange, he thought, noticing the perspiration for the first time then wiping the moisture from his forehead with the back of one hand. Stress.

He tried to block the negative thoughts and imagined himself back on the beaches of Palau but it didn't work. His legs were suddenly tired, as he realized that they too were as tense as every other part of his body. He glanced down at his watch, but the minute hand had hardly moved.

'Damn!' he cursed.

His mind wandered for just a few seconds before snapping back quickly, reminding him of what was happening and why he was there in the quiet house alone.

He rubbed his forehead again, cursing the drops of perspiration that had gathered there to remind him of the danger and consequences of what he was about to do. He played with the head-
phones again, annoyed that they didn't sit exactly on his head as
he'd wanted. He knew that the tension was getting to him. And he
was tired. So very, very, tired.

Coleman willed himself to think of the future, and the lazy days
he would have once again in the sun, lying back on the beach, resting, but the serene pictures would not form in his mind. They were
blocked by a confused swirl of many thoughts, faces and events
which refused to give way to the pleasant and peaceful images of
the tropics. He closed his eyes momentarily and listened to the
silence.

He knew that this was stupid. Open your eyes, you fool!

He fought against the desire to sleep as he went through the
procedures once again. His mind kept repeating its signal, over
and over. Be alert! Wait for the moment! Push the button! The instruments in front of him became hazy as he listened to the commands. He felt even more sleepy and closed his eyes again, for a
few seconds, before snapping back from the drowsy state. Nothing had changed and his eyes closed again as his brain attempted
to reduce the enormous pressure it now experienced.

Be alert! Wait for the moment! Push the button!

Again, Coleman jolted suddenly back to full consciousness and
looked quickly at his watch. The hands showed eight minutes before six o'clock.

Startled, he sat up immediately. It was almost time! Bloody hell!
he swore at himself. He'd almost slept right through.

Coleman removed the headphones and poured the remaining
half bottle of mineral water over his face before wiping his forehead with the used napkin lying on the table along with the other
remnants of yesterday's lunch. Or was it dinner? He didn't care.
Snatching the headset off the table and placing them firmly over
his ears Coleman concentrated on the reception.

Still there was nothing. He played around with the equipment
and decided that, as it had been set and reset, he counted, maybe
twenty times, perhaps he should just leave the bloody gear alone
and wait.

Holding his head-phones with one hand, Coleman bent forward and then back, and then forward again until his head was between his knees. Then he sat up and inhaled slowly, blowing the foul air from his neglected lungs.

He repeated this exercise four times and, feeling the first signs of giddiness, knew that would be enough. He then lit a cigarette which caused him to cough violently. He stared at the smouldering stick and stubbed it out in the overflowing ashtray. Coleman picked up the plastic one-litre bottle of mineral water and, remembering it was now empty, threw it across the room in disgust.

His watch informed him that it was already six o'clock. He sat perfectly still, his expression that of stone. It was almost time.

At any moment now his once dear friend would deliver the brief-case to the one-time General. To his step-brother. And then they would both die.

Stephen sat gazing through the window across at the Embassy as he considered this one final act of retribution. Anderson didn't know. At first, he had not planned to kill Albert but the more he thought about his old friend's actions the more clear it became to Stephen that Albert too should die.

Imagining the two men sitting together somewhere in the os-tentatious building across the road filled him with cold rage. Were they laughing together, at him, at the rest of the world? Did they have any comprehension at all as to the incredible pain that they had inflicted on others? On Louise, on Wanti, on him? No, he was sure, they bloody well did not! He knew in his heart and mind that this had to be fact.

One had killed the woman he loved and the other had killed the woman he'd married. But today they would both pay.

Anderson could do nothing to prevent him from seeking his just revenge from these men who had lied and cheated their way into his life, destroying everything that was good, finally leaving him with nothing.

Coleman's fingers danced almost rhythmically on the table. One touch of the button would send the signal out through the airwaves to be captured by that one designated receiver installed in the brief-case carried by Albert Seda. He knew that they had not reached the Ambassador's private office where the listening device still sent its almost-silent humming signal into his headset. This was imperative to Anderson's plan.

Coleman was to detonate the small charge of plastique by remote, sending the signal across the few hundred metres into the compound, until it found its way into the labyrinth and ultimately into the open arms of the receiver which would, in those milliseconds, activate the detonator attached to the half kilo of malleable explosive.

He wished he could be there to see the expression on their faces as they died. He wished he could let them know in their last seconds of life that he had been responsible for their deaths. He wanted to have the opportunity to tell them that this was their punishment for their crimes against others.

Against him, Stephen Coleman.

The cruel thoughts passed slowly through his mind, only to be displaced by images, firstly of Louise as he had last seen her, and then Wanti as she had been taken away from his home in Jakarta, collapsed and still in trauma, only to be taken back to Australia and violated by the very man who had been given the responsibility to care for her.

Anderson had been reluctant to say, he could tell. When they had discussed Albert's role Stephen felt obliged to ask after her. The older man expressed genuine surprise that Stephen was not aware of his wife's death many years before. And when the unfortunate slip was made regarding her daughter he was incensed with what the man suggested had occurred to the unsuspecting Wanti. Albert had taken Wanti and she had become pregnant while she had no control over her own mind.

At first he had wanted to go directly to Albert and confront him with the evidence. And then kill him!

He felt drained.

Anderson had, he realized, deliberately withheld this vital information from him in order that there would be no disruption in their plans to execute the General. He would not forgive Anderson this one last machination as it was obvious that the Intelligence Chief had known from the very beginning. He wished he could destroy him also.

Stephen felt disgusted with the whole filthy mess and just wished he'd never ventured back into Hong Kong. 'Was it really less than two months ago?' he wondered.

Anderson had shown him photographs of the girl. Stephen had insisted. And the birth certificate when he again questioned the accusations made against Albert. She had been born prematurely, the master manipulator had lied, and her mother had died as a result of the birth, having never recovered from her mental disorder and the trauma resulting from her last visit to Jakarta. Stephen had sat coldly still as the realization of what Anderson had suggested slowly burned deep into his soul.

Unanswered questions immediately became clear, such as why Albert had made no attempt to contact him after Wanti died.

His old friend had been too ashamed.

It was now clear how Anderson had managed to convince the man to do his bidding. Coleman wondered just how long the Director had held this information over the former teacher. Had he threatened him with a charge of rape? It would also explain how he expected to maintain Albert's silence once delivery of the bomb had been effected. Although Coleman knew that this would no longer be a problem.

He just could not understand how Albert could have done such a thing. Stephen felt disgusted to the point he desperately wanted to hurt the man, painfully and slowly. His behavior had been criminal and totally incomprehensible. Now he would pay the price for his abuse of the woman he once claimed to care for, to love. A price, Stephen believed, which would be commensurate with the man's deeds.

* * * * * *

Albert had taken a taxi to the Embassy. At first he had difficulty just leaving the cab as the soldiers manning the gates looked so intimidating. He paid the driver and stood for a moment observing the main gate guards. They were dressed in their parade best, he knew. These were not the ordinary security one would normally see watching over an Embassy he thought apprehensively, recognizing the maroon berets and fierce appearance of the paratroopers. Had he not been so concerned Albert might have been impressed. It was unusual to see foreign military in Canberra, especially armed soldiers. Albert stared across the driveway and lawn at the impressive building and then back at the guards. Unless the occupants position demanded such prestigious attention that relaxation of the Foreign Affairs rulings had been granted, then these men should not be strutting around the main entrance, wearing sidearms. His palms started to feel moist as old memories forced their way back into his mind.

Albert produced his invitation and handed it to the guard on the right, who glanced casually at the gold embossed card and handed it back, coming to attention as he did so. There was no salute and neither had he expected any from the paratrooper. He then proceeded through the huge iron gates unaware that the soldier had waved once towards the embassy building before returning to his previous station.

As he entered the grounds a small elderly Javanese confronted him and demanded to know his business. Albert was suddenly frightened. What if this man insisted on checking the contents of the briefcase and discovered so much money inside? Immediately he started to sweat in the cold evening breeze.

"*I have an appointment with Bapak Seda,*" he said, hoarsely, his voice letting him down right at that very moment. He wished he hadn't come!

Umar scrutinized the man's features. He smelled the fear and was satisfied that this man represented no danger. He was old and it was unlikely that he would be carrying a weapon.

"*Follow me!*" he ordered, watching the visitor carefully as he turned and moved quickly along the driveway then up the steps into the lobby. Umar walked briskly then motioned for the visitor to take the stairs with him.

He followed, trying desperately to keep pace as they climbed the staircase. Albert was frantic. The shorter man moved so quickly! He had difficulty keeping up and, before they had even reached the first level, his heart was already pounding from the exertion. He needed desperately to slow down, yet had to appear casual and mask his difficulty in breathing.

Albert rested at the second level and feared that he had overstretched his physical limits. The giddy spell threatened to throw him back down the steps which doubled as a fire escape. He held tightly to the bannister and breathed slowly. Then he looked up and prayed that it wasn't far to go before he could deliver the briefcase and leave. He didn't particularly want to meet with Nathan but his directions had been explicit. 'Deliver only to the Ambassador, or bring the case back home,' were the instructions the government man had given him. He had been quite emphatic. If he were to leave this delivery with another how could they be certain that the Ambassador had really received the gift and that he had not taken it himself?

Albert certainly did not want these people to think that he had taken the money. He was committed to passing the briefcase and contents only to his step-brother.

He looked at the polished leather Satchi case, its deep, almost maroon color reflecting the value of its contents. The polished brass latches were fastened but not locked as the simple tumbler combination in the centre and under the handle served this purpose. The sealed envelope in his pocket contained the numbers required before the gift could be opened.

Albert had no idea how much money was inside the briefcase. It felt like a great deal. He hadn't expected it to be this heavy. Perhaps there were also gold bars inside, he thought. That would explain its weight!

As they reached the final steps Albert knew that, had there been one more flight of stairs to tackle, then he couldn't have made the delivery. He was becoming dizzy from the exertion when the dark little man opened the heavy access door and indicated that they had arrived at the last level.

Albert breathed a sigh of relief. He paused for a few moments and then continued along the passageway past the lifts, following the other man directly into the Ambassador's private office.

Umar instructed Albert to wait while he went in search of the General, who had last been seen escorting the Indonesian Foreign Minister around the huge reception area in preparation for the formal announcement calling the guests to dinner.

* * * * * *

Seda was pleased to strut around as the visitors admired the decorations and complimented him on the magnificent social event that had been arranged for the Independence Day celebrations. It was obvious from their reactions that very few of those present had ever attended such a function in the capital as grand as this and Seda played the part of Ambassador to perfection.

Umar wasn't happy with having to leave the man upstairs alone, but those had been his instructions. He ran down the steps as quickly as his tired legs would permit.

Albert was also tired. He placed the briefcase on the floor and removed the small envelope from his breast pocket. He wished he could leave. Perspiration added to his discomfort as he sat waiting for the man he had not seen in so many years. He waved the envelope slowly, softly fanning his face, as he had forgotten to bring a handkerchief.

The minutes dragged by and he felt a slow wave of panic descend upon him. His shirt became damp with sweat as he felt the fear grow. He looked up at the air-flow duct but knew he wouldn't be able to see if this was warm or cold air moving through the system. It felt so hot!

Albert glanced at the envelope and was startled to see that it had become damp along the edges where he had held it. Embarrassed, he placed the letter back inside his coat pocket. He looked at his wristwatch and frowned. How long should he wait?

Should he take the money and return?

Where is he?

Albert Seda rose to his feet and stood indecisively as panic engulfed his mind and body causing him to suddenly feel ill. He coughed once and swayed slightly just managing to keep his balance as an attack of nausea threatened to further complicate the moment.

* * * * * *

Coleman had heard them enter the room and then there was silence. He leaned closer to the small powerful transmitting device and raised his index finger. And then he too waited for Nathan Seda to arrive.

* * * * * *

The Ambassador had gestured abruptly at Umar as he attempted to interrupt the Foreign Minister's harangue on the wonders of Sumatran culture. Annoyed, he moved away from the small group and stood alone, waiting for the General's signal to approach. It didn't look good. Within minutes he was joined by other Indonesian dignitaries who had arrived early, all offering their congratulations on the splendid appearance of the Embassy and the evening's preparations.

He checked his watch. The visitor had now been waiting for almost half-an-hour. The reception was about to commence! Guest limousines were already entering the grounds and the short security man shook his head in frustration as the Ambassador continued to ignore him.

Suddenly the foyer seemed to fill very quickly as the Ambassador, accompanied by the Foreign Minister and the Chief-of-Army-Staff, were ushered into position in the receiving line.

Seda remained there surrounded by other dignitaries for almost thirty more minutes, greeting his guests as they arrived in the lavishly appointed lobby.

The large crowd had already spilled out into the garden area where mountains of food had been stacked in preparation for the reception. Laughter could be heard as the guests moved around admiring the effort that had gone into producing the delightful setting and colourful decorations.

The aroma of *saté* drifted into the reception hall, tempting the visitors into the magnificent garden and temporary dining area. The band had been sitting patiently, awaiting the signal for them to play their national anthem, *Indonesia Raya*.

Umar again checked his watch and decided that the man upstairs had been left alone far too long. He went to check on Albert.

* * * * * *

Coleman realized that something was terribly wrong. There had been complete silence for over an hour and he could not understand why the General had not yet entered the room. And then he heard a door opened. Then closed. Followed by more silence

* * * * * *

Albert could not bear to remain any longer. He could hear the band starting up and decided to depart. He looked at the case containing what he thought was money.

Albert thought that he would be conspicuous leaving with the briefcase and decided he had no choice but to leave without it. He would tell the government man that the Ambassador had personally accepted the gift and thanked him for his kind gesture. He left the private office and hurried down the passageway to the elevators.

The lifts had been locked in the ground position to prevent any of the evening's guests from inadvertently accessing the upper floors of the embassy. He took the stairs and discovered upon descending to the lower level that the security doors had also been locked on the ground floor for the same reason. He sighed and commenced the slow climb back to the upper levels.

At this time Umar had used his security key and activated the lift controls. Upon entering the Ambassador's office he was surprised to find the visitor gone. And then he noticed the case.

Umar lifted the elegant briefcase and was surprised at its weight. It was much heavier than he'd expected. He examined the container for a few moments more and, unable to ascertain its contents, decided that he would lock it away until he had either located the missing visitor or had discussed the situation with his General.

Umar Suharjo mumbled '*brengsek*', cursing as his knee caught the side of the sofa and, in the distance, startled by the sudden sound and mistaking the man's voice for that of the Ambassador's addressing the courier, Stephen Coleman panicked and his sweaty hands squeezed the small luminous red button sending the dedicated frequency transmission through the airwaves.

Coleman tensed. He waited for the distant explosion.

Nothing happened. He tried again. Another malfunction! A feeling of incredible disbelief swept over him and he slammed his fist hard down on the table, accidentally knocking the remote control to the floor. He cursed as he had never cursed before.

Coleman pulled the heavy curtains back angrily and stared across at the brilliantly lit building surrounded by hundreds of limousines as the elite of Canberra's society enjoyed themselves inside. Waves of disappointment flooded through his tired body and he kicked angrily at the broken mechanism lying on the floor.

They had failed!

* * * * * *

Umar rode the lift down to the lobby and, in his haste, overlooked re-locking the elevators. The General had moved into the garden area and was already approaching his own table when the Security Attaché gave up any further attempts to call him away. It would now be impossible, he knew, observing the guests filling the marquee and taking their allocated positions. Wishing to avoid the multitude of people now crowding every corner of the Embassy and garden, Umar slipped unnoticed into the empty registry.

Albert Seda had succeeded in slowly climbing the steps once again and rested on the stairs for a number of minutes regaining his wind. He was becoming disorientated and confused as to how he became locked inside the building. He thought he heard the whirring mechanical noise stop and forced his old legs to carry him back into the passageway and down to the lift station.

Relieved to find that it was now functioning, he pressed the button and instantly the strange sounds commenced again signalling that the ten-horsepower electric motor was pulling the wire ropes returning the lift to his floor.

Albert then descended to the lobby and, finding the room completely blocked by hundreds of visitors now pushing past him towards the garden, he decided to wait there until their numbers had thinned just enough so that his exit would not be too conspicuous.

Umar Suharjo looked around the quiet registry and, identifying the switch he sought, turned the lights on in the adjacent room.

Outside, the guests were clapping as the Indonesian Ambassador stood in front of the band and raised his hands over his head clenching them together. They had played *Bengawan Solo* and other favourites, much to the enjoyment of the gathering.

The conductor then waited, his body half-turned observing his Ambassador, poised for his signal. As the General nodded, the baton waved delicately in the air, and immediately the handsome Menadonese drummer commenced his roll calling all present to attention. The guests rose to their feet as the band commenced playing the national anthem.

Inside, having now opened the metal doors leading to his arsenal, Umar Suharjo nonchalantly dropped the briefcase containing the plastique explosive casually into the corner.

The sensitive mechanism, which had been unable to receive the earlier signal, immediately reacted to this excessively rough handling. As the deadly package hit the floor an eight-centimetre detonator activated, causing the highly brisant RDX plastique to ex-

KERRY B.COLLISON

plode. The first and second primary explosions came within a milli-second of each other, as the C-4 exploded directly through the walls into the PETN, which had been prepared inside the van to deto-nate the packed ammonium nitrate after the vehicle was later po-sitioned under its own target.

The first shockwave pushed through into the parked truck and ignited its deadly cargo, activating all of the contributing compo-nents simultaneously.

The fertilizer exploded, cutting through the building like some giant knife, the powerful shock waves slicing their way in all di-rections as the explosives acted on each other creating the moment which would rock the political world.

* * * * * *

The first to die was Umar. Then Albert. And many others as that one enormous burst of energy erupted through the assembly turning the entire area into one massive fireball of destruction.

Figures danced momentarily before disintegrating into heaps of lifeless flesh and bone.

The roar had ripped through the guests, hurling musical instru-ments into the maelstrom of human carnage, decapitating a bands-man. Then, for an immeasurable moment, there was silence.

A shrill cry pierced the quiet, then a cacophony of screams emphasised the full horror of the blasts.

Coleman picked himself up off the floor slowly, not noticing the blood across his face and shoulders which had taken the impact of the imploding window. He wasn't seriously injured. Searching fran-tically around in the dark he located the glasses and wiped them quickly.

Coleman viewed the scene through binoculars. He stared at the scene in confused awe. He did not understand how, finally, the relatively small charge had been detonated with the effect of a much greater explosion. Although he had not seen the bomb Coleman knew that it was contained in the small briefcase as he had ob-served Albert walking through the main gates carrying the deadly package.

He was numb with the shock of what he had done. That he was responsible for this incredible destruction. He raised the glasses once again and was horrified to see that most of the building had

588

been destroyed, while many of the limousines were burning fiercely as fuel tanks continued to explode through the cold night air.

Clouds of black smoke spewed out from where the rear of the building had been and Coleman could see that houses in all directions had also suffered incredible damage. The buildings closest to the blast were burning fiercely.

There could be no survivors he thought, still stunned at the sight before him, as he recognized that there would have been many hundreds of guests caught in the horrific explosion. He had watched most of them enter as their cars arrived to deposit the important passengers at the steps of the mansion.

Minutes passed and he heard sirens screaming as fire engines were first to arrive at the scene. Several loud explosions followed and he could then identify the loud calls being made as the firemen urged the neighbouring Embassies to vacate their buildings quickly. The whole evening sky was ablaze with light.

He could see American Marine Guards running outside their own compound, checking its perimeter. A car horn sounded. It had meant something to him but his mind was still confused with the horror outside and he was unable to unscramble his thoughts. What was it? He tried to remember. The horn sounded again. This time impatiently.

Immediately, then, Coleman remembered. The signal!

He moved quickly, leaving the binoculars and broken pieces of the transmitting device behind as he vacated the premises.

* * * * * *

He entered the black Ford Taurus Ghia and the car moved away slowly from the scene as more fire tenders appeared. Road blocks were already being established to prevent even further casualties as petrol tanks continued to explode into the night.

The gloved driver remained silent, guiding the car swiftly away with increased speed, leaving the disaster and its terrifying aftermath well behind. They continued down the capital's protocol roads winding their way through the startled suburbs and across the lake towards the airport. Fifteen minutes passed when the driver pulled into the government forestry reserve amongst the pines and switched the engine off.

Soon, the faint cooling noises of the hot metal adjusting to the new temperatures were the only sounds evident in the cold night.

The cloud had all but disappeared. They were parked on a rise looking back towards the city proper.

Coleman stared at the man behind the wheel.

"It's finished," Stephen stated simply.

The driver's eyes glazed momentarily as he turned his head towards Coleman.

"Could you be certain that he is dead?" he asked softly as if not wishing to break the silence inside the vehicle.

"Yes," he answered knowing that no one could survive the blast.

They sat quietly, together, observing the bright red glow in the sky.

The other man turned again towards Stephen.

"Both of them?" he asked again, without surprise.

"Yes. Isn't that what you really wanted?"

He didn't answer. Instead he watched the red blinking light move across low in the sky. He could see the lights guiding the late and last flight for the day down the runway. It would be from Sydney, he knew. The last flight was always from Sydney.

He sighed. "Then I guess you're free."

"Free?" Coleman asked, suddenly terribly weary as he looked out across at the bright evening sky. He thought he could still hear some explosions in the distance.

The realization of what he had done continued to numb his brain. All of those people. Dead. Because of him!

"Free?" he repeated, confused.

His companion slowly released the wheel then leaned across and placed his gloved hand on Coleman's. Stephen was not conscious of the gesture and continued to look out through the side window at the distant blaze. They sat in silence, observing the extent of the bomb's destructive power. The moon could be seen fighting its way through the clouds of billowing smoke, casting a ghostly light over the capital.

"Yes, free," the driver whispered softly as he moved his left hand across from behind the passenger seat, pausing as the automatic came to rest against the other man's temple.

Coleman turned, surprised at the feel of the cold metal. As the bullet burst from the small handgun his body convulsed and his eyes registered an instant of disbelief at the final treachery.

As life flowed from his body he recalled images of faraway scenes. Of people and places. And of beaches fringed by coconut palms and, he thought that he could see Louise standing, smiling, calling his name and beckoning him.

And then he was swallowed by darkness.

* * * * * *

The driver wound the window down and sat for a while staring at the view. He felt no remorse. Only sadness at what had taken place. It had to be done.

An owl hooted twice from its perch high up in the branches of the pine trees and the faint mist that had settled across Lake Burley Griffin was now slowly drifting away. The breeze touched the trees and their faint swaying motion created the almost surreal impression that they were dancing and waving at him.

John Anderson sat quietly considering those words he had read many years before, words he had always believed in and had tried to instil into the minds of his young trainees.

'That the justification for the use of force was that Government was force. And that the Government had the right to use force against its own citizens.'

He felt no shame. Just sadness.

The grey-haired Director studied the dead man beside him and was surprised to feel a slight twinge tug at his heart. Sometimes principles had to take a back seat to real life. To reality.

Anderson placed the revolver in the lifeless hand. It had been Stephen's.

"Silly bugger!" he muttered.

And then he left, slipping away silently through the shadows, and into the night.

Epilogue

Canberra

Lightning flashed. A clap of thunder heralded yet another downpour as the young woman sat wistfully looking out at the bleak, wet day. The rain never seemed to cease.

She looked down once more and, still filled with curiosity, was tempted to open the faded envelopes as she held them with both hands. After reading the letter attached to the documents she knew it would be wrong to do so and, with a sigh, set them aside for posting.

Seruni looked at the photograph once again and slowly moved the tip of her finger across the images of the couple as they smiled at each other. On the reverse side there was an inscription and date.

Stephen and Wanti — 1972
Cinta Abadi — Eternal Love

In the year following her fathers' death Seruni's grief had been immeasurable. Most nights she still cried herself to sleep. She felt so alone. Albert Seda had been cremated. She was never sure how they could have determined which body had been his. The explosion's aftermath left little. She had scattered his ashes around her mother's grave. Nobody had asked her to do so. Seruni just felt that it was the natural thing to do.

She sorted through the strange case of personal effects which had been passed to her as heir to her mother's and Albert's estate but there were no answers. Only more questions.

Her eyes returned to the snapshot and, with a gesture that even she did not understand, she raised the picture and placed her lips softly against the faded faces while wondering who this wonderful benefactor had been.

Seruni had counted the cash, still not believing her good fortune. There was almost half a million dollars there. The money had been a gift to her mother, Wanti, from the handsome young man in the photograph.

And now it was all hers!

Glossary of Terms

Although many readers would have visited Indonesia, this simple glossary of the *Bahasa Indonesia* words used throughout the novel may assist others who have not yet been fortunate enough to visit the beautiful archipelago and become familiar with its multifaceted culture and language.

ABRI	Indonesian Armed Forces
adik-tiri	younger step-brother/step-sister
adjal	destiny
aduh	exclamation
ALRI	Indonesian Navy
ANIB	Australian News and Information Bureau
Antara	Indonesian News Service
ANZUS	USA, NZ and Australia Treaty
Apa kabar?	How are you?
Apodeti	Timorese Popular Democratic Association
ASDT	Timorese Social Democratic Association
ASEAN	Association of South East Asian Nations
ASIO	Australian Security Intelligence Organisation
ASIS	Australian Secret Intelligence Service
AURI	Indonesian Air Force
awas!	be careful!
babu	servant (female)
bagus	good
Bahasa Indonesia	Indonesia's national language
BAKIN	Indonesian Intelligence Agency
bangsat	arsehole/louse
Bapak/Pak	a term of respect to an older man
becak	tricycle taxi
beliau	His Honor, Sir
berita	news
bersama	together
bioskop	cinema
bisa	can

KERRY B.COLLISON

bohong	lie
brengsek	something/somebody incompatible
bule	foreigner (slang)
Bung	older brother
bunuh	kill/murder
cepat	fast
cewek	girl
cinta abadi	eternal love
cyclo	tricycle taxi
dia	he/she
jahanam	curse/hell
Dji Sam Soe	cigarette brand
dukun	witch doctor
enggak/tidak	no
fajar	dawn/day-break
FRETILIN	Revolutionary Front for East Timor
gamelan	Indonesian orchestra
ganja	cannabis
gudang	storage room
gunung	mountain
guoilo	foreigner
halaman	garden/court
HANKAM	Department of Defence
hidup	live
Idulfitri	end of fasting period feast
jaga	guard
jangan	don't
jongus	servant (male)
joss	bad luck (Chinese)
journos	journalists
kali	stream
kampung	village
Kapten	Captain
kawin	marry
kita	we
koki	cook
Konfrontasi	War against Malaysian Federation
kongsi	union/company/society
KOPASGAT	Indonesian SAS

Korp Komando	Indonesian Marines
KOSTRAD	Strategic Reserve Command
krait	deadly poisonous snake
kretek	clove cigarette
ladang	arable land
Laksamana Madya	Admiral
langganan	dealer/client
Lebaran	a religious feast
Letnan Satu	First Lieutenant
losmen	housing
lubang maut	death hole
lurah	village head
maaf	apology
mandi	bathe
manis	term of endearment/sweet
Mas	address to an older man
mati	dead
mengerti	understand
Merdeka	independent, free
mereka	they
muda	young
nama	name
nasi putih	steamed rice
nenek mojang	ancestors
njonja	address to an older, or married woman
obrol-obrol	chatting/gossiping
OPM	Free Papua Movement
OPSUS	Govternment Special Operations Unit
orang asing	foreigner
Panca Sila	the Five Principles of Indonesian National Philosophy
panggil	call
parang	sword
Parlimen	Parliament
pasar	market
pemerintah	government
PLN	Electric Company
pribumi	indigenous people — 'sons of the soil'
protokol	protocol

PTT	Post, Telegraph and Telephone
rakyat	people, of the country
Ramadhan	the ninth month of the Moslem year
Ramayana	Indonesian epic originally from India
rambutan	small red fruit with hairy rind
ranjau	land mine
rejeki	good fortune
rendang	spicy meat dish
ringgit	Malaysian currency (dollar)
rotan	rattan, cane
RPKAD	Army Regiment
rupiah	Indonesian currency
sabar	patience
sawah	rice fields
saya	I
sedih	sad
sekolah	school
selamat datang	welcome
selamat pagi	good morning
semua	all
sialan	damn
silahkan	please
simpati	sympathy
sudah	already
sumpah	swear
tamu	guests
terima kasih	thank you
terserah	do as you please
cap	stamp
toko	shop
tua	old
tuan	sir
Tuhan/Allah	God
tukang	labourer/worker
UDT	Timorese Democratic Union
warisan	legal heir